I0650632

2232

CHASE INTO BLACKNESS

KENNETH TAM

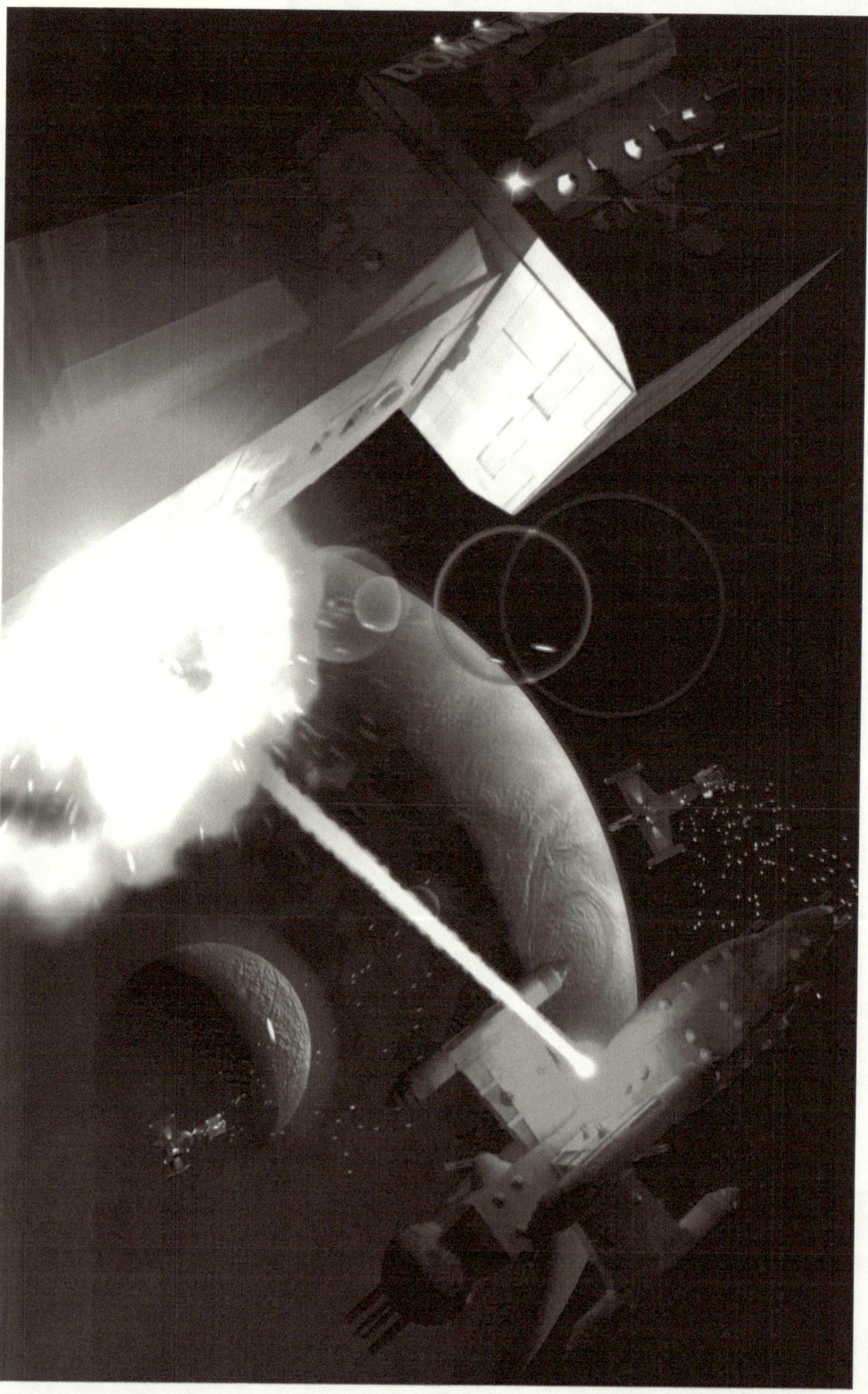

2232

CHASE INTO BLACKNESS

MARTIAN WAR - OMNIBUS 2

KENNETH TAM

ICEBERG

Published in Canada by Iceberg Publishing, Waterloo

Library and Archives Canada Cataloguing in Publication
Tam, Kenneth, 1984-
    2232 : chase into blackness / Kenneth Tam.
(Martian War ; omnibus 2)
Contents: The gallant few -- The Jupiter patrol -- The Sinope
    patrol -- The dark cruise.
ISBN 978-0-9865017-9-1
    I. Title. II. Series: Tam, Kenneth, 1984- . Martian War ; omnibus 2.
PS8589.A7676T843 2010   C813'.6   C2010-900092-7

The Gallant Few first published by Iceberg Publishing in June 2007.
Copyright © 2007 Kenneth Tam

The Jupiter Patrol first published by Iceberg Publishing in June 2007.
Copyright © 2007 Kenneth Tam

The Sinope Affair first published by Iceberg Publishing in December 2007.
Copyright © 2007 Kenneth Tam

The Dark Cruise first published by Iceberg Publishing in December 2007.
Copyright © 2007 Kenneth Tam

2232 - Chase Into Blackness international omnibus first published in January 2010.
Copyright © 2010 Kenneth Tam

NO PART OF THIS BOOK MAY BE REPRODUCED OR TRANSMITTED IN ANY FORM OR BY ANY
MEANS, ELECTRONIC OR MECHANICAL, INCLUDING PHOTOCOPYING AND RECORDING, OR
BY ANY INFORMATION STORAGE OR RETRIEVAL SYSTEM WITHOUT WRITTEN PERMISSION
FROM THE AUTHOR, EXCEPT FOR BRIEF PASSAGES QUOTED IN A REVIEW.

Iceberg Publishing
55 Northfield Drive East, Suite 171
Waterloo ON N2K 3T6
contact@icebergpublishing.com
www.icebergpublishing.com

Cover Image: Wesley Prewer
Cover Design: Kenneth Tam

DEDICATIONS

THE GALLANT FEW
For gallant friends – Mik, Matt, Sam.
Thanks, gentlemen.

THE JUPITER PATROL
For me. Maybe an unusual dedication, but
I needed to write this during some pretty dark times.
It kept me afloat.

THE SINOPE AFFAIR
For my good friend
Peter Caron.

THE DARK CRUISE
"It is the nature of the military that swiftness rules.
Ride others' inadequacies.
Go by unexpected ways.
Attack where he has not taken precautions."
- Sun Tzu

THE GALLANT FEW

THE AUTOBIOGRAPHICAL REMINISCENCES OF
ADMIRAL THE LORD KEN BARRON FOR 2232

THE MARTIAN WAR - 5

KENNETH TAM

FROM THE AUTHOR

Welcome to the second year of the Martian War.

When I started this series, one of my goals was to develop the Martian War in a way that reflected many of the real wars I've studied in history. I might be wrong about this, but I don't think the course wars take after they start is often thought about in popular circles... or explicitly discussed in historical ones. After a war starts, is it just go-go-go until the end? Not usually.

There are many periods during large wars that are relatively quiet, 1915 and 1940 being examples. Don't get me wrong, battles happened in those years of the First and Second World Wars, but they weren't years of constant, large-scale collisions between the central battle forces of the involved countries.

Why do I bring this up? Well, we start 2232 with a bang — Glorious February (named after the Glorious First of June, Howe's victory in 1794). However, the year to come, while full of action, will see a lot of smaller fights, and operations at the fringes of the Empire. In my experience, this is what you often see with wars. The attacking power comes out swinging, but then uses up the resources it had set aside for the assault, and has to pause and take time to build up materiel for a second flurry of heavy attacks. The defender enters the war in a state of shock — they attacked us?! — and then takes time to build up the capability to fight back.

For instance, there was a 'Phoney War' over the Christmas of 1939-1940, as France and Britain waited to see what Hitler's Germany would do next. They dropped leaflets calling for peace out of bombers over German soil. Then, from April to June 1940 (right before the Germans overran France), the British got tied up fighting a German invasion in Norway, essentially a side-theatre of the World War (no offense to Norwegians, there, but France was the Allies' defensive priority).

What I'm getting at is that wars have lulls — times when there are no major clashes between huge fleets over key objectives. You're going to see that later in 2232... though for this book, get ready for a lot of fleet combat.

As ever, many of the characters you'll read about in this volume are based on real-world friends of mine, and these characters will be immune from death for the entire series. Given their immunity, and my desire to create suspense, I'm not going to list who they are — they already know who they are. That said, you can probably guess some of their identities if you really want to. I want to thank all those people who've allowed me to poach their personalities — I hope your characters live up to your standards!

Peter Caron, Wes Prewer and Mik Christensen all deserve special thanks for help with parts of this book, and contributions to the entire series. Extra thanks to Wes for all the work he's done on the covers of both the *Defense Command* and the *Equations* novels.

Finally, the biggest thanks again to my parents, Jacqui and Peter, the best anyone could ask for. And though Atlas has departed, thanks to him too.

– Kenneth Tam

PREFACE

Wait a minute, you've picked up the wrong book! Book five of my reminiscences should be *The Jupiter Patrol*, shouldn't it?

Well, if you look in the back pages of a first edition of *The Hawke Mission* or *The Independent Squadron*, then you'll answer that question with an unresounding (well, perhaps slightly resounding) *yes*... So what the hell is *The Gallant Few* doing here, in your hands?

Go ahead, close the book for a second, check the spine. Yep, says number '5' doesn't it? So is it a gaff?

Well, sort of.

Let me tell you a story.

One bright day I walked into my publisher's cramped offices whistling a happy tune, the manuscript for *The Jupiter Patrol* under my arm. I wandered into the president's office and dropped it on his desk, turned around and left. Job done — I'd delivered another book, I could take some time off before I started work on *The Sinope Affair*.

Thinking just that, I went home, sat down on my couch, and turned on the vid. There was nothing on, so I activated one of my ancient vids from the twentieth century — some of the first days of vid entertainment (then called 'TV') and I still say some of the best. I was watching a fine show from the 1960s called *The Avengers* when my comm chime interrupted me.

Scowling, I paused my show and flipped over to the comm screen. As I did, my publisher appeared, and standing behind him were his three chief editors, all of them looking slightly concerned.

"What, is this an intervention?" I asked, probably not very cordially.

The publisher swallowed (am I really that intimidating?) and held up the manuscript, "This starts in March of 2232."

"Yeah. That a problem?"

He glanced back at his editors and then swallowed again (seriously, do I look like an axe-murderer or something? If you don't know what an axe is, look it up), "Well, that skips Glorious February..."

"I had nothing to *do* with Glorious February," I didn't sound impressed.

"No, but... well... readers will want to read about it. Even if you weren't there..."

I straightened myself up on my couch, "Well then I'll direct them to the excellent naval historian Roger Sar—"

"I'm sure he's fantastic, but they'll want to hear it from you."

"He's the best in the business. I'm a *hack*, he's entertaining and actually informative too. They can read him on Glorious February," I was pretty firm about this.

"Well... see... but... well, people are getting used to hearing *your* voice. No offense to that other guy. Some people who'll never read a history book in their lives are reading your series. Least you can do is fill in the two-month gap for them..."

My publisher was trying to find a convincing angle. I was trying not to budge.

"Look… I mean…" I wasn't as coherent as I needed to be to fend this off.

"You can write your version of what happened, and then that'll get people more interested so they'll go read the proper scholarly version. You know your books on 2231 have made a half-dozen history books into bestsellers, because people want to read more about the events you're describing."

See, that's the button he needed to push — the one that worked. As you know, I'm a big history proponent, and one of the laments of historians everywhere is that people don't always pay attention to good, scholarly history. So sometimes it's up to us hacks to do a respectable job introducing people to an event, getting their appetite whetted so they'll look more deeply into it.

That started to win me over. But my prudence (or laziness) still demanded I put a few more provisos on this.

"If… if I do this… it doesn't mean I'm writing the whole history of the war. I'll fill in this one blank. But I'm not going back and adding volumes about everything else I wasn't witness to…"

My publisher held up his hands, "That's fine, that's what that Roger guy is for. He got a publisher? We should cash in on him."

After a few more minutes of conversation, I agreed to write The Gallant Few, and I must admit, I'm now glad I did. This book is going to be different than any of the others, because Karen, Charlie, Wolf and I won't factor in it much at all.

No, you'll be seeing mostly what was going on with John Fiora, Greg Noyce, 'Mik' Mikaelsen and Marshal Samuels — Wes, Mark, Andrea, Kris… we were all stood down, preparing for our missions coming up later that year. I'll check in with us from time to time, but mainly this is a story about the guys in the first sentence of the paragraph.

Trust me, you're going to enjoy it.

I mean, come on, it's about Glorious February, a month that's been made into six movies.

So let's get into it…

Oh wait, I better provide context. Otherwise my publisher will complain. More.

Alright, this is taking place in January and February of 2232. We had been off Egesta for a month or so, and there's still much fallout from that to be dealt with in both this book and those to come. But that's not important for right now. This was a period in the orbital season when Earth was about to be bracketed by both Mercury and Mars — both planets would be in close range of Earth at the same time.

And, as you probably know, that was going to give the Martians a perfect opportunity to launch their second big assault on the Home Fleet. I still don't know quite why they didn't wait to start their war in February of 2232 — they would have been in a much better position orbit-wise… but anyway.

That's when we are. Let's begin.

CHAPTER ONE

IRELAND

"Are you sure this is the right lane?"

First Lord John Fiora sounded cold when he asked the question, because he *was* cold. It was late in January, it was foggy and damp, and this was Ireland. He was going to be cold, no matter how many fancy heaters had been sewn into his jacket.

Major Carrie Walsh of Special Branch (remember her from *The Almost Coup?*) was his immediate companion; her squad's officers were fanned out in the fields on either side of the lane, creeping forward through the fog, trying to see if they could find a landmark.

How do I put this without embarrassing them...

They had been *misdirected* by the fog.

In other words, they were lost.

"I think... I mean, this *should* be..." Carrie Walsh, remember, had been with John, Greg and Haley Briand when they'd stormed the Emperor's Terra Nova Palace — she was as tough as Special Branch made them.

But even Special Branch is no match for fog. Capital Island and Ireland have very similar climates — they're essentially in the same positions on opposite sides of the North Atlantic — so both places saw plenty of the thick, damp, misty fog. But that didn't help. There is something unconquerable about fog. You just have to learn to live with it.

That fact wasn't helping John or Carrie at this particular moment, though.

"Major, I think I've got something over here — I see a house!" a voice came over Carrie's earpiece and she held up her fist in one of the Special Brancher hand gesture thingies that Charlie Peters uses so fluently.

John, being much more worldly than me, knew what it meant, so he stopped in his tracks, thrusting his hands deeper into his pockets and tried to avoid a scowl, "Found the house yet?"

Carrie nodded slowly, "Think so. Everyone form up on Stacey's position, right thirty from me."

A chorus of 'yes ma'ams' came next, and John turned to his right, took two steps forward, looked down and stopped. At the edge of the lane, there was a grassy mound covered in what looked like frozen mud.

"I'll let you check it out, last thing I need to do is slip and throw my back out. Anne would not be pleased!" He waved Carrie forward, and the Major smiled before leaping over the mound like a cat.

"Ooh, to be young like that again," John muttered and shook his head.

He waited for a couple of minutes, the cold wind picking up and proving yet again that no uniform jacket, no matter how decompression-proof it says it is, can keep out the damp cold of the North Atlantic. As he turned and looked at the lane he'd been walking up, he started to wonder what was taking so long...

And then a deafening whirr started screeching through the air. You probably wouldn't be familiar with the sound, but being a history fellow himself, John recognized it as a *very* old air-raid siren. The hand-cranked type.

Then the thud of a microphone being activated filled the air, and after a second, a thick Irish voice came ripping through the fog, "Who the fuck is out there tryin' to steal my horses?"

John stopped dead in his tracks. No *way* he'd been seen through this fog.

He took a couple of steps up the lane, and the fog — with impeccable timing, as fog tends to have — started to lift a little. The lane definitely curled up towards...

"Stay right the bloody Jesus where you are, dammit! You're in a minefield!"

John stopped dead in his tracks... ooh, sorry about that almost-pun.

The fog was lifting quickly now, and John's eyes started darting around his feet, looking for any disturbances that might have marked mag-mines... or even old-fashioned explosive mines.

"Jesus Mary, that's a Special Branch squad. What in the name of God are you doing out in my field, exactly? I know ye bastards all have the death-wish mentality, but I'd think you'd want to have at least a fightin' chance, yeah?"

Aha, John might not have been seen. He was going to gamble on that, anyway. He started creeping up the lane, and after just a minute the big yellow two-storey clapboard house he'd been looking for came into view.

And standing in front of it with a comm in one hand and some sort of club in the other was the man he was here to see.

Coming closer, John rounded a wooden fence and started up the path towards the house, and then the half obscured figured twitched.

"Oh Jesus!" He dropped his comm and spun the club around, and John realized it was no club. He went to ground with haste, and the loud report of a shotgun — an honest to God cartridge-firing *shotgun* — cracked out through the fog.

The shell was fired high, but that was enough to force Carrie Walsh into action. Braving the mines, she and her squad sprinted towards the fence, sidearms drawn.

But John stood up slowly as the shooter walked towards him, and as he patted his now-damp clothes with one hand, he waved Carrie off with the other, "Nothing to worry about Carrie, that's his way of saying hello."

Carrie and her squad slid to a halt in the field.

"Well Jesus, it's John Fiora isn't it?" the shooter emerged from the last wisps of fog with a grin, and tipped the shotgun back against his shoulder. "And here I thought it was a horse thief, come to steal me ponies."

"You don't *have* horses, Daragh," John tried hard to sound unamused, and the Irishman shrugged.

"I dunna have a minefield either, but that didn't stop me from havin' my fun with your entourage. What the hell are you doing bringing a whole squad out just to find me, man? I swear I wouldn't really shoot you!"

Smiling, John shrugged, "Thought you might need some convincing."

To answer my publisher's question, the real reason was simple: concern that the Emperor or some of Dave Caldecott's old people might use the opportunity of the First

Lord wandering through Ireland on his own to stage an accident. No one was supposed to know he was there, but it was very out of the way, and an ideal spot for a trip and fall down a cliff side. Better safe than sorry.

Daragh grinned and looked back out at the field. The fog had lifted entirely now, revealing the awkward predicament of Carrie Walsh's squad, as they stood tentatively in a seemingly innocuous field.

"Fun indeed, that's true enough... oh Jesus, now that's Carrie Walsh out there, isn't it? Now I've gone and done it, I play cards with her auntie every Thursday. What're you doing getting a good Irish girl lost in a minefield, Johnny?"

Grinning, John stepped forward and patted Daragh on the shoulder, "I'm getting you in trouble with her auntie, what else?"

Snorting a laugh, Daragh nodded, turning and waving towards the house, "There's no mines, Carrie girl. And don't tell your Aunt Mairaid about this, or I'll be killed!"

With a relieved (and I'd expect slightly miffed) sigh, Carrie Walsh started moving her squad across the field towards the yellow house.

John, in the meantime, fell into step next to the man he'd come to see, "So, thanks for not shooting me back there."

"Who says I meant to miss?" Daragh replied with a grin.

"I didn't say you meant to. I'm thanking you for being a terrible shot, as always," John fired right back.

"Jesus, your mother was Irish after all, wasn't she?"

"She most certainly was," John chuckled. "So, do you know why I'm here?"

Stopping and scratching his chin with this free hand (he still had his shotgun against his shoulder and held by his other hand), Daragh looked at John, "You've either come for tea, or you've come to abduct me to fight in this damned war you've got on the go."

John shrugged, "*Fight* is such a strong word. I don't know if that shell thrower would do much good in a fight with the Martians."

Daragh laughed, "Oh come on now, this here would scare the bejesus out of any damned Martie you happened to send my way. So what's it you want of me, then? I'm not commanding any damned carriers, not a bloody chance. You know, I've no more bloody interest in going up into that bloody vacuum. Done my time, so I have. Retired to raise horses."

"You don't have horses, Daragh," John's tone was flat again.

"I did not say I was *good* at raising horses."

"Good," John smiled, "you're coming with me."

"To do *what?*" Daragh's eyes narrowed.

"To be Second Lord of the Admiralty. Go pack your bags, Daragh."

That earned a thoughtful pause, and Daragh directed his gaze skyward for a moment, seemingly thinking it over.

Then the Irishman tilted his head, "You... you're bloody mad. I'm going to do so much damage..."

"I figure you will," John shrugged, "but Dave Caldecott's network of cronies is still messing up our logistics and admin. I want you to clean things up and then get us in shape to win the war. Diane Pena just doesn't have the experience."

"Oh boy," Daragh grinned, turned and walked off.

John never found out just what Lord Ryan meant when he said "Oh boy", but I don't think it really matters.

Because yes, that was Lord Daragh Ryan. *The* Lord Daragh Ryan.

And that's how John got him to be the new Second Lord of the Admiralty.

Not much like Dave Caldecott, surprise surprise.

The wind died and the fog started rolling back in.

CHAPTER TWO
THE PLAN

Belt Two base was busy — very busy — around this time. *Wolf* and the entire Jupiter Force (except for the communications and supply ships) were in orbit of the rock, sitting around while we swapped personnel and got ourselves ready for the long cruise.

Actually, I think that's where I'll start, with me and a friend of mine talking about the decisions that had to be made...

Well actually no, I can't start right there. Let me back up and remind you of all that was going on in Belt Two space. I stopped in mid-thought at the end of the first paragraph.

So to begin with, Admiral Greg Noyce was back in charge, and he was in local space with the battleships *Warspite* and *Goliath*. Then there was newly-promoted Commodore Marshal Samuels, our old veteran friend from the Belt Squadron. He'd taken over the 'new' Belt Squadron, which at present was just three ships — his *Alberta*, Isoruku Togo's *Generous*, and Katya Romanov's *Sackville*.

The Jupiter Force was also at Belt Two, with *Wolf*, *Lion*, *Cheetah*, *Lady Grace*, *Friendly* and *Honesty* — all ships of the old Belt Squadron, now officially reassigned, but in reality still here looking after things.

The Independent Squadron was floating nearby too, each of its ships sporting skeleton crews and the flagship *Nova Scotia* serving as Commodore Wes Pellew's home. A lot had changed.

Wait, there were actually two more warships — and this is where the story of this chapter properly begins — because they were *Cyclops* and *Nanton*. Scratch your head and try to remember those names... that's right, it's Commodore Christian 'Mik' Mikaelsen's flagship, and one of his Hawke Force corvettes. What were they doing here? They had escorted twenty-three Hawke and allied merchant vessels up from the Protectorate to Belt Two in a convoy — part of the patched-together convoy system that Marshal Samuels was establishing.

Anyway, there was a larger point to Mik's presence, the convoy escort being only part of it. So let's pick up with a meeting between him, Greg and Marshal.

Entering Greg's office on Belt Two base, Mik smiled and came to a stop, offering a sharp salute to the Admiral, "Good to see you, sir."

Marshal had been sitting opposite Greg's desk, and now he stood and extended a hand towards Commodore Mikaelsen, "Christian, good to see you again."

Mik and Marshal had been through the Academy together, though they hadn't seen each other often since. Mik took the offered hand as he dropped his salute, "You too, Sam. They still calling you Sam?"

"You can call me whatever you like, Christian, you brought us your battleship."

Expression neutralizing slightly, Mik nodded, "I figured that was why you wanted me here. So what's happening?"

Marshal waved Mik into the chair next to him, and Greg Noyce spoke for the first time, "Well, Mik, you probably know Earth will be bracketed by Mercury and Mars within the next two weeks. We're expecting the Martians to try to launch a heavy assault when that happens."

Nodding, Mik immediately grasped the situation — as any Defense Command officer would. To make it a bit clearer for the non-military readers (no that isn't a derogatory designation!), let me explain. Essentially, in February of that year, Mars' and Mercury's orbits would be such that they'd have Earth sandwiched between them for a solid week. During that time, transit from one planet to the other would be relatively short, and that meant Earth was likely going to get hit hard — from both the Mars Home Fleet and the Mercury Fleet — in the next two weeks.

"So…" Mik began after a few seconds' thought, "We're going to reinforce Home Fleet?"

Greg smiled and glanced at Marshal, then looked back and shook his head, "No, we have something more unorthodox in mind."

"I've got our first convoy to Earth scheduled to depart first thing tomorrow. That means they should be able to make it home before the most likely window of attack," Marshal smiled. "And that will be a perfect, plausible excuse."

Mik's eyes narrowed thoughtfully, and he stroked his goatee, "Excuse? Explain."

Greg sat slightly forward in his chair, "We're taking three battleships and three corvettes out to escort the convoy. It has over fifty ships, and it's going to be passing through some potentially dangerous space, so that will be our cover. But about two thirds of the way to Earth, our escort will peel off, the convoy will redirect away from Earth, and we will go to Mars."

"Really?" Mik's eyebrows climbed. "Objectives?"

"By the time we arrive, the Martian Home Fleet will have left for Earth — presuming they intend to attack. If it hasn't, we'll pull back as soon as our Starlights detect it. If it has, we will go in and bombard as much as we can, and gather more intelligence."

That isn't actually what Greg said. I've talked to Greg, Marshal and Mik about this meeting, and that definitely isn't what Greg said. What he said is still classified. All I'll do is give you a historical hint: during the Second World War, the British broke German Enigma codes, allowing them to know when and where the Martians would be. Er. Germans would be.

But during the war, and for years after, they couldn't reveal they'd broken those codes, even though the immediate threat was passed; they didn't want to let the Soviet Union know they had that kind of code-breaking technology. Even twenty years later, people thought the British had just been very lucky.

Well, I won't elaborate on what that allusion has to do with our Martian War. Read into it whatever you like. If those last two paragraphs actually get printed, it means the Admiralty will have approved of their inclusion, and that means my allusion can't be too close to what Greg was basing his Martian deployment information on… or can it?

Anyway, suffice it to say there was more certainty about where the Martians would be than I can elaborate about at the present time.

That certainty was what Greg really talked about.

"We leave in the morning, then?" Mik was smiling by the end of the conversation that I can't really repeat.

"Yes, you do," Marshal nodded. Sorry, part of that conversation included the fact that Marshal had to stay at Belt Two, to coordinate the nascent convoy system and to have *Alberta* available to escort convoys if necessary.

And to answer your next question, the Jupiter Force was technically not supposed to do any escorting — as I'll talk about in a bit, our crews were changing at this point, and our ships were stocking up for a long cruise to Io. We were thus not part of the convoy system, though if Marshal had needed either us or Wes' Independent Squadron ships (skeleton crews or no), we'd have been there.

But Marshal is a master organizer — he hadn't needed us yet, even though he was running convoys with only a fraction of the escort force he required, and would get later in the war.

So. That was a lot of explaining. I think that's enough for this chapter — you know the plan, so perhaps we should get on to something else.

Chapter Three

Pudding Philosophy

While Greg, Marshal and Mik were meeting, I also happened to be on Belt Two base, arguing (rather fruitlessly) with Lieutenant Commander Fiona Kellerman. Yes, a Rear Admiral was arguing with a Lieutenant Commander, but those of you (well, probably most of you) who remember Fiona Kellerman, either from her moment in *The Independent Squadron* or from her many later deeds, will not be surprised by the fact that she was standing her ground.

"You cannot have those supplies, sir."

It's funny (or not, perhaps): this scene was in many ways the same one she'd faced against Captain Dwight Bahim of the old Independent Squadron — he'd come down to the base for palettes of MAG-90s, and had been met by Fiona at the door to the warehouse. Now that I think about this, our encounter played out with eerie similarity... and a few pathetic differences.

"I'm a Rear Admiral, Lieutenant Commander. Get out of my way!" I probably sounded about as surly as that reads. I'm a sad and pathetic person at times.

"Sir, that pudding is designated for station personnel only. The new shipment for your force will come in with the next convoy."

Yes, she said pudding.

Let me pause while you laugh at me.

Alright, back to it: "That's not going to be for weeks, Fiona! My crews are craving it now!"

You'd be surprised how many written complaints you get when your crews run out of pudding. Defense Command meals are fairly standardized. Some people hate that, some people love it, but all people prefer their meals when they're accompanied by pudding.

Now this isn't blood pudding, or some sort of meat concoction (that I'm sure is wonderful) from the UK: this is North American pudding. This is a paste that tastes like smooth chocolate, or smooth butterscotch. I like the chocolate myself. It goes with every meal, as dessert, and it's surprisingly popular — for pudding.

But the Jupiter Force had none. This was in fact my fault, because while our ships had still been part of the Belt Squadron, I'd let the pudding orders lapse. Yes, I'm terrible. I saved the Empire (with Karen, of course) at least once, but I let the pudding run out. That's nigh-unforgivable...

And my attempts to rectify the problem weren't working.

"Sir, you're not getting this pudding," Fiona folded her arms and stared sternly at me.

At this moment, to emphasize the point, Charlie Peters appeared behind me, "Give it up, Ken. She's just going to be mean."

He patted me on the shoulder and I looked down and shook my head sulkily, "Yeah,

I guess she is."

Fiona didn't budge. Cold-hearted woman.

Charlie and I turned around and started to clomp away indignantly.

"Guess we'll have to buy some privately," Charlie said quietly. "I'll get Carly and the squad together and we'll go to Food Box Plus down in the Capital Dome."

I nodded slowly, "I'll use my signing authority to bill it to Belt Two's discretionary defense fund…"

Yes, I'm admitting that Charlie and I committed fraud in the amount of $31,640 (in today's money, that's like a month's pay for a Lieutenant) to buy a three-week supply of pudding for the Jupiter Force.

Don't worry, we paid it back later.

Come to think of it, though, I don't know if that was actually fraud. We used the fund to buy standard foodstuffs for our crews… I'm pretty sure that *wasn't* fraud. Just very irresponsible.

Anyway, Charlie and I parted company there, Charlie using his ultimate Special Brancher stealth ability to vanish down a corridor. It was probably a little over the top, I'll give you that, but we were extremely happy to be where we were.

Let me put this into context for you: we'd been back from Egesta for about seven weeks, and none of us had put it completely behind us. Charlie and I had bounced back reasonably well, and of course Karen was as resilient and unflappable as ever, but even so, we were glad to be worrying about things as stupid as pudding. The break… well… we *needed* it.

And we were going to milk it for every bit of immature joy we could.

I kept walking for a few more minutes, trying to stay focused on pudding, but I had other, rather important things to work out. All the changes I described earlier required us to shuffle our personnel situation… and that wasn't fun. Karen was tied up in meetings with Sharon Stanton (Captain of Belt Two base, soon to be moving over to the Independent Squadron) so I had to wait for her… but my mind was quickly floating back to the problems.

What was so dreadful about this personnel work? Well, to begin with, one person's situation was really plaguing me: Andrea Kiley.

Ah, now it starts to make sense, eh?

Remember *The Independent Squadron*? Remember how badly she was doing when she got away from Egesta? She essentially appeared 'stable' now, but Karen and I had our suspicions. We couldn't put our fingers on what exactly was troubling us about her… something instinctive was telling us Andrea had changed. We just didn't know how much.

We weren't the only people noticing a change either: Kris Jacobs had seen differences in Andrea's behavior, and Mark Gunney had reported concerns. Again, nothing — *nothing* — conclusive. Nothing we could really ask Andrea about.

It could simply have been stress, and therefore not all that serious… It was, in fact, so much worse. Today I feel quite badly for not having realized how serious the situation was, but Andrea (as I think we saw at the end of *The Independent Squadron*) was expert at hiding her difficult state.

Anyway, all those half-concerns were floating around in my mind. The question they led to was simple: could we trust Andrea with a combat command? Could we be certain that, if she was plunged into the fray, her judgment would be as razor-sharp as it had always been?

Oh, and to answer my editor's question, there was no way in *hell* we were putting her in front of a combat psychologist. That would have instantly torpedoed her career. Things were much different then than they are today — any suggestion that Andrea was losing her grip meant she'd be on a desk, and there wasn't much John, Greg or I could have done about it... at least not until Caldecott's people were cleaned out of Defense Command Medical Services. I'll get into that some other time.

So, I was worried about what to do with Andrea.

And, by very good luck, I ran into Mik. Almost literally.

He was turning the corner coming one way just as I was approaching it from the other, so we did one of those awkwardly abrupt stops you do when you nearly walk into someone, and both started saying 'excuse me' before we recognized each other.

"Mik!" I think I exclaimed first, grinning and extending my hand. "Heard you'd come in. Get briefed by Greg yet?"

Mik took my hand and smiled in reply, "Ken! Yes, I'm just coming from the meeting. You know the plan?"

Nodding, I let go of his hand, "Yeah, Greg ran it by me before he called you up from the Protectorate."

"Ah good, so you think it's practical?"

"If you mean 'survivable', then obviously not. You don't think I'd let glory slip away from my grasp if it was survivable, do you?" I didn't manage to pull that one off deadpan, and Mik laughed generously.

"Right. So I just need to get some pudding for my ship stores..." he started looking down the hall towards the cargo section I'd just left, and I shook my head.

"Sorry, buddy, they're not giving it up. I just tried to pull rank on a Lieutenant Commander and she didn't budge."

"Damn, that's cold. We need our pudding," Mik chuckled. "Vivar's been bugging me about this all cruise..."

I didn't register that comment at first, but as Mik started to stroke his beard thoughtfully, I frowned at him, "Vivar. That irritating Commander from the independent belt?"

Now that's a pretty vague description, so let me remind you of Commander Guy Vivar of *Nanton*, the corvette Mik had brought out here with him. If you remember your *Hawke Mission*, Vivar was the most annoying cretin of a Commander I've yet described in these books, and the dolt's last posting had been out to Caligula, a punishment for bad behavior.

Mik nodded, "Yes, he's out here with me."

"Why?" I blurted out the question, and Mik gritted his teeth in the way someone does when he's getting drawn into a conversation he doesn't really want to have.

"Well, not that I don't appreciate you trying to get him off my plate, but I called him in as soon as I got my promotion. Been keeping him with me since then."

I frowned, "The annoying guy?"

"Yeah…" Mik winced slightly. "Sorry, different style than yours, I guess. I just think it's best to keep the troublemakers close, so I can keep an eye on them. Better than leaving them out on their own to create problems. One of Lia's ships is out there now."

Oh.

See, Mik's a natural at this business — he's a damned fine CO, and by rights he should have been a Commodore before I was. I mean, look at that. First thing he did when John gave him his promotion was to collect the most annoying Commander possible and bring him in (remember, it had been me who sent Vivar to sit on Caligula, not Mik). I didn't get into an elaborate discussion about exactly how Mik reversed my order there in the corridor, but prepping for this book we talked about it.

Arriving at Hawke One, Mik's new base of operations for the combined Hawke Command-Defense Command 'Hawke Force', Vivar had been told flatly that he was going to pay attention to the chain of command, and that if he choked in action, 'the Martians would be the least of his problems.' But he got a chance.

Now, see, I'd have left the guy at Caligula to rot, but that's why Mik, I think, is a better CO than I am. He came up in the Independent Belt, and that makes him a better leader. Let me explain that…

The Belt Squadron, I think it's been made clear by now, was the pinnacle squadron. Every member of its crews — and every skipper — was picked and honed. None delivered less than their best, and if they were off their game, they felt bad about it. Never *once* had I run into a Belt Squadron officer or rating whom I couldn't respect.

There had been some, I've heard of in stories, who slipped through the harsh selection process. As soon as they were found, they were 'exited' — to the Independent Belt cruisers. The Belt Squadron had to be kept in top fighting form at all times, and if that meant excising bad people, then that's what we did.

That's the environment in which I learned to lead. I could send my problem cases away.

But Mik had no such luxury, and more importantly, he had more patience. He made the most of every ship he had — something I'd only do if I was forced to — so he'd kept Vivar close. He'd given him a chance.

Better leader, like I say.

So what's the point of all this rhetoric about leadership style and ability? Well, it probably sheds a little light on why I was having a tough time figuring out what to do about Andrea. If she was unstable, how would I cope with that? I had no intention of 'exiting' her, no bloody way.

But perhaps I could take a page from the book of Mik.

"Keep them close…" was the revelation I had right then, and Mik frowned at me.

"Puddings?"

I blinked and looked up, "Puddings?"

After that we commed Charlie to make sure he bought extra pudding at the Food Box. All chocolate, by the way. Butterscotch is for crazies. Yes, I said it. And I stand by it.

CHAPTER FOUR

NOW INTRODUCING... BANG

"Do you really need to keep carrying that thing around?" John asked the question as he eyed Daragh (for the record, that's pronounced 'Dar-ah') Ryan's shotgun.

The Irish Peer grinned, "I see no reason not to. It's not as though it'll hurt a thing."

"It shoots solid lead, man, of *course* it'll hurt a thing. *Anything.*"

Daragh shook his head, "It's full of blanks, so it is. I'd never be putting lives at risk for the mere pleasure of seein' people wet themselves."

John shook his head slowly, "I suppose there's something noble in that."

They were walking up the path from the landing field to Admiralty House's front door, and word of their coming had preceded them. Of course, John had told no one in Admiralty House just who he was getting to replace Caldecott. There'd actually been a pool going (which John did *not* have money in), and the frontrunners were the Third Lord, Diane Pena, and John's predecessor, Deidre Warsangeli.

Diane, despite her good intentions, had proven over the past couple of months that she wasn't quite up to the job. Nothing against her personally, she just hadn't been in the Admiralty long enough to have the clout, or the thick skin, to deal with groups like the builders' guilds.

Deidre would have been great, but John knew that in the mid-February cabinet shuffle, Prime Minister Pope was going to make her Minister of War, so she was out of the running.

Greg or Marlene would also have been perfect for the job, but both of them were (obviously) tied up in very crucial combat commands.

So then the pool broke down to a smattering of random officers. The longest odds were actually on Mik — yes *Mik*, with the next longest on Marshal Samuels, then Karen, then me. Those were some *long* odds. Foolishly long, really.

Then again, Daragh Ryan was little better, and only one wise young Ensign had picked the Irish Lord for the pool. That Ensign got himself a shiny new hovercar out of this deal.

Anyway, none of that much matters. The point is that the whole of Admiralty House had turned out in the lobby to watch John walk in with the new Second Lord, and there was an air of excitement.

And being true to himself, John Fiora was bound and determined to take absolute advantage of it.

Let me switch perspectives from John's and Daragh's to the security camera inside the lobby of Admiralty House (looking down from top-rear-right of the lobby, with the door at the very top of frame). The crowd had gathered, almost a hundred staffers that Tuesday morning, including ratings and officers, everyone from Sensors and Communications technicians to Special Branchers. Behind the reception desk, Gerald and Betty — the receptionists who had been there forever — took no notice.

Then someone yelled, "They're coming, shh!"

A hush fell, and John Fiora walked through the door on his own, hands thrust deep in his pockets, shaking his head, "He said no."

He walked off.

Just like that.

You can pick out the book-keeper on the vid; she's the one scrolling through her pad, looking to see if anyone had picked 'no one' — to see if 'no one' was even an option she'd allowed. Maybe she got to keep everyone's money. Maybe that flashy red convertible was hers!

Then — and I'm still not sure if I actually believe this (as many times as I've watched the vids, howling with laughter) — Daragh came in *shooting*. Blanks, of course, but my God. Shooting.

I don't know if you've ever heard a powder weapon fire in person, but it's *loud*. The staffers flung themselves everywhere. They piled onto each other like they were taking fire... well, they thought they were.

Now, of course, the Special Branchers and SF in the lobby were well-trained to deal with intruders carrying firearms, but Lord Ryan... well, he's Lord Ryan. The first Special Brancher to have her mag off her hip looked up and found herself nose-to-muzzle with Daragh's 12-gauge shotgun.

And Daragh was grinning like a madman.

"I..." he declared loudly as people managed to turn over enough to look up at him, "...am your new Second Lord. All ye be attentive of that!"

Then he pulled the shotgun back, leaned it against his shoulder, and walked after John.

The funniest part of all this? Gerald and Betty had not so much as budged from their seats behind the reception desk. I don't know if they even stopped working. I truly think they may be cyborgs. Look it up. Cyborgs.

About twenty minutes later, Daragh sat in one of the chairs opposite John's desk and carefully rubbed the barrel of his shotgun with an oily rag. To John it looked suspiciously like the Irishman was not paying attention...

"...so they're demanding more money from us, or they're going to delay delivery of *Hokkaido*..." John was explaining the biggest headache he was having at the moment.

Get ready for a few paragraphs of boring discussion about Naval building practices.

As you probably recall from *The Independent Squadron*, John had ordered a whole lot of new construction to augment the fleet — the *Asia*- and *Australia*-class frigates and corvettes being two thirds of it. So far, both of those production orders were running smoothly — the *Australias* were due to start coming online in July, and the *Asias* were expected by the end of the year.

But to start getting at the headache, let me explain *how* most of them were being built: they were going to commercial yards. You see, the Navy has nine building and repair yards throughout the Empire, eight of them with multiple docks (the ability to build or repair more than one ship at a time). But John had ordered a lot more ships than those Naval yards could possibly build, so to get the rest of the construction going, the Admiralty (technically the Navy Board, but that was effectively defunct and had been since Lord Hawke's days) sent orders out to commercial *civilian* yards for building.

Now, civilian yards love these sorts of orders; the government pays its bills in a timely fashion, and pays handsomely too. There's always a lot of competition for fleet shipbuilding contracts because of that. The process is straightforward: yards hear that we're getting ready to build, we send out the specs of what we want constructed, and they send us quotes telling us how much they can do the job for, and guaranteeing to deliver on our timeline, and to our quality standards.

It's a great system when it works, and it often does work. There are many fine shipbuilders out there, my favorite being Garnett-Wentworth, not that that matters. The problem that arises, though, is that some rather cheeky builders see giant orders like this one as an opportunity to take the Admiralty for a ride.

There were so many ships being built that at least some of the builders getting contracts were inevitably going to turn out to be sub-standard. One of these had managed, through a brilliant acting job, to get the contract for *Hokkaido*, one of the four battleships John had ordered. The other three were in Naval yards. But this firm had put together a great pitch, got the contract, and now was demanding more money for 'unforeseen' expenses, or they weren't going to deliver on time or to quality. With the war on, they figured they had us over a barrel.

This was the sort of problem John needed handled — the sort of thing Diane Pena, for all her good will and administrative experience, simply wouldn't have been able to sort out.

But it wasn't Diane Pena sitting across the desk from John.

"...Daragh... are you listening? They're in the boardroom downstairs right now..."

I know you know how this is going to end. But there's no way I'm giving up my chance to actually write it.

As soon as John said those words, Daragh was on his feet and walking out of the office. Witnesses who saw him on the way say his expression was calm as he walked along with the shotgun leaning against his shoulder.

Now let me cut again to a security camera feed in the boardroom to which he was heading.

Four representatives from the guild of builders we were having trouble with were sitting at one end of the board table, chatting amongst themselves in a quiet and sneaky way. Well it looked quiet and sneaky. They were waiting for someone — my guess is Diane Pena — to come in so they could demand the money.

Daragh — again, my God — came in shooting.

Like a psychopath.

Defense Command officers in the lobby had fallen all over themselves trying to get out of the way. The guilders started screaming. Manic screams. He stormed in, shooting off his shotgun like mad, driving them to the floor in terror.

"My name is Daragh Ryan, I'm the new Second Lord around here and I understand you're trying to *fuck us over for more money?* Is that so?"

He asked the question (complete with expletives, I know) as he came to stand over the lead negotiator — the one who'd been sitting at the head of the table. Leveling the shotgun at the man's face, he crouched slightly so he could press the hot tip of the barrel into the negotiator's cheek.

"Would you be tryin' to take unjust sums of money from us, Mister Negotiator?"

Try bargaining from that position. Well, don't actually try it. But imagine.

"So, here's how it'll be. I'll let you all walk out of here, some of you perhaps to the bathrooms to change your pants, and then I'll send a Special Branch squad to your head offices, where they will follow you around every day until *I'm* convinced you're no longer trying to take what isn't yours. You'll stick to your quoted price, and if you don't, I'll space the lot of you. Personally!"

I personally think the pants thing was a bit much, but he did say it.

"You… you can't…" one of the other guys on the floor eeped (I know, not a word) out the reply. Not wise, but then these people seem adept at not knowing when *not* to push their luck. Er, canceling the double negative there, they didn't know when to shut up.

Daragh grinned, turning the shotgun on the new target, "Do I *look* like a man with sufficient mental health to understand the difference between right and wrong, or to care about the consequences of my actions? And Jesus wept, man, the Admiral commanding SF in the Empire *reports to me.*"

My editor pointed out (after reading that passage) that Daragh had in fact already identified the practice of the guild as 'wrong', and thus clearly did have the ability to distinguish between right and wrong. Nonetheless, it's what Daragh said, and I defy anyone to tell a screaming Irishman with a shotgun that his statements are sometimes contradictory. I mean, he's crazy.

Anyway, I think I can stop the narrative there. Let me just tell you, we got *Hokkaido* early. And the yard building it went out of business shortly afterwards.

All because, to quote someone I once heard (forgive the language), "Lord Ryan? Christ, the man's batshit insane!"

Yep. Yep he definitely is.

CHAPTER FIVE

ARCHITECTURE OF DEFENSE

Later that day, John was sitting down with Daragh again, but this time there was no shotgunning to be done. Nope, no shooting this chapter, I promise. Seriously.

That said, the issues at hand weren't terribly different than those that had confronted Daragh in the boardroom... they were just... well... not shotgun-worthy.

"*Bonnie's* shakedown is going fine, but getting *Terra Nova*, *Bonavista* and *Hibernia* ready to fight is going to be tricky."

I seem to like introducing these shipbuilding problems with dialogue fragments. Look at the last chapter, I did the very same.

And, like last chapter, I'd better follow this one up with exposition. I'm *sorry*, but you need to know.

Of course you're familiar with *Bonaventure*. Laid down as an assault carrier, she (and we tend to refer to it as a 'her' instead of an 'it' because her nickname is *Bonnie*) was converted to a rather huge and powerful battleship soon after her keel was laid. That was a victory for John at the Admiralty; Caldecott had won the first round, getting her laid down as a carrier, but we'd regained control over the project, and turned her into a battleship, then ordered three more.

Now, as I'm sure I've mentioned in at least one prior book, the builders were rushing to get *Bonnie* and her fellow ships out of the yards and ready to fight with all haste, but it wasn't going as well as John had hoped it would.

These, for the record, were all good builders, but they'd been asked to compress as much as six months' of work into as many *weeks*. There were, inevitably, wrinkles.

Unfortunately, the rush was now very necessary — that's what this meeting was really about. Not ships, but why they were needed.

"So if it's just the Heavy Squadron, you think we can hold them off?" Daragh's question came with a frown, and of course, leads me to explain slightly more.

The 'them' he was talking about were the expected Martian attack forces (emphasis on the plural) that were coming for Earth. With *Warspite* and *Goliath* now at Belt Two, the Heavy Squadron of the Home Fleet was now down to five battleships, one of them an only partially-enhanced *Odysseus*-class which had been built back in Daragh's day.

Thanks to sources of information I again can't elaborate on, John expected two assault forces, one from Mars and one from Mercury, each of which would actually outnumber the Heavy Squadron. But being outnumbered didn't necessarily mean defeat was inevitable, obviously... it just meant the cost of a fight could be very heavy.

And the Martians didn't actually have to eliminate us; they could call it a victory if they simply managed to cripple the Home Fleet since that would force John to recall Greg's battleships from the Belt and Marlene's from Venus in a bid to protect the homeworld. That would be strategically disastrous, and a political nightmare.

So heavy losses had to be avoided, and of course, Earth had to be protected.

"Without *Bonnie* and her siblings, I don't know…" John had already explained all this, hence Daragh's question about holding off the Martians.

Nodding at the First Lord's rather unconvinced reply, Daragh continued, "Alright, so we'll be making it clear to the builders, then, that those ships are going out to fight, even if there are workers still aboard."

John winced, "Oh, I'd rather not see that. You ever hear of *Prince of Wales?* A KG5 in the Second World War, went out to catch *Bismarck* with workers still aboard. Was nearly sunk in that fight, and HMS *Hood* was blown up. I think it must be bad luck to have workers aboard."

The story trailed off as Daragh half-scowled, "You're saying you don't want to take everything you have out to meet the Martie bastards because 500 years ago some damned English bastards got themselves shot up with some workers aboard?"

I take no responsibility for Daragh's opinions, by the way. I'm just repeating what John told me about the meeting.

Shrugging, John now nodded, "Yes, I'm saying I'd put the Empire at risk of utter defeat because of my historical superstition."

He managed to say that with a straight face.

The two Admiralty Lords stared at each other for a few seconds, then they burst out laughing.

I guess that was funny. I wasn't there, so I may have missed the funny part in the retelling. You have my sincere apology.

Anyway, returning to the matter at hand, Daragh leaned back in his chair, "I'll see to it the yards speed up, don't worry yourself about that, John-boy. You just figure out how the hell you're going to stop an attack from two fronts. Is there a counterattack in the works?"

Smiling, John nodded, "I suppose you'd expect me to have a plan, wouldn't you?"

"Well if you didn't, I was going to bloody shoot you and come up with one of my own," Daragh grinned, and John chuckled before continuing.

"There's no way we could get away with pulling Home Fleet ships off the line here for a probe at Mars, but our [information suggests] that Mars *will* be open to a strike when their fleet attacks. They're counting on us not realizing that, or being stretched too thin to be able to take advantage of the situation."

The [square brackets] there, I should explain, are from the second draft — his original explanation of how he knew what he knew has been removed for security reasons, and I approve of the removal.

"They're not far from wrong now, are they?" Daragh's grin faded. "You've got nothing to move out against Mars, surely…"

John could now have played coy or done something needlessly dramatic, but real briefings tend not to be coy or needlessly dramatic. Well, unless there's a ham like me involved.

But I wasn't there, remember… not that I needed to remind you, sorry.

"Greg's going to come out from Belt Two with *Warspite*, *Goliath* and *Cyclops*, under the auspices of convoy escort in case anyone's paying attention to his movements. He'll break off on the way and the three battleships and a few escorts will hit Mars."

Daragh's smile returned and he nodded in approval, "Alright then."

In a movie (any of the movies, actually) this conversation drags on a bit more, as John invariably has to explain the reasons behind the attack — you know, the 'we can gather intel and strike back at the enemy, getting some measure of revenge' explanations.

And, of course, Daragh asks some rather unlikely questions — 'well, are we putting Belt Two at risk by pulling its battleships away?'

Yeah, no way LORD RYAN would possibly be able to grasp the strategic consequences of battleship redeployment without asking. Not like his career up to retirement had been eventful or anything…

Sorry, this is turning into a rant, so I'd better just vent now, get it out of the way.

I do *understand* that movies think they need to go out of their way to explain things, and in the cases of movies rated for young viewers, I'm happy about that — I like that the logic behind things can be explained to those too young to necessarily come to it on their own (though most kids, I think, are more than bright enough to figure it out anyway).

But four of the movies on Glorious February were rated for adults only, and yet these movies were just *dumb*.

So here's a question, dear reader, do *you* think it'd be risky to pull battleships off Belt Two station and send them into Mars space? No kidding, so do I!

Yeesh.

Daragh knew it was a risk, and an acceptable one — it was a chance to shake up the Martians, and hopefully damage their infrastructure. And it'd play very well in the media, which would be important.

That's something that isn't often talked about: John wasn't just planning here for a battle or two against Martian ships, he was also coming up with ways to make certain we won the PR battle. It had to look good when we sent them running. It had to look even *better* when Greg reported in and word was widely released that we'd hit Mars while our dear enemy was loafing around trying to hurt us.

"Well, like I said, I'll make sure your *Bonnies* are ready for the fight. We'll talk more about the plans for defense when we're a mite closer to the launch date, eh?" Daragh offered in a manner that would close the discussion, and John nodded.

"Indeed we will. Now take your shotgun and get to work."

With a bright smile, Daragh nodded, "Against my better judgment, I'm coming to appreciate this job."

As the Irishman stood, John chuckled and shook his head, "We both know you don't have judgment."

So much truth in that statement.

CHAPTER SIX

THE SHUFFLING BEGINS

Organizing the Jupiter Force wasn't going to be a walk in the park. The promotion of so many of the Belt Squadron's skippers had hurt us...

Alright, I'd better slow down here. By 'so many' skippers I really mean only two were leaving the force, and others were being promoted to other ships within it. As Karen and I started trying to address our personnel concerns, we had to do so minus the recently-promoted Commodores Wes Pellew and Marshal Samuels. As I implied in *The Independent Squadron*, that was a considerable loss to us.

But — and I suppose this is an aside on something that already felt like an aside — that sort of splitting up is what happens to good units. Once skippers like Wes and Marshal prove their mettle, they get separated so they can positively influence a wider body of personnel.

And the Belt Squadron — now the Jupiter Force, actually — suffers for the loss.

The good news, though, was that we had great depth — we had plenty of excellent people ready to move into command positions.

We just had to figure out who was going where, what promotions they'd need, and so on.

It sounds boring, and perhaps if you're reading this series just because you like, as one reader once eloquently put it to me, "stuff blowing up!" then you may want to skip this chapter. That said, you should probably see what moves Karen and I were planning (or trying to figure out) for our officers — for our *friends*. A lot of what we had to do relied on analyzing character, I suppose...

(Don't worry, we blow up a lot of *stuff* later).

Karen and I were, unsurprisingly, standing in my quarters, and of course I wasn't quite on topic.

"I could have taken her down. But I didn't want to cause a headache for Sharon. That's the only reason I didn't start swinging."

The pudding thing really had wounded my pride. Or at the very least, I was playing it up to an absurd degree in a bid to restore some of the frivolity and generally inappropriate happiness that had surrounded Karen and I before Egesta. In other words, I was overcompensating as I adjusted to the long shadows cast by *The Independent Squadron*.

Karen, because she is made of the same stuff as goddesses and angels, was putting up with me, "Yes, I'm sure it was a selfless act on your part."

Sounded dry, compared to the usual warmth of Karen's retorts, though I don't expect you could blame her for that. It was still a retort, and we were at a stage by this time where the rhythm — if not the feeling — behind our normal repartee was starting to flourish again.

Sharon, by the way, was in the process of handing over her duties as CO of Belt Two base to Commander Scott Liebgott; he was going to take over when she joined Wes' new Independent Squadron as the skipper of *Yukon*. She was having a stressful time passing things over — a hell of a lot of work goes into running Belt Two base, and Sharon's not the sort of person to just let it drop — so my excuse for not physically attacking Fiona Kellerman to save Sharon a headache was, I suppose, plausible.

Of course, you know me; Caldecott or Sean Cook's people aside, I don't think I'd generally be inclined to attack any Defense Command personnel.

"But Charlie's paying for our pudding. I'm going to bill it to the base, that'll be poetic justice!"

Again, overcompensating a bit. What can I say?

What Karen said, maybe, "You don't have to try so hard."

I looked across at her, the mock expression on my face fading to neutral, "Alright."

She smiled — thank God — and nodded, "Good. So. We have personnel to shuffle."

The game started there, and it wasn't easy by any means. We scattered pads all over my bed, then stood around, sort of just staring at them in wonder. Who should go where?

At that point, the obvious job openings we had were for the CO of *Wolf* — Karen was Commodore now, and if she wanted, she could have a Captain under her — and for the top spot aboard *Honesty*, Mark Gunney's former command.

Then there was Andrea Kiley to consider. I don't remember if I mentioned in *The Independent Squadron*, or earlier in this book, but she *could* be promoted. That possibility hadn't been revealed in the meeting that had seen Mark Gunney's rise to Captain, because knowing she'd been on Egesta the longest, John and Greg hadn't been certain whether a promotion would be the right move. They'd left that up to Karen and me — the people who'd spent a week with her on that rock.

Now here's one for the neo-suffragists: *no*, she didn't have her promotion held temporarily because she was a *woman* and it was thought she couldn't hack it because she had two 'x' chromosomes. Sorry to disappoint you.

No, any human being who went through those two weeks (remember, she was there for a week before Karen and I arrived) could conceivably be badly affected by watching tens of thousands of deaths take place without having any recourse. If John and Greg rushed her promotion through and she got up to Captain, but then cracked due to psychological trauma, she'd be finished.

So better to be cautious. We did the same for a lot of officers who were on the colony for both weeks — none of them, obviously, as high in rank as Andrea. But after Egesta, many became alcoholics, and a considerable number have taken their own lives over the past twenty years.

We didn't want that sort of fate to befall Andrea.

Anyway, that was another concern we had as we stared at all the personnel file pads scattered on my bed. Much to consider.

"So, where do we start?"

Seemed like the obvious question, so I asked it.

Karen sighed and stepped forward, reaching down to the bed and picking up a pad, "We need to decide if Andrea's being promoted or not. If she is, we have another slot open for movement."

"Ah, yes..." I nodded slowly, staring at the pad in Karen's hand for a moment. The conversation with Mik was coming to mind again.

"We make her a Captain, where do we put her? I suppose the only opening is right here..."

I was narrowing my eyes thoughtfully, and Karen looked at me with a thin smile, "Yes, she'd have to come to *Wolf.*"

Aha. Mik's solution seemed really quite good at that moment. Actually, it seemed *perfect*, because promoting Andrea to Captain and putting her on the bridge would look distinguished on her record — it'd look like she'd been rewarded for exemplary service in defense of civilians on Egesta.

It would also put her in a very safe environment. If problems started to occur, both Karen and I would be there as backup.

"Three skippers on one bridge... why do I get the sense this will lead to headaches?" I started to smile, and Karen chuckled softly.

"I'll call *Friendly* in the morning, I'm pretty sure she's on leave. Now, that leaves us... everything else."

I nodded, "Uh huh... everyone. So. So. Hmm."

Yes, mark that as some of the most intricate dialogue I've ever put on the page.

"Start at the Commanders of the corvettes and work our way down?" I asked slowly, and Karen offered a nod.

"Seems best."

"Right."

"Good."

We stood at the foot of my bed and stared for about a minute at the many pads.

I then looked at Karen, "Hungry?"

"My quarters?" she replied instantly.

"Well, my bed's out of action. Let's go."

We left the scattered pads. It'd take a while to sort all this out.

CHAPTER SEVEN

DEPARTURE

The next morning, Marshal's convoy had assembled just outside the orbit of Belt Two and was preparing to accelerate. Watching the assembly, Greg Noyce was feeling a little anxious. Now this, of course, is Greg Noyce — victor at Deep Black and at the Battle Over Earth, stormer of Imperial palaces and hero of the Empire, so I can tell you with certainty that he wasn't anxious for himself. This run to Mars would be risky, but for reasons that I obviously can't say, Greg had a very good idea of what he'd face.

No, his concern wasn't for his strike force, but for the Trojan horse they were using to get into range: the civilian convoy. Sending fifty virtually unescorted ships laden with goods out into black space between orbits to just hang around and wait… that was making him anxious. If luck ran against those ships, the Martian fleet on the way back from its failed run to Earth would happen across them, and then it'd be mayhem…

But there was no choice. Greg had risked many things in his life, now he decided he had to risk the safety of these civilians. Some very significant targets needed to be dealt with, so Mars had to be attacked. I'll leave it at that.

Anyway, these were the sorts of thoughts Greg tells me were running through his head as he stood on the bridge of *Warspite*, watching the convoy coalesce. Standing next to him was his veteran Flag Captain, Val Rodriguez, and on Battlelink were Becky Afflighen of *Goliath* and Mik. The corvette Commanders hadn't tied in yet — they were herding the convoy ships together and thus were moving in and out of range — but two of them you'll know quite well: Commander Romanov of *Sackville* and Commander Togo of *Generous*. Both were Belt Squadron veterans who'd been with Greg and the rest of us at Deep Black.

"So total cruise time to Point Fun is thirteen days," Mik confirmed on his screen, having just checked with *Cyclops'* Helm and Navigation Officer. "That'll put us at our final destination in fifteen days. And our best guess is that'll be roughly the same time the Martians will be knocking on Earth's door?"

Greg nodded, folding his arms across his chest, "Yes, that's what we know."

"Alright," Mik stroked his goatee, "we'll be ready to pull out at your order."

The conversation, which again was edited to avoid betraying classified information, (just take it as a given that every piece of dialogue about where our intel came from is edited in this book) died off. Ouch, sorry, those brackets really complicated that sentence.

Greg watched on *Warspite's* main screen as the convoy slowly got into column formation, and after about twenty minutes of side-slipping and some complaining from merchant skippers who either didn't know how to maneuver at close quarters or who were stuck next to ships that didn't know how to maneuver at close quarters, things were ready to go.

"Val, move us into escort position. Christian, Becky, at your discretion," Greg delivered his orders with the same old smoothness.

"Message incoming from *Wolf*, realtime for interface into our Battlelink," *Warspite's* Sensors and Communications Officer reported quickly, and Greg simply nodded to get my signal piped into his grid.

The *Warspite*Net screen buffered for a few seconds, then Karen and I appeared on one of the smaller monitors on the battleship's bridge.

"Good hunting out there, all of you," I said rather formally — looking at the recording of it now, it seems a little awkward.

Because that's clearly important.

"Remember," Karen never sounded awkward, "glory can bleach clothes, so don't roll yourselves in too much of it. Or if you do, get your uniforms washed quickly."

Actually, that also sounded kind of awkward... or at least *odd*.

I looked at Karen, "Was that a domestic joke?"

She smiled and shrugged, "I'm trying to branch out."

Greg interrupted us with a chuckle, "Duly noted, Karen. We'll hopefully be back before you set off for Io, but if not, safe journey. Stay in touch."

"Seriously. Look after yourselves, you two," Mik added with a smile and a nod.

"Same to you," I nodded to Mik (as well as anyone can ever nod to anyone on Battlelink) and then I waved to Jim Hannigan. *Wolf's* signal shut down.

Greg turned to Val Rodriguez and opened his mouth to give an order, but his Sensors and Communications Officer interrupted him, "Uhm. Signals from *Nova Scotia* and *Alberta* now."

Within moments, then, Marshal Samuels and Wes Pellew were both on *Warspite's* screens, the old Belt Squadron veterans sending their luck with their old CO, old squadron mates, and so on. It took another ten minutes for Greg to get clear comm channels, and then at last he looked at Val Rodriguez.

"That should do it, let's form up and prepare to boost. Communications, let's get the three corvettes on Battlelink as soon as possible."

I remember watching them go from *Wolf's* bridge, and for around twenty minutes just about every fiber of my being wanted to be going out there with them. Karen had much the same reaction. I don't know if you'll understand what I'm talking about... probably depends on your own life experience. Suffice it to say my instinct was to be out there with my fellow officers, doing the risky raid on Mars.

But I didn't have that option. Neither did Karen, Wes or Marshal. As much as we'd each have liked to be with them, the war demanded other duties from us.

That's why this book isn't really focusing as much as usual on the three of us.

Well, except for the personnel shuffling. But I'll leave that for a little while, because I should send you back to Earth for a meeting that, admittedly, will come out of nowhere, and may not make any sense at all for many books to come.

But it's a meeting I'd recommend you file away in your long-term memory. 'Cause it's important. So important that I shortened 'because' to 'cause' right there for colloquial effect. So important that the editors didn't even change it.

Um. Here we go.

CHAPTER EIGHT

THE MEETING YOU NEED TO REMEMBER FOR MUCH, MUCH LATER

This chapter starts oddly, and I'll tell you why. One of the editors, reading the first draft of this book, asked a perfectly good question: why, exactly, was Daragh Ryan qualified to be a Second Lord? Well, I just about had a conniption. Obviously, everyone knows Daragh Ryan's history, right? Come on, hero of the Empire, mad savior of Venus, bane of pirates...

When I pointed that out to the editor, he shook his head. He was too young. Hadn't heard much about Daragh's career, and didn't know how our mad Irishman got selected for the job.

So, in deference to those of you too young to remember, Daragh was a troublemaker of John's vintage. While John was the responsible and dashing hero at the Belt and at Earth, Daragh was one of Marlene's predecessors at Venus, and he was brilliant at his job. What he became most famous for, of course, was saving Venus from the pirates in the bad old days.

In payment for his great service defending their rich homes, the Lords of Venus decided to make Daragh a Peer (a fellow Lord), and for that reason (and a number of others that I have no business explaining) he then retired from service, to raise horses. Like he said earlier, he sort of failed to buy the horses, but that's irrelevant.

He and John stayed in touch over the years, and John knew the Irishman hadn't lost the knack for Naval works. Daragh just had no interest in coming back to the service while the politics of men like Dave Caldecott were casting such a large shadow. Now, with Dave gone and a real war on, he'd come back... so that's why he was in Admiralty House.

Now, on with the chapter...

Daragh was pacing the corridor with his shotgun leaning against his shoulder. It wasn't loaded — he'd exhausted his supply of blanks in that meeting with the shipbuilders — but he wasn't going to reveal that to anyone. No, that'd take the fun out of it... and the worried looks off the faces of the people walking past him as he paced.

Now I've never managed to find out *why* Daragh was pacing. It was his second day on the job as Second Lord, and it was mid-morning, so there could have been any number of reasons. There had been some problems with violent strike-breakers the night before; the local waste disposal companies in Terra Nova were on strike at the time, and the municipal government had hired some 'private police' to break it, which ended up with Admiral Hirobumi sending SF in to stop a riot. Over 100 people had been injured, twenty of them hospitalized. Daragh's chair was also reportedly uncomfortable (it had been Dave Caldecott's, and the back-adjusting chairs the previous Second Lord liked tended to cause numbness in Daragh's limbs).

And... oh I don't know, Daragh could be pacing for any number of reasons. That was his business, and I shouldn't allow myself to get too distracted.

What matters is that, as he reached the end of one leg of his pacing, he stopped abruptly, turned on his heel, and came face to face with what he called 'a pretty young lass'.

A delightful young lady (translating from Daragh-speak, that means in her 20s) in civilian clothes with an all-access Gold Pass clipped to her lapel, and a huge, beaming bright smile on her face.

"Uh… er, may I be of some help, my girl?"

The young lady shrugged, "I'm looking for the First Lord. But I hear you're the Second Lord, and that means I can probably trust you too, can't I?"

She was *so* toying with him.

Daragh, not sure what to make of this, just barely avoided a frown, "John-boy and I get along well enough, yeah. He's up at *Bonnie* looking things over right now, though, so it'll have to be me."

"Then we should step into your office," the beaming young lady said, and allowing himself to narrow his eyes at her, Daragh nodded.

"Alright. It's over here."

Now, you want me to tell you who this girl is? Nah, I'm leaving you in suspense. This is one of the few occasions when I get to write something in these books that you haven't seen in movies or read about in other books, so you bet I'm going to milk it for all the suspense I can.

Anyway, back to the narrative.

A moment later, Daragh was rounding his desk, and the young lady was closing the door. As Daragh frowned and laid his shotgun on the desk, he waved her to a chair opposite him, "Please have a seat, lass."

"Thank you!" she beamed and sat with cat-like grace.

Still rather suspicious, Daragh lowered himself into his chair. Then he released a string of expletives as the chair back tried to sever his spine. Standing up, he rounded his desk and seated himself in the comfortable seat next to the girl.

"Pardon me, lass, that chair was bought by my predecessor, and it's bloody deadly."

"No worries!"

I think 'bubbly' might be the best way to describe how she was behaving.

"I have to say, Lord Ryan, I've always been a fan. No one, not even the First Lord or Ken Barron or any of the Belt Squadron… *no one* ever got as wild as you out there. It was inspiring!"

As she said this, she reached into her shirt's breast pocket and pulled out a tiny silver strip, then tabbed an unmarked button on it, and laid it on his desk. You've probably seen enough spy movies to know what that sort of thing usually does.

Typically, the unknown person announces, "There, now we may speak freely!"

But the girl didn't, she just kept beaming at Daragh.

After a moment, it got a little tiresome, "So, lass, why would a sweet girl like yourself need to jam recorders in my office?"

"Basically, I want security to think right now I'm doing something very inappropriate, because I'm a big fan."

Daragh's eyes narrowed right down to slits, "Is that a fact? That's a shotgun on my desk, you know. You're not gonna take me easily."

Now I realize that statement could be interpreted incorrectly, so let me tell you what Daragh was thinking — 'take me' wasn't the inappropriate connotation. He assumed that he'd let an assassin, who was using her looks and her jammer to get a clean shot at him, into his office. He had no idea why she'd do such a thing, but that was the best hypothesis he had at the moment.

"Your shotgun's empty," the young lady smiled, sliding her hand into her pants pocket as she said it, and pulling out a mini-disk. "You need to take this and give it to John. It's his insurance against the Emperor."

Talk about coming out of left field.

"Excuse me?" Daragh's mind — which had been trying to figure out if he could break this girl in two as easily as it looked like he could — changed gears instantly.

"Last fall, when he and Greg went into the Emperor's palace. That's his insurance. Everything I hear says the Emperor's going to try to take him down as soon as this war's done. That'll protect him. And you, by extension, m'Lord."

She extended the disk towards Daragh, and he took it, "I think callin' me Daragh would be fine, lass. This is insurance?"

She nodded again and, I should mention, was still beaming. She's *so* good.

"But if it's not going to be useful until after the war... why are you givin' it to us now?"

The perfect smile twitched just a fraction, "I'm going to the Belt, and I may not come back. So I just wanted to make sure that was in safe hands before I went, because if I do come back, I don't want John in a noose."

"A *noose?*" Daragh was still unsure of what to think, and understandably so.

The girl nodded quickly, "A noose. Now I really have to get going, it's been a pleasure meeting you, Daragh."

She started to stand, but Daragh's hand closed around her wrist. That'll just go to show you that he wasn't slowing down too much as he got on in years — he beat her super-spy honed senses.

Though I'm pretty sure she'd have snapped his head off in a second if she'd needed to. I mean come on, you *must* have figured out by now who we're dealing with.

"I'll ask you once, lass, and I'm willin' to bet I wouldn't be able to force an answer, so I'll *just* ask. Who are you?"

Her smile, according to Daragh, faded for just that one second, and she let out a sigh, the way a normal human might if she were nervous, "Haley Briand. Tell John to watch out."

Daragh didn't recognize the name — he wouldn't, he'd left the service while she was still a kid, if not before she was born. Even so, he had an ability to detect an honest voice, and to read a person — even a superagent as well practiced as Haley.

So he nodded, "I'll personally see to it he's safe, lass. Safe journey out to the Belt, and good luck with whatever mission Thea has you on."

'Thea' was Thea Fostopolos, Admiral of Defense Command's Intelligence section.

Haley forced her smile to restore itself, "Oh Daragh, even Thea doesn't know what I have to do. I hope I'll see you again some day."

And with that, she left.

How's that for cryptic? Remember this meeting.

CHAPTER NINE
BONNIE LADY

There's never been a warship *anywhere* quite so magnificently grand as *DCNS Bonaventure*, or *Bonnie*, as she's known. Yes, I'm sorry this battleship has been labeled a 'she'. Don't know if that's politically correct or insensitive or some such thing, but it's just the way it is.

Bonaventure is the most powerful ship in the solar system — the flagship of our fleet — and… well… she's just incredible. If it's bad to refer to something that formidable and honored as female, then I just don't know what to say. Judge for yourself, I suppose.

Cruising up towards this mighty lady in the second seat of an F-194D Starlight, John Fiora had to smile.

I don't know if words can quite do justice to the experience a fleet officer has the first time she or he sees *Bonnie* up close. That probably sounds incredibly odd to civilian readers, but it's just the way it is. Wait, I said 'it's just the way it is' two paragraphs ago. My editors hate it when I repeat stuff… but… well… it *is* the way it is. Oh great, now I've done it three times. There's a wrist-slap coming…

When any fleet officer sees a Defense Command ship, there's a certain wash of pride — a little bit of breath getting taken away. It never quite gets old, or mundane… there's something powerful, elegant and majestic about Defense Command warships that just inspires awe.

And *Bonnie* was truly the greatest of Defense Command's vessels. Don't mistake me — I love *Friendly* and *Wolf* deeply, they're truly exceptional ships and they were with me through a lot. But seeing *Bonaventure* is like going aboard HMS *Victory* in London, or one of the old United States museum ships. Or for a more obscure comparison, like going aboard HMCS *Sackville* (the namesake of the Belt Squadron's *Sackville*) in Halifax.

There's just a little more magic.

So while I personally would always choose *Wolf* as my favorit*est*-ever ship, no Defense Command officer will ever say a bad word about *Bonnie*.

I don't know if this is getting my point across… alright, one editors says 'HELL YES YOU HAVE HAMMERED IT ACROSS — GET OFF IT ALREADY'. Suffice it to say that John was little short of awestruck by the massive, almost white, shining warship that he was approaching.

Anyway, let's fast-forward past the proud gazes and John leaning forward and tapping his pilot, Commander Sophie Ayala, on the shoulder and grinning, "I'm the one who made sure she happened."

He had every right to take the credit, of course — he was the one who'd taken the situation by the horns, and when Douglas Pope had been elected to office in 2229, had convinced the new cabinet to change *Bonnie* from a carrier to her current form…

Sorry, I said fast-forward, didn't I?

As soon as the space doors closed behind John's plane in *Bonaventure's* landing bay, an honor guard of thirty SF rushed out of the observation lounge to meet him. Ayala easily set the Starlight down on the deck, and then the canopy popped and John carefully climbed over the side, onto the wing and then down to the deck.

The SF snapped to attention and saluted, so he waved back loosely, "As you were. Captain's not here yet?"

The hatch at the far side of the bay seemed to open on cue, and Lennox Williams, Flag Captain to the First Lord, entered.

I probably don't need to introduce Lennox Williams to anyone today, though I will explain who he is just in case someone's been living under a rock in a cave in the unexplored belt or something. You know, like the people who didn't know who Daragh was.

Captain Lennox Williams was one of the most decorated battleship commanders around. Despite having been attached to the Home Fleet for his whole career, he'd always managed to find fights. He'd been out to the Belt and to Venus rather frequently, and he tended to destroy pirates wherever he went.

Now he'd been handed the proverbial keys to the most powerful battleship in the history of the solar system, and he was happy about that.

Quickly crossing the bay, Lennox stuck out his hand for John to take, "Come up to check on me, John?"

Did I mention Lennox is a member of the Fiora ring? And moreover, he's Trinidadian, so he's friendly and relaxed about most things.

"We're going to do some shooting in a couple of weeks, Lennie. I just want to see how shiny she'll be when we go out there."

Grinning very brightly (literally, if you've never seen a picture of Lennox's bright white teeth just think 'reflection of midday sun on field of fresh snow'), Lennox nodded, "She'll be as shiny as you'd like her to be, that I can promise. But Lynn has told me work on *Hibernia* is still behind schedule."

Rear Admiral Lynn Boakai had been appointed to command the squadron of *Bonaventures*, giving up her position as Fifth Lord of the Admiralty to do so. Some people have asked me what a Fifth Lord does, and now seems an appropriate time to explain.

Fifth Lord of the Admiralty is the job given to someone who has reached Flag rank, who is deemed too valuable to lose, but for whom there's no available command. Instead of putting these people on half-pay retirement (usually forcing them to look for other work), you make them Fifth Lord, and they just do odd jobs until a new command rolls around.

Lynn had been headed for the Venus Squadron, though she wasn't one of Marlene Stoll's protégés, or part of the Fiora ring. She'd been elevated to Rear Admiral in 2229, when John was working on increasing the size of the Venus force to two squadrons, but when the parliamentary support for that had fallen through, they'd discovered she'd been promoted out of any job left in the fleet. As the most junior Rear Admiral, she was at the bottom of the list for all possible assignments. Lacking any political allies, she had no way to get bumped ahead in line.

But John didn't want to lose her talent, so he'd made her Fifth Lord.

Now she got official command of *Bonaventure* Squadron (officially called the Assault

Squadron of the Home Fleet, but we all know the force as *Bonnie's* Squadron).

Of course, for the coming mission, John would have overall force control; to avoid the confusion and risk of having the fleet and squadron commander on the same ship, Lynn had elected to fly her flag from *Terra Nova*.

Anyway, that's a whole lot of exposition around just one name. What's critical at this point is the fact that *Bonnie* was pretty much ready to fight, while other ships in the squadron were less well off.

As John and Lennox headed for the exit hatch, the Captain provided the Admiralty Lord with a more complete run-down of where things were in terms of progress. There was still plenty to be done — the installation of showers and kitchen equipment being some of the most important.

What you need to take away from this chapter, though, is what Lennox said to John as they stepped out of the hatch, "The weapons have been fully tested though, John. We're ready with our lasers."

At that remark John smiled, "Then we're going to win this fight."

"Yes, we are."

The pair headed off to tour the decks of the massive *Bonaventure*.

It took over four hours.

CHAPTER TEN

TRADING HUMAN BEINGS — LEGALLY!

Picture a dark room with a poker table in the middle of it. Alright, now turn the poker table into a briefing table, lit from above with no other lights on in the room. All moody and atmospheric, right? Good.

See, if I was an actual writer — not a hack — I could have described that to you without actually asking you to imagine it.

Anyway, at that table sat Karen and I, and Wes and Sharon Stanton, but it wasn't a happy setting. No, Wes and Sharon were on one side of the table, Karen and I on the other, and in the middle were stacks of personnel files.

We were divvying up the old Belt Squadron's people.

Let me explain: Wes had a whole new squadron to put together, and he had his pick of officers and crews from around the fleet. Obviously he wasn't personally choosing every single person — there were thousands of ratings to be brought in — but he was picking certain people he'd met over the years and wanted to work with. The idea here was that he could build a core staff of officers and NCOs he knew and trusted, and those people could help build the cohesive crews needed to run the elite ships of the Independent Squadron.

But there was a problem with this: for much of his career, Wes had worked in the Belt Squadron, and now that version of the Belt Squadron (as opposed to the version Marshal now commanded) was *my* Jupiter Force — he wanted my people!

So we were horse trading. Except for people. So we were people trading. Which sounds much less insulting than 'horse' trading in this context. Whoops…

Alright, wait a minute.

Sorry, I'm sitting here trying to write this as if we were facing off, Wes and Sharon and Karen and me… like it was some battle for people, no-holds-barred and ending in fisticuffs. That's the amusing mental image I always get when I think about this sort of personnel-sharing, but to be honest, there wasn't much drama in it at all.

What was I saying about being a hack?

"So I'm basically going to gut *Cheetah* on you, Ken," Wes sat back in his chair, half-wincing. "Sorry…"

I should probably confess at this point that the room was normally lit, and there was no moody, grim atmosphere… just the usual breathable kind.

"Hey, you'll need them. You're going to have a lot of new faces, it's good you'll be able to keep some familiar ones around."

See, not much drama.

"So who are you leaving us?" Karen asked pleasantly (even though when I read that question to myself it sounds like it has a bit of an edge).

Wes had a pile of pads in front of him, and he now lifted and tossed them casually across the table to us, "Most senior is Kate Levec, my Sensors and Communications Officer. She's great — knows the ins and outs of *Cheetah*... I think she'll be able to keep the ship together for Mark until he settles in."

I've never actually asked Wes why he let Kate Levec stay — I would have brought her with me in a minute, but then I'm very selfish. Wes was leaving us good people, despite his desperate need for experienced veterans in the new Independent Squadron.

"I'll also leave Marcus Atallah for you."

Another huge gift — I don't know if you remember Major Atallah of Special Branch from his brief encounter with Captain Bahim in *The Independent Squadron*, but he was a hell of a good officer. We got to keep him.

"You don't need his experience?" Karen was just avoiding frowning, and Wes shrugged.

"We're getting a company in from Earth that will take over Special Branch operations for all our ships. Single coherent unit if we ever need to put them on the ground at once."

He didn't have to say any more than that — Karen and I both understood. Special Branch units generally operate in twelves or sixes, but they're technically organized into companies of ninety-six. These companies train together at Special Branch schools at Sandhurst and the Sea of Tranquility, and thus can work well together in the field.

Not that Special Branchers who haven't trained together can't be equally elite — Charlie has great rapport with, among others, Marcus Atallah of *Cheetah* and Sandy Korpela of *Lion*, even though I've barely mentioned the first guy up to now, and I'm fairly certain I've not mentioned Sandy at all.

Well, they worked together really well, you've just not had the chance to see it yet. And you won't... I mean... I'll explain later.

"Alright, so we keep Marcus and Kate, you're taking most of the rest?"

Wes nodded at my question, "I'll be spreading them across the squadron. I'm willing to bet they're going to give us a lot of new recruits."

With eight Independent Squadron ships to crew from scratch, Wes was right: it was almost inevitable that he'd be sent a lot of new recruits, wet behind the ears and untested. Many people don't know where personnel come from in the service — when we build a new ship, who crews it?

Well, there's always a cushion of about 100,000 personnel in make-work jobs (like Fifth Lord, actually) — people we don't want to lose from the service, so we stick them in PR roles (they're the ones you see doing military-like things in the recruiting vids) or have them act as liaisons with commercial firms. Those are pretty cushy jobs, so they encourage veteran spacers to stay on with the service, and to wait around for a new ship to come along.

With the war effort ramping up and the four *Bonaventure*-class ships being brought online at the moment, that 100,000 had been used up pretty quickly. The next source of personnel came from the reserves — the 'Saturday night spacers', as they're unfairly called. These are people who, for one weekend a month, go on orbital maneuvers around their home world or station, and who are usually involved in space travel in their civilian lives. They'd be called up, and they'd be alright...

However, with all the new ships being built, these crews were already being trained for specific assignments. They would form semi-experienced cores of personnel for the new vessels that were being constructed, with the rest of the crews around them being filled in with raw recruits — kids who had come through accelerated completion training at the academies, and people who'd enlisted when the war started and who were just coming off their five-week crash course on being a Defense Command rating.

Because the Independent Squadron would already have that core of experienced people (taken from *Cheetah*, mostly), Wes was almost inevitably going to see his own ships topped up with similarly inexperienced personnel. He needed all the experience he could get, so commandeering only eighty percent (or so) people off *Cheetah* was really incredibly reasonable of him. He had a lot of work ahead.

"I'm also pulling some good people off Belt Two base," Sharon put in helpfully at that moment. "I wasn't the only spacer down there who wanted to get back on a ship."

I nodded, "Good. Well, I'll probably draw on some of the recruits coming in to fill the holes aboard *Cheetah*, but we'll be alright…"

I could get into more of what we said to each other, the discussions we had about who might be good in what jobs and such, but I imagine you must already be pretty bored. I mean, this is a boardroom meeting, which I know is automatically boring, and it's about personnel assignments. I find this stuff interesting because I'm a very wrong person. Yes *wrong*.

I give up, next chapter.

CHAPTER ELEVEN

THREE PROMOTIONS

Yes I know, more personnel talk. Sorry. It has just occurred to me that I don't think most people have any idea how folks like us get our jobs, or move between jobs, and some of you might be interested to know. If you're not interested… well… hang in there. I'm sure Martian-shooting will come soon.

Meantime, aren't you just a little curious about who was leaving *Wolf's* bridge crew? Some for the last time…

Karen and I were standing in my cabin again, with the piles of pads still scattered on my bed and a list of open positions in the command level ranks behind us on a screen. This was about two hours after our meeting with Wes and Sharon.

"So Mark's skipper of *Cheetah*, we know that…" I was repeating the most obvious observation. Helpful.

Karen nodded, toying with her ponytail as it sat on her left shoulder, "And his only request to us was that Aaron Ashby be promoted to take over *Honesty*."

Mark Gunney, remember, had been promoted to Captain and was leaving his old corvette *Honesty* behind; his only request was that his former XO, Lieutenant Commander Ashby, be promoted to Commander to take over. That was reasonable — Ashby knew the ship and was a solid officer.

"Done."

I leaned forward, grabbed Ashby's pad off the bed, and tossed it onto the chair.

"One down."

Karen 'mmhmmed' and nodded, "So, logically, we stay with Mark. He's going to need good officers for *Cheetah*, because we'll have to fill out that crew with a lot of recruits."

Since Wes was keeping four-fifths of *Cheetah's* crew for the Independent Squadron, we'd have a lot of recruits in that ship. That meant we'd need good officers over there to help break in the new people.

"So, XO… probably a Lieutenant Commander we should promote to Commander," I glanced at Karen and she nodded again.

This was the sort of question we had to deal with. Mark had filed no specific request for his new XO — he didn't feel too strongly about who he should work with. Mark's the sort of guy who can work with almost anyone, and he trusted we wouldn't give him someone who fell outside the 'almost'.

"Well," I started and stopped. Who would we lose?

Oh, it was *we* — *Wolf* — who would lose, because Karen and I had decided to leave *Lion's* command staff alone. We were already shaking up the staffs of two frigates, we didn't need to mess with a third, especially considering Kris was still only just settling in over there.

"Well, we could give him Jim or Erica, I guess," Karen sounded just as reluctant as I felt.

I nodded. Both of those officers had been with me since my days aboard *Friendly*, but now our classic roles had to change. In past, we'd been able to advance our ranks but stay together — Erica, for instance, had been Helm and Navigation Officer on *Friendly* as a Lieutenant, and then on *Wolf* as a Lieutenant Commander. Now, to advance further, she'd have to take on an entirely new job.

"We also have *Friendly* to consider," that popped into my head too. Andrea Kiley was coming to *Wolf* remember, so there was an opening for a Commander on the bridge of my old corvette.

"Why do I get the sinking feeling that my command staff is going away?" I asked halfheartedly as the reality of who'd need to go where started sinking in.

Karen patted me on the shoulder, "There there."

She sounded *so* sincere, it was hilarious.

Huffing, I grabbed three pads off my bed and glanced at Karen. She then nodded in approval. But that wasn't the end of it. The nature of the promotions demanded we make a big deal out of them. We had to deliver the news in person, over-dramatically if possible, just for pure devilment.

It took us about twenty minutes to draw up the official papers, get them printed off and all the rest of it. Printed, you ask? Yes. It's a Naval tradition. We always give new assignments on paper in folders, never by pad. Some people use pads, but they're just not as classy as Karen and me.

I realized, on the second draft of this book, that I may have offended a lot of officers by saying they're not classy. Sorry.

But you're not classy. So there.

Yes, I said it. Though admittedly in saying it, I probably proved I don't have any class either. Please don't challenge me to more duels, I tire of them. Anyway.

Erica Martin was sitting down to an early dinner when we knocked on her cabin door. She'd pulled the late evening watch shift on the bridge, so she was feeding herself early while she watched her messages from home.

I don't think I've ever had occasion to mention, but Erica was happily married, had been since 2228, when Karen and I had both attended the wedding at Belt Two. Her spouse and their two young daughters were now living on Belt Two, but Erica didn't get down to see them much during the week — while we were in local space, she only went down on the weekends.

When we knocked on her hatch, she quickly came to the door, still chewing. The hatch swung open, Karen and I smiled, and Karen handed her a folder, "Good news is you're a Commander now. Bad news is we're losing you."

She contained what must have been a rush of relief at the prospect of getting away from us with a surprised look, "Really?"

"You're Mark's new XO. Effective as soon as we can find someone to take over for you. He'll need you around to get things organized over there as soon as Wes makes his move to *Nova Scotia* permanent," I imagine I was beaming proudly. I probably haven't conveyed how much history Erica and I had — as an Ensign, she'd been the one who'd flown me over to *Friendly* for the very first time, and she'd virtually been my Helm and

Navigation Officer since then.

She started to smile, and we chatted a bit more, but we left her quickly to think about the implications of what we'd just done. Some implications she'd have no idea about.

Anyway, we'd have to find Jim next.

Jim Hannigan was on the rec deck. He'd taken the morning watch, and because we were in Belt Two local space, there wasn't much reason for him to hang around the bridge when he wasn't on duty. There were far too many ships and sensor arrays around here for us to worry about getting jumped by surprise, so he could afford to relax.

Now, I don't want to, uhm, tarnish Jim's reputation at all.

Well.

I mean.

Sorry, this is awkward for me. When we found Jim, he was sitting in the Officer's Club on the rec deck with a half-interested Lieutenant Commander Adrienne Thompson, of Wolfstar Squadron. He'd managed, through a force of courage beyond anything I could have summoned, to ask Adrienne to have a drink with him, and, well, they weren't a match.

Yes, he had been thinking in terms of *match*.

The conversation was pretty much dead by the time Karen and I slipped into the half-empty Officer's Club — any time Jim brought up something, the subject ended up side-slipping into work.

"Oh yes, I love kittens too... they purr like finely-tuned mags... speaking of which, have you heard about that new tuning configuration. It's supposed to increase efficiency by eleven percent..."

I made that dialogue up, but based on what Jim told me later, it wasn't far off the truth. Ever been in a restaurant or somewhere and watch a first date crash and burn? Hell, ever been on a crash-and-burn yourself? I personally haven't, but I don't date. Poor Jim.

Of course, that's all beside the point, because Karen and I were about to change the complexion of his day.

Karen appeared behind Adrienne in a flourish, planting her hands on the Lieutenant Commander's shoulders in a surprisingly casual fashion, "Sorry, Adrienne, we're going to have to interrupt."

She played it big, so I felt obliged to do the opposite. I walked up behind Jim, came to a stop next to him, dropped the folder onto his table, and said (with no emotion at all): "Congratulations."

I think I sounded unimpressed, and Karen smiled ear to ear to compensate. We may well have scared the bejesus out of poor Jim. Or maybe just freaked him out.

I could just imagine someone asking how the date went.

"How'd the date go? Oh I got attacked by my two Flag Officer COs, one a dead-faced psychopath and the other a smiling lunatic. Went great."

Poor Jim. You'll be hearing those words a lot in the next number of books. That's what happens when someone is stuck too close to Karen and me.

We didn't wait around for a reaction — we were interrupting a date, so we turned and walked away (adding to the freakiness of our delivery, no doubt). I did notice, as we slipped out the door, that Adrienne was raising a glass to toast his promotion. That was something, anyway.

Just for the record, there was no second date for those two. Lovely people, just not quite compatible.

Matt Baxter was on the bridge, talking to Lieutenant Kyle Stranks. Kyle, remember, had taken over for Matt after the Briton's promotion to XO.

So this was appropriate, I suppose.

Karen and I arrived on the bridge and tried to creep up behind our good friend Matt, but he instinctively knew we were there, and he turned with a stern glare, "What the bloody hell are you two at?"

Ah, Matt.

Glancing at Karen with a smile, I pulled the folder from behind my back (where I'd been holding it in a very, very clever attempt to hide it) and handed it to Mister Baxter.

Scowling, Matt grabbed it from me, opened it, read the pertinent few lines, closed it, and glared at us, "You think it'll be that bloody easy to get me off your backs?!"

I actually replied to that with, "Um."

Karen shrugged, "We. Uh. We'll always remember what you said about doing 'stupid stuff'..."

"Yes you bloody well will, because I'll be close. Even if I'm on *Friendly*, I'll still have my people in this crew. You'll never find out who all of them are, until they get in your way next time you try to get yourselves bloody killed!"

Jeeze. I think Karen and I were both leaning slightly backward — the way you do when someone's yelling at you but you find it amusing... does that ever happen in any other context? I don't know. But it was happening here.

"So. You accept?" I asked after the ranting sputtered out.

Frowning, Matt nodded, "I suppose. Just know I'll still be watching you."

In the entire history of Defense Command promotions, two things are reasonably distinct about Matt's appointment as Commander of *Friendly*. First, he'd only been a full Commander for a few months — it was a pretty short period of time at that rank for someone to get moved over to ship command, though not unheard of. Aaron Ashby, for instance, was being promoted straight into it.

Entirely unique, though, was that at the receipt of his promotion, Matt had begun yelling at a Commodore and a Rear Admiral. First of all, most people who've just been promoted are a little too happy to yell, and then it's a rare Commander who can more or less threaten (in a parental fashion) his or her Flag Officers without getting thrown out of the service.

I was going to miss Matt. A *lot*. But it felt good putting him on the bridge of *Friendly*, and Jim would make a very fine XO for *Wolf*.

So there we have it, the first round of personnel shifts. In one fell swoop, Karen and I had sent away our XO and Helm and Navigation Officer, and had promoted our Sensors and Communications Officer out of his job.

When we got back to my cabin a little later, I looked at one of my clocks, "We decided to do all that just over an hour ago. And now it's done. Think we should have put more thought and reflection into it?"

I glanced at Karen as I asked the question, and for a moment she was still.

We looked somberly at each other for a second, and then together we shook our heads.

"Nah."

We started looking at the rest of the pads on my bed.

CHAPTER TWELVE

THE NEXT WEEK

So this feels awkward... I can't really fill in the next ten days of story with much more than little vignettes. Usually in one of these books, I can handle boring long travel by remembering some anecdotes about what Karen and I were doing to pass the time, but we weren't traveling. I can relay some more details about the personnel swapping that was going on at Belt Two, but I wanted to take a break from that for a moment... there was so much of it and I just couldn't figure out what was worth telling you.

So instead of making this chapter a continuous narrative, let's jump around to various places for a handful of short scenes that'll prove important later.

First up, Marshal Samuels getting home after a long day at the office.

I've talked about Marshal plenty in these books so far. But I've mentioned his wife, Mel, just once (I checked) and that was in passing in *The Independent Squadron*.

Well, I've cleared this with her, and with DCI, so now I can fill in a few of the blanks behind who she was.

Anyone who watched the Belt Two news, particularly the sports beat, would know Mel Samuels as the coach of the Belt Two Imperial Games gymnastics team. That was just her cover, her 'legend' if you wish to use the proper term.

Mel was DCI, had been for years. She was well regarded in the service for her ability, like our friend Haley Briand, to play any part, and, if need be, to deal ruthlessly with anyone. She also had, to quote her favorite compliment, the 'stealthy skill of the ninja'.

Marshal had first met her back in the Belt Squadron days, when he'd just taken over *Alberta* — in a raid of a pirate base, he'd personally taken her prisoner. Once aboard ship, she'd revealed that she wasn't in fact a pirate skipper, but a DCI plant. He'd confirmed her story, seen to it that she escaped, and then she'd helped us track down Grant Merger's fleet to start the chase that led to the Battle of Deep Black.

This is, I believe, the first time she's gotten credit for that excellent work. Publicly, anyway. You could say revealing it is putting her at risk, but it's not as though she and Marshal aren't high profile enough as it is.

Besides, she's DCI.

I bring all of this up because it has an important connection to something else. Because she'd been visible as an infiltrator in pirate ranks, Mel had moved into Counter-Intelligence — it was decided it would be too risky to put her deep undercover with pirates again after she'd betrayed the Syndicate fleet, so she was now running Belt Two's Counter-Intelligence Office, making sure pirate and Martian spies didn't get any information out of us. That job made her the top spy in the whole of the Belt colonies, and any good DCI agent on his or her way through would have to at least let Mel know that he or she was coming.

So, as Marshal walked in the door of the house they had on Belt Two (which he usually only got down to on weekends), Mel walked out of the living room, "Just got a call from DCI Central. Apparently we've got a top girl coming through in a couple of weeks."

Just take a guess on who she was talking about.

Marshal, being Marshal, half-grinned, "In a couple of weeks? You're already here!"

Smooth, Marshal. Very smooth.

While Marshal was getting that news, Greg Noyce and Mik Mikaelsen were sitting in their cabins on realtime comm, about four days out from the point where they'd have to split off from the convoy and head for Mars.

"Leaving a ship behind to protect the convoy would probably be the best idea," Greg had been reflecting more on his concerns for the safety of the civilian shipping, and that was the conclusion he'd come to. Mik, being the only other Flag Officer with Greg's force, was the natural person from whom to get a second opinion.

Stroking his goatee (which was fine by regs, by the way, for those who asked after *The Hawke Mission* if DC officers can have beards), Mik nodded, "I can't disagree with that. One of the corvettes?"

Nodding slowly on the screen, Greg looked down at a pad he was holding (that you can't see in the vid), "The most logical choice for that job would be *Sackville*, as it is the oldest and probably the slowest ship we have at our disposal."

Mik narrowed his eyes thoughtfully at that suggestion. There was no question that Katya Romanov's corvette was technically the least-suited ship in the force to include in a raid on Mars — it was quite old, even if it had been overhauled.

But what about Guy Vivar?

I know, I made a big deal earlier about how Mik was keeping that kid closer to *Cyclops* in order to make sure he didn't cause trouble for someone else, but this was different than just a deployment. Mik hadn't known when he'd cruised out to Belt Two that he'd be taking *Cyclops* and *Nanton* into this sort of fight. Attacking Mars, even a relatively under-defended Mars, might be too much for Vivar to handle.

And *Nanton* was only slightly newer than *Sackville*.

What would Vivar do if placed in convoy command? He might screw it up, and put a lot of lives on the line. But if he went into Mars space with the battleships, he might screw up just the same, and in the process he could get some of the battlewagons damaged or destroyed.

Mik had to decide which would be a worse disaster for the Empire: losing all that cargo and the innocent lives of the commercial crews, or losing battleships and crews that would be difficult to replace, and that could turn the tide of the war. Not an easy question.

My first (and ultimately final) instinct would be to protect the battleships. Yes, I'm painfully aware of the lives that would be put at risk, but they'd still have more of an escort than the original plan had called for, and the unfortunate truth was they were replaceable. We needed the battlewagons to win the war, saving a great many more lives than were risked in that convoy.

And Mik agreed.

"Of our three sloop Commanders, I have the least confidence in Commander Vivar... if we're going to send one ship with the convoy, it's probably better that it's him."

It was Greg's turn to narrow his eyes, "Been keeping him close to you to make sure he stays out of trouble?"

See, Greg was a good CO — he understood Mik's progressive thinking.

But when you were flying into Mars space for a gunfight, you had to make tough and merciless calls like this one.

"Yep," Mik nodded his confirmation. "I'll send him orders to that effect."

And that was settled.

Greg and Mik had other things to discuss, but that's about all I need to pass on from them. Well, at least all I can tell you... you know... without revealing state secrets about their sources of information...

I think it was about a day after this that I was walking down a corridor of Belt Two base with Wes. We'd gone for lunch at one of the posher restaurants in the main dome, and now were back and awaiting the arrival of the first of the new personnel who were being shipped in from reserves across the Belt. These were our first new people, and Wes and I had decided it'd be a good idea to welcome them to Belt Two personally, before we started dividing them up into their new assignments.

It was also a great excuse to get a fancy lunch. But then, as Wes and I both discovered (as we do every time we have the brilliant idea of getting an expensive meal on the Fleet's tab) fancy food doesn't agree with us.

Anyway, we were walking towards the receiving lounge in Belt Two base, and our conversation had turned towards the subject of personnel. Being my worrisome self, I'd gotten off onto a quiet tangent about Andrea Kiley.

"...so we're bringing her aboard *Wolf* as Captain, so we can both keep an eye on her," my tone was quiet, as I obviously didn't want what I was saying to be easily overheard.

Wes was restraining his concerned frown to avoid drawing undue attention, "Well, if you're worried about her, you could get her checked out."

I shook my head, "I don't trust any of the doctors around here."

I didn't need to elaborate on that; Wes understood my reluctance. Just to reiterate the point again, a single visit to a fleet psychologist could potentially end someone's fighting career. I know, today everybody goes to see the head-doctors, and they often get important help from them. But the prejudices and politics of 2232 weren't as forgiving. I didn't want Andrea stuck at a desk for the rest of the war if she didn't need to be. It would have killed her.

Actually, when I thought 'it'd kill her' at that time, I'd had no idea how right I was.

Her job, her command, was giving her a reason to *not* self-destruct. Or to do less self-destructing, perhaps. Giving her *Wolf* was in one regard a vote of confidence — something telling her that we still believed in her, that she shouldn't give up.

And Wes, reading into my simple remark, understood all of this. That's one reason I was somewhat *miffed* about the breakup of the old Belt Squadron. Don't get me wrong, I was immensely happy for Wes and for Marshal, but I'd miss the intuitive understanding we shared. That sort of relationship takes the right people and a long time to forge.

But that's not for the moment.

Wes slowed to a stop in the corridor, his face growing grim for just a moment, "Alright. But Ken listen, if you think she needs help, tell her to come see me. We'll talk. If... if it's conscience... if it's guilt. I know how to get through that. And I know what it can do to someone."

I smiled sadly at the words — he surely did. After everything with Sara... But I'm not really sure if I should get into that. I'll have to check with him, and even if he okays it, I'll save it for now.

Anyway, I took a deep breath and nodded, "Thanks. Hope we won't have to send her to you."

Half-shrugging, Wes started to walk again, "Just don't be afraid to. If she needs it, better we help her than someone who'll get her chained to a desk."

That was great advice, as Wes always gives. We walked on somberly, and after a few moments managed to shake the grim subject from our minds. At least for now.

It was three days before Mik and Greg would split off from the convoy and head for Mars.

CHAPTER THIRTEEN
CIVIL DEFENSE

John Fiora and Daragh Ryan were supposed to be meeting to discuss the state of Earth's civil defenses. This made a great deal of sense. In a few days, Greg and Mik would be peeling away from the convoy they were supposedly escorting and would be on their way to Mars. Around that same time, John *guessed* (you know what I mean) the Martians would be boosting out of their local space and coming for Earth.

The climactic battle was less than a week away.

You'd therefore expect John and Daragh to be quite focused — every waking hour being spent thinking through another nuance of the defense of the realm.

Well, not *quite*.

"I told you to order yourself a new coat, man, and yet you didn't when I said to!"

Yes. Coat.

"Well, I've been preoccupied preparing the defense of Earth. *Coat* was low on the priority list."

"And now they're back-ordered through to March. So you're stuck with that shabby old thing you wore when you came to get me at home, aren't you? I'm after forgetting, was that a warm one?"

John harrumphed and shook his head, saying nothing. This subject — that of John's new coat — had come from a perfectly legitimate conversation about supply requisitions. Daragh and John had been discussing how the orders of new war materiel were going.

Actually, this is a good excuse for another one of my patented asides. Today's subject: war materiel.

Notice how 'materiel' isn't spelled 'material' — I don't know how familiar people are with the term materiel, but it essentially means manufactured goods you need to fight a war. Often when I discuss the problems of supply during the war with people, they assume that I'm talking about things like mag cells and torpedoes, combat rations and all the rest.

But it's not just those. Boots, socks, tunics, and of course *coats* are also part of the problem. If you're mobilizing a few million recruits over the course of a couple of years, you need to give them something to wear, right? Yes. You definitely do.

This meant that Defense Command Supply's stocks of things like coats had gone out to the first wave of recruits, and new orders were being put in with civilian and military suppliers to get thousands of replacements.

So now John had to wait to replace his old coat... unless...

"I'm First Lord, I'll just order someone to *buy one* for me. From a store if they have to. With lots of pockets. You should have a pocket for everything, Daragh!"

"They have pockets for egos? I could do to hide mine..."

That drew a laugh from both Lords, which was quite good.

As you can tell, they weren't stressed quite yet. Remember back in *The Almost Coup*, John was storming Imperial palaces without so much as elevated blood pressure. At his level of experience, you're just too cool under pressure, or that's my interpretation of it anyway.

Even so, they did need to consider the defense of the realm. The transition was seamless.

"So the *Bonnies* will be ready in time for the fight," Daragh was repeating what they both knew in that statement, and John nodded at the change of subject.

"Lynn has the builders on a short leash. The ships will be ready."

Lynn, of course, was Vice Admiral Lynn Boakai, who I think I already introduced.

"Got a plan yet?" Daragh had a habit of asking the tough questions quite bluntly, and with a smile John shrugged.

"We're going to beat the Martians."

I laughed when John told me that — if you're familiar at all with your nineteenth century history (you all must be, certainly!), you might remember that a similar quote was attributed to the Duke of Wellington on the morning before he defeated Napoleon at Waterloo. Asked by his second in command — Lord Uxbridge, I think — what his plan was, he supposedly said 'to beat the French'.

John has a great sense of history.

But the joke fell pretty flat, "I'm no damned Uxbridge. You're going to bloody well *tell me* your plan, or I'm going home and puttin' out a real minefield to keep you away this time!"

Dammit. It's fun using obscure historical references until someone tosses them back in your face.

"Alright, fine," John leaned back in his chair (did I mention they were in John's office? I'm sorry, I'm terrible at this scene-setting). "I'm taking the *Bonnies* out to meet the attack force from Mars. The Heavy Squadron is going out on the Mercury vector."

Pulling a pad off John's desk, Daragh looked at some things I can't describe, "Dividing your forces before the enemy?"

John nodded, "Since we [can guess confidently] about the dispositions of the two Martian forces coming at us, yes, I am."

"Putting an awful lot of faith in those [guesses], though. As long as you're comfortable with it, I suppose… you're [probably] going to be outnumbered with the *Bonnies* when you vector for Mars, though. They'll [most likely] come at you with six battleships from their home fleet."

John smiled, "Well, nothing in the Heavy Squadron would keep up with us. And we're all tougher than them anyway."

A fair amount of historical allusion actually went unsaid in that short sentence. If you get a chance sometime, look up a battle called 'Dogger Bank' — or at least that's the English name for it. First World War, Admiral David Beatty of the British Royal Navy against Admiral Franz von Hipper in a battlecruiser fight.

You may remember from *The Almost Coup* that the battlecruisers from our time were lightly armored but heavily gunned. Same story then. But at Dogger Bank, Hipper came with his squadron of battlecruisers *and* a slower armored cruiser… think of that as a big frigate… because it was assumed he needed an extra ship to offset Beatty's numerical superiority.

Well, the extra ship was inferior to Hipper's other battlecruisers, and as such when Hipper had to make a run for it, that ship got left behind. The rest of Hipper's ships got banged up but escaped. This odd ship out, *Blucher* (ironic since I was talking about Wellington up there) was sunk.

What does that have to do with what John said? Well, if he plucked one of the battleships from the Heavy Squadron to join the *Bonaventure* Squadron, it would be slower and lighter — it'd likely get destroyed if things didn't go quite as planned. Better to keep the *Bonaventure* Squadron pure.

Daragh got the allusion to Dogger Bank immediately — I mean come on, he knew John was paraphrasing the Duke of Wellington, do you think he'd miss something as obvious as Dogger Bank? This was one of the reasons John and Daragh made such a great team as First and Second Lord — they were on the same wavelength. And one hell of a wavelength it was.

"So, you do have a plan then. I'm not saying it's a good one, but you have it at least!" Daragh leaned back in his chair and folded his arms.

"Uncharitable," John grunted, leaning back as well.

That's about all I need from this meeting. Let's check in somewhere else…

But where…

Oh! One of my editors pointed out that I never mentioned whether John got Haley Briand's disk. Of *course* he did — Daragh handed it to him first thing the day after she dropped it off, and for good measure, the Irish Lord had made a copy for his own secret hiding place.

The Emperor was going to have a hell of a time if he tried to destroy John.

I believe Daragh's exact words when he saw John — get this — were: "Damned bastard Emperors, what the fuck do we need 'em for anymore anyway?"

Cue the laugh track.

CHAPTER FOURTEEN

BABIES, AND ONE OF THE NEW GUYS

We'd been standing in my cabin, staring disheartened at the stacks of pads still scattered on my bed when the call had come in. The usual routine was followed; my vid screen chimed, we turned around, I activated the link, and then Kris Jacobs appeared.

Our delightful — some say token — Australian (which amuses me, because Kris generally wouldn't be considered a 'token' anything) was frowning rather darkly.

Karen and I frowned back, Karen being the first to ask, "Kris, what's wrong?"

With a sigh, Kris scratched her temple, "I need new Special Branchers."

"A new... er..." my brain was in a quasi-goo state, as I'd been in this cabin spending far too much time looking at pads of personnel. *Still* looking, days and days after we'd started. It was a big job, we had to get the crews *just right*, or as close to that as we possibly could.

And I wanted to have my bed back, dammit. The pads had to be cast out!

So I didn't quite get Kris' problem on first hearing. Karen, always more coherent than me, was able to sum up my stuttering and disgruntled sounds, "Why do you need new people?"

Kris huffed another sigh, "Sandy's pregnant. And so is Siraphun. And Monique."

At first I was almost certain this was a joke — Kris pretending to toss another personnel problem at us by reporting that, somehow, three Special Branchers had all decided to start families at the same time.

I mean, when does that happen in real life? Come on, now.

But think about it for a minute. Wherever you work, ever noticed that pregnancies sometimes — *sometimes* — come in clusters? No? Well then this was just incredibly odd.

"You're *kidding*," Karen's look of disbelief was about where I should have been with my own expression, but I was too slow on the uptake.

Kris shook her head, her mouth a thin line, "No, I'm not. I don't know why or how, but they all seem to have decided at once, and that puts the squad down by a Major and two Captains."

Which meant, in effect, the squad was going to need new commanding officers.

"We're going to have to transfer them all down to Belt Two, otherwise they'll be into the second trimester when we need them to land on Io for us," Kris' words were still grim, and Karen and I both nodded slowly.

You know how you're not supposed to drink, smoke or do drugs while pregnant? You're *definitely* not supposed to get yourself into mag crossfire. Just wouldn't be safe for the baby. And as forward-thinking as Defense Command was, we didn't have maternity-sized combat vests. Sorry, we're terrible.

Anyway, the rest of the conversation is reasonably irrelevant — what matters is that Karen and I now had to scramble, looking for a Major and a couple of Captains who could come in to take over the jobs being vacated.

And that brings me to the second part of this chapter, because the company of Special Branchers Wes had ordered for the Independent Squadron had arrived. That meant ninety-six Branchers, when if you do your math, Wes only needed eighty-four. That's right, a whole extra squad!

A couple of days after Kris' call (and on the same day that John and Daragh had the meeting mentioned in the last chapter) Karen and I waited in *Wolf's* briefing room for the new guy... one of the new guys... who might be able to take over for Sandy.

Some have wondered how we pulled this off — how did we get this guy, and moreover, how did we get him away from his own squad.

Luck was on our side with this one. Major Ruifu Chang (reverse the two names for the proper Chinese order, though he goes with the Anglicized version) had been loathed by Dave Caldecott. I mean *loathed*. Ruifu... 'Rufus' as he's more commonly known... had never been part of the Fiora ring, but John had always kept an eye on him, mainly because his *direct* approach as a Special Brancher had annoyed Caldecott so much.

Indeed, Caldecott had made it his business to *end* Rufus. The Major had been pulled out of his old squad over three years prior, and had been made 'security supervisor' of the Lunar Four Arsenal. It was a guard duty and weapons cataloguing job, and yet while doing it, Rufus had actually broken up a black market arms-dealing ring he'd stumbled upon. That success drove Caldecott nuts, but the old Second Lord had used all the pull he could to keep Rufus up there.

Now, with Caldecott in exile, John took an interest in the Major, got him off Luna, slid him into the last (newest) squad in the company Wes ordered, and sent him out to the Belt, expecting the damage Rufus could do to the enemy would be considerable.

And since Wes was using the older squads that had been together longer to fill up his ships, we were probably getting Rufus. Hence the meeting.

Karen and I were sitting and waiting, both of us rather preoccupied, not thinking too much about Rufus himself as much as the many different personnel shuffles we were doing. We'd already interviewed most of the officers from Erica's Helm and Navigation staff, and we didn't really feel comfortable promoting any of them into the senior slot. There was definitely no one on Jim's staff with enough experience to take over as Sensors and Communications Officer. Jim was apparently working on the latter problem, but we wanted to get Andrea's input on the former... she was just nowhere to be found.

That's interesting, actually — the fact that despite all of the worries about Andrea so far in this book, we haven't actually seen her in person. I'll get to that a little later.

Anyway, when the hatch opened and Ruifu Chang stepped in, Karen and I both looked up sluggishly, then made rather disorganized efforts to stand and extend our hands... before we actually said anything. The days of staring at files had definitely taken their toll.

Rufus took my hand first, because it was closer, and as I was shaking his hand I realized that I should, perhaps, speak, "Major Chang, I'm Commodore Barron."

Chang's eyebrow arched, and then Karen shook his hand and added, "Captain McMaster."

We gestured to the seat opposite our chairs, and as we all lowered ourselves into them and tried to get slightly comfortable, I cleared my throat and laced my fingers, laying my hands on the table in front of me, "So, uhm. Major... anything you want us to know...?"

At this point I realized that Rufus had different colored eyes. That's called 'heterochromia', I just looked it up. Left eye was blue, right eye brown... no that's not right, reverse those. Anyway, that gave his face a slightly asymmetrical look, which I will admit threw me for a second.

So, getting back to my question, Rufus looked between us, "The first thing you should both know is that you are *Rear Admiral Barron* and that you are *Commodore McMaster*."

Depending how you read that, it might sound snide or disrespectful. Didn't come out that way — Rufus has an understated way of saying things, almost like a counselor or something to that effect. Actually, I believe that's his nickname... 'the counselor'. Much better than Charlie's nicknames — 'Charlie' and 'hey you'. Charlie really should get a good nickname.

But back to the story. Karen and I looked at each other, and Karen said it first, "Well, he's already saved us once."

I nodded, "He's hired."

We then looked back at Rufus, and Karen smiled, "You're hired. Need you to take over *Lion's* Special Branch squad, and bring two Captains with you. We're losing *three* officers to maternity leave over there."

Rufus... actually, we were still thinking of him as Ruifu in this meeting, I can't remember when we started going with Rufus, but it must have been early on... anyway, he tilted his head thoughtfully, "Really, three at once?"

"It's been an eventful break since we got back from Egesta," I shrugged.

"Very," Rufus concurred. "I have two officers in mind from my old squad. The rest of that squad will remain with the Independent Squadron?"

I blinked at the question. I hadn't thought to see if I could possibly steal the extras from Wes... I certainly wouldn't mind having nine extra Branchers on the way out to Jupiter.

"I... I'll think about that. See if we can't bring your whole squad over perhaps..." I don't think I sounded nearly as coherent or dynamic as I should have, but, oh well.

Rufus nodded again, "Very good. Is there anything else?"

I looked at Karen, and we both barely contained shrugs, "Uhm. Well. Not... right now."

Talk about awkward. We seriously weren't distinguishing ourselves in the meetings that day. Too preoccupied.

As Rufus got up and walked out, Karen and I leaned towards each other, then made eye contact.

"Should we have prepared for that meeting?" I asked sheepishly.

Smiling, Karen shrugged, "It's done, so does it really matter?"

What a great answer.

We eventually got back to work.

CHAPTER FIFTEEN

SHORE LEAVE

Andrea Kiley had been owed a great deal of leave, and she'd taken it while Karen and I were worrying about the personnel questions. No one knew where she went, or at least I didn't think anyone knew. No one told Karen or me back then, anyway.

Based on what Andrea has since explained to me, though, let me describe just where she was and what she'd been doing while Karen and I were in that meeting.

Already this sounds ominous. I'm afraid it lives up to the way it sounds.

According to what little I understand about dealing with trauma — if that's the best word for being forced to witness what she witnessed — one of the most common responses is to avoid contact with anyone who can figure out that something's wrong.

But let me back up for a minute. The good news was that Andrea had stopped putting a gun to her head every night. That was definitely an improvement. She still did it occasionally, but much less frequently, and she was able to pull the mag away from her temple much more quickly.

She still had nightmares, though. Brutal ones. I don't really need to get into them — just think what it'd be like to be stuck reading and re-reading *The Independent Squadron* every night forever, then make it a million times worse.

Think you'd crawl inside a bottle? Yep.

So it's perhaps no surprise that Andrea was sitting at the bar in a high-end brothel in Belt Two's Dome Four — the 'Pleasure Dome', as anyone who knows Belt Two calls it. This brothel served the elite officers of the fleet, as well as business tycoons, politicians, priests… the usual sorts of clients who didn't want it known that they were going to these establishments.

Karen, Charlie and I had been through the building on various occasions, though despite the rumors, it wasn't to partake of the services. Usually we were recovering either politicians or fellow officers, and on one occasion, we were following a lead on one of Grant Merger's top men.

Anyway, now Andrea was there. And she had been for the past ten days. Not kidding. This was a full feature place — it's like a spa, just with many extra services. It wasn't cheap, and she was running up quite a bill, but she didn't care — she had a lot of back pay, and a lot of credit on top of that.

She thus alternately spent time in her expensive room and at the bar, drinking a great deal, numbing her emotions as much as she could, running from the nightmares. When she was in her room she was rarely alone, but no one was ever allowed to be there with her when she was sleeping. She sent them away before turning out the lights. Her suspicion was that if she'd woken up from a nightmare with someone in bed next to her, she'd kill that person.

Glad she never put that to the test.

The staff of the brothel were good people. That might sound ridiculous — some sort of adoption of the 'noble whore' motif or whatever. I don't know whether you think this sort of work is acceptable or not — the movement to make prostitution illegal was around then as it is now. I'm indifferent, personally, but I do know that these particular brothel workers win my respect. When they saw Andrea in the state she was in, they got on the comm with a contact of theirs in Belt Two base, quietly asking questions.

That's how they found out about her promotion. That's actually how *Andrea* found out, because she hadn't checked her messages since she'd arrived at this place. The brothel staff told her. Congratulations.

I feel rather badly about this; Karen and I, so preoccupied with personnel shuffling, hadn't been paying enough attention to our friends. The fact that we'd sent word to Andrea of her promotion, and that she hadn't replied over a week later, should have been a warning. Especially after the amount of worrying about her that had led to the specific posting she got...

But we thought we had addressed the problem, and our heads were already elsewhere.

Andrea herself later pointed out to me that we knew she was on leave, and letting her have an uninterrupted break shouldn't mean that we were being inconsiderate. That's true, I suppose. I just wish I'd paid more attention then.

Depending on what you think of brothels, high class or low, you may not see anything wrong with Andrea checking into one for ten days. But this is Andrea Kiley we're talking about. This was totally out of character for her.

No, to put it the way she explained it to me, she was making herself numb to the pain, and only very intense feelings could safely cut through that wall of numbness she was building. The brothel helped her build her wall with the booze, and to remind herself of what it meant to feel something in the rest of the hours of the day. Some, of course, would point out that this wasn't effectively dealing with her emotional problems.

No kidding.

And Karen and I weren't paying enough attention to realize what exactly was going on.

But then, full credit goes to Andrea for being able to hide this. Her job, her command, that was something she could fall back on. She had to put on an artificial, cool persona to be able to command. Because doing that was instinctive enough, it was something of a relief — it let her focus on tasks, not herself, and that helped.

That in mind, she packed up and left the brothel the moment the concierge knocked on her door with the message we'd sent to her aboard *Friendly*.

An hour after that, she was knocking on my cabin door aboard *Wolf*.

Karen and I, of course, were back standing in there. This was several hours after our meeting with Rufus, and we were still looking at a number of candidates for Helm and Navigation Officer when the knock came.

Without even thinking, I just yelled, "Come on in."

Andrea poked her head in, and was smiling in a genuine manner. Karen and I both looked back at her, and then instantly we were smiling too. We were too preoccupied to really notice her appearance — she was coming off a lot of drinking (with the help of detox pills, but still) and she hadn't been sleeping. I remain certain that, had we not been wrapped up in our own affairs, we would have realized what sort of rough shape she was in...

Reading this draft, Andrea's told me to stop the self-deprecation, so I'll try.

She stepped into the cabin and traded handshakes with Karen and I, "Sorry I'm so late, didn't check my messages while I was on leave."

"Good policy, I say," being a terrible host, I was already turning back to the piles. "Better to get a real break, come back refreshed."

Karen, being that honestly wonderful person, smiled and kept looking at our new Flag Captain, "Get a good rest?"

I glanced back to Andrea for the answer, and her smile didn't lose any of its warmth, "Oh, I didn't sleep as much as I was planning. But I got a lot of exercise."

I can just imagine the high school and college students yelling "HELL YEAH SHE DID!" and high-fiving each other when they read that. I don't know what to say, really, just that Andrea was clever at telling the truth in such a way that we didn't get suspicious. And that Karen and I weren't on a wavelength then that would have allowed us to pick up the double meaning. One editor pointed out that, before this, we'd never have *dreamed* that Andrea would be where she was, and that's a fair point. We really wouldn't have guessed.

Andrea went on, "But it was good... now I'm famished, though. Could I interest you both in some dinner?"

I frowned and glanced at the chrono next to my bed, then looked back in surprise, "Didn't we get back here at 1400?"

Karen nodded, "Yeah, five hours ago."

"Good God," I frowned, "Andrea, thank you very much for coming to rescue us!"

I don't think I could have picked worse words.

But without so much as a wince at the fact that my saying 'rescue' could recall memories of the people she felt she had failed to rescue, Andrea nodded, "It's part of the job. We should talk, too. I don't know if you have a Helm and Navigation Officer, but I've got a lady over on *Friendly* you might want to consider."

She wasn't just acting unaffected, she was bringing good ideas. She should really get into professional acting.

We all went to get supper on the rec deck.

CHAPTER SIXTEEN

THE HEAVY SQUADRON

Up until now in this series of books, I don't believe I've mentioned Vice Admiral Rachel Butler, which I feel rather poorly about. Honestly, I haven't been asked much about her — we didn't cross paths often, and she wasn't really part of the Fiora ring, so she just didn't fit into the narrative for 2231.

But someone had to take over for Greg when he left the Home Fleet to return to the Belt, and we were trying to ensure we kept Dave Caldecott's cronies out of the top spots. As you probably know, a bunch of them did manage to hang around in secret, and they'd make our lives particularly difficult later on... you probably know exactly what and who I'm referring to.

For now, though, these trouble makers were staying quiet and out of the way, fearing that John would get rid of them if they said a word about his leadership. We were still in the afterglow of *The Almost Coup* — there was no chance of taking on the Fiora ring in the press or in government. That said, many of the Admirals *were* taken out of the equation by the 'purge'. They were getting desk jobs, study jobs, whatever John could saddle them with that would keep them out of combat commands.

So Lynn Boakai had gotten the *Bonaventure* Squadron, but who was to command the five remaining battleships of the Heavy Squadron — the four *Empire*-class battlewagons and one *Odysseus*-class, plus escorts?

That was to be Rachel Butler, a solid Flag Officer who, it has to be said, didn't have the longest history in combat commands. She'd been a skipper in the independent belt for ten years, and she'd won a few actions against the pirates, but you'll probably remember her as a frigate Captain who helped head off the Syndicate fleet during their raid on Earth. That was the action that got her flag rank, but since she'd lacked political affiliations (she sided with neither Fiora or Caldecott — having one on your side was a real necessity in the fleet of those days) she'd been unable to get a squadron command...

Alright, to preempt the inevitable "aha, so it was patronage!" snickers by those who say the service doesn't award merit, just connections, I'd better do an aside here. Look, there's plenty of evidence to say that, in order to advance well, you had to have a 'patron'. Obviously, in the Fiora ring, John was ours. Dave Caldecott had a circle too, and let's be honest, Dave put his circle together first. The Fiora ring was a response to that — John saw that his friends were having roadblocks thrown in front of them by Dave *because* they were his friends. So John decided to play that game, and he ended up becoming First Lord over Caldecott, so John won.

But — and I'm sure the cynics won't believe me — John worked hard not to protect *only* the members of his ring. There weren't that many of us, and he made sure his first priority was to keep us safe from Caldecott's people, but that wasn't all he did. Any good officers were given their chance, whether they liked John or hated him. And sure, cynics will say "yeah right", but Lynn Boakai was given Fifth Lord, remember, and getting back to Rachel Butler, she was given a plum assignment too: Superintendant of the Earth Academy.

Before any of you laugh and say that's a stupid job — something I've heard from a number of civilians — think back to where Karen and I first met John. Oh yes, where was that? Right, he was the Superintendant of the Earth Academy. Funny coincidence, eh?

The point I'm hammering away here is that Rachel Butler wasn't one of our own, but John had seen her talent and was by no means going to write her off because she hadn't joined one camp or the other during the in-fighting. Anyone who doubts John's fairness, then, should keep in mind that both Admirals appointed to the Home Fleet in this period weren't in his ring.

That was a whole long tirade. Sorry. Just gets under my skin.

Back to Rachel Butler. She was entering the lobby of Admiralty House early in the morning (which due to alternate time zones happened to coincide with Karen, Andrea and I sitting down to our dinner on the rec deck). Walking with enough quiet confidence to mask any nerves, she headed over to Gerald and Betty's reception desk and started to announce her arrival for a meeting, but was interrupted.

"Rachel, Jesus wept now it's damned fine to see you again girl!"

Who else could that have been but Pat Conroy?

Well, Second Lord Daragh Ryan, actually. I wonder who Pat Conroy is... name just popped into my head. Sounds Irish. Oh well.

Daragh crossed the lobby with flourish and a big grin, stopping next to Rachel and wrapping his arms around her, "How've you been girl? How long's it been now?"

You have to watch the surveillance vids of this meeting. You just *have* to. Go to the archives and watch them. Poor Vice Admiral Butler's expression is priceless.

Why?

"Um. Second Lord..." she started trying to push him off politely, but his was a big, friendly bear hug, "...we've never met before."

"How're the kids? What's that?"

He actually didn't stop hugging her, which was the fantastic part.

"We've never met before, sir," Rachel assured him, rather confused.

Daragh frowned, though didn't stop hugging, "Are you sure of that?"

"Certainly," Rachel nodded against his shoulder, so he let go.

"Well, thank God for that. I was afraid we'd met before and I'd forgotten. Jesus, *that* would have been awkward!" his grin returned.

As Daragh stepped back, Rachel blinked a couple of times and said what we all probably are thinking, "*That* would have been awkward?"

"Aye, damned right it would have been! Come on to the meeting, then — I know you must've met John, eh?"

They headed to John's office.

"Rachel, how's the squadron?" John was standing and talking to one of his aides when she and Daragh walked into his office. He sent the aide out and then returned to his chair, waving Daragh and Rachel to the seats opposite him.

"We're ready to move at your order, sir," Rachel's answer stuck John as firm but not overconfident — a good combination in his mind. She didn't seem nervous to him either, which was definitely a sign that she was the right person for the job.

"Excellent. So it's about time I explain to you the [guesswork we've been doing], and the assignment you'll be getting," John pulled a pad off his desk and tossed it softly towards her. She grabbed it and turned it around in her hands.

Daragh and John waited for a couple of minutes as she scrolled through the text on the orders screen, then she looked up with a creased brow, "We're sure this is reliable [guesswork]?"

"The best we can get. Thea Fostopolos is willing to bet her life on it, and we'll collect on that bet if she's wrong!" Daragh exclaimed in jest, but Rachel gave him a withering sort of 'you better not be serious glare'.

"What?" he held his hands up. "We have a convenient payment plan…"

"No more jokes for now, Daragh," John cut in before it got any worse, and the irreverent Irishman let it go.

"It's good [guesswork], and we're basing everything on it, Rachel. So when you take the Heavy Squadron out, you either have to find that Martian strike force, or you return to Earth immediately."

Rachel's orders (or at least the convenient summary of them) were simple: she was taking the Heavy Squadron out towards Mercury, on a vector that John and Daragh had determined was the most likely course of approach for the fleet the Martians were *probably* sending to Earth from that side.

Of course, if John and Daragh had [guessed wrong] about the course the Martians were coming in on, there was the potential that our red-hulled enemy could pass Rachel in space, and beat her back to Earth. So there were a whole bunch of tactical safeguards in place to avoid such an eventuality. I'll get into those later.

What John had to be sure of, though, was that Rachel knew to turn around if she got to Point Luck II (as opposed to John's Point Luck on the vector to Mars) and found no Martians after a specified amount of waiting time. The rest of the orders and plans were clear enough on the pad — she could ask clarifying questions if necessary — but that point was critical. She was to go out, and if the [guesses] proved incorrect, she was to come back *fast*.

That was the plan, and of course Earth was at stake.

Since I spent the first half of this chapter hitting you over the head with what a solid officer Rachel Butler was, the next piece of dialogue shouldn't come as much of a shock to you: "I understand, sir."

"Excellent. So, questions, thoughts?"

The meeting continued.

CHAPTER SEVENTEEN

SOUTHERN BELLE

As you're probably guessing by now, once we get into the back half of this book, it's going to be all John, Greg, Mik, and the rest... most of the time. I'm honestly surprised by how much I'm finding to say about what Karen and I were doing, and I hope you're not finding it all frightfully boring. It's what they call the 'character' stuff in fiction, so in non-fiction I suppose it's quasi-biographical...

Well, no matter, this is just about it for the personnel stuff. At least for the moment. You see, this chapter falls on the evening before Greg and Mik were to split off from the convoy, so there's no need for more 'filler'.

Ouch, I just called Shelby filler. Now that's just not polite.

And polite definitely counts with Shelby.

So let me explain what's going on here. At dinner on the rec deck, Andrea had told us she had someone in mind for Helm and Navigation Officer, and as *Wolf* was her ship, she certainly had a say. And Andrea was our friend — no amount of trauma was going to change that — so while she was very much in favor of this candidate, she kindly wanted Karen and me to interview the Lieutenant to make sure we were satisfied.

The funny thing about this meeting, though, is that we were running late.

Actually, I don't see how that's 'funny', in any sense of the word. Let's just switch that to 'Unfortunately we were late.'

We had a good reason, of course — we were running to this meeting from one with our new Sensors and Communications Officer, who Jim had — as promised — secured. I'm not sure if he had to drug and kidnap her, or if Mark Gunney knew yet, but Jim had gotten Kate Levec off *Cheetah*.

You probably recognize Kate's name by now, she was a highly experienced Sensors and Communications Officer, and she was ideal for the position on a force flagship. One thing people rarely seem to realize about that job is how insane it can be — and by that job, I specifically mean the job of Sensors and Communications Officer on a *flagship*. When on a non-flagship, you're only coordinating the information for your Captain. On a flagship, you have one or even two Flag Officers in addition to your Captain to look after, *and* you're in charge of distributing squadron orders.

Not something you can hand to someone with no experience.

Knowing this, Jim had either petitioned Kate's sense of duty, or possibly her ambition, and had convinced her to come over... which meant Mark was down another senior officer on *Cheetah*. I had no doubt that he and Erica — remember, Erica Martin was his new XO — would find a good person to fill that gap, but I did feel slightly guilty.

Slightly. Come on, we got a replacement for Jim who'd been hand-picked and coerced by him. It was reassuring.

Anyway, we'd just had a meeting with Kate, but since she's reasonably familiar to readers by now (check right back through all the 2231 books if you don't remember her), I'm not covering that meeting here.

Especially since it was basically a repeat of the one we had with Rufus — Karen and I sounded rather... er... unintelligent. Me more so than Karen, as ever.

So I'm going to save the scrap of the dignity I'm trying desperately to maintain in these books, and move along to our meeting with Andrea's candidate for Helm and Navigation Officer: the delightful Lieutenant Shelby McLaws. Wow, took a while to get to the point there, didn't I?

For you history buffs out there, you might remember a General McLaws from the nineteenth century U.S. Civil War — I believe he commanded one of Longstreet's divisions at Gettysburg. No idea if Shelby is one of his descendants, though I'm certain she has military traditions running through her family.

But, I really should get to the meeting I'm supposedly talking about. I mean, I do enjoy dragging you around on all my tangents, but...

I swung open the hatch to the briefing room and stepped in, Karen right on my shoulder. As we entered, Shelby came out of her seat on the opposite side of the table, clicking her heels together at attention and snapping a nice salute.

The first thing that went through my head — silly as it sounds — was: *wow, she made that look easy.*

You know how in movies, junior officers snapping salutes to Flag Officers are usually portrayed as going ramrod straight, refusing to make eye contact and so forth? Not Shelby. I'm not sure how to describe it, but she was quite smooth... elegant, even. She had the air of someone who was very comfortable in the service, and not easy to wow.

Karen was equally impressed, but what she told me after (and strangely didn't occur to me at first sight) was that Shelby was a "southern belle".

Can't disagree. Curled golden locks, poise and carriage that would give Lia Hawke (in court mode) a run for her money, and a certain way of speaking... it was definitely all there. The negative connotations sometimes associated with southern belledom (not a word, I know) didn't apply to Shelby, but this was still a bit of a change for Karen and me.

See. Um. We'd never before met anyone from the southern US. I know, I know, it's unbelievable. Seriously, though, we'd worked with people from all over the Empire, we'd just never seen an honest-to-God southerner up close. There are plenty in the service, obviously, we just... well... we'd never met any of them.

Yes, it's weird. Sorry, we were sheltered.

"Sir, ma'am, Lieutenant Shelby McLaws reporting as ordered," she introduced herself softly as her salute dropped to her side, and she remained at attention.

Karen and I — and please remember again that we were *still* being buried by paperwork, and weren't ourselves — actually paused at this introduction. We were both... this is so ridiculous... marveling at her accent. I'm sorry, again, I feel like I'm disrespecting the good folk from Georgia.

"Welcome aboard," Karen finally spoke, which was a big step for the two of us. After that we managed to move to autopilot, waving Shelby to sit back down and then sitting opposite her.

Now, watching Shelby sit — I'm going to be killed for saying this — made me wonder if there was a finishing school that taught proper etiquette for ladies going into the service, because her posture was impeccable. I mean, I can't actually describe the specific rules she followed — how far forward to lean and whatnot — because I don't know the rules. It was quite a switch from Karen's and my usual relaxed sitting style, though.

We both started to feel slightly under-dressed for the meeting.

"So."

Yes, I entered the conversation on that high note.

"Soo…" Shelby laced her fingers in front of her on the briefing table and smiled sweetly. I fear that sounds sort of jaded or something, and I worry that you're starting to see her as a prim and proper snob in uniform. Just the opposite… think legitimately charming professional southern lady… Innocent! That's the word I'm looking for. When I read these quotes back without Shelby's voice in my head, they strike me as perhaps sounding conceited. Not at all, just a plain old southern girl, as Shelby once said of herself. Innocent and charming.

Karen and I looked at each other at that point, then Karen leaned forward, "You come very highly recommended. Andrea wants you to take over at Helm and Navigation for *Wolf*."

Shelby nodded perfectly, "Yes ma'am, Captain Kiley informed me of her recommendation when she made it. It's a real honor for me, being considered for this position."

Perfect cadence and flow.

"And you think you'll be comfortable stepping into the role?" I asked, trying to get myself working properly again.

I'm sorry, haven't you ever met someone and been distracted by their accent before? I expect it happens to everyone at some point… that or I'm just insensitive and foolish.

"I'm sure it'll be a challenge, sir, but it's one I definitely look forward to taking on. And I believe I am well qualified for it. I won't let you down, sir," she nodded again. Perfectly.

We didn't need to talk about qualifications at this meeting — Andrea knew Shelby's qualifications and endorsed her, so that was enough for us. We just needed to make sure we could work with her.

And after the novelty (such a cheap word, again I apologize) of her accent wore off, presumably Karen and I would be able to.

But, being highly intelligent, I had to ask.

"Um, Shelby, forgive my impertinence… but are you always… this… proper?"

Karen's eyes darted to me — one of the 'how could you say that?' looks.

Shelby smiled, looked down and to her left for a second, took her right hand off the table and gently scratched behind her right ear — it all looked very ladylike — then did a half-shrug, "I've always felt myself an officer and a lady. I suppose I always do behave this way."

She handled a ham-handed question with charm and aplomb. Probably meant I wasn't the first idiot to ask it… and, of course, that she was indeed always proper.

"Well. I like to think of myself as an officer and a gentleman," I backpedaled. "I'm just really bad at the second part."

"Yeah, I definitely don't have the lady part down either," Karen said that sincerely, though you and I both know she was just trying to lend me a little support.

Shelby's smile sparkled, "Forgive me, sir, ma'am, but of course we all know better than that."

Cheap flattery? She said it so unassumingly, I'm pretty sure it was honest.

Anyway, by the time this meeting was over, I was certain I was going to feel like a pedestrian guttersnipe for the entire cruise with her on the bridge... but no, of course I grew accustomed to her, as did Karen.

Defense Command Public Relations (DCPR) did fall in love with her, though, and that's why throughout many of the remaining years of the war, she was the face of Defense Command recruiting adverts. Karen, Greg, Wes, John or I would record the 'we need you' section of the ad, but it was Shelby who would be the face of the 'ordinary' Defense Command officers corps — the smiling beauty who told people to go to their local recruiting center.

It's been tracked: application numbers increased when those ads with Shelby started running. That's how good she was then. And of course, later... well. That's for later.

That was Shelby McLaws, our new Helm and Navigation Officer.

Chapter Eighteen
Preparing The Realm

As confident as John was in his… uh… *educated guesses* about what the Martians were sending at Earth from both directions, he couldn't avoid planning for some contingencies. Well, not just planning for them, but publicizing them.

You may have seen much of what I'm about to record in the original press conference, though I'll go back a little further than just the conference…

John was sitting in the office of the Home Secretary, maintaining a neutral expression as she reviewed the information on the pad he'd sent ahead. Those were the plans for meeting the Martian assault; he'd signed off on them at the Admiralty and they had also been approved by the Prime Minister. The Defense Minister, on his way out because of ties to Caldecott, wasn't a concern, but Lori Finigian had demanded to be included after John and the PM had left her out of the press conference before the Battle Over Earth.

I should back up and explain that a little better: Lori Finigian (that's an Armenian name, by the way, not Irish — everyone seems to think Irish) was Earth's Home Secretary, a member of the planetary (not Imperial) cabinet, and in charge of planetary security. Hers was in many regards a redundant position, as security of the homeworld was also a responsibility of the Imperial cabinet, but (not unreasonably) Lori Finigian wanted to do her bit to help organize Earth's defense.

As such, Prime Minister Pope had made it clear to John that she was to be involved in any further defensive plans established for Earth. Otherwise it'd be a war of words in the press, something no one needed while there was an actual war on.

So here John sat, in Lori's office on Capitol Hill in Washington, DC, waiting as she went over his plan.

John's comment to me later: "If she'd wanted to change anything, I'd have said a few choice words and left."

Being inclusive was one thing, but Home Secretary or no, Lori Finigian had less tactical and strategic sense than Dave Caldecott. Her main job was administrative and she'd been put in her position because she was a good administrator.

Now, Lori wasn't a bad sort. I came to know her a bit after the war, and she's definitely abrasive, but I think her heart, if she had one, was in the right place. Well, the autopsy did confirm she had one, I expect. I never actually checked. She died about four years ago — overdosed on heroin, I believe. Left no relations, no family that knew her… she was a professional woman, did her job, retired and took up recreational drug use to speed her passage from the world.

Anyway, I say that she wasn't so bad because from this meeting you'll likely get the opposite impression. John didn't much care for her, and I have no doubt I'd have loathed her if I'd ever had to work with her during those years.

"You've got balls, I'll give you that. You might be a fucking arrogant bastard, but you've got balls."

John smiled — not appreciating the quip, this was an icy smile, "I know my job better than you do. Is there a problem?"

Lori snorted a laugh and dropped the pad on her desk, "Yeah, you probably do. So you're just going to dictate how Earth's defense is going to go and I'm going to go along with it?"

She wasn't a master of phrase-turning, either — note the repetition of "going to go".

John nodded, "Yes."

Just that simple.

"And if I say you're putting our planet at undue risk based on guesswork?"

John's smile didn't so much as twitch, he just reached down to his belt and drew his comm, "In that case, I call the PM, and he'll call the President, and you'll get a message telling you that I know what I'm talking about, and you don't."

Lori laughed harshly, "You get off on this, don't you? Feel powerful and bigger than you are."

John leaned forward slightly in his chair, "I'm big enough, Lori. And I am powerful. More powerful than you, actually."

He didn't say that with a sneer, I'm certain. He said that with the sort of tone a parent might use when reminding a surly teen of who pays the bills.

"Yeah, fine."

So, getting to the press conference then, let me run through some of the highlights.

John and Lori were on the aged white steps of Capitol Hill, with most of the Imperial Parliament press corps in front of them. The reporters had been tipped off by the Imperial Press Secretary that new defense arrangements for Earth would be announced in Washington instead of Terra Nova, so they'd all flown down for the event.

Lori gave a lovely speech about defending the homeworld, how no Martians would ever set foot on Earth and all the rest of the vitriolic rhetoric she'd been itching to spew for some time, and John stood aside with a quiet smile, letting her rave.

Then, after what feels like half an hour even when you're watching a vid feed with a time stamp that tells you it was only four minutes, she introduced John and the real information started flowing. After a five-minute overview, he turned it over to the press corps for questions.

I'll jump around here, go to the key questions and answers.

Jocko Kent (who you'll hear a lot about next book) asked the first good one, "Lord Fiora, you're pulling all our capital ships and many of our frigates out of Earth orbit. Now, I don't have to tell you that many viewers will be asking if that's wise."

John nodded with a smile at the expected question, "Yes, it's definitely a risk, but it's a carefully calculated one. Again, I can't tell you where, but our ships will be very nearby, able to get into orbital defense positions within hours."

Of course he was bending the truth — you think the Martians couldn't be tapping this feed too? He couldn't give away the plan, but he had to prepare Earth for the possibility of going it alone if some Martians broke past the *Bonnie* and Heavy Squadrons. So he said all the battleships would be only hours from Earth, in some hidden position, ready to get the drop on invaders.

By 'hours', he actually meant thirty-six, as opposed to the two or three he implied, but technically he wasn't lying. It wasn't John's fault if people low-balled the expected number of hours.

Jessica Qing (again, wait for next book) also kicked in one of her classic human interest queries, "First Lord, do the people of Earth have anything to fear from this Martian assault?"

See, I'm pretty sure we couldn't have *planted* a better question. Jessica has a long track record of giving good officers their chance to shine on camera — she gained a lot of her early notoriety for proving good officers to be every bit the heroes people wanted them to be, and for that matter, by making bad officers look heroic.

With gusto, John seized the chance she gave him, "The Martians are coming, Jessica, that's always grounds for some concern. But there's no need to worry too much, we have this in hand. I can promise you that the force they're sending will not overcome the Home Fleet, and that they'll regret their visit. Funny, usually I tell visitors to Earth to come back often. Not this time."

Those last two sentences became one of the ten most played sound bites in Imperial history. It became a slogan for the whole war. It became the thing both John's action figures said. It even became a popular ring tone on civvie comm units (with background music added).

Of course, John's answer did more than just sound good: to any spies listening, it implied that he was expecting only one Martian force, and that the fleet was going to sit waiting for that force to arrive.

We don't know if any Martians watched this press conference and passed on intel from it. It wouldn't surprise me if they had.

But as you know, it wouldn't have helped them.

In the meantime, John's smooth, unassuming delivery of this confident statement set Earth abuzz. I should mention that rumors of an impending attack had been floating around — the population of Earth wasn't ignorant, many observers and 'experts' on the vids had pointed out that the Martians would be fools not to take advantage of this season to launch a huge attack on the planet.

Instead of worrying, though, the people now started to feel confident. I know it sounds rather arrogant for me to say what 'people' were feeling, but the polls conducted the night after this press conference put public confidence in Earth's defenses in the eighty percent range. I think you'll agree that's rather high.

So the Fiora ring's media savvy, something Caldecott had never understood or cared enough to try to learn, had very measurable positive dividends.

Earth was ready to receive.

CHAPTER NINETEEN
THE ORDERS

This chapter is about two conversations… it sounds dull, but hang in there. These are two rather important conversations, both conveying sets of orders that will be critical later. I know, there's been a lot of setting up and not a lot of knocking down so far this book. Not too much longer to wait, I promise.

The first conversation (well both of them, actually) was on Battlelink, with Mik on one side and Commander Guy Vivar on the other.

On the bridge of *Cyclops*, Mik was standing and stroking his beard, "Do you understand your orders, Commander?"

Vivar was wearing a very stern expression, "Yes sir, I believe I do… you wish me to leave the attack force."

It sounded like he felt he'd been snubbed — that he wasn't good enough to go in with the battleships and the Belt Squadron corvettes.

Well, that just happened to be the case. Had Mik known why he'd been called out to Belt Two, he'd probably have brought along a different escort, most likely *Amherst*, with Nikhil Jones. But he hadn't known, and there was no point worrying about that now.

But Vivar needed some handling, "Yes, you are leaving the attack force, because Admiral Noyce is getting an earful from the convoy Commodore. If we don't leave a good ship on guard, we're going to be… in trouble."

I don't know if that sounds flimsy to you… strictly speaking it wasn't. The convoy Commodore (not a Defense Command rank, but an honorary title for the merchant Captain elected as convoy controller by the rest of the skippers) had known nothing of the actual mission of the battleships, though I'm sure she'd guessed all this firepower hadn't just been assigned to her because she and her ships were special. She'd be hearing about the loss of her escort soon, and Mik was pretty sure he'd be able to hear her explode despite the thousands of kilometers of void between her ship and *Cyclops*. Merchants, entirely understandably, didn't like to be used as bait or decoys.

But war necessitated extraordinary measures…

"I am therefore being wasted on political operations while you and Admiral Noyce enter the history books?"

I'm remembering why I didn't like this guy. And here's more reason to laud Mik's leadership skills — he was keeping him in check.

"Listen, *Commander*, we all left Belt Two together, all our names will be in the dispatches if that's what matters. But you need to ask yourself what's important now: notoriety or the lives and cargoes of all those ships I just ordered you to take command of," Mik put the question frankly, and Vivar's face tightened.

There was no way command of a big convoy could, in any Defense Command officer's mind, come anywhere close to stacking up to participation in the first raid on Mars. We all wanted to get back at the bastards for their still-unexplained attacks, and even if the risks were high, our pride was higher.

To get this close to being part of the raid and then being left behind, that just couldn't have been pleasant.

I wonder if that sounds strange to you non-military readers... that it was a disappointment to *not* cruise into a heavily defended space on a raid. Ah well. All I can tell you is it was.

Anyway, Vivar was pretty obviously trying to weigh his options at this point — on the vid you can see the gears turning in his brain. He had no choice but to follow orders.

"Very well, Commodore. I'll do as you say."

And with a huff, he vanished.

I feel rather badly for *Nanton's* crew of that time — they must have cursed their luck daily for being commanded by a guy who brought them ignominy.

Sorry, no matter how Mik was able to handle him, I still think Guy Vivar was a liability of the worst kind in this service. Enough said, moving on to the second conversation...

'Commodore' Shazia Batak was incensed.

"We were your Trojan horse, that's it. You put fifty skippers and their crews at risk so you could roll yourself in a shitheap of glory?"

I'm sorry, that's not a tone you take with Admiral Greg Noyce.

Well, I wouldn't stand for it anyway (this chapter must be making me look rather like a reactionary), but Greg's wisdom was more than equal to the task of diffusing his angry response.

He folded his arms as he stood on *Warspite's* bridge, "Commodore Batak, it was necessary. I apologize for having had to mislead you about our mission, but remember that we have protected this convoy for the past ten days. That protection, I would suggest, has been much better than you'd have otherwise had."

"Yeah, but apparently there's a chance of running into the Martian battle fleet out here, and now we won't have you with us. Fuck you, Greg."

She turned and waved her hand to her comm tech to cut the signal, but with a half-bob of his head, Greg ordered *Warspite's* Sensors and Communications Officer to override Batak's control of the conversation (a little ability Defense Command ships had when dealing with non-military Earth-built signal systems).

"Hey, get the fuck off my screen!"

Greg let out a bemused breath, "Commodore, we're leaving *Nanton* with you, and I would suggest that you get your convoy out of the space lanes, and don't attempt to approach Earth for several days. Give us time to defeat the Martian fleets."

"We have delivery schedules, we're going to meet them whether you like it or not."

Sheesh. As if Greg wasn't trying to keep her from getting incinerated by Martian laser fire.

"I would advise you to delay them. And you are to go signals quiet, or your position will likely be tracked by your comm lasers."

"Bullshit, no one can track comm lasers..."

"I wouldn't believe that if I were you," Greg said it with just the right amount of menace, implying that the Martians could track comm lasers when I'm almost certain they couldn't.

Batak's face was a thundercloud, "And where are you going? To sneak up behind the attack force?"

Greg obviously hadn't told a civilian the whole plan, just enough to get her to (hopefully) do as she was told. Ouch, that sounds patronizing… but… well… she needed to do as she was told, dammit. Or she and all her ships would die.

"Something like that. Now do as I've instructed, please, Commodore. Or *Nanton* will compel you to do so."

Ooh, a threat. Sad that it had come to that.

Batak met the order with a sniff — yes, a sniff — and then nearly spat her response, "Fine. But if so much as one of my ships is damaged, I'll take it out of your ass."

She then walked out of frame. Letting go a sigh, Greg waved his Sensors and Communications Officer to kill the feed.

Captain Val Rodriguez stepped up next to him as the screen switched back to a sensor display and shook her head, "Big talker."

"Yes, and not very happy," Greg nodded.

Val chuckled and looked at him, "Seriously, that's all you have to say? Boss, you have the patience of a saint. I'd have taken a shuttle over there and harmed her physically. Hell, I'll do it now if you ask."

Greg smiled, "I don't think that'd be appropriate, Val. But I appreciate your willingness to harm people on my behalf."

Val Rodriguez laughed again… and so ends the chapter.

About four hours after this, the convoy and the battleship raiding force parted ways, and the plunge towards battle began.

CHAPTER TWENTY

THE AUDIENCE

This is probably (I say probably because I really don't know) the last time you're going to hear anything from Belt Two for a while in this book. But I figured I should just set the stage for what we were doing as we waited for word on the various actions that were destined to be fought around Earth and at Mars.

To do this, we're going to have to skip forward about thirty-six hours, to the point where Mik and Greg were a little over half way to Mars, and in Earth time, the early hours of the morning before John and Rachel were set to boost out of orbit.

From this point, we at Belt Two had decided the chances of a Martian encounter were growing more and more likely, so we were set up and waiting.

Now, what does waiting entail?

Well, Belt Two base has what we all like to call the 'war room'. It's basically a command chamber with over 100 screens in it — and no controls. It's not the room you'd go to if the base was actually under attack (you go to C&C then) but it was ideally set up for viewing intelligence and media feeds from a long distance.

As soon as John or Greg made contact with anything, they'd start sending burst logs informing Admiralty House of what they were up against, and what they'd done. Those logs would then be passed along to the major bases so that we were all on the same page. It was all top secret — don't get the misimpression that the reports were simply being released. No, they were going to the Prime Minister's situation room, coming to Belt Two, and going out to Marlene Stoll at Venus, as well as to Lia Hawke. No one else was getting up-to-date information — they'd all have to wait for the after-action report.

To answer my editor's question, the reason we didn't make these data feeds more widely available was because, frankly, it would be too risky. You don't want to publicize where your active formations are and what they're doing live and in realtime for two reasons. First, if everything goes pear shaped, you'll have panic from a lot of people not qualified to deal with the ramifications of a loss. Second, if the Martians intercepted a live feed that told them all the capital ships of the Home Fleet were away from Earth, they might be able to find some way to capitalize. Our *guesses* had told us they weren't in position to do that... but why risk it? So only those secure feeds were going out on highly encrypted frequencies, and only to people we knew we could trust absolutely.

Anyway, this meant the Belt Two base's war room was going to become news central for the battles to come, and since people like me, Karen, Wes and Marshal were all just a teeny bit interested in what was going on, we were rather inclined to spend some time there.

Just slightly inclined.

That's *sarcasm*. Or irony. One of those things where you're understating your interest for comedic effect. And now I've undoubtedly wrecked it. Curses.

I'm pretty sure it would have been a comical sight, though, for anyone watching. Wes had pulled *Nova Scotia* in to dock with the base, and Andrea had pulled in *Wolf* as well. That meant Karen and Wes and I could all spend our days in the war room, but still be just a brisk run away from our ships in case something came up. So now all of us, plus Marshal who was pretty much living on Belt Two, were collected in the war room.

And we were just sitting.

I really need to do a better job of describing this room. It's huge, for one. I think the word 'amphitheater' might give an accurate impression of the height and breath. It was round, and on every wall there were huge floor-to-ceiling screens. *Big*. There were no techs or consoles in the room — they were all next door, so if we wanted to change something on one of the screens, we had to tap the comm and ask.

At the center of the room were a dozen very comfortable spinny chairs (you know, chairs that turn) on stat-grav pads so they could slide around on the floor. I promise, we didn't push ourselves around having races in those chairs. Really.

No, we just sat, staring at screens with nothing on them. Sure, the sensor displays were up, but they were blank. So — and I think this is priceless — anyone walking into that room would have seen Rear Admiral Ken Barron, Commodore Karen McMaster, Commodore Wes Pellew and Commodore Marshal Samuels all sitting in big chairs, facing opposite directions, and staring at nothing.

Yes, ladies and gentlemen, we were the defenders of your realm. Feeling confident?

I will point out again that we were just minutes away from our respective command posts, should evil have come to pass in local space, and out there in orbit the rest of the Jupiter Force was fully crewed, un-docked, and ready to respond to any challengers. So we weren't being negligent.

We were just sitting.

"So. See anything?" Wes asked at one point, and there was a chorus of 'nope' responses.

We sat some more.

"Hey, is that… nope…" I was hopeful there for a second, but the blip on one of the screens was just some sort of comet. Stupid comet.

We sat some even more.

That is so grammatically wrong, but that's what we did. My editors all wanted that sentence changed, but I held out and they finally caved. Just ramming home the point that we waited so long (even more longer!) that we were ready and willing to abandon any concerns for grammar. Well, I was at least.

"So chances are there isn't going to be anything to see today," Marshal said a bit later. "John hasn't even left Earth yet."

"Yes, but as soon as we leave this room, the pickets will pick up something. Fate will bend the fabric of space-time to make it happen," I assured him.

He laughed, "Okay then. Can someone who understands physics please comment on that?"

We all turned our chairs towards Karen, and I swear this is true, she was quietly asleep. Wes and Marshal chuckled and turned back to the screens, though I will admit I watched Karen sleep, until she woke up a few minutes later. Come on, it was a hell of a lot better than watching a blank screen.

And when she woke up, she smiled her unflappable smile, "All this personnel work has been cramping my sleep style."

I chuckled, "Yeah, well it's *my* bed covered in pads."

She laughed, "Tragic."

My expression switched to mock-serious, "For both of us, obviously."

Yeah, we didn't have much else to do. We were waiting for the fights to begin, but of course, we'd have to wait another day.

At this point, I think I can safely say I'll be turning the narrative over to John, Greg, Mik and Daragh — the people I assumed at the beginning would be getting all the page time. Guess I'm too vain, had to include more of me!

But we were finally into the busiest days of February now. Glorious February.

Let the games begin…

CHAPTER TWENTY-ONE

MOUNT UP

So here we are, on the big morning — 12 February 2232, Imperial Standard Calendar — when John and Rachel took their respective battleship squadrons out of Earth space. Once the battleships began to move, Glorious February really got started...

I should take a minute here to *compliment* movies about the scene I'm going to describe. Most actually get this right, even if the critics always assume the scene was just added in for effect. No, this is how it played, and with good reason.

The scene is always a dramatic one set on the bridge of *Bonaventure* — a brand new ship, untested in battle, but with a picked crew of the best women and men available. There were many incredibly able people on that bridge, and every one of them was very aware of the challenges *Bonnie* faced, going into such an important mission so very green. You could cut the tension with a knife, according to everyone I've talked to.

But when, in the movies, the actors on the bridge play their characters as anxious, some critics pounce, demanding to know why an elite Defense Command crew would be nervous. Well, because they knew how big the mission was going to be, even if they didn't know the particulars.

Hell, look at how anxious/nervous/quasi-panicked I got over the course of 2231. Everyone's entitled, as long as they don't let the anxiety interfere with their ability to do their job.

Anyway, at 0700 in the morning — sharp — Captain Lennox Williams appeared on his bridge, and with a warm smile he went from console to console, saying good morning to his new crew one by one. He knew many of these officers — he'd helped pick them, after all — but it was still a new team. He knew they were on edge.

"We're breaking orbit at 0845," he announced to his crew after he finished his greetings, and there were tentative deep breaths and some furtive glances. The bridge was relatively quiet, everyone speaking haltingly in low tones, trying not to seem nervous, but quietly admitting to one another that they were.

And this seemed to drag on. Remember how time moved slowly for me when I was waiting for the action to start? Same sort of feeling: they just wanted to get the mission started, but had to wait...

For an hour they waited. John was actually flying up from Admiralty House that morning, and it took him that long to land and reach *Bonnie's* bridge.

Here again the movies do the scene justice.

The lift doors opened, and John stepped out onto the cavernous bridge. He took a deep breath and, in the same instant, the XO snapped to attention, "His Lordship on deck."

This was tradition — one John wasn't entirely fond of — so everyone on the bridge came to their feet and to attention. At this point the First Lord or Admiral or whomever would generally walk to the middle of the bridge and give a rousing speech that would go down in the history books, get the crew fired up by explaining the importance of the upcoming mission, and all the rest.

That's what was expected.

John went a different direction. He looked around him, smiled, and said, "This is the best crew I could have asked for. Here's to all of you."

Then he started to clap. Clap, you know, slap two hands together in front of you. Applaud. His cadence was slow at first, and he looked around him as he clapped. This confused these nervous officers and ratings — they were expecting a speech, the veiled thrust of which would be that John was great and they were his servants.

Lennox Williams understood, though, so he started applauding as well, and then he and John turned to various consoles, raising their hands slightly while they clapped, suggesting the officers behind those panels should begin to clap too. The senior officers started following pretty quickly, then the juniors and the ratings.

The bridge was, within a moment, swallowed by the roar of applause from fifty officers and technicians (*Bonaventure* has a huge bridge, if you've never seen it), all applauding and looking at each other, John, and Lennox William with mixtures of first surprise and then, increasingly, a little pride. John has a way of making sure the people under his command don't think he believes it's all about him.

And it helps that he doesn't actually believe it's all about him.

He kept the applause going for a minute or two, and then he stopped his own clapping and let the rest die down as he moved to stand next to Lennox Williams, "Lennie, let's mount up."

"Yes sir," Lennox smiled brightly, then stepped forward and started issuing orders to prepare *Bonaventure* to break orbit.

"Sensors and Communications… who's behind the consoles?" John turned towards the bank of panels, identifying the Commander there.

"Jorge Allende, sir."

"He's been stuck running around with me for years, John," Lennox added from behind John, and the First Lord smiled.

"Jorge, you and I are going to be talking a lot over the next few days."

The Commander nodded, "Yes sir, it will be an honor."

John snorted a laugh, "You'll find out pretty quick that it's nothing of the sort. Alright Jorge, let's get Battlelink set up, all ships from our squadron. We're also probably going to get a call from Rachel Butler over on *Empire*."

Nodding, Jorge Allende started passing orders to his huge crew of officers and technicians.

Just to be clear, *Bonnie's* bridge was half-again the size of *Warspite's*, meaning it was just about three times the size of *Wolf's*. This was a ship meant to be a fleet flagship, and the command and control abilities it had in this one chamber (and their backups in the ship's secondary bridge) rivaled those at Admiralty House.

For the next forty-odd minutes, the bridge was buzzing, and the tension dissipating. The combination of John's uncharacteristic entry and the fact that the crew was finally able to get started on their departure jobs had seriously reduced the prevailing anxiousness.

These were fine officers, they weren't going to let themselves remain preoccupied.

When 0840 rolled around, and both battle squadrons were preparing for departure, Battlelink was up with all the ships of the *Bonaventure* Squadron.

Alright, sorry, this is going to get very list-like very quickly, but there's no way around that. Don't worry if you don't remember which name goes with which ship, I'll make sure to mention one in the context of the other any time I bring them up later on.

So, with John in this *Bonaventure* Squadron were obviously the three other *Bonaventure*-class ships: *Terra Nova* with Vice Admiral Lynn Boakai and Captain Alvin Godfrey, *Hibernia* with Captain Tom Flynn, and *Bonavista* with Captain Sheena Sutherland. The escort force for these four ships was relatively light, owing to the need to leave at least a few frigates and corvettes at Earth. Commodore Shamus Czarnecki, George Parks-Dawes' old escort commander, had retained control of the remains of the Light Squadron's cruisers, and now John was taking him along with two *Predator*-class frigates, *Hawk* and *Eagle*, and the corvettes *Charisma*, *Charm* and *Droll*.

So that made five escorts, including two frigates and three corvettes, admittedly still under the command of a loose affiliate of the Caldecott circle. I don't know if you recall, but Czarnecki had been part of 'my' force in the Battle Over Earth, and he seemed solid enough to me. Not worth tossing out over political affiliations, particularly since he'd never been a close friend of Dave Caldecott. He was in charge of the escort.

That was the *Bonaventure* Squadron, then: nine ships, all of whose skippers' faces were now up on some of *Bonaventure's* bridge screens.

"We're boosting in four minutes," Lennox was keeping an eye on the clock, and John nodded.

"Good. Rachel should be calling soon."

A minute later, she did call.

Now, in the interests of getting this all out there right now, here's what she had with her in the Heavy Squadron: the battleships *Empire* (her flagship, under Captain Liam Singh), *Repulse* (Emma Nelson), *Revenge* (Patty Brennan), *Royal Sovereign* (Diana Blackwood), and *Medusa* (Ophelia Zukhov), along with Shannon Hunter's three frigates *Panther* (Shannon's own), *Tiger* (Wen Luong) and *Jaguar* (Conrad Benwah). That's a total of eight ships — the Heavy Squadron was leaving behind two corvettes to add to the Light Squadron's two frigates and two corvettes…

Dammit this is getting confusing. I'd demand a chart, but you and I both know this publisher doesn't spring for that sort of thing.

To summarize, John had nine ships — four battleships, five escorts — and Rachel Butler had eight ships — five battleships and three escorts. They were leaving behind two frigates and three corvettes.

There.

Now, back to the narrative, Rachel Butler appeared on one of *Bonaventure's* screens about three minutes before the appointed launch time, her expression stoic, "We're ready to boost on schedule, sir."

John was standing at the front of his bridge with his hands in his pockets, "Excellent, Rachel. Godspeed out there. Be good!"

He said that with a bright smile, which Rachel didn't feel comfortable enough to return. She offered a conservative nod, "And good luck to you, sir."

"Thanks, Rachel."

The screen (the one with Rachel on it, not all of them, as one editor thought) then blanked. See how quick and efficient communications can be when the people talking aren't old friends?

Turning to Lennox, John nodded once, "At the mark, boost on your own discretion, Lennie."

With a broad smile, Lennox Williams nodded, "Very good, sir."

As the Flag Captain stepped over to the Helm and Navigation consoles to prepare the order, John moved from the middle of the bridge forward to the 'stage' — that's what anyone who's been aboard *Bonnie* knows to call the long, substantially raised platform in front of the big screens.

He watched the clock tick up towards 0845, and he assures me he was beginning to half-panic — to worry about whether he'd be able to manage this, to wonder if the [guesses] could be wrong after all…

I don't believe he was that worried, but he says he was. You decide.

The clock on one of the screens finally did hit 0845.

Looking up at his skippers on the Battlelink, John nodded, "Alright boys and girls, let's get a move on!"

Lennox Williams nodded to his Helm and Navigation Officer, "HNO, make acceleration for 198 kps, watch our formation. Course set for main vector to Point Luck."

Bonaventure is magnificent.

Just plain magnificent.

And watching the feeds from the news cameras that were in orbiting shuttles as the order was given, you get a hint as to why. The four *Bonaventure*-class ships fired their drives simultaneously, as did the escorts, and then with austere grace, they slid off into space, making speeds faster than any battleship before could have made.

From a little further behind in the orbit, the Heavy Squadron made a similar exit.

And that was it, our battleship squadrons were sent out to intercept their Martian counterparts, in an educated gamble to secure our position in the war.

CHAPTER TWENTY-TWO

RANGING MARS

"We're about thirty hours out, now," Val Rodriguez was entertaining Greg in her day cabin off the flank of *Warspite's* bridge. "Still no sign of outer pickets."

While John and Rachel were boosting out to meet the Martian assault forces, Greg and Mik had continued to press on, and now they were well within what Greg would have considered maximum range for outer pickets...

And, of course, I should stop to explain outer pickets.

After the Battle Over Earth, John had been bound and determined to make sure Earth wasn't caught by surprise again, so he'd collected the Admiralty yachts and a number of small logistics ships and sent them out on 'patrol' along the most likely approach vectors the Martians might choose. Starlights and Starbursts kitted out for extra-long patrols were also out running constant recon sweeps between those picket ships. The idea was to maximize the possibility of the Martians being detected well away from Earth, allowing time for the defenses to be activated and for the Home Fleet to go out to meet them.

Greg and John assumed (perhaps wrongly) that the Martians would have thought to do something similar — send out a web of their annoying but unfortunately effective 'scout bombers' (painfully uncomfortable ten-person craft that sometimes carried missiles, but we usually saw them doing simple recon) to guard the approaches to their planet.

Indeed, *Warspite* and *Goliath* were flying heavy combat fighter patrols around Greg's force in case a bomber happened past — the Starlights would jump on the plane before it realized what it had seen and sent warning to Mars... but that was assuming there were any of the damned things around. So far it didn't look like there were.

Of course, Greg's force was coming in on a random vector — not an approach the Martians would expect to see a battleship force use. Space is rather huge, so it's impossible to cover all angles. That was one of the reasons this attack was so brilliant.

Anyway, Greg nodded at Val's observation, "Thirty hours and no sign that the Martians are defending this vector."

Val was sitting behind her desk, and now she smiled, leaning back in her chair and lifting her boots up onto the tabletop, "We're going to hurt them, aren't we?"

Greg stared at the sensor maps on the screen, "I think we'll be effective. But to be honest, I think we have the easy task. I do not envy John's position."

I think we all realize by now that Greg was a big picture sort of guy — he knew that the more critical, and more tricky, part of this next couple of days of action would be John intercepting the Martian assault forces. The raid on Mars was going to be good for morale, but Greg didn't have enough firepower with him to do anything decisive. This was a Doolittle Raid (World War Two, look it up), John and Rachel's missions were Midway (same war and theatre, a number of months later).

"Can the First Lord win the war if he makes contact? That's the scuttlebutt that's been going around the crew, though I've been discouraging it," Val laced her fingers behind her neck and reclined her chair as far back as it'd go.

Frowning, Greg thought back to his communiqués with John. In an ideal situation, the Martians would have sent everything at Earth, and that could mean the annihilation of the Martian battle fleet in a single day. If their battle fleet was gone, they'd call in their other battleships from their scattered posts... presuming they hadn't already...

But that was all moot, because the first scenario was unlikely to the point of being near-ridiculous. I'm sorry, despite what the movies and most strategy sim games might suggest, it's virtually impossible to destroy the other side completely — unless, of course, you're willing to sacrifice everything you have to do so.

And guess what, John was in no mood to sacrifice ten battleships to destroy twelve.

Er. An estimated twelve.

Dammit, I'd be a terrible spy.

So the point of that is to say that the Martians weren't all going to be destroyed in this mess. John's goal was to do something akin to pulling a 'Jutland' — he didn't have to destroy them all, he just needed to bloody their noses so badly that the Martian Naval staff would decide it was too much of a risk to come straight at Earth again. And for you history buffs out there, he was hoping to do that without losing more ships than the Martians in the process (as the British had to at Jutland in 1916).

The plan was, at the very least, to scare the hell out of the Martians — make them think every time they sent their home fleet out, we'd beat it senseless, *and* attack their homeworld. That'd keep them from getting pushy.

So, I've meandered well away from the dialogue again. Sorry, it's necessary...

"I don't think John or Rachel will be able to completely destroy the forces they're going to face," Greg turned to look at Val, and his Flag Captain let out a sigh.

"Figured that'd be too easy. But we're retaking some of the momentum?"

Greg nodded once, "That's exactly what we will do. They won't be able to dictate this war. We'll put them on the defensive, and then attack them in our own time."

Val nodded, "That I can live with."

In his day cabin on *Cyclops*, Mik was still feeling somewhat uncomfortable about having dispatched Guy Vivar with the convoy. The more he reflected on that decision, the more he wondered whether the annoying Commander would do something deadly, and get a bunch of civilians killed.

Mik knew it was too late to worry about such things, but knowing that didn't stop him from worrying anyway. But he wasn't letting it consume him. His primary focus was on other matters: the Mars raid itself.

Greg had planned this operation, so Mik had full confidence that the details had been looked after. Nevertheless, he wanted to study it himself. Well, study it *again*. He was going back over the [guesses] about the expected Martian defense forces on site, and he couldn't help but worry that they were too optimistic.

The best [guesses] still said there would be *no* Martian battleships at Mars. Eight battleships total were expected to be permanently stationed there, but in order for a crushing blow to be made against Earth, all of these battleships were [probably] being dispatched to face John. Two were simply twelve hours behind the six-battleship main force, acting as a rearguard…

To be honest, that was a pretty useless deployment — if the Martian plan went off without a hitch, it'd still put the nearest battleships a day away from the red rock, and it deprived the Martian Grand Admiral (we were already pretty sure it'd be Garvey commanding this attack) of two of his battlewagons during the fight.

But there may have been a purpose or logic to it that I don't see — I am looking back with hindsight, after all.

Anyway, those were the predictions, guesses, *whatever* I keep calling them. Mik knew well that guesses could be wrong, though, and what pleased him most about the assault plan was that Greg was similarly prepared for a surprise.

Greg's assault plan had contingency scenarios built in, one ready in case they arrived to find the whole Martian fleet still at the red world, and one for four Martian battleships, three, two, one, and none. They were all very flexible — Greg doesn't rely on frameworks, he knows well how to improvise — but they laid out guidelines of action in case problems arose.

Mik appreciated this, and he continued to appreciate it as he reviewed the plans again.

The assault force drove on.

CHAPTER TWENTY-THREE
THE PICKETS

Admiralty yachts are beautiful ships. Their hulls are gleaming white with golden trim, they're always polished and shiny, and they completely avoid the hull designs we're used to with military ships, leaving them sleek, almost like sea-going sailing yachts.

But, like so many (but not all) beautiful things, the yachts were about six feet to the left of totally useless. That's an over-clever attempt to say they were actually pretty useless.

Pretty. But useless.

Except for today, actually. John had known full well that the yachts were as much good to him as a decorative shoe rack (no idea where that simile came from), so he figured out what he could do with them. The Admiralty had four, after all.

And since I've already explained this, I won't be coy: the yachts were serving as picket ships. One of them, *Admiral Ku* (they're all named for former First Lords), was pretty much on the base course straight for Mercury, roaming back and forth along the imaginary perimeter that lay about a day and a half out from Earth orbit.

Skippering this lovely little ship was Lieutenant Commander Lisa Sims, an up-and-comer who John had figured for a corvette commander by 2233 at the latest, and whose name you're probably familiar with. She was sitting in a very well appointed (in plainspeak: cushy) 'bridge'.

Sorry, I just realized I've been over-using the brackets, I'll stop.

Lisa was yawning, because her chair was far too comfortable to keep her awake with the usual discomfort and coldness that most bridge chairs provide. Damned comfort.

Sitting around her was a command crew of four, and they were all pretty tired too. Well, tired's nothing new for a Defense Command officer — it's part of the job. But 'tired' may not be the best word here. They were all *sleepy* too, and that was unquestionably due in part to the pervasive over-cushiness around the bridge.

"If we had one of those 'sounds of the oceans' tracks going, I'm pretty sure I'd be snoring," Lieutenant Carmine Hellqvist was XO aboard *Admiral Ku*, and like Lisa Sims, she was an up-and-comer.

Rubbing the back of her neck, Lisa shook her head, "Yes, I suppose so. Just as well we don't then, what?"

Lisa's a Brit, don't think I mentioned that. Carmine's from Luna One.

"You know, I still haven't heard a real ocean. But for some reason the sounds of the ocean put me right out."

This must seem like inane conversation to you (well, if you're from Capital Island like me, the prospect of someone never having heard an ocean verges on the tragic, but moving on...). You have to understand, *Admiral Ku* had been out on this picket job for three weeks now, and the yacht was slated to be out here for another week before they took it in for a tune up and to trade out the crew for the next cruise.

John didn't have enough yachts and other reliable picket ships available to rotate the hulls themselves, so he'd set it up so that each yacht would have two crews assigned to it, and they'd trade every month. Better to keep the crews sharp — and to keep them from getting too comfortable with the cushiness.

The conversation about the sounds of the ocean was ambling along pleasantly when the drowsy tech at the Sensors and Communications station narrowed his eyes at one of his screens, "Wait a minute. I see… six battleships. Plus escorts. Not ours."

"What?" Carmine didn't sound particularly impressed as she asked the question, but then the words started to sink in.

Lisa leaned forward in her armchair, "That'll be the Martian fleet. Six battleships?"

"Plus three destroyers and five destroyer escorts… doing 180 kps. They'll be able to shoot us in about five minutes."

Running a hand through her hair, Lisa nodded, "Alright, send that back to Admiral Butler. Billy, turn us around and get us the hell out of here before they realize they've been seen."

The Helm and Navigation Tech nodded, deftly turned *Admiral Ku* over and then boosted away from the oncoming Martian force. The tiny little ship was tough to see on the best of days, so it got away without being noticed — though I should point out that, hitting 182 kps, it was redlining its small drives. Yachts just weren't fast enough. If *Admiral Ku* had been noticed, one of the Martian destroyers would have hunted it down without much trouble.

I say that with some certainty.

Admiral Hawke was named, of course, for Lord Ian Hawke, though in terms of design it was no different from *Admiral Ku*. I say 'though' because Ian Hawke and 'that little yellow man' never really got along. For instance, Hawke often called 'Wolseley' Weichün Ku 'that little yellow man' — a very old slur used by Caucasians against Asians. Ian Hawke had a sense of history when it came to being a racist sonofabitch. At one point the Tam clan had been so offended that it had nearly — *nearly* — put out a contract to kill him, but eventually the families thought better of it.

You know those Tams, lunatics. All of them.

Admiral Hawke was on the vector to Mars, and its commander, Lieutenant Commander Chad Lerner, was another of the up-and-comers in the fleet — actually more senior than Lisa and Carmine both.

He was pacing around his bridge, far less calm about the impending approach of the Martian forces than Lisa had been, worrying rightly that if his yacht was seen, there wouldn't be much at all he could do to survive the Martian attack.

"Sir, I have enemy forces on my scope… six battleships, six destroyers and nine destroyer escorts."

"Very well, inform First Lord Fiora aboard *Bonaventure*. Helm, turn us around and get us out of here," Chad's orders were even, and *Hawke* turned smoothly and began to accelerate away at 181 kps (the ship wasn't as well-tuned as *Admiral Ku*, appropriately enough, so it was slower).

It was only a moment later that another report came in, "Sir, two destroyer escorts are accelerating to 201 kps, coming right after us!"

From this point on, the panic in the voices on the bridge of *Admiral Hawke* was palpable. Chad took his seat and held onto the arms of his chair as he delivered hurried orders, "Kick everything we can into the drives, prepare our mag to fire."

Each yacht carried one mag, good for blowing up asteroids, and that was about it. It didn't even have a full mount, so it couldn't traverse properly.

"There's a comet seven minutes out… if we blow it we could get lost in the debris, they might never find us!"

That was probably the comet that appeared as a blip on the screen in the Belt Two war room.

Chad took that report from his Sensors and Communications tech with a nod, "Get us there, helm. Start tossing out the furniture if you have to!"

Admiral Hawke poured everything it had into its drives, and sitting at the manual mag controls, a technician looked down the sights at the comet as it got closer and closer to firing range.

It was like one of these movies that are so popular, where the young and innovative officer manages to defy all odds — and I don't just mean steep or difficult odds, I mean *all* odds — and survive thanks to a stunning plan. The officer is invariably played by a young heartthrob, male or female, and tends to risk everything for the love of his or her life, because he or she rather stupidly gets him or herself into a fix. But it works out in the end.

So think of Chad Lerner as that young, dynamic hero with a plan to keep his plucky little yacht alive despite the two destroyer escorts chasing it down… just imagine the movie…

Two minutes into the chase, the Martians got into laser range. While the crew of the little yacht wished themselves forward to the safety of the comet, Martian lasers sliced their ship apart, and killed all of them.

Young Chad Lerner, one of the bright hopes for the future of the service, had died on his first command. I only know what happened on the bridge of his ship because some of the vid recorder logs survived.

I'll be the first to say that it's possible to beat the odds in the real world. But you don't *always* beat the odds, and when you don't it costs you.

It cost young Chad and his crew their lives.

But we knew that the Martians were on their way, and there would be some revenge.

CHAPTER TWENTY-FOUR

SEEING THE ENEMY

Much to my shame, I can't recall the twentieth-century strategic analyst whose book first instilled in me the importance of finding the enemy first. Believe me, this piece of doctrine isn't some innovation I'm the first to write about, it's a well established lesson of fleet warfare... I just can't remember who to credit with it.

Hell, it was probably Nelson himself, in the nineteenth century, but that's no matter.

Anyway, finding the enemy first is considered in Naval circles to be one of the most crucial steps towards winning a fight. This really shouldn't be a surprise, I suppose — in any kind of conflict, the information edge is generally a good one to have. Once you know where your enemy is (and he or she don't know where you are) you have the chance to dictate the engagement. This is critical — you choose where and when to fight, and *how*.

So the pickets that were positioned based on John's [guesswork] had done their job: they'd confirmed the Martians were coming on as expected, and they'd established the timeline for the ensuing engagement.

About twelve hours after each yacht detected its Martian fleet, battle would be joined. Twelve hours after that, Greg and Mik would hit Mars.

It was all pretty straightforward, and I'm not certain just how long I can drag it out for drama's sake... hmm.

Well, here's a simple method: back to Belt Two!

I know, I promised to stay out of Belt Two, but it actually occurs to me as I talk about dragging out those twelve hours, the torturous waiting was something we in the war room were experiencing.

While the women and men cruising to the battle were doubtless anxious in a way that only people going into battle can be anxious, Karen, Wes, Marshal and I were just about losing it in the war room. Well, not Karen, but the rest of us. Well, actually, not the rest of them, just me.

"So, we *know* that's them. Confirmed ID. Looks like *Admiral Hawke* didn't survive the escorts though," I repeated that observation (for probably the fifth time), and I was stared at by the elite officers who were sitting calmly in their seats.

Wes was eating soup, and he looked up at me, "We're not going to know anything more for twelve hours. There's no way John could get to them before then."

I folded my arms across my chest and stopped my pacing for a moment, reading down the list of ship types that *Admiral Ku* had noted coming from Mercury.

"That looks like survivors of the Battle Over Earth, back for more. Anyone here know much about Rachel Butler? What's her style?"

Can you tell I really wanted to be out there with the fleets? This was brutal.

No one answered my question, so I turned around. Marshal was reading a pad and sipping a coffee, paying me no attention at all. Karen was, again, snoozing in her chair. It's a testament to how preoccupied I was by this soon-to-be-battle that I didn't just end up staring at her for a while.

Wes was eating his soup, but as I turned around he looked over his bowl at me, "We already said none of us know what she's like. Ken, sit down. Watch Karen sleep for a while."

"I'm not asleep..." Karen woke up and said that the way someone says she was 'just resting her eyes' when she was snoring away. Karen rarely snores...

"See, can't placate me with that," I shook my head. "Dammit, Wes, how can you just sit there like that, with your soup? You don't even like soup!"

I was getting a little exasperated.

Karen woke right up, and Marshal looked up from his pad, as if I'd just declared that I was a walking, talking, humanoid wolf.

"I *love* soup. Always have," Wes said slowly, lowering his bowl.

I frowned, "No you haven't. That's a lie."

"I think I'd know," Wes' eyebrows climbed just a little.

Karen shifted in her seat, "Yeah, that's one of the first things I learned about Wes. Soup."

Marshal chimed in, "Haven't you ever watched him order at a meal? He gets soup, then he gets more soup."

Of course, I had no idea what they were talking about. Because I'm both an idiot and a terrible friend...

"You're... kidding. You three are all pulling my leg."

"No, I'm enjoying my delicious soup," Wes shook his head before raising his bowl again.

At this point I turned back to the screens with a less than dignified huff, and I was again ignored for a while. After a couple of minutes, though, I heard the door open, and Charlie Peters stuck his head in. Now Charlie has been very poorly served in this book — all I've written about him involves, I believe, a raid on the pudding isles of Belt Two supermarkets.

But although Charlie was a Special Brancher, he was also one of the members of the Fiora ring, and he wanted front-row seats for the battles. He'd thus handed off the next couple of days' training to Carly, his XO, and had arrived to save me.

"Charlie! Quick, does Wes like soup?"

See, because he wasn't there when the joke started, he wouldn't know to lead me on.

Frowning as he closed the hatch behind him, Charlie nodded, "His favorite food."

I stared at Charlie for a minute.

He frowned back at me, "What?"

"That's it, I'm a terrible friend."

Huffing again, I turned and went back to my chair next to Karen, then sat down and glanced at her. She was sleeping again.

Well, at least I had something to watch... because we had many hours left to wait. The long wait before a battle...

Chapter Twenty-Five
The Fools Wait

While I might have been demonstrating how much of a fool I was, I wasn't really suffering from the worst wait of the day. Far from it. The Defense Command officers and crew in the ships cruising into battle were suffering the worst. Yes, they were preoccupied by their duties, but they were also going to be putting their lives on the line.

John was observing many of these people as he walked around *Bonnie's* bridge — stoic people, who were clearly forcing themselves not to react, not to appear anxious. I'm sure I'll never stop saying it in these books: the waiting is the worst.

War or no war, waiting is always a pain; while you wait for something stressful, you can imagine all the ways it might go wrong, all the things you'll have to do… They all seem more daunting than they are, and you can start to move towards panic. Experience helps, but then, no one in Defense Command yet had a lot of experience in cruising into action against an organized enemy with the kind of firepower of these Martians.

Some of us had done it, but doing it once, even twice, even a dozen times, doesn't necessarily quell the anxiety. Because something can always go wrong.

And the people on John's bridge were all more than smart enough to be able to think of hundreds of plausible things that could fail and end their lives, and more importantly (at least to all the ones I've spoken to) put Earth in danger.

"So Jorge, tell me how much longer we have to wait," John directed the question at Commander Allende, and the officer looked from one console to another before returning the First Lord's glance.

"Another six hours, sir."

John nodded evenly, "Alright. If they're flying smart, they'll have pickets out front to watch people like us. Jorge, order Admiral Boakai to launch our combat cover."

This was all covered in the plan, but John half-explained it in his order for the benefit of his bridge crew. Usually he wouldn't be so overt in clarifying *why* he was giving certain orders, but in this case his actions could hopefully assuage some of the waiting pains, at least briefly. They were launching fighters, after all.

Lennox Williams, upon hearing the orders, turned to Jorge as well, "Have Tim launch the Bonniestars."

The Bonniestars were, of course, *Bonaventure's* leading squadron. They'd do the first three-hour patrol, then land to top-up while the Bonnies went out to take the second shift.

With Lennox's orders passed on, and Lynn Boakai issuing similar commands to each of the other battleships, the space before the advancing squadron rapidly filled with fighters. If the Martians had scouts out forward, the Starlights would hopefully deal with them.

Unfortunately, that was about all anyone could do at the moment. There was no way to speed up time, to take the edge off the long wait… they just had to tough it out.

And they weren't the only ones.

Members of Rachel Butler's crew commended to me the steadiness of her presence on the bridge of *Empire*. Liam Singh, the veteran battleship skipper, in particular told me he'd been concerned at first when the newcomer had come aboard — he had been uncertain of this new commander's abilities.

Concerns like that are typical of Captains receiving new Flag Officers — there's always the worry that someone got promoted for reasons other than merit, and that they might in turn give ridiculous orders that got your ship banged up, or your crew killed.

But as Liam Singh kept an eye on Rachel during the cruise out, he was impressed by her calm. Now, he couldn't take calmness during the wait as a certain sign she'd be alright in combat — there's always a chance that people who appeared calm going into the battle are that way because they have no idea what they're getting into. That said, he liked what he saw, and his bridge crew concurred.

Empire was a real tough ship, and had been around the block (cliché, I know) a couple of times. If you recall, it was this ship that had been entrusted with conveying Dave Caldecott to his exile with the Coalition (as well as that went). The crew had excellent instincts, and if I had to pick a battleship outside of *Warspite* to be aboard for a cataclysmic clash of fleets, I may well have picked *Empire*…

Not that any of the other Heavy Squadron battlewagons weren't of high caliber… I'm just going to paint myself into an awkward corner if I start trying to pick battleship favorites — beyond *Bonnie*, of course. So I'll stop.

Anyway, that tangled mess of prose is supposed to make sure you feel alright about Rachel Butler's abilities. While her veteran bridge crew was up to handling the stress of the wait on its own, she wasn't creating problems, and was in fact reinforcing the calm.

In point of fact, just about the only not-calm person in the vicinity of Earth (that I've talked to personally, anyway) was, you guessed it, Daragh Ryan.

Daragh was in the same boat I was — entirely cut off from a battle he felt he ought to be involved in, and not handling it with the aplomb that a grownup should.

In the C&C, in that mysterious underground level of Admiralty House (the one that, if you remember *The Almost Coup*, I can't reveal the actual location of), he was pacing around with his shotgun leaned back against his shoulder (not loaded — too much sensitive equipment in C&C for even Daragh to get that bold) and barking rather sharply at people, sometimes at random.

I'm sure that sounds rather unprofessional and perhaps unkind to you. This is Daragh, are you expecting something different?

"And do *you* have anything to report, then?" he asked a passing Ensign at one point.

The boy paled, then squeaked, "No sir…"

"Ah, that's alright then boyo, on about your business," he let the Ensign wander off.

As the boy cleared the blast radius, Daragh started bellowing again, "Now how long is it exactly 'til the clairvoyant gadgetry in this room tells me something other than *hold please*? I'm sure dying of old age'll be fun, but I'd bloody rather do it *after* the battle, yeah?"

By this time, enough ranting of this sort had been absorbed, so the C&C staff were mostly past reacting to it. Well, the junior ones were still slightly (wholly) terrified of the apparently psychotic Second Lord, but everyone else was fine.

"We wait another four hours, Lord Ryan," Captain Ron Davis, Admiralty House's Sensors and Communications Officer (that is to say, the guy in charge of all sensors and communications for Defense Command *on Earth*) looked up from his place behind one of the many rows of nearby consoles.

"Bah, damn ya."

Daragh continued to pace.

This was the waiting game. If reading about it is frustrating, just multiply that feeling by a billion and that's where Daragh was. We wanted this to get started, and we damned well might clomp around like three year olds until it did.

Seems odd, really. Even inappropriate. I think I'm paraphrasing a Welshman in a fine old movie here, but some might rightly say that only a fool runs towards a battle.

Fools we were. Fools we definitely were.

Chapter Twenty-Six

The First Moments

Rachel Butler's Heavy Squadron was the first to finish its waiting period, and as the Martian Mercury force was sighted by the scouting Starlights she'd sent ahead of her, she headed to the front of *Empire's* bridge, where the skippers of all the battleships along with Commodore Shannon Hunter were waiting for her on Battlelink.

"Looks like they're exactly where we want them. Back the Starlights off, stand by to launch all remaining fighters for point defense cover," Rachel crossed her arms and squared off in a classic command pose, and the fighters were ordered to pull back.

Hopefully they'd gone unnoticed by the Martians...

"Form up the battle line. Shannon, have your frigates ready to move forward to interdict against their destroyers."

Shannon Hunter nodded on the screen, then looked away. She had her own skippers — Conrad Benwah and Wen Luong — up on *Panther's* Battlelink, waiting for orders. As the directives were relayed to those ships, Rachel watched them surge ahead on *Empire's* main screen, and take up station as a vanguard.

There's no way to build dramatic tension now, really — this was going to be a simple encounter, two sides running right at each other, the Martians not exactly sure what they were in for, the Heavy Squadron getting pretty much what it expected.

Captain Liam Singh came up beside Rachel as the icons of the Starlights dropped back across the main screen, "Time until the Martians see us?"

His Sensors and Communications Officer checked with one of her techs, then replied, "Four more minutes to maximum detection range."

We could only really guess what Martian maximum detection range was at that point, but it was an educated guess at least.

Liam leaned closer to Rachel now, "So that's six battleships, three destroyers and five DEs... they have the edge in escorts, alright."

Rachel nodded at the quiet words, her brow creasing as she assessed her options. Her basic encounter strategy was to form battle line and dance the dance of battleship fighting — trade heavy blows and try to hurt the other side faster than it hurt you.

But that wasn't the strategy she really wanted to stick with. It was good enough to serve as the universal fallback — if all the other clever plans didn't work, then a straight gun-to-gun fight would still probably do the business.

That said, she could afford to be a *little* clever. Not too clever — too clever is dangerous — but maybe she could split them up...

How?

"Shannon, I need you to send one frigate forward. Try to bait their escorts to chase you back. If we can get some of their screening DEs moving out ahead of the line, we might be able to level the escort odds for you," Rachel's eyes darted to Shannon as she spoke, and the veteran Commodore tilted her head very slightly before nodding.

"Sounds like a job for you, Conrad," she passed the command along. "Move out there, see if you can drag some Martians back with you. The battleships want to get in some target practice before the main event."

Rachel couldn't see Conrad Benwah's reply, but the feed is in the archives. With a somber nod, the elite Ojibwa skipper passed some orders along to his Helm and Navigation Officer, and *Jaguar's* thrust kicked up again.

"Reduce closing speed," Rachel gave the orders softly. They'd have to wait again — but only very briefly.

See, the idea here — and again, Rachel didn't have to explain it explicitly because the Defense Command skippers she was talking to were well aware of its intent — was to trick the Martians into dividing their force. The thinking goes like this: if the Martians saw they'd been detected by a patrolling frigate — a lone patrolling frigate — they'd probably try to destroy that ship to keep it from reporting in.

The Martian battleships could (despite the stupidity of their turrets) easily do away with a *Predator*-class frigate. However, bait like a single frigate could indeed be a trap, so logically the Martians would send their own lighter ships after it — their destroyers and destroyer escorts.

We've been away from the Martian fleet for a while, so just as a reminder, Martian destroyers were essentially equivalent to our frigates, and their destroyer escorts were on par with our corvettes.

The Martian force from Mercury had eight of those ships — nothing to shake a stick at, that's like having the whole Jupiter Force as an escort — so Rachel wanted to pull some of them out ahead, and then blast them with her battle line.

It was a chance, but she didn't risk too much by taking it — a single frigate would be sufficient bait, and with Conrad Benwah on the bridge of that ship, it was almost a certainty that it wouldn't be lost.

So while the Heavy Squadron battleships and Shannon's two other frigates reduced speed to give Conrad room to play, the skippers and Rachel herself watched with mounting apprehension. They were about to get into this, at last...

Standing in Admiralty House C&C, Daragh Ryan was getting updates on the developments as they took place. It wasn't quite realtime, but every order Rachel was giving was being sent back to Admiralty House as well, so that Daragh would know what was going on. He, in turn, was sending word on to us up at Belt Two, Lia at Hawke One, and over to Marlene at Venus.

We all waited with rather baited breaths.

Taking his time, Conrad Benwah ordered *Jaguar* onto an oblique course... meaning he turned his ship so it wasn't pointing straight at the enemy fleet. That way it'd appear as though they'd happened upon a patrolling ship, instead of having run into the leading vessel of a force coming out to meet them. Smart move — Conrad's a hell of a frigate man.

Closing the range took *Jaguar* about three minutes at cruising burn — again, setting up to look as though he was just on patrol, Conrad had reduced from maximum speed to a healthy (if a tad brisk for patrol) 196 kps. I can only imagine the faces on the bridge of the Martian flagship when the frigate appeared.

The way one movie imagined the Martian perspective has always stuck with me. The bridge is dark and gloomy and red-lit — the way all villains' ships inevitably are. A guy is being shot for insubordination because he stammered somewhere in the background, all the women are in tight clothes that reveal much cleavage, and are fawning over the men like exotic slave-girls in those bad movies from the 2050s. Then *Jaguar* appears on the scope, and the Admiral leaps from his chair, knocking over the two women who'd been caressing his upper arms, "By the red sands of Mars, that's a Defense Command frigate! To battle stations at once!"

And then he pulls out his sidearm and, for no reason, shoots one of the women who'd been rubbing him.

I really don't understand how the movie maker in that case thought that made any sense. I mean… well… I don't know where to start, but then I doubt I need to explain to you that that's probably not how it went down on the Martian flagship.

More likely — and much less entertainingly — the bridge was quiet, with an urgent report being passed up to the Admiral sitting on his elevated dais.

Whatever happened, Rachel got her wish.

There were quiet cheers on *Empire's* bridge when one destroyer and two destroyer escorts accelerated away from their own formation. The telemetry was being fed back to *Empire* from *Jaguar*, and the frigate now turned hard away and initiated a full-thrust burn, trying to keep ahead of the Martians coming after it.

Oh, I say 'quiet cheers' because it was one of those moments of elation during which nobody could yell "huzzah". There were quietly pumped fists, "Yes!" was whispered sharply, and people said things like "we've got the bastards" under their breaths. So there were cheers, but they were quiet cheers. This confused my editors to no end… I don't know if it makes any sense now. Ah well…

They had the bastards, alright.

"There's the first three kills of the day," Rachel looked up at her skippers on the Battlelink screens. "Hold formation in the battle line, but whoever registers the first kill is getting extra beer rations when we get back."

A neat little perk for the ship with the most effective gunnery — not the sort of thing Greg was known for offering, so it was a bit of a change for his old Heavy Squadron.

For the next minute, the ships of Rachel's force watched as the range ticked down.

"As soon as they see us, they're going to try to reverse course," Rachel continued to think on her feet. "All ships prepare to jump forward, full burn."

Remember back in *The Almost Coup*, when the Martian battleships had jumped forward into range of the Light Squadron — when they'd destroyed the battlecruisers and the carriers under Parks-Dawes? Well, the battleships of the Heavy Squadron had found that maneuver to be rather inspiring, and under Greg they'd worked on a squadron acceleration of a similar type. It's a terrifying maneuver to watch, not just because it's dangerous, but because seeing that many big ships coming at you that fast can't *not* be daunting.

The prize here wouldn't be as big as had been the Light Squadron, but it would be significant nonetheless.

"They'll detect us in forty seconds," the Sensors and Communications Officer reported, and Rachel nodded.

"Prepare for a fast-track laser solution on the destroyer, Vera," Liam Singh turned to his XO, and she nodded as she readied her targeting array. Liam's a practicing Sikh, so he wasn't interested in that beer for himself, but he knew his crew might appreciate the reward.

Flagships generally like to try to prove their excellence, I've found. Remind people why they *are* the flagships.

Conrad was playing his role quite well; now he was pouring on another burst of speed, making it look as though he was really trying to run. It'd do no good to make the Martians think he wasn't actually running — they'd get suspicious. And better yet, the faster he went, the faster they had to chase, and the more difficult it would be for them to reverse.

"Twenty seconds to scan range. At this rate, they'll be in our outer fire envelop thirty seconds after that," *Empire's* Sensors and Communications Officer reported again.

The closing rate here was phenomenal.

"Wish I could see their faces," Shannon quipped over the Battlelink with a smile, and Rachel half-shrugged.

"You'll have to settle for seeing them in pieces."

Ouch, cold.

The Martians came into range, and you can almost *see* the panic in their icons on the archived sensor logs. Alright, that's an exaggeration, but I've never seen three ships try to turn around so fast. Going from 'huzzah, we're chasing the Imperial dog' to 'sweet sands of Mars, we're all going to die' in the blink of an eye could *not* be fun.

That's what you get for trying to destroy us. Sorry, but we're not secretive about consequences of trying to attack the Empire. You *die*. Simple.

And die was what these three ships were about to do.

Because of their stupidly-designed rotating drive pods (instead of our pods with multiple directional vents) the Martians had to actually spin their engine pods around to get maximum thrust in the reverse direction. That cost them ten seconds. Their full reverse-drive-stop then took another ten. Then they had to try to work back up to full speed from a standing stop…

The battleships leapt onto them, with no remorse.

"Shoot!" seemed to be barked in stereo on *Empire's* bridge — one of the calls from Liam Singh, the rest coming over the Battlelink.

The Martian ships vanished, just like that, and the Heavy Squadron pushed on through their wreckage. As Conrad turned to rejoin the formation, Rachel turned to *Empire's* Sensors and Communications Officer, "Who drew first blood?"

The Commander frowned, moving around behind her panels before looking up with a nod, "It was *Repulse*, ma'am. Sorry to say."

On the Battlelink, Emma Nelson barked a laugh, "Got it everyone. The beer's ours!"

There were audible cheers from *Repulse's* bridge, and Rachel smiled.

The squadron's spirits were good as they closed for the next phase of their fight.

But before we get to that, the first phase of the next engagement was just getting started...

CHAPTER TWENTY-SEVEN
FIRST LORD, MEET GRAND ADMIRAL

While the Martian escorts from the Mercury force were meeting their unfortunate end, the Starlights John had deployed ahead of his *Bonaventure* force were picking up the Martian home fleet's approach.

"That puts them… four minutes out, present closing speed, sir," Jorge Allende made his report from *Bonnie's* Sensors and Communications post, and John nodded.

"Alright, maintain flank acceleration. Put a full count of the Martian ships up on the main screen."

Remember, John's squadron included the four *Bonaventure*-class ships, as well as Shamus Czarnecki's *Hawk* and *Eagle*, along with the corvettes *Charisma*, *Charm* and *Droll*. That was by no means a weak force, though as John arrived on the stage at the front of *Bonnie's* vast bridge, he admits to have harbored more than a pang of fear that it wouldn't be enough.

Coming to a stop and setting his hands on his hips as he stared at the screen, he let out a quick breath, "Well, that's just great."

When you listen to the bridge log, that doesn't sound like a negative comment or a positive one — it's just an observation. According to John, though, he really wasn't terribly pleased by what he was seeing.

The six battleships were expected — remember, our *guesses* had told us that we were going to see six up front, with a rearguard of two additional battleships mysteriously (senselessly) deployed twelve hours behind, in a no man's land where they were too far from the main fleet to render assistance, and yet too far from Mars to defend their homes.

Still don't know what they were thinking with that… except perhaps that if John blew through the front six somehow, those battleships could slow him down if he counterattacked directly against Mars. They obviously weren't expecting Greg to be coming from the other direction…

Anyway, the six battleships were there, but so was a *huge* formation of escorts — *six* destroyers and *nine* destroyer escorts. I've looked at this deployment a number of times, and never has it looked particularly bright to me. I mean, I try to be fair to the Martians (admittedly, I don't try very hard) but this doesn't make a lot of sense.

The only guess I can come up with is that, if their plan had worked flawlessly and they'd arrived in Earth space with twelve battleships to our nine, those escorts would have been there to defend against fighters, or to shoot down civilian ships trying to escape.

Sounds fair enough, I suppose.

And I should point out that so far all the signs pointed to this Martian operation being *very* well coordinated. Can't fault them on that. If you look at the intercept points — Point Luck and Point Luck II — they're almost equidistant from Earth. In other words, if John and Rachel hadn't been out there to meet the Martians, they would indeed have converged on Earth at essentially the same time.

As much as I routinely slam the Martians, their timing was impeccable. At the Battle Over Earth, it had been foiled by Marlene Stoll using her sorceress powers, now it was coming up against the best [guesswork] network in the solar system.

Thank God.

Anyway, where was I with all of this? Right, John was standing on the stage, not liking the number of escorts he was seeing. That was *fifteen* escort ships, to his five. And while I'll credit Shamus Czarnecki with good skills as a cruiser officer, there wasn't much chance of him winning that fight.

Daragh himself couldn't have made it happen. Even if he'd tried his infamous 'wiggle' maneuver.

"Well, this is going to be interesting…" John looked up at the many monitors showing the faces of his officers on Battlelink. "Shamus, put your frigates in line abreast over our battle line, and put the corvettes below in that same formation. Lynn, form the battle line, and then reduce to stop. All ships hold formation."

Lynn Boakai understandably blinked in surprise, "Sorry, Lord Fiora, was that *slow to stop?*"

He nodded, "Yes, it was. All ships prepare for jump acceleration."

That earned him a frown from his officers, but they obeyed, issuing the orders to the squadron. This, I probably don't need to tell you, was not exactly orthodox. You never stood still in a fight if you could help it — movement was one of the best defenses you had out there, because without it you were, for lack of a better colloquialism, a sitting duck.

So what was John doing ordering his ships to an all-stop?

This was a gamble, a big one, that was based on dramatic effect instead of tactical sense. I'd explain, but this gives me a great excuse to jump over to Venus, to let the sorceress herself (who we've not seen for *two whole books, dammit!*) explain.

While we were in our war room at Belt Two, Marlene was on the bridge of *Sorceress* watching the reports coming in on the battleship's main screen. I should mention that, because of comm lag, she was seeing all this half an hour after it took place… but it's like tape delay — it was still realtime to her.

Kyle Feldman, her Flag Captain, was at her shoulder, and as John's ships slowed to a stop, he looked at Marlene, "What's he doing?"

Marlene smiled, "Showing us why he's First Lord. If that's Garvey leading the fleet, he's going to remember when we stopped him on the way to Earth, and he's going to get nervous."

If you remember your *Almost Coup*, Marlene had been sitting in space waiting for the Martians when they'd come upon her, and after that their entire assault plan had gone right out the window.

"But fighting from a standstill?" Kyle Feldman was asking the questions that any sensible Defense Command officer would ask — the questions John was even asking himself.

Marlene glanced at her Flag Captain, "Garvey will be asking the same question, wondering what John has up his sleeve. Keep in mind, Kyle, the Martians didn't even know the *Bonnies* existed. This is going to be a disconcerting surprise for them."

Kyle took a deep breath, "I hope so."

"Oh, it will…"

Unfortunately that's the only excuse I have to insert Marlene into this book. For you Marlene fans out there, fear not, she and I may not cross paths much in 2232, but you can be damned sure she'll be back a whole lot more in 2233.

Anyway, back to *Bonaventure*.

"The Starlights are forming up with us now. Ready to launch the rest of our fighter squadrons," Lynn Boakai reported over Battlelink, and John nodded.

"Launch them. Now, we have to get our targeting priorities straight: as soon as they come into range, I want each *Bonnie* to line up on one Martian battleship, and one *only*. When I give the order, open them up," John's words were cool.

Now here's a question: wouldn't that have been the plan? Well, not necessarily. I think it was back in *The Almost Coup* when I talked about how just one or two extra battleships should give one side a decisive advantage over the other — remember, the whole 'tag-teaming' thing, where two extra battleships meant two of ours would face two-to-one odds, and thus die twice as fast? With that in mind, the skippers of the *Bonnies* might have, not wrongly, elected to divide their mighty laser batteries between two Martians battleships, trying to compensate for the smaller numbers.

But John wanted each *Bonnie* to focus on one Martian only… which meant each Martian battleship would get four full laser beams in the gut. Oh, don't know if I mentioned that. Part of what made the *Bonaventure*-class so epically powerful was its power grid: while corvettes and frigates could only fire one laser emitter at a time, and all other battleships could fire only two, the *Bonnies* could fire *four*.

That's what you get when you install enough power supplies to operate a carrier and charge all its planes, then remove most of the planes and all the power-hungry support systems that go with them. Lotsa power.

So much that it gets called 'lotsa'.

And if you do your math, then (I had to get the calculator out for this) four beams is the equivalent to two battleships, meaning those four targeted Martian ships would hopefully die quickly.

"They'll see us in thirty seconds," Jorge Allende reported, and John nodded.

"Alright, Jorge, when they get into range, I want you to signal their flagship. Lynn, Shamus, as soon as I give the fire order, we're going to do an acceleration jump."

The Vice Admiral and Commodore both nodded. Yet another benefit of the *Bonnies* was their high speed, and their unique ability to get up to maximum velocity from a standing start with the agility of a frigate.

It'd still take a minute for them to reach 198 kps, but the targeting solutions on the Martian lasers would hopefully be thrown off by the movement.

And it'd be disconcerting to see four massive and previously-unseen battleships leaping forward with frigate-like agility, each firing four lasers at the same time.

The orders had been given, everyone on *Bonaventure's* Battlelink network was now simply waiting…

Twenty seconds. Then ten…

The Martians came into sight range, and boy did they ever slam on the brakes.

I've often wondered what I'd do in their place. Slamming on the brakes is a likely first reaction, though it's in fact the worst choice. Forging on forward and bowling over the standing defenders would be the most tactically efficient, I think, but surprise and fear interferes with that.

Why are they just sitting there? They shouldn't just be sitting there… what's behind them? Better stop and square off with them…

Despite the fact that if you crashed into them at 188 kps (the speed the Martians were doing at this stage) you'd probably do them a lot of harm, and because you were moving fast, you'd probably receive relatively light damage in return…

But John had judged right: Garvey wasn't going to try to jump past him.

"Sending query," Jorge Allende announced.

Lennox Williams stepped up next to John, "They're decelerating very smoothly, no?"

John nodded — you can look up the logs yourself, and you'll be impressed by the cohesion and ease with which the Martian home fleet was hitting the brakes — rather different than the panicked reaction the destroyer and destroyer escorts had when seeing Rachel's battle line for the first time. So either the Martian home fleet was elite, as much of our own Home Fleet was, or the fact that Garvey had the edge in numbers was giving his ships more confidence, letting them do it properly.

One way or the other, they came to an easy stop about thirty seconds beyond *Bonnie's* maximum weapons envelope, and probably forty-five seconds beyond their own.

"Signal coming in now, sir," Jorge Allende reported.

"Whatever screen is closest to me," John nodded with a smile, and then as the *BonnieNet* loading graphic appeared, he shifted his position to be right in front of the appropriate monitor.

What comes next is actually another of the scenes that movies consistently get right — and that critics again dismiss as being 'highly unbelievable'. After all, it's not common for commanders of opposing forces to sit still in space and have a chat. Indeed, it is highly irregular, but John's strategy of just sitting still and appearing entirely undaunted was enough to earn a little face-to-face (via realtime comm) with Grand Fleet Admiral Ezekiel Garvey.

You can get the logs of this conversation at the fleet archives if you don't believe me.

After a short loading time, Garvey appeared on *Bonnie's* screen, and John greeted him with a smile, "You're Ezekiel Garvey, right?"

Garvey, complete with his high collar and head of silvering hair, was playing it equally cool, "And you're Lord John Fiora, of the Imperial Admiralty, I believe."

He got the title wrong — John hadn't yet been made a peer, so unlike Daragh, he wasn't yet 'Lord' John Fiora. 'First Lord' was only his job title. But that's a common mistake (I even do it from time to time).

"Well, we know who we are, that's a start. Now I know we're at war, and I should just start killing your ships without so much as saying hi, but I'm in a good mood today. So I thought I'd give you a chance to turn back first."

I've been asked whether John really would have let them go if Garvey had turned around. Short answer: nope. No, this was a once-in-a-lifetime sort of encounter, thanks to a lot of good [guesswork]. If the Martians had turned, John would have been forced to be dishonorable, and start shooting. His offer had basically been a taunt... a friendly one, but a taunt all the same. He thought it highly unlikely that Garvey was going to concede defeat so handily.

"Your generosity is curious, Lord Fiora," Garvey's painted-on smile remained steady. "Seems to me, the only reason you'd sit out here and then try to talk would be to intimidate me... to *bluff* me, because you actually don't have enough force to stop me. Even though your *Bonaventures* appear to be complete."

Hmm, so obviously the Martians knew something about the *Bonaventure*-class, though we've never found out how much they knew, or where they heard it. As you'll see, we can ascertain that they didn't know as much as they thought they did.

John tilted his head, "Now really, Ezekiel, don't you think I could just be being nice?"

Garvey's smile faded, "I rather doubt any man who takes on the title of a noble Lord has much capacity for being nice. That would get in the way of the hubris and the arrogance that's required for the peerage, wouldn't it?"

Whoa.

I mean *ouch*.

I was at the cinema watching one of the movie versions of this, and someone in the row in front of me at this point exclaimed, "Oh no you did-ant!"

But Garvey did. Had. I mean he had done it.

John's smile faded, "Is that a fact? Well in that case I suppose we'll move over to the 'no mercy' part of the encounter. Goodbye, Ezekiel!"

Hearing those words, Jorge Allende cut the feed, and then John looked up at the Battlelink screens, "Let's shoot them, then back us off."

There were confident nods...

And now it's time to break chapters.

CHAPTER TWENTY-EIGHT

HEAVY ACTION

Rachel was still standing squared-off at the front of her bridge with Liam Singh close by when the Martian Mercury force detected her. Unlike the John-Garvey matchup, though, this one wasn't about to be prefaced by an insulting conversation.

"Weapons range in fifty seconds," the report came to Rachel and she looked up at her skippers on Battlelink.

"Shannon, screen at your discretion, keep them off us. Whoever is finished with their parallel target first opens up on the leftover battleship. Remember, First Lord Fiora's out there winning glory with the new battleships. Let's be sure the Heavy Squadron isn't forgotten!"

Nice little inspirational quote there — first beer, then the promise of glory. Rachel was keeping her already motivated people even more highly motivated.

Liam Singh turned to his XO again, "Solution on our opposite?"

She nodded immediately in reply, and he looked back at the main screen.

The Martians had shaken themselves into a battle line, with their screening vessels moving out ahead to interrupt any torpedo runs Shannon's frigates might attempt. The screening vessels would be ignored, though; that was the nature of battleship fighting, the frigates and corvettes — as big as they are in the context of the Belt Squadron or Jupiter Force — were just pups in a fight like this. Though, in *Jaguar*, *Tiger* and *Panther's* cases, I suppose 'cubs' would be more appropriate.

"All ships be ready to reverse drives on my order, we need to keep the fall-back option open," Rachel continued as the clock ticked down below fifteen seconds.

Retreat was very much an option here. If either John or Rachel's force was eliminated, the other simply *had* to survive, or Earth would be defenseless. Thus you'll see that both actions were fought very, very conservatively.

"In range in four... three... two... ready... shoot!" That was actually Emma Nelson on Battlelink, I just love the way she counted it down.

And as soon as she said 'shoot', every other battleship skipper in the Heavy Squadron was saying the very same thing.

The veteran battlewagons of the Heavy Squadron thus dispatched their dual-laser greetings to the Martian Mercury force. These *Empire*-class battleships had all been at the Battle Over Earth, and they'd all kept up their gunnery practice since. They didn't miss much.

Of their ten laser shots, seven connected — that's incredibly accurate fire, particularly at maximum range with two fast-moving forces. Of the seven that connected, two slid off their targets relatively quickly, flaking off armor and doing considerable damage, but not as much as would have been ideal.

The last five shots, though, focused on the three central ships in the Martian line, and *Repulse* again proved the best of the Heavy Squadron's shooters: that ship's two lasers bored right through the nose turret of the targeted Martian battleship, and caused a slew of secondary explosions in its forward pod.

That Martian's speed sloughed off fast, and it fell out of line.

There was moderate damage with the other two Martians that had taken heavy fire, but they were still in line, their turrets lining up for when the range became manageable.

"That's a hell of a first round — good work leveling the playing field!" Rachel's heart rate was probably way up now, and her voice was showing some of her increased energy. "Emma, move over to tackle that extra they brought."

With that exceptional opening salvo, Emma Nelson and her gunners aboard *Repulse* had ensured the Heavy Squadron couldn't face any of that double-teaming. From here on in it was one-to-one dueling.

"We have incoming fire," *Empire's* Sensors and Communications Officer made the declaration as she gripped the console nearest to her. "Some of it's close!"

"Brace yourselves," Liam Singh followed that thought with his own orders, then he glanced back at his XO. "Vera, prepare for another shot, as soon as the cycle is complete."

The laser fire from the Martian battle line came in fast and scattered — at such long range, their turreted weapons weren't quite as accurate as our larger integrated emitters, and they were weaker as well. That said, it was still battleship laser fire...

Diana Blackwood of *Royal Sovereign* suddenly winked off her Battlelink screen. Rachel was holding one of the nearby railings to keep herself upright as a laser shot skidded across the port side of *Empire's* bridge pod before sliding away, and she had to look away from her screens for a minute to make sure she had the rail firmly in hand.

When she looked back, Blackwood was gone.

"Where's Diana? Status on *Royal Sovereign?*" Rachel's head whipped around as *Empire* started to stabilize, and her Sensors and Communications Officer frowned and stumbled to another console.

"Bridge hit, *Royal Sovereign* is twisting to starboard... dammit, ma'am, their helm must be out!"

"Breaking formation, they're comin' right for me!" Patty Brennan reported quickly then from her own screen, and *Revenge* fired its drives in a 'vertical' direction, elevating itself up out of line to allow the now-uncontrolled *Royal Sovereign* to pass beneath.

"Dammit, close up as quick as you can..." Rachel wasn't sounding terribly calm anymore, but her judgment hadn't been compromised.

So much for the level playing field.

"Shoot!" Emma Nelson was remaining focused on gunnery, as were Ophelia Zukhov and now Liam Singh.

The battle line — the three ships left in it — sent out their angry red lasers again, and one of the previously-damaged Martians took the worst of it. Emma's new target wasn't coming straight at her, so *Repulse's* lasers raked it, but slid off quickly, not doing as much harm.

This time the Martians didn't lose a ship, and Rachel watched this turn of events on her main screen with a grunt, "Prepare to reverse course. Status of *Royal Sovereign's* drives?"

There was no answer to that question — *Royal Sovereign* was twirling away from battle in wide arcs, presumably having lost its bridge and now trying to get secondary navigation back online.

Rachel didn't want to leave the wayward battleship behind — it would be a costly loss, one worth avoiding if possible. But the vector it was spinning away on was not back towards Earth — if Rachel withdrew it'd mean abandoning *Royal Sovereign*, and the Martians would unquestionably come in to finish it off… or capture it…

This is the sort of moment that sifts the fleet commanders, I think. What do you do, and how do you do it? There's no right answer, as far as I'm concerned — every CO will come at a problem like that with their own experiences, plans and expectations. You might find hundreds of different solutions.

But the real sift doesn't come in the answer, but in the decisiveness. That's my opinion at least. A great leader will decide, quickly and clearly — and not outrageously — what to do. A good leader will figure it out without too much ado, and a bad leader won't decide.

I could be getting this all wrong — it is only my opinion, not some absolute measuring scale of leadership, so it's fallible.

Rachel hesitated for about ten seconds. I don't know if that was a long, medium, or short delay. I wasn't there, so I can't fairly judge. As much as all the logs and interviews tell me, I can't really say what that delay said about her as a leader.

I will say, though, that Shannon Hunter proved herself to be truly great.

Shannon had many options at her disposal at that moment. I haven't mentioned it, but she was handily winning the fight against the two destroyers and three destroyer escorts that had been tasked with interfering with her. Between Shannon herself, Wen Luong on *Tiger*, and of course, Conrad Benwah, you had some of the meanest frigate skippers our Navy has ever seen. The Martians weren't even in with a chance. The DEs had been the first to be driven back, and the destroyers were vectoring away now as they realized they were outnumbered, and only the slightest of damage had been done to *Tiger* in the first exchange.

The fact that those escorts had backed off created opportunities.

So while Rachel took those ten seconds, Shannon sent *Tiger*, which had lost four of its bow mags to Martian lasers, on a run against one of the moderately-damaged Martian battleships.

Frigate against battleship? Suicide, surely.

But battleships in the middle of big capital ship fights can get tunnel vision. It happens. And despite the damage to its weapons, *Tiger* was still a *Predator*-class frigate, with a *torpedo tube*.

With more than a little fancy flying, the frigate drove right in on the bottom of the Martian battle line, where the interceptor fighters that habitually stayed around their capital ships took notice and began strafing runs. All the Starlights from Shannon's trio of frigates — some sixty-odd planes — then got in close and started mixing it up with the interceptors.

Remember, those Martian interceptors weren't built to fly far and fast, like our Starlights, but to stay close, and to support point defense… shoot down torpedoes, for instance.

When Wen Luong had the desired range, he gave the order, and *Tiger's* torpedo rocketed from its tube. *Tiger* dove away, but Tigerstar Squadron rode with the weapon, blasting the interceptors out of its way, and then peeling off once it got into point blank range.

The wounded Martian battleship was having problems with its turrets — had it not been damaged by *Revenge's* fire, it probably would have been able to shoot the thing down with its own point defense mags.

But damaged it was, and destroyed it was soon to be.

The explosion is what ended Rachel's ten-second pause, "All fighters, prepare to escort torpedoes in. All ships, launch what you've got!"

The Starlights were cruising in clouds around the battleships, feeling rather underappreciated through the first volleys. This was a very awkward war for fighters — they were on every ship, yet their ordnance was so useless against warships they seemed to have nothing to do... a point I've made many times already.

But escorting torpedoes was something they *could* do.

Empire, *Repulse* and *Medusa* each launched their two torpedoes immediately, and as Patty Brennan managed to drop *Revenge* back into line, that ship fired as well — this all as the explosion was just clearing.

The signatures of the incoming torpedoes were clear on the Martian sensors, though, and their four remaining battleships tightened up and let loose another laser barrage, their interceptors following it out to intercept the torpedoes.

Those lasers came in hot again, and just as *Revenge* got back into line, the fire from the same ship that had wounded *Royal Sovereign* connected with Patty Brennan's port drive pod wing. Bad luck for Patty, they didn't slide off; the wing nearly sheared off instead.

"Dammit!" she erupted over Battlelink. "Cutting speed, we can't maneuver at combat speeds now... we'll go after Diana, ma'am..."

It all happened very fast — battles tend to — but Rachel nodded, "Watch our backs."

With a drive wing burned half-way through, there was no way *Revenge* could continue fighting in the line — it could too easily lose control and veer into *Empire*, the ship on its port side in formation.

So Patty dropped back and changed course, going after *Royal Sovereign*. Perhaps despite the damage, those two ships could pull together and get back into the fight somehow.

Four of the eight torpedoes that had been fired were shot down by the time Rachel's eyes darted back to the main screen, and her grip tightened painfully on the metal railing she was still braced against. She wanted the odds leveled again.

"Maintain laser fire, we have to keep their heads down!" she was sounding hurried now, and she glanced at Liam. "Give me a good shot."

Liam offered a simple nod in reply, then glanced back at his XO again, "Focus fire on the ship Emma is targeting."

Emma Nelson was barking "shoot" on the Battlelink when *Empire's* two laser beams lanced out and slammed into the ship she was aiming for. The four beams were too much, and the ship bucked backwards and well out of line, venting copious amounts of atmosphere.

"Thanks for the assist," Emma smiled on the link, then disappeared from it momentarily — bounced sideways as *Repulse* took another hit. Her picture started to get grainy.

"We're down to our secondary transmitter. Someone over there likes shooting for the bridge," she grunted.

The torpedoes plunged towards point blank range, but the remaining Martian battleships were all healthy enough to shoot them down. And many of the Starlights escorting them, dammit. Like the household cavalry at Waterloo, they'd ridden right up to the guns, and now the interceptors and the point defense systems were coming at them from all sides.

"Get our planes out of there," Rachel's orders had calmed very slightly — it was three-against-three now.

At this point, Shannon had driven back the two remaining destroyers, having inflicted considerable damage on them. Both *Panther* and *Jaguar* thus dove into the fray of the Starlight-interceptor engagement, covering the fighter withdrawal with their mag fire, and lining up for torpedo shots from close range.

That was it.

The Martians reversed drives — just like that, they reversed engines, leaving the frigates behind as they backed off. Interceptors swarmed Shannon's ships, ready to shoot down any torpedoes just after they left the tubes, but the Martians were turning away.

"Reduce speed, let them go," Rachel was quick in giving that order. "Shannon, keep tabs on them. If it looks like they're regrouping and trying to come back, slow them down and we'll come up. Battleships to come to all stop, recover fighters and assess damage. Remain at general quarters."

Those Martians weren't coming back, but as I've said before, there was no way for us (well, in this case Rachel) to know that at the time, so she wasn't going to assume she'd won the battle. Not by any means.

Meanwhile, another nasty fight had already gotten started.

And, intending no offense to the gallant officers and crews of Rachel Butler's Heavy Squadron, this other fight is probably the one you've been waiting for.

CHAPTER TWENTY-NINE

THE MASTER

"Jump *now*."

It sounded like John had just calmly ordered lunch, not an assault. But good God, did those *Bonnies* ever move.

You have never — not *ever* — seen anything like the four *Bonaventure*-class ships leaping off from a standing start in near-unison, and neither had that bastard fool Garvey.

Of course, Garvey's response was immediate: his ships accelerated forward — much more sluggishly, surprisingly enough — and that ten-second gap to firing distance evaporated in less than five.

John didn't even say shoot. He didn't have too. The skippers of the four *Bonaventures* were all picked men and women. They shot.

I wish I could have seen Garvey's arrogant face.

Four — count 'em, *four* — lasers from every *Bonnie*, each slightly more powerful than one of *Empire's*, pounded into the Martian battle line. When those battlecruisers went up at the Battle Over Earth, I'd never seen such big ships die so easily. I never thought I'd hear of fully-protected battleships meeting a similar fate. One did.

Just like that, the battleship on the right end of Garvey's line turned into a small star that burned out rather quickly, and again, the Martians slammed on the brakes.

But John wasn't planning on stopping. Two of the Martians, one under fire from *Hibernia* and the other taking shots from *Bonnie* herself, began losing atmosphere almost immediately, and as they threw themselves into dangerous curves to try to avoid the incoming fire, they lost armor in sheets.

That was the firepower of the *Bonaventure*-class battleships. Bet Garvey hadn't been expecting it.

And to think, Dave Caldecott had wanted them to be carriers. What the hell good would that have been?

Garvey was reversing drives fast now, but it wasn't enough — not nearly enough. So he did the only thing he could: he ordered all those destroyers and destroyer escorts he'd brought with him to attack, and as they leapt out in front of the reeling Martian battle line, they unleashed their missiles.

'Missiles' are what the Martians call torpedoes, and as seems the case with all Martian tech, they were smaller but more numerous than our own. Half the size, but twice as many, and John couldn't afford to overlook them.

"All fighters, advance on point defense duty. Shamus, stay where you are. Lynn, all *Bonnies* to switch firing priority to mag point defense."

If you think *Bonnie* and her sisters had obscene laser power, you're going to think their mag complements were grotesque. The cloud of twenty-one missiles was racing forward, and the Starlights wove in to shoot down six of them, but the Martians sent their interceptors forward as escorts for the warheads — much as Rachel had sent her Starlights forward to escort her torpedoes.

Well, this time our Starlights were on the defensive and the Martian interceptors were the Scots Grays at Waterloo (sorry, I should explain that allusion, but I really don't want to interrupt here, and I still want to use it, so it's not going to be edited out). The Starlights dropped on them with some pent-up anger and anxiousness, and a rather epic dogfight began.

John couldn't pay that any heed though, "Open up point defense batteries."

The mags from the *Bonaventure* battle line began to stream… to pour. It was like watching hurricane rains — the golden energy bolts just seemed to fill the space before the battle line, and the last fifteen missiles didn't make it anywhere near their targets.

"Move forward now," John glanced at his officers on the Battlelink. "Their screening units are going to try to protect their battle line, so we'll have to cut our way through. Shamus, stay tight on us, watch our high and low flanks."

There was no way but forward, and John wasn't about to let a handful… well, fifteen… petty escort ships stand in the way of the mightiest battleships in the history of the solar system. Is that hubris? Maybe. But sometimes hubris is deserved.

The lasers from the destroyers and destroyer escorts began firing, some of them targeting Shamus' corvettes and frigates. In something of a surprise, *Eagle* lost a drive pod, spiraling away from the formation, while both *Charisma* and *Droll* were severely damaged, and dropped out as well. *Charm* and *Hawk* quickly buddied up for protection, but they fell back soon too, completely overwhelmed by the volume of fire the fifteen Martian escort vessels were putting out.

Keep in mind, at the Battle of Belt Two we had *nine* frigates and corvettes, and the fire we put out was daunting. Fifteen is a *lot*.

But not too much for *Bonnie*.

John stood on the bridge stage, hands still settled on his hips, and he watched as Garvey backed his battle line off and turned it around under the cover of the escorts. To the Martian's credit, he'd realized after the destruction of one ship and the heavy and moderate damage dealt to three more that this wasn't a fight he wanted to stay in.

Well, Garvey might escape, then, but John wasn't about to let all these destroyers and destroyer escorts leave with their battleships.

"The battle line's going to get away," John said evenly. "Let's make sure they go home unescorted."

It sounds cold. Arguably, it *is* cold. But the Martians had been coming to destroy Earth's defenses, and that wasn't something that can go unanswered.

So *Bonaventure*, *Terra Nova*, *Hibernia* and *Bonavista* all opened up with their lasers again — this time sending each beam at a separate ship. If you do the math (again with a calculator for me) that means four ships, four beams each… sixteen separate targets could be tracked, and there were only fifteen Martian escorts to shoot at.

If you watch the vids taken by the external cameras on the *Bonnies*, you'll see how close the range was. And you'll see more destruction of warships in a single fell swoop than most people would dream possible. Ten of the fifteen ships — including *all* the destroyers — were cut apart. I've talked about how devastating battleship lasers can be to cruiser hulls, well here was the ultimate proof.

Remember back to *The Rogue Commodore*, when Wes' *Cheetah* had taken that bad hit from a very old battleship laser at very long range? These lasers were at short range, and they were about ten times as powerful.

None of the ships that were hit escaped. Some survived, but none were able to make the cruise back to Mars. The lucky five survivors wheeled hard around and ran — every scrap of energy they had poured into their engines.

"Let those five go," John confirmed his wishes to his officers on the Battlelink. "Use mags to finish off the crippled ones. We need prisoners, and R&D will want to take a look at the wrecks."

The next ten minutes were a fait accompli, to use a non-English expression. Two of the crippled escorts tried to fight back as the mighty *Bonaventures* came to loom over them. Four had been destroyed outright by the lasers, and the last four simply surrendered. The victory is often said to have been one-sided.

But John will be the first to tell you it wasn't. Of five escorts that went out with him, two remained repairable. None of the other corvettes were ever put back into operation — they were so badly shot up that they were deemed unfixable and scrapped. *Eagle* was out of action for almost a year, because a secondary shot to its sensor tower had managed to cook its reactors. Over three hundred of its crew died horrible deaths of acute radiation poisoning, including its entire bridge crew and Nina Angavanakis, its skipper. Both *Hawk* and *Charm* were serviceable, but to get them back to full combat readiness took almost three months.

So the *Bonnies* had proved themselves to be incredibly good — unbelievably so, by some accounts. But it wasn't a good day to be riding *with* them instead of *in* them. John was acutely aware of that.

As he later told me, he guessed that Garvey was calling to the two rearguard battleships that were twelve hours behind him, planning to rendezvous and possibly — just *possibly* — try another attack. John doubted the Grand Admiral would be so stupid, though... Garvey would more likely be worried that the epic *Bonaventures* were going to chase him back to Mars.

John wouldn't be so foolish.

For one thing, he didn't know yet how Rachel was faring. And even if he knew she was holding her own, it would have been ridiculous to continue the chase to Mars.

I was going to explain why at the end of this chapter, but I think I'll cut to a new one instead.

Before I do, let's turn it over to John, as he smiled and turned back to his bridge crew, "Great work, everyone. Let's get search and rescue teams out there. Starlights, start spotting the debris for signs of survivors."

The mighty *Bonaventure*-class ships came to a stop in space, and their SAR teams went out into the debris field to find the living.

CHAPTER THIRTY

THE REALITIES OF WINNING

I've been asked by many people, if this was what the *Bonnies* could do, why didn't we win the war shortly after this? Clearly they were superior to everything the enemy had — Martian battleships had crumpled before them.

I can understand where that line of thinking comes from, but the realities are always subtler that the media makes them out to be.

Let's look at these two battles, first, and do the win-loss assessment that is inevitably done (in the press) after they're over.

Well, we've covered what John lost — his escort force — so let's review quickly what he won. First, one Martian battleship was destroyed completely, two more were heavily damaged, and another one still was neatly scarred. In addition to that, the *Bonnies* had annihilated ten escort ships — six destroyers and four destroyer escorts. That's already a very expensive day for any fleet. John destroyed more ships in ten minutes than comprise the entire Hawke Protectorate fleet.

It's always interesting (in a very morbid way, I'll admit) to compare the significance of a ship like a frigate on different scales. In the Belt, a frigate is a monster of a ship, bane to pirates and re-assurer of allies. A frigate is mighty.

On this day, a frigate, or its parallel, a destroyer, was just a pawn. Well, a rook at best.

Anyway, no question that John had a good balance on the score sheet.

For Rachel, things hadn't gone quite so well.

The Heavy Squadron destroyed one Martian battleship — thanks to Wen Luong's torpedo — and badly damaged two more. The rest of the Martian battle line had received light to moderate damage. In addition to that, two destroyers and four destroyer escorts had been destroyed, which was a total of six and was again a prodigious level of destruction, overall.

This had come at rather a high cost, though.

Royal Sovereign wasn't fully repaired until the last months of the war. The shot that took out that ship's bridge — and which killed Diana Blackwood — had cut the controls to many of its key systems. Three hours after the battle, the reactors went into an overload cycle, and the only way to shut them down was manually. Forty engineering techs died in the process, and the ship was actually abandoned and towed back to Earth because it had been entirely contaminated with radiation.

Revenge did the towing, and that would be the battleship's last activity of the year, because for the next thirteen months Patty Brennan's ship was in for repairs. First the wing that had nearly been lost had to be rebuilt, and then the collateral damage that had been caused needed attending to. That process revealed some serious reactor problems.

Seeing a theme? I'll get back to that in a minute.

None of the ships of the Heavy Squadron had been left unscathed, of course. Shannon's frigates each had at least two week's work to be done on them — *Tiger* was in the yards for two months getting the mags it had lost reinstalled. The other battleships each had about a month's work to be done on them to have them back to full operational status.

So, keep all that in mind when you remember what the newsflashes said.

I mean, it's all good and well to say that John and Rachel destroyed or crippled half the capital ships and two thirds of the escorts sent to attack Earth — they did — but the claim that they did it without losing any ship to outright destruction is a little misleading. It took the Home Fleet a long time to pick up the pieces from this fight.

That all said, I'm hardly saying this wasn't a great pair of wins. Just remember that it wasn't an avalanche of goodness for us.

For one thing, the consistent reactor troubles were worrying, and as you may or may not know, the prevalence of them in this battle led to some investigations. I'll let John explain about that later, but it was definitely significant.

And getting back to the original question I started this chapter with, why couldn't we just end this war now, with the mighty *Bonnies*?

None of us were under any illusions that the *Bonnies* were invincible. Today they'd been horribly underestimated by Garvey, but that wasn't a mistake that would be made again by the Martians. If John had carelessly ridden into Mars space and started shooting, the seven surviving Martian battleships plus all of their static and mobile defenses would have eventually destroyed our prized *Bonnies*. Better to keep them and use them judiciously.

They were powerful, but they weren't magical weapons that would somehow win the war on their own.

But anyway, I'm sure you're waiting to hear about the third event on the calendar for this day, because about ten hours after John's fight finished, Greg and Mik's adventure kicked into gear.

CHAPTER THIRTY-ONE

HELLO THERE

Lieutenant Yevgeny Dongo was the first Defense Command officer to enter Mars space in over twenty years. He was the pilot of Warstar 1004, the Starlight that happened to be on point rotation for Greg's force as it approached Mars, and thus crossed the threshold into Martian space before anyone else.

The rest of Warstar and Warspite squadrons, as well as those of *Cyclops*, *Goliath*, *Generous* and *Sackville*, not to mention the ships themselves, were right on Dongo's heels. As they arrived, Greg was standing on his bridge with arms folded and a slight frown, watching the sensor plot up on the main screen.

So far there were no signs of heavy resistance, and while that was good news on the face of it… well, I don't need to tell you, *too quiet* was almost as bad as busy… even worse in some ways.

"Looks like we're clear so far. Think we have the drop on them?" Mik asked the question over Battlelink, stroking his goatee and narrowing his eyes thoughtfully.

Glancing up at Mik, Greg shook his head from left to right once, "I don't know, Christian. The best way to find out seems to be to press in. We're in detection range of their outer satellites?"

That question was directed at his Sensors and Communications Officer, and she nodded, "Looks that way, sir. The moons didn't see us, but I'm hearing increased comm traffic from their orbital grid. Sounds panicky."

"Guess they weren't expecting a knock at the back door when everyone was out front," Val Rodriguez smiled hungrily, standing a few feet to Greg's left.

Taking a thoughtful breath, Greg nodded, "That's possible. Everyone stay alert on your sensor scopes, though — they could be baiting us in to destroy us."

There were nods over Battlelink and on *Warspite's* bridge — no one was in the mood to turn this mission into a suicide run.

"Time to orbital yard cluster?" Greg put another question to his Sensors and Communications Officer, and she had the answer waiting for him.

"Present velocity, twenty-one minutes."

Now, I should explain the attack plan, because I've been reasonably coy about it all book. If Greg got in here unscathed, his primary objective was to blow the almighty hell out of as many shipyards as he could — to wreck the Martians' ability to build new ships, and to repair the damaged ones that were coming back from the attack on Earth.

In Earth space, most of our yards are orbiting Luna — relatively few are over Earth these days, because it's just too busy with orbital transit docks for moving cargo and passengers. Most of the heavy construction is done at our moon, and our moon is big enough to support that.

Mars' moons are, to be entirely frank, quite pathetic. Phobos and Deimos don't compare at all to rocks like Belt Two, and they're certainly not big enough to safely shelter a large number of shipyards. That being the case — and due to lower volumes of passenger and cargo shipping — the Martians built most of their shipyards over their own planet.

That was fair enough — it put those yards under the protection of Mars' own orbital defenses — but with the Home Fleet gone, Greg had a very clean run at them.

Of course, there were far too many for three battleships to destroy entirely — it'd be patently unsafe to hang around that long — so using some damned near clairvoyant *guesswork*, Greg and John had figured that a large cluster of stations would be over the planet's north pole... a nice juicy target that could allow three battleships to fly past, meeting the minimum of resistance, and blasting as many as *forty* active yards.

Forty. That's a lot. As much as fifteen percent of Mars' local ship production capacity, if you count the multiple slips on some of them. Mercury had its own yards of course, as did the Martian asteroid colonies, but the ability of the Martians to build and repair ships in their home space could be disrupted by just one pass.

That was the plan, since no resistance was evident.

The battleships lumbered forward, and ten minutes went by *very* slowly. No one could relax on the approach, even though there was no resistance — Mik, Greg, Val, Becky on *Goliath*... everyone was waiting for the other shoe to drop.

Then it did. Rather softly.

"Hang on... got it, two destroyers and four destroyer escorts now on scope, coming around from behind the planet. Looks like they're going to try to get in our way," Greg's Sensors and Communications Officer reported it first, and Mik was quickly given the same information by his own Lieutenant Commander Finn Yaalon.

"Think there's more?" he asked quickly, and Greg nodded.

"I would guess there is. If I were defending this planet with limited resources, I wouldn't reveal everything at once."

Mik nodded, "Agreed. We could move to intercept, destroy the defense force and then wait to see what's next, but that *would* slow down our exit."

Greg frowned now, "Yes... I want to be out of here quickly..."

His voice trailed off as he watched the six Martian ships form up and come over the planet towards his force. Given where he was right then — basically in Mars orbit — Greg didn't really want to chance a heavy engagement. Minor damage taken here could be devastating, as they had no friendly port to check into, and a long voyage back to Belt Two.

No, they weren't planning on going to Earth — that might have meant running right into the retreating Martian attack force. Instead, the hero of Deep Black was doing again what he'd done there against the Syndicate — coming from the blackness of space, and returning to it.

The point was that he couldn't risk a toe-to-toe engagement with too much Martian firepower. He'd only need to be a little bit unlucky and he'd be in trouble.

"Alright, Isoruku, Katya, take your corvettes forward, inflict as much damage as possible to the shipyards, but do *not* take any undue risk. Be ready to withdraw to the escape vector on my order. Val, Becky, Mik, we're going to deal with those defenders."

That was the best option Greg could come up with, and I can't disagree with it.

The battleships were by far the least likely ships to be damaged in a gunfight with the Martian destroyers and destroyer escorts, while the corvettes could definitely still cut up the unarmored yards.

And if the Martians revealed heavier firepower once the corvettes neared the planet, Katya's *Sackville* and Isoruku's *Generous* could get away faster than the battleships could.

All in all, a good division of forces.

"All fighters keep close, watch for missile fire," Mik offered his order, and Greg nodded in approval. This could get slightly messy…

It took about five more minutes for the Martian defense squadron to get into range of Greg's ships, or, to put it more accurately, to get within Greg's weapons range of their ships. Destroyer and destroyer escort lasers couldn't fire as far as battleship weapons, of course, so the entire attempt to get in the way of Greg's attack really had an air of futility to it.

"Why don't they change course and go after the corvettes?" Val Rodriguez asked quietly at one point — a perfectly valid question, the corvettes were a clear and present danger to the yards.

Greg leaned back and answered just as quietly, "They're probably under orders to keep us busy. If they leave us alone, we could do a lot of damage to other areas."

"Right…" Val nodded.

Think about it. If a bunch of burglars broke into your house and you had one gun, who would you point it at: the crazy huge guy in the living room with an axe strapped to his back, or his tiny sickly-looking partner who was pilfering the cutlery? Better to keep the gun on the axeman, because if you worry about the cutlery too much, you'll end up with an axe in the back of your head.

Good grief, that was rather grim. Gruesome, in fact. Jeeze. I apologize. But, well, it does make sense to me.

"Weapons range in fifteen seconds," Greg's Sensors and Communications Officer reported then, and Greg nodded.

"Target the destroyers first," he gave the order to Val and Becky Afflighen in particular, and Mik shifted on screen.

"Mind if I jump ahead? My lasers don't have quite your range."

Greg nodded, "Go ahead."

Looking away from the screen, Mik ordered his Helm and Navigation Officer to accelerate, and *Cyclops* began to pull ahead of *Warspite* and *Goliath*.

"In range."

With that, Greg nodded, "Shoot."

Val and Becky both passed that word on to their respective XOs, and four lasers fired from both battleships. A few seconds later, Mik's own guns found their range, and with a stroke of his goatee, he nodded to his XO, "Let them have it."

Within a couple of heartbeats, then, six laser beams of great power were hurtling towards six destroyers and destroyer escorts, and you almost have to feel bad for those little ships. They were what remained of a home defense force that should have been a hell of a lot stronger, but which had been foolishly weakened by Garvey.

Well, I should actually point out that, if not for our excellent [guesses], we'd probably have been overwhelmed, or at least very badly mauled, by his attack. If we hadn't known where and when he was coming, he'd have been lauded as a hero and genius by his own people, and the greatest foe we'd ever faced in Defense Command.

So I don't feel sorry for these guys.

The shooting of our three battleships was good, though the power of their lasers was much less than those aboard the *Bonnies*, so none of the Martians were obliterated by that first blast. Two were pretty badly torn up, though, and one of them began to pirouette towards the Martian atmosphere.

After that, they reversed drives, but released missiles at the same time. That was gallant enough, but the eight warheads were up against some very stiff competition in the Starlight and Starburst squadrons (yes, *Cyclops* still had Starbursts aboard, now flying a combat patrol) that were out there screening. Needless to say, none of the damned little warheads got through.

"They're backing off, and I'm reforming with your line," Mik reported over the Battlelink, and Greg nodded.

"Very good. Adjust course for the yards, see if they tag along with us."

Meanwhile, about ten minutes in a different direction, *Sackville* and *Generous* positively fell on the Martian yards at their northern pole. It was vicious. The yards had some defensive mags (or whatever it is the Martians called them, I always get it mixed up) but they were relatively low-yield, no match at all for the armor of the Defense Command corvettes.

That said, Isoruku Togo and Katya Romanov still took their attack conservatively — they had no interest in stumbling into a trap. But conservative, under these circumstances, was still lethal.

At one point Katya came across six Martian battleship keels, recently laid down and now about a quarter of the way built. Because those six ships weren't armed or commissioned, neither *Sackville* nor *Generous* were credited with destroying six capital ships, but you better believe they carved those keels to bits with laser fire.

There you go, depriving the Martians of six more capital ships for the war. Not bad for two corvettes, eh? Did I mention they're both Belt Squadron officers, not that I'm biased towards that unit for any reason…

Greg and Mik came onto the scene after that ten-minute flight, and here's where, in the movies, the Martian battleship or ships (in one movie as many as, and I still don't get this, *ten* battleships) appear, either from behind the planet or from behind a moon (neither moon orbited over the north pole, so that's a neat trick) and attack.

Unfortunately for people concerned only with drama, but very fortunately for Greg and Mik, no such force appeared. There was no sign at all of the Martians having capital ships in the area, because they didn't.

I know this sounds incredibly stupid, and really it is. But it was a risk taken by Garvey, and as much as I hate to admit it, it wasn't a terrible risk. In point of fact, it was a risk very similar to the one John had taken in removing all the Heavy Squadron and *Bonaventure* Squadron battleships from Earth, and to a lesser extent, that Greg had taken in pulling his battlewagons out of the Belt.

In another ten minutes of intense and expensive laser fire, Greg's forces cut up all forty-two of the yards they found over Mars' northern pole, destroying the hulls (in construction or under repair) of six battleships, nine destroyers, and two destroyer escorts.

After all of this, Greg said the famous (and usually correctly quoted line), "We've finished shooting into the barrel for today. Let's go home."

With a smile and a nod, Mik gave the orders to his crew, while Isoruku, Katya, Val and Becky all did the same. The fighters were recovered, and the five-ship squadron boosted outward, into the black of interplanetary space.

They left a lot of chaos in their wake.

On the first reading of that 'battle', one of my editors conceded to being a bit disappointed — said it 'felt like an anticlimax'. Well, sorry, operations that are carried off without a hitch tend to be that way. I'm sure if I was writing fiction, *Cyclops* would have had engine failure just when the Martians were about to counterattack, Mik would probably be in a love triangle, and Greg would be going deaf or something.

But in reality, it wasn't that overdramatic. It was still dramatic — *hello*, these officers attacked *Mars* within months of the opening of hostilities! But it was well-planned, excellently executed, and has become the textbook operation for teaching fast strike raiding tactics and priorities at the Academy.

John will later be quoted talking about this raid, and as with the reactor thing, I don't want to steal his thunder, but suffice it to say that it went exactly as we wanted it to.

And for those people out there who say, rather emphatically (and incredibly stupidly) that Greg should have just hung around and done more, come off it. Greg didn't know when or where the Martian response would come from, and he was commanding the *only* capital ships available for the defense of the Belt colonies and the Hawke side of the independent belt. He couldn't afford to get caught in a trap, so it was in and out.

Why not just a few more yards? Because discipline in that sort of scenario is key. Just a few more could translate into a dozen more, and any one of those could get lucky, launch a missile or even fire a fortunate mag shot, and change the complexion of the battle. Arguably, even of the *war*.

So it was a clean in-and-out, the objectives were destroyed, and the Defense Command ships came away unscathed.

I once heard a Colonel suggest that this raid could have been like Pearl Harbor — a failure of offensive tactics. He was basically saying that, if Pearl Harbor (World War Two, 1941, when the Japanese brought the US into that war with an attack at the US Navy's base at Hawaii) had been attacked more vigorously, and its fuel depot destroyed, the Second World War would have gone to Japan. His follow-on argument was that, at Mars, if Greg had hit harder, we could have won the war in 2232.

Notice that he was a Colonel. And he happened — this is the rich part — to be an Imperial Army Colonel. In other words, he was (and is) an idiot. Bring on the duel.

Maybe that argument about Pearl Harbor holds water, but Greg had a raiding force, not an assault force proper. He did damned fine work, and I'm very happy to say that he and his officers, Mik in particular, were lauded for it.

And that, I should say rather obviously, was the end of military operations (at least on a grand scale) for Glorious February. Greg and Mik were on the long cruise home, and John and Rachel were heading back to Earth to tend their damage and prepare for any second strike.

But we know now what they didn't know then: there'd be no second strike.

The Martians would never again attack Earth.

CHAPTER THIRTY-TWO

OH, RIGHT... US...

For the record, you never, *never* want to be in the room with four veteran combat commanders and an interested Special Branch Major when they're sitting (or standing, pacing, or hopping up and down) and watching three ship battles of huge importance over which they have no control.

I'll preserve our collective dignity (mainly mine) by not describing just what antics we were up to.

"What's that mean? Was that a hit? Was that a hit? Was that a *hit?*"

We (well, mainly I, I suppose) yelled lots of things like that.

That's the trouble with watching the progress of a battle based on the update bursts being sent by ship Sensors and Communications Officers — it's not realtime, not by any means. You see a flash of action, and then depending on how good the Sensors and Communications crew on a given ship are (and how much they're doing in heat of battle), you have to wait an interminably long time to find out what happens next.

And then just to further complicate things, we were actually watching the first two battles at roughly the same time. Now, that was sort of a good thing, because at times when one battle would seem to freeze, the other one would give us something to pay attention to... but it was hectic.

When *Royal Sovereign* took the hit that destroyed its bridge, we were actually watching John sitting in that standoff with Garvey, so we were all looking at screens on the opposite side of the room. The ping that indicated a new report being posted got Wes' attention first, so he turned and looked, and said, "Bah."

We all turned and let out long breaths. We'd known we'd suffer — of course you always hope your ships will breeze through a battle without being battered up too much, but we never really expected such a fantastically happy end.

Actually, the fact that we didn't lose any capital ships was a pretty good turn of events. But you better believe every one of us felt for Shamus Czarnecki's escorts — the ships lost from John's force. As I said in those chapters about the battles, the escorts with both forces would, in terms of the Belt, have qualified as powerful formations.

But when the capital ships fight, frigates and corvettes don't fare well in the crossfire.

Once the battles were done, we released a collective sigh of relief. Well, more like a dozen sighs of relief. It will sound absurd, but the war room was incredibly tense — again, being the spectators in this fight wasn't easy, and there was no way to ease the tension.

Remember, it was about ten hours after John's battle finished that Greg rolled into Mars orbit and started shooting. That was a *very* long wait for all of us.

We actually had to have dinner delivered to the war room (Wes got soup, because apparently he likes soup) and we sat in our chairs and did what you'd expect over-stimulated and under-active fleet officers to do: we talked.

Backwards and forwards, we talked about those first two battles every which way. We analyzed anything we could. We speculated on what the hell was going on with reactors aboard our ships. We talked over and over again about what our Starlights could do in action these days. We discussed optimum distance between ships in formation to allow for evasion. We talked about who to put on Battlelink with the flagship. We talked about *everything*.

It was nerves, to be honest. Happy as we were to see both the Heavy Squadron and the *Bonnies* cruising home more or less intact (we didn't know how badly shot up the Heavy Squadron was at this point) we were still worried about Greg, Mik, and our former squadron mates Katya and Isoruku.

If you'd asked any of us before that day in the war room, or even up to a minute before we started getting telemetry bursts from *Warspite* and *Cyclops*, we would have told you point blank that the raid on Mars was the riskiest operation of the three, and some of our very good friends — and people we needed to help with the defense of the Belt — were on that mission.

We'd worried about John, sure, but he had *four Bonnies* with him, and was going to fight a similar force in open space. Greg and Mik were riding into the belly of the beast...

But of course, that went well too. We watched the telemetry from Mars come up the first time, all of us standing in a sort of huddle with arms folded as we bounced our weight from foot to foot and held our breath like an election team waiting for the results to start coming in.

"That's it? I was honestly expecting a bit more," Marshal was the first to say what we were all thinking about the small Martian defense force.

Waiting and watching as the strike force headed for the polar dockyards, we all froze when the report showing Martian ships came in, but regained the ability to breathe when Greg sent them running...

You really don't need me to recap the whole battle for you, I know. Sorry. It's just... well, this wasn't fun for us. This was anxious waiting, and by the time I got out of the war room late the next morning, my head was pounding, and Karen actually looked slightly haggard.

Haggard.

It's not easy for us to stand by and be able do nothing, but actually, I should make it clear that we were spoiled. We were getting the news first — anyone not in the Fiora ring or the top levels of government were forced to wait a lot longer for information. So in many regards it's really the height of arrogance for me to presume that we had it at all rough...

But you know me, I'm arrogant. We had it rough. Anyway, time to move on. Plot needs to advance and such.

CHAPTER THIRTY-THREE

THE PRESS CONFERENCE

You've all seen this press conference, or at least clips of it. It was really the first official discussion of the battles of Glorious February, though of course the Imperial Press Office had leaked word and even footage of the battles the night prior. It was broadcast all night long, with rumors and expert analysis, speculation and quite a few jingoistic exclamations of how great the Empire was.

By the time Daragh Ryan gave the briefing in front of the cameras, everyone was primed for some exciting news... and they got it. Like I said before, the spin on these battles was that we killed or crippled half the battleships that came at us, and lost *none*. That always looks good on the screen.

So as you know, Daragh gave the initial briefing, because he'd been in charge at Admiralty House for all of the actions, and thus had the best overall view of the situation. Now, his appointment as Second Lord had never been properly publicized, so believe it or not, many of the reporters in the Parliament Building Press Gallery had no idea he'd be briefing them — they were expecting Diane Pena. Crazy, I know. I would have assumed that news like Daragh's return to the Admiralty would have been picked up by somebody, especially with all the business he was conducting with shipbuilding guilds. Sometimes stories just don't get out, I suppose.

In any case, the press corps' surprise led to an unusual round of applause for Daragh when he walked onto the stage. Even then, you have to understand, his popularity was almost universal. He appeared quite insane, but before he'd become a hermit at this estate in Ireland, he'd never avoided giving the press a good story. They still loved him for it.

With the help of some very slick animations on the screen behind him, Daragh explained the battles that we've already been over. His best line of the whole press conference came after he'd wrapped up the discussion of the three battles.

"Now, to summarize all of that..." he grinned and put his hands on his hips, "...parents cover the ears of your wee ones... covered? They fuckin' well won't be comin' back!"

He half-yelled that, and before they caught themselves, some of the reporters in the gallery let out one of those cheers you give when your team scores the winning goal. Daragh knew how to get people's blood up, even without his shotgun.

The number of people I've met for whom that line from Daragh was the definitive moment of Glorious February is stunning. Not really surprising, I suppose, but for me the real defining moment of that press conference came next, when the Prime Minister emerged onto the stage to relieve Daragh.

Many people today don't know about Winston Churchill. He was a great Prime Minister of Britain, and he was one of the great orators of the twentieth century... who am I kidding, of all time.

I'm sorry, but I think Prime Minister Douglas Pope is better. That's a tall order, I know, and that's taking nothing away from Winston Churchill, but I always thought very highly of Pope's ability to turn a campaign stage into a pulpit, and domestic tax issues into pulsing rhythms that caught the heart of the nation.

"I'd like to thank Lord Ryan for his help in explaining how completely we taught the Martians a lesson yesterday," Pope said in his rich voice. Daragh nodded and waved, then exited stage right to give the Prime Minister room to speak.

"Victory again, my friends. Again the Martians have sent a determined assault force, again they have tried to steal a win. 'Attack the Empire,' their analysts have told them. 'With surprise on your side, you cannot fail.' Well, those analysts should be out of work now. And hopefully, the new analysts will come in with one word on their lips: 'peace.' We did not ask for this war. I don't need to tell you that it came out of a clear sky, at a time when we believed the darkest days of fighting were behind us. But it did *not* come on a day when we'd forgotten how to fight. This should be a clear lesson for every human being in this solar system: the Empire is here to help, but don't mistake our kindness for weakness."

That, of course, was the ominous promise to anyone else out there who wanted a piece of us: don't bother trying.

"Yesterday we repelled two attacks. For those victories, we much first acknowledge the sacrifices of all the officers and crews who gave their lives in battle. They will forever be remembered as heroes of the Empire. We must also honor every woman and man who serves with Defense Command, because it is their hard work and willingness to risk their lives that protected us yet again."

He paused briefly here for dramatic effect.

"Most of all, we must thank the architects of the success: a few fine officers who were responsible for some of the most daring missions in the Empire's history. First, of course, Lord Ryan must be thanked. He slipped quietly into Admiralty House earlier this year, and has tirelessly worked behind the scenes to prepare Earth for this battle. Admirals Rachel Butler and Lynn Boakai have taken command of our battleship squadrons at Earth, and have fought with utmost distinction. And of course, the architect of Earth's protection, the First Lord of our Admiralty, is John Fiora. His masterful control of the Defense Command Navy is peerless in the history of this Empire."

Pope understood that creating heroes not only makes good vid and good politics, but it also improves morale.

"There are also the attackers: our old friend Greg Noyce, Admiral commanding at the Belt, and Commodore Christian Mikaelsen, our officer at the Hawke Protectorate, who mounted the daring raid against Mars. These officers have sent a message to Mars: don't come for Earth again. Because whenever you come for us, you *will* be stopped, and you'll have nothing left to protect yourselves with."

I can just imagine that part of the speech running in the Martian President-for-Life's office. Take that you arrogant bastard.

Ahem.

"These gallant few, and the many thousands of men and women who serve in the ships that yesterday made the Martians think twice about their choice for war, are the heroes of our Empire. They are proof of our resolve, our ability, our *strength*. And today, tomorrow, and for the rest of this war, it will be their efforts that will take the fight to the Martians, and make our former colony realize how foolish it was to attack us."

Hmm, wonder if the book title came out of that paragraph…

"The Empire is strong, my friends, and it's time we showed what 'strong' means to our foes. My message to Mars is simple: we are coming. Sue for peace, because if you don't, your Imperium will regret it."

Big talk — bigger talk than I'd usually approve of — but Pope sold it well. And I'm pretty sure any Martian Naval staff officers who watched that last bit, and saw Pope's confident gaze staring straight out of the screen at them, broke into a sweat.

Because he was right. This was going to be the last time we'd sit and wait for them to come for us. From this day forward, we were going on the offensive.

And believe me, Defense Command's offensive is not something you ever want to find yourself on the wrong end of.

Well, Grant Merger wanted to, but that's a story for later.

The press conference was a huge hit, with Pope's oratory and Daragh's animation pleasing news directors across the Empire. It would be played over and over again during the next twenty-four hours, and it remains to this day one of the most-replayed news conferences the Imperial Government has ever held.

That's possibly because — if you'll pardon my exception to my own rule about swearing here — it wasn't bullshit.

We were going after Mars. It just took a couple of years to get there.

CHAPTER THIRTY-FOUR
EARTH SETTLING DOWN

When John walked in the front door of Admiralty House two days later (after getting back he took two days off to spend at home with Anne) everyone, Gerald and Betty included, stopped what they were doing to give him a big round of applause. There's been a relatively large amount of applause in this book, and I think with good reason. John got a lot of it, and while he'll be self-effacing and credit many other people for the success in Glorious February, a lot of it was his doing.

I've probably done a very poor job of pointing out just how important he was to making it all happen. I've talked about the [guesswork] that went into deploying the Heavy and *Bonaventure* Squadrons to meet the Martian attacks, but do you realize how risky relying on that was? The battle of Midway keeps coming to mind for me on this — hell, right down to 'Point Luck' being the designation of the point where the interceptions were expected. Look that battle up sometime, and you'll find that Chester Nimitz, the American Admiral in charge of the operation, had to take a similar gamble, albeit based on signal intercepts, to go out to meet the enemy.

John demonstrated a lot of personal courage doing what he did, and it paid off.

Because if he'd done what someone like Dave Caldecott would have done, and just sat and waited at Earth, we probably still would have survived (with the *Bonnies* online, the force balance was essentially in our favor) but the collateral damage to Earth, Luna, and all the orbiting facilities could have been epic.

Eventually John got through the throng of well-wishers in the lobby, and deflecting as much praise as he could, he managed to get to his office. Took him about ten minutes, because along the way everyone came out of their offices to shake his hand and say nice things.

When he finally got there, he closed the door behind him and let out a long sigh, then noticed the large piles of pads on his desk (but not spread all around his office, thank goodness) and decided he best to get back to work for a while.

He rounded his desk, pulled out his chair and seated himself, then randomly selected a stack of pads and pulled the first one off the top.

As he started to read it, his door swung open, and Daragh breezed in, shotgun leaning comfortably against his shoulder, and dropped into the chair across the desk from John.

John looked up, "Morning, Daragh."

The Irishman grinned, "What, no complaining that I didn't knock?"

"Would complaining now do anything but entertain you?"

"So you're saying that me being entertained isn't important to you?"

"That's exactly what I'm saying," John smiled and dropped the pad onto his desk. "So, what's new?"

Daragh frowned and laid his shotgun across his lap, "Well let's see, watched you and

Rachel and Greg blow the bejesus out of the Martians, routed damaged ships to repair slips… some of the reactor damage looked bad, I must say… and did a press conference. You?"

"Oh, trying to figure out exactly what to do next. The PM said we were coming for Mars… guess we shouldn't make a liar out of him," John leaned back in his chair and Daragh snorted a laugh.

"I'm sorry, *make* a liar out of him. He's a politician, didn't God make him a liar already?"

Oooh, Daragh takes a swing at politicians everywhere.

Chuckling, John shook his head, "Pope's better than most. What're you hearing from the yards about those reactor issues?"

As promised earlier, here's a talk about the problems our reactors were having. If you don't care, feel free to skip ahead, but the fact that we detected this flaw during this fight meant we could do something about it. Had we not paid attention to the problem, it probably would have cost us many ships in 2233. As it was, the flaw still cost a lot of people their lives in 2232.

"Well, you'll have to forgive my total ignorance to some of what's being explained to me — high-handed technobabble y'see," Daragh began, "but to put it in my own words, our backflow valves just aren't what they bloody well should be. None of the ships that survived the Battle Over Earth got hit badly enough for us to see it, but by the look of it, if a surge of energy goes through the secondary grid, it goes right past the buffers and can cook off the reactor."

I'm going to try to explain this, but I'm probably going to fail. I apologize in advance.

We all know that the reactor sends out power through the power grid. The reactor powers everything — weapons and ship systems included — and it does this on multiple grids. The weapons are all on the primary grid (actually there are two primary grids, 'A' and 'B', but don't worry too much about that) so, when a ship does a laser shot, all power from the reactor gets poured into the primary.

If something happens, and a hit connects with the primary grid (imagine if someone fired a laser shot *into* one of our laser emitters) there's a failsafe at the reactor that keeps all that energy from surging back through the grid and overloading it. It's sort of like grounding a house against a lightning strike.

But the secondary grid didn't have that same shut-off valve, to mix metaphors. If a shot went into that grid, the failsafe wasn't there to keep the energy from running right into the reactor and causing unpleasantness. Now, that sounds pretty stupid — why no failsafe? Well, no one had ever been able to get a shot into the secondary grid in any of the fights we'd been in before.

Keep in mind, the secondary grid powers internal systems. Unlike a laser emitter, which is partly open to space, there's no easy way to get laser or mag energy through the armor of a ship and into the secondary grid. Unless you have heavy firepower, like the Martians did. But we'd never faced quite that kind of firepower before, at least not enough of it to realize that it could do this.

"Alright, so R&D is coming up with a fix?" John asked the important question, and Daragh nodded.

"They'll have something soon. Apparently the way the *Bonnies* are wired, it's not a problem for them. But we'll have to cycle the fleet into dock for upgrades to get most ships fitted out," the Irishman replied with a nod.

The *Bonaventure*-class, having originally been developed as a carrier, shunted all its grids through the same failsafe 'valve' that the laser grid went through. It hadn't been planned as an extra safety feature, it'd just been easier to set it up that way during the construction process.

Definitely paid off though.

The mention of yards triggered another thought in John's mind, and a small smile crept onto his face, "Speaking of yards, I hear Greg took out forty-two. And six battleship keels."

Grinning, Daragh shifted excitedly in his seat, "That he did. Very expensive day for the Martians, they'll have a hell of a time fixin' the damage you did, and their replacements will be another year later than they'd planned for. Unless they have more on the go, but even if they do, that's six less we'll have to worry about."

"That Mars raid," John started shaking his head, "was the real success of the day. We got hurt out there, Daragh, but Greg made it worth it."

Daragh nodded, understanding John's thinking entirely. For a couple of moments, then, the two were silent, before something else came to the Second Lord's mind, "Oh, and another bit of excitement: Greg's convoy came in last night, with a surly Commander called Vivar complaining about not having been contacted with orders or some other damned thing. He's one of Mik's boys from Hawke, annoying little bastard."

John frowned now, "Not one of his best?"

"Not bloody likely. I bet Mik was keeping him close to keep him out of Lia Hawke's hair. Dumped him with the convoy when the actual fighting was to begin."

John narrowed his eyes thoughtfully, "I think the name is familiar. Might have been a troublemaker during Ken's Hawke mission or something. Alright, let's promote him to Captain of Convoy Operations for... Luna. That should keep him out of the way. Lisa Sims back from picket duty?"

Lieutenant Commander Lisa Sims, remember, had been skippering *Admiral Ku* on the Mercury picket. As I said before, she was an up-and-comer, and she'd done a fine job out there. Lieutenant Commander Chad Lerner had as well, but he'd been obliterated because he didn't live in a movie wonderland.

Daragh nodded, "She's back. Promotion?"

"Her and everyone from that crew goes over to Vivar's frigate, she's appointed Commander. Send her out to Hawke One as soon as that's done," John nodded slowly as he thought that through.

"Right. But we'll need more corvettes for convoys over at Belt Two. Could send her there," Daragh flipped the shotgun over in his lap as he thought aloud, and John frowned.

"Alright, I'll apologize to Mik, but you're right, the convoys are critical."

"Good man," Daragh nodded as he made a mental note of the transfer. "Now, I have a crackpot scheme for you to buy into. I want to build the Forge back up..."

John looked surprised at those words, and Daragh started explaining his thoughts about strengthening the Defense Command presence at his old base. The Forge, to answer my editors' questions, was a DC post built on a vulcanoid asteroid that circled the sun between the orbits of Venus and Mercury. In the old days, it had been Daragh's base of operations, though it had been largely demilitarized during the twenty years prior to the war... alright, this is all information that can wait for future books, so let's move on...

The discussion went on for two hours. Obviously the subjects continued to change as they thought of new issues to deal with, but this process of sitting and talking things over took time. Many important evolutions in Defense Command operating policy would come from this talk, and others just like it.

The quiet and settled manner of changing the Empire — not as exciting as blowing things up, but a hell of a lot more productive.

CHAPTER THIRTY-FIVE

HOMECOMING: HAWKE ONE

Mik peeled *Cyclops* off about three days out of Mars space, setting course for Hawke One so he could return to his squadron. That was a bit of a disappointment for all of us back at Belt Two who wanted to say hi and congratulate him, but he wasn't really needed at Belt Two. Hawke One, though, needed to have its battleship back.

So it was about six days after he'd split from Greg's force that Mik pulled *Cyclops* into Hawke One space, and the avalanche of congratulations messages started coming in. There'd been about two weeks for word of what had happened to get around, so everyone at Hawke One was waiting to give Mik a hero's welcome.

Hell, even Lord Hawke (whose doctors had put him on reduced court hours because of a heart problem that was starting to get serious) was pleased to see Mik back in his zone of space.

But I know what you're thinking: you don't care about them, you want to know what Lia Hawke was doing.

Come on, admit it, you've missed her. Don't worry, Charlie won't hunt you down and harm you for thinking it. If you say it out loud he'll come for you, though. Like a monster in the dark, he'll come for you...

As *Cyclops* edged up to the usual dock at Hawke One's government dome, Mik and his command staff received a summons from the Hawke Court — or at least that's the digital letterhead the message came on. Mik expected there was going to be some sort of parade or something (he didn't want one, but he wasn't naïve — he knew he was going to be HawkeGov's PR golden boy for a little while, and there wasn't much he could do about it) so he figured this was a ruse.

Smart. Mik's always on the ball about these things.

"Alright lambs, the slaughter is down that chute, and we're all going," he said to his officers as they collected at the airlock leading down to the Hawke Government Dome.

They descended the zero-gee chute with a level of somberness appropriate for lambs going to the slaughter, too. Some of them were just playing along with the gag, Mik himself was tired and more concerned about finding out what he'd missed while he was gone. Before he took it easy and raised a beer with his fellow Captains, he wanted to be sure things were indeed going as well as they seemed to be going.

Reaching the bottom of the chute, Mik didn't really know what to expect. Well, he expected almost anything except what he got, actually.

Stepping out into the docking lounge (one identical to the one Karen, Charlie and I came through in *The Hawke Mission*, but actually a few doors down from that one) Mik looked left, then he looked right, and then he stroked his goatee.

The only person in the room was a janitor, who looked up once with half-interest and then got back to his mopping.

"Something doesn't add up here," he said, glancing at Georgina Yamagawa, still *Cyclops'* Chief Engineer, who was standing next to him.

"I don't know, one janitor plus zero screaming lunatics equals me not getting a headache," she shot back with her usual brusqueness, and Mik nodded.

"Mmmhmm."

"Guess the summons was legit," Finn Yaalon, *Cyclops'* Sensors and Communications Officer suggested from behind, and Mik sighed.

"Probably. Well everyone, prepare to get criticized for turning up in Hawke Court in ship fatigues. This way…" Mik didn't own court dress, though he'd been to court a few times in his dress uniform since *The Hawke Mission*.

He hated it.

The courtiers were 'forgiving' of his attire because of the war, but boy were they ever a bunch of, um, well, asses. Mik didn't approve of them much at all.

Anyway, he led his officers out the left side exit — the fastest way to the lift that would take them down to the ground floor, where presumably vehicles would be waiting.

They passed one docking lounge, then another. The place seemed quite empty.

But the door to the next docking lounge was open, and there was the sound of a party inside.

You can see where this is going, can't you?

A couple of drunk Hawke Command officers then stumbled out the door and started groping each other, doing the classic drunk-couple things — you know, backing up against a wall, half-unbuttoning things and constantly kissing. Classy.

Mik slowed to a stop behind them, and his officers — many of them no doubt quite amused by the show of undisciplined amour — formed a half circle around him. He then tapped the woman on the shoulder, and her hand flailed at him, "Busy."

"Mmmhmmm."

She actually paid him no more heed, that's the really funny part. I'd have expected these two junior Hawke officers to get red-faced and embarrassed when they realized what they'd been caught doing, by whom, and in what context.

But no, these two had their… okay, I was about to say hands full, but that'd be too much of a groaner.

"This one's ours, I think," Mik glanced back at his crew, thumbing them in the direction of the door to the arrivals/departures lounge.

They filed in slowly, while everyone was more or less focusing their attention on the chute on the room's far side. Some people noticed the *Cyclops* officers enter, but there was already a mix of Defense and Hawke Command officers present, and Mik wasn't leading the officers in, Finn was. No one clued in to the fact that they'd set up their big to-do in the wrong arrivals lounge.

Mik kept to himself, and his officers stood quietly around him, all trying to figure out how best to utilize their surprise. Everything felt a little too obvious — to just declare their arrival would be too up front, to try some sort of gag would be a little too slapstick.

"Just give me a minute," Mik nodded to his people, then slid stealthily — and unnoticed — through the crowd, spotting Lia almost immediately.

She was up near the chute, standing on her own, arms folded, gaze locked on a patch of floor in front of her — she was in thinking mode, she hadn't turned on her courtier's charm yet. She was in her Hawke Command uniform, by the way.

So Mik silently came up behind her, then leaned in slightly, "You set this up in the wrong lounge, we docked in number eight."

Somehow not even missing a beat, and not changing expression or direction of gaze, Lia shook her head, "But this isn't a party for you, Mik. Haven't you heard the war's over?"

Now, Mik's nobody's fool, but the way she said it, he had to stop for a minute and study the half of her head that was visible from his angle. Lia can lie with the best of them, you see.

Then she turned, pushing a beer that seemed to appear in her hand from nowhere at him, and raised her arms, "They parked at the wrong dock, but they're here!"

The crowd cheered, and Mik smiled at Lia.

She was instantly smiling, the way Lia can, and she elbowed him as soon as her arms came down, "See, had you going there didn't I? Wasn't that fun?"

Mik laughed politely, "No."

Lia's smile melted on command, "You were hanging out with Ken, weren't you? He's taught you his meanness."

"No, I'm mean enough on my own," he assured with a smile.

So altogether, the surprise party fell flat by being at the wrong dock, and there were no laugh-out-loud moments in the setup, but Mik and Lia agree that this little shindig was appreciated on both sides.

In Mik's words to me when we talked about this years later, "It was just right. I didn't like the parade later, but this was just right. No hero worship, a bit of booze, and a good time. And then we all got back to work."

The Hawke sector was being well taken care of.

CHAPTER THIRTY-SIX

HOMECOMING: BELT TWO

There wasn't much chance of Greg's return to Belt Two being so modestly handled. The number of media shuttles floating in massive hordes in orbital space to catch the arrival of *Warspite, Goliath, Sackville* and *Generous* was insane.

Just plain insane.

There were near fatal collisions out there. In *space*. Space shouldn't be small enough for accidental collisions, but there were nearly several. Damned media.

Er. I've been advised by the editors to water down that insult. Damned media… shuttle pilots. Yes. Reporters are fine, their pilots are freakin' maniacs.

Oh come off it, you'll find out what I really think of reporters in *The Jupiter Patrol*, since we hosted two for that entire mission.

Anyway, suffice it to say that the fanfare of those four ships pulling in after their attack on Mars was pretty damned big. Wait, can fanfare be big?

Alright, this is going nowhere fast… changing scene to something I *can* describe.

My editors let me get away with literary murder.

Because four ships were docking at Belt Two base, there couldn't be a party for the officers in the arrivals lounge — there would have had to be four separate parties. And while there would have been more than enough celebrants to fill four parties, it made more sense to just have one huge one.

The Governor of Belt Two actually decreed 26 February (the day they arrived) 'Mars Day', and made it a colonial holiday. This was an excuse for a huge street party in the main dome, sanctioned by the Governor (and I always thought politicians didn't want huge numbers of people in the streets, drinking and trashing things), which was pretty much in full swing by the time Greg, Val, Becky, Isoruku and Katya got down to the base.

Wes, Marshall, Karen and I were there to meet the returning skippers. Sharon Stanton would have been too, but she was slightly preoccupied with trying to make sure the main dome wasn't going to be torched by rioting mobs of celebrants. She wasn't pleased by this party idea.

Pulling rank, I advanced to shake Greg's hand first, and then everyone shook everyone's hand in a bit of a messy but well-meaning tangle of hand-shaking.

"So no big party for us? I'll admit I'm not disappointed," Greg asked, looking around as we finished our greetings.

Karen, who'd come to stand next to me, traded one of those 'which one of us is going to tell him?' glances with me, and while we both said nothing, Marshal cut in with his usual promptness, "Actually, the Governor declared today a holiday, and there's a party in the streets outside. You're expected to say a few words."

Greg tilted his head slightly, "Really?"

I nodded, "Mars Day."

"Drinking and partying in the street," Wes' dry tone revealed his own dislike of the entire concept, and Karen finished up our peanut gallery commentary.

"The good news is, by the time you get out there, they may be too drunk to actually listen, so you'll be off the hook."

Greg blinked once, "Well."

That was about all he could figure to say, and who could blame him? Leading the Captains of the strike force, he headed for the lift that would take him down to the party. Under no obligation to follow, Wes, Marshal, Karen and I all exchanged glances.

"So, um. Anyone *really* want to go down there?" I asked coyly, and looked between them.

You know what Karen and I think of parties, eh. So giant street parties? Nah, not fun.

"Well... it can't be all bad. Sharon told me they have a carnival area set up for the kids. Merry-go-rounds, a Ferris wheel... there's some good wholesome fun out there..." Marshal did *not* sound convinced.

Wes shook his head, "I hate Ferris wheels. Can't stand heights."

Karen and Marshal nodded, and predictably, I looked at Wes, "What do you mean you *hate* heights?"

Yeah, apparently I'd never met Wes Pellew before. I'm a terrible friend.

Greg spoke to a crowd of over a million people — that's almost an eighth of the entire population of Belt Two — from a podium on a tall stage just outside headquarters. Well, the million or so people weren't all in one place, obviously, they were spread through the nearby streets and parks, and it was just a hook into the colony PA system that let Greg talk to them all at once.

But there was so much cheering when he talked that I worried the asteroid's orbit would shift due to all that vibration.

Marshal went off to find Mel, because she was apparently meeting someone in this crowd (yes, it's exactly what you think), and Wes stayed backstage somewhere, having been hooked into a conversation with Sharon Stanton, who was slightly on edge and needed the company.

Karen and I went looking for Charlie.

Poor Charlie, all he's been doing this book is showing up at odd times to steal pudding and insult me. Now he was being tasked with crowd control, because Sharon was desperate for every body in a uniform she could get, and he'd been too nice to say no.

Of course, he and his squad weren't just standing at barricades or anything mundane (but important) like that. No, when one of the hovercar-mounted patrols of the dome detected some looting, Charlie's squad was the unit that was going to drop on the looters' heads.

So Karen and I shanghaied one of the hovercar units to pick us up, and take us out to wait for Charlie to get a call. We were going to go out of our way to mess him up. Why? Because we were bored. If you'll recall, the last time we were bored at a Belt colony, it was Belt Nine, and we paid a visit to an informant, found him dead, and then ended up uncovering both the new Syndicate and the Martian plans against Earth.

We weren't aiming that high this time.

So Charlie got a call — some Belt Widows (the local chapter) breaking into an electronics store. Pretty typical behavior for the cretins. With that, Karen and I looked at each other with big smiles, tapped the driver on the shoulder, and hurtled down to the target area.

Marshal found Mel at one of the playgrounds, sitting on a bench with an attractive young woman, having one of those conversation that spies have — the ones that involve no eye contact, and few signs that the two participants are even aware of each other. Had he not been wed to a DCI superagent himself, he may not have realized what was going on. But as the unknown young lady stood up and walked away, he realized that she'd probably handed off something to Mel.

Approaching with as much stealth as a regular fleet officer can muster, Marshal seated himself on the bench next to his wife, "So, who was that?"

Marshal had high enough clearance to hear whatever Mel wanted to tell him, so she pulled mini-disk out of her pocket and held it up, "That was Haley Briand. I'm supposed to give this to Greg... insurance in case the Emperor comes after him."

That drew a frown from Commodore Samuels, and he paused as he recalled the name... "Briand, went into the palace with Greg and John, right?"

Mel nodded, "Yep. And now she's disappearing out here somewhere. Can't tell me why, but I don't think she believes she's coming back."

As a superagent, Mel knew the signs her kind gave off when they were going deeper than deep. She'd felt that way once, when she'd infiltrated Grant Merger's organization. That man's ability to smell a spy was legendary, and only because Mel was a truly special superagent had she remained undiscovered, and become one of his skippers.

Wherever Haley was going, Mel was sure it was at least that dark. But she didn't need to know.

Marshal and Mel sat on that bench for a while, tucking the disk away and just relaxing as the party went on around them. Greg got the disk later that night, and it, along with a copy, were locked away immediately thereafter.

Charlie had his MAG-90 raised and was speedily moving up the street towards the electronics store, with one of his Special Branchers next to him. He saw two Defense Command officers standing outside the store, and four Belt Widows lying face down on the street with their hands on their heads.

Now, he didn't recognize us instantly, possibly because we were both covered in powdered plaster, so he came closer, frowning, "This is Special Branch, you have them all?"

I turned and waved, "Hey Charlie!"

"We got them all!" Karen leaned out from behind me and waved too.

Then the building, full of over $40 million dollars (in 2232 money, so about $228 million today) worth of mobile electronics... well, it didn't quite collapse, or explode. Sort of crumpled, really.

Charlie lowered his MAG-90 and started shaking his head, "What are you two doing out here?"

He asked it in that exasperated way the serious guy in a comedy sketch asks things.

Karen and I looked at each other sheepishly, and Karen said it: "Um, surprise!"

The rest of his squad then seemed to appear from buildings all around us.

"We had this handled," he assured Karen and me, and we nodded.

"Yep. Yep, probably would have gone better if we hadn't shown up."

Charlie nodded, slowly rubbing his forehead, "How exactly did the building fall down?"

A ridiculous quote came to mind, from a centuries-old television show, "Well. First it started to fall down. Then it fell down."

Letting his head slump forward, Charlie sighed, "Plant some sonic grenades on the kids."

"Hey man, we'll take the fall for this if we can get some pics with you! My girls'll think it's hot that we got taken down by Charlie Peters!" one of the kids looked up from the street, smiling her best smile at him.

His jaw dropped, which was bloody hilarious.

Seeing this, I stepped closer to Charlie and patted him on the shoulder, "No worries, buddy. I won't tell Lia."

He came *this close* to killing me right then. I'm sure of it.

So that was how we spent the party for Greg's return. We got our little break from the war — our chance to collapse a building again. For reasons other than it having housed a rape room. That was a change from Egesta.

And don't worry about the store owner. Because of the government sanctioning of the street party, he was compensated by Belt Two Colonial Insurance on the Governor's dime. He got about twice what the store and its contents were actually worth, too, as a compensation for the trauma.

He then opened a bigger store, Mason's Electronics Shed, a few blocks over, and as an apology, Karen and I taped some ads for him when we got back to Belt Two after the Jupiter mission. You may remember the commercials:

Me: "Hi, I'm Ken Barron!"

Karen: "I'm Karen McMaster!"

Me: "A while ago, we blew up Ahmed Mason's electronics downtown store. We were apprehending some bad guys and gals at the time."

Karen: "Now he's put up a new one, and you should shop there. The prices are fantastic, and the new all-alloy construction means even we couldn't collapse this building on you!"

Me, suddenly deadpan serious: "Unless we tried. Because face it, she and I could blow up just about anything."

Karen, also sounding sort of like a hit woman: "That's true. You just have to know how to do it."

Cut to the logo, and the voice-over specialist, "Come down to Mason's Electronics, before Ken Barron and Karen McMaster blow it up again! Best deals in Belt Two!"

The ad, creepy as I've been told it was there at the end, was a *huge* hit, and he made enough money in the next four years to start a chain. That's why every Belt colony today has a Mason's.

So we didn't save the Empire with this one, but we did save the citizens of the Belt colonies from unreasonable prices on electronics!

Wow.

CHAPTER THIRTY-SEVEN
MY BED RESTORED

I had to stop and appreciate the fact that my bed was no longer covered in pads.

It was later that evening, Karen and I having returned to *Wolf* (under close guard by half of Charlie's squad) and we'd showered off the plaster and sent our uniforms to be cleaned. Now she was lying on my bed again, in her typical pose, waiting for supper.

So some would argue that I wasn't marveling at my bed, but the person on it. No comment.

But I had my whole bed back. We'd finished our personnel shuffling, or at the very least had handed off what was left to unlucky subordinates. The Jupiter Force was more or less sorted out, and we'd be boosting for Earth (our waypoint on the run to Jupiter, because of the way the orbits worked that season) in about a week.

"Admiring something in particular?" Karen smiled devastatingly as she asked the pointed question, and I just shrugged.

"Good question."

Terrible answer, but very good question.

She shook her head and looked at her hands, "I'm still hungry."

"That's tragic," I answered with a grin, then grudgingly turned for the kitchen.

Our usual meal didn't take long to prepare, though our normal potatoes had been replaced by rice. We'd made the switch from one form of carbohydrate to the other because rice was simply easier to store in vast quantities, and since we were getting ready for a very long cruise, rice was going to be our starch staple.

It was a difficult change to accept, but after much heartache we went along with it.

Not to over-dramatize or anything.

Emerging from the kitchen with two trays after a couple of minutes, I discovered that Karen was again *asleep*.

Turning back into the kitchen, I laid both our trays on the mag counter and stepped back out, sitting on the bed next to her and expecting the dip to wake her up. It didn't.

So I shook her slightly with one hand, and she woke with an "mmmm".

"We really need to do something about this narcolepsy," I said half-seriously. "Last thing I'll need is to be on the bridge getting an earful from Matt about being irresponsible while you snore in your chair."

Karen rolled onto her back and stretched her arms over her head, "Well first of all, I never fall asleep somewhere important..."

"Oof," I smiled.

"...second, Matt isn't on our bridge anymore..."

Oh right. See, that would take getting used to.

Then she patted the bed: "...and third, now that we've cleared all these, I'm sure I'll be able to sleep easier tonight."

My editors all hate that last sentence. You can read it so many ways. One editor assumed that meant I'd been bunking with Karen while my bed was being eaten alive by personnel pads, another that Karen didn't sleep well unless she was sleeping in *my* bed, and a third that Karen was simply glad to have the personnel work behind her and was enjoying her usual supper position, now that it was unfettered by annoying pads.

The best part was when, at an Empire Day party during the editing of this book, two of these editors got into an argument — which turned into a minor brawl — about whose interpretation was correct. I enjoyed that.

"Well, we have a long boring cruise ahead, so you'll have plenty of time for sleep," I smiled, standing up again. "For now, your supper is getting cold."

Rolling back over with a satisfied exhalation, Karen nodded, "Then bring it to me, sir, for I am hungry!"

We ate our supper, happy to be back to our old routine.

Seven days later, *Wolf* and the Jupiter Force boosted out of Belt Two, and the book that I already wrote (but that I'll now have to rewrite because I covered so much of the background in this book) can come into play.

In other words, buy and read *The Jupiter Patrol* next!

Afterword

So that's *The Gallant Few*. I have to say, I'm glad I listened to my publisher and went back and wrote it. It was *fun*, and I realize now that if I'd tried to explain all those personnel shuffles in the first couple of chapters of *The Jupiter Patrol*, it would just have been chaos.

Hell, looking at the old first draft of *The Jupiter Patrol*, it was chaos.

There was a flow chart.

Not any more though (sorry to people who like flow charts), now it's all going to be me complaining and railing about various things, as you either love or hate.

But enough about me, this was a book about some great officers, like John, Daragh, Greg, Mik and Marshal. We're not going to see much of them for a while now, so if you're a big fan, my apologies.

No, on the cruise to Jupiter, we were working mostly without a net. That's always dangerous…

So anyway, thanks for hanging around, and next time I promise it'll really, truly, honestly be *The Jupiter Patrol*.

I think.

THE
JUPITER
PATROL

THE AUTOBIOGRAPHICAL REMINISCENCES OF
ADMIRAL THE LORD KEN BARRON FOR 2232

THE MARTIAN WAR - 6

KENNETH TAM

FROM THE AUTHOR

And now, *The Jupiter Patrol*.

This book deals with questions of leadership, and specifically how much one should detach oneself from the people one is leading. There are countless fine works out there about theories of leadership, principles of good command, and so forth. I haven't read any of them. Ken Barron hasn't either. For better or worse, we both learned the style of command he practices from the study of history — from looking at commanders in action in wars past.

One thing those experiences have taught us is that detachment is a good quality for a commander. A leader in combat needs to be able to compartmentalize her or his emotions. Friends and loved ones might die, but the leader has to keep a clear mind, stay rational, and keep making decisions to best deal with the crisis at hand. This is a great principle of leadership in war, as far as I'm concerned, but from the outside it can inevitably make a commander seem uncaring, cold or even vicious.

Well, as far as I'm concerned, commanders are only uncaring, cold or vicious if, after the dust has settled, they don't feel the weight of what they've done. When there's time to safely feel pain, a good leader will feel it. A bad one won't.

That's what my theory says, anyway — and Ken Barron's too. This book really explores those theories. I was dealing with two deaths in the family when I wrote it — one a couple of months prior to me starting the first draft, another just weeks after. I imagine that influenced the way I was looking at things then, and still do now. Ken Barron was at the same time dealing with the fallout from Egesta. I think we were both spending a lot of time reflecting on grim business during this adventure.

And it inevitably had an impact on the writing..

As you probably know, many of the characters you'll read about in this book are based on real-world friends of mine, and these characters will be immune from death for the entire series. Given their immunity, and my desire to create suspense, I'm not going to list who they are — they already know who they are. That said, you can probably guess some of their identities if you really want to. Thanks to all of those fine people — I hope your characters do you proud!

My good friends Peter Caron and Wes Prewer must be thanked particularly for the advice they've given and the suggestions they've made on this series. Wes must also be specially recognized for his brilliant work on the covers of both the *Defense Command* books and the *Equations* novels.

As ever, of course, the greatest thanks of all go to my parents, Jacqui and Peter. Without them, there'd be no Iceberg, and no Defense Command.

And thanks to Atlas, my absent friend.

— Kenneth Tam

PREFACE

Well here we are, in the long-anticipated book, *The Jupiter Patrol*. 'Long' because you were expecting this for book five, but instead you got *The Gallant Few*. Sorry about that. The story of why *The Gallant Few* made that unexpected entry into the 2232 cycle is told in the Preface of that book, and I really don't need to repeat it here.

So with *The Jupiter Patrol* we're into March of 2232, a part of the year where we (Karen and I, along with our skippers Kris Jacobs, Mark Gunney, and Matt Baxter, among others) were finally getting back into the war. And thank God for that — we'd been going stir-crazy.

Our mission wasn't going to be as intense as any of the battles of Glorious February, though; we weren't going out to raid a Martian base, or to stop Martian assault forces. John had something else in mind for us: a long haul to Jupiter that would probably lead to action, but which wasn't exactly going to be an explosion-a-minute romp. Hopefully.

Just to review, I'd been put in charge of the Jupiter Force, a new squadron destined to make a long cruise to Io, and our orders were to discover just what was going on out there. Communications hadn't been successfully restored with the moon base around Jupiter; the communications ship we'd dispatched had vanished.

With that in mind, the rest of 2232 was consumed (for us, anyway) by this mission — we weren't out there for the whole year, but aside from this operation, we really did very little. You want heroes for 2232, you need Wes Pellew, Marshal Samuels, Christian 'Mik' Mikaelsen, Greg Noyce and Marlene Stoll, not to mention John Fiora. You've already read about some of their titanic efforts in *The Gallant Few*, and there were more exploits to come. You want to find out about the Jupiter mission, this is the first of what I'm guessing will be three books that explain it to you.

Now, two reporters came aboard *Wolf* for this patrol, and you may know parts of the story I'm about to tell from their coverage. The first, of course, was veteran war correspondent Jack 'Jocko' Kent, whose contributions from this entire mission are perhaps some of the most memorable journalism in history. Representing his rival network (you're nuts if you think I'll name either network in this day and age — I'm not willing to fight the army of professional duelers they'd send after me!) was none other than Jessica Qing, just then making her mark on the industry, trying to work her way into the top echelons of Imperial journalism.

Permission has been given by all involved for me to be frank about the experiences of both those journalists — a testament to journalistic desires to be honest and to project the truth, I'd say. That might sound cynical to you, but in Jessica's case I know it to be fact: she may not come off in the best light, but even with her present status, she's willing to let me tell the story the way it happened, without editing her part in it.

Anyway, I shouldn't preface things too much more. Let's get into it: *The Jupiter Patrol*.

···

Aha, it's happened again. The publisher wants more background — more information on how Io became a base of the Empire, and about why we'd be committing a force of elite frigates and corvettes to investigate its silence. This is important information, I must admit.

Brace yourself for a history lesson.

So, to begin with we have the Io base, on that moon of Jupiter. It was founded in 2186, after a suggestion by the board of directors of EM Weapons Limited made it through both houses of Parliament. What was the plan? Basically, EM Weapons Limited thought having a distant, faraway base would allow for the assessment of a plethora of weapons that couldn't be tested closer to home — weapons too dangerous, too *evil* to ever unleash in the asteroid belt, or on Luna.

Well, good idea in theory.

The reality's been much less... how shall I put this... dramatic? The bottom line is EM Weapons Limited never came up with a weapon that could be such a considerable threat to public wellbeing — nothing so daunting or powerful to make it too dangerous for the asteroids. That was problem number one.

The second was the practical one that Defense Command officers in 2186 screamed about at great length (sometimes literally) when the proposal was ratified: this new base needed to be protected. Now, EM Weapons assured the government that Io's remote location would somehow render it impervious to attack from the outside, that the pirates would never bother flying that far just to raid some poor base.

Think about it this way: a facility is set up far from any other Defense Command support, and it contains the most advanced experimental weapons in the solar system. Doesn't that sound like a rather convincing invitation for pirates to come calling? Indeed! So immediately Defense Command had to jump on board with the base project, to provide protection for the weapons we might ourselves never buy, but that we couldn't afford to turn over to a bunch of enterprising pirates.

So far, so bad. Strike three comes next: setting up a base that far out in the solar system was hugely, hugely expensive. For the ships of the time, it was almost a three-month cruise to Io, and the number of engineers and the amount of digging equipment that was needed to establish the base was considerable. EM Weapons Limited found its $950 trillion (not adjusted for inflation) development budget emptied before the first tunnels were dug, and sure enough, they ran to the government for financial support. The Parliament, having agreed to back this venture, contributed $3.8 quadrillion over the next year, and the base was set up, though it could hardly be mistaken for a shiny glowing science facility... more like an independent mining camp with some fancy gear.

Now, all of this wasn't supposed to be a problem — as soon as the big scary new guns EM Weapons had in development went to market, the profits would *easily* make up for the losses, and then the facility could be expanded and brightened while all the EM Weapons' execs bought new wives and mistresses and smoked cigars in celebration.

And guess what happened?

None of their new weapons were worth much, at least not to us — too unreliable, too exotic, not military spec. Over the next twenty-five years, Io produced nothing but white elephants. Brilliant.

EM Weapons Limited folded in 2216, with the huge corruption and price-fixing scandals that you've probably heard about. The last order of weapons we made from them was a massive EP-5 contract for over 6 million units, most of which were still in use in 2232. After they folded, we topped up our EP-5 stocks now and then with orders from smaller companies building to the same pattern, but ultimately Defense Command moved all its contracts over to MAG Corp Weapons, and its *asteroid based testing facilities*.

Hence the new MAG-90, and the fact that all the lasers and mags on the *Predator*-class frigates are from MAG Corp.

The important thing for the moment is Io. We couldn't simply abandon the base — there was too much expensive research equipment out there, too many projects in the works. Such a huge capital outlay couldn't simply be abandoned… or at least Parliament wouldn't allow it. Defense Command tried to pull out twice, but the government blocked us. Defense Command R&D took over the base in 2218 (after a chaotic couple of years where control over the base was fluid), then built a proper dome so that we could actually use the place. I have no idea how they managed out there for so long without Earthgreen accommodations, but then I suppose I'm a prejudiced Earth-born.

Over the thirteen years between us taking over and the beginning of the Martian War we'd made the facility at least somewhat productive, researching comm and weapons technology there.

None of it was particularly revolutionary, but we tried.

The bottom line is we were still out there, and there was enough sensitive military and communications technology — not to mention expensive research equipment — that we couldn't just abandon.

Hence the Jupiter Force. Hence our mission.

Sorry, that was quite the history lesson (I know, I can ramble!). Anyway, after that incredibly lengthy foreword, we get into the book… on to *The Jupiter Patrol*.

CHAPTER ONE
REVISED

In the first draft of *The Jupiter Patrol*, this chapter rather ambitiously attempted to explain all the changes to the command structures in the Jupiter Force. I was laying out who went where, why they went to those places, and so forth. In *The Gallant Few*, I expanded all that information into, oh, *half a book*, so I'm glad now that I don't have to squeeze it all into a single hectic chapter.

With a flow chart. The old version of this chapter had a flow chart.

I think this is for the best...

But now I have to figure out something to put in this chapter. Actually, I should probably review the personnel swaps, because they may not be fresh in your mind.

On *Wolf*, Andrea Kiley was skipper, because we were looking out for her after her traumatic Egesta experience (though we still had no idea how bad off she was). Jim Hannigan had taken over as XO, which meant Kate Levec had come over from *Cheetah* to be our Sensors and Communications Officer, and Lieutenant Shelby McLaws was our new Helm and Navigation Officer.

Mark Gunney was now Captain of *Cheetah*, with Erica Martin, *Wolf's* old Helm and Navigation Officer as his XO, and Matt Baxter, *Wolf's* old XO was now skippering *Friendly*.

See why I needed the flow chart?

Look, you probably remember much of this from *The Gallant Few*, and even if you don't, I'm willing to bet that me running over it again here is only going to help a very little, if at all. I figure the best way to remember who's where isn't by doing a list or a chart — rote learning is evil like Lucifer — but by reading about people doing their new jobs. So by the end of this book, things will hopefully seem more sensible.

If not... well... they will. No room for failure. Yikes.

That still leaves the question of how to fill the rest of this chapter. I've been trying to think of something clever or quippy — something Karen and I were up to on the cruise from Belt Two to Earth in March of 2232 (that was the first leg of our trip out to Io) but I can't come up with anything.

We were just our usual selves. How terribly uninteresting.

Just so you know, we *were* on our way. Cruising Earthward with the Jupiter Force, making about 190 kps.

Hmm. Nothing exciting coming to mind.

This isn't easy.

I mean, when I write a book (and keep in mind I'm a retired officer here, not a writer by trade) I get a story in my head and just run with it. The editing process, as you've probably figured out by now, isn't one I'm really comfortable with. That's not to criticize my editors, just to say that... well... me and editing don't get along.

So coming back to this and having to throw out the existing chapter, then somehow integrate an entirely new one into the start of this book is just awkward. I need to do it, because... well... that's a good question, why do we need it?

According to my editor, it's to keep us on track with our 60,000 word target for the book. But why 60,000?

Because. *Because?* Because isn't an answer!

No it's not!

Sorry, readers. This is a conversation I'm having over the course of three days of sending the draft of this chapter back and forth to my editors. As you can see, we're entirely mature and professional.

No *your* momma!

Look, if you want the book to be longer, I'll expand my discussion of what happened when we got to Io, it's not so complicated. Satisfied?

Yep, they were. On we go.

CHAPTER TWO

THE NARRATIVE BEGINS, ON EARTH

Alright, so we were about two days out of Earth when, with a sense of triumph, John Fiora finally saved the file he was working on: the paperwork was done. That's not to say *all* of it was done — far from it. The paperwork of a First Lord of the Admiralty, even a 'fighting' First Lord like John (who had now turned most of his administrative duties over to new Second Lord Daragh Ryan) was endless.

Literally *endless*.

But this particular slice of paperwork was done… and, of course, I bring it up because it was related to the Jupiter Force. My command was now official and proper — all promotions were signed off on, all necessary supplies for the long haul out to Io were aboard *Artemis Agrotera*, the Defense Command Communications (DCC) ship was preparing for its cruise… all the paperwork was finished.

Of course, as John has pointed out many times, paperwork is only one third of the battle to getting things done. Nonetheless, it was an important third.

And with the wash of triumph that was gripping him, he decided to take a break. Standing up behind his desk, he maneuvered his way around the piles of pads sitting all over his day cabin (the floor of his office looked like a mini-city with sky scrapers built of pads) and went through his hatch, out onto the bridge of his flagship.

He was working today from everyone's favorite ship — *Bonnie!* That's DCNS *Bonaventure*, of course, and she's still the fleet flagship today. *Bonnie* and her class of battleships remain in a league of their own, and they'd proven their quality in February of 2232 when, thanks to orbital seasons, Earth had been sandwiched between Mars and Mercury. You read about Glorious February already (I hope) so I won't go into how John and Admiral Rachel Butler had gone out and stopped Martian attacks from two sides, while Greg Noyce and Christian 'Mik' Mikaelsen took a run at Mars, and blew up many shipyards.

After Glorious February, John felt quite at home on *Bonaventure's* bridge, and now as he paced to the forward screens he smiled at the Captain of the Fleet (the Flag Captain of the First Lord gets that fancy title), "I finished the paperwork for the Jupiter Patrol."

Lennox Williams is a Trinidadian, and he smiled back at the First Lord, "Glad to hear that. Only a hundred thousand pages to go?"

John grinned and shrugged, "One day at a time. What're you looking at out here?"

Williams raised his hand and pointed at *Bonnie's* fourth screen (each one about as big as the average corvette's *main* screen), "The communications ship for the very same force, in fact. Looks to be having some helm trouble."

A frown slowly formed on John's face, "Really? Not what I wanted to hear."

"Yeah, seems the yards put it back into space a bit faster than they should have. I was just on with its Captain, an old friend of mine, and she says it's handling like a pig."

John's good mood didn't exactly die, but it was tempered, "Send it back to the yard. I don't care who's on the schedule for the next servicing. Ken's going to have to take this one out with him, and I want it running properly when he gets here."

The concern inherent in that statement wasn't specifically for me, though don't misread that as John being uncaring about the Io mission. No, John was expressing the same sorts of concerns that all experienced spacers felt about long trips out into the black. *Nothing* could be allowed to malfunction on the way to Jupiter — it was nearly a fifty-day cruise, and there was no help out there beyond the squadron you were flying with.

A comm cruiser with a bum drive pod could be in dire straights on the long flight, and no amount of patching-up might save it. Better to get it fixed properly the first time.

Lennox Williams nodded in reply to John's orders, passing them on to his Sensors and Communications Officer, Jorge Allende.

John folded his arms and frowned at the vid feed of the comm ship. It could be quite a complication, indeed...

Time would tell.

CHAPTER THREE

THE TWO CORRESPONDENTS

Journalists. Some people hate them, some people love them, and people like me judge them one by one. I'll likely get slammed by some of the media for saying this, but a good percentage of journalists out there today are sensationalist fools, desperate for as bloody or as sexy a story as possible, and none too concerned with the cold reality that's separating them from it.

But I will say that most journalists are not so shallow, and indeed, I've been lucky enough over the years to deal with many who are in fact quite reasonable, and I'd even say honorable.

I'll let you decide what I think about the two correspondents who were joining us for this trip. I'm actually going to be intentionally coy about this, because the relationship between me and Karen, our crews and these reporters has never accurately come to light.

Well, I'll say this much: the movie that featured the love triangle was totally wrong.

As for the rest of our relationship, I'll try to build cheap suspense for you. I doubt it'll work, but it's worth a try.

So here goes.

The day the Jupiter Force pulled into orbit over Earth, two correspondents sat in the lobby of Admiralty House, waiting to talk with John. Now, John was in orbit aboard *Bonaventure*, a fact that we weren't publicizing because we've always liked to avoid broadcasting the exact location of the Commander-in-Chief of the fleet during wartime. Call us paranoid, but there it is.

Anyway, neither of these correspondents seemed particularly amiable to the officers and ratings around them. I'm getting my account of their presence from a couple of people I know who were there that day (one Irishman in particular), and of course from the security camera feeds of the lobby.

Suffice it to say they didn't look terribly friendly.

But then you wouldn't expect them to be.

You know who I'm talking about (I think I already mentioned them somewhere): they were the now-famous Jessica Qing, at this point still building her reputation, and the much more established Jack 'Jocko' Kent, the correspondent who'd covered the Battle of Deep Black from the cockpit of a yacht that he'd hired and used to followed us.

Quite the pair, you must agree. And yes, to the makers of that stupid romance movie, they were both attractive people — imagine, correspondents who look good on camera! Shocking!

As you also probably know, Jessica and Jocko represented rival networks. I can't tell you which networks, because then anything I say might be construed as slander under Imperial Defamation Codes, and I'd have to fight a duel with one of their hired guns. That gets tiresome. But suffice it to say they were both there to one-up each other on this trip…

which is in itself a remarkable goal.

"Ah, so that's the reporters, is it?"

Jocko and Jessica looked up simultaneously at the words, and both appeared miffed. I can't really blame them for their mood since, I should add, they'd been made to wait (with no explanation at all) for about, oh, three hours. Probably should have mentioned that at the start.

Now they came to their feet in a race — who could stand up first — and whirled on the speaking officer, probably expecting it to be John.

It wasn't John, it was Daragh Ryan, the new Second Lord and the generally mad Irishman who the media tended to love for his open and shameless conduct. If John wasn't around, there was no doubt that talking to Daragh was the next best thing — apparently it was believed that he and John had some sort of science-fiction-like telepathic ability to know the same things at once, or something.

And there was no way in *hell* the reporters were getting up to *Bonaventure* to see John Fiora when his day cabin looked like a miniature model of Manhattan. No, it was Daragh who would talk to them, and they really shouldn't have been disappointed by that.

But, on this occasion, Daragh's usual ability to melt angry stares didn't quite work. They just stood there, glaring at him for about a minute. If only he'd had his shotgun with him — he'd left it behind to avoid appearing intimidating. Ah well.

"So, I'll have to use my Irish charm to get you both to stop attempting to kill me with your stares? Now what's old Daragh done to you two? Not like you've had to wait three hours, yeah?"

At this point, Gerald (of the eternal Gerald and Betty receptionist team in Admiralty House's lobby) caught Daragh's eye and nodded once.

Daragh's mouth dropped open a little, "Oh… so you have been waiting for three hours. I see. Well… dammit this is awkward. I suppose pretending that we're happy to have you here isn't going to work after that, now, is it?"

He then flashed his charming Irish smile, and Jocko cracked a smile of his own, "You tried, I suppose that's worth something. Good to see you again, m'Lord."

"Oh watch your fuckin' tongue, Jocko. People who call me 'm'Lord' tend to get shot at," Daragh grinned, approaching the veteran correspondent and shaking his hand.

Daragh then turned to Jessica Qing, "My pleasure to meet you, Miss Qing. If you'll pretend I didn't swear just then, I'd be obliged, as I make a point of never cursing in front of a beautiful woman. Well, at least not one who happens to be the fastest rising star in broadcast journalism."

Jessica started to smile just a little as Daragh shook her hand — the Irishman had cracked her stern veneer with his charm, "You're lucky I had my pills this mornin', though, my dear. You'll probably never hear it from anyone, but when I first met Rachel Butler right out here, I gave her a great hug. You'd be in for the same treatment, but I'm behaving myself today."

Jessica's smile broadened just a tad, and Daragh then waved the reporters to follow him, "Alright, so I must brief you on where we're sticking you. Come to my office with me."

The tension of their long wait having been melted by Daragh's friendliness, they followed, and minutes later they stepped rather gingerly into Daragh's incredibly messy office. There was as much stuff in there as there was in John's day cabin, but Daragh had a philosophical dislike of piles. Piles are the devil's candy, he once told me.

No of course that doesn't actually make sense. Doesn't have to — it's Daragh!

"You'll have to excuse the mess," Daragh seated himself in his chair and then grunted as it tried to destroy his spine. "We're so busy I haven't even had time to get rid of Dave Caldecott's chair. That little man apparently liked to have spikes in the spine, dammit. But sorry, we're failing on the niceties."

"I don't think either of us came here for niceties," Jocko's words came off like those of a personable battle veteran, and if you think about it, he had in fact *seen* combat, if not been a part of it. So he did have some grounds to make that claim.

"No, that you didn't. You two came for the thing my predecessor with the liquid back was most paranoid about: a story," Daragh grinned. "I'll say it plainly to you both, though, both John and I like you. And yes, I'm saying that to suck up to you so you'll be nice to us… but it's not all lies. And if you don't believe me, just wait until I tell you where we're sending you…"

And I just realized I haven't explicitly explained to you what Jessica and Jocko (and their networks) had been promised. Simply put, John had agreed to attach correspondents from the two leading networks to a mission of 'high importance', so they could get coverage from the front lines.

The problem with that, of course, is operational security. The number of times reporters had compromised Defense Command missions since the era of Ian Hawke was startling. Irresponsible reporters looking for a scoop had, in the past, been prone to broadcast locations of Defense Command ships *while they hunted for pirates*. Famously, Vera Nash had reported her position from a yacht shadowing the independent cruising frigate *Wyoming* in 2225. After the pirates maneuvered to escape, they made a point of capturing her yacht and raping her to death on camera.

Since then, we'd been doing everything we could to discourage correspondents from attaching themselves to our heels. With the defeat of the Syndicate we'd finally seen some success — peace wasn't exciting enough to justify the expense of sending reporters out after our active squadrons. There were none in position during the start of the war, so as you doubtless noticed through the first four books in this series, there were none following us around.

Things were about to change. Fearing that, with a full shooting war underway, correspondents could become an even larger security risk, John had gone to the two news networks that had the money to send reporters out on their own and had struck a bargain: correspondents got full access to Defense Command ships *if* they agreed to leave their transmitters behind.

In other words, we would broadcast their stories, but only when we knew it was safe.

The networks resisted at first, but John used a few subtle threats and a number of large incentives to get them to play ball. This mission to Jupiter was going to be a test project…

"You're both going to be boarding *Wolf* tomorrow, for a mission to Io that will likely take at least four months," Daragh's forthright introduction of Jessica and Jocko's mission was a little more abrupt than either was expecting. They'd figured on some token assignments on ships doing regular local duties, perhaps battleships of the *Bonaventure* squadron if they were lucky. But no action... no missions...

In other words, they'd expected us to stonewall.

Nope, we were taking them to Jupiter.

"That's Ken Barron's new mission, isn't it?" Jocko asked quickly, frowning and not managing to reveal how eager he was about the prospect of joining the Jupiter Force.

I'll sound like I'm blowing my own horn here, but our force was certainly a plum assignment. Remember, Karen and I were two of the hottest celebrities around, weird as that was to both of us. And the rest of the squadron was made up of other exciting people, like the beloved Andrea Kiley, the much-lusted-after Kris Jacobs, and the ever-popular Mark Gunney. The possibility of doing feature reports exploring the realities of our military life was just too good to be true...

But true it was. When John drives a hard bargain like he did with the networks, he knows to deliver on his end. Keeps them playing ball.

Jessica leaned forward in her chair, modulating her voice very carefully to contain her own eagerness, "So, we're going to have *full access* aboard the most famous ship in the fleet?"

Daragh smiled, "If you mean *Wolf*, then yes. It's a fifty-day cruise to Io, so if you're thinking Rear Admiral Barron's somehow going to be uncooperative, you've got over a month to wear him down. And I don't think he'll be uncooperative to you, dear Miss Qing."

Both reporters sat perfectly still. They'd heard rumors about the Jupiter Force — the reports from Belt Two had basically uncovered its six-ship makeup, and some carefully controlled leaks from Admiralty House had revealed to the press that we were headed for Jupiter (well, basically it was leaked that the six-ship formation was called 'the Jupiter Force', and the journalists had been able to put those oh-so-subtle clues together).

"You'll receive all the fun details tomorrow, but for now I suppose you better call your news directors and your families and tell them you're running away for half the year. Report back here tomorrow at 0900, we'll fly you up. You get a camera crew each, three people with pre-approved general clearance and at least three years' experience. As much luggage as you like, though you may have to carry it yourself if you get some spacers at the docks who don't think reporters have any business on ships of war."

Jocko and Jessica paused and stared at Daragh's grinning face — both of them trying to figure out what the catch was. The cagey Irishman had to be leaving something out. Surely we weren't honoring our word and putting them on a plum ship assignment...

Daragh laughed and prodded them on, "*There is no catch.* You both might want to go start packing."

Exchanging a quick, surprised glance, Jocko and Jessica rose to their feet, each stepping forward to extend a hand towards the Second Lord. As he shook each presented hand in turn, Daragh smiled and nodded, "I'm sure you won't get yourselves killed! Hopefully, at least!"

Ouch.

The correspondents nodded back wordlessly, and then they filed out of Daragh's office, both still somewhat surprised by their success. In terms of postings, this was an unbelievable stroke of luck.

Both Jessica and Jocko were on their comms as soon as they cleared the secure jamming of Admiralty House.

Then they went to pack.

CHAPTER FOUR

ARRIVING HOME

All the command officers were on the bridge for *Wolf's* return to Earth orbit — I was there, Karen was there, and Andrea was there, and technically we each had a different set of orders to deliver. I was to order the Jupiter Force to maneuver into formation with the Home Fleet, then Karen was to actually order each ship in the squadron to do that, and with those orders in hand, Andrea was to instruct Shelby McLaws (the new Helm and Navigation Officer, remember) to get *Wolf* into position.

So juggling all those orders took a little getting used to. It'd be slightly different when the other ships joined our formation — the supply ship and the DCC ship would be under my orders, not Karen's, so there *would* actually be a point to having us both here.

I don't believe I've really explained why John needed to send a Rear Admiral on this job, but you've suffered through enough exposition already, so let me keep it as short as possible: they needed to make sure I was more senior than any commander we found at Io. The CO out there was a Commodore, and as a Rear Admiral I could officially take over the situation without any regulations-based resistance.

That was painless enough, wasn't it?

"Into our parking slot, Shelby?" Andrea's quiet question came with a relatively neutral expression, one that wouldn't suggest our dear Captain was at all troubled. Actually, during moments like this, when work was at hand, Andrea tells me she was indeed fine — she had things to focus on.

"Yes indeed, Captain. Holding altitude and in formation behind *Jaguar*, making easy orbit speed of 50 kps," Shelby McLaws' reply came in that southern accent that makes the media go wild.

"Very good, we're in parking orbit," Andrea confirmed the report and nodded Karen's way. "On station."

Karen nodded, "Very good."

She looked at me, "We're all in position."

Now, that must read rather absurdly, and rightly so, since Andrea, Karen and I were standing next to each other. We'd all heard the first report from Shelby, and the reports over Battlelink from our five skippers on other ships stating they were in position.

Essentially, we were just trying to get ourselves used to our new roles on the bridge — to become accustomed to what orders we were supposed to be giving by repeating things a lot. And, to be honest, we were also being slightly absurd, just for kicks. That really shouldn't surprise you.

"I prefer these circumstances to the last ones," Karen looked back at the vid of Earth on the main screen. "No plans to visit the set of the Geraldine Coilier show."

I smiled, "You're not kidding."

If you don't know what we were talking about, refer to *The Almost Coup*.

"Comm grid meshing with Earth standard, and a signal's coming across from *Bonaventure*," Kate Levec was pacing behind the Sensors and Communications consoles.

I bobbed my eyebrows at the words, looking eagerly at Karen and Andrea, "Who wants to see the new flagship!"

That was in the voice of the eager young boy who wants to see the fast car. You know the voice.

Karen and Andrea both gave me the deadpan 'grow up' glare, then I shrugged and looked past them to Sensors and Communications, "Kate, can you indulge me with some pictures? Screen... four. Put John on screen two."

With a smile, Kate Levec nodded, "Gladly, sir."

I turned back to the wall of screens and took a couple of steps forward, staring at screen four as it buffered and the mighty *Bonaventure* appeared, glowing in all 'her' glory. Once again, about the 'her' thing: *Bonaventure*'s nickname was *Bonnie* — I believe I've already used it in this book — so she's always been known to the fleet as a 'she' instead of an 'it'. I think that's fair enough. The fact that the toughest ship Defense Command has ever put into space happens to be considered a 'female' should please the neo-suffragist movement... right?

I am *so* going to get letters.

Anyway, *Bonnie* completely filled screen four — she was nearby in formation, so our own cam lenses were getting great beauty shots. Big ship — *huge* ship. New sloping sides on her neck, as opposed to the triangular projections from the necks of ships like *Wolf*... well, if the publisher would spring for a diagram, I'd show you that. Never mind for now.

Karen stepped up next to me with arms folded and a charmingly surprised expression, "Didn't realize she'd look *that* good in person. Wow."

Of course, we'd not seen her in person, even though we'd watched her icon smash the Martians during John's engagement in Glorious February (the one we watched from the Belt Two base war room).

I grinned, "John personally had a hand in her redesign. And the Martians have already felt the sting."

"I like to think so!"

Those words, of course, came from John, because while Karen and I had been ogling *Bonnie* with the maturity of kids staring at a supercar, John had appeared on screen two with a smile.

"Well, rightly so," I looked at the First Lord without quite missing a beat. "How're you keeping, John? We're definitely glad to see you... well, I am. Karen was saying some nasty stuff about you just a minute ago."

Karen elbowed me instantly, then flashed a bright smile, "I was, but he shouldn't have told you."

John laughed, "I'm sure! Well, my office looks like Manhattan, I've got so many pads in skyscraper piles, but if that doesn't bother you then I'd be very happy to have you and your Captains over for dinner. You should come first, though, so I can share some news."

"Of course, we'll be over presently," I nodded, and Kate Levec immediately forwarded the invitation to the other skippers, who'd probably overheard it on their Battlelink comms anyway.

"Looking forward to it," John nodded again, then cut his feed.

I turned from the screens and smiled broadly at Karen and Andrea, "Now we get to go aboard!"

Karen shook her head (in that tolerant way you shake your head at someone's overexcitement, not in a refuting manner), and Andrea simply nodded.

We headed for the flight bay.

Andrea felt a little out of place arriving in the Admiral's dining room aboard *Bonaventure* with us. She was definitely one of the Fiora ring, owing to her elite service with the Belt Squadron, but she wasn't nearly as close to the First Lord as Karen and I were.

John admitted to me later that it had honestly slipped his mind that Andrea was now *Wolf's* skipper — he'd thought he'd only been inviting Karen and I to *Bonnie* early, not Andrea as well, but he didn't show any surprise at all when she followed us into the room. He got out of his chair at the head of the table and came right over to us, grinning ear to ear.

"Home again, at last!" he shook Karen's hand as soon as she offered it, then took mine. "And extra rank bars all around!"

I grinned as he shook Andrea's hand and greeted her too with a genuine smile, "Yeah, don't make it sound like you had nothing to do with the promotions. You've got thanks from all of us, from Wes and Marshal… I think you're pretty popular at the moment."

Chuckling, John waved us into chairs around the table, "It only takes a little bribing to win over the Belt Squadron, I hear."

"We're cheap," Karen nodded, choosing a chair next to the opposite end of the table and seating herself. That wordless action reminded me that I was supposed to sit at that opposite head — I was the second most senior officer in the room, and would be for the dinner.

Andrea lowered herself into the chair next to Karen and I sat down, and we all looked to John, now leaning back in his own seat.

"I finished the paperwork for your operation yesterday, it's all ready to go," he slipped into business talk quite handily, and I nodded. "There are a couple of bits of news you're not going to be crazy-nuts about, though…"

His warning brought that sinking feeling — the 'I think I hear the other shoe dropping right on me' feeling.

"Your comm cruiser isn't exactly up to maneuvering spec. Seems DCC's been cutting back on maintenance funding to try to balance its budget, and just about everything they have in the yards right now is in rough shape. *Semaphore* is the best they have to offer, and one of its drive pods is acting up. I've got it in for servicing again," John's first warning wasn't all that bad, then. Sure, DCC cruisers were known to be slower, much less flexible ships than the DCC relay ships that plied the space between the Belt and Earth, but I could live with that.

John turned his chair slightly and tilted his head, "And you're going to be taking Jessica Qing and Jocko Kent aboard *Wolf*."

Now, how do you react to that change of pace? I mean, you go from a minor technical issue to 'oh and you're going to be under close press scrutiny for the year'. What do you say to that?

"Oh," I looked stupidly at John. "I see."

Karen glanced at Andrea and bounced her eyebrows, then looked back at me with some concern.

I blinked a couple of times, "When do they come aboard?"

John leaned forward in his chair, lacing his fingers and laying his hands on the table in front of him, "Tomorrow. And I know it's a bad deal, but I had no choice. I can't have reporters flying around out there in private yachts — we'll have dozens of them killed by Martians or pirates, and as much as they might hand out awards for that sort of dedicated journalism, I'm not willing to risk their lives."

Yes, that's actually what John said. Some people seem to think his reason for trying to control the movement of reporters in a warzone was evil — he was trying to crush the free press or some such thing. Well *no*, that wasn't the case at all.

That's not to say John (or I, for that matter) always likes what goes to air on the news, but he's not a fool — he's never entertained any notion that the media could or should be repressed and replaced with a propaganda machine. He was trying to protect lives, and I couldn't disagree with that.

"So. Reporters."

As you can tell, I was still assimilating this concept.

"On *board.*"

John nodded, "Two of them."

Karen leaned forward slightly, "Well, I suppose we'll have some fun, then."

"Yes," Andrea added with a tone that was conspicuously somber, "we're likely to."

John nodded slowly, and I let out a long breath. Reporters on *Wolf.* Well then.

We chatted a bit more before dinner, though the bombshells had been dropped. The rest of the conversation focused on things we needed to get up to speed on… for instance, John told us for the first time about the plans to build up strength at the Forge (that base on the asteroid inside Venus' orbit). He'd just decided to promote Shauna Cass — one of our counterparts from Marlene's Venus Squadron — to command there… but more on that in 2233. You probably know the story already… moving on…

CHAPTER FIVE
WELCOME ABOARD

Dinner turned out to be quite delicious. Mark, Kris, Matt, Aaron Ashby and Elise De Winter all arrived in turn, and we sat down to an excellent meal by John's cook, then called it an early evening. It was Friday night, so John was flying home for the weekend.

I should elaborate on that, actually: since Glorious February, John had begun to allow himself the luxury of working from home on the weekends... he was just required to keep his two-seater F-194D Starlight on his lawn at all times, ready to carry him up to *Bonnie* if anything entered Earth local space.

The presence of that Starlight — Commander Sophie Ayala's plane — wasn't good for the health of John's lawn, but that was a sacrifice he could afford to make if it allowed him to spend the weekends at home.

Anyway, John was actually celebrating his wife's birthday that weekend — he and Anne were going to a nice resort near some falls in the North American Great Lakes (and Sophie Ayala's Starlight was traveling with them, of course) so I'll move along to our entertainment of the next day.

Ah, the arrival of reporters aboard ship.

Wolf was abuzz. Probably the first time I've used that word in these books, but it seems the only one to accurately describe the crew's state of mind. None of our spacers were particularly awed by someone like Jocko Kent. Sure, at a dinner party he could (and did) wow the guests with his tales of watching the Battle of Deep Black from the cockpit of a hired yacht. But most of the crew then aboard *Wolf* had seen that fight from their *battle stations*.

No, it wasn't awe the crew was experiencing, but anxiousness. By and large, we Belt Squadron officers knew how to deal with the press — it was part of the 'cavalier' persona we maintained. Even the non-commissioned officers and ratings were generally quite adept at it.

But this was different. This wasn't just putting on a show at a press conference or an interview and then heading home to unwind... these journalists would get to watch us unwind.

The air felt a tad electric as a large Admiralty shuttle lumbered into *Wolf's* Bay Two, lowering itself right in the middle of the usual small craft landing lane (there was no traffic due in, and the shuttle was just making a drop, so there was no point hauling it over to a landing slot).

Karen, Charlie and I stood in the waiting lounge, watching through the glass as the space doors closed behind the big craft.

"Anyone thinking the plan to bring Andrea over here to give her some quiet time was a bad idea?" Charlie Peters — yes, good old Major Charlie Peters who's gotten no page time up to now — asked the prudent question in a low tone. We had a squad of SF with us who didn't need to overhear this.

It was a worry that had occurred to Karen and me too. We'd brought Andrea aboard *Wolf* so that she could re-discover her space legs without putting her in a position to do much damage if she happened not to be herself.

But what if she snapped at one of the reporters? Spaced one of them? Shot one of them? The list of things she might do could border on the humorous and absurd, but we were legitimately worried that they might see her out of sorts, still a little out of character after Egesta, and that they would report it and end her career.

And we didn't even realize how badly off she was. None of us knew where she'd taken her leave in Belt Two. None of us knew that her sleep was torturous. We'd been bad friends and comrades: we weren't noticing the clues we should have been noticing… or we weren't reading enough into them. Andrea says she'd have done what we were doing — give her distance to settle on her own… but… well… I can't help but think we should have realized what was going on with her.

But if this trip to Jupiter proves anything, it'll be how well she hid her pain. That's not an excuse for our inability to see through her mask, just a statement of reality.

You'll see.

The space doors closed too quickly, and the three of us had to file out into the landing bay and head over to the still-closed shuttle hatch. We were all trying to act natural, to play it cool… and we all probably looked like we were trying to play it cool.

Of course, the reason the three of us were out here was because we were some of the most media-savvy on the ship. That and, us being the commanding officers, it was also sort of our job. Behind us, the squad of SF we'd brought along fanned out and tried not to look too imposing.

It didn't feel like a very long wait before the hatch of the shuttle swung open and people began climbing out. First were a couple of spacers from the craft, helping transfer baggage down to the deck, and then came Jocko Kent, sauntering down the grated ramp with a little too much swagger.

A camera crew followed Jocko, and then a second camera crew came, and then another two spacers. After another pause, Jessica Qing descended the ramp, walking with what I can only describe as over-sold purpose. You know when someone's trying to project confidence to hide fear, and it's not working? Yeah, Jessica was nervous. This was her first trip out of Earth space.

Yes, her *first*. Hard to believe, eh?

As the reporters and their crews came to a stop at the bottom of the ramp, they began to size us up. They'd seen and sometimes questioned us before at press conferences, in media scrums or on vid, but here we were, facing them on the deck of our own ship, welcoming them.

Right, *welcome*.

I think we stood there staring at each other for a solid three minutes. It was highly awkward, but, well, it could have been worse. There was no shooting, or more realistically, no snide or passive-aggressive remarks from either side. That was good.

"So," I said finally, again demonstrating my excellent command of English.

"Yeah," Jocko replied without missing a beat.

We stared at each other for a minute longer, and then Karen did what Karen always does — make something that's stalling fly again.

Stepping forward, she extended a hand to Jocko, then to Jessica, then to the members of the camera crews, "You all know who I am, I guess."

There were nods as she introduced herself, and following her example we all introduced ourselves properly. Jessica's camera crew consisted of Sal, Joanne and Ray-Ray, while Jocko had Bunny, Summer and Destiny. I don't know if those were given names, or if the ladies had changed them after becoming part of Jocko's crew... but it was certainly an interesting set of names.

So we all introduced ourselves, and then with continued presence of mind, Karen waved towards the SF squad, having them advance.

Watching the reporters visibly stiffen at the move was quite entertaining — thoughts of 'oh no, a trap' and whatnot must have been coming to mind. But no, as Karen helpfully explained, the SF were just here to help with luggage and to show the reporters to their cabins. Karen was really making this work — without her there might have been mild gunplay.

Charlie and I shuffled closer to each other as the camera crews and the reporters began to collect their gear, and as our intrepid Major narrowed his eyes and sized up the new arrivals, he began shaking his head, "I think this is trouble."

My tone was deadpan, "Gee, think so?"

Cracking a smile, Charlie nodded slowly, "You know, I do."

"Aye..."

Our words trailed off as Bunny and Summer both bent over to pick up heavy crates. Yes, I'm sure that sounds crude, but we weren't looking at Bunny and Summer, we were watching the six male SFs from the squad as they all rather comically stopped what they were doing to watch the two women.

"*Gentlemen*," I cleared my throat instantly, "perhaps you could *assist* instead of just staring."

Oh they all turned red. Well, one snorted a laugh (he was probably a womanizing bastard), but the rest of the men seemed embarrassed.

"Don't see many people dressed like that aboard a warship, I guess," Charlie offered quietly again, and I nodded.

I don't think I was clear above, but suffice it to say that Jocko's camera team was a point of pride for him. I'm not sure if he was sleeping with one or all of them, but he definitely seemed to believe that, on a long trip, he should have three overtly beautiful women with him.

Who knows what mischief he'd gotten up to in his hired yacht back during the chase before the Battle of Deep Black.

Anyway, Charlie was right — Bunny, Summer and Destiny all gave that first impression of being bubbly and beautiful. You'd think that on a ship with a crew that was some fifty-five percent female, the men aboard wouldn't be affected by that. But, well, these women weren't dressed regulation style.

So there could be trouble.

You'll see in a little while why I'm driving this point home.

In the meantime, I needed to do something — I had to seem at least a little bit like I was happy to have Jessica and Jocko aboard.

"Miss Qing, Mister Kent, a word please..." ouch, that came out formally.

Karen — who was herself trying not to gawk at the Bunny-Summer-Destiny spectacle — turned to give me a 'relax quickly or disaster will follow' look, and I nodded to shoo away her concern. I could handle these two...

"Look, it's probably no surprise to you that I don't really want you aboard."

Or I could insult them.

Jessica and Jocko came to abrupt stops in front of Charlie and me as I said that, both sizing me up instantly. I don't think that frank introduction was actually what they'd been expecting — they were probably looking for the polished 'welcome aboard... full cooperation... pleased to have you...' line that would be followed by no cooperation and much misery for them and their crews.

"Good," I forged ahead, "now that we're not playing games, let's be honest. You're both after life-on-the-front stories, right? Want some human interest and probably a little gossip and intrigue for the viewers?"

Neither actually answered that rather abrupt challenge of their intentions — they were too busy trying to figure out my angle.

"Well, do it. You get the run of this ship, you get to ask anyone anything you like. We actually don't have anything to hide, and the sooner you figure that out, the more pleasant this flight is going to be for all of us."

I'm really not sure if I was making any sort of point with this introduction, but at least I was being honest.

Jessica's eyes narrowed the furthest, "So... all-access?"

I shrugged and nodded, "Yes. Knock on my door any time you like, though I don't promise I'll be in a good mood if you do it in the dead of night or something. And stay out of the crew showers, that would just be creepy. But you have the run of the ship."

Jocko's eyebrows were starting to climb in surprise, and he took an extra-manly step forward, "So why are you being so accommodating, sir?"

Ooh, the 'sir' was classy.

Glancing back at Charlie, I shrugged, "I think we're too lazy to do the usual song-and-dance pretense of cooperation." I looked again at Jocko, "It's a long flight to Io. I'm willing to bet the novelty of all-access will wear off quickly anyway. You're going to find out just how boring long haul transits can be!"

I don't know if I was taking the best tack with this approach, but it was certainly fun — and honest.

"We'll see, Rear Admiral," Jessica Qing said then, rather menacingly. "We'll see."

"Good... now dinner tonight. I'll bring my senior officers from the XO up, and you can bring yourselves and your crews. You'll outnumber us two to one. And the chef's pretty good."

I hadn't planned any of this ahead of time — I was thinking on my feet.

Yes, that usually *does* end badly.

Somewhat surprised nods were the only response, and I grinned, "Excellent! Isn't that excellent, Charlie?"

Charlie was standing slightly behind my right shoulder, so I couldn't actually see his expression, but I'm sure it was golden, "Not particularly, no. Do I have to be there?"

That earned him a rather sweet smile from Jessica — trouble, *trouble* — and I kept my painted-on grin firmly in place, "Of course you have to be. And you have to pretend to enjoy it! Now, if you fine reporters will excuse us, we have to go hide from you while pretending to be busy with something! Karen!"

We left the flight bay.

Chapter Six

Trouble, Oh So Much Trouble

Wolf wasn't due to leave Earth space until the following evening, so I had plenty of time during the rest of that day to take a quick flight down to Capital Island to see my folks. Karen came with me, and we then stopped by to see her mother before heading back up to *Wolf*.

Karen still wasn't convinced my approach with the reporters had been the right one — go figure, she was the smart one after all.

But as we landed our planes in bay two upon our return, we both immediately noticed a different... *electricity*, I suppose is the word, in the air. The crew seemed a little more lively, as if the anxiousness of earlier in the day was beginning to give way to excitement. Two reporters aboard!

Karen and I shared a couple of frowns as we left the flightdeck, and as we entered the lift to our quarters, we stared at each other for a dozen seconds.

"What *is* that?" I asked after that pause, and she shook her head.

"I don't know. Think the reporters have already started poking around?"

I half-shrugged, "Maybe."

We really weren't sure what was going on — things just felt different. Trouble.

As the lift arrived on the deck that held our cabins, we stepped out a little tentatively, looking both ways as the doors closed behind us, making sure no cameras were lurking. We proceeded down the corridor almost as cautiously as if we were storming a pirate fortress, and we found ourselves clinging to the wall — the way you do if you're expecting some shooting to start.

And then we came to the intersection that led to our cabins. We needed to hang a left, and we were walking along the left wall. Rather dramatically I stopped right before the turn, flattening my back against the side of the corridor and looking at Karen, "This is way too overdramatic. I feel like I'm about to rush into a shootout."

Smiling oh so brightly, Karen shrugged, "If that's so, I think it's noble you're leading the way."

I grinned, "Of course, Admiral's prerogative you see. Greg and John did it at the Emperor's palace."

"Who am I to argue with that?" she continued to beam, backing up to the wall and sliding right up next to me. "Well, noble Admiral, unto the breach..."

I stared at her smile, "In a minute. I'm distracted..."

"Do you two flirt like this a lot?"

I nearly hit my head, I jumped so high in surprise at Jessica Qing's rather frank question. She was standing around the corner — she later told me she'd been wandering the corridors with her camera crew and had stopped when she heard our voices. I still believe she was lying in wait for us.

The good news was she didn't actually see me jump — and she definitely didn't get it on vid.

Karen turned a slight and very charming shade of red, "Only when we're teasing reporters."

"Uh-huh," I added with authority.

Jessica Qing poked her head around the corner, "I see."

"Yes, you do," I said it far too quickly. "Now, if you'll excuse us."

Ignoring the fact that we were still in our flight suits, Karen and I turned and headed the other way. I'm sure Jessica gave us a nice stare as we quickly walked off.

Jocko Kent was the man's man of reporters. That wasn't just his persona — he wasn't just playing at being macho when he was recording his reports, he acted the part all the time.

So when Charlie was drilling his squad in the gym that afternoon, and Jocko showed up, it was… um… interesting.

At first Charlie didn't notice the reporter and his camera crew, but when Destiny shoved her small field-cam in a little close to Carly Henderson's face and in turn nearly lost an arm, Charlie realized his hand-to-hand session had an audience. He called a halt immediately.

Turning to Jocko, Charlie donned the most artificial smile he could and paced over to the tall reporter, "Mister Kent, how are you?"

"Sorry, Major," Kent said with practiced bravado. "You know how editors are, they love to see the visceral stuff. Your squad shit-kicking with hand-to-hand techniques is what we want to be able to show off."

Charlie was actually impressed, to some extent, by the frankness of the reply. He told me later that he'd been expecting the usual huffy 'well you *said* all access' reply, but instead he got a straightforward admission of what Jocko was doing here.

"Be careful about where you line up for shots, then," Charlie said evenly. "I take it you don't want to do one of those reports where the journalist tries what he's covering, to add to the authenticity?"

Jocko grinned, "What, like when Sandy Sheppard volunteered to be shot with a mag, to see what it felt like?"

Charlie cocked an eyebrow, "Well, I wouldn't actually shoot you."

The reporter's grin expanded slightly, "So you'd just shit-kick me…"

Jocko glanced back at his camera crew and shrugged before looking at Charlie again, "Yeah, alright, I'll take my lumps. Just don't do anything irreversible, I'm really a big pussy under the attitude."

Whaah?

Charlie told me that's exactly the word (or perhaps sound) that played on the laugh track in his head, but he didn't let it slow him down.

Instead he led Jocko out onto the sparring floor, pointed to Carly Henderson, and smiled, "Captain Henderson, don't do anything he can't recover from."

Carly smiled and nodded, leaving her sparring partner and coming over, "I've been a fan of your work for a while, Mister Kent."

Jocko sized up Carly with a glance, "I'm *very* glad to hear that."

He was on his back with a flat thud a few seconds later, Carly's knees pinning his arms at his sides as she sat on his ribs. The camera crew was laughing happily, and Charlie was smiling — as was the rest of the squad.

But the happiest person in the gym seemed to be Jocko, who was laughing more heartily than most people who'd just been tackled could ever manage.

Carly leaned down, "Enjoying yourself?"

"Honey, if you're not married or involved, I want to have a drink with you later."

Charlie frowned instantly. *Whaah?*

Carly's eyes narrowed, "I'm sorry, what?"

"Come on, now you know I'm harmless. I have to eat dinner with the Admiral, but let's you and me have a drink later."

Carly looked up at Charlie with some surprise, "I, uh…"

Trouble. Like I said, trouble.

And there was more to come.

CHAPTER SEVEN

DINNER – AND TROUBLE

Karen was sitting at my right hand, and Charlie at my left. Andrea had the opposite end of the table (even though Karen should have been sitting there according to protocol) and Jim Hannigan was at her right. Bunny was sitting opposite him.

Arrayed along the sides of the table between me and Andrea were the reporters and the rest of their crews, and the chef was sending in courses of food at a breakneck pace — trying to end this quickly for all concerned.

It was a noble sentiment, but it wasn't going smoothly — the table was getting over-crowded as we eaters couldn't keep up with the pace.

As the main course arrived and discovered no room to land, I looked up at the head steward, "Vinny, tell Buck to *slow down*, will you? It's not going so badly that we need to rush out of here. Yet."

I smiled as I said it, and I got some curious glances from people again.

As Vinny headed back to the small kitchen next door, Jessica Qing's eyes settled on me, "Do you think you're going to irritate us with that sort of commentary, Admiral Barron?"

"It's Rear Admiral," I said quickly, stabbing my salad again. "And no, I really don't know what I'm accomplishing. There's no nefarious plan, if that's what you're thinking. But let's be honest, Miss Qing, I'm not wild about having you and Mister Kent aboard for this trip."

"You don't have anything to hide, though?" Jocko ate as fast as a man's man should, so his salad plate was already empty.

I shrugged, "Not really. I mean, I'd make a joke about us having an alien crew member or a secret weapon or something, but you'd probably take me seriously."

With a laugh, Jocko shook his head, "Come on, I can smell bullshit."

I stopped stabbing my salad for a second and looked up at the man, "Alright, don't take this the wrong way Mister Kent, but quit with the language please."

Looking up the table at my less flippant words, he nodded, "Fair enough."

Jessica Qing was looking not-so-subtly at Karen now, "So, Commodore McMaster... how do you feel about having us aboard?"

Karen was sipping her water when the question came, and as she lowered her glass to the table, she swallowed slowly, "I'm not particularly enthusiastic. I'm sure we'll all settle in though, get comfortable with each other... more or less."

Jessica's eyes jumped from Karen to me and back, "Yes, I shouldn't speak for Jocko... but I think all us lowly reporters want is for you to be able to get back to your jobs, so we can see what it's really like out here."

"Oh hardly *lowly*," Jim Hannigan cut in almost immediately, flashing a smile at Bunny.

"Certainly," Andrea followed up — those two had quickly developed a great Captain-XO rapport. "We know your reputation, Jocko. I was skippering *Friendly* when you cruised into the Battle of Deep Black under my port drive pod. I nearly blew your yacht to bits… rather glad I didn't though."

She smiled at Jocko Kent.

An awkward silence threatened to descend at that moment — no one at this stage knew much about Jessica's reputation, she hadn't been out of Earth space by this time, and we had been with the Belt Squadron, after all.

But Charlie rode to a prudent rescue, "And Miss Qing, I understand you're the rising star of your network. My papa raved about your reporting on conditions for retirees in Germany last year."

Talk about a good save.

Jessica smiled at Charlie.

"So there," I said quickly, detecting the overtones of that smile. "We don't think poorly of you. This'll just take a bit of getting used to."

Quickly restoring her slightly terse look, Jessica nodded and glanced back at me, "Good. We'll just want you to be behave naturally… act as if we aren't even here. And we'll report on that, the real day-to-day goings on."

The words were neutral enough, but Jessica locked first me and then Karen with her gaze as she said it. Do you think something was being implied?

Wait for it.

Anyway, loaded comments notwithstanding, the conversation seemed to be lightening. We were clearing the air about the awkwardness of the situation, which was key, and it seemed the moment to push the table along to fluffier, brighter conversation.

Speaking of which, there was a rather shocking question: "So Commander Hannigan, you were the SCO last time you were in Earth space, right? Was it you who developed the combat ranges ring we saw on the Admiralty sensor data we got for the Battle Over Earth?"

This was a smart question — remember back in *The Rogue Commodore* it had been Jim who'd developed that simple but revolutionary dashed-line ring around a ship's icon to show its weapons range? Well, if you wanted to get the conversation moving away from awkward matters, that was one way to do it.

But poor Jim was in shock. He had his mouth full of salad, and had been chewing, but now he stopped and stared. Andrea had to kick him subtly to shake him out of his static state.

"You see, I'm the one who usually has to go through and explain the sensor data when the package comes in. I'm the only one on the team with experience with that sort of info."

Who do you think was saying that? Why was Jim frozen in somewhat rude (and amusing) surprise?

Because it was Bunny who was talking to him. The absurdly gorgeous blonde sitting opposite Jim Hannigan was asking him about Sensors and Communications. That sort of thing generally doesn't happen.

Jim started stammering out an answer, which Bunny seemed incredibly interested in, and Karen and I shared a glance.

We both had one word in mind: trouble.

We continued to eat.

Now, my editor read this chapter and commed me. He said a few things that didn't make a whole lot of sense to me, but after a few minutes of subtle prodding, he finally gave up and asked me point-blank, "What the hell is this, a high school romance?"

I started laughing when he asked the question, and then I had to shrug. I really don't know what the hell was going on during (or in this case *before*) that outbound trip to Jupiter, but there was a good deal of romancing.

For members of *Wolf's* crew, I can understand a certain desire to find companionship, particularly with all the stress they'd been under. Jim deserved to find a good woman, that was for sure... operative word there being 'good'. Meanwhile, Andrea was running from Egesta, and as we've seen, just about anything she could do to distract herself was being done.

But what about those reporters and their camera crews? Alright, so Jocko was a known womanizer, with a couple of divorces under his belt, but for the rest... well, no idea.

All I can tell you is that this trip out to Jupiter was one of the few not-so-boring long hauls I've ever done aboard a warship. And a lot of that had to do with the fact that the fresh civilian faces aboard had tickled the fancy of the crew, and the result was... colorful.

You'll see what I mean soon enough... so let's move on to the departure.

Oh right, the rest of the meal was fine. Buck was a great chef.

CHAPTER EIGHT

DEPARTURE

The next day wasn't particularly exciting — there was more hiding from reporters, much more subtle concealment of that hiding, and then time for departure rolled around.

"We're receiving an all-clear from Admiralty House to break orbit," Kate Levec was pacing behind the communications consoles with her hands behind her back.

I nodded, "Alright Kate, let's signal the force to break orbit in pre-established cruising order." Then, with a smile, I looked from Kate to Karen standing right next to me, "Commodore, I believe you're leading us out?"

Karen's eyebrows bobbed, "Of course! Andrea, Wolf leads the way. Mark, Kris, Elise, Aaron, Matt, follow us out in squadron order."

We had Battlelink up for this little bit of theatre, and the skippers on the screens all smiled, enjoying the awkward happiness we seemed to be projecting from Wolf's bridge. I'll explain that in a minute (though you can probably guess what was causing us to behave so... properly).

Andrea was standing at Karen's other side, and now the Irishwoman took a step forward, "Shelby, mark course for the first waypoint, accelerate us to 170 kps."

"Yes, ma'am," Lieutenant McLaws' southern drawl contrasted delightfully with Andrea's Irish brogue, and I actually noticed Destiny — the sound technician, apparently — smile at the effect that had on the audio feed.

We were all being recorded.

Two camera crews were running what they call 'B roll' (a term that throws back to the days of video tape) of our departure, so we were all dressed up, with tunics on and buttoned right to the top, arms neatly held behind our backs, and so forth.

"Signal coming from Bonnie. Venture..." Kate simulated a half cough after she realized she'd nearly addressed the flagship by its nickname on vid. How unprofessional! "First Lord for you, Rear Admiral Barron, sir."

I didn't know Kate as well as I knew Jim, but she already had permission to call me whatever she wanted to — 'Rear Admiral Barron' being one of the less common choices.

"Put it on screen eight, please, Kate."

I sure wasn't going to start addressing people by their titles just because a camera was sticking in my face... literally, Jessica's camera crew was pushing in a little too close.

Charlie was standing next to me (on the opposite side from Karen) and now he cleared his throat deftly and bobbed his head, "Might want to back up a little. Nostril shots aren't appealing."

The operators backed off — a little — just as John appeared on screen eight with a smile, "I'm taking Bonaventure out as far as Luna's orbital plane as a sendoff, Ken."

"Excellent," I smiled. "More camera time for the shiny new flagship?"

I pretty much forgot the cameras when I asked that frank question, but John didn't seemed to mind, even if Karen and Charlie both gave me urgent 'watch it!' glances.

"I'm always happy to show off the achievements of the Empire's mighty industrial capacity," John's politic answer as much as revealed the fact that I'd let him know we were being recorded during departure.

"All ships from the squadron now maneuvering under cruising power," Kate Levec reported carefully as soon as John finished those words. "*Artemis Agrotera* is now breaking orbit."

I nodded, "Thanks, Kate."

We all fell into something of an awkward silence then, not sure what to say (or what we *could* say) with the cameras running.

"Receiving realtime feed from *Artemis Agrotera* now," Kate stopped behind one console as the feed came in. "Captain Patel on screen nine for you."

Looking to the screen under John's, I watched Zail Patel appear. The pleasant Indian fellow nodded, "Good day sir, we are pleased to join your force."

So much artificial pomp and ceremony. I'd cruised with Zail once before while commanding *Friendly* and there was absolutely no reason for us to appear to be meeting for the first time.

Except that it looked good on camera — and I'd commed Zail earlier that day to let him know we'd have an audience.

Now we all began to wait again, the Jupiter Force pushing away from Earth in a long line with *Bonnie* cruising comfortably on our port quarter. The last ship to come out was *Semaphore*, the communications cruiser.

"Signal from *Semaphore*, Captain Kinder," Kate continued with her string of reports, and I nodded again.

"Screen ten," I made a point of visibly moving my head to indicate I was turning my attention to another screen, and then I waited long seconds as the message buffered. Sela Kinder appeared after that delay, and the DCC skipper nodded to me with some half-hidden consternation.

Let me pause to explain: Defense Command Communications section employed Captains from Defense Command Navy for their cruisers, so Sela Kinder was indeed a combat officer. She'd taken this post when she'd been a Commander in order to get a fast promotion to Captain — the only reason a Naval officer would really be tempted to join the slow-moving ships of the DCC.

However, with the exception of some specialist positions, most of her crew were, in fact, DCC personnel, with nothing even approaching combat experience... and on stressful days (like all the days in time of war) that could be a challenge.

"Rear Admiral Barron, we're coming out with you at best speed."

'Best speed' in this case seemed a politic way of saying 'as fast as we can manage'. No matter how bad a skipper's crew was, Captains didn't blame them for ship performance in public. It just wasn't done.

"Glad to have you with us, Captain," I nodded back, and she rather obviously let out a relieved breath.

"Alright, Jupiter Force, our course is marked, we'll cruise in order as established by this morning's dispatches, *Wolf* in the lead. Kris and Matt are rearguard."

There were nods on the realtime screens — this obviously wasn't new information to anyone, we'd set our cruising order ages ago. This was for the benefit of the cameras.

"We'll be off your port beam until Luna," John repeated on screen eight, and I nodded.

"Excellent," I paused and took an overdramatic breath. "Well, we've officially begun the Jupiter Patrol!"

We had indeed.

CHAPTER NINE

NO DANGER ON THE HORIZON

I don't think I've written about too many occasions when time wasn't a crunch factor in our long ship transits — *Wolf* has always been rushing to get somewhere, be it to Belt Two in *The Rogue Commodore*, to Earth in *The Almost Coup*, a whole bunch of places in *The Hawke Mission*, or Egesta in *The Independent Squadron*. Cruising to the clock is a very stressful pastime; cruising for short periods with no pressing timeline is boring.

But what about a sixty-day trip (that's right, thanks to *Semaphore's* slow cruising speed, we were looking at as many as sixty days out in the black) into the unknown? Well yes, there was some concern about what we'd find at Io — would it be a serious communications error, would the colony be occupied by Martians...

Somehow, none of us cared.

I don't say that lightly — it was a time of war, there were serious affairs at hand, and yet we didn't give a damn at that point in the mission. And that wasn't just because we had reporters aboard... come to think of it, we'd probably have made fewer attempts to *look* as though we cared had we been free of the camera crews.

So what manner of monsters were we, you ask? Well, I'm sorry, but we had *sixty days* to figure out how to deal with what we found out there. In the first week of that eight-week trip, it really wasn't too easy to focus on what might happen at the end. Any elaborate plans we made about what to do upon our arrival could be wrecked if one of the ships of the force had mechanical trouble, or some other such thing.

My only goal for the first *month*, then, was to make sure crews didn't get too rusty. They were encouraged to relax, of course, but not to the point of losing their combat edge. That's hard to explain, I suppose, but we wanted them feeling rested, but not sloppy.

That in mind, there was one drill a day that first week, all of them run by Andrea and Jim Hannigan. But Karen and I had nothing to do.

Yes, we were flag officers on a long cruise in the blackness.

So what was Karen doing the first Friday night of the cruise? You guessed it, that thing readers have been sending me much mail about: she was dancing. To all you eager readers out there who've demanded I insert more of Karen's dancing, here you go!

She was ten minutes late for dinner and I decided I'd better check on her — it was entirely possible that Jessica was questioning her or that Jocko was propositioning her. I expected him to try that in the first week... I mean, to attempt to step into his mindset for a moment, Karen was likely quite the... how do they say... prize... score? Anyway, if he tried to 'score' her, I was certain he'd end up requiring considerable medical attention, and that wouldn't be good for our coverage, so I'd have to rescue him (and perhaps hurt him myself).

Ha, as I read that, I have to laugh — I really didn't understand Jocko well in the first week.

Anyway, I knocked on Karen's hatch door, and after almost a minute without answer I coded it open and stepped through.

Yep, she was dancing away. I shut the hatch quickly — the loud twentieth-century music pouring out into the corridor was a dangerous thing with reporters aboard.

"Ken!" she was beaming. And in case I haven't said it this book, Karen's broad, bright smiles essentially disintegrate my ability to reason or word properly sentences.

I used incorrect syntax there in an attempt to demonstrate my incoherence when she's beaming — clever, eh? Apparently my editor doesn't think so, which is unfortunate. Gave me quite a lecture, he did. Though he did leave it in, so perhaps I'm wearing him down…

Karen danced her way up to me just as I locked my legs and folded my arms — yes, once again, I was going to play the fop without rhythm.

"You danced with me at the party on Belt Two, I *know* you can do it!" she began swinging her arms around me and doing some hip-wiggles or some such, while I continued to stare straight at her eyes.

"Yes."

That was my very thoughtful answer. I'm really hopeless, don't you know?

"So then you'll dance with me now," she rotated slowly around in place right in front of me, her body wiggling and shaking delightfully, while I stared strictly at her head.

I really must be coming off as a bit of a shallow bastard, but I defy any man of similar inclinations to do any better than I did.

Well, I don't really defy any man to do so — they'd have to have seen Karen dance like this to be able to compete, and had they seen Karen dance like this, I'd have probably killed them in a duel.

"Supper's getting cold," I remembered at last why I'd come in here.

"Oh, well I guess we can move the party to your cabin," Karen stopped her rotation as she came to face me again, and as the song began to wind down, she stopped her dancing with a satisfied sigh, her smile remaining full-on.

Grabbing the remote from her bed, she paused the music on her screen and turned back to me, abruptly donning an air of mock formality — chin up, shoulders back, arm held out ladylike for me to take, "Admiral sir, if you'd be so good as to escort me to your cabin."

I couldn't help but smile at the theatre, "Of course madame, my pleasure!"

I did a parade ground step forward, turned on my heel, linked my right arm around her outstretched left one, and we moved to the hatch, which I leaned forward and opened. Karen half-bowed to me, then stepped out first… and managed to stumble on the door frame.

I should mention, she was wearing her usual undress cabin wear — long baggy sweats, a t-shirt and socks, the most casual attire one could get that still had pressure bags to deal with decompression. The baggy sweats and the farce we were putting on combined to interfere with her usually graceful carriage, and down she went in a heap on the deck.

She was laughing so hard by the time I realized what happened that I didn't know what to do… so with a bit of vaudeville acting, I stumbled and ended up on the deck next to her. She laughed harder, and I started to chuckle, both of us half-lying on the corridor deck, laughing ourselves to tears.

You know what's going to happen, of course.

First though, let me just defend our behavior — yes, we were both acting as though we'd gone to the Lia Hawke school of insanity, but it was the first week of a long, uneventful haul to Jupiter. We both knew there was a war on, we both knew this was serious business... we just needed moments like these, *evenings* like these, to remind ourselves how we wanted to feel — in a word, *happy*.

And what else were we going to be doing on a Friday night with no battle prospects?

"Come on, you," I managed to regain some composure after a minute or two, just as my chest was starting to hurt from the laugh-fest.

I started to push myself up onto my feet, then reached around Karen's waist and started to pull her up with me, and she made a surprised sound.

For a second I thought I'd accidentally grabbed some part of her anatomy that really wasn't to be *grabbed*, but then I realized that my grip was good and gentlemanly-placed, which meant...

Of *course* Jessica was standing about ten feet from us, her eyes just a bit wide and her mouth hanging open.

See, this is a lesson to all of you men and women on spaceships with reporters: don't be happy when others can see you, because of course it becomes *news*. As Karen forcibly calmed herself, I helped her up and we quickly made ourselves stand properly side by side, though I'm pretty sure we looked as sheepish as teenagers who'd been caught fumbling.

Which, to be honest, is almost how I felt at that moment. It's not every day a Rear Admiral and a Commodore are found laughing themselves to tears while lying on the floor of a corridor.

That said, we were flag officers now — that supposedly meant they could no longer fire us, only retire us...

But that wasn't going to be an issue, or even a worry, I realized, because Jessica's camera crew wasn't with her.

I cleared my throat, "Aha, Jessica. Can we do something for you?"

Jessica Qing closed her mouth, her eyes darting from me to Karen, and then up and down Karen.

Right, Karen looked like she was heading to bed. I could pretty much *see* Jessica reading into this — she was probably seeing headlines in her mind's eye. Great.

Karen repeated my question, "Need something, Jessica?"

Jessica blinked, and I could just about hear what she must have been thinking: 'Yeah, I *need* a camera.'

But she didn't say that, because Jessica Qing is a smooth and capable reporter — she was watching our body language and figuring out how embarrassed we were, "Sorry to interrupt, I didn't realize it was *that* late..."

It wasn't said unkindly — she sounded genuinely sorry, but knowing Jessica, I'm pretty sure the emphasis on *that* was a little test. Was this something we did every night, just not always on the floor of the corridor?

I felt a need to deliver a deflecting reply, but none seemed to come instantly to mind. I glanced hastily at Karen, and she wasn't quite able to say anything either. This really wasn't panning out well for us.

Thankfully, a white charger arrived. By which I mean Jim Hannigan came around the corner just behind Jessica, "Miss Qing, I lost you there. Dinner's served."

No, they weren't having a candle-lit dinner; Andrea was entertaining Jessica and Jocko at the Captain's table, with Jim as backup. Apparently, Jim told us later, Jessica had heard something and discreetly 'gone to the washroom'. I'm willing to bet that 'something' was screaming about a 'Boogie Fever' during the few seconds it took me to enter Karen's cabin before I closed the hatch.

Correspondent Qing had some damned good hearing.

Anyway, Jim paced up to Jessica's side, "If you'd be so good as to join us, Miss Qing, the Captain is most eager to begin dinner."

Jessica's eyes were still fixed on Karen and me, but she nodded slowly, "Of course. Rear Admiral Barron, Commodore McMaster, enjoy the night."

Another carefully-crafted probe of our embarrassment level. Jessica's quite good at her job. But now she turned and went around the corner Jim had just come up, and for a second I thought we were off the hook.

Then Jim stormed up to us, "Before he left, Matt ordered me to keep you two out of trouble!"

Karen and I both slumped meekly — yes it sounds absurd, but it's what we did.

"You've heard about putting a sock on the doorknob, or shoes outside the door?!" Jim hissed loudly despite his attempt to whisper.

"Now wait a minute–"

"It only works if you're *behind the damned door!*" Jim barked sharply. "Get indoors, then do whatever you want to!"

With that he stormed off too, and Karen and I stood rather shocked in the corridor for a moment.

"Did Matt infect him with parental responsibility or something?" I asked after a moment's silence.

Karen shook her head slowly, "I don't know. But my feet are cold, so my socks are staying on."

We started laughing again almost instantly. Some grownups we were, I know.

Yep, a Rear Admiral and a Commodore, laughing like maniacs as we stumbled to my cabin for food.

CHAPTER TEN

MORE SERIOUS BUSINESS

It was early the next week that word came across to *Wolf* that *Semaphore* had drive problems — of course, as John had feared, the DCC cruiser wasn't up to the cruise for which it had been so hastily prepared. This reality was proving more than a little frustrating for Sela Kinder.

"My engineer's trying everything he knows, but his staff is usele… isn't having much luck…"

Karen and I had joined Andrea in her day cabin for the realtime conversation with Sela Kinder, and Sela was in her own day cabin, so we could presumably talk openly. Even so, being a classy fleet officer, Sela managed to avoid saying that her engineer's staff was 'useless'.

Though the implication was coming across pretty clearly.

"What do you need, then, Sela? Stop for a break?" I asked with a slight frown, leaning back on the desk that a year prior had been mine, and six months prior had been Karen's.

Sela Kinder let out a long sigh and rubbed her forehead, "I really don't know yet, Admiral. I'm sorry, my engineer's only been able to promise 150 kps… I think he's afraid that if he shuts down the port pod for servicing, it may never start up again."

I cocked an eyebrow at the frank assessment — it wasn't the sort of report that anyone in the Navy would be inclined to take lightly.

"Alright," I glanced at Karen, "we're just beyond the Belt perimeter now, right?"

Karen nodded, "Yep, we cut through the unexplored Belt on the far side of the Coalition… nearest friendly port is four days behind us, at Bataan II."

"Four days is better than thirty. We should stop here, I think," Andrea said in an unusually firm voice. I was starting to detect something then, but I couldn't put my finger on what — something about Andrea Kiley's tone, its texture, its *feel*… was just off.

Well, as long as I was the only one who noticed…

As I glanced at Karen, I realized she was giving Andrea a half-hidden look of surprise. She'd heard the same unnaturalness in the Irishwoman's tone that I had. Great. Well as long as only we two noticed…

No, Sela Kinder didn't see it — she didn't know Andrea as well as Karen and I did, and besides, a vid comm call doesn't tend to carry the subtle cues.

Anyway, Andrea's idea was sound enough: if a ship was facing critical mechanical failure, better to have it occur close to a friendly port. Stopping now made sense.

"I think that's best," Karen was still looking at Andrea as she concurred, then she glanced back at me. "We wait here, get Starlights out on patrols to make sure we don't get jumped."

"Exactly my thinking," I nodded. "Alright Sela, call the all-stop, we'll form the squadron around you. We'll use this time to make sure all ships are doing fine for stores. Your engineer has forty-eight hours, then let us know your status."

Nodding slowly, Sela Kinder let out a sigh, "I'm really sorry about this, sir. My fault entirely."

It was her job to say that — as it was any Captain's job to say that.

Remember what I think of job descriptions, at least on some occasions?

"Sela, if you had a crack Navy crew aboard that tub I'd be displeased with your news. You've got what, thirty DCN specialists?"

Another slow nod was Captain Kinder's answer, and I smiled, "Indeed. I'm impressed that you've come as far as you have without breaking down — I have no idea how you put up with the DCC flunkies."

Kinder cracked a tired smile. Hopefully I'd relieved some of the pressure she was feeling just then. She had my understanding, which meant her reputation was safe, despite her ship's inability to fly properly.

"Alright, come to all-stop, Sela. We'll form the force around you," I straightened up, and with a final slow nod Sela Kinder vanished.

Karen was frowning as she turned to me, "Sela looks like hell."

"Can't blame her. We're spoiled with the best crews around, I can't imagine what it'd be like to put up with a bunch of cast-offs."

I sounded very uncharitable there, and that wasn't fair of me... mild frustration was slipping out when it shouldn't have been. There's no question, the crews aboard DCC cruisers were some of the least efficient in Defense Command as a whole; the DCC ships that plied the space between Earth and the Belt always got the best DCC personnel, as they got a million times more signal traffic than the cruisers, and were required to move much more often.

The *cruisers* were the dregs. There were six in total, of which half were probably serviceable at any given moment, and they operated beyond the Belt only, channeling traffic to and from Io base... and that was it.

That made them the dumping ground. DCC cruiser command was the place that all the hard cases and 'slow ones' went to find work — they were put in ships that did nothing but sit in the pitch black for months. So *Semaphore* only had thirty Defense Command Navy specialists to herd the rest of its crew of flunkies. The only way to get proper fleet personnel onto these dreg-laden ships was to promise short-order promotions; Sela Kinder had been a Commander for four months before taking the post, now she was a full Captain, and was to be given a frigate upon her return from this cruise.

A professional bribe, you see.

Anyway, that all said, the men and women crewing a ship like *Semaphore* were still volunteers, even if they included some of Defense Command's worst scum and least qualified people. They were *our* personnel, and in time of war especially, I shouldn't have been so callous about them.

"The bastards'll put the pod to rights or I'll bloody well board them with SF and shoot every DCC woman and man on that engineering staff," Andrea's remark... perhaps it's better to call it a 'threat'... caught both Karen and me by surprise.

Neither of us could keep ourselves from turning abruptly to look at our Captain, and she was immediately aware of the attention, so her winningest smile came out — the captivating one that had, over the years, attracted many marriage proposals from complete strangers.

"Now you two really need to relax. You think I'm mad?"

The question was light and airy enough to disarm my concern, at least for that moment, though I think Karen's intuition was still tweaked.

"We're being careful about relaxing. Jessica Qing got an eyeful of misinterpretable-information when we relaxed on Friday," I changed the subject quickly, offering a smile of my own.

Andrea laughed once, then passed us heading for the door, "Well, not to worry… we can take care of her if she decides to get out of hand with unfounded assumptions!"

See, if Charlie, Mark, Matt, Jim, Kris… *anyone* else had said that, I'm sure it would have come off like a joke.

But as Andrea stepped out onto *Wolf's* bridge to order our deceleration, Karen and I stood anxiously in the day cabin. We looked at each other once, took simultaneous deep breaths, and followed.

We were (finally) getting worried about Andrea Kiley.

CHAPTER ELEVEN
OPPORTUNITY EXPLOITED

Being stopped in the middle of nowhere for two days was itself an opportunity — or at least that was how Jessica and Jocko saw it. Since we weren't moving, why not collect all Karen's skippers together aboard *Wolf* for dinner and interviews? I don't even need to suggest to you how *thrilled* about that particular prospect those skippers were.

Zail Patel and Sela Kinder were excepted, of course — they weren't celebrity heroes (much to their relief, I do believe). But the rest of us were on the hook, so the evening after we stopped in space the invitations went out, and Commanders and Captains began turning up on *Wolf*.

Karen, Charlie and I could have gone to meet each CO as he or she boarded *Wolf*, but since the camera crews were down in bay two watching their arrival, we'd elected to stay away; we were waiting in my cabin for the call to dinner. I won't lie, we weren't at all eager.

"Is putting all the squadron commanders aboard one ship while we're sitting out here in the middle of nowhere really *wise*?" Charlie asked the question again, his arms folded as he paced.

Karen was in her usual spot on my bed, staring intently at the end of her ponytail, and she didn't even bother attempting to answer, so I did.

"If we're going to do it, here is as safe as anywhere… and frankly I look forward to seeing Jessica deal with Mark Gunney."

Yes, that promised to be entertaining…

"Well I don't know, it sounded like a plausible excuse to me. Come to think of it, though, I'm the only Special Brancher invited — you can afford to do without me, can't you?" Charlie stopped and turned to Karen and I with a rather hopeful expression.

Karen didn't even look up, "You're coming. If you don't want her to try to flirt with you, sit next to Jocko."

Jessica Qing had definitely taken an interest in our Charlie — not too forward an interest, but she was attempting to become quite friendly with him. Just a *tad* too friendly, all things considered, but a tad was enough to wrong-foot Charlie. As far as he was concerned it was like being propositioned by the enemy — the *media* — and that didn't even account for the more obvious reason it'd make him uncomfortable: he loved Lia Hawke.

Sure, they hadn't seen each other since *The Hawke Mission*, which was in chronological time just about five months before this, and they didn't trade messages as often as anyone might expect… but that didn't matter.

So Charlie wanted to have dinner with Jessica as much as we did. But duty called, we had to be there.

◆◆◆

Twenty minutes later, we were at the table, and again food was coming from Buck's kitchen. The salad passed uneventfully — there were somewhat anxious glances darting back and forth between our skippers, but nothing overt — and as the main course arrived, I started to hope we'd escape this without too much consternation.

This is a good time for me to impart an important life lesson: never *hope* things like that.

"So Captain Gunney, how's the promotion treating you?"

An innocent enough question from Jocko.

Mark was in something of a press conference mindset, "The chair isn't as worn in as my old one on *Honesty*, but I'm loving the bigger cabin."

Jocko smirked, "I'll bet you are."

When I heard Mark's reply, I'd read nothing into it, but then Mark had something of a reputation as a ladies' man (perhaps it wasn't undeserved, but he was no malicious womanizer). Jocko, however, seemed to be thinking in terms of Mark being a kindred spirit — a man who'd try to sleep with any woman he set eyes upon.

"So, any appealing officers over on *Cheetah*? I might consider moving if you can promise me good scenery..."

I stopped chewing at Jocko's question, as did every officer at the table, and Jessica too. I thought first the question was asked in jest, or perhaps it was a test — perhaps Jocko was just trying to see whether Mark's reputation held true.

But there's one thing people need to understand about Mark Gunney: his duty is his *duty*, no one toys around with that.

Lowering his fork to the table, Mark stared at the correspondent, "My *officers* aren't sport, Mister Kent."

Jocko grinned and nodded, "Duly noted. Guess I won't be moving..."

He glanced then at Andrea, "...things are good enough around here as it is."

Andrea had been trying to ignore the exchange, but now her eyes widened considerably, and she dropped her fork to her plate, "Excuse me, what are you implying about *my* crew?"

Jocko was pushing buttons here, and he obviously wasn't winning any friends as he did it.

"Nothing that isn't based in truth," Jocko's tone was playful. "I like the hospitable reception I've gotten here. Long trips demand distractions, you know, and I've found..."

"We don't give a God damn what you've found, sir. Oblige us by being silent before one or all of us finds a manner in which to *shut you up!*" that, of course, was Matt Baxter. Oh how I missed having him aboard for moments like that one. Sure, Jim Hannigan could offer a great scolding, but there was something incomparably sharp about Matt's clipped British tone.

Jocko simply smiled and nodded, "Yeah, I think I've seen what I need to see."

I still wasn't chewing, and now I looked sideways at Karen. She didn't look impressed. And I certainly wasn't impressed.

So I dropped my fork, which was probably a bad idea.

"Look, Jocko, I don't know you by much more than reputation, so let me be even *more* open with you than I've been. I think you're quite possibly a bastard, I think your womanizing is a disgrace, but I think you know that and I think you know I know that. I think you're purposely trying to push our buttons here, because watching us close ranks to shoot down your supposed propositions gives you some insight into what we're actually like."

There you go, if the bastard is trying to play your Captains against each other, *call him on it*. His smile faded, and his eyes narrowed slightly, "That's your interpretation?"

"It is. I'm sorry, but there's no way you got to where you are professionally by trying to bed every subject of every story you ever did. No, you're a cool professional, I think. You know the rumors about Mark, and you're wondering if on a long cruise our professional camaraderie becomes more than professional, so you're seeing how casually we can talk about some breed of sport sex, and how defensive we get."

Jocko's head tipped sideways slightly, "Is that so?"

"It is. And I think you have your answer."

A thinner smile curled the corners of Jocko's mouth upward, "Well, the people want to know. You're all celebrities, and as my editor has said to me, who celebs fuck, and how freaky they can get in bed, that's news."

Every Defense Command officer at the table sat back in some surprise at the commentary. I mean, obviously we'd heard that sort of comment before — we lived in an Empire where the Geraldine Coilier show was the most watched live program on Earth — but we weren't accustomed to hearing it at the dinner table.

Before any of us could react, Jessica leaned forward with what I'm told was a disapproving stare (she was sitting nearer to me, so I was seeing the back of her head), "You really think insulting the integrity of a table full of heroes is going to get you what you want to know?"

Jocko's smile widened, "You know, Jesse, it already has."

"You could have just asked, you know," Karen offered quietly, her tone being forcibly leveled as she kept herself civil.

"What, like this: Karen, how many times does Ken fuck you in a week?"

I was on my feet instantly, and so was Karen, Mark, Matt, Andrea, Aaron Ashby and Elise De Winter. Charlie, however, was sitting next to Jocko, and it was his hand that clamped down on the reporter's shoulder.

Jocko started to laugh, "See Jess, you start attacking the leaders, then you see what happens. You want to find out what sort of unit you're dealing with, you test 'em with some fun questions."

"Seems counterproductive to me," Jessica leaned back in her chair and folded her arms, and Jocko laughed and shook his head slowly.

"You'll get it when you've done this a few more times, Jesse. You know I once asked that very question to Commodore Cook, when I was doing a feature on the Independent Squadron. He and one of the skippers from the squadron were making eyes at each other all dinner long, so I threw it out there. And you know what, he answered straight up, gave me a number of times for *that* week, and then he got heckled by his Captains for not having enough staying power."

I'm not sure that bringing Sean Cook's name into this room was a good idea.

Andrea leaned forward from her end of the table and *slapped* Jocko — an open-handed, ladylike slap, the sound of which actually made me wince.

He laughed, "I think I'm being too subtle. You all passed this test, you're classy officers, not like Cook. I could have told you when I did that feature with Cook that he was going to be trouble. The man bragged about bedding one of his Captains, not a whole lot of morality there. You, on the other hand, seem pretty proper..."

His gaze shifted up to Andrea as he said that last bit. I looked directly at her then too, and realized she seemed to be... vibrating. Not trembling, not shaking. Vibrating. It was as though there was an immense wave of rage pumping through her, and it wasn't far from breaking her self-control.

"You've gotten what you wanted out of this dinner, Jocko. Now stand up and leave this room," Charlie said quietly, leaning close to Kent's ear. Our elite Major was watching Andrea too, and he wasn't about to have to wrestle her off Jocko's bloody corpse.

Nodding, Jocko slowly stood, "Yes, I have what I need. You all don't like what I did here, but that just means you'll like what I report. Wait and see. Oh, and if I can get the rest of my food delivered to my dog house in a doggy bag..."

Normally one of us might have quipped something as he turned and exited the room, but we were all beyond speaking. Jessica also elected to be quiet, realizing she'd won many points with us — she was the *good* correspondent, it seemed just then.

"Excuse me for a moment," Andrea's voice was sharp, and as the rest of us began to sit, she slipped out the opposite exit door, and didn't return for some long minutes.

I don't know where she went, but her calm was restored when she got back. She might have taken a tranq, or maybe she'd just screamed at some cabin walls or something, but she had vented sufficiently to be able to finish the meal.

Karen and I ate in silence, our minds whirling. You can probably guess our frustration at the continued scrutiny of our personal lives — the constant assumptions and the determination of so many people to confirm or refute them.

But something else was nagging at us both.

Exactly what the *hell* was going on with Andrea?

CHAPTER TWELVE

AFTER DINNER

After the Captains and Commanders headed for the landing bay, Andrea Kiley vanished before either Karen or I could so much as have a word with her. Jessica disappeared too, leaving us to stand and stare at each other, completely baffled again.

"This is getting tiresome," I said quietly after a moment.

"Oh no, I *love* being microscoped..." Karen's sarcastic words came out less smoothly than they usually would have. She was clearly irked.

We left the dining room and ambled slowly down the corridor toward our cabins, looking at the floor before us as we walked.

"Do you think we should try to sit down and talk to Andrea?" I asked in something just a bit louder than a whisper. That wasn't a question I wanted heard by any of the crew.

Karen had thrust her hands into her pockets, and now she slowly shook her head, "I don't know. I don't know if anything's really wrong. But if it is, we might make things worse, if she thinks we're losing confidence in her..."

I nodded at that. It's funny, I'd have expected myself to be better able to handle concerns about a colleague like Andrea... but I wasn't. How do you deal with someone who *might* be falling apart? Or someone who might just have been changed by her experiences, and was moving on? Would going back and addressing what she'd seen on Egesta make things better or worse?

You're probably thinking we should have done the wise thing: called the ship psychologist. Get professional help, right?

No, not that easy. Andrea was the Captain of this ship, she couldn't go to the Lieutenant shrink — that'd end her career. Doctor-patient confidentiality? Not in the service, not then. The Lieutenant would be required by regs to report to DC Medical — and no, we wouldn't try to convince him to do otherwise. That would put his neck on the chopping block, and look like we were trying to cover something up... actually, that's exactly what we'd be doing. There were too many Caldecott lackeys still around for Andrea to survive his report — she'd be transferred to a desk job as soon as we got back. Even John wouldn't be able to protect her.

I wasn't about to lose Andrea to a desk.

"Maybe we can talk to Doctor Morgan, get some input on post-traumatic stress symptoms," I suggested quietly, but Karen shook her head again.

"Andrea passed the psych debrief at Belt Two with flying colors. If she's going through something, she hid it from them. I don't think book work is what we need... we need her friends to start looking for differences..."

A new voice interrupted our conversation, "I've got a few of those for you. But I'm not her friend."

Karen and I stopped instantly and our heads whipped up.

Jocko Kent was leaning against the corridor wall ahead of us, facing Karen's door in fact. My hand actually jumped down to my hip, to where the handle of my mag would have been, had I been wearing it. Karen took a step forward and squared herself off, "What exactly is that supposed to mean?"

"It means we need to talk, behind closed doors. Either of your cabins will do," Jocko came off the wall, stepping towards Karen's cabin.

We stared rather incredulously at him, but he shook his head and pointed at Karen's door, "Look, you can *space me* if I irritate you again, but hearing what I have to say isn't going to hurt."

I wasn't sure what to think. This could have been a ruse to get into Karen's cabin — to look for evidence on my presence in there or something.

Karen glanced back at me, and half-shrugged.

"My mag's in there," she said finally. That qualified as a yes, so she moved over to her hatch, coded it open, and then we all entered her cabin.

As the door shut behind Jocko, Karen and I turned on him simultaneously, standing tall and close, backing him up to the door with our bearing.

"What do you have to tell us?" my question was blunt, as was appropriate, I think.

"Andrea Kiley. I don't know her well, but I do know her reputation. And I know people. And I think she's having... difficulties."

My eyes narrowed — I wasn't sure what his angle was here, but I wasn't about to admit that the Captain of *Wolf*, one of our Belt Squadron elite and one of our friends, was having difficulties of any kind.

Jocko detected that stubbornness on my face and on Karen's, and he elaborated, "Look, I know neither of you trusts me, but I'm trying to help. Whatever she must have seen on Egesta hasn't left her. I can *tell*."

"I'm sure you can. You have excellent observation skills, don't you?" Karen's sharp question lacked her usual smoothness.

"I do. Why do you think she slapped me when I said Cook's name? Come on, you two must understand people better than *this*. She was there for an extra week. Now you all have classified footage of the horrors, but I know there were horrors, and she saw more of it than any of you, yes?"

Neither Karen nor I so much as blinked. This would undoubtedly end up on the news as it was...

"I'm off the record, here. Really off the record. Look, I'm not interested in discrediting your people, especially not after what I saw at dinner. All the buzz about your Belt Squadron being the real deal... well it's true. You *are* a 'band of brothers', or whatever they call it these days. You all look out for each other, and now I'm telling you that you need to look out for Andrea."

Yeah, sure. I wasn't buying this.

"Making one our best out as someone suffering from post-traumatic stress would be good news, wouldn't it?" Karen folded her arms, then leaned in a little closer to Jocko.

Unphased, he shook his head, "You think making Andrea Kiley out to be a whore would get me traction in the news? She's the sweet, bashful one, the one who gets all the marriage proposals! Even if I got a lot of up-front air time, I'd become the reviled ass who destroyed a sweet innocent Captain, and Defense Command wouldn't let me anywhere near a battle ever again, would they?"

My eyes were narrowing now, and Karen took a short step forward, just about seething the word: "Whore?"

"That's how she'd look, if I spread word about what we've been doing. She's been in my cabin three nights so far. Hasn't spent the whole night, but it's been... memorable. Don't worry, I'm not spreading the word. Despite what you might think, I'm good at being discrete."

Interesting how his choice of words changed from dinner, isn't it?

Karen's hand found his throat instantly, and I stepped forward now too, "I think you were assuming too much when you thought you'd make it back to Earth *alive* after calling Karen's Flag Captain a *whore*."

Jocko managed not to gurgle as he rasped out the words, "She came to my door. Three times. Wasn't being coy about it. She needs *help*."

Karen's grip loosened slightly, much to Jocko's relief, and she leaned in even closer, "Help you gladly provided, I suppose."

"Look," his eyes grabbed Karen's, "don't you think I got the hint in there? Why the hell would I come find you and subject myself to *this* sort of reaction if I didn't want to help her? If I was going to broadcast the fact that Andrea Kiley and I were playing, wouldn't it have been smarter to keep it under wraps until I sent the report back to Earth, so you couldn't kill it?"

Neither Karen nor I had been thinking rationally enough to process that reality ourselves — until he pointed it out to us.

Karen's hand came off his throat and she backed off just a little, "So you're confessing to taking advantage of our friend... to get our good will?"

"That's exactly what I'm doing. When a woman like Andrea shows up at my door and tells me what she wants, I'm going to enjoy the ride. But I'm not an idiot. It's getting pretty clear to me that she's not just looking for a good ride, that's not *her*. She's running from something. My *sport*, as Captain Gunney calls it, doesn't involve taking that kind of advantage. So I'm here, because I'm legitimately worried about your Captain. And you two should do something about it."

Karen and I exchanged a glance at those words, and Jocko pressed a little further, "I only know Andrea's reputation, but I take it she didn't do this much before Egesta?"

No, no she hadn't. I mean, sure, it wouldn't have been something that Andrea would have publicized, but shipboard rumor mills and loose-lipped Belt reporters would have let hints out...

"So do something. Because I don't want you to lose your Captain."

With that, Jocko opened the door and slipped out of Karen's cabin.

We remained inside. My skin, I have to say, was slightly crawling.

CHAPTER THIRTEEN

INTERVIEW PREP – AND COMPLICATIONS

Over the next week, the Jupiter Force got going again. Sela Kinder's engineer had delivered full functionality from the port drive pod in forty hours, with the help of some volunteer engineers from *Lion* and *Friendly*, who'd gone over to provide support (since the DCC engineering staff aboard *Semaphore* obviously lacked some of the necessary knowledge to get the job done).

Twenty days into our trip, we were making 168 kps and we were well beyond the Belt, pushing out into the black the way ships of the old days sailed out into the vast unknown of the Atlantic or Pacific. Too much romanticism? Sorry, but it's a different feeling when you're beyond the Belt. The sun is smaller, the stars seem brighter, and there's a feeling of being alone — *very* alone.

There's no real trade traffic out beyond the Belt, and only rarely do the pirates venture that way — it's generally considered to be too dangerous a place for any lone ship to be. A communications failure, a drive malfunction, anything out of the ordinary and you might *never* be found.

I'm sure I could stop and insert some metaphor here about how losing a ship in the blackness could be like us losing Andrea… but that'd be tacky. And probably not accurate either. No, I'll avoid stupid metaphors, and just explain what we were thinking after that charming meeting with Jocko.

If this was an after school special, or some sort of movie with an important message about family or some other damned thing, our immediate course of action (after we finally decided Jocko wasn't lying) would be to race to Andrea's cabin and stage an intervention. We'd demand that she talk to us, tell us all that was wrong with her life, hug and cry and hug some more. There'd be touching music and we'd let Andrea admit to us how hurt she'd been by Egesta.

To quote Andrea herself, when she talked to me about this later: "If you'd done that, I might have shot myself."

Karen and I were by no means experts on psychology. All we could do was try to put ourselves in Andrea's place, and as we talked about that for many hours after Jocko left Karen's cabin, we started to piece together a rough understanding of what was happening with our dear Flag Captain. We didn't really comprehend it all, but we figured out enough to guide our approach in dealing with her for the rest of this mission.

You see, Andrea was doing exactly what Jocko said she was: she was running. She was numbing herself to the pain in her dreams by simply shutting down most of her emotions, and cutting through that haze with some recreational activities with a certain journalist. I think I explained the psychology of all that when I talked about Andrea being in the brothel in *The Gallant Few*. Well, now Karen and I were at last starting to see that this was Andrea's situation.

But what do you do in response to that sort of activity?

Well, *nothing*.

I'm sure psychologists who know how to treat people with these conditions would disagree, and perhaps they would be right. But to Karen and me, sitting in a ship that was days beyond the asteroid belt, it seemed the only thing we could do was give Andrea her space. If she wanted to have lusty encounters with reporters, that was her business. She was doing nothing that we could see to jeopardize the safety of the ship, and while as friends we were definitely *disturbed* by the change in her character, what would be accomplished if we went to her and told her she had to stop?

We'd perhaps make it appear that we were losing confidence in her. And what would happen if she thought our confidence in her was wavering? The only thing that was consistent in her life now — the only thing that seemingly hadn't been changed by Egesta — was her duty. She was an officer of the Defense Command Navy, and a damned good one at that. That was something she could hold on to.

Karen and I hoped that, as time went on, Andrea would be able to sort out her problems — as long as we kept that confidence in her. That confidence gave her a reason to mend herself... something to live for, if that doesn't sound too overdramatic. We'd just have to make sure any odd personal behavior didn't bleed over into her duty.

Now, to answer the question of one of my editors, we certainly could *not* tell anyone else in the squadron about this. None of the other skippers, none of the crew of *Wolf*. We trusted them all, don't get me wrong, but what could they have done? If Andrea started to get out of control — if, despite our hopes, her turbulent personal activities started causing her to make bad command decisions — no one other than Karen or myself would have had the power to stop her. If we told Jim to make sure Andrea didn't do any harm, what exactly could he do if she tried? Nothing that wouldn't actually be insubordination or *mutiny*.

No, one of the reasons that Karen and I had brought Andrea aboard *Wolf* was to make sure she had a safety net — us. We'd deal with her troubles, no one else could.

She was our responsibility, and there was a long road ahead.

Anyway, this was in the background (because if it had been in the foreground it would have been a serious problem); what was front and center on day twenty was the beginning of the *interviews*. Let's talk about those.

Big news networks are notoriously impatient. They hear a trip will take sixty days, but they want the story in half that. Actually, they wanted the story in twenty-seven days, because that was the day of the journey on which we were scheduled to leave *Semaphore* behind — that was when we'd reach that ship's patrol station. Once set up, the communications cruiser would be able to connect us to the Admiralty again, and of course we could send back news stories.

Thanks to our two-day pause to fix *Semaphore's* drives, we were a little behind schedule, so it would be day twenty-nine before we made the stop. Even so, that left the reporters aboard nine days to construct their feature reports. Both Jessica and Jocko were getting full-hour specials on their networks; they had to pick story angles and then work up sixty-minute pieces about their experiences thus far, and about shipboard life.

Since it was operationally safe for them to file these reports (we weren't in the process of chasing an enemy, or whatever) we didn't have any power to censor them unless they tried to reveal classified information... which they didn't.

So this was going to be a stressful nine days, as the reporters started doing interviews and recording segments to tie together the B roll they'd shot during the first third of the trip.

If *Wolf* was abuzz before, the atmosphere was sizzling now.

Which was why I was going from compartment to compartment — literally — talking to every one of the crew on that twentieth day.

Many of these spaces I hadn't been down to in literally years — I'm talking way belowdecks here, places where Captains, Commodores and Rear Admirals rarely visit. I was going through the weapons pod at the front of the ship, and Karen was starting down in the engineering section. We'd work our way towards each other, meeting in the middle.

At this moment I was standing before a team of mag-calibrators. These seven women and men kept our port side mag batteries firing cleanly, made sure no relays had melted, and so on... they fixed broken mags.

"...So I don't know if they're coming down here, but I'm guessing at least one of them will," I was finishing my explanation of the interview procedure — or at least of what I predicted about it — and the crew was nodding slowly.

"And you wants us to be perfectly honest, yeah?" one of the women on the crew asked somberly, wiping some sweat off her brow with the back of her sleeve.

I nodded, "We've got nothing to hide. Well, don't tell them about the moonshine the engineers make on that still, and the ridiculous price they charge for it. But other than that."

The crew chuckled, one of the other women piping up, "We got their price down with the war, 'cause they're producing more on the long hauls now, sir."

I grinned, "I can see the headlines: 'Price War in Moonshine Divides *Wolf* Crew.'"

"No price war, skipper. We're divided 'cause the engineers are a pack of assholes, if you don't mind me saying," one of the men asserted with a smile.

"And right now Karen's down in engineering hearing what cheap bastards the mag crews from the weapons pod are," I persisted, and the mag team laughed.

The spirits aboard ship were very good indeed — we'd all been together on this crew for years, and there were many friendly (and even some unfriendly) rivalries. By and large, though, *Wolf* wasn't beset by the bitterness that many independent belt cruisers faced belowdecks. That was one of the benefits of being an elite Belt Squadron, now Jupiter Force ship: you got to pick your crew, and to make sure the belowdecks life was happy.

A happy ship fought well.

"Alright, I'm going over to talk to the flightdeck hands, but you're all set?" I finished the levity with serious words, and the crew members nodded in turn.

"Good to see you down here again, sir," one offered with a smile and a nod.

"Shit, yeah sir, we were afraid the sun on the collar would have made you into an asshole," another offered with a grin, and then she got a nervous whack on the arm from the tech standing next to her.

"You don't call the Admiral an asshole, Kyla," the second tech hissed, and Kyla reddened.

Of course I didn't care — as stated above, it was pretty clear this was a happy ship, which was all I could ask for.

"*Make me* a what?" I boomed, overdramatizing transparently. "I take offence, Kyla. I've always been one. Back to work now!"

There were chuckles at my barking, and as the crew got back to their daily servicing, I left them to their work, heading to the number two flight bay. It was a quiet walk, and I passed no one along the way. I spent much of the quiet walk pondering things — pondering my ship... *Andrea's* ship, that was...

Arriving at the hatch to the observation lounge that looked out onto bay two, I wasn't even paying attention to what I was doing; I opened the door, stepped through, and bumped right into Destiny, who in turn bounced into Summer, who stumbled into Bunny.

I'd walked right into a camera crew. How's that for luck?

"Oh I'm terribly sorry," I stammered, stepping away from the trio of camera operators rather more awkwardly than I should have. I didn't want to look like I didn't want to see them or anything...

Bunny pounced, "Perfect! Rear Admiral, we wanted to shoot some B roll of a pilot checking out an F-194, but Lieutenant Commander Thompson's saying none are available. Could we steal you — it'll only take a few minutes."

I said no... well, in my head I said no.

But as my mind slipped into 'media relations' mode, I somehow smiled brightly and nodded, "Well actually, my plane's over in bay one, but if you don't mind the walk..."

"Of course we don't, come on girls!"

We trekked back out of the lounge, then up the stairs to go over bay two and then down the stairs to the between-the-bays section that housed most of *Wolf's* sensor gear.

I played tour guide rather too well, "That hatch coming up on the left leads to the main sensor suite. It's pretty impressive in there, if you want to get some B roll. Nothing classified as long as you don't go through the second hatch on the inside..."

"He's right, girls — get some reccies and then meet us in bay one!" Bunny bubbled.

'Reccies', I learned, is the short word for 'recordings' — it's pronounced 'reck-ees', and in fact is also an old British slang for 'reconnaissance'. More dinner party facts from your friend Ken Barron...

As Summer and Destiny (I'm sorry, I never get used to typing those names, not that that really matters to you) peeled off, Bunny hopped along with me (sorry, the puns are irresistible).

"You've seen the sensor suite before?" I asked in a friendly fashion as we turned a corner and headed for the hatch to bay one.

"Yep, Jim took me down here last week, showed me all the gear, and the Mark Fourteen array you have. That's one *sweet* rig! I mean..."

I stopped, "Excuse me, he showed you *what?*"

Whoops, my media relations mode had jammed.

Bunny stopped in mid hop (oh I know it's bad, but it's sooo good too!), her face flushing instantly, "Oh my God. I mean. I didn't see anything."

Right.

I frowned now, and I'm pretty sure I put my hands on my hips, which is odd for me, "You saw classified equipment... Jim Hannigan showed you classified equipment?"

"I begged him. I'm so sorry, sir... I just, well, I like that sort of stuff. And I promise it's off the record. Please don't get Jim in trouble, he was just being really nice, and I... er..."

Bunny was stumbling over the words here, though by the tone of her voice I could tell she was genuinely worried about what was going to happen to Jim Hannigan. He'd shown off classified gear, that was generally a no-no.

But strangely — or not so strangely — I didn't care. Part of that was because the latest commercial sensor suites being fitted publicly to merchant ships were as good as the Mark Fourteen, so it wasn't exactly a big security breach.

Another, stranger part of it was the way Bunny was trying to cover for Jim. I mean she wasn't distinguishing herself with her repartee, but she genuinely seemed to be worried. That struck a cord with me, particularly set in the context of that time — when I was already worrying about the potential loss of a good Captain.

Was I going to do something unspeakable, like fire Jim, because he showed off his big sensor suite to Bunny?

Bunny was studying my face, "Seriously, Admiral, I only got a peep through the door, and he said I wasn't supposed to see it..."

I turned and kept walking, and Bunny was left in my wake. When I got to the corner where we needed to turn to get to bay one, I looked back, "Coming, Bunny? Fighter check-out B roll awaits."

Swallowing, Bunny nodded.

CHAPTER FOURTEEN
CONSEQUENCES

Some hours later, after Karen and I met up and headed back to her cabin to review the day, I passed on the little bit of information about Jim's tour-guiding. Karen's eyebrows shot up at the news, "Bunny? Jim and Bunny?"

Of course, the shock for Karen wasn't about the tour, it was that Jim was spending off-duty time with Bunny.

"Well... I suppose..." she shook her head in that way people shake their head when they're resigning themselves to something that doesn't quite add up to them.

I nodded, "So what do we do?"

Karen didn't answer for a moment, her mind still trying to put Jim and Bunny together in some way that made sense. After failing again, she blinked, "What?"

"What do we do?"

I folded my arms and began to pace back and forth in front of Karen's bed, "I mean, it's a breach of classified information. By the book he gets demoted by a rank and transferred out to a garbage scow or something..."

Karen frowned, "It's sensor gear. The latest commercial kit is just as good. No, we just do the usual — I'll sit down and tell him to tell her not to tell the Admiral next time."

I stopped pacing and looked at my dear Commodore, "But you can't talk to him."

Karen's frown deepened, and she tilted her head sideways, "Why not?"

"Commodore. That's the job of the Captain."

Within a second, the expression on Karen's face changed — from a playful frown to a dark one. Little breaches in security like this only ever went to courts martial if you wanted to railroad someone off your ship. All we wanted to do was tell Jim to be more discreet next time — or to remind Bunny, if he insisted on associating with her, to be a little less brazen with her boasting.

But what would Andrea do? Here was a test for our cavalier 'give her space' approach.

"Oh my," Karen's words quieted. "Well... I guess this is another chance to see her state of mind."

"Yeah, and if she tries to throw Jim out an airlock, we'll have to have Charlie ready to intervene..." I tried to make that sound sort of like it was a joke.

I don't think it was a joke.

We didn't waste any time on this, we went directly to Andrea from Karen's cabin, told her the news, and waited with bated breath.

Well, that's overstating matters a little — we went casually, almost jovially, implying that we'd just heard this amusing thing and wanted to share it with our good friend. Under different circumstances, that would indeed have been the case.

As it was, we hoped our anxiousness about Andrea's reaction wasn't obvious.

Andrea had been sitting in her chair beside her bed when we arrived, apparently reading a book. I found out much later that, until she heard the knock at the door, she had actually been studying her mag rather intently. But her mag belt was hanging over one side of the chair back, and the mag was put away as the door opened.

It really scares me when I think about it — the number of times she did that, the number of times her will to live, or her belief that she was obliged to win, nearly lost the battle in her mind.

She's a strong woman: I have no doubt that if she decided she had no obligations worth filling, she'd have shot herself through the temple. Makes me glad we went to all the lengths we did to show confidence in her, in fact.

But now, as she rested her book in her lap, she frowned, "Jim did what, you say?"

Karen shrugged and smiled a genuine smile, "I think he's smitten, Andrea. He gave a tour of the Mark Fourteen sensor suite to Bunny."

Andrea lifted the book off her lap and tossed it on the bed, stood quickly, and stepped right past us, out the cabin door.

Karen and I looked at each other, noted that she'd left the mag on her chair, and followed.

Emerging onto the bridge three minutes later, Karen and I stopped just inside the door and seriously contemplated getting some SF to the bridge. Jim was standing in front of the Sensors and Communications consoles, chatting with Kate Levec. It was evening shift on a long cruise, so there were only a handful of techs on duty. That was good… unless we needed many warm bodies to restrain Andrea…

Andrea sauntered quietly up to Jim's side, not drawing any attention to herself until she wrapped an arm around her taller XO's shoulder and gently pulled his head down close to hers.

"Hi there, Kate," Andrea's first words weren't to Jim at all. The next ones were, "So, Jim, I hear you've taken a certain very pretty lady called Bunny into our classified sensor suite."

Her words were quiet, and she spoke (according to Kate) through a clamped jaw — you know, the way anyone who's trying to look like they're not saying anything talks.

Jim's eyebrows went up and he stumbled to say something, "Uh… where… um…"

Kate, for her part, put on an astonished look, leaned forward, and whispered, "Bunny?"

Andrea nodded over-enthusiastically, "I know!"

"I always figured you for a brunette kinda guy, Jim," Kate whispered with full-on mock astonishment.

"And there's not even a comfortable place to lay her down in there, Jimmy," Andrea shook her head. "I swear, Kate, did he never date at the Academy?"

Kate just stopped herself from snorting a laugh, "Come on, skipper, we communications types were the innocent ones at the Academy. I swear, I only took a ride on a console once. Well, twice."

You know, I usually don't condone that sort of talk. In this book there seems to be a lot more of it than I generally like, but all in all I try to stay away from it. Karen and I don't use it at all.

But this, I thought, was *brilliant*.

"So, Jimmy, if you like the girl, stay in your cabin, not in the classified compartments. Okay?" Andrea said it sweetly.

Letting Jim go, Andrea was smiling that mischievous smile as she walked back towards us.

"Dealt with," she chuckled as she went by.

Karen and I just looked at each other, and then back at poor Jim, beet red and turning away from Kate while she tried to keep from cracking up.

"Well, that looked like it went well..." I said quietly. We hadn't overheard the low conversation, I should point out — we were just watching the fallout.

As Jim went back to his operations consoles, we headed quickly over to Kate, then tried to avoid laughing as she told us what had been said.

It wasn't easy, so we left the bridge.

We were feeling pretty good about the 'give Andrea space' plan.

CHAPTER FIFTEEN

INTERVIEWS AND FEATURE REPORTS

I contemplated providing a whole lot of coverage of the interviews in this book, but then I realized that didn't make any sense — you've probably already *seen* the interviews Jocko and Jessica did with many members of our crew in those nine days before their deadline. So instead let me give you snapshots of what happened, and what I heard happened.

First, both reporters talked to all the senior staff — Andy Jenson, Alicia Morgan, Adrienne Thompson, Kyle Stranks, Shelby McLaws, Kate Levec, Jim, Charlie, Andrea, Karen and me were all interviewed. And from what I understand, there wasn't anything too unusual about any of the interviews.

Well, Bunny took a long time getting Jim wired for sound. Hehe.

Sorry, that was juvenile. But then so were the rumors Jim had spawned — and the good-natured jeering he'd started receiving from the crew.

I really shouldn't put this in, but I recall passing Jim as I was looking for Karen on the rec deck one day (she was punching a bag looking goddess-like again). Just as I passed him, Shelby McLaws stuck her head out of the door to the pool, and with her irresistible southern charm, had a go: "James, you never told me you preferred blondes. I'd have tried my luck!"

Poor Jim, it really wasn't fair. But he was smitten with *Bunny*, so I think he had it coming. It all turned out for the best anyway… well… no, I won't over-qualify that remark. Sorry, way off track here. Interviews.

There wasn't much out of the ordinary in our interviews — that is to say, we talked a lot about ship operations, about how we kept the crew sharp on a long jaunt, a bit about how we passed the time. Both Jocko and Jessica played by the rules pretty nicely when we sat down with them — they knew we had a long flight ahead, and probably each decided that trying to probe us for more intimate answers would be counterproductive.

So after all our careful preparation, our fear of insidious probing, our consternation, our… well, I'm too lazy to get a thesaurus open, so if you want more words for fear and consternation, look them up yourself. Come to think of it, I could have looked them up in the time it's taking me to tell you do it. But, well…

Let me give you a snapshot of the reports we saw on day twenty-nine, as *Semaphore* set itself up for comm traffic with the Empire, and the rest of the Jupiter Force sat around Sela Kinder's ship.

All of this is a description of a slice of what you've probably seen on screen (and my editor says I have to thank the networks for letting me include it, so *thanks*):

"…it really doesn't come as a surprise to find a real camaraderie aboard Ken Barron's flagship," Jocko said as he walked though the crew mess. "Ask anyone in here, they can tell you about the Battle of Deep Black, the Battle of Belt Two, the Battle Over Earth, and Egesta. These are some of the hardest-fighting spacers in the Empire, and they're all fiercely loyal to their commanding officers."

Cut to Spacer First Rate Jimmy Boyle, a native of Capital Island (who I think they picked because his 'Newfoundland' accent, still unique to that island, makes for great vid): "I've been shipping out with Admiral Barron since he was in *Friendly*, and sure enough he's the best in the business. Him and Commodore McMaster, yes my son. Best around, wouldn't ship out with nobody else."

Cut to Ensign Eileen Wang.

Jocko: "This is your first tour, Ensign, and already you've seen more battles than any surviving senior officer in the Caldecott circle. How's that feel?"

Wang: "It does not feel like anything I could easily describe. I joined to protect the Empire, and providence placed me on this ship. I am grateful for the leadership we have had."

Jocko: "Being led by celebrities?"

Wang, smiling: "We here never think of them as celebrities. Admiral Barron and Commodore McMaster were both our Captains in their own times, as Captain Kiley is now. Outside our hull they may be celebrities, here they are our leaders, part of our ship family, our squadron family."

Let me interrupt here. I never know how to respond to comments like that. The word 'flattered' seems inadequate… I just, well, thank you seems all I can say. Don't know if any of the old crew is reading this book, maybe you are, and if you are, ignore the terrible grammar of this sentence, and *thank you*.

Anyway.

Cut back to Jocko, standing in the corridor that held my cabin, Karen's, Andrea's and Jim's: "The officers here aren't just celebrities, I've found that out for certain. All the integrity and good grace we see in the press isn't just a show. *Wolf's* officers, and the leaders of this mission, have been the face of Defense Command in the Belt for years, and they are exactly what we all hope them to be."

That was flattering.

Cut to Karen, sitting at her interview.

Jocko: "I believe you're blushing, Commodore McMaster."

She was. And so you know, the first time I watched this feed I stopped thinking for a while, and marveled at the ability of modern vid to capture just a slice of Karen's personal magic on a feed that would spread it to the Empire.

Karen smiled: "Well to be honest, I don't take praise all that well. I mean, Ken and I didn't do anything any other officers wouldn't have…"

Jocko: "You crashed a highly-rated network program and faced certain death in a gunfight with the Imperial Army. I can't think of many officers I know who'd do the same."

Karen's smile persisted and she looked down and then back up: "You need to meet more officers, then. Because I can guarantee every officer in this Jupiter Force would have done the same, or something *smarter*, with the Empire on the line. It was only us because of pure luck…"

Jocko: "You really won't accept accolades for saving the Empire?"

Karen scratched her eyebrow: "Well, um… not if I can help it."

Cut back to Jocko: "I came here intending to remove the mask from these officers — my goal in joining this mission was to find out the truth behind the recruiting vids. If I wanted to condemn any of those vids as propaganda, then I came to the wrong ship."

Cut to B roll footage from around *Wolf*, and Jocko's voiceover: "For just under a month now, I've lived with the crew of DCNS *Wolf*, I've tested their minds and their characters, and I've probably won some enemies in the process. But what I haven't found is a black mark on the reputation of the people on this ship. Whatever we find at Io, I'm confident in the abilities of these women and men to deal with it."

Back to Jocko: "This is Jack Kent, posted to DCNS *Wolf*, a month outside the asteroid belt. Have a good night, Empire!"

End of feed.

Watching that for the first time, Karen, Andrea and I looked at each other with some surprise. I'm sure you'd expect us to be elated with such a positive story. Cynics back home called the report propaganda. But it was accurate, I think — *Wolf* was a happy ship, a very good ship. Of course our fleet had many not-so-happy ships, and we were going to be adding more with the new construction John had running.

But this Jupiter Force had no unhappy ships.

Maybe that's why you're reading a book about it.

Jessica's report had a different look and feel — Jessica Qing started as, and remains, a human interest reporter, not a reporter looking for the war story. Coming aboard *Wolf*, she'd decided to focus not on our mission and reputation, but on the very personal aspects of our job. How did we get along every day?

"I don't have a military background, I didn't know what to expect when I came aboard *Wolf*," Jessica was standing in an engineering bay. "To live under the stresses that our Defense Command personnel live under, one would almost expect a crew of superhumans, or a crew of people constantly in a state of despair, or somber near-depression. This is far from the case."

Cut to footage of one of the crew galleys during a meal, and the uproarious laughter and good spirits there.

Jessica: "Looking at this crew, you'd think of peacetime, a pleasant cruise between Belt colonies, or perhaps shore leave. There is no melodrama here, there is no dark cloud hanging over people. And yet these are by no means naïve individuals."

Cut to SF Guard Eugene Sengooba, a large African fellow with a brilliant smile, "Yes I was on Egesta, ma'am."

Jessica: "Did you witness atrocities."

Sengooba, with pain flashing into his eyes: "I did, ma'am. Not as many as some, but they have stayed with me."

Jessica, with a very soft tone that has served her well all her career: "Would you be willing to share any of them, perhaps just briefly."

With a stiff, somber nod, Sengooba: "A particular incident that I continue to remember came with the death of a woman near Government House. She was killed in a friendly-fire accident after we had rescued her. It was the fault of no one involved, but she died within reach of safety because the fighters of the Guild had put our position under threat. I often remember the look on her face as she died."

Sengooba had been one of the SF Guards on Government House's terrace when Mark Gunney, armed with a borrowed mag, had accidentally killed that woman to save the ceasefire.

Jessica: "That's terrible…"

Sengooba, smiling sadly: "Forgive me ma'am, but you have no idea how terrible."

Cut back to Jessica, standing in the engineering space again: "The crew of this ship have seen battles, atrocities, and triumphs. And yet if you visit any of them — and we've visited many — they welcome you with a sort of warmth that is frankly surprising."

Cut to the SF Guards' mess, with Sengooba sitting at a table releasing a rich belly-laugh without pretension, and the women and men around joining in. Jessica: "Instead of dark moods and sorrow, here we've found people being happy. Perhaps they are forcing themselves to be happy, to fight pain that is building within them, or perhaps they are truly remarkable individuals who can put the horrors and pains of the past behind them. Either way, they make a ship like *Wolf* a welcome place. And an effective combatant."

Cut to Andrea in mid nod: "Oh definitely, a happy ship is the best kind out here. We're almost a month out from the Belt, you see. If you're out this far with a crew that isn't happy, you're in for a rough cruise."

Jessica: "So your opinion as a commander is that a jovial ship is good for combat effectiveness?"

Andrea: "Oh it's good for everything, Jessica, it really is. Discipline remains, of course, but on a happy ship you don't need discipline much at all. We're so very lucky with *Wolf*, to have the same crew aboard now that started with Admiral Barron years back. There's been turnover in personnel, of course. I've come over from *Friendly*, for instance, but all the crew from our old Belt Squadron, we're like a family you see. We get along really really well. I don't know how it is for other squadrons' ships, I've always been with the Belt Squadron, but we have elite crews who really click. And we're happy."

Jessica: "So that helps you get through crises like Egesta?"

When I first heard that question, my breathing halted and I studied Andrea's face for any hint of her state of mind.

Andrea: "Yeah. Em… yeah. It helps. Egesta was a nightmare, there's no other way to say it. A nightmare that many of us keep having every night. But every day when you get to be around your crew, you remember that you're still out here, that you still have a job to do, with people who are important to you. And with Egesta we're lucky to know that we solved the problem there, so we can all sleep a little easier."

Handled so well by Andrea — the woman is a master of concealment.

Cut to Jessica walking through the corridor where she caught Karen and me on the floor: "And what about the two most famous officers in the force? Admiral Barron and Commodore McMaster have been grabbing headlines for years, and speculation has been rampant as to the nature of their relationship."

Cut to Karen, smiling again… Jessica: "So you and Admiral Barron seem to make quite a good team."

Karen: "We get along really well, yes."

Jessica: "You know what I'm going to ask, of course. The viewers want to know, Commodore McMaster. What exactly is the nature of your relationship?"

I get perverse pleasure from thinking of viewers sitting on couches all across the Empire, hearing the question, stopping whatever they were doing, and sliding to the edges of their seats. Well, that's probably a lot of ego on my part, but it's an entertaining mental image.

Karen, her smile solid: "It's a good relationship."

Cut to me: "I'd say it's a good relationship, Jessica."

Jessica: "Well I think the Empire would agree. Let me ask you this, there are no regulations against fraternization between officers, correct?"

Me: "No regulations, no."

Jessica: "In fact, Lord Hawke, during his time at the Admiralty, was well known for carrying on highly visible relationships with officers, wasn't he?"

Me: "Well, I wasn't alive for some of his reign at the Admiralty, so I couldn't comment."

Jessica: "Fair to say. But after Lord Hawke, First Lord Deborah Warsangeli had several during her years. There was the famous press conference incident."

Me: "I recall that."

Jessica was referring to the day Deb Warsangeli had held a press conference in her home's living room, responding to the reports about another Syndicate attack on an allied colony. The press conference had come up so unexpectedly she'd simply rolled out of bed, dressed, and headed down to it.

She didn't tell the man in her bed, Commander Walter Bouvair what was going on, and five minutes into the press conference, he wandered through the living room, half asleep, wearing a bathrobe. He got his breakfast without even realizing what he'd done until he turned on the kitchen vid.

Anyway, it wasn't much of a scandal — Deb was a good First Lord, and the media was more entertained than anything else. Walter Bouvair was embarrassed out of the service, of course, it being decided that he was sleeping his way up the rank ladder. He resigned, and after that became a successful game show host.

It was a well known incident back in 2232 — less so now.

Jessica: "So, there's nothing at all to keep officers from having intimate relationships?"

Me, tilting my head slightly: "No regulations that I'm aware of."

Jessica: "Have anything to add about your relationship with Karen, then?"

Me, smiling: "Ah Jessica, you know I don't."

Cut to Jessica, standing in the corridor again: "Mysterious as ever, neither Admiral Barron nor Commodore McMaster offered any insight, on the record or off. But what did the crew of *Wolf* have to say?"

Cut to the mag crew — yes, they got interviewed!

Kyla Delancie (the one who called me an asshole): "Oh I figure they're in love. Definitely. We don't see them much down here, but when we were down on Egesta you could see from the way they looked at each other. They just had that look, you know?"

Another of the techs, Xin-Chu Fu: "That doesn't mean love though. That's friends, whatever else they do we don't know. Ain't our business."

Jessica: "So like the public at large, you have your own theories about the nature of their relationship?"

Kyla, offering a lopsided grin: "Gotta be careful theorizing about a commanding officer, ma'am. Bottom line is when they say do it, we do it. I've just seen the two of them making eyes at each other. They're in love, I figure. Not in the sappy movie way, but they're in love. And damn, if Commodore McMaster ain't all over him she's... well... I don't know what I can say without getting myself brig time. She oughta be though."

Watching that, I think I turned many shades of red. Karen smiled at me, just to make it worse.

Cut to Charlie, sitting awkwardly in his interview. Jessica: "It's widely believed that you're Admiral Barron's best friend."

Charlie: stares at Jessica.

Jessica: waiting for answer.

Charlie: "Um... that was a question? Oh, yeah, I'd say best friend. One of them anyway. We've been through plenty of scrapes together."

Charlie was trying to sound at ease, and it wasn't working. He still felt awkward being in the room with Jessica, and I can't blame him for that.

Jessica: "Some of the crew has characterized his relationship with Commodore McMaster as a love relationship. Do you think that's fair?"

Charlie: "Oh it's definitely love. The question you should be asking is what kind of love. The Greek philosopher Plato believed in two sorts of love, agape and eros. The first one is sort of the love between close friends, the other is pretty self-explanatory."

Jessica: "And you won't tell me which sort you think it is. Or if it's both."

Charlie: stares at Jessica.

Jessica: waiting again.

Charlie: "Oh, was that a question? No, not a chance."

Charlie's a good man.

Jessica went on from here to talk about crew respect for their officers, and to cover some of the same territory Jocko covered, but that's about as much as I'll repeat.

Watching these feeds in Andrea's day cabin, I had to be pleased — things were looking good for *Wolf*. Andrea had come through untarnished, and Jocko — true to his word — hadn't so much as hinted about their liaisons.

I was grudgingly beginning to respect that man, and Jessica was really proving herself to be... well... the reporter we all now know her to be.

So that got the first hurdle with the media out of the way... now we had another month of flying, and Io to visit.

Let's start a new chapter.

CHAPTER SIXTEEN

SO LONG, SEMAPHORE

"We're ready for thrust," Shelby McLaws turned from her bank of consoles to make her report.

"Thanks Shelby," Andrea nodded in reply, then glanced sideways at Karen and me, "we're ready."

"So are we," Mark chimed in on the comm, and then the rest of the skippers of the Jupiter Force added their own confirmation.

I nodded slowly as they all reported ready, then stepped to my right a little ways to come to a stop in front of screen eight, to face Sela Kinder.

"Well, Sela, looks like we're set."

She nodded evenly at my words, "Yes, sir. We're going to miss your company."

I smiled, "Likewise..."

We were getting ready to leave *Semaphore* behind, to continue on to Jupiter to deal with the Io situation.

"Still nothing coming from Io, sir," Sela offered as I paused. "We'll keep our ears open for any comm traffic from that vicinity, and we'll have it for you when you check in."

Io was silent. Up to this point, we hadn't been sure whether the colony's lack of communication with us had been due to the loss of the previous DCC cruiser out here, or if it meant foul play at the colony itself — though (obviously) we'd expected the latter.

Now we could be fairly certain that our expectations were right — *Semaphore* was all set up but nothing was reaching the ship's receivers.

"Very good," I nodded again, "we'll be in touch."

I stepped back from screen eight and turned to Karen, "Let's move out."

Offering a bright smile, Karen looked up at her skippers, "You heard the man, fire drives and form up in cruising line, same as before."

"Zail," I nodded to Captain Patel of *Artemis Agrotera*, "you've got the same spot in line."

The Indian man nodded, and with that all of the ships of our Jupiter Force began to push away from *Semaphore*. As was the tradition of the time, the comm ship was being left to work on its own.

"Make speed 185 kps, if that's fine on your drives, Zail," Karen was looking up at the skippers as I returned to her side.

Zail Patel smiled, "Commodore McMaster, my ship can cruise safely at 190 kps, if you wish."

With *Semaphore* and its bum drives out of the formation, we could kick into gear and cover the second half of this trip at a speed considerably higher than the one that had brought us out to this first waypoint in twenty-nine days. The sixty day trip would be shortened.

Smile broadening at Patel's enthusiasm, Karen nodded, "Correction, 190 kps please, everyone."

More smiles came to the faces of the skippers on screen, and I certainly wore one — the Belt Squadron of old had never liked slow cruising. We were elite, fast, ships and it felt wrong to make long hauls at below cruising speed.

Alright, I should stop here briefly to describe *Artemis Agrotera* to you — it's rare that combat storeships get any attention whatsoever. Essentially, these ships do what their names suggest they'd do — they carry stores into combat. Every ship in the Jupiter Force had supplies aboard to sustain its crew for four months, but if you look at our transit times, four months was just about as much time as it would take us to get out to Io and to come back... allowing for no time over the base.

What sort of supplies am I talking about? Well, water was reclaimed in these years, though we always like to be able to top up on the fresh stuff for drinking, so there were many tons of water aboard *Artemis Agrotera*, along with thousands of MREs, soap, boots, uniforms, spare parts, and weapons. That's just some of what the ship had, and if you looked at the grand total of everything in the vessel's holds (it was, for reference, about the same size as Greg's *Warspite*), it extended the cruising life of our squadron by *three months*.

May not sound like a lot, but think: that single ship could support its own crew for seven months, and the crews of six other warships for three months. Nothing to shake a stick at, so to speak.

And having been built to follow and support Defense Command warships, *Artemis Agrotera* had sturdy drives that could push it up to military cruising speeds without too much difficulty — unlike poor *Semaphore*.

So, with that little review in mind, you can perhaps see why we were all smiling. It wasn't anything against Sela Kinder, she was one of our own Naval officers who'd just been unlucky in her new ship. We were just glad to be accelerating to a respectable speed again.

"Reaching cruising velocity," Shelby McLaws reported from her consoles.

"We're leading out," Kate Levec added, then strummed a few keys on her master control panel to switch the main screen over to a cruise scan display.

"Excellent. Here we go again..." I said the words quietly, and Karen glanced at me with her smile.

"Another month of fun nothingness," she said equally softly. "I'm looking forward to it."

Of course, it wouldn't be nothingness — she and I both knew that we seriously had to start analyzing what we might find at Jupiter, so there'd be more work and less frivolity... but there'd still be frivolity.

Karen was smiling, of course there'd be frivolity.

Chapter Seventeen

Insight On The Process

About a week after we left *Semaphore*, Karen and I started to seriously consider what we might face at Jupiter. We had very little to go on, of course, but by now you'll probably realize that's nothing new for us. Flying blind is a specialty of just about every Defense Command officer you'd care to name, I think.

Lack of information just led to extreme contingency planning — we had to have ideas about what we'd do under just about any circumstance. Io could have been taken by Martian or pirate attack... it could have been blown apart by the testing of some experimental weapon we'd never heard of... it could have been overrun by aliens — monstrous mutants, perhaps, who looked like wolves and cats and bears...

Yeah, right. That'd be believable.

We had to look at all the possibilities, or at least as many of them as we could dream up. There was an open chance that none of what we expected would be what we actually encountered, but then there was just as good a chance that we'd get out there and find that one of our scenarios was indeed what had happened.

Actually, this is a good place for a little rant: movies seem to have trained the viewing/reading audience to be cynical about this sort of preparation. In a movie or a novel, the characters inevitably have some foreshadowing of the climax of the movie, or sometimes they guess exactly what's going to happen. Now, in fiction this might just be bad writing, but I have to say, in life it *happens*.

Look, we're professionals, we're good at our jobs. You send us to a place like Io and on the way we will (as you're about to discover) come up with many possible scenarios for our arrival, and all it takes is for one of them to be correct. The problem with movies and some fiction, I find, is that it shows the audience only the prediction that proved correct in order to avoid confusing viewers about what's coming.

This makes people cynical about what really comes from long hours of work. They think 'Oh wasn't that convenient?' It *isn't* convenient; figuring out what the future might hold is never easy, so when we get it right, we're proud of it.

With that out of the way, let me explain to you what Charlie, Andrea, Karen and I were doing: we were sitting in the briefing room, with Jocko, Jessica, and the camera crews.

Yep, we had an audience — though this was an audience I was rather hopeful about. My thoughts on this were pretty simple: show the media how long and boring the process is, and they'll be able to tell viewers across the Empire how unglamorous and how difficult the job of mapping out contingencies can be.

Instead of doing that, Jocko and Jessica both simply cut most of the footage — it was slow and boring.

I probably should have seen that coming, but now I get my revenge: I get to subject you, dear reader, to our planning!

Well, not all of it. I don't even need my editor to tell me not to include it all — some of it was incredibly dull. But the highlights, how about those?

"So, best case scenario is they had a transmitter malfunction and they sent a ship to tell us about it… but it didn't make it…" Charlie, as usual, offered the sober assessments of possibilities.

I nodded at his words, "Exactly… though we lost contact with them when we lost contact with Earth, so I'm thinking that's a very slim chance."

When comms between Earth and the Belt had gone down in the fall of 2231, we'd lost contact with Io as well. That had been almost seven months ago, which would have meant that their courier ship would have arrived probably around the time Karen and I were on Egesta… unless it was destroyed on the way.

But the people on Io wouldn't have known the ship was destroyed… they'd have waited, seen that no help had come, and then sent another ship… which still probably would have arrived…

No, no it didn't seem likely they were sitting on a dead transmitter.

"Best case scenario if the Martians or the pirates hit them is that they fended off the attack, but lost their transmitters in the fight, and didn't have any ships fit to make the cruise to Earth," I added my own thoughts on the matter. This was a more likely scenario — the Martians attacking, but being fended off…

Well, it was more likely than the blackout simply being caused by a mechanical comm failure. It wasn't as probable, though, as the Martians attacking and *taking* the base.

"Ctirad Prazsky is Commodore of the Jupiter Squadron," Karen leaned back in her chair, eyes narrowing thoughtfully.

For the benefit of the cameras, that probably looked like a fact just being thrown out for digestion. In fact, that was Karen saying 'there's no way in hell Io was successfully defended', because Commodore Prazsky was almost Ian Hawke's age, and the only reason he was still in the service was because no one else wanted his job at Io. He stayed out there on a mission *worse* than Sela Kinder's, enjoying the control he had over a tiny rock in the far reaches of nowhere.

He was not an elite combat officer. Far from it, actually. His last engagement against pirates had been in 2207, and he'd commanded three old Defense Command 'cruisers' (the predecessors to our frigates) that were slotted for retirement at the time. He'd managed not to lose any of his ships in the fight, but the pirates had strutted away too.

And that was when Prazsky had been in his prime.

Andrea, Charlie and I all recognized the context of Karen's comment, and the tone she delivered it with, so we didn't need to point that fact out to the cameras — it was bad form to pan officers on camera, unless you had a very good reason (as with Sean Cook) or were part of the defunct Caldecott Circle (those Caldecott sorts loved to hold press conferences, remember?).

"Worst case?" Charlie decided to carefully turn things towards the negative.

Leaning forward, Andrea interlaced her fingers and laid her hands on the table before her, "I'd say that's pretty obvious. Io belongs to the Martians, and they're fortified and using experimental weapons… probably even sending weapons back to Mars so they can reverse-engineer them to use against us."

"Think they'd want to keep the base, or just empty it and leave?" Charlie offered another prudent question.

"Hard to say," Karen tilted her head. "If they had any sense, they'd realize what a huge liability Io is to their Imperial security — they can't afford to protect the Asteroid colonies, they'd have no hope of looking after Io…"

We all started to nod, and I followed up Karen's suggestion with the counterpoint she'd set up for me, "But 'common sense' and 'Martians' don't always go together. They might keep Io for a PR victory, or whatever they'd call it in their haughty verbiage."

Charlie grinned at the word choice, "Bravo on 'verbiage.'"

I smiled — you don't often get to use a word like that in a sentence.

"So worst case, we're looking at a dug in Martian force equal to our own… or stronger… and lying in wait for us, because destroying the force sent to investigate the loss of Io would be another big feather in their cap," Andrea's tone was frank.

"Yep," I nodded.

Karen folded her arms, leaning back in her chair, "And since we weren't terribly secretive about heading out here, they *could* know that we're coming for them."

She then looked down the table at the camera crews, "No offense."

Jocko smiled and held up a hand, "None taken."

That bastard. I was starting to like him.

Bastard.

"Well, we're officially going to need sixty days to get out there, but without *Semaphore* we'll do it in what, fifty-five or so?" I asked quietly, and Karen nodded.

"Just over fifty-five at present speed, we might catch them by surprise if they're expecting us later. And if we increased to 198 kps, we could arrive a whole week early. Shake up any plans they had waiting for us…"

"Leave *Artemis Agrotera* behind?" Andrea asked with a frown.

"Only two days behind. We could set a rendezvous point with them just short of Io, then rush ahead and get a look at things," Karen might as well have been crawling around inside my mind.

Which is my strange way of saying I was thinking the same thing.

"I like that option," I nodded. "We'll set that up when we're done here, but we better get some possibilities between 'best' and 'worst' onto the table first. Anybody else here think the Martians would need some sort of local base of operations to pull this off?"

I'm going to stop this talk here — I've shown you best and worst, and you know we'd talk about things in between, but I just scrolled back up through the pages in this file, and I'm pretty sure this chapter is long enough already.

So let's skip ahead a week.

CHAPTER EIGHTEEN
ANOTHER WEEK GONE BY

The trip was starting to come to a close. Think summer vacation for a school kid — it seems like it'll last forever at the beginning, but before you know it…

At the end of week two of our post-*Semaphore* leg, we were forty-three days from home — pretty much ten days from arrival. *Artemis Agrotera* was a little ways behind us, keeping in regular comm contact. I didn't like leaving Captain Patel in the rear, so at the very least I was insisting that we keep in touch with him, in case something unexpected came up.

We spent a great deal of time working on contingency plans, coming up with possible scenarios and problems, working through solutions, but the bottom line was we had no idea what we'd be running into when we got out there. Preparation was done as much to give us all some comfort as it was to get us ready for whatever Io yielded.

During all this, Karen and I managed to stay reasonably relaxed. The reporters aboard no longer felt like an imposition — we were getting to know them and their camera crews… and getting to like them, honestly. Even Jocko had somehow reversed all expectations for his character, now that he was done pushing buttons.

We were also feeling pretty confident in our approach to dealing with Andrea.

She was continuing to do her duty without any sign that her experiences were negatively affecting her judgment, so our only concerns were really for her personal life. Jocko wasn't sharing her bed anymore, at least from what we could tell, so it seemed that perhaps she'd gotten it all out of her system.

Oh wow, how many times have you heard that sort of stupid assessment of someone's situation? Of course she was still hurting, tied up in a dark place. We'd just stopped hearing about the symptoms, and were perhaps too optimistic in assuming she'd worked through it so quickly. Wishful thinking instead of worrying about her wellbeing… well, even if we had worried, our approach wouldn't have changed. She still needed her space, and we'd give it to her.

Instead of crowding Andrea, then, we read and re-read reports that we'd gotten from the Admiralty through *Semaphore's* uplink; Wes Pellew's Independent Squadron was out on the hunt for that pirate base that had plagued us through *The Hawke Mission* and *The Independent Squadron*, though he'd been out of touch for a while, so no one knew if he'd gotten it yet.

And as far as I was concerned, it was a question of 'yet'… or more grammatically correct, of *when*. I knew Wes was going to nail those bastards — he commanded specially designed pirate-hunting ships, and he had some great officers with him, not least among them Captain Sharon Stanton, back on space duty with her recovery finally complete.

So Wes' exploits made for some excellent reading (I'm trying to convince him to write his own memoirs about them — feel free to flood him with fan mail), and Karen and I thoroughly enjoyed them.

Another set of interesting messages came out of Hawke One, where Lia had taken over as provisional head of state when her father had been confined to his bed after a minor heart attack. And yes, for the bitter cynics reading, the heart attack had occurred while he was in the presence of Shauna, Emily and June — three of the mistresses whose names you might recognize because he named corvettes after them.

Lia was under more than a little stress, then, as she was expected to be the Lady Governor and the commander in chief of the Hawke Command forces, and she didn't really trust any of her then-staffers to take over either job on an interim basis. She'd learn to delegate... eventually.

Working closely with Lia, though, was Commodore Mik Mikaelsen, who was still riding a wave of glory after his participation in the raid on Mars during Glorious February. Mik has never been a huge fan of the spotlight, but he hadn't had much choice since he made Commodore. He was just too good at his job for the media to ignore him.

And the Martians were sending large groups of pirates and warships into the independent belt he and Lia were looking after. We still aren't certain about their motives, but my best guess is that they had counted on taking our Belt colonies at the beginning of the war, and had probably pegged all their resource and production hopes on the extra capacity the captured industry would provide them. Since they didn't take our colonies, they had to strong arm the independent belt to get extra resources out of those rocks...

Or try, anyway. Lia and Mik weren't having any of it — and they had a powerful Hawke Force with which to hurt the raiders.

So that was more interesting reading.

Marlene Stoll, who I haven't had the chance to mention enough lately, was holding the fort at Venus, and was coordinating with John to build up our forces at the Forge. Commodore Shauna Cass (not related to Ian Hawke's Shauna, obviously!) had been promoted to Rear Admiral and was put in charge. We'd been close to abandoning the Forge by 2231 — it had been built by First Lord Boscawen on that 'vulcanoid asteroid' (one that circles the sun entirely inside Venus' orbit) decades prior, to serve as a forward post in the fight against the Venusian pirates. Daragh had launched many victorious missions from there, but when Marlene arrived later, she'd been able to deal with the pirates from Venus. As such, the Forge — with its hugely unpleasant radiation levels — was looking like a needless expense by the start of the war.

Now John and Daragh were planning on using the old base as a launch pad for the attack on Mercury that they were planning for 2233. The Martians would expect the attack to come from Marlene at Venus, but if Shauna Cass (who was to Marlene's Venus Squadron what I was to Greg's Belt Squadron) could get the Forge ready, we could hit them from an unexpected quarter, or even from two fronts.

Or so the plan went, anyway. Even this early — a year before the projected operation — the buildup to that attack was beginning.

Meanwhile, in Belt space, Marshal Samuels was streamlining his convoy system. The Martians wouldn't have a chance to disrupt our trade thanks to Marshal's efforts. As that was going on, Greg was reorganizing the defenses of the Belt Sector around his battleships, trying to make sure that Marshal got the escorts he needed for his convoys while still retaining a heavy enough hitting force to do some good if a Martian Squadron attacked. It was a tricky balancing act, but when has Greg ever *not* been able to balance forces?

All told, it sounded like plenty was going on back there, and I do regret in some ways not being present to see it all, and to be able to tell you about it. As I say, I'm harassing some of the fine officers who were front and center for those incidents to get to their keyboards and to start writing, but many of them are stubborn. I mean, Marlene's and Greg's papers are already out, but the rest of the officers... well, we'll see. Who knows, depending on when you're reading this, there might already be new accounts out for you to peruse.

Meantime, we were ten days out of Io, and waiting...

"Sounds like Lia's having a tough time," I was talking to Charlie as we walked back to our cabins from the rec deck. We'd been shooting targets, and as usual, I had embarrassed myself next to Charlie's lethal aim and precision.

Yes, I *could* hit the broad side of a barn. Charlie, however, could hit the ant crawling across the broadside of the barn. Poor ant.

My comment, probably not the most jovial I could have come up with just then, sucked the smile from Charlie's face, "Yeah... yeah when she sends me a message, you know it's not going well."

In order to keep their relationship under wraps, Lia and Charlie seldom traded comm traffic. Only when things were serious did they exchange messages, so the very arrival of a message for our gallant Major was a bad sign.

"Indeed... is she alright? When we get back we could... well... I could definitely get you posted over to Hawke One as a consultant or something."

Charlie shook his head, "Not necessary. Not yet."

I tilted my head slightly as we turned a corner, "Well, I didn't mean *now*. But by the time we're back, it could be right... not that I want to lose you to Hawke One..."

"Charlie's moving to Hawke One?"

Okay, remember how I said we'd gotten comfortable with the reporters aboard? That comfort led to lapses in judgment — talking about Lia and Charlie in the middle of the corridor, for instance.

So when Jessica Qing appeared on the opposite corner of the intersection Charlie and I were moving through, I mentally kicked myself.

Charlie had gotten more comfortable with Jessica after the last chapter — sometime over the week in between, they'd had a sit-down chat, and that had seemed to put things to rights.

Now, though, we had to be careful — Lia needed to keep her father from realizing just how close she and Charlie were, because if he figured out the depth of their relationship (as opposed to thinking they just had the odd illicit rendezvous), Charlie would probably be outlawed from Hawke space, at least until Ian died.

Bottom line: we couldn't have Jessica Qing reporting that Lia and Charlie had *any* sort of relationship whatsoever.

"No, of course not," was my obvious and rather bland reply.

Jessica frowned, "But it just sounded like you were offering to post him to Hawke One... to help look after a *woman*...?"

A *woman*? I'll say it again, I don't know what about this long cruise predisposed everyone to think about romance...

"Well... I..." I stopped in my tracks now, and glanced nervously at Charlie. He hadn't told me exactly what he'd said to Jessica to get her off his back.

Charlie stopped too, and I swear he almost sorta looked a little panicked (Special Branchers never *actually* look panicked), "Yes, Jessica. A woman..."

"You said your woman was on Belt Two. Why would you be going to the Hawke Protectorate to see her? You said she wasn't in Defense Command, why would *she* go to the Hawke Protectorate in wartime?" Jessica's tone was on the line between personally hurt and rather confused.

Charlie managed a dignified, "Uh..."

"Honestly, Jessica, look at him. You think there's *one* woman?"

Well, I bailed Charlie out of that one with that comment, didn't I? I just made him look like a scumbag in the process. So... well. Yeah. Um.

Jessica's mouth thinned into a narrow line, and she folded her arms instantly, "Ah, of course."

She didn't say more than that, she just went on her way, leaving Charlie and I standing at the corner of the corridor, staring at the piece of wall that had been behind her.

There was a long, awkward silence.

"So," he said after the pause, "I'm a womanizer and a liar?"

He said it half-amusedly. I think.

"Well..." I scratched my head precariously, "...well... Lia will be happy. See, we deflected any chance of your relationship hitting the press."

"Isn't that like keeping people from finding out you killed a doctor by blowing up the whole hospital?" Charlie looked at me.

I swallowed, "Well. Imagine how grateful the woman who wanted the doctor dead will be."

I looked at him, and we both shook our heads.

"That analogy's just *wrong*." Charlie said and started walking again. "You're right, though, when Lia finds out, she'll probably offer to start wearing a blond wig half the time, so I can be seeing two different women."

I frowned as we headed up the corridor past Karen's cabin door, "Don't you hate blondes?"

Charlie shrugged, "Hate? No. They're just not my thing."

Of course, Karen was coming out her hatch at that moment, and she cleared her throat behind us. Charlie and I stopped in place again, refusing to turn around.

"You just keep walking me into minefields today," he said with a smile. "I'm going to go clean my guns."

With that he was off, and Karen and her lovely blonde hair appeared next to me, "Lia going to dye her hair?"

I grinned and glanced at Karen, "I might suggest that to her, just for pure devilment." We chuckled.

CHAPTER NINETEEN

GETTING BACK TO BUSINESS

Skipping ahead another week, we start to see the seriousness setting in. Think of it as the last week of a long vacation — just before going back to work, people really start focusing on what will happen once they're back on the job, and at times also curse the lax approach to prep work that should have been done long in advance of going back. Well, I don't know if you could call our attitude during the cruise 'lax', but we were definitely back to work.

Andrea was running long drills beginning five days from Io — these weren't single drills, but complicated battle-evolution sessions, that ran through the entirety of an action, from the sighting of an enemy through blowing them to hell and finishing with damage control. They were time consuming and tiring, but the crew of *Wolf* took to them quite well; after so much downtime, the men and women aboard didn't mind the chance to stretch their legs before the real fight came.

As Andrea had said in the interview, a happy ship was important.

While the drills proceeded, Charlie took his squad and ran the SF guards through a fresh clinic on base-storming — we'd decided that one thing we might find at Io was a Martian-occupied dome, so it made sense to get our landing forces back up to their peak preparedness.

Other skippers in the squadron were doing the same, too, I should mention — Mark, Kris, Matt, Aaron and Elise all had their own styles, but their mission was essentially the same. The Jupiter Force would be ready to deal with whatever it found.

But I wasn't so sure I'd be.

What's that? Me worrying? Surely not.

Sorry, that was a pathetic attempt at sarcasm: you know by now in this series that I've got the penchant for worrying a whole lot about things, and three days before we arrived at Io, I certainly wasn't breaking with tradition. Sitting on the bed in my cabin, I was staring at the screen that reviewed the ships in the Jupiter Force, their crew complements and armaments... facts I knew by heart, of course, as all of my fighting ships here had been with us since the Belt.

Six ships... what would we find out here? Surely it didn't make sense that the Martians would have sent a battleship to capture the base? The original Jupiter Squadron had a battleship...

That made me think (hardly for the first time) of the composition of Commodore Prazsky's squadron, so grabbing my remote, I called it up on screen next to the list of Jupiter Force ships. This is going to get expositional, so strap in — it won't take too long.

Prazsky had ten ships in his original Jupiter Squadron (make a note, I'm trying to differentiate between his ships and Karen's and mine by referring to ours as the 'Force', his as the 'Squadron'), including the *Empire*-class battleship *Dominator*. *Dominator* is an impressive ship, the same make and model as Greg's *Warspite*, and the rest of the squadron was, on screen, nothing to shake a stick at.

One *Noble*-class corvette, *Trusty*, was the newest vessel in the Jupiter Squadron's formation — it was only slightly older than *Friendly* and *Lady Grace*. Beyond that, the squadron featured four first generation *North America*-class frigates (*Idaho*, *Iowa*, *Kansas*, *North Carolina*) and two last generation *North Americas* (*Quebec*, *Manitoba*), along with two middle-aged *Canada*-class corvettes (*Pictou* and *Taber*). That was a grand total of a battleship, six frigates and three corvettes, not too bad at all.

On screen, at least.

The problem with that lineup, though, had nothing to do with the hardware — the ships were good, well-designed, and at least until they'd come out here, had been well looked after. No, it was the human equation that concerned me, because as was the case with Commodore Prazsky, many of the personnel sent to Io weren't our best... they were the ones who wouldn't be missed.

Now there were exceptions to that rule, but on the whole I simply couldn't expect the ships of the original Jupiter Squadron to be well-handled.

So why was that occupying my thoughts while I was sitting on my bed cruising out to Jupiter? Because the disposition of the Jupiter Squadron had hardly been a well-kept secret. In fact, we routinely leaked its force count to the press in the old days — when they printed that a battleship was looking after Io, it was solid dissuasion to any pirates who might try to attack the base.

But that meant the Martians would probably know how many ships they'd have to overcome when they attacked the base, and that meant they probably dispatched equivalent force.

So our new Jupiter Force might indeed find itself facing a battlewagon. Wouldn't that be a hoot.

Of course, another question was what the ships of the original squadron were up to, presuming the Martians were over Io. Would they have fought to the death, would the throwaway officers commanding some of these ships have run, would they be fighting guerilla-style in and around the many moons of Jupiter?

In other words, would we have other ships out here to augment our strength? For instance, if *Dominator* had escaped the Martian attack, we could add a battleship to our force.

And if we could, would those ships be useful, or would I have to exchange their crews with some of my own? Would they fit, or would it be like trying to cooperate with one of Dave Caldecott's ships?

I was asking myself many questions like these. It's been a while since I've explained this, so let me go over it again: I panicked and worried before major actions. I had to — I had to map out the possibilities, review and re-review everything I could imagine going wrong and come up with contingencies. It was stressful as all hell but it was the way I worked.

The key was simply not to let anyone else know I did it. Well, anyone else but Karen — Karen instinctively knew.

And that's about when there was a knock on my hatch, and the door opened and

Karen stuck her head in with a smile, "I sense panic."

I smiled halfheartedly, "My, Karen, what a sense you have."

Stepping into the cabin, she closed the hatch behind her and then came to sit next to me on the bed. As she settled down, I leaned over against her shoulder and sighed, "You'd think I'd be over the panicking thing by now. It's not like we haven't saved the Empire once already this war."

Karen's smile broadened just a tad, "I count it as twice, myself. We discovered the war was about to start, *and* we warned Earth in time."

A playful frown crossed my brow, "Well… I guess…"

"And panicking is part of your charm. I'm glad you do it," Karen looked sideways at me, and I lowered my head onto her shoulder.

"I'm glad one of us is."

We sorted out my panic.

My editor pointed out to me around here that I may have left the impression now that all was well with Andrea Kiley — I haven't mentioned her contemplating suicide at all for a while. Well that same evening, three days out, Andrea Kiley sat without eating a meal, alone in her pitch black cabin, mag hanging from her chair back.

I cannot imagine what she saw in the darkness — she's told me it was all the horrors of Egesta, they never left her alone. In particular, there was a certain rape room she'd stormed with Captain Jameson and Lieutenant Hong of Special Branch — one full of civilians in need of rescue, who she hadn't been able to help. That one stuck with her, as did a couple of incidents I didn't describe in *The Independent Squadron*, involving spaced school children.

I never saw those sorts of things on Egesta. I may have seen some slices of horror, but she had the whole cake, if you'll forgive that rather pedestrian metaphor. And I don't think I've mentioned this so far, but three of the crew of *Friendly* who'd been with Andrea for that first week before the rest of us arrived had suicided in the five months before the launch of the Jupiter Patrol. Another dozen had chosen to be invalided out of the service on psych grounds in that same time.

Among those remaining with the ships of the Jupiter Force, many were far from alright. Captain Gwen Jameson, of Special Branch, had given up sleeping, or so the rumor went. So — and I should have made this clear earlier — please don't think that Andrea was the only one having a rough time with the shadows of that first week on Egesta. Many were faring much worse that she was.

To answer my editor's next question, a 'big deal' wasn't being made of all of this because, simply, that wasn't how we did things. Those who wanted to leave did, and did so with a quiet dignity that is to be commended. Those who stayed did so because they didn't want to abandon their crews in the middle of a war. No one was going to second guess them, and many of them had the silent support of their friends and shipmates, just as Andrea did. It wasn't a perfect solution, but few solutions are. We'd look after our own the best we could, and we wouldn't trumpet the fact that good men and women who'd saved lives on the ground at Egesta were still being haunted by what they saw. If that doesn't make sense… well, I can't explain it any better, I'm afraid.

I've focused on Andrea because she wants me to — she wants her story out there so the many other veterans from that first week still living with her sorts of symptoms can know they're not alone, and so they don't feel they have to come forward themselves. She's told the true stories, so no one else needs to feel obliged to put themselves in the harsh spotlight to uncover what happened to all those innocent people. It's a sacrifice for her. Every year as the Egesta anniversary rolls around, she's the one the media wants to hear from, to relive a lot of pain all over again.

Sorry, drifted off onto a tangent there.

Andrea sat in the blackness with mag at her shoulder, thinking God knows what.

Reading the first draft of this passage, one of my editors put to me an interesting question: was she crying? I can only guess he wanted to know because a crying Andrea would perhaps seem more vulnerable, more sympathetic, or some other such thing. To be honest, I never asked Andrea whether or not she was crying right then. I don't care to know.

I know on some occasions there were tears, but I very much doubt there were sobs.

Real crying requires a lot of feeling, and Andrea was getting to the point... no she was *past the point* where everything inside felt dead. That's a scary place to be, when you stop feeling.

And when you don't feel, you don't really cry. Your eyes water now and then, but other than that, you are dead inside.

Andrea felt like that. And let me tell you from personal experience, it's a bad place to be.

Enough dwelling on it, then.

CHAPTER TWENTY

FIRST CONTACT

A day and a half out of Io, Jim Hannigan had the watch. This day was to have no long drills — we were close to Io and Andrea didn't want to risk tiring out the crew just before a major engagement — so it was quiet on the bridge.

Kate Levec was pacing silently behind her bank of consoles, Shelby McLaws was at the helm, and Jim was moving between them, hands linked behind his back and eyes drifting from screen to screen in the dull, robotic, repetitive way of any good officer keeping watch. You don't even think, you just do it...

"Ma'am! Battleship on scope, two escorts!"

The report was barked by one of Kate's technicians, and Kate was immediately standing behind that tech, then leaning over his shoulder, "Confirming, Jim... definitely. It's *Dominator* and two corvettes."

"Battle stations," Jim's tone was tight, as was Kate's, for that matter. "Shelby, stand by for deceleration."

"Yes, sir," Lieutenant McLaws nodded.

"All command officers to the bridge, Kate," Jim looked back to his successor at Sensors and Communications, and she sent the internal mail to Karen, Andrea and myself just as the battle station chimes began to sound.

"They're turning to match course... we'll have interception in... six minutes. They're working up from less than 100 kps..." Kate was almost thinking aloud, but because Jim was himself a Sensors and Communications specialist, he got rather a lot out of her words.

For the benefit of those of us uninitiated into that particular club, allow me to translate: it looked as though *Dominator* and its consorts had been cruising away from Io at far less than 100 kps, and had been heading Earthward on a base course not far off our own.

We'd appeared on their scopes, and they were turning to intercept us, accelerating as they did.

"Anything to suggest their intentions?" Jim asked firmly, coming to a stop before the main screen just as it lit up with the sensor feeds.

"Nothing... Battlelink activating with the rest of the squadron," Kate was a blur behind her consoles now.

Matt Baxter popped up on screen one, "Jim, anything to suggest their intentions?"

Managing a smile, Jim shook his head to the black Briton, "Word for word what I just asked, and no, no idea."

Mark Gunney was up on screen two next, "They still ours?"

Jim shook his head again, "Don't know, Mark."

As Kris and the other skippers appeared, they each essentially repeated that question

— they wanted to know if *Dominator* was still a Defense Command ship, or if it had been taken in battle with the Martians and was now being used as a Trojan horse or a Q-ship (two historical analogies, neither of them perfect, I know).

Basically, the Martians could have taken *Dominator* by boarding, and now might try to fool us into believing it was still one of ours… because if a hostile *Empire*-class battleship got into range with our squadron, we'd be finished.

Karen and I had been in her cabin, Andrea had been asleep, or so she said. We arrived on the bridge within a minute — no mean feat considering we'd come all the way from the crew decks through the weapons pod and then up.

Coming out onto the bridge, I manage to repeat the question of every CO on the Battlelink — who did *Dominator* belong to, us or the Martians? Jim gave me the same answer everyone else had gotten, then retired to the operations consoles at the back of the bridge.

Karen, Andrea and I stood before the main screen with matching frowns.

"Time to weapons range, Kate?" I folded my arms as I asked the question, and Kate Levec tapped a tech on the shoulder to have Jim's innovative rangefinder rings displayed around the icons on the main screen.

She followed that action with words: "About a minute."

I took a second to blink, "All ships reverse hard, I want to hold that distance until we get comm contact. Kate, keep an ear open."

Kate Levec nodded at that, though really it was a redundant order. Of course she was going to be listening for signal traffic…

And for the record 'reverse hard' is in fact (and I'm not being sarcastic) a technical term, a different wording for something like 'full ahead' or 'full astern'. What it means is hardly gentle, though — it's one of the things engineers hate to hear ordered, because it can strain a ship's engines quite spectacularly.

Basically, you completely reverse the direction of thrust coming out of your drive pods… in a single second. Think of driving one way at sixty kilometers an hour, and then without slowing down, throwing it into reverse at the same speed. Now, in a hovercar that might break your neck, but aboard a large warship the artificial gravity plating makes it feel more like you're on an ocean-going ship on a relatively calm day.

No, the problem isn't with staying standing, it's with putting that much strain on all the drive systems.

That all should highlight, then, just how cautious I was being — I didn't want to take any chances here. *Dominator* could now be a Martian ship.

"Send a query, see if you can get someone up on screen for me. And stand by fighters, a close visual sweep might be in order," I followed up my orders quickly, trying not to listen to the strained vibrations running through *Wolf* as our drives reversed.

Kate tapped a tech on the shoulder and a query was sent. We stood in suspense for long seconds as the laser crossed space and found the receiver array on *Dominator's* bridge. Who were we dealing with…

Time was moving quite slowly. Come on come on come on…

Wolf settled into its reverse pace, moving backwards with the rest of the Jupiter Force, and keeping about a minute outside of *Dominator's* weapons envelope. A minute passed, and then another, and we continued to stand silently.

"Return signal with DC tags," Kate looked up from the console she was hovering behind. "They look authentic, putting it up."

Screen nine glowed to life, and the *WolfNet* buffering display seemed to be lumbering along. Either I was very anxious and I was perceiving a slowdown in time, or *Dominator's* grid had been damaged and the signal was having trouble getting through to us.

Finally a face appeared — and not a face I recognized. There was a fizzle of picture dropout, but as soon as it cleared I started to study the young woman who was wearing one of our uniforms, and who had Commander's bars on her collar.

"This is Commander Maryna Mazur, commanding officer of DCNS *Dominator*, calling DCNS *Wolf*. Please close to realtime range, we need to conference immediately."

The signal cut.

I stood frowning on *Wolf's* bridge, then glanced at Karen, "Think it's a trap?"

Karen's eyebrow climbed, "Could be... pre-recorded with a surviving officer, or one of theirs in our uniform, attempting to draw us into range..."

I nodded slowly, then glanced at Andrea, "Let's send Adrienne out for a look. See if she can get someone on realtime."

"Another feed coming in now, this one from *Trusty*," Kate interrupted quickly. "Screen ten."

I looked back up at the screens just in time to watch Commander Nancy Whitehorse appear on that display, "*Wolf*, it is very good to see you. This is Commander Whitehorse of *Trusty*, I am sending a second signal to you because I fear Commander Mazur's may appear a trap. I... have just suggested to Commander Mazur that she decelerate and allow me to take *Trusty* into realtime range, to safely confirm our identity."

Nancy Whitehorse should never have been sent to Jupiter. She was given *Trusty* fresh out of the dock, and was expected to join Marlene's force at Venus. Instead Caldecott (yes, him again) had screamed in his high-pitched way about the lack of new ships out at Io, and had managed to get her ship reassigned for a five-year cruise.

I think, personally, Caldecott was being sour — Whitehorse had beaten out Dave's niece for command of the ship, and she'd ended up in DCC as a result. Nancy's assignment to Io was revenge for that — and reversing it was a battle John couldn't afford to fight at the time. We were keeping all of our political sway focused on getting the *Bonaventure* deal done, so while we succeeded, Nancy Whitehorse got stuck.

Anyway, her caliber as an officer was shining through in this instant — the first of many — and her recommendation was quite apt. Of *course* we wouldn't let *Dominator* into range under these strange circumstances, but one corvette was no threat to our six-ship formation.

"Record me," I glanced back at Kate and then stepped in front of screen ten's viewfinder. "Nancy, good to see you again. This is Rear Admiral Barron aboard *Wolf*. Bring *Trusty* up and we'll be glad to have a realtime chat, but you're right, we're going to need *Dominator* to stand off until we can confirm your identities. Send it."

Kate ordered the message on its way, and then we all waited for a handful of minutes and watched *Dominator* and *Pictou* (the other corvette) decelerate, while *Trusty* held range.

"Alright, slow our engines, let *Trusty* into range," I nodded to Karen, and she in turn nodded to all our skippers on Battlelink, while Andrea passed on the commands to Shelby McLaws.

Wolf began to slow its retreat, and over the next few minutes *Trusty* edged into realtime range. Kate nodded to me as soon as she established a link, then screen ten flashed to a loading graphic again.

Karen and I shuffled sideways and got into ten's viewfinder just in time to see Commander Whitehorse reappear, "Rear Admiral Barron, Captain McMaster, it is a pleasure to see you."

We didn't correct her on the 'Commodore' McMaster error — there was no way Nancy Whitehorse could have heard that we'd both been promoted, as the promotions had come during the comm blackout. She only knew I was a Rear Admiral because I'd identified myself as one in the message I'd sent.

"Good to see you, Nancy. We've been worried about the silence out here... I take it you've had visitors?"

The Commander nodded evenly, "Io has been overrun and captured by a Martian squadron. I will not attempt to trouble you with the details over Battlelink, but perhaps I could come aboard *Wolf*, along with the Commanders of *Dominator* and *Pictou?*"

I nodded, "Of course. We'll close range with your ships again... though if you wouldn't mind telling Commander... who was it... Mazur... tell her to keep *Dominator* out of weapons range. She'll have a longer flight over here, but I still have to be cautious. You understand, I'm sure."

"Of course," Whitehorse nodded. "I will make the arrangements, and we will be over directly."

One of my editors pointed out here that I hadn't mentioned Jocko or Jessica. They were (obviously, since you've probably seen some of the footage) on the bridge, but to be entirely honest, I forgot their presence then, as I did just now writing about it all over again. It's easy to remember they're around when nothing else is going on, but when you're dealing with something major like this, you can forget they're even there. This is probably going to happen a fair bit as I get into describing what comes next... and probably a whole lot in the next book. I apologize in advance.

But then I suppose this is what they wanted — to see us unscripted, in our element, and doing our jobs. Kinda creepy how good they were at getting into my blindspot like that... anyway...

CHAPTER TWENTY-ONE
WHAT WAS GOING ON

I would have preferred to put all my COs together in a room with the three commanders of the Jupiter Squadron, but I couldn't risk stripping my Jupiter Force's six warships of their skippers when we weren't certain of the situation. Instead we had to virtually add them to the meeting through the use of realtime vid link windows on the conference room screen. It's never an ideal solution, but I certainly wasn't going to leave the skippers out of the meeting altogether.

The Commanders had come over separately, of course, and it had taken an hour for them all to arrive. Nancy Whitehorse, a pilot like Karen and myself, had come over first in her Starlight, and shaking her hand in the number two flight bay, I'd felt a little relief — this *probably* wasn't a trap.

Karen and I had personally led the fatigued Commander to the briefing room, and on the way we'd convinced both Jessica and Jocko to give us a private first meeting — the two reporters smelled a story, and there indeed was one to be told… I just didn't want three Commanders who were probably in rough shape to be put on the record. Not yet, anyway. Jocko and Jessica were both very good about this — a combination of genuine sympathy and faith that the goodwill they'd earn by playing ball would pay off… if that doesn't make them sound too bloodthirsty.

Commander Giovanni Calzatti was next aboard, being escorted to the conference room by Andrea; *Pictou's* skipper was unknown to me, but based on the calm familiarity he had with Nancy Whitehorse when he arrived, I could only assume he had her respect. That was a good start in my book.

Commander Mazur arrived last, and she came with a different air entirely. She was now the skipper of a battleship, at least in her own mind, and a squadron commander — that much I realized as soon as she walked through the door. Talk about a sense of entitlement, she'd actually come aboard with two SF Guards, as if she needed an escort.

As she seated herself at the opposite head of the table in the briefing room — remember, that's the seat reserved for the second highest ranked officer in the room, though Karen never uses it — she laced her fingers and laid her hands in her lap.

"Rear Admiral Barron, I'm glad you've brought reinforcements."

Interesting way to put it.

"We'll talk about that in a minute, Commander. Would one of you mind telling me what exactly happened here? We're officially at war with the Martians back home, and they attempted to attack Earth last October, after trying to snatch the Belt colonies. Last month there were more attacks on Earth, none successful, and there's been plenty of scrapping in the free belt, and attacks on trade," I got the quick 'what's been going on in the Empire' summary out of the way up front, and the three Commanders exchanged glances.

"Well, last October we were hit by a surprise attack, which destroyed the frigates *Manitoba* and *Iowa*, and captured the frigate *Quebec* by boarding. I was forced to cut locks and escape without Commodore Prazsky or Captain Clive," Commander Mazur began regally. "Commander Calzatti and Commander Whitehorse were able to keep up with me as we escaped, and since that time we have been doing our duty, harassing enemy positions. I decided an attempt to return to Earth under these unknown conditions would be too risky, so we remained to observe the enemy."

I'd deal with the self-important tone in a minute, there were more pressing questions about what was going on first.

Karen started the questioning, "The other ships of the squadron?"

"They fled into the moons. They've been hiding, we've seen nothing of them since the attack."

"Have you *looked?*" I barely contained my frustration with that question — I didn't like this woman's tone at all.

"No, *Dominator* is not designed to play hide and seek in amongst moons. We would be at undue risk."

"You have two corvettes," Karen's comment was sharp. It's funny, though none of the Commanders had actually identified who was making the decisions for their force, Karen and I had both zeroed in on Mazur.

Calzatti looked from Mazur to us and then nervously at Whitehorse. Whitehorse nodded at him, and then looked at me, "Commander Mazur has appointed herself in command of our remaining ships. And she ordered us to stay with *Dominator*, to help protect her command."

"Has she indeed?" I leaned back in my chair. "And I take it neither of you could do much to argue, owing to the size of her guns?"

That last question came out sympathetically, as it was meant to — the two corvette commanders were doubtless much better officers than Mazur, but that meant they weren't fool enough to get into a fit of arguments with the CO of a battleship...

"Yes sir," Calzatti nodded quickly. "We've been sitting out in the space on the approaches to the Belt for four months, our supplies are virtually gone but *Dominator* has a large surplus. Because Commander Mazur broke dock with only half the crew aboard."

That last little jab wasn't really professional — a Belt Squadron officer probably wouldn't have added it to the end of the comment. Nonetheless, it was important information, and after months of being stuck with Commander Mazur, I could guess that tolerance and etiquette would be in short supply.

"And why did you boost with half a crew, Commander?" Karen leveled a steely stare at Mazur, who seemed unmoved.

"The attack force was coming in, there was no time to waste. We could not meet them while docked."

"What were you facing, Commander Whitehorse?" I turned the question to the officer I felt was best equipped to answer it.

Nancy Whitehorse leaned forward, "We saw one small Martian battleship, five destroyers and four destroyer escorts, along with seven armed pirate ships of moderate size."

"And you engaged them?" I asked the question to Whitehorse, then turned my eyes to Mazur.

"We did," Whitehorse glanced back at Mazur. "Commander Calzatti and I had the picket duty at the time. Our corvettes engaged the enemy vanguard, destroying four of the pirate vessels and damaging another."

"Reducing them to twelve effective vessels," Andrea leaned forward slightly. "Then what, Commander Whitehorse?"

"*Iowa*, *Idaho*, *Kansas*, *North Carolina* and *Manitoba* broke dock. *Quebec* did not respond, I do not know why. *Iowa* and *Manitoba* were the first ships clear, and they rendezvoused with us, and we attempted to attack again. Both frigates were targeted by the Martians, and were destroyed. At that point we withdrew, having destroyed one destroyer escort."

"And where were the other frigates?" Mark Gunney interrupted quite appropriately over the comm (remember, all the COs were watching, they were just being unusually quiet). "And where was *Dominator*?"

"*Dominator* was withdrawing from action, it did not attempt to engage. The other frigates approached the vanguard, but fled after witnessing *Manitoba's* destruction. *Taber*, the other corvette, was destroyed at the start of the action — it was that ship's destruction that first alerted us to the attack."

You see, this is what an unpolished, poorly-unified unit looks like — and this is how badly it performs. The Belt Squadron, with only *nine* ships as it had at Belt Two, could have crippled that Martian force. We would have found a way.

But these ships were poorly crewed and badly coordinated, and the one ship that should have rallied them and led them into the attack had *run*. Mazur's battleship was the *only* unit in her squadron that could have gone toe-to-toe with the Martian capital ship. With it fleeing, the aged frigates of the squadron had no hope, and had been forced to withdraw or die fruitlessly. And Mazur hadn't even tried to connect with them?

"Io is now occupied and guarded by three Martian destroyers and two destroyer escorts," Whitehorse added after a moment's pause. "We believe there is a large contingent of Martian soldiers in the dome, and that the science crews are being required to continue their work on experimental weapons, we suspect to make them feasible for transport to Mars."

An apt assumption. Life is seldom like you see in the movies — you can't, for instance, just waltz into a protected experimental weapons facility and take all sorts of highly destructive kit with you. New weapons aren't always stable, sometimes they're downright dangerous. Making them safe for transport would take time — a lot of time perhaps — and if the Martians had indeed been watching our vid feeds, they'd know that they had over a week left before the Jupiter Force was due to arrive…

Wait a minute.

"The Martian battleship isn't protecting Io?" I blurted out the question a little more hurriedly than I'd have liked.

Whitehorse's mouth stretched to a thin line, "No sir, it isn't."

"So why haven't you taken back the dome? You have a capital ship!" I turned to Mazur with that question, and the Commander cocked her eyebrow at me.

"It would be too much of a risk to my ship. Now that reinforcements have arrived, I will be happy to–"

"You'll be happy to be confined to your quarters, Commander Mazur. I'm not sure if you'll be going to the gallows for dereliction or if you'll just be drummed out of the Navy, but I'm done talking to you. I'll put someone else on your bridge, and your ship is going to join my Jupiter Force in attacking Io immediately."

I snapped, that's the only way to describe it.

The Commander kept a cool look on her face, but she sunk back in her chair as I erupted, "Commander Calzatti, Commander Whitehorse, thank you for hurting the enemy before you had to pull out. You're going to get the chance to do a lot more of that in the next few days. Now, do you have any idea where the Martian battleship went?"

Whitehorse looked from Mazur to me, probably unsure of whether I'd snap again and brig her. Of course I wouldn't — she had nothing to be ashamed of. No, it was the commander of a battleship who ran from a fight when fellow ships were dying who got my wrath. The officer who didn't counter-attack, didn't go for help, and who kept other ships from doing either. Not the commander of a plucky corvette who did all she could before being forced to withdraw.

"We believe the Martians must have a small base of operations on one of the other moons. We've not been allowed to search for it, but I believe given a few days of looking, we can locate it," Whitehorse answered my question evenly, and I nodded.

"Very good, that'll be our second priority. First is to get those bastards out of Io dome."

We talked through a few more aspects of the upcoming operation, with Mazur shrinking deeper into her seat.

When it came time to end the meeting, I got an evil idea, and thumbed the comm on the table top, "Lieutenant Stranks, I need two SF in the briefing room for prisoner escort. And call Jessica and Jocko and their crews. They're going to want to see this."

Five minutes later, Mazur's hands were bound, and before the cameras of two powerful networks, she was led to the brig as an officer derelict of her duty. I then introduced Commanders Calzatti and Whitehouse to the cameras, explaining their heroism in the face of the overwhelming enemy, and what they'd accomplished with only two small ships — an interesting contrast to what Mazur had *not* accomplished with her very powerful battleship.

You hopefully know by now that I don't expect miracles from Defense Command officers — I know all too well that sometimes nothing can be done, and no one is to blame. But I had never in my life to that point seen such galling cowardice. A *battleship*, a modern, *Empire*-class battleship, not even stopping to do so much as trade shots with the vanguard of the Martian force? I'm not saying she had to go toe-to-toe and fight to the death, but she shouldn't have simply started running, leaving the frigates to fend for themselves.

No, that was about as professional as... well, I don't even know how to finish that. I've seen pirates with more courage and responsibility.

After the circus was over, Jessica and Jocko left to start compiling their stories — we'd be able to send them back to the Empire soon enough. The Commanders returned to their ships, and Karen, Andrea and I sat alone in the conference room, with all the other Jupiter Force skippers still on the comm.

"That was a little harsh, wasn't it, Ken?" Kris asked her question with a frown, and I sighed and shrugged.

"Probably. But if a lot of the officers out here are like dear Commander Mazur, then setting an example is for the best. It's our only shot at scaring them into doing their jobs."

Karen was nodding slowly, but then she looked at me, "So... who's taking over *Dominator?*"

Oh. I hadn't quite thought about who would take over the battleship as Captain.

I looked up at all the faces on screen, all of them looking away awkwardly. None of them wanted to leave their ships — to have to go take over a vessel with a questionable crew...

"I'll take care of it for you."

Of course you know who said that.

"If you don't mind stepping back in part-time as Captain, Karen."

Andrea Kiley was smiling. She wanted the job.

CHAPTER TWENTY-TWO

HOW DO YOU SAY NO?

You know that moment in every cheap horror movie (and even some good ones) when you yell at the screen: "DON'T GO IN THERE, <INSERT GENERIC NAME>, THE KILLER'S IN THERE!". Ever wonder why <insert generic name> don't listen to you? Well, probably because it's a movie — being pre-filmed, the characters can't listen to your advice, and in point of fact, they wouldn't even hear your words through the screen if it was a live broadcast (that's why your sports teams of choice never listen to your advice when they're losing).

In real life, similar 'don't go into the house' scenarios definitely do happen. One of them was happening when we handed *Dominator* to Andrea. Now, I shouldn't actually compare that handover to a murder movie, as we know how it turns out... but I think if anything really revealed how edgy Andrea was in her job (not just her personal life) that was it. I don't know, maybe it was for the best... but, well, I'll let you decide. Though I can almost hear you screaming at me through the page: "DON'T LET ANDREA LEAVE *WOLF*, KEN! DON'T DO IT!"

Sorry, I can hear you now (which possibly means I'm insane) but I didn't then, and neither did Karen. We'd taken Andrea aboard *Wolf* in order to make sure she was bouncing back from her experiences on Egesta, and as far as we knew she was doing that — she was joking on the bridge with Jim about Bunny, she wasn't some sort of raging disciplinarian, she was... well... pretty much herself.

That's what we saw, that's what we believed.

We'd also looked at the other choices to take command of the battleship... well, there weren't any. Sorry, that's not true, there was one: Karen. See, *Wolf* was the only ship in the Jupiter Force with three past or present Captains *of that same ship* aboard. Uniquely, then, we had enough command officers aboard to be able to lose one.

But realistically, it couldn't be Karen, because she still had a squadron to look after. She could hardly do that job properly if she spent all her time aboard *Dominator* trying to get the crew to click.

No, the new Captain of the ship would have to constantly focus on the crew's performance... it had to be Andrea. And who knew, if we lucked out and found that the Martians hadn't executed the officers on Io, the old Captain might come back... though I'd never met Captain Jonas Clive, and I couldn't speak to his ship-handling ability. Time would tell.

So Andrea was getting ready to head over to *Dominator*, and we were sending a detachment of crew with her. *Dominator* only had 466 people aboard — that was just under half its full crew complement. In order to give Andrea the numbers she needed, and to provide a nucleus of reliable people for her to work with, every other ship in the Jupiter Force, including *Trusty* and *Pictou*, were sending twenty volunteers to augment the crew.

That meant Andrea was getting 120 veteran Belt Squadron personnel to work with, as well as forty fresh faces from the Jupiter Squadron. We hoped that'd make things easier on her.

Meanwhile, *Pictou* and *Trusty's* crews were remaining unchanged, except for the volunteers they were sending to Andrea. We wanted to welcome those ships into the new Jupiter Force, knowing that the celebrity status of many of our ships would mean acceptance came with a feeling of accomplishment. To put that more clearly, our ships were all Belt Squadron veterans, and were the famous victors of the Battle of Deep Black. For us to welcome these ships and crews into our ranks unchanged was a strong vote of confidence — one that we hoped would help them integrate into our force a little easier.

In the case of *Trusty*, I'd have welcomed the ship under any circumstances. The crew had been top notch from day one, hand assembled by Marlene Stoll for service with her squadron, and only stolen away at the last moment. I was less certain about Commander Calzatti's ship; *Pictou* and its crew seemed well-meaning enough, but I couldn't be certain of how effective they'd be in action.

Nevertheless, they were to be proudly welcomed.

So as Andrea hurried around *Wolf's* bridge and shook hands with her senior staff, a duffle slung over her shoulder and her mag at her hip, Karen and I were more concerned with what she'd find aboard *Dominator* than how *Dominator* would find her. We needed that battleship…

Coming to a stop in front of Karen and me, Andrea smiled a true, calm smile, and shook both our hands, "I hand this fine frigate back to you. Maybe I'll be back one day, but right now the flagship needs our very best, Karen."

Karen shook her head as she smiled, "That's you, Andrea, not me…"

No, that wasn't Karen laying it on thick. That was Karen being honest — or at least being honest from her own perspective. She never agreed when I told her she was the best skipper in the fleet, she's too self-effacing for that. But that's really not on point right here, is it?

I took Andrea's hand with a smile of my own, "We'll miss you, but thank God you'll be over there. I wouldn't trust that ship without you on it."

I said that quietly — I didn't exactly want to be overheard by the two cameras rolling at the back of the bridge. Even though both camera teams' parabolic microphones picked up the words anyway. I got challenged to a duel when that footage ran, though the coward who issued the challenge — a Lieutenant off *Dominator* — backed out on the day.

I mean really, it's not like 'to the death' means anything anymore anyway, resuscitation being what it is…

Andrea offered me a last nod, then headed for the bridge hatch, the camera teams following her.

As they all left the bridge, Karen and I shared a long glance and a sigh, and then we both oddly felt like doing the 'home sweet home' stretch — you know, the one you feel like doing when the inlaws leave after staying in your house for a week, or something like that?

Don't get me wrong, we'd been really happy to have Andrea aboard *Wolf*… it was just less complicated this way. Not better or worse, just different.

Oh screw it, it was better, and Andrea knows it and isn't offended by it. We were just happier to be on our own again for a while, even if it wasn't going to be a permanent arrangement. It wasn't exactly too many cooks in the kitchen with her aboard... it was two ex-cooks and a cook in the kitchen, and that dynamic was one that took a while to get used to.

Now we had a break.

A break that came about by isolating Andrea from her friends and colleagues when she probably needed them most.

Top marks, Barron. Top marks.

CHAPTER TWENTY-THREE

BORING PLANNING

We turned back for Io as soon as Andrea took over *Dominator*, nine ships in a two-column formation moving at 191 kps, the maximum acceleration *Dominator* could pull for the time required to get back to the moon.

That evening, about twenty-four hours before we were set to arrive at Io, we had another vid conference with all Jupiter Force COs, to try to figure out just what we'd do when we arrived. Hold onto your chair, this is going to be exciting.

Sorry, I really shouldn't be derogatory about this — the planning was crucial, I just know some readers out there aren't going to get the same sort of kick out of it that I do. Please don't throw the book, though. Throwing is wrong.

Look at that, I've wandered off the narrative again. Wonder of wonders.

"So, we don't know where the rest of the ships they hit Io with have gone," Andrea was in her new day cabin aboard *Dominator*, and she started off the discussion.

"Could be a trap — they could be hiding their battleship behind Io, trying to draw us in..." Matt Baxter pitched in from *Friendly's* bridge.

"Yeah, we get the party started and they crash it. It's not as much fun when you're the one being crashed," Mark Gunney was sitting at his desk in *Cheetah's* day cabin.

"What about this idea of a Martian base out here — a staging area. They could be orbiting that," Kris tossed out another possibility.

"Or they could have headed for home already," Karen was sitting in her chair behind her desk, toying with her ponytail on her left shoulder.

Silence followed her remark, all the veteran skippers on the screen sifting through the possibilities in their minds... and coming up with nothing more conclusive than a 'maybe'.

"So," I was sitting on the corner of Karen's desk, "we basically have no idea. We know what *Trusty* and *Pictou* saw over Io last time they were in range, but even those ships could have been reinforced or reduced by now, and we have no idea where the Martian heavies are."

Everyone in the meeting shared silent nods of agreement — we were still basically flying blind.

"Alright," I folded my arms across my chest, "so let's work this as if we know nothing more, what the Martians sent out here — the battleship, the five destroyers, three DEs and two pirates."

Those, of course, were numbers that took into account the damage Commander Whitehorse and Commander Calzatti had inflicted before beating their retreat.

"And let's also assume that to coordinate their operations out here, they set themselves up an outpost, or have a combat supply ship like *Artemis Agrotera* that would be reasonably stationary — a central operations point," Matt Baxter added with a thoughtful frown.

I nodded, "Sounds fine. So we can assume they're reasonably well-established."

Everyone nodded again. Because of our lack of information about the enemy's disposition, we had to set up an imaginary board on which to strategize. Yes, there was an open chance that some of our fundamental assumptions about the Martians' disposition could be wrong, but we wouldn't be building iron-clad plans, just flexible ones.

"Seems the first step in this little operation needs to be a hunt for information," Andrea folded her arms across her chest.

Another series of nods followed that remark; it wasn't a surprising suggestion, but it wasn't exactly an easy one either.

"So, we board a Martian ship and rob its logs?" Kris' question came next, and I started to frown thoughtfully. Getting information from Martian computers would probably be like getting a transplant liver from a donor tree. Yes, it would be as muddled and awkward as that metaphor.

"How about the base? If they've been occupying the place for months, they'll probably have been using the comms. If we could get into their signals database, we could figure out where they've been sending what," Aaron Ashby weighed in for the first time, and I perked up at his suggestion.

I didn't really know all that much about the internal working of comm grids — certainly wasn't my specialty — but I did know I'd heard Jim Hannigan speak many times about the signals database.

I looked down at Karen almost instantly, but her thumb was already on the comm, opening a link to the bridge.

"Bridge," Kate Levec picked up the call before looking at the origin. "Um… what can I do for you skipper?"

Kate Levec's station was about ten feet outside the door to this cabin, so she was understandably a little surprised to have us calling her as opposed to one of us sticking our head out the door and yelling.

"Send Jim in, or come in yourself… or both of you come in!" I interrupted Karen rather rudely, and she frowned at me.

"Hey, wait your turn," her tone was rather parental. "Kate, could you and Jim join us please?"

The comm cut one second later and the door opened a second after that, Kate and Jim stepping in together with solemn faces.

I looked back at Karen, "You want to ask or should I?"

"Oh, be my guest," Karen smiled.

Turning back to the two Sensors and Communications specialists, I literally rubbed my hands together, "We're thinking that we might want to rob the Io base comm logs to figure out what the Martians have out here, and where it is. That possible?"

"Commander Ashby was mentioning a signals database," Karen added.

Jim and Kate looked at each other thoughtfully, and they were silent for a few seconds as their minds worked. During that time, I subtly hopped off the desk, put a hand on each of their shoulders, and gently pushed them into range of the screen's viewfinders, so everyone in the conference could see them.

"I think we could do it. The messages sent by Io's comm grid should be stored in its outgoing signal banks in the base command and control…" Jim was starting to think out loud. I don't even think he noticed that I'd moved him.

"But they could have wiped the banks, and deactivated the blind copy functions," Kate was sounding equally thoughtful.

"Yes and I doubt we can do a remote tie-in because they'll have changed the codes, so the interrupters will block the override."

After this, they started exchanging strings of technobabble, and I have no idea what most of it meant. I think I heard the word 'buffer' in there a couple of times. I know what a buffer is. Just don't ask me to explain how it works.

This is why I studied history for my academic component at the Academy.

After about five minutes of them going at it, they both looked back at me. Being specialists in communications, both knew that they had some clearing up to do if they wanted to *communicate* anything to us lay-people.

"We think, if you could get us into the communications center at Io HQ, we could get you what you need."

"We sort of need this info to get us into the dome, though, Jim," Mark Gunney put in over the comm. "Any way to get to it from outside?"

Looking at the screens, Kate Levec shook her head in answer to the question put to Jim (eerily enough, the two were seemingly of one brain), "Afraid not, sir. The databanks will be on an internal drive, and that's only accessible through the IoNet system. Well I presume it is. That's the way it's done at all of our installations, and it'd be rather convenient if it was different here."

"It isn't," Nancy Whitehorse offered from her piece of the screen.

Damn.

All the skippers were quiet for a moment, trying to figure out the solution to this little problem. We wanted to get the cart firmly in front of the horse, but how?

"We could insert Special Branch into the dome," Kris suggested after a moment. "They might be able to infiltrate…"

I shook my head, "Nah, I'm not sending them in without any idea of what's down there. Is there a way we could go after the transmitter itself… hack in from there?"

Jim was frowning at that question when Nancy Whitehorse half exclaimed, "Aha!"

We all looked instantly at her, and she leaned towards her screen, "The old control center might still be hooked into the comm grid."

Usually I'd say here that the speaker didn't need to elaborate any more because we were all on the same page, but that'd be a bit of a lie in this case. Aside from Commander Calzatti, none of us had a clue what she meant.

"We need a little more than that, Nancy," Kris said gently, and the Commander nodded.

"Of course, of course. The old control building… it was the exterior structure that connected the old complex to space, before Defense Command built the dome out here. It's not particularly new, but it may still be connected to the communications grid by hard wire. It had its own transmitter for many years…"

Alright, that was starting to make sense to me. Before Defense Command had completely taken over here, EM Weapons Limited had set up the research and experimentation/testing facilities in tunnels dug into Io's surface. That had been costly, but the result had been a large complex beneath the surface, with separate quadrants for living, testing, and researching. These sectors were connected to ships in space by a command building (pressure tight) that sat on the surface, with its own airlocks, transmitter, and so forth.

The arrangement was very cumbersome, and as it wasn't Earthgreen, it wasn't pleasant living for anyone involved. When Defense Command took over, we'd demanded an Earthgreen dome be erected, and a small one was. This dome was not directly over the old subterranean complex, where testing and research was still carried out. As such, the old command building was still sitting out there, not used, but perhaps hooked into the grid.

And that meant it was possibly the perfect target.

"Sounds like a plan. Get us in there, we read their mail, then figure out how best to smack 'em around," Mark Gunney was his usual, brusque self.

I smiled and nodded, "Let's build a plan around that. The word 'feint' comes to mind..."

With that, we figured out who would do what next.

CHAPTER TWENTY-FOUR
OPERATION READ THEIR MAIL

We actually started calling this plan 'operation read their mail'. We didn't hyphenate 'read their mail', or capitalize it, we just called it that. Which strikes me as kind of funny, actually. Or rather pathetic.

About four hours before the operation began, the ships of the Belt force were edging into the space around Io, and preparing to split up. It's generally a bad policy to split your forces in the face of an enemy whose disposition remains a mystery, but it's good policy to take advantage of surprise.

And preferably, not to get caught at all...

The plan — and this took us a couple of hours to iron out, be glad I didn't bore you with that — was for Andrea to take *Dominator*, *Trusty*, and *Pictou* forward to demonstrate against the Martians, while we slipped strike teams onto the base without revealing the presence of *Wolf* and the other newcomers.

Sounds simple, and really, it was. The only tricky part would be slipping us in unnoticed... and yes, I said 'us'. Come on, do you think making me an *Admiral* would stop me from doing stupid stuff?

The time to head for the surface hadn't come just yet, however; *Wolf*, *Lion*, *Cheetah*, *Friendly*, *Lady Grace* and *Honesty* were creeping up behind Io, having made a wide approach to stay away from the sensors of any Martian pickets. Andrea had *Dominator* moving directly for the moon.

Io's a big rock, and when a rock is big enough you can creep up right behind it — even with six ships — and not be seen. It's not so easy if the rock is like Belt Two or Hawke One; places that important have sensor grids that cover all directions. However, Io was never equipped with that sort of kit — would have meant more money being thrown into the seemingly bottomless pit.

So that gave us an approach vector, presuming the Martians hadn't already hidden ships behind the moon.

We really didn't know what to expect as we closed with the dark side of Io — that's why Karen and I weren't in our cockpits, we didn't know if we'd be actually launching the landing operation, or if there'd be a fight against a Martian warship... or four.

"Still no emissions from the dark side," Kate Levec was keeping us regularly updated, and I nodded in reply.

"Very well. Continue silent running."

We had our emissions turned way down, approaching not on steady drives but on irregular drive bursts that pushed us along at roughly 168 kps. We hopefully wouldn't be detectable to the Martians, should they be waiting at our destination.

We continued to close for long minutes, with Kate Levec pacing just a little anxiously behind her consoles, and with Karen's eyes and mine glued to the main screen. Would we be able to pull this off…?

Now, I'm going to say this again, and I know I've said it a lot over the course of these books so far: waiting is part of this business. These long minutes stretched right out, and every time I looked up at the monitor I was convinced a Martian battleship was going to appear because I was positive we were flying right into the upper jaw of their trap.

Nope.

"I'm still not seeing anything here, skipper," Kate stopped and leaned over the console of one of her techs, both camera crews zooming in on her face as she did.

Oh, sorry, I probably should have mentioned that the camera crews were up here recording all of this. I hadn't let Jessica or Jocko in on the planning sessions, but there was no way I could exclude them from the entire operation — especially not this part, the *safe* part.

"Think we're clear to launch, Kate?" Jim Hannigan asked for the confirmation from behind his operations consoles.

Nodding and looking across at her predecessor, she nodded, "Yes, we'd see energy tweaks by now. There's nothing hiding back there."

I think I understood what that meant, and Jim nodded slowly, "Alright. I concur."

"Excellent!" I said it immediately, clapping my hands together and then rubbing them against each other in a theatrically over-eager manner.

Like I said, cameras.

Karen looked at me with a blank expression, then turned to the camera crews, "Alright, he's never this excited. He's doing this for your benefit."

I huffed and donned a scowl, "Well sure, go ahead and wreck it…"

Smiling now, Karen shrugged, "The viewers deserve to know the truth. Kate, you coming?"

Kate Levec would be the communications expert to land at the transmitter base with us — Jim Hannigan would have volunteered, certainly, but he was the XO now, and so he had to stay to command the ship.

With a nod, Kate pointed to one of her junior officers, "Take over, Felicia."

We then left the bridge, camera crews in tow.

Kris Jacobs took squadron command while we headed down to the flight bay; she was the next-most-senior skipper in the squadron, since Marshal Samuels and Wes Pellew had gone off to command their own forces. We didn't have Battlelink up to avoid the considerable comm emissions it gave off — Battlelink was incredibly easy to detect, so it didn't make sense to have it online while we were silent running.

I include that information for no particular reason, just… well… so you know.

Karen, Kate and I arrived in flight bay one after about five minutes in transit — silent transit, as none of us felt particularly conversational while we were crammed into the lift with two camera crews.

Charlie's squad was kitted out and waiting for us, the pilot of their special ops shuttle already warming up its engines. Lieutenant Kyle Stranks had another thirty SF guards ready to transit in two of *Wolf's* other shuttles, and we'd be getting support from both Rufus Chang's Special Branch team from *Lion* and Marcus Atallah's team from *Cheetah.*

So that's a total of thirty-six Special Branch Officers, and thirty SF... we hoped that'd be enough to take an old abandoned command building.

And if not, *Friendly*, *Lady Grace* and *Honesty* had their Special Branch teams on standby.

Adrienne Thompson, who I really don't get to mention nearly enough in these books, was standing with Charlie, hands on her hips and a typical smile on her face. As Karen, Kate, the cameras and I approached the pair, they both nodded to me.

"We're ready to cause some mayhem," Charlie smiled at my approach. "All clear?"

I nodded to Charlie, then looked at the Lieutenant Commander of fighters, "Looks like. Adrienne, you're hopefully going to have a quiet flight."

Adrienne tipped her head, "We don't get much fun anymore, but that's fine. Wolf and Wolfstar Squadrons will look after you though, sir."

"Never doubted that," I smiled. "Alright, let's rock, as they say."

Charlie's eyebrows shot up, "Excuse me?"

Karen leaned into the conversation, "Camera crews, he's trying to jazz up his dialogue."

"Oh. You're a ham," Charlie left it at that and turned to his team, doing some hand gesture things that translated into 'get onto the shuttle.'

"Kyle, mount up!" I called down the deck to Kyle Stranks, and with a nod and a wave he motioned his guards onto their shuttles.

Turning back to Kate, I bobbed my head towards the Special Branch shuttle, "You might as well ride with Charlie."

Nodding, Kate Levec smiled, "Going in with Special Branch; they didn't teach this in Comm 101."

"There's really nothing to it. Just don't die," I chuckled. I probably shouldn't have chuckled.

Kate nodded with a smile, then stepped away, leaving Karen and me to stare at the cameras.

"And no, you don't get to come along," I said rather parentally as I turned to the camera crews. "You have to stay here. We'll see if we can't get some surveillance vid footage for you to run with, but I can't put you at risk in a close boarding action like this one."

Bunny, who'd emerged as the leader among the camera crews, took a tentative step forward, "It's safe enough for the Admiral to go..."

"No, it's not. I'm just incredibly reckless, Bunny. No arguments, now. We'll see you when we get back."

And with that, I turned on my heel and headed for my plane, which the deck crew was preflighting along with the rest of the F-194 Starlights in the bay.

We launched minutes later.

CHAPTER TWENTY-FIVE

TO PLAN

Twenty-six F-194 Starlights and five shuttles (one from *Lion* and one from *Cheetah*) were hugging the surface of Io, weaving between plumes from the erupting volcanoes of the moon, watching for sharp rises in the terrain, and keeping an eye skyward for any sign of Martian fighter patrols.

I was piloting one of the planes towards the front; Karen and I weren't going to get in the way of Adrienne's well-oiled squadron when it came to flying escort operations. As I've said before, I wasn't a fantastic super-pilot. Karen was, sure, but not me. Better to let Adrienne's top-notch personnel see to security.

As it turned out, though, security wasn't a huge deal at all. We rounded the surface of Io at over 190 kps, and had a quiet ninety-minute flight. The Martians didn't seem to be worried about dark side attacks.

"We're coming up on the base, throttle back to 85 kps," Adrienne's voice came over the comm. "We'll peel off now, skipper. Good luck."

There was no way we could slip all twenty-four planes of Adrienne's two squadrons into range of the dome unnoticed — it'd be a minor miracle to get the three shuttles and two Starlights into range unseen.

That was the point of Andrea's distraction…

"Alright, shuttles into hover. We're waiting on *Dominator* now."

About ten minutes later (not perfect coordination, I'll grant you), *Dominator*, *Trusty* and *Pictou* lumbered into sensor range of Io's long-range grid, their weapons fully charged.

Andrea tells me that the crew of her new ship *hated* her, and I can guess why. First of all, she was making them work, making them be *real* spacers, and thanks to the experienced crew she'd taken with her, there were Belt Squadron veterans in every department to make sure the work Andrea demanded got done.

Second, though, I think she was on a bit of a power trip. She had a project, a place to vent her anger. I don't think she consciously knew it, but I'm pretty sure she adopted *Dominator* as a situation she *could* control. Here she could make a difference — make a *fighting ship* — and she could rage all she liked. Aboard *Dominator* she had reason to vent; she'd never have reason to aboard *Wolf* because the crew was just too good.

Anyway, her bridge was a sullen place as she drove *Dominator* into action.

Watching the sensor screen below my HUD, I noted the reaction of the Martians — the ships Commander Whitehorse had said were over Io were still there, and they now started pushing away from the single Io dome, power levels spiking.

Noble of them — the three destroyers and two DEs were going to try to scare away a battleship, but then again, the last time they'd seen *Dominator*, it'd been commanded by a coward. And in point of fact, Andrea was going to have to pretend to be a coward herself — try to get them away from the dome so Kris could slip in behind with ships they hadn't known were out here.

And while all that happened, we hovered over Io, waiting.

It was quite the wait. I'd forgotten how *tiring* waiting for hours in a cockpit could be. Not that the cockpit of the F-194 is uncomfortable — just the opposite, it was very well designed in ergonomic terms. No, it's a matter of the tension… the waiting and wondering, keeping an eye out for patrols and whatnot.

I still wasn't sure why the Martians weren't flying fighter sweeps of the surface of Io until I was talking to Wes months later. He pointed out that the Martian interceptors didn't actually have a strong atmospheric capability (unlike our Starlights) and like it or not, Io has a thin atmosphere. Toss in all the particles being spewed into that atmosphere by the many volcanoes all over the moon and you probably had a very, very dangerous environment for the Martian Interceptor. While perhaps a good plane for defending its mothership in space, the Interceptor wasn't suited to this sort of mission. At least that's our best guess.

Advantage to us.

After twenty minutes of hovering and hiding from base sensors behind plumes of volcanic smoke, I watched on my HUD as Kris started bringing up the Jupiter Force. They'd need an hour to get the rest of the way around the moon to the space over the dome, so Andrea needed to keep the Martians' attention for at least that long.

Over the next half hour, the Martians kept pushing out to meet Andrea's advance, and to keep them coming, Andrea continued her approach. Here I (despite myself) have to credit our enemy; this wasn't a flim-flam group of Martian ships like the one we'd faced at Belt Two. These had to be professional spacers of a high caliber — they were cruising out to meet a battleship with no capital ships of their own.

Now that might sound stupid, but remember back in *The Hawke Mission* how I was talking about Defense Command ships joining a battle even if the odds were stacked against them? That's the sense I got from this. Better yet, remember how Nancy Whitehorse and Giovanni Calzatti had stood their ground for a while against the Martian battleship force? Same idea: you don't just turn and run because things look bad. The Martian CO knew it was his job to protect Io, and was determined to show teeth to *Dominator*, in a bid to scare it off.

Of course, he was doing that assuming *Dominator* still had a coward for a skipper…

After fifty minutes of waiting, then, I gave the order: "Alright, let's go."

Without need for reply, Karen hit her burners, and so did I. We raced out ahead first, weaving around volcanic plumes while the shuttles surged forward behind us. We were still staying low in a bid to remain off the base sensor panels. They'd just spent that last hour staring at the arriving battleship, hopefully that meant they weren't paying attention to ground-scan passive detectors. If they caught a heat spike from our burners and hit us with a lidar ping, we were finished.

Well, not finished, but things would be very, *very* complicated.

But they *didn't* see us. Thanks to Io's latent volcanic activity, the heat of our burners simply got overpowered. We raced up on the base quickly, while all Martian eyes were turned skyward.

So far so good.

The old command center outside the dome was a modest affair, an unimpressive grey building with small pressure windows and all the hallmarks of the previous century's overbearing construction. Its airlocks were designed to accommodate small craft *only* — cargo ships coming out here in the old days had to move everything down to the base in large shuttles, which was obviously much more awkward than simply docking a ship with a dome. The only large entry point the building had was a 'garage' — essentially a landing bay for shuttles that were too large to dock. It was a logistical transport nightmare... that's why we demanded our dome when we took over.

In any case, the airlocks gave us our very obvious access point. Hopefully the Martians wouldn't even have paid attention to this old dump.

Special Branch was going in first. Charlie's team would clear the building with help from Rufus Chang's officers from *Lion*, while Marcus Atallah's team from *Cheetah* secured the subterranean access points into the old complex.

Once the building was swept for any Martians (we had to make sure they hadn't outsmarted us) and was deemed secure, we'd open the garage and Kyle Stranks' two shuttles of guards would enter. Kyle's job was to help fortify and hold the subterranean access points that Marcus occupied; there wasn't just one subterranean access point, it was more like a parking garage with many exits down there. Marcus needed the support of the regular SF to cover all angles.

While all of that was being looked after (in just minutes), Kate could work her magic, we could find out where the other enemy ships were, and we could (maybe) even secure the building as a foothold from which we could launch incursions into the dome. Charlie wasn't wild about that prospect, though, since we'd have had to go through the underground research complex to get to the dome from the building, and just like you see in every space horror movie, research complexes, particularly underground ones, can be meat grinders.

Alright, all that exposition sound good?

Good. And things were going smoothly.

"Peeling off to join Charlie now. See you inside," I was looking out my canopy at Karen as I said it.

"Listen to Charlie for once, will you?" she replied with a smile (well, it sounded like she was smiling, because I couldn't see through her helmet), before peeling off to join Marcus Atallah's landing shuttle — there was only one fighter docking chute per shuttle, so she was going in with *Cheetah's* Special Branch.

I waved, then jinked into position behind Charlie's shuttle, and began the docking sequence with the soft chute that had been extended behind it for my benefit.

The passive emissions sensors on the old building had to be picking us up by now — we were coming in much closer than any volcanic plume would have, so there was nothing more to mask us. Speed was thus of the essence; that whole plan I just described needed to unfold within bare minutes, before any Martians who might have been there figured out what was happening.

Charlie's shuttle nearly *rammed* the airlock as it came down on the landing pad, and I dropped my Starlight's landing feet onto the same pad immediately after it. Charlie didn't wait for me before launching into action; while I was still popping my canopy and floating through the chute into his shuttle, he was clearing the second floor of the building — the floor we'd docked with.

It took me a minute to clamber through the soft chute to the shuttle. As I put my feet on the small craft's floor, I found Kate Levec smiling nervously, mag in hand.

"Major Peters told me to wait for you," she was managing to cover her anxiousness pretty well. Sensors and Communications Officers generally didn't join assault missions, and unlike me, Kate Levec was sane, so it really wasn't her cup of tea.

With a nod and a smile that I hope came off as confident (not as *trying* to appear confident), I waved towards the exit lock, "Well then, after you Lieutenant Commander."

I said it with flourish, and she smiled, turned, and stepped into the lock. I followed.

The next thing I knew, I was being sprayed with her blood, and she was falling back into me.

CHAPTER TWENTY-SIX

NOT A GAME

Karen heard my roar on the open comm. She was on the other side of the building, breaking into the basement with Marcus Atallah's Special Branchers, and she swung back into the cover of a doorframe and slammed her comm's key hurriedly, "You alright up there?"

I didn't answer, which probably served to cause some panic. But Karen never lets panic take over. She swung out of the doorway and started shooting, and advancing, with a vengeance.

The pilot of Charlie's shuttle was a Special Branch officer, Lieutenant Chet Srisai, and he had his MAG-90 out of its cradle next to his seat and was spraying energy through the open lock before I knew what was happening.

I was flat on my back with Kate bleeding out all over me.

"Christ, we've got *Commandos* in here! *Watch your angles!*" that was Carly Henderson, Charlie's XO, making a grim declaration over the comm.

It took a very long second for me to realize what was happening, and as soon as I did I sat up with some difficulty and started firing wildly into the corridor as well. Using my free hand, I grabbed Kate's collar and dragged her back into the cabin of the shuttle.

"I have you covered, sir," Srisai must have seen who'd done the shooting, I certainly hadn't. He then very prudently reported that we were taking fire, and called for the medic with Charlie's team.

I dropped my mag onto one of the nearby seats and then knelt next to Kate, trying to see where she was hit. I didn't have to look hard: just above her left hip, the flesh at her waist had been punched out. It was a gruesome wound, revealing the white of her lowest rib on that side, but it looked like it had missed the key organs.

Kate was conscious, too. Mag blasts — or whatever the Martians call them — cauterize wounds, and while they definitely throw the victim into shock, they can do enough critical damage to a nervous system to actually fail to knock someone out. Think of trying to overload something with a power surge, but then burning away the conduits before the energy can be shot through them. It's a cruel fluke when it happens.

"Watch it, we've got regular Martians down here in the complex... pull back, *pull back*," Marcus Atallah's voice came over the comm. I'm sure there were more exclamations on the comm, but I wasn't hearing them all, and I'm not remembering any more now.

I was staring at Kate, lying there awake, with a piece of flesh the size of grapefruit missing from her left side.

"What was that?" Kate asked the question in a surprisingly strong tone.

"You took a hit at full power," I was sounding ridiculously calm.

"Really..." she tried to sit up, to look at the wound, but there was no way letting her see it was going to improve the situation, so my hand pressed her flat against the deck again.

"No, you stay down. Medic's on the way."

"It's starting to hurt..." her voice began to falter.

"That's the shock wearing off," I said without looking at her; I stood up quickly and looked for the first aid case. There it was. I grabbed it in a blur and cracked it. Charlie had explained to me how to deal with these sorts of wounds — we'd seen them on some grizzly occasions in the old days.

"Withdraw to second floor, we need to get to the databanks, forget the rest!" Charlie declared over the comm.

I had to pack the missing area of Kate's stomach; you didn't want anything falling out, gruesome as that might sound. I tore open a gauze pack — foam sealers just wouldn't work on a wound of this size — and started unceremoniously stuffing in the pads. Charlie's advice was not to worry about being too gentle — sure you could push a rib into a lung, but that's why she had two lungs...

A hand came down on my shoulder, "I'll take it, sir. Good work..."

Charlie's medic was Terry Schroeder, and he politely but firmly pushed me out of the way.

I stood up slowly — watching as Schroeder rolled some bandages and drove them into the gaping wound, then started to wrap her waist.

"They must have figured we'd try this," Charlie came in over the comm again. "Garage won't open for you Kyle, but we'll need you in here to secure a route to the comms room."

The plan was going pear-shaped, alright. The Martians had invested this place with some of their troopers, and according to what Carly had said, some of their *Commandos* too. That's the Martian word for Special Branch.

"I need to med evac her now, sir, with your permission," Terry Schroeder looked up at me. I just nodded.

"Chet, break dock," Schroeder looked at the pilot. "Sir, you need to get your plane off our shuttle."

I blinked. Right.

"Charlie, this is Terry, I'm breaking dock with a critical casualty, the SCO. Another shuttle can land at this pad."

"Roger that, Kyle you coming in?" Charlie replied instantly. I don't remember this now — I'm going on log recordings.

"We're on our way," Stranks came back.

In a blurry few moments, I hauled myself through the soft dock chute and closed my canopy, then broke dock. I think I did that all within a minute, and then I watched the boat race away, leaving the lock empty.

My mind was lagging, or at least it felt like it was — seconds were very long at that moment.

"Jim, Kate's down. I need you to be ready to talk one of us through whatever we have to do. And fast."

That's my voice on the recording, though I don't remember saying it. I sound assured enough — I was on total autopilot now, shocked by what I'd seen but still doing my job. I'll get into whether or not I should have been shocked in a little while.

After a hesitation, Jim Hannigan came over the comm, "We'll have to go full comms, the Martians will see us coming up…"

In other words, instead of just firing brief comm bursts back and forth as we were doing at that moment, we'd have to keep a channel open, and with the ruckus we were already causing, there was no way the Martians wouldn't track that signal back to *Wolf* and the Jupiter Force. The Martian ships we were hoping to catch in a vice would be warned before we could get into position.

"We're not going to get the ships anyway, Jim. But we need this intel. Kris, bring the squadron in fast."

The plan was gone to hell.

About ten minutes later, I'd docked with Kyle Stranks' shuttle after it had hooked up with the now-empty lock. Kyle waited for me to come through the chute before moving to the door.

"Is Kate alright, sir?" he asked with a frown, and I half shook my head.

"Don't know, Kyle…" I drew my mag.

Letting out a breath, Stranks nodded, then drew his comm from his belt, "We're at your old lock, Charlie. Are we clear to come in?"

There was a long pause, then the sound of firing in the background, "Get in here, Kyle. Second floor is about as safe as it gets — be careful!"

Kyle was still quite young for this job, and his nerves hadn't yet hardened to days like this, so he took another deep, reassuring breath before he palmed open the hatch and led the way out into the second floor corridor, trying to cover all angles.

Drawing my sidearm, I went out after him, and the SF guards behind me all followed quickly. This wasn't a Special Branch team — the SF were trained in some close-quarters combat, but they were also the people who broke up fights, stood guard at dignitaries' doors, and did all those sorts of less combat-particular jobs. Each of them knew they'd be outclassed by Commandos, but they were moving carefully, looking out for each other.

A figure swung around a corner ahead, and three of their MAG-90s (they were all carrying MAG-90s now, by the way) swung to face the newcomer. None shot Karen, and that's good (for a lot of rather obvious reasons). As she came down the corridor I was suddenly so very happy to see her. I almost smiled slightly.

Well, nearly almost. I must have been in shock, even though I shouldn't have been.

"Kate got hit?" Karen's question was level as she stopped next to me.

I must have given her quite the dark stare, because her eyes fell in a way I'd hoped I wouldn't see again after Egesta, and she sighed, "Alright. Alicia will see to her. We have to do this now."

How very right she was. Doctor Alicia Morgan was, in my estimation, a medical miracle worker. She'd take care of Kate Levec. We still had to get the information from the comm buffer and get out.

"Status in here?" I asked the question, making no effort to sound untroubled.

"Charlie has pulled back to the second and third floors, but it's dicey. These old buildings are loaded with ventilation ducts and tubes and all sorts of ways around our hold points. We're not secure, and I don't think we can be. They had this place pegged for the prime target it was," most of Kyle's SF had passed us now, so we turned to follow.

"Jim's talking Carly Henderson through the download, we need to make sure the way out stays clear," Karen went on. "Two Officers were hit, both took it in the vest so they'll be alright. Rufus has them in his shuttle, and is waiting to evac. Charlie says he'll spread his team over all the shuttles so we don't need to bring one back to pull him out."

I was barely keeping up — Karen and Charlie had this all under control, which was good, since I'd completely screwed it up. It was my call to come in here to begin with, and now I was seemingly in shock. *Shock.* Just because I'd had someone shot in front of me.

Not effective. I wasn't being effective. I remember thinking that.

"Kyle, hold this floor. Six people watching that airlock, the rest of you find a wall with good sightlines and lean back," I barked those orders, trying to regain some control of myself.

Looking back at Karen, I let out a sigh, "I called in the squadron. You knew that. Sorry... but I called Jim. We're not going to get the Martian ships out there because I tipped them off."

Karen frowned, "That was a long shot anyway."

I frowned too, then shook my head and elected not to say anything more. Something wasn't feeling right in my head. I'd screwed something up, I felt it.

"Alright, I've got the buffer, we're getting the hell out of here," Carly Henderson came over the comm after a moment of silence.

At that same instant, the sounds of mag fire came from around our airlock, and there was a grunt as one of Kyle's SFers dropped to the deckplate. One of the other SF started hauling her fallen comrade, and Karen and I didn't even think as we rushed back that way to offer covering fire. Kyle and the half-squad he'd kept to hold Charlie's route to the shuttle started to join us, but I waved them back.

"Stay put, don't let Charlie get cut off!" I hissed.

Another SF dropped — some of the Martians were shooting very cleanly — and Karen was the one to drag him into the shuttle's lock.

"We need to go," I was saying into my comm, leaning around a corner and shooting. It's all still a blur. "Karen, can you get to your plane? Marcus is going to have to get rid of it when he blasts off."

Sorry, I remember asking that, but I can't contextualize it. I just remember Karen nodding and running the other way. Charlie then arrived, with three of his team, and Kyle fell back to the shuttle.

And then I was again in my Starlight, releasing myself from the shuttle, and following it as it raced away.

I'd screwed up somewhere or somehow, I knew that much. But I couldn't keep a clear enough head to figure out what I'd done wrong.

That was probably the problem.

Chapter Twenty-Seven

The Space Fight

As it turned out, there had been around fifty Martians in the building, including fifteen Commandos. The one who'd shot Kate had come down a vent on the second floor after we breached, and by luck had been missed by the sweep Charlie ran before moving on. Charlie has always felt quite badly about this, though I don't see why he should. The nature of traps is that you don't see them coming... the fact that we got out is a testament to his fine work, and the efforts of his officers and Kyle's SF. I always say they should be proud that they stymied some of the elite Commandos of Mars.

And me? I was furious at myself. And still am, when I think about it.

I should have been more alert, less cavalier. I should have known that we weren't playing games with pirates. I should have expected them to be waiting for us. I should have done something a little bit more tactical than saying 'after you'.

But I didn't. And I couldn't stop thinking those things as I cruised back to *Wolf*. Kris Jacobs had accelerated the squadron to 198 kps and was coming around Io on a wide arc, cutting down the distance to the dome to only fifteen minutes by the time I was on my way. As soon as I boarded the ship, I headed for the bridge.

No, I didn't check on Kate. I thought about it... but I *shouldn't* have even thought about it, dammit. You're not supposed to think about that sort of thing until the battle's done, and it wasn't.

The camera crews met me in the bay, and they followed discreetly. More importantly, they didn't try to cram into the lift with me. They waited for the next one. Looking at my expression on the vids they took, I'm pretty sure I know why Bunny kept her distance. I was armed, and I definitely looked dangerous.

Jim Hannigan turned to face me with a nod as I arrived, then pointed somberly towards the main screen, "Andrea's coming in hot, the Martians are reversing course and heading back here. They definitely sent a signal to somewhere else around Jupiter when she turned up."

I nodded, "Fine. Carly got the buffer information. She send it on yet?"

He nodded, "I think she lost some of it during extraction, but she sent through enough. Kate's... um... Felicia's people are working on it now."

"Good. Get Battlelink set up. I want to kill some Martians, Jim."

That was better. I had to be focused.

The camera crew arrived on the bridge as the Battlelink came online. I think everyone's first instinct was to ask after Kate's condition — the old Belt Squadron really had been a family of officers — but every one of the Commanders and Captains had enough sense to keep their minds on the situation at hand.

And come to that, I doubt my appearance inspired questions: I was still in my flight suit, and it was covered in drying blood.

"Go to general quarters, everyone. I'm not waiting for the data from the buffer, I want to take out some of that squadron out there."

I could want whatever I liked. Wouldn't make it happen.

"Damned straight," Mark Gunney voiced his approval first, and the rest followed in due course.

Jim started giving the requisite orders on *Wolf's* bridge, and I stood with my arms crossed for five minutes or so, watching the main screen as our ships went from the standby alert they'd been on to full battle readiness.

"Sir, we've tracked the signal being sent from the array," Lieutenant Felicia Khalid was standing behind Kate's consoles, and I turned to her, probably looking like a thundercloud. She wasn't phased, "Signals have been sent to a relay point between here and Mars, and to another moon around Jupiter... our charts call it Sinope. No signals to any points closer than Sinope, and at present orbit Sinope is a day away, on the far side of Jupiter."

I nodded, "Good."

Perhaps the plan had worked after all: we could be reasonably confident now that the Martians here weren't about to be reinforced.

"Shelby, take us out towards our friends out there. Felicia, get me a link to Adrienne Thompson please."

I don't think I'd spoken directly to Felicia Khalid since her interview for the Sensors and Communications Officer job. Karen and I had passed her over on account of limited experience, interestingly enough.

"Yes sir," she pointed to one of the technicians as she replied, and then sat in her own seat. She still ran one of the consoles up here, at least for now.

Adrienne Thompson's audio comm came live over the bridge speakers a moment later, "We're here skipper, what do you need?"

"I'm going ship-hunting, I want you to strip Io of all shore batteries. They haven't started charging them yet, but I don't want them to get the chance. We'll launch all squadron fighters to give you a hand."

As I said those words, the skippers of the Jupiter Force listened and then in a single motion began to give orders to their own bridge crews. Within minutes, the squadrons from *Lion*, *Cheetah*, *Friendly*, *Lady Grace* and *Honesty* would be in space.

Now I know what you might be thinking: it's been well established that fighters can't do much harm to armor. That's true, ships were by this time pretty much impervious to fighter ordnance. However, static ground defenses lacked the ability to maneuver, and when they were as old as some of the ones on Io, they might indeed be weak enough to get chopped by fighter missiles. And we'd put more than a hundred fighters over them — eventually they'd be overwhelmed.

Karen appeared on the bridge just after I'd given that order, having been the last to dock after the recovery of the strike team. As she came to a stop next to me, I glanced at her, "Karen, do the honors of taking us after them?"

She managed to contain her frown this time, nodding instead and looking up at the main screen to make sure she was properly oriented, "Maximum burn, let's get after them."

As she said that, I folded my arms across my bloody chest and waited.

+++

It was no use. Andrea came in towards Io with all the speed she could muster, but it didn't help. The Martian ships were well-led, and they recognized the vice we were trying to close around them. After we'd been accelerating for about ten minutes, they sidestepped and escaped, heading for Sinope at 196 kps. They had enough of a head start, thanks to their position directly between Andrea's ships and the Jupiter Force, to make an interception virtually impossible.

Karen and I watched them run, watched them *escape*, without a word. I tried to tell myself that they probably would have escaped anyway, but I was just too loaded with frustration and anger. I wasn't myself at this point, it's pretty clear. I knew I should have been, I knew I wasn't, and that was getting to me.

I don't know if I can adequately or rationally explain what these internal problems were, or where they were coming from. Or why we haven't seen them since Egesta.

Who am I kidding, of course I can. And I will. But as we watched the Martians run away, the battle essentially ended. That gave me a little license to admit to myself how bad I was feeling about Kate's situation. And I didn't even know if she was dead.

I had to find out about that.

I needed to tie up the loose ends first though, so I looked up at the Battlelink screens, "Alright, let's see if we can get an idea of what he has out at Sinope. Matt, Aaron, Elise, get after them. Don't pick any fights you can't win, but see if you can get a look at what they have at Sinope."

Matt Baxter was the first to nod, "We'll track them. You'll look to Io then, Ken?"

He had the tone of a concerned parent. It was pretty evident I wasn't in proper form.

I nodded, "Oh, I will."

With a few more words of acknowledgment, Matt, Aaron Ashby and Elise De Winter took their ships out of formation with our force, heading after the escaping Martians. I looked back to Felicia Khalid, "Order the rest of the force to concentrate over Io. What's the latest from Adrienne?"

Khalid turned her chair and looked over one of her tech's shoulders, "There are two batteries she cannot crack, the rest have been eliminated."

"Right. Mark, deal with those batteries," I looked up at Captain Gunney, and he nodded.

"Roger that."

I paused again, then looked at Karen, "Alright. Get us all parked up over the dome, then we'll figure out how to take it. I'm going to go to the infirmary now."

Karen's head tipped ever so slightly, "Want me to come along?"

"I really don't," I nearly whispered.

She understood.

I then turned back, realized the camera crews were recording me, and sighed, "You cameras. Come with me. And Bunny, call Jocko and Jessica and tell them to meet us down there."

I left the bridge with the camera crews.

CHAPTER TWENTY-EIGHT
REALITY VID

Jocko and Jessica were at the door to the lift when it opened, both of them looking quietly shocked that I'd told them to come. I don't really blame them for their surprise — I suppose the expectation at a time like this is that I wouldn't want a camera anywhere near me. I suppose on one level I didn't, this wasn't exactly my finest moment.

But on a deeper level, this seemed incredibly necessary.

The sickbay was a long way from the lift we'd taken, and I walked slowly.

"Ask your questions," I offered quietly as we went.

You've probably seen a lot of the footage that came next. Some say it made Jessica Qing's career.

"You have an officer seriously wounded," Jessica was asking the question in her serene tone when her eyes drifted down to the red splotches on my flightsuit, "and that's her blood?"

"It is," I nodded and replied softly.

"What's her status?" Jocko's question was much more abrupt.

"I'm going to find that out now. She didn't look good when I last saw her."

Both reporters were very good about handling their questions, I should add: neither asked for confirmation of her name, though both knew who she was. It wouldn't do to send a report to Earth with word of Kate Levec's death, and have it broadcast before we got to inform Kate's family. It was respectful, and showed integrity.

"The mission didn't go off as planned... was that because your judgment was affected by your proximity to the officer when she was hit?" Jessica's question was a potentially damning one. Could I confess to the entire Empire that I'd screwed up a perfectly good plan just because I'd watched one of my bridge officers get shot?

Hell, I hadn't actually *seen* it. She'd just landed on me.

"I'm rather certain it was, Jessica. I called in and gave up *Wolf's* position too soon, and the Martians got their chance to escape. They're getting away as we speak."

"You think you screwed up?" Jocko's question was literally one of disbelief, and I nodded.

"I did. Me alone, make sure that's on the record. But right now I'm more concerned with the state of my officer. I'll worry about correcting my mistake after I know her status."

There it was. That was my problem, see. Too focused on Kate's status. Too worried about one woman who I didn't know very well, just because she'd landed on me when she'd been shot. That's why I was angry with myself. I was certain of it.

The questions had stopped, the cameras and the reporters simply following me the rest of the way to sickbay. I entered silently, drawing a surprised stare from two of the orderlies who were on duty in the receiving area.

One came to her feet, "Sir..."

The cameras and reporters followed me in, and stopped her words.

"Orderly, I'm inquiring into the state of the wounded officer..." I let my voice trail off, and the young woman nodded.

"Of course, she's in surgery now. I'll take you into the observation bay, though I'm afraid there won't be room for them."

"We'll wait," Jocko said instantly.

With that, I left the reporters behind, and followed the orderly into the surgery bay. It didn't immediately occur to me that, for Kate to be in surgery, she presumably had to be alive.

The bay itself was a sealed chamber inside the sickbay (sorry about the double 'bay', that's just what they call it). Within the surgery area you could fit three patients at once, and there was a large window looking into the space from *Wolf's* sickbay. Alicia Morgan and her staff were in their ship scrubs, working quickly and precisely over Kate Levec's torso, while in the next two beds, wounded SFers were being patched up. I'm no medical specialist, I had no idea exactly what they were doing.

But I had to interrupt them, if only briefly.

Keying the intercom, I spoke quietly, "Alicia, give me her status in five words or less."

Looking up without any indication of surprise at the sudden question, Doctor Alicia Morgan delivered her answer: "I'm not going to let her die. I can't do the reconstructive surgery she'll need here, but I can fix her organs. When we get her back to the Empire some specialists can fill in this hole with new flesh."

Yes, that was more than five words. No, I wasn't going to complain.

"Other casualties?" I asked that question tersely. I couldn't become so fixated on Kate that I didn't ask about the rest.

"Moderate. The two in here will be off their feet for a while, but I've heard nothing serious from the other doctors."

That meant she'd checked with *Lion* and *Cheetah* — their wounded Special Branchers would be fine.

With those answers I nodded, "Thanks."

I started to feel slightly woozy with relief. Again, that angered me. I should have been more detached.

Despite that, I stepped out of the observation bay, and headed right back to the cameras, "Doctor Morgan assures me she will recover. Considerable reconstructive surgery will be necessary. That'll wait until we get back to the Empire."

"Very glad to hear that," Jocko did sound legitimately relieved.

"Definitely. So the Martian ships managed to slip away, but we've suffered no fatalities?" Jessica's question was soft again.

"There were other casualties. All will recover. We were lucky," I started with that, then said the famous line, "And I let the Martians escape, yes."

Jessica frowned, "Could you have guaranteed they'd be trapped if you hadn't called this squadron when you did?"

That question should have tipped me off to where this was going. I'm actually rather glad I was still oblivious, "There's no guarantee, no. At the moment I've sent three corvettes out to chase them. We may at least get some intel regarding the Martian base."

Jocko was standing off now, because he sensed Jessica was leading up to something, and his camera was going to get the same answers anyway.

"So, by ordering your ships forward early, you saved the lives of your officers wounded in a daring landing operation, one of whom, it's quite clear from the blood you're wearing, you helped save. And you didn't lose the Martian ships, because there was never any guarantee you'd get them in the first place. Instead, they're leading your ships right to their base. Isn't that the case?"

I blinked, "What?"

Jessica took a step forward, making sure to frame herself in the shot of me standing in my bloody flightsuit, "You personally saved the life of one of your officers, and still accomplished as much as you could have had you been given the chance to spring your trap."

I didn't know quite what to say to that, so I stammered, "Well... I mean... no I don't..."

"Alright, that's a wrap. Let's get some shots through the window of the doctor working," Jessica ended the interview just like that, her instincts about these things being impeccable.

Bunny now looked quickly to Jocko, "Us too?"

Jocko was grinning, "Yes, definitely. That girl's going to put me out of business..."

I didn't understand what was going on, but as Jocko walked by he patted me on the back, and Jessica patted me on the shoulder, "Thanks, this is going to be great."

I still didn't get it, so I left the sickbay, and went to my cabin to change.

Before I continue with the narrative, I might as well discuss what came of that footage, and why. Basically, there are a couple of ways those enterprising reporters could have spun the story. The way I would have gone with it is probably of no surprise to you: Ken Barron at last reveals himself to be a hack, loses his detachment, screws up operation.

But that, of course, isn't the spin Jessica took.

She got footage of me that was unlike anything the public had ever seen: they saw me in a frame of mind that only Karen and sometimes Charlie had witnessed up to that time. She got the exclusive first look behind my good PR face and my bravado, and gave the public a glimpse of the real me — in her words, "the noble warrior who cares deeply for every man and woman under his command, and who will put their lives above his own glory... without forgetting his obligations to the Empire."

I grew more popular than ever when the story ran, and so did she.

Quite the effective load of bullshit, wouldn't you say?

I don't know if Jessica believed what she said about me in that report. I'll never ask her. I do know that I disagreed entirely with the conclusion she came to.

I should have been able to shake off the shock of having Kate Levec land on me. I should have been able to get on with my job and to do so without blundering and letting the Martians get away. I shouldn't have been so damned fixated.

I feared this may have been a shadow of Egesta. I feared I'd lost my ability to detach after seeing what I'd seen. After all, this was the first serious fight I'd been in since Egesta, and I'd cracked… a fact that few seemed to realize.

I don't know anymore. Whatever you think is your own business. I've been accused of being too self-critical, of underestimating the importance of saving lives… of many such things.

But I still had a job to do, and that's what I was going to focus on.

Arriving in my cabin with that on my mind, I quickly pulled off my flightsuit and got into my ship fatigues. The bloodied garment went into the laundry chute for my steward to deal with, and then I went to my fridge to grab water. I needed to drink something.

I didn't hear the hatch open, and I didn't hear Karen come in. I simply turned around from the fridge with my unopened water and suddenly her arms were wrapped around me. Let me tell you, if there was one thing in the universe that could help my state of mind at such a moment, this was it.

I dropped my bottle of water and let out a very long, pained sigh, my chin settling onto Karen's shoulder and my hands pressing against her back.

I closed my eyes, "Kate'll need reconstructive when we get home. But Alicia says she'll live."

"I heard," Karen squeezed me a little tighter.

The serenity that I felt right then was a marvel. It was something that I desperately needed, and Karen had known that, because she was Karen.

We held onto each other for another moment, and then we left for the bridge.

There was still work to be done.

CHAPTER TWENTY-NINE
IO NEGOTIATIONS

When Karen and I got back to the bridge, I must have been carrying a different air about me — the bridge crew seemed relieved somehow. Well, I shouldn't be so arrogant as to take all the credit for that: word had spread that Kate would recover. That probably had a good deal more to do with the relief than my improved mood.

Andrea was still half an hour out, so it was just the three frigates floating over Io; Matt was leading the corvettes out after the Martians, having just finished recovering his fighters. Mark Gunney had done his job, killing the last Io shore batteries and thus leaving the colony open to our attack.

The Martians down there had to know they didn't have a hope.

But if they didn't know, I had to explain that fact to them.

"Alright..." I nearly said Kate "...Felicia, signal Io and request realtime comms."

Lieutenant Khalid nodded and keyed the commands into her panel, "Signal sent."

"What're we going to offer them?" Mark was still on Battlelink, as was Kris.

"The usual, death or the brig," I looked up at him and answered with a dry tone.

He was frowning, "Yeah, but where do we put 500 prisoners?"

Dammit.

That sort of problem I should have thought about sooner. We'd figured we'd have killed many of the Martian troops in the dome when we attacked, and whoever was left could be spread between the ships of the Jupiter Force. But if we got a straight surrender, that'd be a bit more challenging.

"Well, we'll see how many there are. We might just have to maroon them out here, take all the important kit with us and leave them with enough rations to get by on," I was thinking out loud, and Mark snorted a laugh.

"We'll be popular."

"We always are," I nodded sardonically. "Anything back yet, Felicia?"

The Lieutenant shook her head, "Nothing yet, sir."

We waited for about ten minutes, during which time the camera crews returned to the bridge. The Martians were probably discussing their options. They were now in an unenviable situation: no matter how strong their position was on the ground, we had the orbital trump card.

Of course they could do what people in that sort of inferior situation tend to do: take hostages, or in the specific situation here, threaten to kill prisoners. That wasn't exactly sporting, but it was their only real chance to equalize the odds.

Not that it'd do them any good.

"Signal coming now, sir. I'll put it on screen five," Felicia reported quickly, then keyed her panel and moved the feed up to that display.

Karen and I shuffled sideways to get within the screen's viewfinder shot, then watched as a red-clad, pale-complexioned Martian officer appeared, "This is Colonel Felix Branx, of the Martian Republican Army. Who am I addressing?"

Karen and I looked at each other, and then sensing we could wrong-foot this guy, we looked back at the screen and said simultaneously, "Us."

The Colonel frowned, "Excuse me?"

I looked at Karen, "Well, I don't see anyone else here. He's addressing us, right?"

"Most definitely," Karen's expression was priceless, just the right amount of amusement and mock confusion. She was still on game.

"Names. I want, names," Branx insisted gruffly.

Karen and I were still looking at each other, and I frowned, "I thought he already had a name."

"He does indeed," Karen nodded emphatically.

We looked back at the screen.

"Colonel Branx," I began, "I'm Rear Admiral Ken Barron, and may I present Commodore Karen McMaster. We're the people to whom you're going to surrender."

His eyes narrowed, and I could see the defiant words welling up in his mind. I could just *see* them.

"Now now, don't threaten to kill prisoners. Our orders out here are to make sure you don't carry away any experimental technology, and if we have to sacrifice that base and everyone on it, we will. In other words, we'll slice the dome right off that rock before we let you escape. Better you save the lives of you troops," Karen sounded so pleasant.

Branx was grinding his jaw, his scowl deepening, "I'm sure you would. You people have no souls…"

I really wasn't sure how to take that, it was a pretty cold insult. One that I'd just proved quite wrong by nearly going derelict of my duty.

"Of course we don't. That's why we'll kill you if you don't lay down arms. Don't make us kill you all just to save our secrets."

Smiling slightly, Branx as much as revealed the fact that secrets had already been carried off Io. To his credit, he didn't say it.

"How many troops do you have on the ground, Colonel?" I asked plainly, my tone becoming rather more serious.

Staring at me for a moment, he seemed to be weighing his options — could he lie to us and get away with it? Could he set a trap and somehow turn this situation around?

No.

"A hundred and fifty."

Of course we couldn't be sure that he was being honest.

"I'm afraid I have no reason to believe you. I won't get overdramatic here by ordering my flagship's XO to target the dome to scare you, but you do realize that I'll kill you all if you don't surrender, right?"

One of Branx's eyebrows started to climb, "You think we're not willing to die for our state? If you destroy this dome, you lose all the secrets held here too."

Again, he managed to stop himself from saying that the Martians had already stolen them.

"That's fine, we'll drill through the dome, decompress, then come down in EVA gear and pull the files. Look, Colonel, we don't doubt your devotion. I'm sure you'd die for that God-president-overlord fellow of yours, but wouldn't you rather live through this?" my tone was getting franker.

It was a good argument, I thought. And Branx seemed to agree.

"Yes. Alright. We'll surrender."

Too convenient? I wasn't convinced either.

"Well, that's fair. I want you to get the most senior Defense Command officer in the dome and bring that person to the comm. I then want you to turn over all your weapons to Defense Command personnel, and once I hear from our officer that all's well, we'll…"

Branx held up his hand, "We don't have Defense Command prisoners."

That stopped me talking, so Karen picked up in my silence, "Excuse me?"

Had they shot all our officers? Their POW experience was going to get a whole lot rougher if they had.

"We moved your military cohorts to… a ship. They're on their way back to Mars for interrogation."

Again, I didn't know if I could believe that ambitious little claim.

"Well," my mind routed me to plan B, "the senior prisoner you do have. And understand, I'm going to confirm your story with that person. If I even *think* they're being intimidated by you when they're talking, I open the dome. Clear?"

Branx nodded slowly, "Yes, clear. Give me ten minutes."

"Fine. Leave the comm up."

We waited.

Chapter Thirty

Scientists, Majors, and Afros

We waited for about ten minutes, and by the time chief scientist Forrest Douglas — with his trademarked frizzy grey afro — appeared on screen five, Andrea Kiley was on Battlelink on screen six. She wasn't looking calm.

"I take it spacing all those bastards isn't an option?" had been her first question, and I'd just shook my head.

Had I been in a proper state of mind, I might have read more into Andrea's words. I might have realized that having people she considered part of her family ambushed and grievously injured was going to force her mind back to where it didn't want to be — to the belief that she should have been able to do something.

A belief I may well have been entertaining myself.

But I didn't notice.

Anyway, it was a few minutes after that exchange when Forrest Douglas appeared with an eccentric, rather studied gaze, "Hello? Hello Defense Command?"

He was looking right at Karen and me, and we were looking back at him. This man was the smartest person in the Empire, no question, but he was… well… he was eccentric. I mean, grey afro?

"We're here, sir. This is Rear Admiral Ken Barron, and Commodore Karen McMaster."

He squinted, "Barron? Any relation to old R.J. Barron, the engineer?"

"My grandfather… but please Mister Douglas, can you tell me if there are indeed 150 Martians down there, and if they're surrendering their weapons?"

"Oh yes yes, certainly. One of them gave me a magnetic disrupter, as though I'd know how to use it!"

Typical scientist — Douglas began a slightly wheezy belly laugh at his joke, his jowls shaking in a good natured sort of way. Strange fellow.

"That's good to hear. I'll need your scientists to keep them covered, we'll be coming down with Security Forces and Special Branch to evacuate the base. Can your research be transported?"

"They already took it all. And wiped all our records. I have a few secret backups, of course. But they took all the prototypes. They were getting ready to take us away too, I really am glad you arrived when you did, certainly…" he looked like he'd be going for a while unless I stopped him.

"I am too. Listen, sir, I have to go get in my plane to fly down to you, and Commodore McMaster has to join me. I'll leave you on the line with one of my officers, though, so that you can tell them if the Martians do anything suspicious. Sound fair?"

Douglas nodded emphatically, "Of course, of course, certainly!"

"Good, I'll shake your hand soon. Just a moment now, there'll be another officer to talk to… in a moment."

Karen and I shuffled out of the viewfinder's range, trying not to seem too eager. Don't get me wrong, Forrest Douglas was a genuinely nice person… he was just an eccentric scientist. Take them in controlled doses.

I pointed at Jim and then pointed to the screen. Jim's eyes got rather wide, and he shook his head emphatically. I pointed at him again. He scowled and pointed across the bridge at poor Shelby McLaws.

She looked at Jim, then at me, wearing one of those 'do I *have* to' expressions.

I nodded. The privileges of rank.

Taking a ladylike breath, Shelby nodded once, put on a charming smile, and with the carriage of the belle of a southern ball, waltzed over to the screen's viewfinder.

"Hello Mister Douglas, my name's Shelby, I'm an officer here on the bridge of *Wolf*. So how has your day been?"

That got him talking, and I could tell right then that Shelby had a dangerous future — she had the evil instinct for theatre that we all seemed to need.

Karen and I headed for our planes.

As I got to the ladder next to my cockpit, Charlie slid to a halt beside me, "Hey."

I turned and nodded to him, "Hey… what's up?"

High language skills I was demonstrating there.

"You… alright? With Kate and all. I'm sorry about that again — I should have double swept… I still can't believe we missed that guy…"

"Hey, you got us out of there with no fatalities. I sent her through the hatch first," I protested.

"Yeah, but I–"

Karen suddenly had a hand on both our shoulders, "Break it up, neither of you was responsible. Move on."

Charlie's a great friend, trying to take the blame off my shoulders, where it rightfully belonged.

"But you're alright? I mean *alright*?" Charlie was trying to make sure I wasn't still burning inside, the way Andrea was (even if we didn't realize Andrea was at the time).

Karen leaned in and smiled, "I hugged him earlier. He's fine."

"Oh," Charlie's eyebrows went up, but he contained his smile as he looked back at me. "So you're feeling so good you think you could single-handedly take all those Martians prisoner down there?"

I shrugged and nodded, "I am feeling pretty good, sure."

"Well you *can't*, so don't get any ideas just because Karen rubbed some magic essence on you," Charlie had started to check his gear as he said that, but at the end he froze and winced at his choice of words. "That sounded a whole lot less crude in my head."

"I'll bet it did," I managed to crack a smile.

"Get on your shuttle. We're going to go meet Forrest Douglas," Karen pointed sternly at Charlie's assault craft. He started to nod meekly, but again he stopped. It seemed that in this conversation, Charlie could *not* finish any gesture he started.

"Wait, *the* Forrest Douglas is down there? I didn't realize he was out here… you're serious… Forrest Douglas…?"

Charlie, if you don't already know, is something of a technofile. Certain kinds of computers and the possibility of constructing AIs, machines with souls, and all the rest of it, really interest him. So for those of you playing the home game, the two personal characteristics of Charlie that most people didn't know until this series of books are:

1)   He hates raccoons. A lot. He wants them all dead. He wants raccoon armageddon.

2)   He likes computers and technology, AIs and stuff. He's read everything Forrest Douglas ever wrote — *and* he understands it.

"Yes, we're serious," Karen was now thrusting her finger at the shuttle, trying to get Charlie moving.

"Yes. Black guy. Big grey afro. He's down there. And if we stopped talking about it, we could go meet him!"

Charlie grinned, turned, and ran to his shuttle. Yes *ran*.

As we watched him go, Karen stepped closer to me, "Well, looks like we've found our way out of having to chat with Mister Douglas."

I nodded, "Yep. And we'll be able to say that the latest breakthrough in the evolution of AI technology happened while those two were helping move Martian prisoners."

With a grin, Karen nodded.

We lifted off shortly thereafter.

CHAPTER THIRTY-ONE
ACCEPTING SURRENDER

Special Branch teams from all the ships over Io save for *Dominator* landed along with Charlie, Karen and I, and then Kyle Stranks came down from *Wolf* in a shuttle with six SF and the reporters and their camera teams. It was probably a little premature to be bringing reporters down to Io — we didn't know for certain that the Martians were surrendering, after all — but Jocko and Jessica insisted, and for some reason I acceded.

Damn me, I was getting to trust and respect those two.

"Stay with Lieutenant Stranks. I mean that, no cowboy documentary filming — you stay with the guards until we know it's safe," I'd said over my headset comm, having already departed from *Wolf* in my fighter.

"I'm no cowboy," Jocko replied instantly.

"We promise to obey," Jessica added.

They wanted footage of Special Branch officers surrounding Martians, taking their weapons, the Martians sitting in large dejected groups… the usual POW fare. I was fine with that.

Coming in to land at the dome (not the building from before) wasn't too exciting. Charlie's team went in first, their shuttle docking at one of the locks near the dome's shuttle bay. Storming across to the landing bay controls, they met one Martian (with a mag being trained on him by a twitchy looking physicist), who obligingly unlocked the doors to the main flightbay.

"Main bay is open for business," Charlie announced over the comm. "There's room for everybody, drive defensively."

Shuttles from *Lion, Cheetah, Trusty, Pictou,* and Kyle's craft from *Wolf* filed in neatly, then Karen and I slipped in just before Charlie started to close the doors. Once the bay sealed and repressurized, there was a flurry of unloading — just over thirty Special Branchers exiting their craft to join Charlie's dozen.

Karen and I stayed back as Charlie started barking orders about how they were going to secure the complex, and how we weren't going to worry about the rest of the dome at the moment. We'd come in through the Io base complex… think of it like Belt Two base, it's essentially a fortress within the dome that also has locks connecting it to the space outside.

We'd collect all prisoners and scientists in that base, secure it against attack from the city, and go from there. Yes, of course we knew that meant some Martians might escape across the dome, but we were more concerned at this point with getting the larger force under control, and the scientists out of harm's way.

I have to be honest, what followed wasn't terribly eventful. Charlie and his Special Branchers went out into the base, doing their tactical hand gestures and checking rooms carefully. Kyle and his guards took the reporters in after them, all the SF holding their

MAG-90s at the ready, just in case.

Karen and I were left on our own to march through the mostly empty corridors of the base, occasionally coming across a Special Brancher. The quiet was nice, if a little eerie.

"I'd expect a science facility to be cleaner," Karen was frowning as we turned a corner to find more dirt and grime climbing the walls.

"Let's just blame the Martian landlords, I'm sure our scientists live cleanly," I found I was paying a little extra attention to every door we approached.

Of course, both of our mags were out of our holsters — we were ready for trouble.

No, we didn't find any. Remember I said this was uneventful?

"There's the C&C, right up there," Karen had recognized the heavy pressure hatch that was the standard for all Defense Command base command and control centers, and we quickened our pace.

Having glanced quickly at the comm logs of the Martians, we did know something of their disposition. Checking sensor logs would give us an even better idea.

Of course, neither Karen nor I were yet convinced that the Martians weren't going to try something fishy, and booby-traps are pretty fishy.

Flattening ourselves against the wall on either side of the hatch, we held our mags at the ready, and then Karen popped the hatch and swung through, covering right. I went left, as always, and we scanned the room over the barrels of our sidearms.

"Looks clear to me," Karen concluded after a moment.

"Yep," I lowered my mag and started heading for the plot table at the middle of the C&C. This place wasn't brand new — it had received very few upgrades since it had been built — but the plot table looked familiar enough. "So let's see what we can find."

"I'll check Sensors and Communications, you look for logs," Karen slid her mag into its holster and headed to the appropriate consoles.

We started searching for information.

Colonel Branx offered his sidearm at just about the same time, and Charlie took it with a nod, "Thank you, Colonel."

The Martian soldier was dressed rather finely — not tactically at all. Martian professional soldiers are, in many respects, a lot like Imperial Army blockheads, tripped up on ceremony and pomp. Charlie's rather the antithesis of that.

"A gentleman would offer me the pistol back, and ask for my parole," Branx grunted in a low tone.

Charlie's eyebrows went up, "Yes, but the last war of the gentlemen was 230 years ago, Colonel, or so our history says. I'm not giving you a weapon. Please sit down with your men."

This seemed to be a great offense to the Colonel — I can only presume because officers and crew were not supposed to sit together in Martian military circles. That was Charlie's guess, and if you haven't already figured it out, it's Charlie's version of this little scene that I'm using.

Handing the Martian mag (or whatever they called it at that moment, since they seemed to like to change the names of their weapons) to Carly, Charlie slid his hand back around the handle of his MAG-90 and turned to see if he could locate Marcus Atallah.

Cheetah's Special Branch commander was nearby, talking to Rufus Chang from *Lion*. Charlie presently joined the two Majors, "We have a count?"

Rufus nodded, "I have 112 here, including some wounded from our attack at the communications building."

"Only 112?" Charlie frowned, glancing from his counterpart down at the large number of sitting Martians. I should have mentioned this earlier, but they were in the lobby of the base — a large, open space with enough room for everyone.

"Indeed. I thought we were supposed to find 150... perhaps the scientists overestimated..." Atallah suggested in a rather unconvinced tone.

Charlie nodded slowly at the Major's words, "Perhaps..."

He looked back to the Colonel.

"Or not."

Without another word, Charlie left the two Majors, walked to the Colonel, grabbed him by the collar, and hauled him to the proverbial woodshed.

"Alright, according to the last log I have, the Martians landed with 500 originally, and the SF tried to fort up here. That lasted for about six hours before they surrendered," I was reading the logs of a Major Brant.

"They pulled out 350 of theirs last week, along with all the Defense Command personnel... Looks like they took more prisoners than they expected, I've got back-and-forth traffic here, asking what to do with them."

It was rather obliging of the Martians to fail to clear their comm logs — I hadn't really expected us to be lucky enough to get that sort of traffic. Actually, as it turned out, the redoubtable Colonel Branx had attempted to delete everything on the hard drives, but he'd been in such a rush that when he punched in the order and followed it with the authorization code they'd stolen, he'd failed to realize that two codes were necessary for that sort of wipe. All Karen had to do was hit 'cancel' and we were in business.

You have to love it when things work out in your favor.

"It says here they're moving them to Sinope. The Martians are going to redirect a transport out here to pick them up... about 400 survivors."

Io base had a full complement of 436 Defense Command personnel. Throw in half the crew of *Dominator* that had been left behind and you'd get roughly 850. So evidently half had died defending the base.

Now, the first question that came to my mind was why move them at all — that many people would be tricky to transport, even on a short haul to a nearby moon. There was a definite threat of some of the prisoners trying to take over one of the warships they were aboard, or something such.

"Looks like they were supposed to pull the scientists out this week... two days from now. They were going to abandon Io, wait for us at Sinope with everything they had while they packed up, and hope we didn't actually find them before they left," Karen was using that instinct of hers — the one that let her find the information we needed right when we needed it.

I know, I know — if this were fiction, you'd be up in arms about how 'impossibly convenient' that is. Calm down. First, this is reality, and second, you just don't know Karen. She has a way with information.

"Alright, so us showing up early was a good thing. Yay for publicizing military operations…" I turned from the plot table. "We'll just have to see what the Martians do, now that they know we're here."

Karen's eyes had been flicking back and forth across the large comm screen she'd been working on, but now they stopped, locking in place as a frown creased her brow, "Hang on… alright, they already sent all the research and prototypes back to Mars. Those left last week on some sort of military transport. Taking prisoners is just the mop-up."

I grunted, "Damn. Alright, we have a base course in there?"

Karen shook her head, "Nope, just word that they left… six days ago."

"Great," I let out a sigh. That was a lot of experimental kit we really didn't want the Martians to get their hands on — even if they didn't have the scientists to help them decipher it. "Well, I guess we'll just send to John and let him know we need them stopped. We can guess on a base course, get a squadron out there hunting."

Nodding, Karen started shifting her gaze. After a couple of moments more, she stopped, shook her head and looked up, "I could do this all week. We can get this copied up to *Wolf* later — probably better get the Martians under lock and key first."

"Ah right, priorities," I grinned sheepishly.

We left the C&C.

By the time we reached the lobby, the Martians were all disarmed and sitting… with a notable exception.

"Branx? And Charlie?" I frowned as I came to a stop next to Marcus Atallah.

The Lebanese man smiled, "The woodshed, as Charlie likes to say."

"The woodshed? Why?" my frown didn't go away.

Atallah leaned closer to me, keeping his voice down, "We're missing thirty-eight Martians. But this was supposedly all of them."

"The other thirty-eight are their Commandos, and they apparently want to either stay unnoticed, or start a little guerilla fight."

I turned at Charlie's voice, just in time to have a groaning Colonel Branx land at my feet.

I looked down at the Martian officer, "Isn't kicking the crap out of prisoner a violation of the Ceres Accord?"

Charlie came to a stop opposite me with a grin, a single line of blood trickling down from the corner of his mouth, "Would have been, if I hadn't convinced him to take a swing at me first. He's got a pretty good right cross, but after that it was self-defense. Nothing that won't mend itself."

I chuckled and nodded, "Alright, and so there are thirty-eight Commandos out there?"

Nodding, Charlie subconsciously brought his hands to rest on his MAG-90, "Yep. I'd say don't let anyone but Special Branch out of this building. We'll clean it up here while you deal with the Martians at that other moon. We can keep the scientists with us, keep them out of your hair."

Karen appeared next to Charlie with a smile, "So are you going to be hunting Martian special forces or talking computers with Mister Douglas while we deal with their squadron?"

Charlie frowned thoughtfully, "I can multi task."

We all shared a light-hearted chuckle.

Then the same question occurred to all of us at the same time.

Karen had her comm out and to her mouth first, "Kyle, report location."

There was a pause, all of us holding our breath, and then Lieutenant Stranks got on his comm, "We're about a block outside the base. The cameras wanted to get some footage of the abandoned city."

I had my comm out by this time, "Kyle, there are Martian Commandos hiding out in the dome. Get back here."

After a brief, bewildered pause, "Understood."

"Better go make sure they get back," Charlie nodded instantly, then looked to Carly and did some hand gestures. His squad was heading for the doors within seconds.

Marcus Atallah was right on Charlie's heels, "We'll watch your flank."

"We'll keep an eye on the prisoners," Rufus Chang added immediately, nodding to his squad to stay in the lobby.

I looked at Karen and she smiled and shook her head, "We'll let the pros handle this one, I think."

I sure wasn't going to argue with that.

CHAPTER THIRTY-TWO

LINING UP THE PIECES

Charlie walked Kyle, Jocko and Jessica back into the lobby and then let out a sigh, "They were definitely marked for the taking."

Kyle, with some appropriate pride, looked at the Major, "Yes, but my guards were there. We wouldn't have gone quietly if they tried."

"No doubt about that. But I'm happier you didn't have to go at all," Charlie nodded diplomatically, and Kyle couldn't disagree.

"So they were lining up for the attack?" I put the question to Charlie with a frown, and he narrowed his eyes, then shook his head.

"Maybe. I think I saw a spotter on the roof on the far end of the street, probably keeping an eye on all foot traffic coming in and out of the base. I'm guessing they have a squad nearby, trying to figure out how long we'll stay. But they won't know for certain that we know they're out there... so I'm hoping to use surprise to our advantage."

In other words, he wanted to make the Commandos believe he didn't know they were out there — if Branx hadn't given them up, we wouldn't have known, after all — and lull them into a false sense of security.

It was good idea, so I nodded, then glanced at Karen, "Well, it seems we have two problems to deal with."

She bobbed her head once, her gaze shifting to the windows at the front of the building, "We should get the prisoners out of the base, move them up to *Artemis Agrotera* as soon as Zail pulls in. Double his SF to look after them."

"Indeed, don't want the temptation here for the Commandos," I agreed, glancing back at Charlie.

Our line of thought was pretty uncomplicated: if we kept the Martian prisoners in Io base, the Commandos would only have to free them to put us in trouble. Open the brig doors and hand them guns and suddenly it's a company-sized action in the streets of an empty dome.

Not something any of us wanted to see... particularly those of us who'd been at Egesta.

So move the prisoners up to a ship, like *Artemis Agrotera*, lock them in a storage hold on the outer side of the hull, and if they attempted to take over the ship, blow their cargo bay's locks and suck them into space.

It sounds vicious, but as last resorts to save one's ship go, it's pretty effective.

More likely than not, though, the Martians would remain quiet and simply get carried back to a POW camp on Luna, safe and not decompressed.

"Move the scientists up there too? It could be safer." Rufus Chang joined the conversation, and his question was an apt one.

"If Zail can make the room, I'd say yes. And then leave you down here with whatever you need to find and get rid of these Martians," I was looking directly at Charlie as I said it, and he smiled.

"Ooh, a tactical battle royale between two special ops forces in an abandoned city. That's my number two favoritest dream of all time!"

I didn't need to ask about number one, I just *knew* it had to do with Lia. And that was *all* I needed to know.

"Definitely..." I was beginning to nod when I realized Jocko Kent was suddenly standing next to me.

"Now *this* the public is going to want to see."

Charlie's smile suddenly disappeared, "Sorry Jocko, a special ops battle isn't a place for civilians..."

"We'll stay out of your hair. Locked in a brig if you want... just let me get some footage," Jocko's protests were prudent enough, but Charlie continued to shake his head.

"We probably won't be stationary, we'll be moving often, and you'll slow us down."

"You'll have to have a base somewhere though, right? We could be there. It'd probably be in this base, which would be pretty secure. And if you told us it was getting too hot, we'd go immediately. Take a shuttle from the bay if it came to that, go up to *Artemis*..."

"If he gets to be here, I get to be here," Jessica stepped forward to cut him off. "No way he's getting an exclusive."

"Now wait a minute, he's *not here*," Charlie tried to cut in again, but I didn't help.

"Hold on, Charlie's going after thirty-eight Martians and suddenly our squadron mandate to attack an equal force in an epic space battle is chopped liver?" I protested.

Ah, you see, confuse them by pointing out that, while Charlie was cleaning out Io, Karen and I would inevitably be dealing with some sort of Sinope affair — a space battle royale between professional Martian and Defense Command forces in uncolonized space. As you can see, the next book is going to be one that the tactical readers really love (but there'll be stuff in there for non-tactical readers too, of course).

Jessica and Jocko both donned thoughtful expressions as I introduced the conundrum. Hopefully they'd both decide the battle in space was more 'epic', as I'd said, and thus they'd get out of Charlie's hair. I know, I sound conceited saying a space battle is epic while implying Charlie's chess match against the Martian special forces was not, but it was for effect — I didn't want Jocko and Jessica to die.

Charlie and I exchanged hesitant 'oh no did we dodge this one or not' glances, feeling somehow powerless about our impending fate. I know that's ridiculous — we had the guns... er, I mean, *authority*... we could tell Jocko to shut up and go to his room...

But how would that play in the press?

Suddenly Jocko and Jessica were whispering to each other, and my heart rate climbed fast. I had a sixth sense for trouble after all those years storming pirate houses and whatnot... and occasionally that sense was right.

Jocko and Jessica whirled on me all of a sudden, "We've come to an arrangement."

My eyebrows went up, "Really?"

"Yes," Jessica was speaking for them both at this moment. "I'll stay aboard *Wolf* with Jocko's camera crew, Jocko will stay here with my camera crew. We'll share footage, and get both stories."

Interesting — they'd protect their own interests by pairing off with each other. I'm not sure how their networks felt about that setup when they heard about it, but of course you probably have seen one or both of their reports coming from what will be the next book. Interesting stuff, I'd say.

Of course, there remained the minor issue: "What makes you think we're going to let you stay in a hot zone, Jocko?"

The correspondent smiled, "Because you'll want me to do the same sort of story about Special Branch that I did about *Wolf's* crew. What better testament to Charlie's team's skill than to have four civilians kept safe from the Martian elite?"

"Yes, but what if you die?" I was pretty pointed with the question.

"I'll go on record saying I shouldn't have been here in the first place, that I got here by… oh… threatening to go out into the city unescorted if I wasn't allowed access, and that you grudgingly complied. I'll assume all the risk."

How nice of him.

"Well, if I'm not going to get blamed when they shoot him… alright…" Charlie didn't sound overly convinced, but Jocko had a point about the type of coverage we could get.

Better not to argue this too much then, so long as Jocko was indeed promising to stay out of Charlie's hair.

"We can assign some dedicated guards for him, Charlie, so you don't have to worry about keeping one eye on him," Karen put in, glancing then at Kyle Stranks.

The Lieutenant nodded, "Now that we know the score, we can keep him safe."

"Excellent!" Jocko gave a manly thumbs up, then turned back to his camera crew. "Now let's talk shots…"

The reporters moved away to another part of the lobby, leaving Karen, Charlie, Rufus Chang and me together in a loose cluster.

"You know what they say about bad ideas?" Charlie asked, watching them go.

I started to nod, but then stopped, "Actually, no."

He frowned, "Really, the road to hell?"

"That's *good intentions*," Karen was looking at the backs of the reporters too, her arms folded.

Charlie nodded, "Right, whoops. Well, I'm sure Jocko has those too."

This was going to be awkward…

CHAPTER THIRTY-THREE
MOVING THE PIECES

I seem to have adopted a 'pieces' theme in my chapter titles. Just thought I should point that out to you. No good reason to draw your attention to it, really. It's not like I'm overly proud of the theme... I just noticed it... thought you might too. You know, in the interests of openness...

Anyway, while Charlie was in his cabin quickly packing up the last of the gear he'd need to deal with the Martians in the Io dome, Rufus Chang was overseeing the move of the Martian prisoners up to *Artemis Agrotera*; Zail Patel had pushed his drives a little and arrived about ten hours early. Moving the supplies from one of his many cargo bays into the holds of the Jupiter Force ships (and thus replacing stores we'd consumed on the trip out here) he'd made room for the captives.

And yes, he'd made the preparations to blow them into space if they got ambitious. We'd moved an extra seventy SF guards from across the squadron onto *Artemis Agrotera* to assist.

That ship was filling up fast, actually, as the scientists were next to go aboard. They absorbed all the guest quarters and some of another cargo bay, but at least up on the ship they'd be safe. We wanted as few complications as possible on Io to give Charlie a clean board on which to 'play'.

Yes, calling it 'playing' might seem a little crass, but what else would you expect from me?

While all of these important things were happening, Karen and I each had some housekeeping to attend to. I probably should have called this chapter 'Housekeeping', but that'd break the pieces theme, and it'd also sound rather pedestrian.

Stepping into the sickbay was not something I did eagerly — not at all. You may have noticed that I haven't mentioned sickbay much through the first four books of reminiscences... through all of 2231, Doctor Alicia Morgan barely got mentioned. This isn't a comment on her character — Alicia is a professional, very kindly person.

No, I just don't like hospitals. It's not a mortality thing, but a dignity one — believe it or not, I don't like to impose on people, at least not on people I care about. Visiting them when they're at their worst, so to speak, makes me uncomfortable, because I always fear my presence makes them feel uncomfortable. I never like seeing people when I'm badly laid up in a hospital — I don't want them to see me off my feet. Vulnerability issues, you see.

But that said, many people aren't like me. Many people are glad of company when they're feeling poorly. Many people don't have my ego. Kate Levec was such a person.

Now, if this was a movie, Kate Levec would have magically been fixed up by this time (about eighteen hours after her wounding) and to be honest, I wish it had been a movie, because, well, you'll see.

She was lying on a bed in the main sickbay compartment, looking tortured. Not necessarily in pain, though I'm sure there was some of that, but mentally agitated. As I stepped in, she was on her back with her gaze locked on a bulkhead in the corner of the bay, and she didn't look at me as I entered.

Her left hand was lying on her ribs, but I watched as she slid it down over the blanket to her waist, and then she shivered as it passed over the *hole* where flesh should have been. She hurriedly replaced her hand higher up on her ribs, biting her lip and closing her eyes.

"So it'd be pretty stupid of me to ask how you're doing, wouldn't it?" I really had no idea how to open this conversation, and it showed.

Kate's eyes flew open and she looked down past her feet at me, "Uh. I'm… I've been better."

Not what I asked, but imagine how much I didn't care.

"Last I heard, you'll make a solid recovery?" I was too blunt with that question, I know.

Kate tried to smile, "Well, yeah. I… there's nerve damage. I've got problems with both legs, so Doc Morgan's using some regenerative drugs on the nerves, and she figures I'll be in zero-gee physio for at least eight months. And once we get home, I'll get reconstructive surgery to…"

Understandably, she didn't want to finish that sentence.

"Right now, there's arti-skin in there, keeping it closed. It looks pretty… well… disgusting, sir. Having a hole like this… I won't be wearing a swimsuit for a while. Hell, maybe ever, because I'm probably going to have a pretty messy scar when they rebuild it. But at least then I'll be able to wear a belt again…"

I don't think I was able to stop myself from wincing at that comment as I moved to the side of her bed, "Yeah. I can't even imagine what it's like. And forgive me, I sorta don't want to."

"Believe me, it's not worth imagining if you don't have to," she tried another smile, then bit her lip.

I didn't know what to say. Really had no idea. I imagine some of you reading right now would have great and profound words, or better yet, simple and sweet words. Mine always lean too far towards the intellectual, the cerebral — that's my safe zone. I don't mean that to sound arrogant… hell, I count it as a curse. Seeing a good officer like Kate Levec laid up with this sort of wound was terrible, horrible… and yet even now as I describe it, I feel like what I'm writing comes off as a computer spitting out descriptors for pain.

Karen's ability to simply know what needed to be said and done wasn't one I shared.

So I pushed on to things I could safely talk about.

"Do you need me to get in touch with anyone back home for you?" I asked quietly. The Navy would be letting Kate's designated contact person know she'd been injured, but out of necessity, there was never much detail in the form letter message carrying that news. When you deal with a lot of wounded, it's simply impossible to be specific in the first notification.

Kate sighed slowly, "I… um. My mom and stepdad. I don't think my dad will care, he hates that I'm DCN…"

She was blinking thoughtfully, so I tried to help her along with as gentle a tone as I could muster, "Siblings, significant other..."

"My brother, he's a Lieutenant in *Terra Nova* now. And no significant other. Not likely to find one, now that I have extra *curves*."

You know, from the way the first half of this book went, with all the fraternizing and whatnot, you might think that comment to be a light one. It wasn't. It was a real concern for Kate, and I could understand that. Everybody had the right to worry about such things, and someone in her state had more right than most.

"Well," I began to nod slowly, "I'll put those calls in for you, let the family know what's going on."

Kate nodded slowly, "Thanks, skipper."

"And I'll get you moved over to *Artemis Agrotera*. We're going to be going into combat, and I don't want you at risk down here."

Kate actually managed to get a smile to work this time, "Don't need to spare my feelings, skipper. I know you don't want the bed occupied in case a battle casualty needs it."

I matched her weak smile, "See through me, go right ahead..."

I looked away for a moment, then looked back, "Look, Kate, I'm..."

"Hey, we don't need to have this talk, right?"

I stopped and frowned, "Excuse me?"

"The one they have in all the movies, where the guy who hasn't been shot apologizes to the guy who has been shot for something he didn't do... you know... always ends in a touching moment from a buddy-cop movie?"

I think I might have started to turn slightly red, "Of course not."

Kate's smile firmed up a bit, "Thanks for coming to see me, Admiral. You come back to see me again once you kill the Martian squadron, I'll want to hear what I missed."

I grinned, "Gladly."

With that I left Kate Levec, and she probably dropped the brave front she'd donned for my benefit as soon as I left. I felt bad for making her waste energy in an attempt to assuage my guilt.

While I was talking to Kate Levec, Karen was taking a silent tour of *Dominator* with Andrea Kiley. She'd made up some excuse to go over and look in on Andrea, I honestly don't know what... perhaps just a 'visit'. I don't know everything they talked about, and even if I did my attempt to transcribe it would probably come out sounding rather cybernetic and inhuman. Karen's emotional power, one of the greatest powers she carries in her back pocket at all times, defies the ability of my flimsy words.

When she got back, Karen and I talked again about Andrea, and it seemed that our Irish Captain was a bit more worn than when she'd left. I can't tell you how Karen came to this conclusion, but I obviously don't doubt it. It seemed to Karen that, outside the comfort zone of *Wolf*, the troubles Andrea was facing in her personal time *might* be gaining a little more purchase in her professional time. But that was a 'might', and Andrea was still settling in. We decided to give her more time and more space to work on it.

We didn't feel as comfortable about that option as we had when Andrea was with us on *Wolf* though. And with good reason.

Karen had noticed that most of Andrea's crew despised her — it was pretty obvious as the two went through the mighty battleship that virtually all the personnel (except the crew we'd transplanted from other ships of the force) were about ready to spit when they saw our dear Andrea.

Now part of that has to be chalked up to the fact that, with few exceptions, the crew of that ship was comprised of incompetent slackers who, at certain times in Defense Command's history, might have been hung for dereliction of duty. Lucky for them this was no longer First Lord Alexis' time.

Part of it, though, was Andrea's hot anger and cold approval (to answer my editor, that's when the only praise you get is a cool 'good' or 'acceptable', not a warm compliment). She saw the *Dominator* crew as her enemy, with the exception of the familiar faces from the other ships. And while she was increasing efficiency aboard the battleship, it was *not* a happy ship.

Remember the interview Andrea did about the importance of a ship being happy? *Dominator* really wasn't.

But we hoped that, with time and space, she could work through it. If the crew would prove themselves in action for her, then she could perhaps get herself back on track. We should have realized that the odds of anything positive happening were slim, though: we were pinning our hopes on a Jupiter Squadron crew. It should have been obvious to us that being out of the comfortable environment of *Wolf*, Andrea would spend more time staring at her mag with a longing that's scary.

I really don't know how Andrea lived like that. From what I understand — though I'm no expert, and I might be wrong — the persistent contemplation of suicide isn't too common.

Usually, I'd guess the urge comes and goes, or it's powerful, continuous, and it's acceded to.

However you slice it, I think Andrea's survival of all that we've read already, and all that's to come, marks her titanic sense of duty, and her big heart. She told me much later that the one excuse she could always use to keep herself from finishing her own life was the obligation she felt to us — to the Jupiter Force.

I suppose I should feel flattered by that. Being me, I tend to be more terrified. We, a group led by my not-so-brilliant self, were what was keeping her alive? Rather glad I didn't screw that up. I was sure destined to mess up many more things...

But anyway. That was the housecleaning done, so to speak.

Though to call either of these encounters 'housecleaning' seems an insult.

I'm not going to dwell on semantics, let's move on.

CHAPTER THIRTY-FOUR
LOOSE ENDS IN THE EMPIRE

I haven't taken us back to Earth often in this book — not since we did our comm check-in after dropping off *Semaphore*. I should correct that oversight… so here goes.

There hadn't been any more attacks on the homeworld in the two months since we left. John had been able to focus on getting the first of the *Australia*-class corvettes out of the yards (admittedly they were so quickly and poorly finished that they had to go back in, thanks to the civilian contractors who built them) and to redeploy many of his recommissioned frigates and corvettes to Marshal Samuels' command.

Marshal, I should mention, had really refined the convoy systems over those two months. Using many old ships that, under any other set of circumstances should *not* have been flying, he developed an escort force that looked after Imperial commerce between the Belt and Earth. The strategy was replicated for Venus and eventually for our allies, but it all started with Marshal.

Wes Pellew was homing in on that pirate base he'd been hunting, and the reputation of the new Independent Squadron was already making the Sean Cook era in command a distant memory. With skippers like Sharon Stanton working for him, Wes had a good slate of officers, and of course he had his own instincts, which certainly helped him run down the pirates. He'd always been good at finding the bastards.

And while Wes was dealing with the pirates in the Belt, Mik Mikaelsen had faced down a concentrated Martian force that had attempted to strike Hawke Six. He and Lia Hawke were getting along as famously as ever — so much so that she'd accidentally let slip about her relationship with Charlie to him. Of course Mik was as trustworthy as… um… something or someone incredibly trustworthy, so that didn't matter. But he and Lia were definitely making great strides towards securing the independent belt in that sector against further Martian aggression.

Commodore Nora Xiang was doing a fairly similar job in the independent belt over on the Coalition side, but I didn't get to know Nora particularly well, and since I haven't mentioned her at all so far, I'm just going to leave that thread hanging. There are good books you can consult for more on that matter.

Marlene Stoll had Venus buttoned up tight, and was working with Shauna Cass to allot enough shipping and SF to the Forge to really make it formidable again. That was a tricky process — the Venus Squadron was going to contribute many of the first ships to the Forge, but Marlene couldn't afford to weaken her position too much at that stage of 2232. It wouldn't be until later in the year, and early into 2233, that the Forge would be built up properly. We'll get to see more of that next year, so stay tuned.

Finally, Greg was sitting in some enjoyable quiet at Belt Two, taking the opportunity presented by the lull in activity to build his new *Warspite* Squadron (Marshal's escort group had retained the name of Belt Squadron). You probably know the battle honors of the force; this was the quiet time when he started putting it together. Again, stay tuned.

And so that was the update. The immediate little scene I want to mention here came when Daragh Ryan, our dear, insane Second Lord, walked into John's office with a bit of a grin. Yes, if you're Daragh, you can have a 'bit' of a grin.

John was down at Admiralty House for the week, and of course was tackling recruiting paperwork. Parliament had voted to increase the incentive package for people who signed on with Defense Command for two-year terms (the controversial short-service personnel, a concept the Fiora ring opposed in principle, but could hardly turn down in wartime).

Rubbing his eyes, John looked up, "Have you come to end my misery, Daragh?"

Chuckling, Daragh located the remote on John's desk, then turned on the First Lord's screen and switched the station to one of the affiliates carrying Jessica's stories.

Jessica walking in one of *Wolf's* corridors: "…so for all the cool, collected projections of charisma and heroism Rear Admiral Barron presents, it is clear that within lies a man who cares enormously for the men and women under his command."

Cut to me, standing blood-spattered in the sickbay: "Doctor Morgan assures me she will recover. Considerable reconstructive surgery will be necessary. That'll wait until we get back to the Empire."

Intercut of Jessica asking her question (which she had evidently re-recorded after the original interview): "So your operation captured the transmitter, secured the necessary intelligence, and incapacitated over 100 Martian soldiers, at the cost of a few injuries, one of them somewhat serious. And the Martian ships have fled?"

Me, answering the original question, not the re-recorded one: "I let the Martians escape, yes."

Jessica (again re-recorded): "Aren't you being a little harsh on yourself, Admiral? Was there ever any guarantee that even your elite ships could capture them? And haven't you made the most of this opportunity anyway?"

Back to me: "There's no guarantee, no. At the moment I've sent three corvettes out to chase them. We may at least get some intel regarding the Martian base." She cut my reply off there.

Jessica, being framed into the shot by now so she couldn't re-record the question: "So, by ordering your ships forward early, you saved the lives of your officers wounded in a daring landing operation, one of whom it's quite clear from the blood you're wearing you helped save, and you didn't lose the Martian ships, because there was never any guarantee you'd get them in the first place. Instead, they're leading your ships right to their base. Isn't that the case?"

Me: "What?"

Jessica, back in the corridor: "That footage makes a powerful statement about the human being beneath Rear Admiral Barron's reputation. Every officer I speak to on this ship sees the action at Io as a great victory, and yet he is humble, even self-critical."

Cut to Lieutenant Sengooba, who evidently became popular after his first interview appearance: "Of course we would have liked to have captured some of their ships, but as I understand it, there was no way for us to close the range on them. Sometimes luck provides a way, but today we did not get that luck. Instead we captured Io without losing a single man or woman."

Cut to Charlie standing over files of prisoners, talking to Carly and Marcus Atallah, with Jessica's voiceover: "Indeed, 112 prisoners taken without a single Defense Command member fatally wounded, and those wounded in the earlier raid will make a full recovery."

Cut back to Jessica: "When I boarded this ship two months ago, I expected to be greeted by arrogance and self-important conceit. There was caution, but no arrogance. By the half-way mark of the trip I found I was greeted by warmth and true friendliness. Today I have discovered that beneath it all, the core here is one of humanity. I would have expected Rear Admiral Barron to be smiling before our cameras today, speaking of the great victory, of the triumph here at Io. Instead he was covered in the blood of one of his colleagues, unwilling to call the operation a success even though it clearly was. Beneath the celebrity and bravado, that is the Rear Admiral Barron his officers and crews have always seen. That is the reason so many are so loyal to him, and perhaps the reason that he is among the foremost leaders in Defense Command. Reporting from Io base, this is Jessica Qing."

John sat bewildered for a moment. Who could blame him?

"Do you think he saw that before it was sent?" John grinned up at his friend.

A broad smile formed on Daragh's face, "Why, you think he had a hand in it?"

John chuckled and shook his head, "No, because he'll probably shoot Jessica Qing — or at the very least throw her in the brig — if he ever sees it."

Daragh laughed. And both Jessica's celebrity and my own grew massively.

I feel dirty writing about it.

CHAPTER THIRTY-FIVE

THE BREAK

As you've probably figured out from the small number of pages that remain, I'm saving all the battle-royales for *The Sinope Affair*, book seven of these reminiscences. So instead of thinking about the war as I finish off this book, let's see if I shot Jessica — or at least brigged her — after seeing the report.

I hadn't been on the bridge when Felicia Khalid and Jim Hannigan had sent the report down to *Semaphore* — by this time I, perhaps foolishly, had begun to trust Jessica and Jocko. And I was distracted too... and perhaps I didn't really want to see the report until it was sent. Not that there was anything I could really have done about it, one way or another. Before seeing it, I'd still expected it to be a shot at my poor leadership. My inability to detach myself from one person being wounded.

Believe me, that was all I could think about. My emotional connection to my crew was too strong for me to overcome, and because of that we'd let the Martians get away.

And then there was poor Kate. I was rather conflicted about all this, I won't deny it, and I'm sure the good officers out there are scolding my inability to get a better grip. Some are probably saying 'told you so — get that friendly with your people and you'll pay the price'.

Well if any of you thought I was under the impression I was a perfect CO, you were wrong. Perfect might be the word for Karen, but not for me.

Speaking of perfect... sorry, I mean speaking of Karen, she was lying on my bed in her usual pose, smiling at the display as Jessica wrapped up her report. The vid froze as the last seconds ticked by, then went to a black *Wolf*Net screen.

"Jesus, I'm going to shoot her. Or lock her in the brig..." John had that much right, amusingly enough. "Or maybe I could sue her."

Yes, these were actual thoughts going through my head, and words coming out of my mouth. No sarcasm.

Karen rolled onto her side and propped her head up on her hand, "You need to stop this. You're reopening wounds I was supposed to have closed with a hug. I didn't think bigger guns would be necessary to reset your brain, but if you're going to..."

I wasn't quite listening (probably should have been), "But... I mean. She's spinning this to make me look the hero. I'm going to be her cash cow — she gives everybody a reason to like me again, and then she becomes the heroine who discovered it. Every famous scumbag in the Empire's going to want her to do a report on them, to reveal the inner humanity under the incompetence."

Karen's smile was gone when my eyes next darted to her face, and I stopped.

"You finished?" she asked quietly.

"No. But I'll pause so you can say something."

"You have to stop this. The only thing wrong with how you reacted to this whole shooting is that you're *obsessing over it*. If anything's damaging your ability to command right now, it's that. I don't care what you think you turned into when she got hit, you still were shoulder-to-shoulder with me in a firefight minutes after. You were still giving good orders. You were still *you*, and still doing what you needed to do. It's alright that you were thinking about Kate. Stop condemning yourself for it."

A long speech, and one that sounded oh so wonderful coming from Karen. Her soft words were warming. My chin sunk, and I nodded once, "Alright."

I was lying to her, of course. It wasn't alright. I didn't even believe *her* just then, and that should tell you something about the epic scope of my own self-critical nature. One talking to doesn't sort me out. Not even from Karen.

But part of Karen's magic at times like those was that she knew I was stubborn and stupid... and she had God's own patience. She didn't expect me to hear it once and be done with it, she just made sure she kept reminding me of what she thought. And that... that saved my life many times.

I know that sounds overdramatic, but it's true. I've said it before, I'll say it now, and I'll say it again and again before we get to... well... to that dark time: Karen saved my life many times during the war.

So she knew my nod was a lie, but she accepted it with a smile.

Turning over sufficiently to sit up on my bed, Karen's warm smile shined, "And yes, Jessica's over the top. But she's not wrong: everyone on this ship would die for you, you know. Probably everyone in the squadron. They know you care about all of them. She's *not wrong*."

Now Karen was lying. Well... dammit, I don't know if she was or wasn't. I was so tied up in knots. She was saying this to try to lessen the strain, so I lied in return, with another nod.

Though with her smile beaming like the sun, I wasn't in much of a position to argue.

"Don't you think that sort of loyalty is more important than being overly detached, particularly when, being true to that loyalty didn't have any ill effects this time?" she asked softly, and I let out a long sigh.

"Next time, or the time after... I'm going to get people killed if I don't start getting a better grip..."

"After Egesta, you're never going to be completely detached again. And I think you'll be hard-pressed to find anyone in this squadron, and after this story, in the *Empire* to tell you that doing everything you could for one life was the wrong move."

The scary thing about that statement is how true it proved to be, under certain circumstances, in the future.

Rubbing my forehead and sighing, I shook my head, "I don't know. I... don't know."

Karen was abruptly crouching next to my chair, "Yes, you do."

Well I didn't, but I wasn't going to argue any more just then. So I backed out of the argument, leaving it unresolved in favor of the more immediate satisfaction of her proximity.

"What would I do without you?" I smiled as I asked the cliché, predictable, and yet painfully honest question.

Karen smiled, "Probably nothing very different, you'd just sleep better."

I chuckled and let out a long breath. That wasn't true, but, well, as you can tell, there'd be no resolution to this. I'd have to face the loss of so much more before I found an end to these problems, and you'll just have to wait to read more about that. Wait a while indeed.

We stopped trying to confront my self-absorbed, self-critical, self-pity and got some food. We had big days to come, but for now *Wolf* just floated easily over Io.

AFTERWORD

So two classic battles are to come in *The Sinope Affair* — both of which are now tactical scenarios used at the Defense Command Academy to teach cadets some of the basics do's and don'ts. Not to worry, though, if you're a non-military reader, there are all sorts of other things happening, as you can probably guess.

I have to admit, I'm rather surprised by how this book ends. Until I sat down to write about the incident with Kate at Io, I'd almost forgotten the considerable impression those events had on my psyche back then. In retrospect it makes sense — coming from Egesta, Andrea wasn't the only one bearing scars. My editors think I'm drumming this point to death, that I'm over-doing it. I probably am. I suppose as I look back now, I see this incident with Kate as the first sign of much trouble to come... my reaction then seems a bigger problem in retrospect than it was at the time.

But you and I both know what comes later, and you can probably understand how, looking back, I see Io as the first airing of issues that would later be so dangerous. I suppose I'll wait to talk more about those when we get to them. It'll be a while yet.

Anyway, *The Sinope Affair* will introduce the very famous battles we fought out around Jupiter, of which there have been no fewer than five vid and movie versions. Battle-royales do seem to be popular on the screen, and I have to say, two of these movie versions weren't terrible. Coming from me, you realize that's rather a compliment!

Anyway, I'll see you in the next book. Keep well until then!

THE
SINOPE
AFFAIR

THE AUTOBIOGRAPHICAL REMINISCENCES OF
ADMIRAL THE LORD KEN BARRON FOR 2232

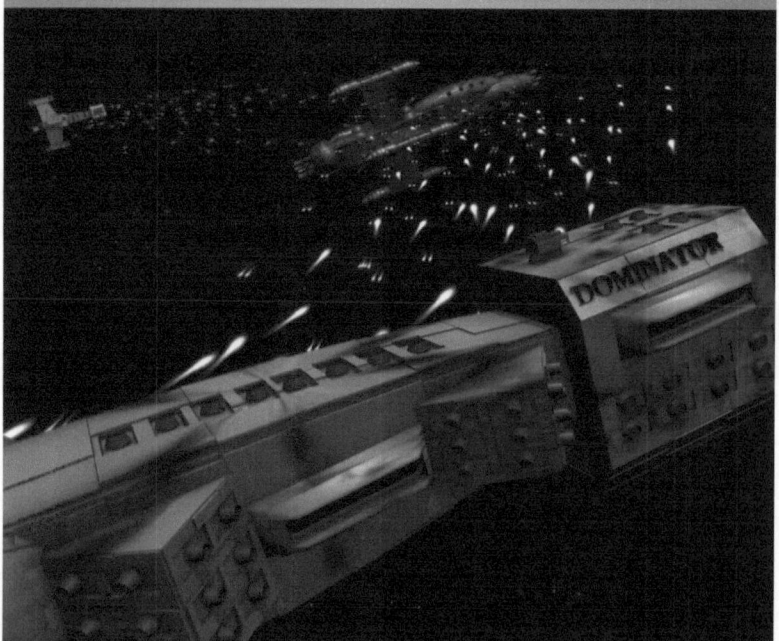

THE MARTIAN WAR - 7

KENNETH TAM

FROM THE AUTHOR

Here we are, at the big battles promised at the end of *The Jupiter Patrol* (or *The Jupiteer Patrol*, if you got your hands on one of those 'special' first editions!). This book marks the first time our characters really tangle with the Martians on level terms, and you can be sure the Jupiter Force is not going to come away unscathed. As much as I wish all these great men and women could get through this book without a scratch... well, that just couldn't happen.

The Sinope Affair moves fast — it moved fast when I was drafting it, and when the editors and readers were preparing it for release, and I think it still must now. The story, with its concurrent battle plot lines, just keeps sprinting along... and I'm very glad it does.

One thing I find repeatedly when I study records of engagements is how quickly time can pass once battle is joined. If anything, I hope this book captures how impossibly quickly things can appear to happen when an engagement begins, and how little time there can be to make decisions that will affect the lives of men and women under your command.

Anyway, on to the usual thanks.

To repeat from previous books: many of the characters you'll read about in this book are based on real-world friends of mine, and these characters will be immune from death for the entire series. Given their immunity, and my desire to create suspense, I'm not going to list who they are — they already know who they are. That said, you can probably guess some of their identities if you really want to. Thanks to all of those fine people — I hope your characters do you proud!

This book would not have happened without the excellent advice offered by my good friend, Peter Caron. All the brilliant moves you read about in the battle for the Io dome can trace their way back to his recommendations (any bad ideas were entirely mine!). Charlie Peters' fight against the Commandos is really a tribute to Peter.

Particular thanks as well to Wes Prewer, for the fantastic artwork that you see on the cover. Wes' images have really helped give an identity to the *Defense Command* series, and there's no better demonstration of his skill than in the battle scene he's produced for *The Sinope Affair*.

Last, and most important, thanks to my parents and Iceberg partners, Jacqui and Peter. One problem I have with a series as long as Defense Command is I'm running out of different ways to articulate how great they are... because... they're... great.

They are, for instance, much greater than the language skills I just demonstrated.

And Atlas... as always, thanks buddy.

– Kenneth Tam

FOREWORD

So we find ourselves at Jupiter. We traveled here during *The Jupiter Patrol* (which, if you got a first edition, was called *The Jupiteer Patrol* on the spine… allow me to pause and shake my head at my publishers for a moment… and on we go…). That trip, as you know, was interesting. Reporters and bad command decisions on my part and such. There was a lot of romancing, too, which was a bit of a surprise. But now we're firmly invested at Io, and our Jupiter Force is ready to tangle with the Martians.

Welcome to *The Sinope Affair*: a book of battles royale. Or is that battle royales? I suppose it doesn't matter.

Sinope, for those of you not familiar with the infinite minor facets of our solar system (for shame!) is the twenty-fourth, or twenty-fifth… I should really check my facts before I write this… moon of Jupiter. It's a tiny rock, only about thirty kilometers across. That means it's just big enough to hold a miniature dome full of supplies to support the squadron the Martians had put out at Jupiter.

But that's not the only interesting fact about the name 'Sinope'. In Greek mythology, Sinope was a virgin who tricked both Zeus and Apollo out of sleeping with her (not bad, tricking two gods like that). Much more topically, Sinope is also a port city in Turkey, sitting on the coast of the Black Sea. Why is that relevant? Look up the Sinope affair of 1853, you'll see it was the site of a nasty Naval battle between the Russians and the Ottoman Turks — a battle in which the Russians massacred the Turkish frigates. Unpleasant. It was such a bloodbath that British newspapers picked up the story, and it's considered to be part of the reason the British and French launched the Crimean War against Russia in 1854.

Sinope seems to have quite a legacy.

And in keeping with that tradition, there's going to be a lot of ship fighting in this book — we're going after the Martian squadron that hit Io, and the prisoners they took from our dome. In a situation with no civilian traffic to worry about, no strategic bases to protect, and no reason *not* to trash the local environment, this is (according to tacticians) a perfect sort of scenario.

And of course, it isn't just perfect in space: Charlie Peters also fights his exemplary anti-Commando action on Io in this book. Once again, with no complicating factors like civilians or a need to protect property, Charlie is free to do whatever he needs to do to get those Commandos out of the dome. Another ideal setup in the tactical books — a real chess game. Just straightforward fighting, us versus them, with no one pulling punches because there are no civilians around to get caught in the crossfire. It's rare in history that you get these sorts of 'perfect' campaigns… only one I can think of at the moment (though there are almost inevitably more) is Montgomery's desert campaign against Rommell, in the Second World War.

So to wrap this up, this is going to be a book full of shooting — what Charlie Peters recently assured me was 'destined to be a page turner.' But then what does he know — he thinks raccoons are a threat to Imperial Security!

CHAPTER ONE

A SLOW START

Charlie had a small duffle in his hand, and his MAG-90 was dangling from its vest clip as he walked through the last few corridors to the lock that was connected to the Io base. His squad was waiting for him as he arrived, each of its eleven other officers carrying a similar duffle, and keeping their MAG-90s equally accessible.

"Alright," he nodded to them as he stopped, "we all set?"

The officers looked at each other and started nodding, and then Captain Carly Henderson, Charlie's XO (who we've seen many times in these books, I believe) spoke for the group, "Ready to go."

Not too flashy or flowery, I'll admit, but these weren't people prone to overly romanticizing things. And more to the point, they were Special Branch officers going into a situation that even they weren't entirely accustomed to.

Think about it like this: Charlie's Special Branchers were some of the most elite special forces in the Empire, but their missions so far had mainly seen them taking on untrained, poorly-trained or regularly-trained adversaries. Now they were going after Commandos... other special forces. This was going to be a fight between two forces who knew many, many, *many* ways to kill.

For the first time, I believe, some of the Special Branch officers on Charlie's team actually thought they might *not* come back from an op. Of course, none would admit to that, but it was the sense I got when I studied their faces.

I managed to look at their faces, by the way, because Karen and I turned up just after Carly spoke. They looked less relaxed than I'd ever seen them... though let's not kid ourselves, they still looked pretty relaxed.

"Alright, get going. I'll be down as soon as I talk to Ken," Charlie bobbed his head towards the airlock, then turned around.

I failed to set that up well enough, I think: Charlie shouldn't have known we were behind him — we hadn't intentionally snuck up, but we weren't very loud in our approach. A mere mortal probably would have turned around and been surprised to see us, but as a Special Brancher, Charlie had 360-degree vision.

It'd come in handy on Io.

"You're all set?" by this time Karen had bribed me through much of my mental tumult with her warm smile, so my tone was less grim than it would have been hours before.

Charlie nodded evenly, "We're going down now. I checked with Captain Patel and he has everything we'll need. Marcus is already there with his squad, too, and with the extras you got us. Any SF I need I'll take from *Artemis* when the time comes. Only thing I'm not sure of is where Jocko is."

Whoa whoa whoa, slow down.

Um. That is to say: I better dissect everything Charlie just said to make sure it's clear

— I followed what he was saying because it was in context, while you might need to be brought up to speed because it's entirely out of context for you.

First, 'Captain Patel' is, of course, Zail Patel, of *Artemis Agrotera*, the combat storeship that had accompanied the Jupiter Force out here. His ship was sitting over Io now, holding more than 100 Martian prisoners as well as the scientists who'd been recovered from the Io dome. Zail also had all the supplies Charlie could possibly need — readily-available supplies were one advantage Charlie had that the Martian Commandos didn't — and extra SF, if Charlie needed them.

Next, 'Marcus' was Marcus Atallah, the Major commanding *Cheetah's* Special Branchers. Marcus was going to be down there with Charlie for this operation, and though they were the same rank, it was tacitly understood that Charlie had overall command. Marcus was a great officer, but Charlie had more experience, and this was going to be his mission.

Moving on, the 'extras' weren't extras like on a movie set, they were the nine Special Branchers who'd been brought in from the company that had provided us Rufus Chang… sorry, I'm going to have to ask you to remember back to *The Gallant Few*. If you recall, *Lion* lost three Special Branchers to pregnancy during February of 2232, so we'd brought in Rufus Chang and two officers from a company of Special Branchers that had arrived in the Belt to supply Wes Pellew's new Independent Squadron with its elite strike capacity. That company had nine more people than Wes needed to fill his squadron, so I'd managed to get those extra officers for our mission out here. Now they were proving useful — Charlie was going to have almost a whole extra squad on the ground.

Spinning off from that, while Charlie landed with thirty-three Special Branchers, Rufus Chang would take over as senior Special Brancher in the Jupiter Force, so he'd be leading any attacks on the Sinope base, with the forty-two officers left on *Lion*, *Friendly*, *Lady Grace*, *Honesty*, *Trusty* and *Pictou*. We were dividing our Special Branchers, which wasn't ideal, but it was very necessary.

Finally, going back to Charlie's dialogue, the question of where 'Jocko' was… well, of course, 'Jocko' was Jack Kent, one of the two reporters who'd come out to Io with us, and who was (despite everyone's better judgment) going to be covering Charlie's op from the (hopefully) safe base we were setting up in the Io dome's HQ building.

"Well, it won't be a tragedy if he misses his chance to get down there," Karen offered a tight smile with those words. She knew how much Charlie *didn't* want to have a reporter on Io with him — one burden he really didn't need.

But the media had 'full access', and if Jocko wanted to get himself killed, who were we to try to stop him?

Sorry, that was in bad taste.

"We'll be up here for two more hours, and then I'm going looking for the Martians," I followed Karen's words quickly with my own. "If he's not down there in that time, he's stuck with us."

Charlie nodded slowly, "Yeah, I'd say go sooner, but…"

There was no real 'but' he could append to that. We couldn't have left sooner: we had to get our SF back aboard, make sure that the scientists and prisoners had moved safely up to *Artemis Agrotera*, and finish emptying the Io base computers of any useful information. I think I set some of that up at the end of *The Jupiter Patrol*, and it was still being done at this stage.

"So…" I let the word hang out there for a moment after Charlie's last comment had trailed off, and then I glanced at Karen and looked back to Charlie.

"So…" he repeated the word and nodded slowly, the way you nod when you have no way of saying what you're thinking… the philosophical, slow nod.

"So…" Karen's smile loosened a bit, and she (being made of the stuff of goddesses) was much more able to follow that syllable with language, "…you be safe down there, Charlie. Safe as you can."

He nodded, "We'll see how that goes. You two look after each other. Particularly if you're landing on Sinope, because I know if you can, *you* will. Go down there with Rufus, and do what he says. I hear only good things about his abilities. Listen to him."

At that point Karen and I got the sheepish 'aw do we have to?' looks on our faces, and rather paternally, Charlie nodded, "*Yes*, you listen to Rufus."

Trying to lighten the moment, Karen and I both heaved overdramatic sighs, then nodded in a sullen fashion. It was probably a little too much for the occasion, but Charlie took it in the right mood, and smiled.

Then I realized I actually *did* have something important to tell him, "By the way… on the subject of collateral damage…"

Charlie stopped his nod and half-frowned, "Yes?"

"Have fun. If we can't reoccupy this base, I don't think the Admiralty's going to complain too much. If you know what I mean."

This was my bright idea of the moment. We hated having to defend Io, and there was nothing critical out here that couldn't be done in the asteroid belt, so if collateral damage incurred while the base was recaptured happened to render it uninhabitable without a great deal of financial investment, we'd probably be allowed by Parliament to abandon it. Finally.

If Charlie wanted to flatten everything in the dome, that was alright with me. And now that I was a Rear Admiral, it 'being alright' with me was actually official authorization.

Scary thought, but so it was.

Smiling at the carte blanche I'd just handed him, Charlie nodded, "Excellent. Alright, I'm going to go. You both be good…"

He extended his hand to Karen, and after she shook it, he turned it towards me. We both smiled as we shook hands, and then he turned and entered the airlock.

It was going to be weird, cruising into battle without Charlie, but it was something we needed to get used to.

As the lock closed behind Charlie, I glanced at Karen, "Any sinking feelings that we're never going to see him again?"

It was a legitimate question. At that point, I was still too preoccupied with my own deficiencies and inabilities to detach myself from my people, so I couldn't tell if I had a bad feeling about Charlie's mission.

Karen frowned at me, "Don't say things like that!"

"But…"

"Shh!" she held up her hands. "We're not going to give fate any ideas, right?"

Shrugging, I nodded, "Alright then."

We turned and walked away from the lock.

Chapter Two

Dominator

Before I start this, I just want to say that Andrea Kiley has approved and encouraged everything I write about her in this book. I say this for two reasons: first, because I want to make sure you don't think I'm attacking her, because of course I'd never do that. Second, I think it's important you know that she's willing to be open and honest about these things — things that the media never really paid attention to or heard about, but things which continue to haunt her.

With that ominous introduction, let's begin...

Few would suggest that Andrea Kiley is *not* a lovely woman. Since she'd joined the Belt Squadron years prior, and particularly once she'd taken command of *Friendly* after my promotion to Captain of *Wolf*, she'd been very popular in the media. She was known as the bashful Irish girl, with the raven black hair and the bright smile. Every time she was seen in public (on red carpets at our annoying PR parties or wherever) men showed up to propose to her. Just like that.

As one press observer said, "She's the girl you want to take home to meet your parents."

Now, why do I introduce her in this book that way? Just to remind you of where she had come from.

What you see if you watch the surveillance vids from the corridors of *Dominator*, the battleship she'd taken over in *The Jupiter Patrol*, will scare you — if you remember that innocent Irish girl.

I mean, it's not that she's grown horns... it's much worse than that really. She still looks like herself, but then she doesn't. It starts with her eyes, because though physically they haven't changed, they're darker. Much darker. And everything about the way she carries herself has an edge. No longer does she seem innocent, she seems... dangerous.

She hadn't been like this when she'd been on *Wolf* on the cruise out to Jupiter — she'd hidden her edge, knowing we'd have panicked if we'd seen it. No, she saved this new, vicious persona for the mainly incompetent crew of her new ship. They would learn to be good at their jobs, or the slight little Irish girl would personally space them.

"Who exactly was it who taught you how to prepare a mag for fire, Chief?"

While Karen and I were seeing Charlie off, Andrea had been touring (or storming) around *Dominator*, checking in on maintenance as the battleship prepared to boost with the Jupiter Force. The port side mags, though, weren't being properly serviced. And Andrea wasn't going to stand for that.

The Chief, whose name I will leave out, bristled, "I was in this Navy before you were born, don't tell me how to run my fuckin' mags, miss!"

A Jupiter Squadron (not Jupiter *Force*) Chief, this non-com had less respect for an officer than she should have. Remember, the Jupiter Squadron had been the dumping ground for many of our worst personnel, and Andrea's crew on *Dominator* was composed mainly of these bad sorts.

It wasn't helpful.

Now, you have to appreciate this scene as it appears on the surveillance record: Andrea is standing on her own, looking up almost a foot at the very tall NCO, and this older, thickly-built woman is glaring back at small little Andrea. The rest of the mag crew's members are standing behind the Chief, with a variety of grins and satisfied expressions — to them, their Chief (their ring leader) was putting a bitchy and jumped-up little officer in her place.

Andrea's response?

She leaned forward slightly, gesturing the Chief to lean in too — as if to quietly say something. As the Chief turned her head slightly to one side to hear what Andrea had to say, our innocent Irish girl jabbed the Chief in the throat with an open hand, and as the bigger woman's knees buckled in surprise, Andrea took her by the lapel and twisted her around, dropping her onto her back on the deck.

The shock of the harsh landing caused the Chief to gasp in surprise, and as the NCO's mouth opened, Andrea drove the barrel of her mag right in there, then planted a knee roughly on her ribs.

"I didn't ask you when you were born, *Chief*, I asked if you have a fucking clue about how to go into combat. And being that a wee little Irish girl could blow the back of your head off right now, I'm willing to bet you haven't a sweet fucking clue, now have you?"

Wide-eyed, the Chief didn't respond, so Andrea smiled in a sweet, sinister fashion, then twisted her mag in the woman's mouth, driving it down a little further and causing the Chief to gag and start to flail.

"What's that, Chief? Is that you agreeing with me?"

Panicking completely now, the Chief bit down on the barrel of the mag, chipping two teeth on the alloy casing. Trying unsuccessfully to scream out in pain around the gun, she gave up and started nodding as best she could.

Andrea continued to lean on her chest, considering the woman's desperate state with very cold amusement. The mag crew stood by in shock. They weren't going to interfere, no matter what — if the Captain was this insane, she'd kill many of them herself if they tried to jump her, and if she survived their attack, she'd have them all dead. No, they weren't budging.

"I think you're saying yes. I hope you are," Andrea slowly pulled the mag out of the Chief's mouth, and then wiped the blood that had smeared on it off on the woman's tunic. Standing slowly, she shook her head.

When she looked up at the mag crew again, every one of the spacers took a step back. Under different circumstances it would have been funny. But it wasn't funny this time.

"By the Articles of Empire, and by regulations pertaining to a fleet at war, any disobedience or disrespect to a senior officer can be considered mutinous, and is grounds for execution. You will *obey my orders*, or by God I will space all of you," she said those words in a soft, cold, matter-of-fact tone, and the crew didn't know what to do.

Some people have a tough time understanding their reaction — if these were rough and tumble spacers, couldn't they just have jumped her? Well, possibly, but they weren't rough and tumble. They were mostly incompetent and cowardly, and having just watched their ringleader get broken put a certain fear into them.

Andrea appeared insane. They believed she *would* space them, so they quietly shuffled back to work.

The Chief on the ground started to recover from her shock, and began to wail. Andrea looked down with what I can only describe as disgust. Holstering her mag, she shook her head, "Get yourself to sickbay."

She then left.

Andrea was *not* herself. As she'd told the mag crew, her actions were legal under the more archaic tomes of the Articles of Empire. Remember, the Articles still allow torture and murder, under certain circumstances, so it's not as though she was bending the letter of the law against the spirit of the law. Ian Hawke had loved to do things like this back when he was commanding cruisers… but the fact that I'm comparing something Andrea did to something Ian Hawke would have loved to do is itself almost inconceivable.

This was *Andrea*.

No, this was Andrea without a net. Without her good officers and crews around her, without her friends keeping her on the level.

She still couldn't sleep properly. She was still keeping herself as numb as she possibly could so that she wouldn't remember what she'd seen on Egesta, just half a year prior. And aboard *Dominator*, that meant she was focusing on the job of turning a poorly-crewed battleship into an effective combatant.

After all she'd seen, shoving a gun into the mouth of an NCO was nothing. Nothing at all.

Word spread fast among the *Dominator* crew about this incident. If you recall from *The Jupiter Patrol*, 120 of the women and men aboard the ship had actually been sent over from Jupiter Force ships, so they were mainly Belt Squadron veterans and part of our extended 'family'. Those people were worried about Andrea — they didn't lose faith in her, they worried for her. And not because they realized how badly she was affected by the memories of Egesta, but because they assumed (understandably, but frankly incorrectly) that for innocent Andrea to go off like that, the provocation must have been considerable.

In other words, they were worried that the 466 spacers and officers who'd been aboard *Dominator* before were turning on Andrea, and were going to try to mutiny, because Andrea was demanding they work to high standards.

This was not good for the ship. As Andrea said in an interview last book, a happy ship fights well. But now 120 members of *Dominator's* crew were suspicious of most of their shipmates. These Belt Squadron spacers figured the Jupiter Squadron people were lazy, and were going to rebel…

See how this is stacking up? Andrea had gone overboard, but the Belt Squadron protects its own. And frankly, no one aboard the ship would have believed that Andrea struck without sufficient provocation. So the crew grew even more divided as the blame was passed around.

Think this was good news for *Dominator*?

Yeah, exactly. Andrea's ship was not in a good way.

And neither was she.

CHAPTER THREE

THE MARTIAN SKILL

If you'll recall, the three original Jupiter Force corvettes (*Friendly, Lady Grace* and *Honesty*) had been sent out after the fleeing Martian ships at the end of *The Jupiter Patrol*. They were still in pursuit about an hour after Charlie had headed down to Io, and after Andrea had been… short-tempered. I shouldn't play coy about that, an hour after she'd nearly killed one of her NCOs.

Anyway, Matt Baxter was standing on Andrea's old bridge (and my old bridge too, I suppose) aboard *Friendly*, and was getting a bad feeling about the chase. He couldn't put his finger on why, because generally gut feelings don't come with explanations, but he just didn't like it.

The Martians were running so *neatly* — they didn't seem panicked to see us… it felt to him as though they'd been expecting to do this.

"Anyone else getting a bad feeling about this?" he was in front of the Battlelink screens at the head of *Friendly's* bridge, and he glanced up at Elise De Winter of *Lady Grace* and Aaron Ashby of *Honesty* as he spoke.

Technically speaking, Elise was the most senior of the three, and was thus in command of the mission. Her frown was the deepest, "I'm not sure, Matt… they do seem to be running quite… well."

"Very organized. Very disciplined," Aaron Ashby nodded in agreement.

Matt nodded his head slowly as well. The Martians were conducting themselves with a great deal of professionalism. They were behaving as well as we'd have behaved — as the Jupiter Force would have — under threat. They were in close formation, keeping their speed at a precise 196 kps and not doing anything that would suggest panic or surprise.

Elise had ordered the chasing corvettes to remain as far back as possible, to stay out of what we assumed was Martian detection range. But did our red enemies know they were being followed? Did they realize they were leading Defense Command right back to their base?

"Something…" Matt said the word under his breath, then folded his arms across his chest. "Marie, where's the nearest rock they could use for an ambush?" he addressed that question to Lieutenant Marie Gavet, *Friendly's* Sensors and Communications Officer (who'd been an Ensign in my last days aboard the ship), and she looked up from behind her consoles.

"I do not see anything in local space that could *hide* an ambush force… the nearest moon is four hours ahead," she answered quietly.

"Four hours. I think we need to be watchful of that moon. Seems to me an ambush would suit them," Matt looked back to his fellow Commanders, and they both nodded.

"We wait," Aaron Ashby agreed.

But they didn't.

A moment later the Martians reversed course — quickly.

"The Martians are coming around!" Marie Gavet's alert was urgent, and Matt moved over to the main screen, watching as the Martian ships he'd been chasing — three destroyers and two destroyer escorts — reversed their pods and spun in space, then fired their engines to reverse their course.

In other words, they turned around to see who was following.

"Reverse drives *now,*" Elise De Winter barked on the Battlelink, and, with a frown, Matt issued the same order to Tony Zhow, the Helm and Navigation Officer who'd taken over on *Friendly* when Shelby McLaws had moved to *Wolf.*

Friendly's drive thrust reversed direction almost immediately, my old dapper little ship vibrating as it was asked to perform the violent maneuver. Matt squared his feet shoulder width apart but stayed ramrod straight, not letting the shaking affect him as he watched the turn.

Of course the Martians didn't have to wait to ambush them; with five ships to Elise De Winter's three, they already had quite an advantage in firepower.

But they *didn't* have an advantage in speed.

"We're at full reverse," Tony Zhow reported to Matt with a nod, and on the monitors, Elise De Winter and Aaron Ashby soon announced the same.

The three veteran corvettes began backing away as the Martians started to accelerate in their direction.

"This doesn't look terribly good, now does it?" Matt shook his head with a sigh. "Are we staying out of their sensor range?"

Marie Gavet shook her head, "I can't tell, sir. We have only guesses about their maximum detection range…"

"They could just be checking to see if they're being followed," Aaron Ashby suggested on Battlelink, and Matt nodded.

"A crazy Ivan, yes," the black Englishman concurred. "Well, they won't be able to catch us. But I'm damned if I want to let them chase us all the way back to Io."

A 'crazy Ivan' is an old Cold War submariner term for a Russian submarine turning through 180 degrees to check to see if it's being followed. I learned it from a very old, excellent movie about a fictional Soviet sub called *Red October*… but I think Matt actually read it in a book or something. It's a reasonably well known expression among fleet officers, from one source or another.

The other two Commanders recognized it, and again nodded. Matt rubbed his chin thoughtfully, "Shall we see how long they chase, then decide if they can see us?"

Elise De Winter looked off screen for a moment, thinking things through, then nodded, "That's what we'll have to do."

The corvettes continued to reverse towards Io.

Back at Io, we were wondering how the corvettes were faring. They'd been out chasing for several hours and we hadn't had an update from them yet. The silence could be taken as good news — Matt or one of the others would definitely have commed us if something untoward was happening. Assuming, that is, he could.

"Still nothing from Matt," were Jim Hannigan's first words to us when we arrived on the bridge.

Karen and I looked at each other, raising our eyebrows briefly.

"Alright," I headed for the screens at the front of the bridge and turned to Felicia Khalid, our provisional Sensors and Communications Officer (Kate Levec, remember, was very much out of action), "Felicia, signal all skippers, I want a realtime conference in an hour."

Lieutenant Khalid was in slightly over her head. As I think I mentioned in *The Jupiter Patrol*, she'd been passed over for the job of *Wolf's* Sensors and Communications Officer during our first round of selections because she'd lacked overall experience. Now there was no choice but to appoint her — Jim was in a critical role as XO, so he couldn't return to his old post, and Kate wouldn't be able to walk again, let alone do that job, for weeks.

"Yes, sir. Does the conference include Captain Patel, sir?" Felicia's clarification question was a fair one, but it was the sort that Kate or Jim wouldn't have had to ask. Lieutenant Khalid had a lot of on-the-job learning to do to get comfortable in the SCO position.

Karen fielded that question for me, and her understanding tone was just right under the circumstances, "No need to call Zail, Felicia."

The Lieutenant nodded, then hesitantly started giving orders.

Oh, to answer a question from one of my editors, Felicia hadn't actually applied for the Sensors and Communications Officer job — no one had. Karen and I passed her over without her ever knowing we'd considered her, so this wasn't a situation where she'd finally gotten the promotion she'd been chasing.

Anyway, despite being flung into the deep end now, she was learning on the fly, and doing her job. You can't ask for much more than that.

"Jim," I turned to him now, and he managed to neutralize what I think was a concerned expression at Felicia's question when I looked at him. "We need to evac Kate over to *Artemis Agrotera*. We may need her med bed if we get into hot action."

With only a nod, Jim turned back to his operations consoles and began delivering orders. I turned to the main screen and looked at the ship dispositions in the space over Io, taking a deep breath as I did.

Karen appeared next to me, "Think the scouts are alright?"

She was referring of course to Matt, Elise and Aaron, and I glanced at her with a half-shrug, "Those ships can sidestep any sort of hell the Martians can send at them. I just need to know what sort of hell the Martians have to send…"

With a nod, Karen folded her arms, "We'll have to wait and see how good they are."

"Yes, we will."

A few hours away from us, our corvettes were running…

CHAPTER FOUR

SETTING UP HQ

Wolf undocked about an hour later, just as we were getting online for our realtime conference. I'll talk about that conference itself next chapter, but first I think checking in with Charlie would be a good idea.

He'd just finished pacing around the 'secure area' they'd set up in the Io HQ building, looking to see if there was anything he'd missed — any way in, any access point or vent, duct or window… anything that could have given the Martian Commandos a way through the perimeter.

Charlie had become somewhat weary of Io's buildings during that raid on the old command structure outside the dome, when Kate and a few other SF had taken hard hits. The Martians on the ground here weren't incompetent, they were *Commandos*. If there was a way in, they'd be able to find it, as sure as he'd have been able to.

But there wasn't, so now he was addressing his people in one of the level's open areas: "Alright, I think we're fine here. We'll hold this sector, and make the airlocks on fifteen our secure access point for runs to *Artemis*."

The area he'd designated really was quite secure: it was on the fourteenth floor of the Defense Command Headquarters tower that jutted out of the HQ building on the 'north' side of the dome. If you can picture it, floors fifteen and above stood on the outside of the dome of the colony, allowing ships and shuttles to dock and move supplies down to the town. Fourteen and below remained inside the dome.

With all the lifts to ground level under control (and rigged to be blown if they were taken by enemy forces), this floor was more or less secure from attack from below. Lifts aside, there were only two stairwells to hold, and they were being barricaded even as he spoke. There were no large ventilator shafts — since part of the building jutted into the void, large ducts would have been a huge decompression risk. Instead the area had the same sort of narrow, higher-pressure atmospheric systems found on DC ships, which were perhaps less fresh than outside Earthgreen air, but which were still more than adequate.

The fourteenth floor also had a medical triage center (it was the floor to which, after action, casualties unloaded at the airlocks on the levels above would be brought for first aid) and some food and sleeping setups. Perfect all round.

The rest of the HQ complex would be considered unsecured, since it'd be altogether too simple for the Martian Commandos to slip in on a lower floor and hide until they could pounce.

'Unsecured', to Jocko Kent, meant *off limits*… wait, you say. Jocko? Yes, remember that Jocko was down there to cover Charlie's operations? Well here he was, with his camera team recording this briefing.

"We take the elevators from here to the ground floor, then send them back up. No stops along the way. Keep the stairs barricaded at all times," Charlie gave his orders, turning now to address the assembled group of Special Branchers and SF he had collected around him in the large triage bay. There were nods among the SF — the regular security personnel, to whom these orders were mainly directed. The Branchers didn't need to be told.

"Good…" Charlie stopped, letting his hands rest on the MAG-90 clipped to his vest. "Now, we think the Commandos out there are trying to lay low. As far as they know, we have no idea they're here. If Branx hadn't given them up, we may not have known. To me that suggests they're going to stay quiet, not set any traps or do anything to draw attention to themselves *unless* we discover them."

This explanation wasn't entirely for the benefit of the cameras — Jocko's crew (actually it was Jessica Qing's crew, since they'd swapped as insurance that they'd share footage) was rolling, but Charlie was also going through these points for the benefit of the regular SF in the room.

The twenty guards from *Wolf* and *Artemis Agrotera* were experienced — some, like the charismatic Eugene Sengooba, (the African fellow who'd been very popular in the interviews in *The Jupiter Patrol*) had even been on Egesta. Even so, some of them wouldn't know why Charlie was operating the way he was, and our intrepid Major Peters does like to make sure everyone is on the same page.

"My plan is pretty simple," Charlie went on. "My squad and Marcus' are going out there in teams of four. We're going to commandeer hover vehicles and do flyovers of the dome, see if we can figure out where they're holed up without tipping them off. Meantime, Captain Bertram's unit will hold the ground floor here, with some vehicles handy in case someone needs to be bailed out."

Pretty straightforward.

"Once we know where they are, we come back here and figure out how best to deal with them. But it is *critical* that they don't realize we're looking for them. As soon as they know we're onto them, they'll start setting ambushes and booby traps. They'll have no reason not to. And the last thing we need is mines and IEDs."

The idea here, and I suppose I don't need to elaborate too much on it, was that the Martian Commandos were probably going to wait until the squadron overhead left to start attacking any Defense Command presence in the dome… and until they had a better idea of what Charlie had available on the ground. They might not even attack at all — they might hide somewhere in the dome and wait until he left, then start preying on whoever we left to occupy the city. If we abandoned the dome, they could reclaim it for Mars.

So they weren't going to be setting traps and ambushes yet. As long as they were trying to hide, they'd be keeping a low profile — and blowing up a bunch of Special Branchers is *not* keeping a low profile. That gave Charlie a little time to figure out what the situation was, and to see if he could locate their hiding spot before they realized he was looking.

"Once they figure out we're on to them, we're going to have to move fast," Charlie finished, and a wave of nods was his answer.

There really wasn't a lot more to say — even Jocko didn't have any comments or questions. There was a great sense of foreboding in this room, partially because it was a triage bay and thus carried a certain atmosphere, and partially because they were coming to terms with the serious threat they faced.

Thirty-eight Commandos were out there somewhere. This was going to get messy.

Chapter Five

The Conference

That poor day cabin off the back of *Wolf's* bridge had been through many owners in a relatively short span of time. A year prior to this, it had been mine. Half a year ago it had been Karen's. A week ago it had been Andrea's. Now it was Karen's again, but of course I always found myself in there, so it still probably had some nostalgic memories of me...

Well, I mean, if four walls, a ceiling, a floor and some furniture can have nostalgic memories...

It was a popular place to be, though — it was, as is every day cabin, conveniently located, and its screen was quite handy for having realtime conferences with our skippers. As such, while Charlie was setting up his battle royale with a briefing to his Branchers and SF, we were setting up ours with a chat between our COs.

On the day cabin's screen were several faces: Mark Gunney's (from *Cheetah*), Kris Jacobs' (from *Lion*), Nancy Whitehorse's (from *Trusty*, formerly of the Jupiter Squadron), Giovanni Calzatti's (from *Pictou*, same story), and of course, our dear friend Andrea Kiley's.

And Andrea, in case you're wondering, appeared to be in the same state of mind she'd been in when she first left *Wolf* — perhaps a bit frustrated, but not particularly unwell. Obviously word had *not* made it to us about the incident with her mag chief.

"We've still heard nothing from Elise, Matt or Aaron," I started the meeting with a statement of the obvious, and everyone nodded.

"So what's the plan? I don't like the idea of us just sitting here and waiting for the report on Sinope. Seems to me we have the initiative right now, we should do something with it," Mark Gunney was his usual brusque self, and he made an excellent point. If we waited too long to move, we'd lose the initiative. The Martians could decide how they wanted to deal with us, instead of us dictating the terms of combat.

So that's point one for anyone reading this plan from a staff college or academy: maintaining the initiative is critical in combat.

"I'd say that's about right," Kris nodded. I think by now you'll remember that she's our redheaded Australian, though my editors suggest that I tell you again. As if you'd forget!

"We go out after the corvettes, then," Andrea sounded relaxed as she said it. "I don't know what I can get the drives up to over here, but even if it's only 180 kps, we should follow our scouts. They run into something, I'd rather be closer than not."

Nothing at all in that sentence to suggest she'd nearly blown away an NCO hours before.

"Can we afford to leave the dome, and *Artemis Agrotera*, unprotected?" Nancy Whitehorse asked the prudent question. Unlike some Commanders who'd recently joined a new unit, Nancy had no reservations about voicing her own opinions, and rightly so. She had, after all, been hand-picked by Marlene Stoll to join the Venus Squadron —despite being sent out to the Io dumping grounds by a vindictive Dave Caldecott, she'd lost none of her touch.

And her question, getting back on point here, was a very good one.

"It could be bait…" I said the words quietly and thoughtfully, letting them trail off so someone else could pick up on them. But no one did, so I continued, "We have no way to know."

We were all silent for a few minutes at that thought — could we risk *Artemis Agrotera* and Charlie's mission by leaving them undefended?

"Would leaving one or two ships behind solve that problem?" Calzatti asked the well-intentioned question, but we all shook our heads simultaneously.

To leave one or two ships behind, tied to the defense of a moon, would be quite bad indeed. You see, those two ships would become easy pickings if the Martians showed up with superior force, and they also weakened our own battle line. Leaving them behind would accomplish nothing.

The Martian squadron out here, I should repeat (since I don't think I've said it this book) included one battleship, five destroyers, three destroyer escorts, and two pirate ships. We had one battleship, three frigates, five corvettes, and a combat storeship that could probably hold its own against pirates… probably.

As you can see, the table was reasonably level — technically they held the edge in size, but we were essentially on a one-to-one basis. The differences in firepower and armor between a destroyer and a corvette are much less significant than the differences between a battleship and a frigate or destroyer, so we weren't too bad off…

But what to do? I had to decide — contemplating wasn't going to get us anywhere.

"We'll have to take the risk, Nancy. I don't like leaving Zail and Charlie behind without top cover, but we can give them a squadron of Starlights for some long range patrols. Bottom line, though, I want to be in the Martians' faces at Sinope with the whole Jupiter Force as quickly as possible. If we give them time to set up, they'll be able to get hidden out here among the many moons."

That was my decision. Our space situation and Charlie's ground situation were very similar in many regards — there was the prospect of a nasty, drawn out raiding fight if we weren't able to crush the Martians at Sinope, just as there would be booby traps and ambushes in the Io dome if the Commandos realized Charlie was onto them.

The difference in space was that the Martians knew we were onto them, so there was no time to waste.

"Alright, so we'll follow the corvettes' base course out, and when they check in with *Artemis*, we'll have Zail let them know we're on our way up in their wake," I said with some finality. "Get your ships ready to boost. I want to be out there in an hour."

There were nods, but Karen cleared her throat before anyone moved to disconnect, and I glanced at her. With a quick smile, she leaned forward in her chair, "Just a reminder, too, that there may be other survivors from the old Jupiter Squadron out there, hiding behind the moons. We need to keep an eye out for them, but beware if any of them show up and act strangely. Some could have been captured."

"Ah, right, I was supposed to bring that up, wasn't I?" I smiled sheepishly, and Karen shrugged at me.

"I reminded you to do it so I'd remember to," she started coming to her feet. "Now you can all disconnect."

With smiles from Kris and Mark, and less comfortable expressions from Calzatti and Nancy Whitehorse, the links started winking out, until Andrea alone was left on the screen.

"I'll see what I can do to keep this bucket in formation," she said sweetly. "I know it's bad form to talk poorly of one's own crew, but the people over here... well... I don't need to tell you."

It was indeed bad form to criticize one's own crew... though that was more of a gray area in a situation where you'd really just taken over the ship, and couldn't be held totally responsible for its personnel.

Even so, it wasn't the sort of thing we'd have expected from Andrea, so when she smiled sweetly — *perfectly* sweetly — and then closed her connection, Karen and I looked at each other with narrowing eyes.

Karen, who if you remember had visited *Dominator* at the end of *The Jupiter Patrol*, tugged her blonde ponytail over her left shoulder and started fiddling with the end, "I'm... I don't know. She admitted to me that she's on edge..."

I nodded slowly, "We'll keep an eye on her. Frankly, I might have said the same thing if I'd been stuck with that crew. As long as she doesn't start shooting them, though, I think we're fine..."

Ha. Oh that was terribly funny. Or was it just terrible and ironic?

The latter one, because I didn't know about what had happened earlier. And to be fair, she hadn't actually pulled the trigger...

To answer the question that must be in your head: no, I have no idea how I managed to be so completely blind to what was going on with Andrea. And as you know well by now, I still believe it was my fault, and perhaps Karen's, for not paying more attention.

But that wasn't the concern for now — for now we had our plans, and we would soon be bound for Sinope.

CHAPTER SIX

RECON

"We're on our way out, Charlie. Good hunting down there."

As my words came over Charlie's comm, I cut my connection, and Charlie nodded to himself. He was on his own now, and that was fine by him — the Jupiter Force would deal with Sinope while he got the ball rolling on Io.

Lowering his hand from his earpiece, he took a breath of the artificially windy 'outside' air and nodded to Carly Henderson. Now, I have to deal with something before we go any further: Special Branch officially calls a second in command a '2IC', whereas the Navy calls a second in command an executive officer, or 'XO'. I'm certain I've called Carly the XO of Charlie's squad on a number of occasions (even earlier this book, I'm just leaving it that way for effect now), but as he pointed out to me when we sat down to talk about the particulars for this book, she was his 2IC.

So I will *try* to refer to her by that acronym from now on. It goes against the grain, but Charlie asked, so I'll try.

Anyway, that's another of my patented asides; let's get back to the narrative...

Carly was sitting in the driver's seat of a Defense Command hovercar, with her team of officers around her. In the next car over, Charlie's other Captain, Raza Weiss, had his team ready to go, and... well, I'm not going to go through and list every car. There were six in total, including the one Charlie was about to climb into, and they each held four Special Branchers.

Looking up and down the line of cars, Charlie gave a satisfied nod, then glanced back towards the lobby doors that led into Defense Command HQ. Captain Bertram was standing just inside, and she waved Charlie on with a smile. Her nine Special Branchers (the 'extras' mentioned earlier) would look after the building while he was gone.

All set then.

Turning once again to look at the cars, he did a hand gesture that even I understand: the 'spin up' one. You know, point at the sky with your index finger and rotate it around, silently saying 'let's get moving'. He then headed for the car he'd be taking and hopped into the passenger's side, getting his MAG-90 ready to fire out the window.

"Alright, let's keep things high but not too high. If they decide to start shooting, we don't want to have too big a fall," he ordered into his headset.

The others didn't acknowledge verbally, but as the cars started to move, it was clear they were keeping their altitude at rooftop height. If someone shot the pad of one of these hovers, it'd drop hard, but at that low height, the passenger cage would keep the crew relatively intact.

I know, 'intact' isn't a glowing state of health, but it's better than falling from ten or fifteen stories up.

The scouting routes had been pre-established, but they were entirely flexible. Special

Branchers often operate that way, I find — when you get to their level of elite, you learn to rely on your instincts as much as your reason. In this context, that meant established scouting routes could be adjusted on the fly.

Charlie's driver was Lieutenant Ben Belete, and with a nod their car was airborne and heading 'west'. For the record, these are arbitrary directions — it's standard practice in these sorts of situations to establish a 'dome north' (which has nothing to do with a magnetic pole) to make deployment clearer. In a Defense Command dome, the HQ building is always considered 'north', and all the other directions thus fall into place around it.

Yes, we're all aware of the potential prejudice the assignment of 'north' to Defense Command could suggest. 'What, is DC too good to be south?' is a question we hear a lot. Some people think that we're saying that 'north' is better than 'south' by always being there. Well, we don't care about politics or prejudices: the rule was set a long time ago, and it makes deployment clearer. Clear deployment saves lives, so we don't give a damn about the politics of it.

West, in this case, took Charlie's car towards the industrial sector of the dome — the manufacturing complex, and the agribuildings. Sorry, I know this chapter has already been heavy on exposition, but it's necessary for me to set these things up now... so we can shoot them up later without me stopping to give the song and dance. Bear with me!

So, manufacturing building? Pretty straight-forward, it's full of various types of machinery that can make anything from toothbrushes to quick ovens. That sort of manufacturing plant is a marvel of Imperial industry — it's really designed for the job of colonization, because it can satisfy virtually all the manufacturing needs one comes across in the dome, at a reasonable (though not *cheap*) price. That said, you don't see them much in the Belt anymore; that close to the big manufacturing plants of the Empire, it's generally cheaper to import.

The agribuildings are a little more common, of course — they're the five-story massive box buildings, and on each floor they grow food. Five stories of wheat fields, or corn, or hydroponic fruits and vegetables, or clonestock. Io dome had two of these huge buildings, and Charlie hoped desperately that the Martians weren't hiding in them.

"Battles in industrial parks are so cliché..." he muttered to himself as he eyed the buildings through the windshield.

I might as well continue describing the layout of the rest of the dome. I'll again try to get a map, but who are we kidding? Not with this publisher.

If you think of the dome as a circle, and then divide it vertically into three strips, the western one is that industrial park. On the eastern strip are about eighty houses (many of them built but never occupied) and the four high-rise apartments (again, built but only sparsely occupied). The Defense Command base is at the top (to the north), of course, and then there's the middle.

The middle is the 'fun' (most dangerous) part: it's the commercial sector. Despite its tiny population, Io dome was built with a big stadium, a big mall, and a number of warehouses and smaller store buildings. At the southern end of that commercial strip stood a hospital and a connected medical research facility.

It was the mall that could be the very worst. Just think about your local shopping

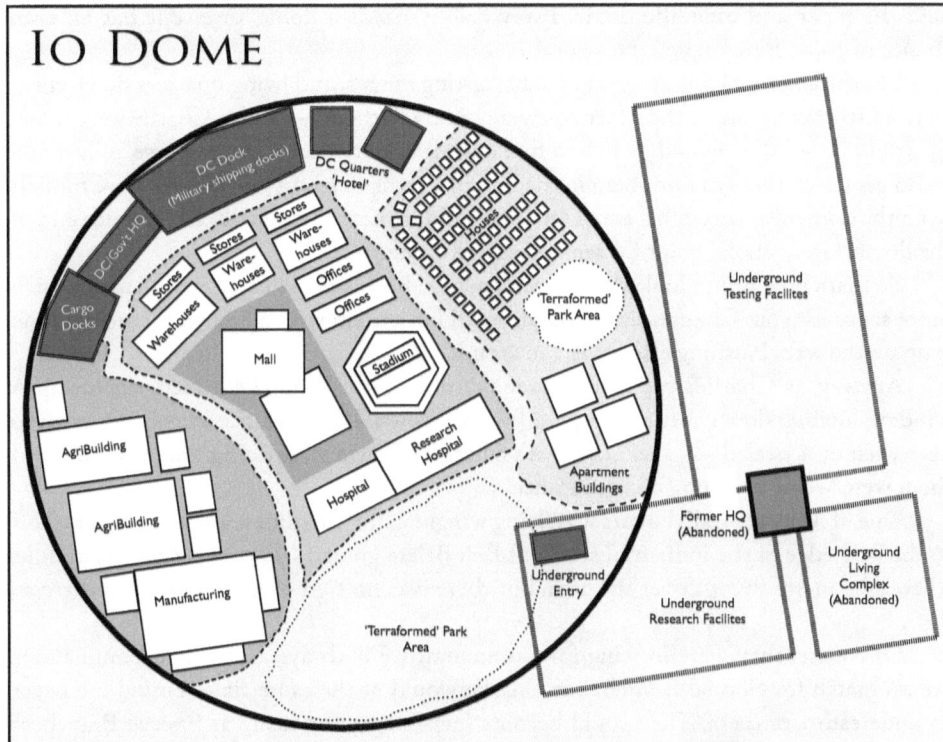

Io Dome

Oh. My. God. A map! A map a map a map! They put this in after the text was finalized, so I couldn't refer to it in the book... but it should make things easier to understand. Don't get used to having these, though... I think they're putting this one in out of guilt after the screw up with the first printing of The Jupiter Patrol... *when they spelled it 'Jupiteer' on the spine. But really, who cares why... we have a map!*

—KB

mall... with all the places in there to hide, to booby trap, to stage ambushes... it could be mayhem. Now, the Io mall had never been filled — only about a third of the retail spaces in it were ever used, owing to the small market and the distance from the trade routes — but that still left a structure that could be hell to secure.

The stadium was connected to that mall by a tunnel, which made things all the worse — it wasn't a huge stadium, but it was still big enough to be a nightmare all its own. The hospitals too... dammit, the whole dome would be a quagmire, to be honest.

But there's more! At the extreme south of the dome, there was a very large 'park' that had been planted but never maintained, so it was full of dead trees and plant life, and was overgrown with many weeds. Snipers could find excellent cover in that patch.

Worst of all, though — the part that Charlie *really* didn't want to think about — was the network of underground testing, research, and living facilities. These were the sections of the 'old' Io base that EM Weapons Limited had dug before it had gone bankrupt and Defense Command had taken over. As soon as Defense Command assumed control, we paid the piper and built the dome. Every colony needs a dome, or else it has an even chance of going Pion on you. Not good.

But the abandoned underground labs, testing ranges, and living quarters down there were all still accessible. If the Martians were hiding in them — and if Charlie were them, he would be — they would be hell to find and clean out. That was, of course, only if you could get down there to find them in the first place: the only way to get into those tunnels from the dome was through a small security building next to the 'park' at the south end of the dome. Great choke point for ambushes and carnage.

So that's how things looked. If there's a map in here somewhere, it will all make much more sense for you. Chances are, though, you'll have to do with a mental picture, or look it up on the web. Nothing else for it, I'm afraid.

Anyway, as Charlie's car floated over the first agribuilding, he leaned out his open window, looking down at the empty roof with a frown. He didn't need to tell his team to keep their eyes peeled — obviously that's what all of them were doing, and so far none of them were seeing anything of significance.

One of Marcus Atallah's cars was flying wingman for Charlie's team, and it banked off to the very edge of the industrial sector as Ben Belete guided Charlie's car up the middle. There'd be many sweeps over the area, but there was no sign of anything down there so far...

Of course, they were looking for Commandos. I'll always assert that Commandos are no match for Special Branch, but Charlie would at the same time remind me never to underestimate them. They could become invisible just as easily as Special Branchers could.

"Looks like they're going to stay out of sight," Charlie said into his comm after a few minutes of overflights of the agribuildings.

"That a bad thing, Charlie?" Carly Henderson came back over the comm almost instantly. "They won't realize we're looking for them if we don't find them..."

"Yeah, but if we're pretending we don't know they're out here, we only get to do one recon flight before we move out of the HQ. If we do more they'll think we're out here actually looking for them, and then the fireworks could start," Marcus Atallah added from his own car.

It was a tricky situation — there were many ifs, many possibilities. And Charlie's gut was telling him it was going to get very messy before it got cleared up.

Lovely.

"For now, keep sweeping... we'll just look like we're being thorough. Hopefully we see something. If not, tomorrow we'll have to start creeping around on foot... dammit," he ended the conversation on the comm with those orders.

There were some sounds of agreement on the comm, and the Special Branchers continued with their flights.

Down there, somewhere, the Martians were watching them.

CHAPTER SEVEN
GAMBITS

"We're going to be back in Io space soon at this rate," Elise De Winter observed dryly on one of *Friendly's* bridge screens, and Matt Baxter let out a long breath and nodded.

The Martians were still pushing directly back towards Io, and there was no way to know for certain whether the corvettes had been detected. What were these bastards playing at?

"Alright, alright..." with arms folded, Matt began to pace back and forth before the monitors, "what could their motives be? Presuming they didn't see us chasing them, they could be pressing back to Io for reasons all their own..."

Matt was working through quite a conundrum here: why would the Martians turn around and keep coming? If they were following the corvettes, why would they go all the way back to Io with them? These Martians had seen *Dominator* and the rest of the squadron arrive, they had to know they'd be outgunned in Io space.

Were they hoping to catch the corvettes before they got to Io — to destroy the smaller Defense Command ships short of the moon? Well, that was unlikely, as nothing the Martians had done so far suggested they had the ability to catch up to the corvettes. And these Martians had been too crisp in their formation to pass themselves off as fools... that is to say, they were acting too intelligently for Matt to be convinced they were stupid enough to chase *Friendly, Lady Grace* and *Honesty* without a good reason.

But what if they *hadn't* seen the corvettes? What if, as Matt had hoped, the Jupiter Force ships had effectively tracked the Martians from just far enough behind *not* to be noticed... and the Martians were turning back for reasons all their own?

"They want to recon our position at Io?" Aaron Ashby asked with a frown from the Battlelink screen, and Matt began a slow, thoughtful nod.

"Maybe that..." his words trailed off.

What else could it be? The Martians wouldn't attack with only five ships — not when they'd seen how much firepower the Jupiter Force had brought in. So the Martians couldn't be attacking... unless it was...

"Oh bloody hell. Marie, get a signal to *Wolf!*"

Wolf wasn't over Io when *Friendly* called in, but *Artemis Agrotera* was in position to pick up the signal. On his bridge, Captain Zail Patel received Matt's message, watched it, and then hastily ordered it passed on.

You see, Matt didn't know where we were so he couldn't send it directly to us, but thanks to Io's long-range detection grid, Zail still had the rest of the Jupiter Force (now outward-bound) on scope.

+++

About six minutes after it was sent, Felicia Khalid reported the arrival of Matt's message on *Wolf*, "Report from Commander Baxter, sir."

I'd been sitting in my chair next to Karen, beginning to realize how fatigued I actually was, when Felicia spoke. With some difficulty I pushed myself up to my feet and nodded, "Screen two, Felicia."

Karen stood as well, and together we paced up to the front of the bridge, not particularly concerned by the prospect of what we were about to see. I mean, it was probably just a progress report, a course change... something not terribly dangerous.

I'm not entirely sure why I assumed that, but I did.

The *Wolf*Net buffering screen scrolled past quickly, and as we settled ourselves into standing positions, Matt appeared, looking about as concerned as he always did.

"About two hours ago the Martians reversed drives on us. We suspected at first they'd seen us, or thought they were being followed, but they've continued on. They're coming right back to you..."

My brow instantly creased, and Karen frowned.

"...and the only reason I can imagine they'd do that is if they're coordinating an attack with the rest of their squadron."

Whoops, there went the heart rate through the ceiling.

"Shelby, reverse drives," Karen gave the order even as I turned to Felicia.

"Get Battlelink online, order all ships to reverse course for Io," I added my own commands. "Send to Zail, get *Artemis Agrotera* ready to receive. How far out was Matt according to the signal stamp?"

Jim or Kate would have had that answer right at their fingertips; it took Felicia a few seconds to get it for me, but get it she did, "About two hours, sir."

I nodded slowly, turning back to the screen, then glanced at Karen, "Ambush?"

She tipped her head sideways and let out a sigh.

Here's what we thought was going on: the Martians probably had some sort of preset plan for the arrival of the Jupiter Force. Remember, thanks to the media, they knew we were coming, but we'd shown up a week before the media had said we could. That probably had screwed up the plan somewhat, but not entirely.

So, a powerful Defense Command force arrives, what does the outgunned local squadron do? It runs. Perhaps leads some of our scouts away, but even if it doesn't, it falls off the sensor panels and goes out of sight and out of mind.

But then four hours out, it reverses course and comes back, hopefully unnoticed, to...*attack?* Certainly, but not on its own. Have you noticed in the war so far how the Martians seem to like complex, coordinated plans that come from multiple vectors? Timing is always critical to the way they approach a battle.

This led us to believe that if the ships Matt had been chasing were going to be at Io in two hours, the rest of the Martian squadron would likely be lining up to attack at the very same time. Indeed, the Martians' original plan may have been to ambush us at Io when we first arrived — to have their main force hiding on the dark side of the moon, as we'd feared (near the end of *The Jupiter Patrol*), but our early arrival could have caught them out of position.

Now, though, they could be closing the jaws of a trap — an attack from two sides...

The Battlelink screens activated one by one, and Mark Gunney was the first to comment as he appeared, "They planning something?"

I nodded, "I'm thinking their main force is on the dark side of Io right now. The ships Matt was chasing reversed drives and will be in Io space in two hours... could be a pincer."

Mark grunted and nodded, "Great. Alright, we double back? We're only an hour out."

We'd come about an hour from Io, and thus were only an hour from Matt's position as well.

Andrea Kiley, again proving she was quite good at concealing — if not containing — her problems, shook her head on screen, "We'll need to be careful, though. If we start reversing course and the Martians are waiting behind Io, they might attack early, realizing they've been found out. *Artemis* wouldn't stand a chance."

Me and my risk-taking... not that leaving one or two ships with *Artemis Agrotera* would have saved the large ship if it was hit by a strong Martian force.

"We'll have to go back. But we need a good reason..." Kris Jacobs put in thoughtfully, rubbing her temple.

We fell silent for a moment again, but Karen, unflappable as ever, asked the brilliantest (yeah I know, not a word — my editor actually groaned when he read it) question that could right then have been asked: "Nancy, what can you see from the dark side of that moon without being able to plug into the Io sensor grid?"

The Martians couldn't take advantage of Io's long-range sensors — the grid was under Charlie's control now.

Nancy Whitehorse frowned on screen, then shook her head, "Not a great deal..."

Sitting close to a rock or moon, your passive sensors can be obscured. Active sensors generally provide a clearer picture, but if you're trying to be stealthy, you aren't using active sensors — they give away the fact that you're there.

If you think back to the end of *The Jupiter Patrol*, when we crept up behind Io, we couldn't see anything either. I was able to tell you what the Martians were doing because Andrea had been coming in with active sensors blazing from the bright side of the moon, and because when we made our strike landing on the old control building, our Starlights had been able to scan the bright side.

But if the Martians were waiting behind the moon in ambush, and were planning to coordinate their attack with the ships Matt had been chasing (and was now running from), they'd be blind.

They wouldn't know exactly what was going on out here.

In other words, we could turn around and head back, hopefully without being noticed.

"Full burn for Io, everyone," I said the words coolly. "Felicia, send to Zail: Lionstar needs to have a look at the dark side of Io... might tip them off that we know they're there, but we need to find out."

We'd been outplayed in our first hours out here, and I didn't like that. Hopefully the Martians would come to regret their elaborate little dance.

CHAPTER EIGHT
THE CONNECTION

"Whoa, whoa, Captain, slow down…" Charlie was pressing his earpiece right into his ear, trying to make out Zail Patel's words.

"I am sorry, Major. I believe that Io might be attacked from space in a matter of hours. It may have been a trap here all along. I thought it best that you were made aware of this possibility."

Charlie's brow creased into a deep frown, "Ken knows about it?"

"He is on his way back as we speak."

"Well, I'll let him worry about it…"

"Very well, Major. We will keep you apprised of all happenings!"

The comm cut, and Charlie shook his head, tapping his comm to open the channel to his people, "Looks like the Martian space kids are coming back, part of a planned counterattack."

It had only been an hour since we'd pulled out of Io space — as you can see, these first hours were all very eventful — so Charlie's six cars were still buzzing through the dome, looking for any visible sign that the Commandos were here.

And they'd found nothing.

"Wait a minute, the Martian ships coming back… would that be a good time for them to counterattack against us? Try to get the dome back?" Marcus Atallah asked the question at the very same moment it popped into Charlie's head.

For a second, our intrepid Major Peters said nothing. He sat still and thought about everything they'd seen — and not seen — so far today. The Martians were keeping a low profile, he'd assumed because they were hoping to go unnoticed. He'd thought they weren't picking a fight so they could outlast the DC occupation, or at least be in position to harass DC personnel and processes when normal operations resumed.

But if the Martians had a planned counterattack, the Commandos could be staging a counteroffensive… they could want to seize the dome out from under the Jupiter Force while we were preoccupied with a space fight.

"I think you may be right," Charlie replied to Marcus' suggestion after that delay.

"What's our play, boss?" Captain Weiss asked the tough question, and Charlie's mind started turning over options.

They were sitting ducks in these cars — one shot to the hover pad and down they'd go. But if he could stay airborne, at least with part of his force, he could drop them into better tactical positions to counter a Martian offensive, if one came.

Tough call.

But there had to be more.

"If they're coming for us, they're hitting HQ… we didn't clear the bottom floors of that building, so Gina, start doing that," Charlie shook his head as he realized his mistake there. He should have spent more time checking out the Headquarters building — what if a squad of Commandos was hiding in there, waiting to spring out during an attack?

But perhaps there were tools that could help, "Actually, Gina, get to base C&C. Check to make sure the Commandos haven't patched into the sensor grid, and then use the base surveillance cameras to look for movement. It'll be safer than going room to room."

Gina, sorry, was Gina Bertram, the Captain in charge of those nine extra Branchers left in the HQ building.

"They could have overridden the feed on the surveillance cameras, looped through some recordings..." Bertram came back over the comm, and Charlie nodded to himself again.

"Yes, they probably would have. So use the central light control and flash the room lights on and off in every room from floor thirteen on down. If the cams are showing a room without flashing lights, that's the one."

See, that's Charlie Peters for you right there — thinking on his feet, ready for counter-*counter*-strike operations. I'm sure you've seen in the movies what Bertram was worried about — the good guys or bad guys override a surveillance camera, record some footage from it that shows everything is quiet, and then feed that recording up to the screens on a loop.

Well, that worked as long as the picture wasn't supposed to change. But Charlie had a fix for it — because that room, with that unchanging looped feed — would stick out like a sore thumb when the lights started flashing.

The other important thing Charlie did was to make certain the Commandos hadn't rigged something that would actually allow Martian ships on the dark side of the moon to patch into Io's sensors. That whole discussion we had last chapter about being blind back there would be irrelevant if the Commandos patched their ships into our grid.

And Charlie wasn't done, "Alright, all cars drop to ground level. I don't want one sniper to be able to take out a whole car, so get those pads down low. It'll hopefully look like we're just taking our sweep lower..."

As Ben Belete guided Charlie's own car lower at those words, our intrepid Major turned his head and let his eyes sweep over the whole dome. Where would they come from?

"My money for attack would be on the commercial district. They'll come right up the middle to hit the HQ, so keep yourselves in positions to pounce."

At this point one editor asked, "Was this really all just Charlie talking?"

The question is understandable (although the editor who asked it was summarily called an idiot by another editor, which I enjoyed). But there were over thirty Branchers down on Io, was Charlie the only one giving orders?

Yes.

Yes, Charlie's hopefully proven his insane abilities to you by now in these books. At Egesta for one, and every time he's saved my life for another. That's a lot of times, let me tell you.

Marcus Atallah? Top officer, no doubt, but he was 2IC overall to Charlie, and Carly Henderson was 2IC in Charlie's own squad... they weren't going to be giving the orders. No, Charlie had command, and he had their collective trust. They were listening to him.

I suppose they would have said something had he seemed to miss the mark, but Charlie rarely misses the mark. Actually, the only times I can ever remember Charlie missing anything were those occasions when he actually meant to miss... I might be forgetting something, but I doubt it.

Anyway, he was on top of this, and his teams were listening.

"One more thing. Marcus, can you get a team into the cargo receiving building, and open the outer doors? I'll tell you why..."

I am *so* leaving that explanation out of the narrative. Cheap suspense building, you see!

So as Charlie's cars reduced altitude and started moving around the streets of Io dome, one vehicle headed for the cargo docks (like the Defense Command headquarters tower, they jutted out of the top of the dome too, but instead of being set up for military docking, they were built to receive freight). The mayhem was coming soon... presuming the Martian Commandos were doing what Charlie expected them to.

What do you think — was Charlie right?

CHAPTER NINE

SCOUTS

The Starlight force we'd left to run long-range patrols from Io was Lionstar Squadron, under Lieutenant Commander Yang Salleh Omar. The twelve planes of that wing scrambled at just about the same time Zail Patel warned Charlie of the incoming danger, and twenty minutes after that warning, ten of the Starlights were weaving through the volcanic plumes in the thin atmosphere of Io, heading for the dark side of the moon at full burn. Two were otherwise occupied.

Salleh Omar (that's his full surname, if you're unfamiliar with Malaysian naming conventions) was a good flight officer — I'd known Yang for a number of years, and he'd always proven himself quite capable in combat scenarios. He was going to need every scrap of that ability if the Martians were really heading for Io.

Ten Starlights against a battleship and escorts… well, I don't even need to editorialize that one: it was bad.

By the time we were half an hour out from Io, his Starlights were approaching the dark side of the moon, and he was on the comm with Zail Patel, while Zail stood on *Artemis Agrotera's* bridge.

"We will pass into the night side of the moon momentarily," Yang was saying, and Zail paced with his hands linked behind his back.

"Very well. I hope you do not find anything."

"I hope the very same," Yang concurred, and then his planes dove into the shadow of the planet.

Zail continued to wait on *Artemis'* bridge, having ordered the combat storeship to battle stations, and seen to it that the scientists being kept aboard — arguably the ship's most valuable cargo at that moment, if the scientists don't mind being called 'cargo' — were placed in the most secure armored areas of the hull.

I think I mentioned in *The Jupiter Patrol* that *Artemis Agrotera* had been designed to keep up with a combat force, in order to provide supplies on long operations like this run out to Jupiter. It was also armed more heavily than you might expect, though that's not to say it was comparatively powerful. All told, Zail had twenty mag batteries to cover a ship the size of *Dominator*, and had no lasers whatsoever.

Being at battle stations thus meant that Zail's crew had the mags up and ready to fire, but the Indian Captain was under no illusion that he'd survive a toe-to-toe fight if the Martians began to engage from laser range.

"We still are not detecting anything. Continuing around the arc of the planet," Yang's reports were coming over the bridge loudspeaker as Zail paced.

The waiting, as ever, was painful, though it wouldn't last as long in this book as we perhaps would have liked.

"Lieutenant Connors here… I think I've got something…"

Yang had his squadron fanned out in a broad line to maximize the breadth of its detection net, and sure enough, one of the planes on the left was seeing something.

"Close in, Connors. What's out there?" Yang came back over the comm.

Zail stopped his pacing and looked up at the speakers in the ceiling of his bridge, waiting. It was tense, *very* tense. What had the Martians done, what had they sprung here?

"Closing in, I see one battleship… three destroyers… two unknowns… last two must be the pirates… incoming Interceptors!"

As scouting reports go, they don't get much clearer than that. It's a testament to the professionalism of Lionstar Squadron that they relayed such a clear assessment of the enemy before about forty Interceptors charged into them.

Zail was now forced to stand and listen to the dogfight.

"They're dropping on us! Connors—"

Connors' plane, Lionstar 909, was the first to be destroyed, jumped by an entire squadron of the Martian craft.

"—dammit get low! Get into the atmosphere!" Yang's command was urgent enough, and I can just picture what he was seeing.

Remember, this was the dark side of the moon, and it's all the way out at Jupiter — it's pitch black. As the Starlights rolled and dove into the atmosphere, it was sheer blackness. Flying on instruments, they danced their way between the huge plumes of volcanic eruptions, trying to lay themselves down as close to the deck as possible.

Lionstar 904, Julia Hunt, went straight into a cliff face when the plumes scrambled her instrumentation.

The Interceptors dropped into the atmosphere after them, but as I think I pointed out in *The Jupiter Patrol*, Interceptors are space planes — in atmosphere, they lose a great deal of their handiness. Now, Io could never be accused of having a heavy atmosphere, but even so, the minimal drop in performance those fighters experienced gave Yang's squadron an edge.

"Cut and run, don't get tied up in a dogfight if you can avoid it!" Yang's orders were barked over the comm, and they would be his last. His plane was clipped, and he went down hard.

Zail directed his eyes to the main screen on *Artemis Agrotera's* bridge, watching as icons of planes winked out. Of ten planes deployed, six were still coming back…

Five.

There were too many Interceptors. Even in the atmosphere, they were able to concentrate the fire of their EM strafe cannons on the rest of the Starlights, and they were proving very effective indeed.

"Boss is down, we need to bug out! Burn burn burn!" Zail had no idea who the speaker was, but she didn't survive long.

Only three of Lionstar's planes managed to dive into plumes thick enough to allow their escape, and as they hit their burners and raced through the thin atmosphere at a full 201 kps, their instruments started to jam from the dense particulates they'd rammed through.

"Three of us coming in, think we're away clean… Jesus they dropped on us…" the last three Starlights had indeed escaped. "*Artemis Agrotera*, be advised, the Martians are coming around the planet after us. I'm guessing thirty minutes until they're in range of the dome, if that."

Zail took a deep breath, brought his hands around in front of him and wrung them together nervously. *Wolf* and company were half an hour out as well… this was going to be very very close…

Now, I've been questioned at times on the seeming perfection of the coordination of offense and defense during this engagement. How did we manage to turn around at just the right moment, or how was it that the Martians came at just the right moment for our purposes?

One word: luck.

Sorry, I know it seems convenient. If this was fiction, I might raise an eyebrow too… but no, I don't suppose I would. I know from history and from my own life that there a great many occasions on which timing worked out exactly as a movie scriptwriter would want it to. Luck does work that way at times.

I think one of the biggest frustrations I have with movies is that they over-use the lucky timing. It becomes a regular convenience instead of something that happens now and then, often due to a great deal of skill and planning. People see it so much on screen that it becomes cliché, and so they just start to assume that timing never works out.

But trust me, it does. Look up Admiral Doveton Sturdee sometime (no I didn't make up that name). One day in 1914, all things went right for his battlecruisers. Just one example of many.

Those examples always give me a little hope…

Today, we'd be relying on luck. But trust me, the coincidence of timing that was occurring over Io — the fact that our squadron and the Martians would arrive over the base at nearly the same time — was not going to make the subsequent meeting any easier.

And speaking of meetings…

CHAPTER TEN

BERTRAM'S MOVE

Gina Bertram led her three teammates into the C&C in the DC headquarters building, sweeping the room with her MAG-90 before lowering her guard.

"Think we're clear. Brad, have a look at the sensors panel, make sure they're not sharing our grid. Watch for booby traps. Racine, get the light flashes ready. Niels, get the surveillance feeds up on the main screen."

As Bertram gave the orders, her officers jumped to action. This squad had been hastily assembled months before to serve under Rufus Chang in the company that had been dispatched to Wes' Independent Squadron, but they'd gelled well (as Special Branchers tend to do) during the cruise up to Jupiter. While they were three bodies and a Major light of full squad status, they were still incredibly capable.

In just short minutes, the main screen was glowing with thirty smaller windows, each showing one feed, and switching that feed every four seconds. There were over 300 cameras covering this building's rooms and corridors, so even with thirty windows up it'd take forty seconds or so to cycle through.

"Sensors are untouched, near as I can tell," the Officer checking that panel reported quickly, rejoining the rest of the squad (the five people Gina hadn't brought into the room with her) outside the door now that his task was done.

Bertram nodded, "Good. Flashers set?"

The Officer at that panel nodded, "We are prepared." That Lieutenant then took her MAG-90 in one hand and waited to push the appropriate button with the other.

"All the feeds are up, ready to go…" the last Lieutenant reported, and Bertram offered her own nod, then backed up to the door as well. "Alright, get ready. We see something, we go fast — it won't take them long to figure out what we're doing when the lights start flashing."

There were nods all around, and then Bertram took a breath, "Hit it."

Keying the light controls, the Lieutenant (Racine, I think, but to be honest, I don't know many of the names of the people on this team) immediately moved to join the squad, while the last Lieutenant (Niels, I think Gina called him) stared at the main screen, his hands on the controls, ready to halt the picture in any window if the flashes weren't showing.

The lights in C&C, and out in the corridor, started to have a conniption. Off-on-off(for a longer time)-on-off-on(for a longer time)… it was relatively random, having been set up as a rough sequential program and then looped. Hopefully it would flush out any Commandos.

The squad waited and watched, the windows on the main screen cycling through new camera feeds at the painfully slow interval of four seconds…

"There!" one of the Officers saw it first, barked it out, and then Niels (I'm assuming that's his first name) at the controls quickly isolated the feed in which the lights weren't flashing — the looped feed.

"Fourth floor… right next to the western stairwell. Locker room next to the gym."

"Let's go," Bertram nodded immediately, and the squad started moving.

Niels came away from the console, but Bertram whirled and stopped him, "Wait a minute, make sure there aren't any more."

He nodded and turned back to the screen.

Descending through the eastern stairwell, the squad hoofed it, as they say, to get to the fourth floor before the Martians displaced.

"We don't know how many yet, sir, but we're taking care of them. I'll let you know," Bertram was reporting quickly to Charlie as she went down.

"Watch yourself, we don't know how good they are," he came back, and left it at that.

Gina Bertram nodded simply, and then she came to a stop as she reached the fourth floor landing, "Four, right here. Room's on the right side of the hall. We go in stacks of four, watch your angles."

Thanks to Charlie's seminar on room clearing, I finally understand some of that jargon. I fear that, in earlier books in this series, I've gotten some of it wrong, but now I'll try to make amends!

With Niels up running the console, there were eight people ready to deploy here, so they were going in 'stacks' of four people each. A 'stack' is the term Branchers use when referring specifically to a team being detailed to clear rooms. Not sure where it comes from, but it sounds slick.

The room was on the right side of the hall, so the two stacks of four filed down that wall — if someone was looking out the door of the locker room, their approach wouldn't be detected. They moved fast.

"Niels here, Cap'n," the Lieutenant's voice came into Bertram's ear. "They're in the next room over from the lockers now… looks like they cut through a wall or something. Watch it."

"Numbers?"

"Four, you have the edge."

Only four? That's what I asked Charlie when I was going over this with him. Wouldn't you put in more?

He shrugged and pointed out that, with the advantage of surprise, four could do a lot of damage, particularly if they attacked when Bertram's squad was facing assault from the outside as well. Also, four was easier to hide than eight or twelve — four could disappear in a small room.

"Shit… Cap'n, they're shooting out the camera… and they're through the next wall too. Are you hearing any demolitions?"

She wasn't, which was curious. As it turned out they were using laser torches with surprising speed to cut through the prefab alloy walls of the fitness section — probably one of the reasons they'd holed up here was because, in a pinch, they could cut their way out.

"Camera in the next room is gone. How far are you from the main entrance to the gym?"

Stopping her stack with a hand gesture, Bertram knelt down, "About ten meters."
"They're in there."

She did more hand gestures, telling the second stack (which was following her own)
to move up behind her, and take position right in front of the door to that gym, while her
stack tried moving *past it*.

If she was lucky, the Martians would think their tormentors (Bertram's stack) had
passed without realizing they had changed rooms, and the Commandos would then
come out in the corridor to jump them from behind. If the Martians did that, though, the
second stack would surprise them.

Don't know if that made sense... hope it did...

More hand gestures were thrown before Bertram started moving; she ordered the last
two officers in the second stack to keep an eye to their back — to look towards the eastern
stairwell in case the Martians didn't take the bait and just made a break for the stairs.

With that, she moved up, took a breath, and walked right past the door to the gym.
If the Martians had wanted to drop her, they could have quite easily. She was gambling on
them wanting her to walk past them...

And they let her go. They were presumably in there, but wanted to go unnoticed, at
least until they got the drop on her. As such, the entire stack went past that door without
event, and as they got clear Bertram stopped them and turned them around, just a couple
of meters down from the doorway.

Now two stacks of Special Branchers were lined up facing that door, ready in case the
Martians sprang.

Instead, a grenade rolled out.

"Cover up!"

"Grenade!"

Too late. It was the Martian equivalent of a magbang, and it went off strong, knocking
out two of the Branchers in Bertram's stack, and one in the second stack.

Bertram had been last in line, and thus was unharmed by the blast. Now she gestured
to her people to launch a replying grenade, and the first officer in the second stack flung
herself off the deck, pulled a magbang of her own, tossed it into the gym, and backed off.

In the second it took to detonate, Bertram waved that stack in — they had three
upright, hers was down to two. As they rolled into the gym, she and her other remaining
officer pointed their MAG-90s down the corridor, in case the Martians made a run for the
stairs.

The sounds of mag fire came from the gym, but Bertram didn't let herself get
distracted. She lined up her gun...

A Commando raced out of a doorway far down the corridor, near the entrance to the
stairs. As soon as he came out, he dropped to one knee against the wall and started firing
short mag bursts in her direction. Gina and her fellow officer replied, and both of them
managed to hit him square in the chest.

He slumped back, but evidently his vest had absorbed the worst of the shots, so he
kept firing sharply. Bertram was forced to roll low, and the second and third Martians burst
into the corridor at the same moment, dragging the fourth, who'd clearly been stunned.

Realizing the Commando who was giving cover had been hit, they dropped the fourth man, turned and started much more accurate cover fire, and Bertram's other officer was knocked backwards and rendered unconscious when one of those shots slammed into her vest.

Bertram tried to keep firing, but she had to dive sideways to try to cover up, and as she did, fire from the second stack started to come out the doorway the Commandos had exited through. Hustling now, the two standing Martians grabbed the two downed Martians and dragged them out, tossing a grenade into the room behind them.

That gave them enough time to haul their stunned comrades out into the stairwell, and then as Bertram got herself to her feet, they hefted the wounded onto their shoulders and started descending as best they could.

Bertram raced after them, and as she closed the distance, one of the second stack's officers tossed a magbang out through the door and into the stairwell. Bertram skidded to a halt as it went off, and then heard several thuds.

"On me," she called to those left standing in the room. All three of the second stack's officers who'd stormed the gym emerged into the corridor, and following her closely, they moved to check the stairwell.

Three of the Commandos were out on the stairs. Number four had slipped away...

"Major Peters," Bertram keyed her comm, "we have one runner, probably half stunned. Half my squad is down, checking them out now."

I wondered if she should have gone after that runner, but Charlie seemed alright with her stopping to check the wounded. After all, there were six cars outside, right?

Well, things were about to get even more complicated.

CHAPTER ELEVEN

COLLATERAL DAMAGE

While the Martian squadron and the Jupiter Force were still about ten minutes away from converging over Io, this runner burst out the front doors of the HQ and made a break for the stores across the street.

One of Marcus Atallah's cars came flying around the corner, the passengers leaning out their windows and firing, and for a moment it seemed inevitable that he'd be taken down. Then the vehicle started taking fire from hidden Commandos, and the driver had to swerve and come to a stop, letting the Branchers out as a withering fire enveloped the car.

The four Branchers scrambled for cover and managed to make it there unscathed, the Captain who was leading them reporting immediately that they were meeting heavy resistance. The fire was coming from a storefront next to an alley that led towards the shopping mall, and as the Commando who'd escaped Bertram made it into that alley, the Martian fire disappeared.

They were all running for the mall…

As that report came in, Charlie's car was coming up to a cross-street that would hopefully let him head off the Commandos.

"Take a right, get ready to jump out," Charlie shifted in his seat as he said it, getting ready to leap from the car if circumstances demanded.

At this stage, the hand had been tipped… er… more clearly stated, there was no more pretending that the Special Branchers didn't know the Commandos were there, so it was just a matter of trying to stop, stun, or kill these bastards before they could find a place to hide or set up an ambush.

Charlie keyed his headset again as the car raced down the street, "Have any prisoners, Gina?"

There was a brief pause, then Bertram replied, "Yes sir, have three."

"Strip their gear and then start working on them. I need to know if they have a base of operations somewhere."

"Roger that."

Things were happening very quickly, as you can tell. I suppose that shouldn't be a surprise, given the fact that this was a case of special forces facing off. Neither Commandos nor Special Branch tended to do things ploddingly.

"Coming up on the alley," Ben Belete pointed ahead and to the left, towards the entrance to the alley the Martians were using to escape from the HQ building, and just as he did, five Commandos exploded out of it — and started firing at the vehicle.

Ben Belete hit the breaks, and the anti-grav pad locked the car in place sharply. Charlie swung his door open and darted out, getting low and shooting as he raced across the open street to the median, then taking cover behind some landscaping. The other three officers in his team each found cover, and the Martians realized they were in trouble as soon as another car raced into the battle from the other direction.

Marcus Atallah had been on the other end of this street and, like Charlie, had directed his driver to come up this way. As he and his team sprung out of their vehicle, the Martians found themselves caught in a crossfire in open ground. Behind them, at the other end of the alley, the team that had been shot up in the street in front of the HQ was blocking that end…

So the Commandos retreated back into the alley, and then blasted their way into the store building next to it.

"Dammit, we're going to have to clean out every one of those warehouses," Marcus Atallah came in over the comm. Charlie frowned and leaned up from behind his cover for a brief second, examining the building a little more carefully before dropping his head again.

Well, this was the sort of situation for which he'd put an ace up his sleeve.

"Not necessarily. Find cover across the street. Keep an eye out for more Commandos coming from… anywhere. They could be all around…" Charlie rose to his feet and started to back his way towards the car, tapping his comm with one hand to change channels while he kept his MAG-90 trained on the alley entrance with the other.

"Dave here, Major. Our turn?" a voice came into his ear, and as he got himself around behind the car, Charlie stopped and kneeled.

"Yep. Get rid of the stores facing the HQ building. Drop them."

"Roger that. You're sure it's fine to do that kind of damage?"

The question was asked in the tone that one asks a question to cover one's liability. In other words, the 'well *Charlie* said it'd be okay' defense.

"Yes, go to town," Charlie nodded, then tapped his comm to switch back to the Brancher channel. "Cover up, everyone."

There was a thunderous explosion — one of the sides of the cargo dock tower burst outward, the debris crashing into the street below with a rumbling thud. Then the loud whine of engines, and two Starlights floated out.

These two planes hadn't been with Yang's squadron when it had been jumped by the Martians. Charlie had decided to cheat, and had called them into the cargo bay, figuring if he needed heavy support (obviously no tanks were available) he could use some hover-and-shoot backup from Lionstar Squadron.

Strictly speaking, bringing Starlights into a dome is a no-no — they're very loud in even this large enclosed space, and their weapons aren't subtle. If there was actually a civilian population in the Io dome, having Starlights engage would be mayhem.

"Eight Commandos heading into the mall!"

Charlie didn't recognize the voice of the Officer who bellowed that over the comm, but he turned around instantly and looked past the warehouses on the left side of the road.

"We're going after them," the voice continued.

Marcus cut into the report, "Don't pursue, we can have the Starlights flatten the place…"

"Not before they get through it, if someone doesn't slow them down!"

Charlie was about to join the 'discussion', and to tell whichever of Marcus' Captains that was to wait, but he was drowned out by the whine of the Starlight mags as they began strafing the stores the first batch of escaping Commandos had fled into.

"Carly here, my team is watching the west end of the stores in case they run for it."

"I have the east end," Weiss followed up instantly.

That was a lot of effort for five Commandos, but at least they wouldn't get out. The buildings started to fly apart under the torrent of mag fire, and everyone watching had to shrink behind cover and protect their ears against the huge noise. Starlight mags aren't necessarily big in the ship combat realm, but against buildings, they're positively apocalyptic.

As he pressed his comm headset further into his ear, though, Charlie heard just what he hadn't wanted to hear from the over-eager Captain: "Shit, mall parking lot... north side... they have us pinned down. Sniper from the stadium, they're flanking us!"

Shaking his head with some frustration, Charlie did some hand gestures and got his team back into the car.

The buildings behind him continued to collapse.

CHAPTER TWELVE

MEANWHILE, OVERHEAD

"They're going to be in weapons range at least five minutes before we are," Karen observed quietly, and I nodded.

We were on the bridge (where else would we be?), standing before the main screen and watching the range tick down between us and the Martian ships now rounding Io.

"Dammit they planned this bloody well, didn't they?" Andrea's question was not delivered with her usual smoothness, and I glanced back up at her face on screen four.

"Can't disagree with that."

She wasn't wrong — if Matt hadn't guessed their plan, and Lionstar hadn't found them, these ships would have emerged out of nowhere at the same moment their cohorts (the ships chasing Matt back here) appeared on the edge of our sensors. It would have been quite the surprise, as we'd have been scrambling to break orbit heading in one direction while they fired a slew of missiles into our surprised backsides.

It was around this time that I decided my Martian counterpart wasn't to be trifled with.

"Send to Zail, get him to retreat in our direction. I'm going to bet the Martians won't waste any attention on Io until we're taken care of," I folded my arms across my chest and frowned. "Hope I'm right, wasn't last time…"

Felicia Khalid sent the order on to Zail Patel, and *Artemis Agrotera* fired its drives and began to push away from the oncoming Martians.

"So…" Karen glanced at me, and I started to nod slowly. We were now at the mercy of the Martian CO's decision making.

Coming towards Io over the past hour, we'd talked about our options. Several factors were important; we had the numbers on them, after a fashion — they had three destroyers and a battleship, supported by two *pirates*, while we had three frigates and a battleship supported by two *corvettes*. I was willing to bet those pirates weren't going to be much of a match for Nancy Whitehorse and Giovanni Calzatti, though of course I wasn't going to build a plan around that fact.

However, that force balance was entirely better than it might have been; had the Martian group chasing Matt been on scene, they would have a marginal advantage in gun power.

But we had an hour's grace before they arrived, and Matt, Elise and Aaron would be with them.

As such, we could fight this skirmish on equal terms.

"Andrea, come up the center. Corvettes to hold on the port and starboard quarters of *Dominator*, frigates forward. Stand by torpedoes, prepare to launch Starlights."

We were five minutes from combat; it was time to shake us into formation.

The Martians could see us now, and we could see them, and their own destroyers were clawing their way ahead of their battleship, probably figuring our intent was to try to torpedo their capital ship.

How perceptive of them.

"Looks like they're expecting us to torpedo the battlewagon," Mark Gunney grunted on screen three, and I nodded. "They have our number alright."

"Plan still on, then?" Kris followed with her own question, and I sighed, frowned, and for a split second thought through our options.

We could either play by the logical rules, and do everything possible to blow up that big gun, or we could get some guaranteed kills…

"Launch all Starlights. One squadron from each ship to ride with our torpedoes, try to keep them from getting shot down," I looked up at the Battlelink screens. "Target the lead destroyer. *Only*. Let's get a kill. Andrea, hold your tubes for the moment."

Mark cracked a smile, "I love it when you fight dirty."

The orders were issued, and targeting sweeps were run. At the back of *Wolf's* bridge, Jim Hannigan helped the experienced gunnery crew with their calculations, and soon enough a ping rang out, "We're locked onto their leading destroyer. All Starlights are up."

"Felicia, patch Adrienne into the bridge comm, I want to talk to her," I nodded to Jim and then passed those orders on to Lieutenant Khalid.

Replying with a nod, our new Sensors and Communications Officer pointed to one of her techs and, just a few seconds later, the comm gave an introductory static hiss, then cleared, "Adrienne here, sir. What's the job?"

"We're going to take out the lead destroyer. Escort the torpedoes, but don't let the Interceptors jump you. If we're lucky, they'll be stacked up to protect the battleship, your way should be clear."

"Roger that. Just say when."

We had to wait another four minutes to reach extreme torpedo range, and in that time it became quite clear that the Martians were planning on bypassing Io to get to us. Kind of them — Charlie's day was going badly enough as it was, without having heavy fire or more Martian troops dropped on his head.

As we got to extreme range, I had to stop myself from holding my breath. With some effort, I pulled my eyes away from the screens and glanced at Karen, "Your squadron, your order."

With a comfortable smile, she nodded, "Why thank you. Squadron, fire torpedoes."

"Shoot!" Jim Hannigan's voice erupted from the back of the bridge, and from the line of three frigates at the front of our formation, three torpedoes raced out.

The Martians had been expecting that, I think — they'd evidently been sent the same sorts of reports after Glorious February that we'd seen. Torpedoes were deadly if they connected, but they could be shot down. Interceptors had already swarmed from the bays of the Martian ships, now they formed into giant deltas and prepared to receive…

But they were all forming *behind* the destroyers. This sounds foolish, of course, but think about it from their perspective: they assumed we'd fired at the battleship, so they'd positioned two lines of mag fire between our torpedoes and their heavy unit. If the destroyer turrets missed the torpedoes, then the Interceptors could finish the job. Not a bad plan.

If we were actually shooting at the battleship, I mean.

Our three torpedoes raced ahead at something like 200 kps — not quite terminal ballistic speed yet, as they'd only leap up to 225 kps when they were in closer range. Wolfstar, Cheetahstar, and Lion Squadrons hurtled out after them, while the rest of the Jupiter Force's Starlights (and some Starbursts from *Pictou* and *Dominator*) formed up around our ships as a combat patrol, ready to intercept any missiles the Martians fired back.

The distance between our forces continued to close, "Laser range in thirty seconds."

I nodded. If you think back to Glorious February, you'll probably remember guns engaging first. Those were battleship lasers, though — much longer range than those aboard a frigate — so for us it was torpedoes first, then lasers. *Dominator* was further back in our formation, so its lasers wouldn't be able to engage for another fifty seconds.

As the range ticked down, the torpedoes began to angle rather overtly for the leading destroyer in the Martian formation, and our enemy realized this. Must have been a terrifying moment on the bridge of that ship.

From everything we saw of the Martian attack force, it appeared disciplined and well-crewed. I imagine the officers and crew on the bridge of that ship thus faced the three warheads racing towards them with the aplomb of a good Defense Command crew... though I don't know that for a fact.

The mag turrets... EMP cannons or whatever the Martians call them... started to spin and fire rather hurriedly, and the other two destroyers began to push forward in an effort to lend fire support. Three laser shots actually cracked out, but the three torpedoes — each one lethal by itself — were dividing the fire of those gunners.

In other words, they had too many things to shoot at, and they couldn't just focus on hitting one or two.

The Interceptor squadrons at the back end of the destroyer line realized they were in the wrong spot, and they started to race forward, but it was too late.

Adrienne Thompson peeled away from the torpedo she was escorting, as did the rest of Wolfstar Squadron, and the other two squadrons that had gone forward with them. They raced back towards us, and our torpedoes kicked up to 225 kps. An EMP bolt finally slammed into one as it entered point blank range, but that was it.

Fearing for damage from the inevitable explosion, the other two destroyers reversed drives and slid sideways out of formation, while the targeted destroyer began to jink. It was coming to its maneuvers too late — it couldn't out-fly our torpedoes.

The first one didn't connect properly — a last-minute maneuver had nearly allowed the destroyer to avoid it, but nearly wasn't enough. It clipped one of the drive wings, and seconds later that entire wing was off, spiraling away from Io at high speed.

The second one hit amidships, and that explosion did much more damage. Flames billowed out of the shattered hull for just a moment before all the air was consumed by combustion and vacuum, and pieces of the ship were scattered across orbital space.

"Laser range... now..." Felicia Khalid had done well to avoid being distracted by the explosion, and now she gave the good news.

Jim had already calculated a good firing solution for us, and on the bridges of *Lion* and *Cheetah*, the lasers were equally ready. I nodded, "Let them have it all."

"Frigates open fire," Karen repeated instantly.

"Shoot!"

Ah, the complex but satisfying layers of Naval order-giving.

Wolf's number one laser howled silently in anger for the first time in months, and *Lion's* roared with equal muted gusto. At that same moment, *Cheetah's*... um... what sound does a cheetah make? Hmm. *Cheetah's* laser 'whooshed' silently as it raced away at light speed, and the Martian destroyers that had been withdrawing felt the heat.

All our laser shots connected, but only very briefly: the Martians were backing off fast, and they slid off our beams easily enough. Bastards.

"Missile separation, four incoming," Felicia Khalid then reported, and I nodded.

"Sounds about right," Karen looked up towards the ceiling speakers, "you hear that Adrienne? Take everything forward."

"Roger that," Adrienne Thompson replied over her voice comm, and the horde of Starlights and Starbursts that had been sitting around our force leapt forward.

"Switch fire control to mags, let's shoot down anything that gets through," I glanced up at the faces on Battlelink, and Mark and Kris both nodded.

Our frigate line closed up, our mags preparing to swat any of those undersized torpedoes that got into range. We weren't going to be caught by surprise — not after what we'd just done.

Then, in a space of time so short that I couldn't quite believe it (though I should have been ready for it), the Martian battleship leapt into range. Well, *its* own range — its lasers, though not as powerful as one of our battleship's lasers, had greater range than *Wolf's*. Barely.

"Incoming laser shots!" Felicia Khalid did not sound calm, and understandably so.

I don't think even Karen had a chance to give evasive orders, I just remember hearing Shelby McLaws' voice erupting from behind the Helm and Navigation consoles, "Side step and z plus five clicks, *now!*"

I could see why Andrea had recommended the southern belle for our bridge — she was on top of this with blinding speed. *Wolf* 'sidestepped' by firing its port side vents simultaneously, then quickly climbed up out of position on the z axis — had any lasers been coming for us, they would have slid off in just milliseconds, thanks to the fast reaction.

Cheetah moved with equal speed (appropriate, given the name), with Mark Gunney calling out orders just as Shelby gave hers, "Drop us low!"

Kris was fast to react as well, but it didn't matter: *Lion* had been the target of all the battleship's forward turrets. I could almost imagine the Martian commander saying 'Attack my screening vessels? Two can play at that!'

Lion was attempting to climb away from the shots, but the Martian, being a smart bastard, had predicted Kris' planned evasion, and his turrets had *Lion* bracketed — any way she tried to escape, she'd run into one beam. And so it was: a battleship laser chomped through the lower half of *Lion's* bow pod, opening the port flight bay to space and blasting out the relays for the three lasers the pod held — just for starters.

The Battlelink connection crashed, and Kris vanished from our screens, but rather surprisingly, *Lion* held formation.

This happened while the Starlights, focused on their own job, shot down the missiles that had been sent for us.

"Dammit," was about all I could say, and then I looked up at Andrea, "we need to answer."

She was nodding, and then she stepped out of range of her screen's viewfinder. We didn't hear what she said, but if you consult the bridge camera feeds from *Dominator*, you'll hear the best in Irish cursing. *Dominator* was plodding, as far as she was concerned. If you can think back to Glorious February again, remember how quickly Rachel Butler had been able to get the battlewagons of the Heavy Squadron moving? How nimble they'd been?

Not *Dominator*. The engine and steering crews were *not* of that quality, and Andrea was livid. One of our elite frigates had literally taken one on the chin, and yet our battleship — the heavy hitter that was best suited to respond — wasn't accelerating quickly enough to reply.

"They're pulling back… think they're going to run for it," Felicia reported. She'd inserted her own interpretation of the Martian intentions there, which was a good sign. She was settling in.

"Reduce speed, get SAR prepped to assist *Lion*," I wasn't going to pursue them, not just now. We'd killed one of their ships, but if we stopped, we had a chance of keeping the casualty they inflicted on us from being a fatality.

"I can bloody get the bastard," Andrea appeared on the viewfinder again, and for once her acting wasn't covering her acute anger.

I shook my head, "Not yet, Andrea. We've won this round, and they're still going to have to go around us to get back to their base."

There would be more fighting soon enough, but for now, we let the Martians back away and then retreat into open space. Starlights followed them, to make sure they didn't turn around.

We stopped to lick our wounds.

CHAPTER THIRTEEN

SHOPPING

Charlie's car swerved and came to a sharp halt just beyond the entrance to the mall parking lot, and as it did, he leapt out of the passenger side, leveling his MAG-90 and opening up a withering fire on a team of Martians who were about 400 meters away.

Coming to a dead hedge, he dove behind it, and the rest of his team quickly joined him.

"This is Peters, where are you?" he demanded into his comm as Martian mag fire started to shear branches off the dead hedges over his head.

He was inquiring, of course, about the position of that impetuous team that had tried to slow down the retreating Martians short of the mall. Sure, that Special Branch car team had kept the Martians stuck out in the open parking lot, but now they were pinned down… somewhere.

"Just saw you pull up, sir," the beleaguered Captain replied quickly. "We're about 300 meters ahead of you… around 100 meters from those bastards who are shooting at you now. Ready to coordinate fire."

"Status?" Charlie shifted the position of his legs so that he could spring forward and over the hedge.

"All fine, we're just pinned tight…"

"On my word, cover us. We're going to flank the shooters. Clear?"

"Yes, sir."

This all sounds like it was going very quickly, eh? Well that's one thing Charlie's really impressed on me about this fight: it moved fast. And I mean *fast*. I've seen fast-moving fights before, but when it comes to a special forces against special forces battle, there's no time to think. These are two groups of women and men who are trained to be the elite fighters of their armed forces, and to act instinctively.

Charlie wasn't going to get too comfortable in any one spot right now — he needed to keep moving. A stationary target is much easier to hit, and more than that, every second the Martian Commandos had to prepare for an attack by his Branchers was a second in which they could set up another booby trap.

If he had his druthers, Charlie wasn't going to stop moving until he'd cleared this dome… though that sort of objective was perhaps unrealistic. He'd worry about it later. At this moment he had a team to get un-stuck, and hopefully he'd keep the Martians out of that mall. If they got into the building, that would be troublesome…

Doing hand gestures to the effect of 'leapfrog on the right flank in open order' he got set to move, then patted Ben Belete — on the right end of their four-person line — on the shoulder. Ben nodded, and that was it.

Into his comm, Charlie said one word, "Now."

The pinned-down Branchers, however foolish their judgment had been in coming into this little quagmire of a parking lot, were still very skilled, and rolling very slightly out from behind cover, they started a vicious and accurate fire. The Martians Charlie had been firing on when he hopped out of his car — one of the two Commando teams that had the pinned down Branchers in a crossfire — had to stop their advance again to cover up, getting behind an abandoned car and some more dead landscaping.

Charlie patted Ben Belete on the shoulder again, then leapt past him, running twenty meters in a low crouch before stopping behind another burned-out hover. He was firing controlled bursts all the way, of course, and as soon as he got anchored the next member of his team came up to him, doing the same.

They almost had a good angle to get the crossfire going, Charlie just needed to move another twenty or so meters towards the mall. For now they all hammered the Martian team with mag fire, keeping the Commandos' heads down.

"We're going again, keep them covered… where's the second team gone?"

There was no more crossfire — the Commandos who'd had the Brancher team pinned from the other side must have pulled out.

"No idea, sir," the Captain came back over the comm, and Charlie swung himself down to sit behind the vehicle for a minute.

"Where are they?" he asked, crouch-walking down to the end of the vehicle nearest the mall itself. "Could they have gone into the mall?"

There was a pause, then, "Sir, they were closer to the stadium. Might have gone in there."

Charlie had to lean forward as a heavy barrage of mag fire slammed into the car his team was sheltering behind, sending painful vibrations through its frame.

"Alright, I'm not going into that mall, no way…" he said that rather determinedly, then tapped his headset and switched over to the Starlight frequency. "Dave, you have those buildings flattened?"

There was a pause as the Lionstar pilot looked over the destruction he and his wingman had wrought, then a cheerful sounding reply, "You bet. Leave one of your teams down there to make sure survivors don't crawl out, but I'd guess they're pancakes. Need something destroyed?"

Charlie almost smiled at the particular wording of that question, "Yeah, I don't like shopping malls. Can you eliminate this one for me?"

"Gladly!"

Again, everything was moving fast — I hope that's coming across.

Charlie tapped his comm back to the Special Branch frequency, "Marcus, Carly, get over to the far side of the mall, but everyone cover up. Our airborne friends are going to do some remodeling of the place."

"Roger that."

"On our way."

The whine of the Starlight engines, which had been left somewhat in the background when Charlie had raced away from them to come to the mall, was suddenly overhead. Within just a few seconds, the planes were over the parking lot, locked into a hover and lining up on the large shopping complex.

"This'll be loud," Charlie warned his team, and they all shrunk down behind the vehicle.

Then there was a sound Charlie wasn't expecting.

"Shit, shoulder lasers… three of them! Coming from the stadium!"

The much throatier scream of shoulder lasers — essentially anti-tank weapons (though at the very start of *The Rogue Commodore*, you might recall one was used for home defense) — managed to remain audible over the din of Starlight engines. The loud explosion that followed them blanked Charlie's hearing for a moment, despite his headset earbuds.

He leaned away from the vehicle they were crouching behind, then raised his eyes just high enough to see that the second Starlight in formation had black smoke spewing out of its fuselage.

Tapping his headset back to the planes' comm frequency, he realized he could barely hear what was happening. The explosion had left his ears temporarily deafened, though he knew that'd clear in a few seconds.

If you listen to the recordings, as I have, you'll know that the second pilot had taken three anti-tank laser shots down the throat of her plane, and her reactor was about to give out. With the calm of a professional, she yanked her stick sideways and raced away from the mall parking lot, settling back into a hover and then dropping heavily to the street just in front of the HQ, where Bertram's officers — those left standing — collected her and got her inside.

As she did that, almost simultaneously, Dave banked his Starlight around and edged it towards the stadium, blazing away at the great building with his mags. The building started to collapse, but not before the determined Commandos in there lined up on him with their shoulder lasers again.

The shots this time went right through the cockpit, blasting Dave to pieces, and sending his out-of-control plane sideways and down into the parking lot. Glass shattered and Charlie went even deafer as the plane crunched into the deck, and the Martians they'd pinned down used the opportunity to make a break for the mall, right around the wreckage.

Using hand gestures, Charlie got his own team moving after them, though he himself had to detour to the crashed plane. The fire was hot, but he slid in close to confirm that Dave hadn't survived the shooting. Putting that loss out of his mind, he checked to make sure the Starlight's wing pods were devoid of ordnance — he'd specifically instructed that there be no Apocalypse missiles on the Starlights that came in here. One of those cooking off inside the dome would have been disastrous, and might even have cracked the dome with its atmospheric concussion. The deck chief on *Lion* had evidently paid attention, so right then Charlie decided he'd buy that deck crew in *Lion's* port bay a round of beer when he got back.

Unfortunately for all concerned, the deck crew was dead.

With the lack of warheads established, Charlie moved on to the mall entrance, where his team was waiting. Some of his hearing had been restored, so he tapped his comm again, "Marcus, get into that stadium, take that team that was pinned in the parking lot with you. Clear it."

Things were moving so fast that Charlie couldn't think of the pinned-down Captain's name.

"Carly, come into the mall from the far side, we can't let them get set up in there, or we'll never get out!"

"On our way."

Charlie took his hand away from his ear, then looked at his three other officers. With a dashing bob of his head, he thumbed towards the doors inside, "Time to go shopping."

His team lead the way in.

CHAPTER FOURTEEN

LION'S HEART

"Looks like they're taking a broad arc around and out — they're going to vector for Sinope, once they're well clear of us," Karen was pointing up at the main screen as she said it, and I nodded.

The Martians were running away from Io on an angle that didn't take them in the direction of Sinope, no doubt because we were in the way. With that in mind, the Martian CO was flying far enough out from Io to get around us and then past us, and our Starlights were dogging him the whole way, making sure we knew where he was.

"I don't want to sit here and let him get back to Sinope to set up for us," Mark's tone on the Battlelink was more terse than usual — he, like the rest of us, did not like the look of *Lion*, or the fact that we still hadn't been able to get through to Kris.

"We can stick with him, make a running fight of it. We have them on the wing, they're nothing if they can't form up…" Andrea's suggestions now weren't particularly calm, though the fire of just fifteen minutes prior — that's all it had been since the end of the engagement — had cooled.

"Takes a day to get there… that's a day for us to hurt them all along the way," Mark agreed immediately.

"Yes, we'll be boosting shortly, but let's give Kris ten minutes to check in. We'll leave *Lion* behind, of course. *Artemis Agrotera* should hopefully be able to patch up the damage. Prepare your ships to get back on the cruise, though…" I said that to the eager skippers then turned to Felicia Khalid. "Anything from Matt?"

The Lieutenant looked up and shook her head, "Not yet, sir."

"Let me know if anything comes in. He's going to have to know where we are…"

As I was speaking, Felicia's hand flew up to her headset, and then she snapped her fingers and pointed at one of her techs, "Screen two."

That could only be one thing — *Lion* — and Karen and I turned to screen two quite hurriedly… only to be greeted by a slow-moving *Wolf*Net loading screen. For the first time that day, I really noticed that my heart rate was up… for some reason, this call, more than any of the trading of shots that had happened just moments prior, had me anxious.

When Kris appeared on the static-ridden screen, I had to stop for a second just to absorb what I was seeing: her usually carefully-managed red hair was matted and falling across her face, she was dripping with sweat and there looked to be burns on her cheeks. And she looked pale… well, I may not have noticed that at the time, on the static-laden feed…

"My engineering crew is dead. Lost port flightdeck. Lasers are offline. Just shut down reactor. All hands abandoning ship."

She then bent down out of frame to vomit.

Karen and I stood frozen as we watched the screen, and then Karen — who'd skippered *Lion* until just before *The Rogue Commodore*, stepped forward, "Kris? Kris are you alright?"

Kris leaned back up into the viewfinder, "I've had 2,000 REM. Maybe more. Our sensors are dead, I don't know for certain."

Karen and I were already frozen, but we somehow became even more frozen.

"Get Zail on the line, I need his medical staff ready for radiation decontamination procedures *now*. We need treatment for all of *Lion's* crew," I whirled to face Felicia as I said it.

"Abandon ship, Kris. We'll tow *Lion* home and let the yards decontaminate it," Karen said smoothly, reassuringly. Kris was still upright, somehow, but Karen couldn't imagine that *Lion's* skipper would be standing for much longer. She *had* to get off that ship.

Now, I don't know if you know anything about radiation poisoning. A lot of myths are still left over from the dark old days. Interestingly, much of what was first claimed in the twentieth and twenty-first centuries has kept a hold on the popular imagination, in part because much of it has remained unchanged.

The human body can recover from radiation poisoning, even up to 1,000 REM (REM is just the unit of measurement we use). Generally there are a host of post-recovery complications like genetic faults, cancers, and then birth defects for offspring — those need to be ironed out with about two years of genetic therapy, that itself can have unpleasant side effects.

Over 1,000 REM of radiation used to be a death sentence, and anything over 5,000 still is. Over 5,000 you're dead, it's just a matter of time.

You see, radiation is… well, this is not a perfect analogy. Indeed, I'm probably getting it quite wrong, but it's the way I've come to understand it. Picture a wooden cottage. That's one of your cells. Radiation comes in like a flaming arrow shot by one of Robin Hood's bows. It flies in through the window, and obviously could burn down the cottage. Now, one arrow probably would go out before it burned the cottage to the ground, but if enough arrows were fired in, there'd be a big fire in no time, and the cell would collapse.

It's a delayed-reaction death, and it's a horrible one.

So as I talk about the number of REM of radiation absorbed, think about the number of fires being started inside the cottages that made up Kris' body. Too many and there'd be nothing you could do to save the place.

Getting back to those numbers, then, between 1,000 and 5,000 REM, many factors come into play, including how soon the victim gets to a doctor who can start pumping her or him full of the latest drugs. Our present drug cocktails are a lot more effective than many people realize — we have particular chemicals that hunt down radioactive cells in the body and neutralize them, and some that increase white blood cell production for damage repair. Others fortify undamaged or moderately damaged cells, and hopefully allow them to remain uncontaminated, or to heal where they might have otherwise collapsed.

All of these drugs do roughly the same jobs that drugs of bygone centuries have done, but 2232's versions were much more effective than those of times gone by. Hopefully they could help Kris.

According to the stats I looked up (admittedly for last year, so about nineteen years after 2232) over forty percent of people exposed to 2,000 REM now can survive. That's up from *none* a century ago.

But Kris needed to get started on the drugs immediately. And I mean that quite literally.

"Doc Burke's dead," she coughed on the screen now, "but she and her medics dosed everyone with… with…"

She collapsed — or almost did, as Lieutenant Omar Cunningham, *Lion's* head of SF, stepped into the viewfinder's range, put his big arms around her waist and looked at us, "I will get her out of here. We have all been dosed with a pre-exposure cocktail, though only 312 crew members were alive at last report, two thirds of them contaminated. We are going to *Artemis* now."

He didn't wait for us to say anything, he just pulled Kris' limp body away, and escape pods started launching from *Lion*.

"Jesus," Andrea was the first to rasp that out over the comm, and Mark added the other half of the blaspheme.

"Christ."

"Captain Patel signaling," Felicia Khalid preempted any exclamation on my part, and I nodded, pointing to one of the unoccupied screens.

Zail appeared quickly, "I have my decon teams ready, and we can accommodate the entire crew of *Lion*…"

"You'll only be getting 312… or fewer…" I cut him off rather rudely — it was a function of some shock at the rather terrifying sight of Kris in that state, and my imagination showing me the scenes of a frigate dying of radiation…

"We will be able to support that many," Zail continued, unphased by my interruption. "I would point out, though, that there is a full hospital facility on Io, and a research hospital attached. I have officers checking with the medical scientists aboard now, there may be resources there that could better treat ARS than my medical facilities can."

That's Zail Patel, ladies and gentlemen. Whoever says non-combat skippers in this Navy aren't up to scratch can go to hell. In that thought — one that had yet to occur to me — Zail Patel saved about 200 lives. A full hospital trumps a sickbay any day.

My mind started racing, "Right. *Right.* Kyle, round up every SF you can, Charlie's not going to have enough bodies to hold that building on his own."

Kyle Stranks, our chief of *Wolf's* SF, was at the back of the bridge, and he simply nodded, "Yes, sir."

Off he went.

"Excellent idea, Zail. Even if there's nothing experimental, their facilities will be much better suited to that many patients. You're converting a cargo bay?"

Cargo bays could serve many purposes — that was one of the reasons combat storeships could fill so many roles. They had the floor space.

"I was, and I can still decontaminate and provide first treatment to the crew as they come aboard. I will then ferry them down to the dome by shuttle, with my medical staff. Critical cases can come to my own sickbay."

I can't begin to give Zail enough credit here.

"Excellent, excellent," I just repeated that word. "I'll get on the comm and let Charlie know his life is getting more complicated. We have to go out after these bastards, but Zail, you keep things in hand here?"

"I will most certainly," the Indian skipper said with some determination, and I think I may have managed a smile at him, strange as that would be under the circumstances.

"Good, I'll get Charlie to call you. Out for now."

Zail nodded and blanked his screen.

Moving fast… everything was moving so fast.

And I couldn't let this slow me down. No. As much as I loved Kris like a sister, I had to kill those Martians. My reason had gotten twisted when Kate Levec got shot, I couldn't let the same happen again.

"Andrea, Mark, Nancy, Giovanni…" I looked from the now-blank screen Zail had been on to my other skippers, "…mark a course to run parallel to the Martians, and boost at 190 kps. *Wolf* will catch up as soon as we deliver our SF to the dome."

There were nods, and Mark took the reigns from there, "Alright, I'll lead us out, if you don't mind, Andrea…"

They made their arrangements. I called Charlie.

CHAPTER FIFTEEN

COMPLICATIONS

"Charlie, sorry to interrupt…"

As I cut over Charlie's comm feed, he was diving behind a fountain in the mall, narrowly avoiding being pounded with full-power mag bolts from a Martian shooter who was well planted in the front display of the New Army fashions store.

One of the officers from Charlie's team lined up with her MAG-90 and, at full power, sprayed back. The sight, caught on the mall security cameras, was impressive. We seldom get to see MAG-90s doing 'the business', as I've heard it called by Matt Baxter, but they can.

To translate that somewhat, we rarely see what a MAG-90 can do at full power. Imperial Army blockheads often laugh at the composition of our Special Branch and even SF teams — they often decry our lack of heavy support weapons. No one in Charlie's squad carried anything other than a MAG-90 and a sidearm (in terms of energy weapons, I mean). There was no 'squad assault weapon' that was clearly designed to lay down heavy cover fire. The blockheads assume this is an oversight, when it's actually a testament to the power of the MAG-90.

When you turn off the safeties and are willing to drain your power cell, a MAG-90 turns from a surgical weapon that causes comas into a shredder.

So as this officer poured the golden mag bolts into the front of the New Army store, the explosion of glass and mannequins was terrific. The flames that broke out in the jeans section were also quite considerable.

Anyway, Charlie landed on his chest with a thud, but somehow wasn't winded, so he tapped his comm headset before rocking up onto one knee and spraying more fire down the broad corridor towards the Asteroid Crater Company department store.

"I'm here Ken, slightly busy…"

I remember hearing the intense mag fire over the comm on *Wolf*'s bridge, but for some reason I was neither surprised by it, nor worried.

My voice came back into his ear, "Sounds lively down there. Sorry I have to do this, but I need you to take and hold the hospital. All of it. *Lion*'s entire crew was just irradiated, I need good facilities for them… and Io has the best available, so Zail's going to decontaminate and do first treatment on *Artemis*, then the shuttles are coming down."

Charlie was listening to that, and processing it, at the same time that one of the Commandos who'd been making this advance hell poked his head up from behind a bench. Just like that, Charlie lined up on this guy, and from fifty meters away, blew his head clean off.

Do not *ever* piss off Charlie Peters.

The rest of the Martians started to displace again, but it was Ben Belete's turn to move up first, so Charlie continued to lay down a base of fire as the rest of his Branchers advanced after their prey.

"I hear you. The cargo docks are out of action, I had to use them to get some Starlights in here so they're damaged. Send them through the DCHQ… and you have what, Kyle's SF coming too?"

Even while he was in the middle of one of the hottest firefights of his life, Charlie was able to coordinate the logistics of a massive crew landing. That's Special Branch for you. Hell, that's Charlie for you.

"Yes to everything you just said. I'm going to go kill the Martians now, I'll see you in a couple of days."

"Have fun. Bring me back a t-shirt," Charlie watched the last of his team get past him, and then Ben Belete started laying down the next batch of cover fire.

Without another word to me, he tapped his comm off, got instantly to his feet and was running up the corridor.

Now, about this mall fight: you never, ever see it in the movies. Why? It'd cost too much money to set up a mall full of stores (complete with products) and then shoot it up. No movie that's covered this time at Io has ever had enough of a budget to do it, so (much to Charlie's frustration) the mall is often replaced by a warehouse. Warehouses are cheap, they're just full of boxes. Malls are expensive, because all those stores are full of millions and millions and millions of dollars of merchandize — even more.

So use your imagination. Think of your local mall, and just picture what that'd look like with fire raking through every store.

Yeah, that's both colorful and morbidly entertaining, eh?

Come on, you know it is. Unless a shoe store was under attack. My mother tells me that would be monstrous and unforgivable.

Back on point: Charlie tapped his comm again as he slid to a stop next to a sporting goods store, "Marcus, take your whole squad and secure the hospital, we're getting SF reinforcements to hold it. There have been serious radiation casualties on *Lion* and they're going to need the facilities."

There was a very brief pause, then, "We'll hold it."

Without a doubt, holding a hospital of that size could be *incredibly* difficult, but the Special Branchers were not the sort to complain, particularly not when the reason for their mission was so important.

But for just a moment let's forget *Lion*. I don't say that easily, but I want to give full credit to the way Charlie and his officers dealt with these Commandos.

They'd chased four Martians into the mall, and inside the mall those four had been backed up by another four. But despite being outnumbered two against one, Charlie's team had continued to push forward, and three of the Martians now lay dead. No comas here, Charlie wasn't taking any chances — and if you think that's cold, I'll give you the cliché (but true) answer: this was war. More specifically, Martian vests had already proved capable of keeping their wearers awake when they got hit point blank, and Charlie's team couldn't risk shooting a guy, passing him, and then having him wake up to attack their rear.

There was nothing especially flashy about how the Special Branchers were getting these kills, either. It wasn't as though they were running around and doing power-slides across the polished floor, blazing away like maniacs. Not at all. They were being smart, laying down good cover fire with one MAG-90 while the other three advanced, and taking clean shots when they had the chance.

Now they'd reached the last long corridor of the mall — this driving firefight did *not* take long. Again, special forces moved fast, it was inevitable.

But now the complexion of the engagement was about to change. Five Commandos were being herded up the corridor for a particular purpose — a certain rendezvous.

As Charlie blasted apart a cookware store to keep one of the Commandos from trying to duck in there, the clanging of the pots and pans filled the corridor with so much noise the Commandos didn't even hear the mag shots erupt from behind them.

Carly Henderson, remember, had been sent in the back, and as her Branchers now opened fire, these Commandos were going to be caught in a vice.

The Martians didn't realize they were taking shots from another direction until one of the Commandos, who was behind good cover against Charlie's fire, had a leg shot off by one of Carly's full-power mag bolts. Screaming over the dying clangs of the pots Charlie was now beginning to melt, this man swung himself around, and with another Commando began to drag himself to cover from the other direction, firing at Carly as he did.

Carly and one of her other officers were in a spa bath store, using the giant tubs as cover against the Martian shots. The other two members of Carly's team were in a bookstore directly opposite the spa tub store, and they now opened up from the opposite angle, producing a very nasty crossfire.

The Commando who'd lost his leg now lost his head.

The other Commando managed to get enough cover to be safe from both Carly's store and the bookstore, but when he popped his head up to fire back, Charlie removed it with another clean, full-power shot.

Three Commandos remained.

One of Charlie's officers leapt out from behind her cover and moved up, but the Martians saw her in time, one of them popping up and putting a full-power bolt into her. She was moving forward with proper body positioning — that is to say, she was approaching with the front of her chest presented to the Martians, instead of turning her torso to present the side. That might sound odd — Charlie says it sure feels odd — but when a Special Brancher is in a close firefight, she or he will advance presenting the broad front of her or his body, because that's where the vest plates offer the most protection.

If you turn your torso, presenting a smaller target, any shot that hits your upper body will go through the much weaker protection of the vest's sides, and will probably punch right through.

So she took a hard hit that broke four of her ribs and caused cardiac arrest, but Terry Schroeder, Charlie's medic, defied the fire and leapt up to immediately resuscitate her with his portable defib pads. As the Martians climbed out from behind their cover to take a shot at the medic, Ben Belete knocked down another one.

Seeing the way things were going, one of the surviving Commandos picked up one of his fallen fellows' weapons and started covering fire in both directions — one arm's mag going after Carly, the other firing at Charlie. Under that cover, the last Martian tried to get out, heading for the store next to the bookstore — one that sold lingerie, which is (for some stupid reason) quite funny to me.

The Commando firing with both hands deserves some credit — he succeeded in keeping Charlie and Carly both from stopping his friend's escape, but as soon as he started backing towards the lingerie store, Terry Schroeder stopped what he was doing, raised his mag and fired a single shot that, because of the angle, sawed right through both the man's knees at once.

In a gruesome sight, the Commando's upper three quarters dropped heavily to the floor, while his shins and boots stayed standing.

But the man didn't stop firing, even as he screamed in pain that I don't even want to begin to imagine.

Without a second thought, Terry then put a shot through the Commando's neck, finishing the job.

Special Branch medics are not doctors. They have never sworn any Hippocratic or Corpsman oaths to do no harm... just to help people who need helping. If that requires some killing, they aren't going to wring their hands about it.

Terry went back to work on the downed officer, and Charlie, Ben, Carly, and the rest of the squad lunged for the lingerie store. Carly got into line first, and as the Commando was rushing for the door behind the counter that presumably led to the stock room, she dropped him with another headshot.

Have I mentioned it's a very bad idea to piss off Special Branch?

Charlie swept into the lingerie store right after the shot, checking to make sure the headless body was in fact dead. Hey, can't be too careful. Carly followed, and then all three of her team members — all women — sauntered in behind her. This next part might seem ridiculous to you, but it happened.

Carly flashed a big smile as Charlie turned back to her, "Can we have a minute to shop? I usually can't afford this fancy stuff!"

Raising his eyebrows, Charlie shrugged, "I doubt anyone's coming back to take inventory."

"Lia might like some of this stuff too... come on, you know you want to get her something..." Carly was already behind the counter getting bags. "I'll pick some stuff for you..."

Charlie, usually not the sort of fellow you'd find anywhere near a lingerie store, just shrugged at what he thought was a joke, and walked back out the front. Much to his surprise, Carly presented him with a bag exactly forty seconds later (she wasn't kidding when she said 'a minute to shop') and, much much later, Lia got that bag. I'll let you read about her reaction in a future book.

After that minute-long break, they stripped the gear off the Martians and moved out the far mall entrance, heading for the hospital.

CHAPTER SIXTEEN

THE DETERMINED RUFUS CHANG

"Kyle's shuttles will all be on their way in another two minutes," Jim Hannigan announced from behind his operations consoles, and Karen nodded in reply.

"Good. Shelby, let's get ready to boost," she turned to Shelby McLaws then, and our southern belle nodded.

"Very good, ma'am."

I was standing silently as all this happened, watching on the main screen as the rest of the Jupiter Force, led by Mark Gunney, continued to pull away from Io at 190 kps. We'd catch up to them at full burn with a little time, but it was still an odd feeling to watch them go without *Wolf*.

Matt had just checked in, and sure enough, the Martians he'd been chasing (or fleeing, I suppose) had changed course — they were angling to match course with their battleship group. If we could keep them separate, we'd probably have a better chance at cleaning up these bastards.

"Torpedo tube reload complete," Jim reported again, and Karen nodded.

Wolf, remember, carried two torpedoes — and two only. All we had the room for. It took quite a lot of work to move the second torpedo into our single launch tube, but since we'd been sitting and waiting, Karen had ordered the operation to be carried out. Now we had a new warhead in place, and hopefully it'd pay off.

"Whatcha thinking?" Karen was suddenly right at my shoulder, asking a playful question to try to lighten my mood. I must have looked rather over-intense right then.

I blinked a couple of times, "A lot of things. I need to figure out how to win."

She smiled, "Well, I leave that up to you, 'cause I have no idea."

"Mmmhmm, I know how you work. You'll feign ignorance and then suggest the winning play, and then never take credit for it," I smiled back, and she chuckled.

"I wish."

"Riiight…"

"Um… we have an unscheduled shuttle trying to come into bay two."

That was neither Karen nor me — that would have been a rather odd progression of our conversation. No, that was Jim again, and he was frowning as he leaned over one of the operations consoles, "It's from *Artemis*. I've stopped its clearance for the moment and it's waiting…"

"We supposed to be expecting anyone?" I shifted my expression to a frown and glanced at Karen.

Shaking her head, she leaned forward and looked around me at Felicia, "Signal the shuttle."

Lieutenant Khalid nodded, and after a few seconds screen eight lit up. The loading screen flashed through quite quickly, and then there was Rufus Chang, *Lion's* Major of

Special Branch, with his mismatched eyes and a deep frown.

"Requesting permission to come in," Rufus' tone was flat.

"Ruifu, shouldn't you be in for treatment?" for some reason I addressed him by his proper name, probably making me sound slightly parental — not something I strive for.

He shook his head, "We were lucky. Very lucky. We were actually heading to the bay to our assault shuttle, because I believed the Martians might attempt a landing on Io. We didn't get there, or we would have been dead. Instead we were trapped in one of the sections between bays, sealed off from the rest of the ship. We had to blow our way through several bulkheads to find an escape pod, but we were isolated from any reactor radiation."

Rufus, by the way, is an explosives enthusiast. If you're ever trapped in a steel maze, he's the one you want with you — because he'll pick a direction and blaze (blow up) a trail through every wall in the way.

But that wasn't the most important thing to take from what he said. Actually, there were two very important things: first, he'd been lucky. Some have implied that he was unusually lucky — that perhaps the real story was that Rufus and his squad had been cowardly and avoided running to assist with the reactor shutdown that had irradiated so many of *Lion's* crew.

Well, you go ahead and think that. I invite you to say it to Rufus' face sometime. He was stuck, believe me. Stuck and just plain lucky, which as I said before, happens sometimes. Most of *Lion's* crew, Kris included, had not been so lucky.

But another item I should highlight here is that the reactor issue that had been identified during Glorious February was still a problem. We'd known about it, of course, but between the end of the battles in February and the launch of our mission in March there simply hadn't been time to put into dock for upgrades. Some safety measures had been added, but none that I could explain to you in anything less than twenty pages, and none of them, evidently, too effective.

Then again, considering *Lion* hadn't simply exploded when hit by the battleship laser, perhaps they had helped.

A bit.

Anyway, Rufus wanted to come aboard.

"Well, we're glad to have you. We just sent all our SF down to Io, and we'll need someone to lead the landings on Sinope," Karen nodded to Rufus. "Come on in. But if you don't mind, Rufus, get a checkup from Doctor Morgan when you land. Just to be sure."

With a nod, the Major disappeared from the screen.

Wolf had some Special Branchers again. That was good, because we'd need them, and Charlie had his hands quite full.

CHAPTER SEVENTEEN
THOSE APARTMENTS

The Martians seemed to thin out over the next half hour. There were twelve confirmed dead, seven presumed dead, and three captured... so that's... twenty-two out of action, out of thirty-eight. Not bad, even Charlie would admit, though the cost had been high.

While the Martians in the HQ had only been using mid-level power on their mags, five of Gina Bertram's people were down and out. Charlie's squad had lost two to serious injury, though both looked like they'd recover. Marcus' squad had three casualties, two of them fatal.

So twenty-two had been taken out, at the cost of ten — a fair trade? Well, yes and no. This is almost directly what I heard from Charlie. The balance of losses was good on the ground, but he'd also used up his heavy fire support — remember both Starlights of Lionstar Squadron had been shot down, with one dead pilot there. And if you look at it, most of the Special Branch casualties had come in that hallway in HQ — in very, very tight quarters. If the Martians got down into the old base tunnels of the research facility, Charlie would be facing more losses like that.

Things had gone well in the running firefight, in part because Charlie had been able to flatten buildings on top of Commandos, at least while the Starlights were up. In the mall it had gone well because, though it was close-ish, it wasn't nearly as tight as a fight in a base corridor, or an underground tunnel. Room to maneuver is critical. When there isn't any room, it doesn't matter how good you are: you're going to lose people.

Gina Bertram's experience demonstrated that well enough.

But all that was unimportant for just this moment. About half an hour after Charlie got out of the mall, he was crouching in front of the hospital, looking carefully over the concrete rail that ran alongside the stairs going up to the entrance to the research offices. Marcus' squad had been through both floors of the regular hospital in a fast sweep that had confirmed it was apparently clear, but he was still sweeping through the research side of the building.

This was not 'good' clearing, by the way. There wasn't time to be thorough — as soon as the survivors from *Lion* started arriving, they'd need immediate treatment. Charlie didn't like the thought of people on gurneys dying from radiation poisoning because his teams were taking their time. That said, it was a risk to be cavalier about the clearing operations...

But Charlie had a hunch that the Martians didn't give a damn about the hospitals. They'd already absorbed heavy losses, and frankly, the hospital buildings wouldn't be great to defend.

No, if he were the Martians, he'd ignore the big structures with their large windows and generous ventilation, and drop immediately into the tunnels.

Which was why Charlie was peering over this concrete railing. He was looking about 900 meters down the street, to the small building that held the entrance to the underground complex. And then he looked up past that building, at the four apartment towers that could provide snipers with a rather fantastic shot at anyone going for the tunnels.

Yes, this qualified as troublesome.

Dropping back down and turning to Carly and the rest of his squad (nine people with the two casualties, and with Terry Schroeder off looking after them both), "If I were them, I'd have a sniper with escort in one of those apartments. And I'd have that access point rigged to blow as soon as enough bodies got in there to maximize the effect."

Carly nodded, "So how do you want to play this?"

Charlie frowned and let his mind seize the problem. He'd give an entire minute over to thought — that's a lot of time in a special forces fight.

He needed to deal with those apartment buildings, but he didn't want to sweep each one. The number of booby traps set up in there over just this last half hour could be devastating. And it was such a perfect position, too... even though they were 1,500 meters or more away, a sniper could start picking off SF guards looking after the hospital from up there.

"First the apartments. I'm trying to decide if trapping the Martians in that old base would be a problem... might be the easiest way to secure this dome. But for now, the apartments..." Charlie let his voice trail off.

Another ten seconds of thinking, then he tapped his comm headset, "Marcus, have you heard anything about the condition of the Starlight that landed down in front of HQ?"

A pause, "Nothing."

Charlie nodded once to himself, then looked at Ben Belete, "We're going to our car, and I need you with me, Carly. Might have to do some jury-rigging."

As his officers and he got moving, Charlie tapped his comm a couple of times again, finding the frequency with *Artemis Agrotera's* Sensors and Communications Officer, "I need someone who knows how to repair F-194 Starlights."

Lieutenant Rona Brown was the pilot of the Lionstar plane that had managed to land in front of the HQ building, and as Charlie's car came to a sharp stop on the street next to the still partially-smoking plane, she was descending the steps from the HQ building's front door with one of Gina Bertram's officers as escort.

"What tha hell are ya' gonna do to my plane?" she demanded as soon as Charlie exited the car, and he actually stopped in surprise at the thick Scottish accent.

Anyone who knows Charlie knows that, at least in his slightly younger years, he'd been quite proficient at mimicking a Scottish accent, though he'd come across only a few Scots in his years in the service. It didn't take him long to shake off the surprise, of course, and he smiled, "I'm going to turn it into an artillery piece."

Rona Brown stopped right in front of Charlie, "Well, I dunna know if I'm goin' to approve of that, sir. But I suppose yer not givin' me a choice, then, are ya'?"

Charlie shook his head, "Afraid not."

The pilot backed off and Charlie then pointed at one of the cars parked as a reserve vehicle in front of the HQ, "We need one of those, then we need lots of rope. I want one car under each wing, lashed tight. We need to get this thing onto the roof of the HQ offices.

I didn't fully describe the Defense Command headquarters complex before, unfortunately, so I'll have to do that now. Between the tower that reached out of the dome and the cargo docks the Starlights had come through was a five-storey building of offices for Defense Command personnel. It had a nice flat roof, and would thus make a perfect artillery position.

"I'll get the car," Carly was already dashing across the street to one of the vehicles, and Ben Belete disappeared into the rubble of what had been the stores (the first buildings the Starlights had flattened, remember) looking for cordage.

In Charlie's ear, a new voice then sounded, "Master Chief Hollings, here, Major. What can I do for you?"

"Hang on, Chief, I have a pilot I'm going to patch in. We need to jury-rig a dead Starlight to fire its mags from the ground."

Rona Brown frowned at Charlie's words, as she hadn't heard Chief Hollings' introduction of herself. Charlie pointed to his headset, "*Artemis* channel."

As a pilot, Rona of course had her own comm headset, but she'd pulled it off her head in anger when she'd heard that Charlie was planning to mess with her poor plane. Now that she was obliged to play ball, she put it back in, "Chief, who is this?"

"Kim Hollings, ma'am. You want to reactivate mags? What's the state of the plane?"

They started talking in techno-terms that I could try to explain, but would take some time to translate in their entirety. For once I actually understand the concepts they were discussing, though, having come from a pilot's background. Charlie, being a technophile who has an instinct around machines, was also able to keep up.

Essentially, the three shoulder laser shots had hit the Starlight's small powerplant, and punched right through it. That sort of shot just rips the guts out of a plane, and leaves it without energy to do anything. Charlie wanted to hook an external power source — like a hovercar engine — into the Starlight, and use it to power the mags. Bang, artillery.

In movies, I often find the technicians who get called in to jury-rig things like this start freaking out. You know, the 'oh it was never designed for that, how could you!?' song and dance. Most of the good techs and deck crews I've come across in my years in the service have had quite the opposite reaction to such challenges, though — they're always happy to try to make something work.

Kim Hollings, one of the Chiefs on *Artemis Agrotera* who'd been patching up fighters for twenty years, was just like that.

Again, I won't get into the details. Charlie, Ben and Carly got the cars strapped under the wings of the battered plane, then gingerly lifted it up to the top of the roof of the office building. Aside from looking funny, that wasn't too exciting.

Once up there, the cables started to come out, and Ben actually had to run into the DCHQ building to rip some relays out of rooms on the first floor, just to transfer the power.

In what amounts to one of those montage scenes from a movie (you know, the ones where the dialogue is replaced by music, and they fade from short scene to short scene, with everyone hunched around, plugging something in or splicing something... the ones that usually have one or two funny scenes inserted, where they're trying to fit the square peg in the round hole, and that end in a handshake and smiling?) they managed to rig the engines from both cars into the Starlight's mag array.

Gee, does that look like I copped out on explaining how they did it? Do you care? Hehe.

Shaking hands with Rona, Charlie was smiling, then he pointed Ben to one car and Carly to the other, "Alright, we aim this thing with the cars."

With the Starlight being immobile, the cars were the only way it could be turned, so Ben and Carly fired up the hoverpads of the vehicles, and then watched as Charlie walked to the edge of the roof and pointed right at those damned apartments.

Carly backed her car up ever so slightly, and Ben stayed right where he was, and with a bit of a screech, the feet of the Starlight dragged across the roof, until the plane's nose was lined right up.

"Rona, if you'd be so kind," Charlie was pleased with the rig they'd put together, and was justifiably smiling about it.

The Scot nodded, then bounded up the side of her plane's fuselage and hopped into her seat. She had no instruments working, but the fire control for the mags was still rigged through her control stick. As long as the mags had power, and they did now, the trigger would work.

"Fire at your discretion," Charlie waved to her, then walked out of the way. Good thing, too.

Without delay, she clamped down on the trigger. Carly and Ben aimed well; the apartment nearest the hospitals was suddenly being riddled with mag shots, and the top half began to cave downwards onto the lower sections almost immediately.

The whine had Charlie plugging his ears again, and he didn't look back at the Starlight until the roof shuddered — not the apartment roof, the roof of the building he was standing on. That got his head to whip around, and he realized both cars had dropped from their hovers simultaneously, as soon as the mags had fired.

Apparently, firing the mag took so much out of the engines that the hoverpads couldn't run while they were shooting.

It struck Charlie as funny then, and I think it's funny now. Didn't matter, though. Between shots, the cars could turn the plane, and then the plane could blaze away. Not ideal, but a hell of a lot better than nothing.

"Take that, snipers..." Charlie smiled to himself as he watched that first apartment drop.

Then a sniper shot took him square in the chest, and knocked him off his feet.

Oops.

CHAPTER EIGHTEEN

THE HOSPITALS

Zail Patel had an excellent medical staff, and he'd made sure to train forty of his spacers to be able to assist that staff in case of a large number of casualties. The result was very fast turnaround.

Lion's pods would head to *Artemis Agrotera*, or be pulled into the combat storeship's landing bay by shuttles out there recovering them. Owing to the amount of cargo a combat storeship moves, its landing bay actually has a dual airlock system; on both ends of the bay, there is an inner and outer door, and a chamber in between, so that people can be working in the bay without EVA kit while shuttles and pods are coming and going. This makes loading and unloading cargo much easier, and is a Godsend in a situation like this. The medical team and volunteers could literally do triage right there in the flight bay.

The process was well established, essentially being the same radiation decontamination protocol seen on most ships, with just a few adjustments. As soon as a pod was opened, medical personnel in anti-rad gear pulled the *Lion* crew out of it, took them behind some curtains, stripped them, hosed them down with decon foam and water, and put them in medical fatigues. They were then taken to a rallying point on the far side of the bay, where they were scanned to check for internal radioactive toxicity, and were injected with a new cocktail of anti-rad drugs, then prioritized for shipment down to Io.

Really bad cases, and those who were 5,000 REM or over, were sent to one of *Artemis Agrotera's* own sickbays, to die.

I wish I didn't have to be that blunt, but that was the way it was. Over fifty people, including the remnants of *Lion's* engineering staff, the XO (Melanie Powell, who I have never mentioned in these books, I'm sad to say) and any of the ship's medical staff that had somehow not died in the first fifteen minutes (most ended up in the reactor room with the engineers, injecting them with cocktails every few minutes to try to keep them alive long enough to finish the shutdown, and thus died themselves) were now going to die on *Artemis Agrotera*.

I don't believe I need to explain just how much heroism, gallantry, and noble sacrifice these women and men exhibited, but I will comment on it anyway: it was awe-inspiring.

This was a crew Karen had built, this was a crew Karen had loved, in the way that any Captain loves her or his crew. It had been her family for years. I don't think I've been able to do as much justice to *Lion* since the war started as I'd have liked, but in the books that I'll hopefully write to tell the pre-war story, I'll be able to capture just how amazing *Lion's* crew was.

Well, they proved it, didn't they? Shutting down the reactors, many had died, but the ship had been saved.

The concern right now, though, had to be with the survivors.

I've just talked about what was happening on *Artemis Agrotera*. While Charlie was setting up the artillery piece on the roof of the DCHQ offices, the first shuttles were landing on level fifteen of the Defense Command tower, and the first twenty members of *Lion's* crew were unloaded into Kyle Stranks' care.

His SF, sixty women and men in total, were spread from floor fifteen down to the street, and Marcus Atallah had sent two cars down to act as escorts for the convoy up to the hospital. Cars for those convoys had been rounded up quickly by Bertram's Special Branchers — again, you can see the blinding pace at which everyone was working — and ultimately, between the cars her team had brought in, and the extras that had already been sitting in front of the HQ, there were seven.

Kris was in the first shipment of twenty survivors, I should have mentioned, along with Omar Cunningham. Omar had been Lieutenant in charge of SF under Karen, and he'd personally taken it upon himself to look after Kris since she'd taken over the ship. Now he (who'd taken only — *only* — 800 REM) was somehow walking next to her stretcher as it was carried down the steps to one of the cars.

He sat in the front seat of the car, which Kyle Stranks himself drove, while Kris' stretcher was laid across the wide back seat.

Along with the six other cars full of patients, and Marcus' escort, the convoy made the run on down to the hospital, and they pulled up at the Emergency entrance (facing the mall) just as the first apartment tower dropped under mag fire.

The first doctors, actually, to meet the incoming patients were Terry Schroeder and Marcus' squad medic. Now, these two knew how to patch up people in a firefight, but they'd be the first to tell you they didn't know how to do a full spectrum anti-radiation treatment. Not in the Special Branch training guide.

Artemis Agrotera's first batch of doctors was coming down on the next shuttle, but for now the Special Branch medics did what they could — specifically, they organized the allotment of beds in the hospital. Critical cases (anyone in the 1,000 REM plus range) were going to the first floor, four to a room (the rooms were built for eight, so it was actually the opposite of cramped, even if 'four to a room' sounds cramped). Anyone between 300 and 1,000 REM was going upstairs to be similarly allotted, and below 300 REM, they were going to the cafeteria to save bed space. Under 300 REM, the drug cocktails could actually reverse the damage before it manifested itself in symptoms… you know, stuff like vomiting and hair loss.

The system was carefully thought out — despite the haste of its implementation — and the medical staff of *Artemis Agrotera* would go on to credit the Special Branch medics with excellent thinking.

When Charlie slowly sat up and unzipped his ruined vest (if he'd left it on and been shot again, fragments from the plating would have blown right through him), he was greeted by the sight of the second convoy, including doctors from the combat storeship, heading to the hospital. Shuffling back from the edge of the roof (in case the sniper tried again), he rolled onto his stomach and then crawled back behind Ben's car.

"So… I hate getting shot," he said lightly into his comm, and Carly gave the most brilliant answer I could have imagined.

"You got shot?"

"What do you mean? Of course I got *shot!*" he purposefully exclaimed, but in a playful way. "You didn't notice?"

"Nope," Carly said it just before the mags fired again, dropping her car roughly to the deck. In the next few seconds, she swept the nearby rooftops with her eyes, looking for a shooter.

Charlie tapped his comm to make sure he was sending to everyone on the Special Branch frequency, then issued a quick warning, "Just got a hit from a sniper. Long range, I'm fine, but watch out. I think he was in the apartments, but I could be wrong."

"Nothing on the agribuildings... don't see anything in the industrial zone at all. Probably in the apartments. Won't be for long."

The apartments were the best vantage point for a sniper, certainly — that's why Charlie was knocking them down without remorse. Pulling off his vest as he thought that, he dropped it on the roof next to him, and started pulling the useful stuff out of it.

He tapped his comm at the same time, "I got shot, Gina. Could you send a new vest up to the roof of the office block when you get a minute."

There was a pause, "Sure thing. You alright, sir?"

"Yeah, surprisingly so, for someone who's been shot. That'll teach me to stand boldly on a roof like an idiot," he finished emptying the vest, then took it up and laid it in his lap. The protection had, of course, worked, and because the mag bolt had come from all the way across the dome, it had evidently lost enough intensity to not punch through, or break ribs. For comparison, by the way, he was kilometers from the likely location of the shooter; the Brancher who had her ribs broken by a similar shot in the mall had taken the hit from, oh, twenty meters. Ten, probably.

Even MAG-90s lose some of their kick over those sorts of ranges, though make no mistake, if not for the vest, Charlie would be very dead.

He tried not to dwell on that right then.

Behind him, Ben and Carly reset their car positions to drag the nose of the Starlight around a couple of degrees more, lining it up with the last apartment. Charlie didn't dare look — he was unprotected now, so he wasn't going to get ambitious — but after Gina's officer had run up a new vest for him, he did look to see the results of his innovation.

Four apartment blocks were now four piles of rubble. That still meant they offered cover, but they were much easier to sweep — there were no rooms to clear, and any pre-set booby traps had been cut apart or crushed.

"Alright, good shooting," Charlie said after seeing that. Now that the shock had worn off, he started to realize he probably had some pretty impressive bruises on his chest, and was in a bit of pain, but he wasn't too concerned.

And no, that's not an ominous setup to us discovering later that he had more serious injuries. Charlie's tough, but he's not stupid — if he'd thought something was seriously messed up in his chest, he really wasn't going to stay on his feet to eventually die, just because he wanted to appear macho or whatever.

As I once put it to him, "Being a man's man is apparently great — it leads to being a zombie's zombie!" My editor didn't get that... I mean that if you go nuts with bravado, you'll likely end up dead. A zombie is an animated dead person... follow now? Oh well.

Once the apartments were knocked down, Charlie left Rona and the cars on the roof with two of Kyle's SF — the new artillery crew, should that fire support be needed. He, Carly and Ben headed down the stairs into the building, and then moved out for the hospital with the next convoy.

The last thing Charlie wanted was a Commando raid on that place.

Kris was in a room on the first floor, and when Charlie walked in she was passed out in her bed.

There is no way to make radiation sickness sexy.

I chose that last word carefully, because I find movies try to make a lot of illnesses look 'sexy'. One movie producer, dealing with a much later case of very serious ailment connected to another Belt Squadron and Jupiter Force woman, essentially told me that in film, everyone (particularly the 'hot women') had to look 'sexy', no matter what they were dying of.

Or not quite dying of, hopefully.

Reality isn't that sexy, I'm afraid. Kris, at that moment, looked like a woman who'd personally hauled four people out of the engineering section (three of whom had lived, and went on to have families, each with a daughter or son named for her). After a dose like hers, the books say there'd be a period of brutal fatigue, due to the radiation's effect on the brain, and then, she'd supposedly appear to be somewhat healthy for a few days — they call that the 'walking ghost' phase, apparently. Then her cells would start to melt.

That's what would happen if she hadn't gotten treatment, but because she'd been pumped full of multiple drug cocktails, she had a chance. If they'd circulated enough before and after the exposure, they could have absorbed radiation and fortified against the very worst of the damage wrought by the blast of REM she received. Her white blood cells were still there, and they were being produced in increasing numbers thanks to the impact of the drugs. Her bone marrow had mostly been preserved, and what was missing would hopefully be rebuilt by those huge numbers of white blood cells.

She was sterile, though. And if she lived through it, she'd face two or three years of genetic therapy, based on the DNA sample taken at her last annual physical. Those things couldn't be helped, and if you look at all of that, it's pretty obvious that she was out of the war for a while.

People often assume that anyone not killed in a battle is okay. Well, Kate Levec hadn't been okay, and Kris *really* wasn't. We didn't have to have ships destroyed or people killed to lose them, believe me.

Even under the best-case scenario, Kris had a long, hard road ahead of her.

Charlie knew all of this as he walked up to her bed, swinging his MAG-90 out of the way to his left side and stopping to look down at her.

Again, probably something I haven't explained enough in these books (for those who don't know our pre-war history) but Charlie and Kris had been quite close — like brother and sister, really — while Kris had been my XO on *Wolf*, and before that back on *Friendly*. Again, the war, and the fact that we'd been separated so much over 2231, has kept me from really demonstrating that for you.

But Charlie was very, *very* unhappy to see her in this condition. Reaching down, he took Kris' left hand in his right and gave it a gentle squeeze, "Hey."

Kris actually managed to open her eyes and look up. She didn't say anything — the fatigue was far too intense — but she curled her lips up in a small, painful smile.

In the movies, I'm sure she'd look like an angel doing that.

Charlie's description to me: "The way she looked made me want to kill people."

Fortunately, our big-brotherly friend Charlie Peters had plenty of killing left to do, because as he said his goodbyes and left Kris to rest, there was the sound of a mag shot, followed by screaming and then mag counterfire.

"Taking fire from the subterranean access building!" someone — one of the SFers, probably — exclaimed over the comm.

Swinging his MAG-90 back to its central position on his vest, Charlie stepped out into the corridor, waved his squad (who'd been waiting for him) to follow, and then headed through the corridors of the hospital at a run.

The Martians were going to pay, you see.

And Charlie Peters is not someone you want to have coming to collect.

CHAPTER NINETEEN

BEGINNING TO SLOW DOWN

If you were to read this book right after finishing *The Jupiter Patrol*, you'd perhaps realize that Karen and I hadn't slept in... oh, a while. Insane as this sounds, if you look at the course of events, our arrival at Io had only been about fifteen hours before Charlie blazed out of the hospital looking for some mayhem.

In that time, Karen and I had stopped to eat a meal — let's call it lunch — and to watch the report Jessica Qing had very hastily assembled and dispatched to the Empire in a comm burst, but we hadn't really taken any down time.

As soon as we'd sent that story (along with our report of arrival) and deposited Charlie on Io, we'd gone after Matt. I hadn't wanted to go to bed as soon as we left, in case anything went awry, so I'd spent two hours on the bridge, at the end of which we'd reversed course, to get back to Io to stop the Martians, and since then it had been steady going.

With the adrenalin running low, I started to recognize how tired I was becoming — and tired wasn't good when I had to face down this crafty Martian commander in the near future. Realizing this as *Wolf* boosted from Io orbit yet again, I looked back at Jim Hannigan, "We're going to get an hour's sleep, you keep watch until we're back, then we'll relieve you."

"You'll take at least three hours," Jim Hannigan didn't even look away from the console he'd been working on, and his tone shared a lot in common with the one Matt had so often used to try to keep us from doing stupid stuff.

I managed to crack a smile, "Is that a fact, Commander Hannigan?"

"Yes it is, don't test me," he still didn't look away from the panel he was working on. "I'll call you if anything happens."

Jim, of course, had been up just as long as we had, but while there was a moment of quiet, he thought it best that Karen and I rest. I had to agree with him — our decisions were probably going to be the ones that won or lost the upcoming battle, not Jim's. I know, I know, that sounds awfully egotistical. But it's not wrong.

In battle, Jim's job was to make sure *Wolf*'s combat systems are operating at full potential, while Karen and I decided what *Wolf* and the whole force were going to do. If we made a mistake, it would potentially endanger more lives — though don't take that to mean Jim didn't have lives in his hands too...

Aw dammit, there's no way I'm going to make this one work, so you know what, I'm just going to say Karen and I left the bridge with small smiles at Jim's persistence, and with exhaustion setting in fast.

Entering the lift, I leaned back against the wall, closing my eyes for just a minute and letting out a long breath. Karen arrived next to me and did the very same, sliding herself sideways so that our arms and shoulders were pressed into each other.

"Kris looked bad," I said after a few seconds of silence, opening my eyes as I did.

Karen didn't answer for a moment, and I glanced at her. Her chin had dropped and her eyes were burning a hole in the floor. I didn't need to ask: *Lion* had been her ship, her crew. She was aboard *Wolf* now, and she loved this ship as much as *Lion*, but then all our old Belt Squadron ships and crews were part of the same family — just different houses, I suppose.

Now, so many of the brave men and women Karen had served with for years were dead or dying. It's hard to describe what Karen was feeling in those moments — what she'd been holding in and was now letting out in grim, blackest silence.

I reached around her arm, lacing my fingers into hers and squeezing her hand. I didn't say anything more — what could I say? You know how terrible I am at finding the right, sensitive, consoling words. I always lean towards the over-intellectual, the comments that are too carefully thought out and never honest enough to help.

So I just shut up, and squeezed Karen's hand. She squeezed back.

Andrea Kiley was not being silent, not at all. She had the engineering crew lined up in the outer reactor bay, and with her sidearm clipped to her hip, and armed with all those rumors about what had happened to the mag tech, she marched back and forth before the ranks of spacers.

Her Jupiter Force personnel were all standing in the rear rank, farthest away from her venom, because she knew *Dominator's* poor performance during our little engagement — its inability to close quickly and bring its powerful lasers to bear — had not been the fault of those imported people. No, the crew members who'd been running *Dominator* for years were the ones Andrea blamed. They should have known how to fight their ship.

And she was conveying that to them.

I'm not going to repeat everything she said. Hell, I'm not going to repeat any of it. You don't need to actually hear it, at all. I am not kidding or exaggerating when I tell you that four of the spacers from engineering were in tears, though.

No word of a lie.

Andrea's sharp, sweet voice, her dark eyes, the anger that seemed to be pulsing off her… it all made everything she said just *hurt*. It comes through on the surveillance feeds. It's not all insult and attack, some of it is describing what I've already talked about regarding radiation sickness.

She wasn't just telling them what they'd screwed up, she was telling them what could happen to even the best spacers if they were caught off guard. Alright, I'll actually quote her on this, because it really is shocking and powerful — it really hits home, I mean. At least it does with me, but then, Kris was lying near death. Perhaps that means I was more receptive to what Andrea was saying. Judge for yourself.

"That's the crew of *Lion*, isn't it? That's one of the best crews in this fleet, you all know that. Some of you in the back were over on *Lion* up until this ship. And you know they were bloody well the best. And look at that, best or not they were still able to go and get irradiated, weren't they?" Andrea kept pacing back and forth, the anger that was burning deep in her starting to emerge with her words. Well, some of it.

"Now forgetting for *just a minute* that we might have been able to do something about that if we'd closed faster, just a bit faster, what would you do, hmm? Three quarters of the ship's crew is going to be irradiated, or *four* quarters will be. Which do you pick, hmm? Because you're bloody *dead* either way, aren't you? Because you're sitting on the irradiator, right through that goddamned wall!" she stabbed her finger at the back of the compartment.

"Why did you join, hmm? Well, I know some of you signed on for hot food, or to get away from creditors, or some other damned thing. But now you're all here, and what's more, this is war. And you're all sitting on your asses saying 'not me'? 'No not me'? I'm taking this ship into the fight against those bastards that crippled *Lion*, and they may well cripple us. Our reactors may fry — we may be irradiated. And what will you do then? Will you die like a bunch of fucking kids who're too lazy or too scared to wear their uniforms with pride? Or will you actually do something, do *something* to try to save a life? Just one damned life? You probably don't want to make that choice, do you? You probably don't want to have to melt from the inside, and die throwing your guts up and shitting yourself. Well then get off your asses, start putting some effort and some *professionalism* into your work. You fight this ship bloody properly, and then *maybe* we won't all die because you lot failed to get our engines up to speed on the fucking double!"

I don't know, I thought that was pretty strong reasoning, language forgiven.

Of course, listening to it now, I can hear the many layers of pain in Andrea's voice. There was a lot going on under the surface, and I don't need to hit you over the head with it again just for effect.

Our dear Andrea Kiley was not herself.

Wolf rejoined *Dominator, Cheetah, Pictou* and *Trusty* about an hour later, while Karen and I stole some sleep.

CHAPTER TWENTY
BUT NOT SLOWED YET

Charlie had found a window in the end of the research hospital that gave him a perfect view of the underground access building. There were four Commandos in the entrance and windows of that structure, not doing too much to hide their presence.

Charlie smelled a trap instantly.

Fifty of *Wolf's* SF were on the ground now, one of them down with a wound that looked like it'd be fatal, and Kyle Stranks was itching to take that building from the Martians. There were only *four*, after all... but were there only four? Charlie doubted it. These four were the bait — their job had to be to draw an attack, because as soon as SF or Special Branchers got into the open and moved against the structure, any number of evil things could happen...

If it were Charlie, he'd have that building rigged to blow.

"Come on, Charlie, we can dislodge them..." Kyle, situated in a room further back in the hospital, was eager to get his own back against the Commandos.

"Not happening, Kyle, it's a trap. I know it looks good, but that building's rigged. We get enough bodies in there to clean them out, they'll blow it. We die, they secure the entrance to the underground installation."

"But that wouldn't make sense — they'd be sealing themselves in," Kyle came back quickly over the comm, and Charlie nodded in reply, even though the Lieutenant of SF couldn't see it.

"I'm all for blowing the building, I just don't want to be inside when it goes," Charlie brought his MAG-90 up as one of the Commandos started to shift positions.

Charlie put a full-powered mag bolt through the man's face. This at about 300 meters away, making good use of the MAG-90's sight.

"Getting any detonator frequencies?" Charlie glanced back at Carly Henderson, who had hooked her comm into a Special Branch frequency jammer/rammer, a handy tool when it worked.

Essentially, the ja-rammer (that's what everyone I've talked to calls it) can stop radio or other signal-based detonation signals — so if someone has a remote control for a bomb, this thing can jam the 'explode' command. Much of the time anyway. Alternately, it can also act as a detonator, figuring out what the carrier signal for an 'explode' command would be, and sending it. Like I say, a very handy tool... when it works.

Normally, Charlie would take a little more time (a whole minute maybe) to think about whether to blow that building, but with this many critically wounded patients in the hospital next door, he wasn't waiting. Kyle was right: blowing the building would seal the Martians in down there, and he'd rather do it from outside, than waiting for the Commandos to do it for him... with him *in* the building...

The immediate priority was to secure this area, so those patients would be safe. As much as he didn't want to face Martians hiding in the old complex's tunnels, he had no choice. It'd be messy, but he'd deal with it later.

But as he glanced back at Carly he found the ja-rammer wouldn't help, because she was shaking her head, "I'm getting nothing. It might be a physical trigger. Trip wire or something."

So they couldn't just blow the place up from long range. Dammit.

"They're falling back!" that call came from someone nearby, and wasn't over the comm.

Looking back out the window, Charlie discovered that the Commandos had indeed displaced, leaving their dead comrade behind on the entry veranda.

"Definitely a trap," Charlie repeated into his comm. "Everyone stay put, my squad will check it."

Gulp.

No, Charlie wasn't looking forward to getting anywhere near that building — he had no interest in becoming a zombie's zombie, to revive that bad analogy. But he also wasn't going to let Kyle rush in with guns blazing and get a lot of people killed.

"Kyle, get ready on cover fire, we may need it," Charlie was already following his squad (still just nine, including him) out of the room they'd been in, then around a corner and out a side door. They left the research hospital, fanning out in three teams of three, moving again with chests to the enemy and eyes looking down the sights of their MAG-90s.

No activity as they got onto the street and closed the first twenty meters. Nothing.

At 250 meters range, Charlie stopped his people with a hand gesture, and they knelt behind the cover on the opposite side of the road. They may not be able to trigger the explosives via comm, but there were other ways...

"All safeties off, Kyle, I want every gun we have drilling that thing. My squad, hold for anyone making a break for it."

Instantly, Kyle's SFs — spread between the windows of the hospital Charlie had just come out of — let loose the power of their brand new (to them, anyway) MAG-90s, and as was the case in the shopping mall, the weapons proved their ability to be physically devastating, instead of precise.

The subterranean access building, sturdily constructed of alloy prefab sheets, was riddled with holes after just a few seconds of barrage, and then its façade literally started to sheet off.

"Alright, hold," Charlie interrupted as the front of the building fell off, revealing the rooms that had faced it.

Charlie and his squad were squinting now, checking to see if they recognized anything explosive or dangerous. Nope.

"Magbangs, Carly's team," Charlie said it quietly, and slinging their MAG-90s, Carly's trio moved forward at a run, covering the 200 meters to throwing range in just over twenty-five seconds (quite fast with all gear). Three grenades were lobbed, and she and her people were running back to their place with blinding speed and precision.

The grenades went off, flashing in the rooms open to the front, and nothing happened. So far so good.

But, of course, Charlie wasn't satisfied.

Tapping his comm again, he switched to Starlight frequency — well, *artillery frequency* now, "Rona, Charlie Peters. Can you take a shot at that building we just blew the front off of, please?"

There was a pause, "I think so. We're going to have to cut it close to that research hospital, though. I'll lean to the left, minimize the risk. You get outta the way too, if that's your squad in the road."

Charlie wasn't about to disagree with advice like that, so his hand went up and the gestures started flying, ordering his squad back into the research hospital again.

Tapping his comm back to Kyle's frequency, Charlie issued the warning, "We're about to get some hot fire from our artillery. Everyone cover up."

The few SF who were in plain sight hustled to get themselves behind cover somewhere, and Charlie followed his team back into the room he'd been occupying before. He tapped his comm yet again, "Rona, we're in that research hospital, so don't miss, please."

She was lining up the shot by eye, looking down the nose of her plane and calling to the drivers of the two cars to back up or move forward just a little to traverse her around, "I *said* I'll lean the other way, didn't I?"

Oof, Charlie got told.

He tapped back to Kyle's frequency, then, "Any second now. She's leaning left with her shot, to make sure she doesn't clip the hospital."

That was just to keep the SF informed, so they wouldn't jump to any conclusions if the shot actually missed its target…

The roar was again deafening, and a stream of golden mag bolts ripped through the air about ten meters to the left of the research hospital, slamming straight into the building. Charlie's first thought was something like 'Only ten meters from the hospital? Glad she leaned left!'

His second thought was 'holy four-letter-word'.

The ground shook as the building went up like a pyre, the blast wave shaking the walls of the hospital. He was definitely glad he hadn't been kneeling out on the street for that one.

Kyle quickly came in over the comm, "Great call, Charlie. Definitely glad we didn't go in…"

Charlie, without realizing it, had fallen onto his back, so he sat up and shook his head once, then pushed himself onto his feet, looking out the window again.

Yep, giant crater — at least forty meters across — filled with rubble. Would have been bad to be in there when the Commandos pressed the 'boom' button.

"That should seal it," Charlie didn't miss a beat in his tactical analysis. "Kyle, get a checkpoint set up across the street from it, somewhere with lots of cover in case some of them were trapped in the dome and want to start sniping. Marcus, your team can secure the hospital buildings along with Kyle's guards… Gina, keep HQ shut up. I'm taking my squad back to you. Need the HQ computers to check out what our counterparts have access to down there."

Just like that, Charlie was on to something else entirely. That's just the way he can be — and the way Special Branch in general can be, I've found. They move fast and hard, they don't tire, and don't screw up.

Knock wood.

Sorry, that's Capital Island superstition — if you say something like 'they don't screw up' you knock on a piece of wood to keep fate from taking your assertion as an affront and going out of its way to prove you wrong.

Moving tactically (but not as tensely) back out the research hospital's side door, Charlie sent Ben and one of the other officers from his squad to get two cars for their trip back to HQ. He was smiling somewhat tiredly at Carly, and was about to mention that they were all due for a half hour's rest, when something rather unpleasant happened.

Night fell. Just like that.

Fell like an axe.

Day. Night. No in between.

That wasn't supposed to happen.

In fact, there were only two reasons it could happen: either someone in the HQ building had decided it was time for the sky simulations to go away and for the dome to go translucent... or...

"What the hell is this?" Charlie blurted the question before he stopped himself. Then he let out a sigh and shook his head, glancing back at Carly. "Ten bucks says we just sealed them in with the reactor that powers this place."

Carly had been smiling, and now that smile was sort of stuck — the way some expressions get stuck in place by surprise.

"Great," she said dryly.

"Not the word that I was thinking," Charlie shook his head, then cupped his forehead.

Pick your four letter word and insert it here. The day... night now, I suppose... was not going swimmingly.

CHAPTER TWENTY-ONE

ALRIGHT, WHAT HAPPENED?

The first half of this book is one big rush, and that's what that first day (loosely speaking) was like out at Io. It was a mad rush, where we were attacked on multiple sides, and fought back, keeping as much of the momentum as we could by just pushing forward. The Martians gave a very good account of themselves overall, but now we had them back on the defensive, and that meant we had to move from reacting and counterattacking into planning and assaulting.

So the tone started to change just a bit, and that was very good for us, because it meant we had a chance — a real chance — to catch our breath, and to plan based on the circumstances we were facing.

First, though, we slept. Karen and I each had about three hours, as per Jim's instructions, and Charlie had a whole twenty minutes. No wait, half an hour! Special Branchers are insane that way — they have the ability to say, "No worries, I'll sleep next week!" and not be kidding.

Yeah, bastards.

Anyway, the long and the short of it was that a few hours after night fell rather rudely on Io, we were all able to stop and ask the question that's become the chapter title — what happened?

And then the next question: what now?

We'll start in space, where *Wolf*, *Cheetah*, *Dominator*, *Trusty* and *Pictou* were tailing the Martian battleship force. We'd collected our Starlights after we'd closed sufficiently with the Martian force to keep it on the edge of our sensors, so it was just a stern chase for now... sort of. Matt, Elise and Aaron were still out ahead of us, and I'll turn you over to our briefing dialogue from there.

"...so I don't *think* they know that Matt's out there," Jim Hannigan was sitting in on a briefing with Karen, me, and the other Jupiter Force skippers on Battlelink, in Karen's day cabin.

Jim's instinct about sensors and the ability of enemy forces to see or not see things was pretty damned good, and the officers of the old Belt Squadron had long ago learned to trust them. Though that didn't mean we believed that he couldn't be wrong... we just trusted that he was right.

"If they don't know Matt, Aaron and Elise are between them and the other half of their force, that puts us in an interesting situation, doesn't it?" Mark Gunney asked the question with a slight frown. "They think all we have is chasing them."

I started to nod, glancing first at Karen, who was sitting behind the desk that I was leaning on, then looking to the screen again, "It creates options."

To bring you up to speed, the Martians had adjusted course while Karen and I slept. Nothing drastic, and frankly nothing unexpected; the battleship force had redirected its base vector for Sinope, and we'd finally received a signal from Matt, saying the force he was tracking had turned in the very same direction.

Now, this may be hard to visualize, but with this turn, we'd essentially strung ourselves into a line of four separate units. In first position was the Martian formation that Matt had been chasing — the two destroyers and the three destroyer escorts. They were just in front of Matt, Elise and Aaron in *Friendly, Lady Grace* and *Honesty*, but as Jim had said earlier, he didn't think our corvettes had been noticed by any of the Martians.

About five hours behind Matt was the Martian battleship, along with two destroyers and two pirates, on the very same course, moving at roughly the same speed. Then, just off the starboard stern of that battleship force was us, with *Dominator, Wolf, Cheetah, Pictou* and *Trusty*.

It was clearly a very unusual arrangement of forces — not the sort of thing you'd expect to be set up for you, and definitely not a scenario for which academies had strategies.

"Well, we have about... what, twenty hours to Sinope?" Mark asked his next question and glanced off screen to confirm. "Yeah twenty. So that's time to hurt them some more, wouldn't you say?"

"Always a good idea to hurt them," Andrea's tone was sharp but steady again on the link, and I nodded and glanced at Karen.

"Ever think you'd see a line up quite like this?" I asked quietly.

For once, Karen seemed disconcerted. She'd come through Egesta, she'd saved the Empire, she'd done countless adventurous things and been *un*flapped through them all. But watching *Lion*'s plight had been worse than all of that for her, because that was her family...

Well, I don't need to explain it again, and I very much doubt you'll hold her reaction against her.

Anyway, as I glanced at her, she looked up slowly, face very slightly drawn, and shook her head, "Never thought I would, no. But we should take advantage of it."

"Listen to the nice lady," Mark grinned on screen.

"I tend to," I smiled as I looked back at him. "Alright, we have the battleship force bracketed, but I have no interest in jumping them until we're a little closer to Sinope. We'll get Matt and Elise to start dropping back to join us, give us the edge. Aaron will stay out there with the other force. We'll leave one corvette forward to keep up appearances, in case the Martians can see them."

In other words, if the Martian force Matt's group was tailing could actually see one or more of Matt's ships, then one corvette could hopefully take the place of three. If those Martians had noticed they were being chased, and the chase force vanished, they'd probably try to warn their battleship, ending our advantage of surprise.

But if we played this right, two corvettes would attack the battleship group from the front, and the rest of our force (which the Martians certainly knew about) would come from the rear... and then we'd smack their battleship, to use a rather pedestrian term.

"I'll make sure we're into it this time. I've bloody well had enough of this mess..." Andrea was starting to look somewhat agitated on the screen.

If you're wondering, these were all signs that Karen and I were taking and filing away for later reference — things we'd remember after the dust settled, and then use to fuel our concerns about Andrea. For the moment, though, we didn't have the luxury of worrying about her; we were really too deep into this fight.

"I'll have Felicia send the signal back to Zail, and have it forwarded from there to Matt. If we sent it direct ourselves, the Martians might grab it, or at the very least see it and realize there's someone up there to coordinate with," I finished off the discussion. "We'll aim to attack in... oh... seventeen hours. I want to be close enough to Sinope to follow up with a strong strike if we do well, but far enough that we can bug out if things go poorly."

There were nods on the Battlelink, and then a chorus of verbal approvals. I looked again to Karen, and she nodded too.

"Alright, then goodbye for now, all of you get some sleep before the battle. I mean that," I said it to the skippers on the screen while looking at Karen.

Links started to cut, and Jim Hannigan rose from his chair opposite Karen and quietly excused himself.

"Send those signals to Zail to forward to Matt for me, will you Jim?" I asked as he left, and he nodded without stopping.

I think everyone had realized I was staring quite intently at Karen, and she looked back with tired eyes. Long day.

I extended my hand to her, "Come on, we need to get your mind off it."

She didn't react at first, then she blinked, "What?"

"Come on, you need to stop thinking about *Lion*. Just for the next twenty-four hours I need you to be mean and cold, like me. Come on," I waved my hand slightly to emphasize its outstretchedness, and Karen took it with a slight frown.

"I don't see what..."

"You will."

What comes next verges on the unbelievable again, I know. In my experience, some of the craziest things you hear — the things movie producers scoff at as unrealistic — are in fact quite true. I think I've said it before, it's just a matter of reality often being truly stranger than fiction.

The rec deck has a 'multi-purpose studio'. Gymnasts could use it (you'd be surprised how many gymnasts we had on the crew), as could martial arts practitioners, fencers, and a host of other groups — it was, as the name suggests, multi-purpose.

When I led Karen in there she really wasn't sure what to think — it probably wasn't what she'd been expecting — so I just pointed her to the middle of the empty floor and said, "You'll see."

With the crew either at standby action stations or feeling the fatigue of the past day and sleeping, the room was indeed abandoned. That was just good timing on our part, though I must admit, had anyone been there I would have pulled rank and tossed them out.

As Karen reached the center of the floor and turned to look at me, I smiled and went to the room controls. The lights were dimmed with one tap, and the music started playing with the next.

Real music. If you'll recall from the end of *The Independent Squadron*, the kind of music with instruments, and melody, and harmony.

It was soft enough not to be intrusive, but with the lights lowered, it was somehow relaxing. I turned and walked towards Karen with a smile, "No how's that for original thinking?"

A tired smile formed on her face by the time I arrived, and she shrugged, "It's pretty good."

Then we danced. I don't remember how long, and it wasn't like some flashy, fancy-footed ballroom affair. I think we just leaned against each other, heads on each other's shoulders, and rotated around for a while, weight going from foot to foot with slow regularity.

We shut the world out for an hour or more. We had to do that — for once Karen needed it. And you know what, battle to come or not, I was going to make damned sure Karen had what she needed.

Wolf and the Jupiter Force raced on, getting prepared and in position to do harm to the Martian battleship formation.

CHAPTER TWENTY-TWO

THE DEADLY DETAILS

"The temperature outside this dome is 173 degrees below zero," Carly Henderson was standing at one of the consoles in Io DCHQ's C&C, reading the exterior thermometer.

The building was still operating, despite the power cut to the dome, thanks to its backup generator. Every major building in the dome had one, hospital included, which meant that for the moment the landing force's ability to move and operate wasn't compromised. But this dome was going to lose its warmth eventually, and that would be a problem. Backup generators on buildings were meant to keep things running long enough for reactors to be repaired, or for evacuation to take place... but at the moment, neither was an obvious option.

Charlie was standing with his hands folded over the stock of his MAG-90, the weapon pointing down as it hung from his vest.

"Well. Dammit."

He'd left that one detail out of his planning, and now he was paying for it. He and everybody else, that was.

"All those volcanoes out there... could we use some of them to geo-thermally power this place?" Captain Weiss asked, though Charlie could tell from the tone that the question wasn't really very optimistic.

Shaking his head, he looked up at one of the C&C's screens, now showing a surface map of Io, "Nearest one is hundreds of clicks away, and I wouldn't have any idea how to build a geo-thermal power station on it."

There was mostly silence as Charlie's squad stood with him in the C&C. Occasionally a wild idea would be tossed out, but mainly that was because every one of his people was making a half-hearted effort to come up with a reason *not* to have to do what they all knew they were going to have to do.

That's right, they were going to have to go down into the tunnels, shoot their way through between eleven and eighteen (depending on whether some of that day's probable kills were actual kills or not) Commandos, and restart the reactor. And somehow destroy the controls, to make sure it couldn't be turned off again.

Options? That's why they were standing around — they were desperately trying to figure out other options, any options...

Yeah, there weren't so many of them.

"Within a day, this dome is going to be too cold to live in. It'll be zero degrees in about eight hours, at the rate we're losing heat," Carly turned away from the panel she'd been standing at.

Charlie sighed and nodded, "Alright, Raza, you get some demo charges and light up all the houses in the residential zone. Hopefully they'll burn nicely, get us some extra heat for a while. Make sure the backup generators on the atmospheric plant are running first, though… I don't want to smoke us out just to keep us warm. Meantime, we need to find a new way down to the tunnels."

As Captain Weiss nodded and led his team out of the C&C, Charlie and Carly stood next to each other and stared at that surface map of Io.

Kris Jacobs woke up in her hospital bed and realized it was night outside. She had no idea where she was, and was having a bit of trouble in that moment figuring out *who* she was. One of the doctors from *Artemis Agrotera* was across the room, pulling a sheet over a 13,400 REM patient who had just died, and as he was turning away in frustration, he realized she was coming around.

This was Doctor Conrad Rhee, and he approached Kris' bedside, forcing himself to smile as warmly as possible as her discolored and burned face turned towards him. Kris was hardly the worst-off patient he'd seen today, after all. In fact, she wasn't even the worst-off patient in this room.

Talking, Kris discovered, was difficult, because her tongue was swelling, bleeding, and coated with some sorts of welts, "Doc… how's crew…?"

Yes, good Captains always do inquire after the state of their crews before themselves.

"Sixty-one of the survivors have now died, Captain," Rhee said in a soft tone. Rightly or wrongly, the Korean didn't believe in withholding that sort of information from his Naval patients (something we officers rather appreciate). "However, only seven remain who we consider to be in danger of death, based on their exposure. You are unfortunately one of those."

Kris let out a breath with great difficulty, and then forced herself to nod, "I reckoned."

"I think you are more likely to survive than some of the others," Rhee continued, speaking softly still, and leaning in a little to make sure his smile was visible to her damaged eyes. There was literally nothing in Kris' body that hadn't been affected by the radiation, but believe it or not, the brutality of her condition at that moment was a good thing. It meant she wasn't a walking ghost.

Remember I mentioned that 'walking ghost' phase when I was first explaining this delightful radiation sickness? From what I understand, that's a 'latent phase' that comes with all radiation sickness, but for those who have doses under 1,000 REM (much less than Kris' exposure), our drugs can essentially fix the damage before the end of that phase. They don't lapse back into symptoms and illness again… though they obviously still need gene therapy and monitoring.

As I understand it (and I'm quite willing to be corrected on this by a specialist) what happens during this 'ghost' phase, if there's no treatment, is simple: the radioactive material is either gone or almost gone, but the cells are all dead. Go back to that cottage analogy I used earlier; it's like the fire being out, but the building collapsing a few days later because the support beams are all cooked.

The drugs the *Lion* medical staff had been shooting into Kris and everyone on the crew had been designed to keep cells alive and protect them from damage — to reinforce them so that the radiation wouldn't do as much harm. The cocktails that came later then repaired as many cells as could be saved, hopefully leaving enough healthy ones to replenish her body when the poisoned cells collapse.

But there was another complication: a cell that had been irradiated and poisoned by radiation could do one of three things: it could simply fail to reproduce (and thus the body dies), reproduce a cell that couldn't reproduce itself (delayed action death of body), or multiply in cancerous style. Any of those things would be bad, so our drugs tried to purge the poisoned cells quickly, replacing them with new ones that were being created by those healthy cells that had survived.

Make sense?

There's a lot more to it than that, but the bottom line is that instead of having a period of 'ghost walking', Kris was going through a long period of nasty symptoms while the irradiated cells were quickly purged. It would hopefully end with her body being restored by new cells.

If it worked, it'd take about a week, after which a long and painful recovery could begin. If it didn't, she'd die miserably within ten days.

Charming.

Kris wasn't completely up on all this — I've talked to a couple of specialists to get to a stage where I can half-competently explain it to you, though I'm sure any doctor would scoff at my crude attempt.

"So... it's good that I feel like hell, right?" Kris knew enough to rasp out that question, and Doctor Rhee nodded once.

"It is a sign that your body has not surrendered. I have high hopes for your recovery, Captain," his tone was soft.

Kris, bless her, actually managed a single sharp (and painful) laugh, "So do I."

Our very own Kris Jacobs.

It was still night outside in Io dome. And it was getting chilly.

CHAPTER TWENTY-THREE
OPTIONS

The situation on Io was handled before we got to our fight near Sinope, so now I'm going to stick with Charlie while he deals with it, before I swing back to space to look at the Sinope aspect of this Sinope affair.

"There's no real alternative… we need at least one reactor back online."

Charlie said that after no shortage of reflection. He was in the hospital again, this time discussing the needs of the *Lion* survivors with the medical staff from *Artemis Agrotera*. The long and the short of it: the hospital couldn't keep looking after these people on generator power alone.

As Doctor Rhee had said before, there were seven remaining critical patients, Kris included, but there were another sixty women and men who could become critical if they weren't kept under observation and if their drug cocktails were interrupted. And indeed, if the power behind the chemical synthesizer failed, many of the stable patients could become quite sick.

There was no other option: the power needed to be turned back on at the source.

"Alright," Charlie nodded a last time to the doctor he'd been speaking with and turned back to Carly, Marcus Atallah and Kyle Stranks, "we need a way down there, and nothing on the maps we were looking at seemed promising."

The maps told a difficult tale; when Defense Command had moved in to put a dome on Io, the engineers had understandably decided to take advantage of the extensive tunneling that had been done for the original EM Weapons base. Instead of digging a new chasm and sticking the reactors in it, they'd simply extended the EM tunnels and put the reactor under the stretch of dome where the dead park was now — through about 100 meters of rock.

As far as any of the maps showed, there were only two access points to that underground complex: the building we'd stormed at the end of *The Jupiter Patrol*, and the building the Martians had rigged and Charlie's artillery had flattened.

"Can we dig our way down?" Kyle frowned, folding his arms across his chest.

"Nothing we have could do it," Carly shook her head, then started drumming her fingers on the butt of her MAG-90. "I don't know… we need a way down…"

"Yes, but once we get down there, it'll be a mess too," Marcus said in a somber tone.

Think of all those movies you've seen, and games you may have played, where the unit of elite troops heads into some mysterious complex full of experimental research and is duly ravaged by either some rather unlikely monsters, or more likely, by booby traps, ambushes, and various other mundane but deadly things. Now think of the little fight Gina Bertram had in the DCHQ building — it had been quite a mess, and they'd *known* where the Martians were.

An entire underground complex? And one where the Commandos would know exactly what any invading Special Branchers would be going for? Nightmare. It had already been demonstrated that the former HQ building outside the dome was not an easy one to storm, and then to have to go through an entire underground base to get to the reactor…

Yeah, the Martians had themselves a good arrangement here.

Unless…

"Well, what if we space them?" Carly asked the question while her eyes narrowed in thought.

All the other officers frowned, and Kyle was the first to pose the obvious question, "But… they're a hundred meters underground. And we don't have any ships handy."

That was a problem — the only vessel with lasers in local space was *Lion*, and there was no way to get its reactors online. Even if there was, the ship's only surviving laser (on its stern) wouldn't work again without yard time… not to mention a complete decontamination of the ship to allow anyone to work on the problem.

Artemis Agrotera, as I believe I mentioned before, was armed only with mags, and those weren't weapons ideal for punching through rock that deep. Presumably it could be done, but the Martians would have plenty of warning.

No, if they were going to try opening the tunnels to space, they'd have to do it in such a way that there'd be no chance of the Martians sealing themselves in with the reactor controls.

"Some experimental high explosives would be handy," Carly glanced at Charlie after another pause. "I think I saw some on the manifest for items being worked on out here."

Charlie tilted his head sideways, "You probably did… but the Martians removed all that stuff to Sinope already. And even if they hadn't, it'd be down there in the research labs."

No magic bullet then. Damn…

"There must be something…"

"Well, wait a minute, they get power up to this dome somehow. There must be a shaft or something… something full of power cables, right?" Kyle frowned, drawing on his experience with ships and the transfer of power from reactors to systems.

Charlie frowned, "You'd definitely think so, but we didn't see anything on the schematics… I suppose it could be missing from the plans…"

"The reactors are right under that dead park. There could be a hatch cover under some of that dead wood," Marcus bobbed his head in the direction of the park, and Charlie nodded.

"Alright, let's sweep it on foot. See what we can find."

Crawling through a matted field of weeds, dead vegetation and dried wood was not fun at all. As Charlie gingerly stepped around the more impassable obstacles, he kept his eyes on the ground, thinking (not unwisely) that the Martians may well have mined this area.

In the dark, though, looking for booby traps wasn't easy, even with night optics. Under the starry sky, the weeds and woods were very ominous, not so much in themselves, but in the long, dark shadows they cast. What if some of the Martians had been left in the dome, hiding out after buildings had dropped (or almost dropped) on them? They'd come here, perhaps, and lie in wait… using the new night shadows to prepare a counterattack.

Lots of grim possibilities.

But, fortunately, the many possibilities didn't turn into realities right then. Instead a voice sounded in his ear, "I have something here. Looks like a hatch!"

The word 'here' wasn't much help to Charlie — there were a dozen Special Branchers and twenty SF in that big park, and he could see maybe three of them. Fortunately, the SF who'd found the hatch aimed his MAG-90 to the sky and started letting off short bursts to allow people to locate his position.

It took a few minutes, but the search parties collected around the find. Sure enough, it was a large round cover with a Defense Command seal on it — the cables that ran power from the reactor up to the dome grid had to be running through this shaft. This was their access point.

"Well, shouldn't we open it?" Kyle asked, leaning down and reaching for the handles of the hatch.

At that moment, bells went off in Charlie's head, and he stopped Kyle with a hand on the shoulder, "I don't think so. No, this is too obvious for them not to have noticed while they were occupying the dome. It's a trap."

Of course it was a trap — it was obvious in that moment. Charlie scolded himself mentally — he should have known better than to think he could just find a magical access point and make everything better. That'd just be so cliché.

"No, they want us going down this shaft…" Charlie's voice trailed off, and he knelt next to the hatch. The cables had to be running under the dirt around here — they weren't jutting out of the ground next to the hatch, so they must have been in the ground. "We need to find the cables. I have a new idea…"

A very mean new idea, in fact.

"See if you can dig up some of the cables. They should be about fifteen centimeters thick, maybe more," Charlie stood up and looked at the officers and guards around him. He was getting a number of quizzical looks.

"Just trust me," he smiled, then he turned away, tapping his comm to get onto *Artemis Agrotera's* frequency.

"*Artemis Agrotera* here, go," the combat storeship's Sensors and Communications Officer's voice came into his ear.

"Hi, I need Captain Patel. And tell him I'm going to need a good engineering crew." This was going to be very unkind.

CHAPTER TWENTY-FOUR

THEIR OWN MEDICINE

Charlie Peters earned some scoffs from human rights activists for what he did two hours later, but you know what, he saved many lives through his actions. You judge for yourself whether it was right or wrong.

"Well, we've figured out which cables are hooked to reactor one, and we're ready to feed it back… if you're still wanting this," one of the engineers who'd come quickly down from *Artemis Agrotera* dusted her hands off and stood up.

They'd uncovered a number of cables running into the shaft, digging enough space around them to allow patch lines to be attached. Two cars and a generator pulled from the wreckage of one of the apartment towers were sitting on a hastily-cleared patch of ground next to the unearthed cables, and the engineers had hooked the car engines and the generator into the grid through a buffer 'valve' and those exposed cables.

You can probably see where this is going.

Charlie wasn't going to back down. He had a hospital full of Defense Command personnel suffering from acute radiation syndrome — he wasn't going to let a dozen Commandos hold them hostage. Even if it meant playing dirty.

"We're doing this. How's that hatch coming?" Charlie turned from the people working on the power setup to the Special Branchers who were carefully disarming the anti-personnel mines the Martians had set on the hatch.

Carly looked up and gave a thumbs-up, "We can open it any time."

"Good," he tapped his comm, "Gina, you have the channel for their intercom down there?"

Back at the DCHQ building, Gina Bertram had been working through a list of internal comm channels, looking for a dedicated line down to the reactor rooms.

"It looks like it's supposed to be 114.9, but I think it's a hard line. I may only be able to reach them from here."

Despite what the movies might prefer, there was no way Charlie could directly patch his own voice in to talk to the people down in the reactor room — the only comm line from that chamber to the surface ran up to the C&C and Defense Command Headquarters. It was supposed to be a security measure, though Charlie wasn't entirely sure what aspect of security was improved by it. Didn't matter, though, he could speak through Gina.

"Alright then, get that set up, then call all the Commandos there to the reactor room. Tell them we want to talk."

Gina started calling down to the chamber (Charlie could hear her words because she left her comm to him open), and Charlie turned back to the engineering crew, "Now, you think you can do the job? I don't like bluffing…"

The head engineer nodded, "Yeah, we can do it, should be just what you want. All we do is pump the power in from all three of those little buddies, store it in the valve and let it go. Boom, it'll be like a mag shot."

Right into an idling reactor.

"Just got an answer. Someone down in that chamber wants to know what we want," Gina's report came over the comm, and Charlie nodded to himself.

"They probably aren't sure what to make of us. Tell them we have 250 people up here suffering from serious radiation poisoning, and we need at least one reactor turned on so we can treat them."

He glanced back at the engineers, and then over to Carly, who wasn't at all concerned by what they were doing. She was ready to open that hatch.

Kyle had his arms folded and was standing behind Carly. As Charlie looked to him, he half shrugged, "We're giving them the chance to do the right thing."

That they were.

Charlie let his hands come to rest on the stock of his MAG-90 as it hung from his vest, then looked up at the stars and started tapping his foot while he waited. They were taking a few seconds to consider his words, at least.

"Casualties from the space battle," Gina's voice came into his ear again — evidently she was answering the Commandos' question.

Though really, the Commandos had probably already figured out the answer.

Charlie continued to wait, then Gina's words came again, "Well, tell me your terms, I'll ask my CO... mmhmm... so you want us to surrender the dome to you? I'll ask."

Somehow, through force of will, Gina managed to sound genuine with that answer.

Charlie didn't even need her to repeat what she'd said, he just glanced back at the engineering crew, "Do it."

He wasn't playing games now. Well... no I won't qualify that, I'll let you see.

The head engineer did one of those half shrugs that generally means 'if you say so', then nodded to her team. Techs fired up the engines of the cars, and the generator, and the buffer valve they'd connected started to hum. A panel was hooked into the valve, and the head engineer had it in hand, watching as the power in the capacitor went up to full.

"Ready to shoot," she said, giving Charlie one last chance to say no.

"Do it," he repeated the two words evenly, and she hit the button.

There was no really dramatic 'whoosh' or any such thing, the humming just stopped — and a powerful bolt of energy was sent down the cables into one of the two reactors in the chamber below.

Charlie figured that reactor had to be idling, not shut down, and he was right. An idling reactor is still active, and it can still overload if hit by a large enough surge. The pulse they'd just pumped in the 'out' should have been enough to get the lights down there flashing red, and the sirens going. Now he just had to play his hand...

He couldn't hear or see what was going on in the chamber below, but a moment later Gina came back over the comm, "They want to know what we just did."

"Tell them to check their rad readings. There should be... oh... 600 REM exposure in that chamber now," Charlie was keeping his voice cool. "Hit them again."

Charlie had no sympathy in his tone, and with another half shrug, the head engineer charged up the buffer again, "You're going to cause a spill if you keep it up..."

Charlie didn't respond, but Kyle did, "That's the point, to make it look *real*. Do your job, spacer."

Of course, there weren't actually 600 REM in the chamber — it takes a lot more than two cars and a generator to cook off one of our reactors. Sure, if they'd sat there pumping in these bursts for several hours, they could cause a radiation leak, but even that would probably only be rather slight.

But the radiation and overload lights and sirens would be flashing, and since there were hopefully no trained reactor technicians down there to tell the Commandos it wasn't as serious as it looked, they'd hopefully heed his ultimatum.

If not, at the very least they'd hopefully clear the chamber, so Charlie and crew could go down there...

The engineer sent another pulse down the line.

"Tell them they're now over 1,000 REM, and that's going to start spreading through the entire complex. They can run and hide if they like, but they're going to start getting sick real soon," Charlie passed the words onto Gina, and she repeated them.

There was another pause, and the air seemed to grow colder... both because of the gambit Charlie was giving the enemy, and because the dome was actually continuing to lose heat. The residential district, by the way, had not burned well — most of the houses had been empty, and as they were mainly alloy constructs coated in flame-retardant plaster, there hadn't been enough fuel to get a substantial blaze going.

"They want to know what we want," Gina relayed the question with a little bit of satisfaction.

Charlie smiled, "Good. Tell them to turn on the other reactor, then to come up the maintenance shaft into the park. They have to come unarmed — otherwise, we shoot them on sight. And it better still be day when they arrive... or we leave them down there to melt."

This felt like it was working a little too well, and Charlie was becoming slightly suspicious of the ease of the Martian surrender.

Gina passed on his words, and again there was a delay.

Everyone — Charlie especially — now held their breath. If these Martians decided to be stubborn, or if they realized all this was a bluff, they were going to be even harder to remove from that base. But Charlie was willing to take the risk. If this little role-play could get them out of that complex with no losses among his people, it'd be worth it.

"They're coming up," Gina reported over the comm.

Charlie smiled and gave the thumbs up, "Here they come. Let's get in position, I want them covered when they get out."

The daylights came on, all of a sudden, and everyone winced.

"Damn... a day is supposed to start with a gentle sunrise," Carly protested with a smile, then began making hand gestures to get her people under cover.

Kyle did the same, but by barking orders to his SF to get them moving.

Charlie turned back to the engineering crew, "Leave your kit, I want them to see it when they come up. Go take cover."

The engineers nodded and left the area, not interested at all in becoming part of a firefight. Getting his grip around the handle of his MAG-90, Charlie squared off, and then waited.

It took about ten minutes for the hatch to raise off its locked mooring and slide sideways over the ground, then the first Commando climbed over the side and raised his hands in the air. Another followed… and another… eleven men (yes, all men — Martians, remember?) eventually were lined up in front of the hatch, hands raised.

"You're all unarmed?" Charlie was the only Defense Command officer in plain view — a risk on his part, certainly, but one he was willing to take.

"We are," the lead Commando said. "None of us have vomited yet."

Weird comment to make? Well, 'time to first vomit' is actually an indicator you can use to determine the severity of exposure… if you don't have Defense Command's irradiation sensors, and the Martians seemed not to. Poor fellows.

"Take them," Charlie nodded in their direction right then, and Carly and the rest of the team, along with a number of Marcus' officers, sprang out from cover, keeping MAG-90s pointed at them, and with ties ready to bind their hands.

"Anybody stay down there?" Charlie knew the answer he was going to get before he asked.

The lead Commando shook his head, "No."

"Mmhmm. Carly, once they're hooked up, let's head down for a look. You lead with the mine sweeper…" Charlie started moving towards the hatch, and the Martians exchanged glances.

Charlie just smiled, he'd let them figure that out on their own.

A couple of minutes later, his squad was descending into the reactor chamber.

CHAPTER TWENTY-FIVE

CLOSING UP AT IO

Not much more to be said about the securing of Io, really. The reactor chamber was empty when Charlie and his people arrived, and both of the mines in the shaft had been deactivated by the Commandos on their way up. Charlie wasn't sure if that was sloppy or not — if they believed the reactor was leaking, they may have thought there was no reason to reset the mines when they passed, as no one would go down anyway.

But the chamber was empty, and Charlie wasn't going to look that gift horse in the mouth.

"Weld the door," Charlie waved a couple of his officers toward the heavy hatch leading into the complex. Then he turned to look at the two mighty reactors, one with lights flashing,

A lot of lights, actually.

"I can see why they would have bought our little ruse," Carly came to a stop next to her Major. "That's a lotta lights."

"It really is. Get a rad sensor going, will you? Make sure we didn't accidentally irradiate them… and us…" Charlie tugged at his collar, and started to feel uncomfortably warm for a moment. "Oh and sweep for sabotage or explosives on both of them. If they thought we were bluffing, they probably left a charge to ruin our fun."

But, to avoid needless melodramatics (and a lot of description work), we can cut to the chase: there were no explosives on the reactors, and the radiation level was nominal. The Martians had truly just surrendered.

Charlie was certainly surprised by this — he'd expected the Commandos to put up more of a fight. While we were chatting about the way this ended, I did suggest a couple of reasons to him; they had, in fact, lost seventy percent of their Commando force to Charlie's day of blazing and flattening, and perhaps more importantly, radiation sickness is no way to die.

It's my belief (for which I admittedly have no evidence whatsoever) that the Martians were looking for a good reason to give up. I think they'd lost their appetite for the fight, elite or not, and that the threat of being irradiated had given them enough of an excuse to surrender — one even their fascist bosses could understand. No one likes to be irradiated.

But that was the end of it. The last Martians (we presume) surrendered, and any of them who'd decided to fight on or wait us out were sealed into the rest of the complex when Charlie's officers welded that hatch shut.

I really can't say a whole lot more about that…

Approximately two hours later, as actual night was falling in the dome (and as one of Marcus Atallah's teams was babysitting the reactor room, making sure no one tried to break in and do anything funny), Charlie was in the hospital, sitting next to Kris' bed.

What Charlie has yet to admit, but other witnesses swear to, is that he dozed for at least twenty minutes while he sat there, and on one of these occasions, Kris caught him.

Kris looked like all the worst kinds of death. I'm not even going to try to describe her at this stage — no matter what you think of, it's probably not going to be bad enough, unless you've seen radiation poisoning yourself.

But there was good news in her looking so deathly: it meant her body was forcing out the irradiated dead cells, and hopefully replacing them as well...

Only time would tell.

Anyway, the fatigue had begun to wear off from the massive radiation dose — her brain was clearing up enough for her to be awake — and as she came round, Charlie was sleeping in a chair next to her bed.

It's a testament to her nature that she, despite the illness, wanted to take advantage of that fact. Unfortunately, she couldn't really do anything entertaining — she was bedridden to the extreme — so she simply hit the 'nurse call' button on the remote next to her hand, and then when the orderly came in, she waved her arm in Charlie's general direction.

"Poke him," she rasped.

The orderly frowned, but did what he was told, poking Charlie on the shoulder.

Not a good idea to wake a Special Brancher who's asleep while sitting, because the next thing the orderly knew, he was on his back with a boot on his chest.

Typical Special Forces, always jumping at people when they wake up. So cliché... oh damn, I just said Charlie did something cliché. He's going to kill me... which is also cliché! Ha!

Great, now I'm a dead man.

Realizing what he'd done, Charlie helped the orderly up and dusted him off, reading the man's name tag, "Sorry about that... Steve..."

The orderly nervously exited, and Charlie turned back to Kris, "You taking advantage of innocent young orderlies?"

Kris cough-laughed, which under the circumstances was a very good thing.

Charlie sat back down, and continued to keep his old friend company.

Chapter Twenty-Six

A Little Later On, In Space

A few chapters back, we saw the meeting with the skippers, where we'd decided we were going to sandwich the Martian battleship force about three hours outside of Sinope. Well guess when we're jumping to now... that's right, a position in space about four hours out from Sinope.

Karen and I were standing on *Wolf's* bridge with Battlelink connecting us to Andrea, Mark, Nancy Whitehorse and Giovanni Calzatti, and we were watching on the main screen as the Martian battleship force held its course.

Had we gotten them? That was the question going through my head over and over, and it was a tough one to answer. It appeared that the Martians were continuing their flight, knowing we were onto them, and perhaps expecting that when they recombined with the force Matt had been chasing, they could whup us.

'Whup' being a technical term.

If they didn't know Matt was in front of them, then they could well be thinking that... but these Martians had proved themselves quite astute. I had to wonder... were they seeing right through us... did they know what we were trying to do... did they have a counterstroke for it?

Worrying. Go figure, I was worrying. It was part of the job — I had to be paranoid about the Martian abilities, because if I wasn't paying attention to all the things that could have gone wrong, something would have.

But then, on the flip side of this, sometimes things are indeed just as they seem. The movies don't often like that — they prefer to twist and turn, and insert dramatic last-minute revelations that can undo entire plans. Sometimes that happens in life, but so far as I've seen, it doesn't *always* happen.

Even the smart enemy only has so many options.

"Well, I think we're ready," Karen folded her arms and glanced at me. She didn't mean we were supposed to move right now, of course — she was referring to the more general sort of 'ready'... the kind that means our ships were probably where they needed to be to make this work.

The question none of us dared ask out loud was 'do you think Matt and Elise are in position?'. It would have been wrong to doubt our veteran colleagues, but we had no way to contact them. We were too far from Io to pass our signals back and forth through Zail Patel, and if we tried signaling up directly in front of the Martian battleship force, they might notice our comm laser and thus be warned there was a surprise in front of them.

We had to have faith, and this was just not one of the occasions when relying on faith was our preferred course.

They say good communications is the key to the success of many strategies. I'd have to agree with that — being able to coordinate with different forces that are distant from each other is imperative. That's one of the reasons we have Battlelink, in fact. It's a system that allows all the skippers in a squadron to communicate, leaving little room for misunderstandings or accidents. I'm sure Nelson would have sold his good eye to have that sort of coordination ability.

Well, I'm not actually *sure* he would have, but he's been dead 400 years, so I might as well just claim I'm sure. If he haunts me, that'll just be my bad luck.

Anyway, we had long been spoiled by close communication, so the occasions when we didn't have access to it were difficult, particularly on the nerves. We were getting ready to run an ambush here, after all...

We stood and waited.

Honesty, Aaron Ashby's corvette, had been five hours ahead of us, but now if you do your math, you'll see that we were only four hours from Sinope. Yep, Aaron was now keeping a discreet distance from the Martian-occupied moon, with his systems powered down for stealth running, and his passive sensors taking in all the information they could.

These were the first bits of information we got out of Sinope.

The moon itself was essentially misshapen, very small, and none too impressive. It wouldn't make a good site for a long-term investment, but that fact made it perfect for a short-term base. It was one of the last places we'd have thought to look for a Martian dome... and yes, there was a Martian dome.

By all standards, it was tiny — just two kilometers across, and probably only twenty stories tall at its highest point, it likely wasn't good living. But it was undoubtedly useful for holding prisoners, for staging equipment and supplies, and for warehousing all the goodies you robbed from Io, at least until they could be loaded up and shipped back to Mars, as many already had been.

There were no fixed defenses, either — there couldn't have been enough power plants on that miserly rock to run defensive batteries. What that left was a simple dome with a tower sticking out of it, and five escort ships now floating around it — two destroyers and three destroyer escorts, if you recall.

As Aaron and *Honesty* watched silently, small craft from those warships were racing up and down to the dome, and Aaron could only guess at their contents. My thought, looking back, is that they were loading up supplies and personnel for a long cruise, just in case they lost the battle they had to figure was coming and needed to retreat all the way to Mars.

It's contingency planning — as proud as you might be, and however unlikely you think it is you might lose, you have to be somewhat prepared for it.

Of course, that left the question of what might be going on with our people. There had to be hundreds of Defense Command prisoners down there — people from the Io dome, and from *Dominator* (remember, Commander Mazur, *Dominator's* XO, had abandoned half her crew when she ran from the enemy). Add to that the thousands of civilians who were supposed to have been on Io — the people running the shopping mall, the manufacturing plants, the agribuildings and so on, not to mention the families of some of the Defense Command personnel.

According to Colonel Branx, that talkative Martian officer who'd told Charlie about the Commandos on Io (after persuasion, that is), all of those people had been loaded up on a cargo hauler and sent to Sinope, and then that hauler had been sent on to Mars full of our experimental kit.

So were they just planning to abandon those people in that dome? Seemed cold, but I couldn't make any assumptions. Not yet. There might have been another ship coming, they might have been ferried back to Io after it was stripped, or they might have been abandoned, and the dome blown so that there'd be no evidence.

We couldn't know. Aaron couldn't know. For now he was just sitting and watching. And he was hoping none of the Martians had realized he was out there.

CHAPTER TWENTY-SEVEN
GETTING ON WITH IT

That last hour of waiting for battle to commence was, unsurprisingly, a long one. By now I don't need to beat the point to death — you know it's never fun to wait to go into a shooting match.

I continued to worry. I looked at that Martian formation over and over, examined the way they'd laid out their ships and tried to figure out if it meant anything... if they had an ace up their sleeve that I wasn't seeing. I couldn't imagine anything they could have that would give them an advantage... but then that was the worry, wasn't it? That they had something more or less invisible...

While I was still silently (and unnoticeably) panicking, Karen was doing nothing of the sort. Pacing around the bridge with a warm smile and unflappable calm, she visited each bank of consoles, nodding to Shelby McLaws, Felicia Khalid, and Jim Hannigan in turn. The staffs at the consoles, already professionals who were quite able to handle the stress of the waiting game, were buoyed by her presence. Best skipper in the fleet, bar none.

Eventually she ended up next to me again, "We've got about ten minutes now."

Her soft words temporarily jogged my mind out of its worrying, and I nodded, "We'll go to action stations in five."

She nodded back and stood silently next to me, staring at the main screen, occasionally glancing across at the skippers from the squadron, all up on Battlelink and waiting for the fight to begin.

My worries reached their apex in those five minutes — they became as large and spectacular as they could, and as soon as they reached maximum, my mind thrust them aside. It was time to focus, so the many things that could go wrong no longer mattered.

We'd just have to deal with whatever came our way, and if it killed us, it killed us. No more time to fret over it.

Once the countdown reached five minutes, I looked up at the Battlelink screens, "Alright, we have five minutes. Move to general quarters."

"General quarters, all hands to action stations," Karen announced smoothly from beside me, and Jim Hannigan hit *Wolf's* action stations alarm.

All the ships in this formation had been at standby alert, meaning their crews were at action stations, but were also being rotated out from those stations for rest and replenishment — they slept and had food breaks. Now any of the people who'd been on sleep or meal rotation rushed back to their posts, and on Jim's main operations console, a schematic of *Wolf* went from white to green as each section of the ship reported itself crewed and ready.

It took us forty-three seconds to reach action stations, and by any account that's *fast*. Contrast that with *Dominator*, where it took two minutes — and contrary to popular belief, battleships don't take longer, not if they're elite, anyway.

"Ship ready to fight," Jim announced with a hint of pride penetrating his voice.

Karen nodded, "Very good, Jim."

Now it was my turn — I had to give targeting priorities, not just to Jim, but to the whole squadron.

What was I going to do… what could I use against them…

Over Io we'd succeeded by hitting their screening units when they'd expected us to hit their battleship. Now they'd have to be cautious, guarding against both possibilities as much as possible. Their formation suited that purpose, too; the two destroyers were flanking the battleship like two wingmen, one on each aft beam of the battlewagon, forming a delta.

The two pirates were chasing along in irregular order behind this trio, looking like small dogs sticking around for scraps. Hell, no 'looking like', that's what they were.

But what should we focus on…

"All fire, all torpedoes to focus on the battleship," I said it with some finality, and on the Battlelink, both Andrea and Mark smiled, Andrea rather more viciously, somehow.

"I like the sound of that," she said.

"Think they're going to be more cautious with their screening this time?" Mark asked the question in far less hungry tones, though make no mistake, he wanted to get at the enemy.

I nodded slowly, "I think they're smart… they'll know we could go after either the heavy or the lights, so they're going to stay close in. Now, hold your torpedoes until we slow them down. Focus laser fire on the battleship's drives, I want to make sure we keep the speed advantage."

Speed advantage… don't believe I've ever explicitly explained that concept. It's an ancient Naval understanding that's as true in space as it was on the sea: the faster ship controls the engagement. If you're faster, you can fall back or attack at your discretion — you choose when you're fighting and when you're not by simply keeping the range at whatever distance you desire. Admiral Togo (no relation to our Commander… I don't think) used this to devastating effect in 1905 at the Battle of Tsushima… hell, Nelson and his compatriots often used it, by simply gaining the 'windward' position in a battle. By being faster than the Martians, we would get to decide how and when the fight would begin.

Because (as I should have pointed out sooner) the Martians were only doing 190 kps, we were doing the same. Now, *Dominator*, our slowest unit, could work up to 198 for short bursts of speed, and of course the *Predator*-class ships, and the corvettes, could do even more. To mount our attack, we'd simply have to leap forward, claw at the battleship's engines, and try to slow our adversaries down.

"If Matt's in position, he'll know what to do," I went on, slightly more quietly. "If not, it's up to us to close this. Corvettes, we'll need you to kill or scare off those pirates, then help with the destroyers so that we can get as much fire onto that battleship as soon as possible."

Calzatti and Whitehorse, to this point quite silent as we old Belt Squadron veterans talked, nodded in turn.

"Hold all fighters until we get them to slow down. There's not much a Starlight could do to help us at these speeds anyway."

Hell, at these speeds it would be tricky to get them out of the launch bays without ramming them as soon as they left.

"And if you're going to take a hit, take it on the wing… we don't want to have a repeat of what happened to *Lion*," they didn't need to hear that from me, but I needed to say it, both for my own peace of mind, and because this was one of the few moments during the day when I recall noticing the presence of the cameras.

This is the point in the book where I stop and say 'oh crap, I forgot Jessica and Jocko' — as if I'd left kids I was responsible for in the shuttle terminal on Luna One or something. Whoops.

Well, it's not all my fault… remember, from the beginning of this book to now has been about a day — and quite a busy day. Jocko and Jessica, the former on Io and the latter here on *Wolf*, had been observing our various operations, rolling cameras and taking notes.

They had *not* been getting in the way, or even asking questions. Answers could be gotten after we were done blowing up the Martians, so they decided to let us work, and had completely slipped my mind while I was dealing with this rather important chase, among other things.

So let me just quickly review where they had been and currently were.

Jocko, trapped on the fourteenth floor of the DCHQ building through all of Charlie's fight, had gotten some great footage (through a window) of Starlights hovering over a city and strafing it. Actually, while we were in this battle with the Martians, he was conducting interviews in the hospital, but as promised, he'd stayed out from underfoot until the situation was stabilized.

Jessica was on *Wolf*'s bridge, and I repeated that warning about not taking hits on the central core of the ship for the benefit of the camera because it was one of the rare moments that day when I actually noticed she was there.

Everyone on the Battlelink nodded, as did Karen, and perhaps most importantly, Shelby McLaws. Our southern belle had already proven she knew how to get a ship out of the way of an incoming laser… though she'd agree that we were still very lucky we hadn't been the focus of the shot that took out *Lion*.

Anyway, now we'd send some lasers back to the Martians.

"Alright," the clock was down to one minute, "on my order, we boost up to 198, and take out those battleship engines. Set?"

"Roger that," Mark Gunney replied with a smile.

"Yes, sir," was Nancy Whitehorse's response, and Giovanni Calzatti's as well.

"The bastard is all mine," Andrea's smile remained hungry. Yes, I know, not a good sign. More on her later.

The clock started running down to zero.

CHAPTER TWENTY-EIGHT

THAT FIGHT

Mayhem in space comes in silence, and I have always thought that rather strange. Surreal, perhaps. You expect all five of your senses to be able to take part when you're witnessing the destruction of something so large, powerful and expensive as a warship, but they don't. You don't hear it, taste it, smell it or feel it, you just watch it.

Well, unless you're on that ship. Then everything changes.

But I get ahead of myself.

When the countdown reached five seconds, two Defense Command corvettes swooped in from their position ahead of the Martian force. *Friendly* and *Lady Grace* were evidently operating from a clock that was faster than the one on *Wolf*... that or Matt was just irresponsible and over eager. Yeah right... it was obviously the clock.

Matt, as I expected, knew precisely what to do when he attacked: he lined himself and Elise De Winter up against the destroyer on the battleship's port side and then threw everything the two corvettes had at that lone ship.

Two lasers, not as powerful as those from frigates, but not weak either, cut into the destroyer's forward weapons pod, and before it could even get its turrets spinning, its heaviest forward lasers were out of action.

But that wasn't all: *Friendly* and *Lady Grace* were moving like the long-time partners they were (they'd been fighting alongside each other since Karen and I had commanded them). They came in at over 150 kps... which doesn't sound like a lot until you realize they were traveling in the opposite direction to the Martian force, which was doing 190 kps. Combined approach and passing velocity was thus 340 kps, which is obviously very, very quick.

And the fire control officers on both corvettes were excellent. Again, here is the advantage of having truly elite ships; only one ship in ten in our fleet could have targeted, fired and re-targeted again in the time it took speedy little *Friendly* and *Lady Grace* to pass over the battleship, but of course, Matt and Elise's crews did.

Their second targets were the pirates, who still had no idea what was going on, I'm sure. They were out here because the trip was paid for by the Martians, and because the loot was supposed to have been good. They were *not* elite ships, they were riffraff that Martian Fleet Command must have hoped would somehow make up the difference.

You don't bring the local farmer and his buddies with their shotguns to a tank battle. You shouldn't bring pirates to a fleet battle. Well, the Battle of Belt Two excepted — the Belt pirates of the new Syndicate were much more sophisticated, a legacy of their time with Grant Merger.

Who knew where they'd found these poor rogues... *Lady Grace* took the one on the right, *Friendly* took the one on the left, and both were blasted apart by laser fire before they could react.

And that completely changed the complexion of this mess.

Now we had seven ships, the Martians had three, and one of theirs was hurting. The aft laser turrets on all three of the Martian warships began spinning up — quite quickly and efficiently, I must admit — but *Friendly* and *Lady Grace* slid out of range.

All that took about twenty seconds. Not kidding at all, just twenty seconds from first laser shot to exit. You can see what I mean about the quick re-targeting.

Because Matt was diving into the fray, I left my order to leap forward until about five seconds after the appointed hour… so for the last ten seconds of Matt's run, this is what happened for us.

"Move it," I gave the informal order, and every skipper, Karen included, looked to his or her Helm and Navigation Officer, saying something appropriate to get things rolling.

Wolf and *Cheetah* kicked forward with practiced ease — Belt Squadron veterans, we had no difficulty getting a move on. *Trusty* was next, moving just a little behind us, not as used to coordinating as the Belt Squadron veterans. *Pictou* was slower, less agile both in terms of hull design and crew, so it brought up the rear.

Well, discounting *Dominator*.

The big battleship lurched forward with difficulty, its drives boosting from 190 to 192… to 194… to 195… Andrea looked off screen and demanded more speed, but didn't say anything to us about the performance. She was, as she later told me, actually impressed they hadn't started going backwards. Her yelling and jumping up and down (and earlier threats at gun point) seem to have had at least some effect on her crew's efforts.

We crossed the threshold into firing range quickly enough, and *Wolf* and *Cheetah* each fired their laser number one at the same time, Mark smiling on screen as he did, "Almost beat you that time, Karen."

She smiled but didn't get a chance to reply, as a destroyer laser abruptly cut across *Wolf's* high engine wing — one of the rear turrets from the destroyer Matt had left alone had found us.

Fortunately for us, Shelby McLaws has a sixth sense for these sorts of things — instead of having to wait to hear from Felicia Khalid that we were taking fire, and certainly before anyone could issue any sort of order, her smooth, ladylike commands were given to the helm ratings, and it was their privilege to oblige the lady by moving *Wolf* out of the way.

"Flaked off our outer armor," Jim reported immediately from behind us. "No performance loss, though I'll want to patch it before we head home. Our shot did about the same to the battleship."

It had no reason to slow down, then…

"My laser bounced off too, I'm shocked," Mark's smile was gone, and he said that to us between quick orders to his own crew. "Lining up again."

"The Martian battleship's aft laser turret is preparing to fire," Felicia Khalid interrupted with that important report, and I looked up at Mark's screen.

"We have heavy shots coming in, ready to dance?"

"I thought you'd never ask," Mark nodded, his sense of humor not failing him.

Karen passed on a warning to Shelby McLaws, and despite everything that she was dealing with, our Helm and Navigation Officer managed to stop, turn to Karen, and nod perfectly, "Thank you for the warning, ma'am."

If you read that as condescending or somehow impolite, don't — the way she delivered it, with grace and a smile, confirmed it was an actual 'thank you'. Damn that girl's proper.

The battleship's lasers opened up; four pairs of beams on converging paths, trying to bracket both *Wolf* and *Cheetah*. However, since only two pairs were being aimed at each of our frigates, we had more room to escape than *Lion* had (remember, Kris had been confronted by five pairs).

That wasn't foolish shooting on the part of the battleship; the Martian heavy was making full speed, and it didn't need to destroy us, just shake off our laser tracks. Killing either of us would have been a bonus, but wasn't really the immediate objective.

And they didn't kill us, of course. Shelby threw us high, *Cheetah* ducked low, and the lasers missed.

Dominator was still coming up, and was just out of range, but Nancy Whitehorse drove her *Trusty* right after the destroyer that had targeted *Wolf*. Her ship's laser number one fired as she got the range, and then raked across that destroyer's lower drive wing… but to no effect. It was quite difficult to shoot effectively and do significant damage in a stern chase.

Pictou came up, and I suppose you may have been expecting what happened next. The determined little ship got into range of the destroyer as well, and fired, missing the Martian to the port side. It was a noble attempt, and I say that without mirth.

The Martian laser shot that punched right through *Pictou's* laser one was better aimed, though, and because *Pictou* was an older corvette with much less internal compartment-to-compartment protection than a ship like *Trusty*, half the forward weapons pod decompressed. The people and anything that wasn't nailed down in that section were sucked out *through* the ruptured laser emitter, only to be splattered against the hull when they were spewed out into space with insufficient velocity to stay ahead of their speeding ship.

The corvette listed hard to starboard and began to spin, and as it was about to fall out of range, a second laser shot punched right through its port engine pod. The spin became a three dimensional twirl, and we had to leave the ship behind.

Friendly and *Lady Grace* had by this time reversed course to follow us, and running at full acceleration, they burst past *Dominator* at 203.5 kps, their lasers targeting the destroyer they'd engaged on their first pass. I don't mean to sound self-aggrandizing, but watching those two ships fight in tandem always reminded me of Karen and I storming a house together. One covered the other, and vice versa.

Friendly took a glancing hit from one of the rear lasers as that Martian destroyer realized they were coming back, and as Matt's crew course corrected and maintained their high acceleration, one of the broadside lasers from the battleship cut right in front of *Friendly's* bow. Well, not *right* in front, but so close that the only way my old little ship could avoid losing a wing was to rotate and 'dive' relative to the other ships.

Lady Grace tried to climb up and out of the way, but too late: the gallant ship's low drive wing was chopped off without ceremony. Being an elite crew, Elise De Winter's people managed to avoid going into an uncontrolled tumble, but *Lady Grace* fell back, out of the fight, unable to maintain enough speed.

Matt must have seen this and been rather displeased — neither Commander, by the way, had linked in with Battlelink yet… too preoccupied in those forty seconds, I suppose. *Friendly* came up again, still doing at least 203 kps, and put a laser shot right through the low pod of the Martian destroyer, and as that ship lost speed, Matt directed *Friendly* to pass below it, unleashing a torrent of mag fire. The Martian began to twirl away as well, and we never saw it again.

Speaking of mags, or whatever the Martians call them, as *Wolf* and *Cheetah* surged up behind the battleship again, a massive barrage of mag bolts began to come our way, and at least a dozen connected with both hulls.

"This'll test the armor," Mark Gunney grunted on the Battlelink. It's been a long time since I mentioned it, but new Defense Command ships still had that lining under the armor that could absorb mag shots into our power system in a good way — the power was absorbed and sent back out through our own mags or lasers on the next shot, instead of getting a free ride to the reactor to overload it on us.

It worked against mag bolts, but not against lasers that punched through the central core of the ship…

Nancy Whitehorse's *Trusty* shifted sideways to get a better angle on the destroyer that was again lining up on *Wolf* and *Cheetah*, and her laser number one fired once more, this time managing to just melt part of the turret cowling on the Martian's rear pod. Atmosphere started to spill out of the destroyer, and that turret jammed.

Then came the main event.

Just as *Wolf* and *Cheetah* were taking mag fire, *Trusty* was doing some damage, and Matt was peeling *Friendly* back to make certain that destroyer he'd wounded didn't regain some control and go after *Lady Grace* or *Pictou*, two massive lasers cut through space and connected with the low drive wing of the Martian battleship.

That was the end of it.

Not the ship, I mean, but the chase. Because with *Dominator* in range, there was no reason for the Martians to allow the stern chase to continue — the Defense Command battlewagon had slightly better range with its lasers, so it could just stay far enough back to hammer at the Martian for hours until one shot got lucky. The Martian's only option was to turn and fight.

With all the speed I remember seeing from Martian battleships at the Battle Over Earth, this one now shifted to the right and hit its reverse engines, letting *Dominator* race up alongside it more quickly than Andrea would have liked.

"Reduce speed to match!" she barked that order to her Helm and Navigation Officer, but we heard it over Battlelink.

"Mark, let's deal with that destroyer, then we can line up to assist," I let my eyes dart from Andrea's face to Mark Gunney's, and he nodded.

"Already there…"

Cheetah didn't even change course, Mark just angled his ship slightly, kicked up to full acceleration, and then number one laser spoke again, aiming for the same general area on the destroyer's hull that *Trusty* had hit. Mark's hunch was that the armor in that region would have to be vulnerable, and vulnerable it was.

The entire rear weapons pod seemed to light up, flame bursting out of seams that shouldn't have been open. But the ship kept up its speed…

"They're trying to divide us," I shook my head. "Let it go for now, you've crippled it."

"Cripples aren't incapable," Mark pointed out with some politically incorrect humor, and I nodded.

"But I want this battleship *dead*. Prepare to launch Starlights, get your torpedo ready," I'd made my decision.

Karen nodded to Shelby at that moment, "Back track towards *Dominator*, 100 kps."

Dominator and the Martian battlewagon were now circling each other, not in perfect arcs but in irregular swoops and z-axis shifts, trying to throw off fire control officers. We had to approach cautiously — *Wolf*, *Cheetah* and especially *Trusty* would be in serious trouble if we got caught in the crossfire of the two heavyweights.

What we saw, and what some of our Starlights actually caught on camera, was something I don't think had been seen up until that time: a battleship duel. If you think back to the Battle Over Earth, or to Glorious February, you see battleships going toe-to-toe only in the company of other battleships… those are what I call 'battle line contests'. See, it's different when you have the assistance of other heavy ships at hand.

This was a slogging match. Our *Dominator* was more powerful, but the crew wasn't as sharp as a Heavy Squadron crew. The Martian battleship (like all Martian ships, if you ask me) was under-gunned, but the crew had already proved itself quite capable.

Mayhem ensued. Mayhem we could only watch as we tried to circle, looking for an uncovered angle to launch our torpedoes. These were our last torpedoes and we didn't want to waste them, but the battleship seemed to have realized that fact, and wasn't about to let us in close.

So it was down to Andrea to end this. To the abused crew that hated her, to the ship she'd been on for just a few days, and to the mind that was full of torment and anguish.

I watched her on Battlelink — I'm sure I was giving orders to get us into range and all that, but all I remember about this part of the fight is watching her. She was mainly looking away from her viewfinder, so her face was often in profile, but she was yelling — things that I couldn't make out because she was directing them away from the mics. Her eyes, whenever they turned towards the screen, were full of death.

At one point I glanced at Karen and nodded towards the screen, and with a sigh, Karen whispered, "I know…"

That wasn't cool, calm, surgical Andrea Kiley. Not the woman who'd commanded *Friendly* to great effect. This was someone harnessing many dark personal demons to unleash hell.

Dominator's two broadside lasers would fire, slamming into the heavy side armor of the Martian, and the Martian would reply with ten much smaller lasers, cutting at *Dominator's* engines. The Martian wanted to deny *Dominator* the ability to chase, that was its way out.

Andrea wanted the battleship dead, because it had hurt her family.

"Torpedo range… yes, we have torpedo range!" Mark Gunney had been watching his approach carefully, and finally *Cheetah* was close enough to the Martian to empty its tube for the last time. "Shoot!"

The torpedo burst from *Cheetah's* tube, and Mark kept driving his frigate forward, with *Trusty* lining up on his port quarter.

Shelby was taking us in a different way — from below. She'd studied the logs from *Glorious February* very closely, and if you recall, Shannon Hunter's frigate squadron had been quite successful in closing range with Martian heavies when they came up from underneath.

"Rolling ship to present our tube," Shelby now reported, and I zoned back in.

The titans continued to clash as we got into torpedo range, and as our great warhead was flung from its port, Shelby rolled us back to present our laser.

"Shoot," Karen looked back to Jim, and our XO nodded, the laser cutting out. It did nothing to the Martian — nothing compared to what *Dominator's* beams seemed to be doing.

Our torpedo was shot down, and then Mark's was — tantalizingly close to impact, too. Martian Interceptors began to swarm us, and our Starlights fought like demons to drive them back.

Like demons.

I'd stopped paying attention for just a few seconds when I realized that *Dominator* had turned directly for the Martian. The lasers weren't stopping on either side, and as the range closed, showers of mags began to rain either way. Both ships were about to start flaking apart...

As soon as Andrea had her ship's bow pointed right at the Martian broadside, *Dominator* fired its two torpedoes. Then the battleship chased those warheads, protecting them with so much mag and laser fire that no Interceptors could get near them.

Both hit, and the explosion bent the back of the Martian battlewagon.

And then *Dominator* rammed right into the broken back. *Wolf*, *Cheetah* and *Trusty* had to break off very quickly to avoid the debris.

CHAPTER TWENTY-NINE

THE PIECES

Andrea had destroyed the Martian battleship at the cost of her own.

We spent the next hour trying to collect all the lifeboats we could find from both ships, while *Lady Grace*, flying quite gingerly on three pods, arrived to assist. Matt had gone after *Pictou*, but by the end of the hour had returned without luck — the older corvette which had spun off was now missing, and while there was still a coherent Martian force at Sinope that might come for us, he couldn't justify going on a long search just then.

It wouldn't have mattered, of course. The poor little ship's reactors went nova about twenty minutes after it was hit, and only half the well-meaning and noble crew got to their life pods. Commander Calzatti went down with his ship; we picked up the rest three days later, finally having tracked down the debris.

While our search and rescue shuttles combed the wreckage of the two battleships, one thing quickly became apparent: there were no Martian survivors from the ship itself. People have on occasion suggested that this was because we didn't take prisoners — that either our planes shot up their pods, or that we just didn't recover them when we found them — but that's not at all the case. We looked for two hours, and then left *Lady Grace* there to continue the search.

No Martians.

Dominator's crew was better off — only 100 dead, despite the carnage, because even in ramming, the ship's hull had stayed mainly in one piece. Andrea, of course, was quite alive.

We evacuated the ship in that hour, and we left it there for *Lady Grace* to oversee. I should clarify: *Lady Grace* was missing a drive pod, but the shot that had taken it off had been clean, and the corvette was in remarkably good condition otherwise, so Elise was able to continue operating to a limited extent. We took aboard the *Dominator* survivors, dividing the 500 or so people among our five ships (*Wolf, Lion, Friendly, Lady Grace* and *Trusty*), and then we set off after the destroyer that had escaped, and to Sinope.

We were four hours away.

About twenty minutes after we left the area... sorry, 'we' being *Wolf, Lion, Friendly* and *Trusty*... Andrea appeared on the bridge. She was not injured — there were no burns on her skin, no bruises or blood. A fair amount of sweat, certainly, and her hair was no longer neatly affixed in its ponytail.

But she looked wounded.

Alright, this is going to be tough to describe: she wasn't physically injured, and more than that, she arrived on *Wolf's* bridge with a neutral expression, and a sigh of relief at coming back home.

But something about her seemed heavier — darker. She told me later that those moments after she'd gotten off *Dominator* were something of a blur… that she'd started to realize she'd lost most of the cool, sharp reasoning that had made her so effective before. She'd replaced reason with anger, and a hunger for revenge… and she was realizing that she found satisfaction in the idea of inflicting harm. It was *good* to hurt the other side.

Good, yes *good*. I understand what she was saying, though that doesn't mean what she was enjoying was actually 'good'. Far from it — she was literally sharing her pain by inflicting it, and I probably don't need to tell you that was not a good state of mind.

Part of her seemed to know that, but it was reasonably ambivalent about the revelation. She wasn't ready to start fighting herself… not yet, anyway.

That state of mind wouldn't last too much longer…

As she came onto *Wolf's* bridge, Karen and I looked at each other rather furtively. What were we to do? From a neutral standpoint, Andrea had lost a ship, but had done so in a gallant last act which had destroyed her enemy. And at best, she was *acting* Captain of that ship — it hadn't been assigned to her by the Admiralty. As Rear Admiral, I could decide if her conduct warranted a court martial.

Or a commendation.

What was I to do? What would you do? She was not herself, but she'd done well, really, in that fight — and she'd kept most of her crew alive. She was also one of us, part of the Belt Squadron. The Jupiter Force now, of course.

A court martial would end her, and I think it would have been cruel to hold her accountable for the loss of a ship she'd volunteered to take even though it was a problem case. No, as far as I was concerned then — and I stand by this now — the only thing to do was to keep Andrea upright and close enough that Karen and I could l look after her.

In a second glance, Karen gave me a look that told me she agreed with this. Sometimes, Karen and I just had the exact same mind… but we couldn't say anything, couldn't so much as whisper anything, because as I'd again noticed, Jessica's camera crew was here with us. At this moment, Bunny (remember Bunny?) was framing a shot of us with Andrea.

We had to play this very gently.

"So, Andrea, you can take over here again?" Karen asked with a warm smile, and Andrea looked up (I don't think she'd been paying us much attention). Approaching Andrea, then, Karen took her hand, "Good job. Most of the crew safe, and there's nothing left of that Martian. Sky's clear for us to finish this."

Andrea started to nod slowly, "Yeah… yes. Yes right."

I made sure I was smiling too, "Excellent, it'll be good to have a Captain back on deck, Karen can get a break from the two jobs."

That was, obviously, a lie — the sort of gentle lie you tell to try to make sure someone feels valued. It was pretty clear to everyone on the bridge just then that Andrea was only half into this conversation. I think many of the crew wrote it off as her simply being a little shook up after that epic battleship fight. Any that didn't just wrote it off as one of the family still having a bad time — but they'd say nothing about it. The old Belt Squadron stuck together.

"Listen, you just got off a wrecked battleship," Karen said quietly, letting go of Andrea's hand. "After what happened to Kris, I'm a bit paranoid, so why don't you go get checked out by Alicia, and then get an hour's sleep before we hit Sinope. That way we'll all be up here when we crash their base."

Brilliant play — Karen's usual — to get Andrea to take a break, and to justify her lack of charm and charisma before the cameras.

"Alright," Andrea just turned and left.

As the hatch closed behind her, Karen looked at me with eyebrows up. We avoided commenting with the cameras around, though neither of us was entirely pleased by what we'd just seen.

Unfortunately, there was no magic bullet to fix Andrea's problems. Hell, I didn't even know if her problems were something that could be metaphorically shot at. We'd have to muddle through, as we always did.

The Jupiter Force... what remained of it... cruised on for Sinope.

CHAPTER THIRTY

CAUGHT

The Martian battleship force had notified Sinope of its position before it had been destroyed, and what I failed to predict, but should have predicted, happened: the Martian ships stationed there came out to assist their flagship. Granted, the battle was three hours away, but the Martians seemed to be operating under the premise that, if the engagement had gone in their ships' favor, or if it was a stalemate, it was best for them to be out there to possibly be of help.

So while we chased that wounded but quick destroyer towards Sinope, two more destroyers and three destroyer escorts were coming out to meet us, and on the way they noticed a Defense Command corvette (which I suppose by their lack of earlier reaction, they hadn't yet seen) hanging around their moon.

This was Aaron Ashby, and *Honesty*.

And it was a problem.

I'd say it's been established by now that these Martians were good at their jobs, and so as they boosted in Aaron's general direction (but on a course that wasn't directly towards him) he assumed that battle had been joined, and that they were going out to reinforce the Martian battleship group. That gave him options: he could go in and take command of the space over Sinope, or he could follow them and assist us.

He went for the second option — the one I'd prefer — and figured he'd follow the Martians from afar again. He didn't think he'd been noticed, you see.

The entry was already made into the log, stating his intentions, when the Martian force passed him.

And then, with no warning, the three destroyer escorts peeled off and came right at *Honesty*.

Under normal conditions, *Honesty* may have been able to back off fast enough to get out of the way of these three marauders, but the ship was under silent running — it'd take about forty seconds to get reactor power up enough to do a full reverse burn on the drives, and after that it'd be a battle against inertia to get up to speed.

Aaron ordered general quarters, and from standby alert his crew — Mark Gunney's old crew — went swiftly to their action stations. I don't know exactly how long it took, but that was a fine crew, a crew of many veterans from Egesta, in fact. While the drives began to reverse slowly, the weapons were armed and crewed, and the targeting sweeps began.

The Martians came in firing, all three of the DEs spraying their small, quad-turreted lasers simultaneously. The first barrage — before *Honesty* could get up any speed to maneuver out of the way — was devastating.

Aaron Ashby and all of Mark's old bridge crew died at their posts, and the bow pod was carved up like a roast. Sections decompressed, armor flaked off, mags were torn right out of their casings.

It was almost as bad as it possibly could have been.

But it wasn't fatal to the ship, and there are a couple of reasons why.

First, the lasers came in from the top, so the sensor array was shielded from most of the force of the laser shots. Why does that matter? After this was all done and we started assessing what had happened to *Lion*, we realized the cause of the massive radiation spill had been a surge through the sensor array — the ultimate secondary system. If you remember Glorious February, it's the secondary systems that were the problem for our reactor overloads at that time.

In this case, then, the sensors weren't hit, and *Honesty's* reactors didn't go critical. There was no terminal radiation leak.

Importantly, and luckily, the laser power conduits were not hit either. The starboard emitter was shorn off, but that left three, and they all could be fired from secondary control centers.

The Chief Engineer, Lieutenant Trevor Herrickson, took command of the ship even while he was getting the engines up to speed, and by orders over the comm to each auxiliary control section, he fought the ship.

Sensor operators sitting next to the array would report what they were seeing to him over the comm, and Herrickson would yell to his engine crew to get maneuvers carried out, and he'd direct fire based on a 'picture he had in his head'.

In other words, he was visualizing what it must have looked like outside based on what he was hearing, and managed to track three corvettes this way.

Manually targeting the stern laser, the weapons crews caught a destroyer escort completely by surprise — the DEs had flown past, assuming its job was done, until that shot carved one drive wing right off the first bastard.

Getting the engines up to full speed, Trevor then turned and headed for Sinope, reasoning that he'd either be abandoned by the DEs (who would be under orders to rejoin their destroyers) or that he'd pull them *and* the destroyers back, keeping them from reinforcing the battleship force, at least for a while.

As it happened, the Martians did neither. It wasn't a bad gambit, by any means, but the DEs kept coming, and let the destroyers go out ahead. The Martians doubtless decided that it would be a bad thing to leave a still-active corvette alone over their undefended base.

Trevor wasn't too disturbed when the Martians played it smart, though — at this stage he was already certain he was going to die, he didn't have much else to lose by being daring. He launched his Starlights, because the twelve planes *Honesty* held were still intact. He wasn't sure what good they'd do him, but it seemed to be worth the effort.

As the destroyer escorts came around again, they sliced viciously across the high engine pod, and it came off after a few seconds of intense barrage. Responding immediately, Trevor Herrickson killed the low pod to keep a tumble from occurring, then used his two remaining pods to lever *Honesty* around and to get the port side laser lined up with one of the two DEs.

The shot was an angry one, gouging a long deep trench in the light armor of the DE's side, and decompressing a few sections. But the Martians weren't backing off; the mag bolts started raining on *Honesty* at almost the same time, and the ship's armor and filament net struggled to withstand the onslaught of EM energy.

Firing without central coordination, *Honesty's* mags lashed back, focusing as much as they could on the ship they'd clearly already wounded. That DE began to suffer from the weight of mag fire coming from the irrepressible corvette, and it twisted away with difficulty.

So far the impossible: *Honesty* had survived two quick rounds with three destroyer escorts, and had reduced them to one effective. Unfortunately, the surprised skipper of the last Martian DE wasn't about to make another mistake — *Honesty* was as dangerous as a wounded predator... no pun intended... and closing to energy range was not wise.

Instead, the DE fired its missile. Now, corvettes don't have torpedo tubes, but Martian destroyer escorts each carry one missile. That's one design advantage... probably the *only* design advantage that I'll concede to them. This missile was not expected, so the Starlight squadron that was turning to strafe the active DE watched it fly right through their formation before turning over and chasing it.

But the range was tight, and the missile was flying at the back end of *Honesty*, where there were few mags. Without central fire control directing the shots, there was little chance of the missile being shot down.

It wasn't.

Reaching point blank range, it did what all powered warheads do: it accelerated. Ramming up into the rear laser emitter, it detonated, and the explosion surged up the power grid and blew the engine section of the ship clean apart. The 'neck' and forward weapons pod, still intact save for the earlier damage, somersaulted away slowly, bleeding atmosphere from many points. Escape pods started to launch.

At this point the DE had a choice. It could either stay and try to eliminate the Starlights and collect the life pods, or rejoin the destroyers for the battle it expected to come. It went with the second option — a dozen Starlights were of no great consequence, and there were two damaged DEs here that could pick up survivors, once control was restored. It thus turned away and boosted hard in pursuit of the two destroyers that were moving to meet us.

But those Starlights weren't so helpless. Lieutenant Corey Byng had command of the wing, and as soon as the first wounded DE — the one missing the drive pod that Trevor Herrickson had removed with his first laser shot — came towards the pods, the Starlights fell on it. The ship was already limping after its damage, and its power systems had evidently been disrupted by some fused relays due to the loss of the pod. The strafing runs the Starlights did were thus surprisingly effective.

Now, don't mistake me: the mags they were using for strafing weren't punching through the hull or anything quite so dramatic, but thanks to a weakened power grid, the energy spikes were playing merry hell with the Martian's ability to operate. Instead of one larger power grid that could simply absorb mag fire, the grid was in pieces, with relays blowing out all over the place.

The ship turned away and retired, not damaged but frustrated and ineffective.

The other damaged ship came for the pods too, and the pilots of HonestStar Squadron jumped on it, closing fast and finding that gap in the ship's armor plating — the gash left by the laser shot. No armor there, so suddenly the fighters' mags, and their Apocalypse missiles, could actually do some harm. Without mercy, they dropped ordnance into that trench, and one warhead must have found the missile storage on the DE.

It *blew up*.

That was the only occasion in the war when a force of F-194 Starlights had been able to destroy an enemy ship (admittedly with the help of *Honesty*, who created the opportunity). It was quite an achievement, though it hardly replaced venerable little *Honesty*.

That ship had been with us for years in the Belt Squadron, it was one of the best… now a wreck, but it had taken one DE with it, and crippled another. At the cost of a little more than half its crew…

This was a very expensive day for the Jupiter Force. A very expensive day indeed.

CHAPTER THIRTY-ONE

THE LAST ENCOUNTER

Two hours after *Honesty* died, *Wolf, Cheetah, Trusty* and *Friendly* were still chasing the destroyer that had escaped, our crews back at standby alert. We were moving in groups of two — *Cheetah* with *Trusty* off its starboard port quarter, and *Wolf* with *Friendly* off our port quarter. Karen and I were still on the bridge, while Andrea was presumably still sleeping.

We hoped, anyway.

There wasn't much ceremony or worry about what came next — to be honest, we were all surprised by it, though we shouldn't have been. What can I say, it had been a long day, and we made another mistake.

"Three destroyers and a DE on scope, coming this way *fast*," Felicia Khalid had settled in well behind Jim and Kate's old consoles, despite her inexperience. That was good.

Of course, what she was saying wasn't.

I whirled to face the main screen, then mentally kicked myself, "General quarters, fast as you can. Time to weapons range?"

"About... forty-five seconds..." Felicia paused to calculate, and already Karen was giving the next order.

"Reverse drives, let's buy some more time to get to action stations," that was both to Shelby McLaws, who was already cordially inviting the helm crew to do a crash reverse, and to the faces on the Battlelink screens.

Almost in unison, our four ships began doing a full reverse burn, again putting some strain on our hulls, but nothing we couldn't handle.

"Matt, you finish off the wounded destroyer... it must be one of them. Mark, we'll take on the healthy destroyers. Nancy, the DE is yours," I was giving the orders quickly, watching the range drop.

"Here we go again..." Karen said softly.

And then the remarkable happened: the Martians reversed their own drives, altered course, and fled.

No kidding, they just ran. Turning onto a vector that looked like it was heading back to *Mars*, even if that'd be a sixty-day flight. Remember, Aaron had watched them running flights to and from the Io dome (probably to take aboard cargo for a long cruise)... I suppose this was why.

They could have stayed and fought, but more likely than not, they would have lost, though both sides would have been badly battered. And they'd never have been able to get home. What about the two damaged destroyer escorts they'd left at Sinope? Must have given up on them.

Alright, I'll stop pretending like I'm guessing about this in a minute, but for now let me finish the scene.

Karen and I stood shoulder to shoulder on *Wolf's* bridge, gazes fixed on the main screen as the icons of the Martian ships turned away. It was, in that instant, just too good to be true. We kept watching, and they kept leaving. It was weird.

Weird, I mean it. We were ready to go again — to take another shot at the bastards. We weren't looking forward to it, or eager to engage them, or anything ridiculous like that... but we were ready. And now we didn't have to do anything?

No, no we couldn't be sure they were actually running. Where were the other two DEs?

"Alright, this is disturbing," I actually had to say what I was thinking, and Mark was the first to come back.

"Yeah, I'd love to assume they got scared of our big bad... oh wait, we don't have any big bad left. Just regular bad."

I nodded, "Exactly. Lost their CO on the battleship, maybe?"

"Not much spine to the bastards if they're not going to fight without their CO," Matt observed unsympathetically. "We should check in with Aaron, see what they've left at Sinope."

Again I nodded... but what would we do in the meantime? We couldn't let them go and just assume they were running home... they could be planning to double back, or go around... something.

We had to keep an eye on them.

"Nancy, keep tabs on them, but watch for them trying to turn and jump you. We'll proceed on to Sinope, collect Aaron, and deal with whatever's left," I said after that pause, then turned to Felicia. "Warn *Lady Grace* they might be running around us. If SAR operations are complete, Elise should head for Io, best speed. She can carve up *Dominator* before she goes, make sure there's no salvage."

Lieutenant Khalid nodded and got to work, and I looked back to the Battlelink screens, "Nancy, get after them. Follow them for a day, and if they're still heading out, return to Io. Keep in touch with us — one way or another, we should be at Sinope."

I don't know if that looked like I was trying to get rid of the 'new' girl, or if it seemed like a vote of confidence in her abilities to keep tabs on the enemy. Some have suggested that early Belt Squadron elitism made me want to send away the unfamiliar person — send her on that dangerous job — so I could keep my favored ships close.

Could be a fair assessment, could *not* be. I really don't know, I just made the decision, and you know damned well Nancy Whitehorse was up for it.

"We'll be in touch, sir," she nodded, then she closed her Battlelink and veered away from our formation.

"Alright, on to Sinope for us, then," I said, letting out a long breath. "Hopefully Aaron took care of the last two DEs for us."

Mark Gunney grinned, "Sounds like something my old ship would do."

Well, that grin wasn't destined to last... but for now we let ourselves feel a slight bit — just a slight bit — optimistic.

When we pulled into Sinope space two hours later, we were quite silent. Andrea had joined us on the bridge, and she was back to... well, not *normal*. But she was basically the way she had been on *Wolf's* bridge before moving over to *Dominator*.

Arriving on the deck an hour after we'd left the Martians and Nancy Whitehorse behind, she smiled at me with an artificial smile that had been harder to see through before we'd seen her condition on *Dominator*, and said softly, "It's really good to be back home."

Something about the way she said it implied a certain amount of pain, but then she started settling back into her groove, and she made sure to chat with Felicia, who she didn't know very well, to start building a rapport there.

She was actually chatting with Felicia right up to the moment when our new Sensors and Communications Officer reported Starlights on her scope; it was Lieutenant Byng's squadron, flying broad sweeps towards our intended approach vector, hoping to find us.

Those Starlights, it must be said, had scared off the Martian DEs trying to pick up survivors out of what some might call spite, but I'll call pride. The pilots, and the surviving crew of *Honesty*, believed we'd rescue them before they ran out of power, and here we were.

We arrived at Sinope, we collected the life pods, brought aboard about thirty survivors each, and found room for the extra Starlights on our decks. I should have mentioned, actually, that *Dominator* hadn't launched its planes, or we'd have had to find space for them as well. Andrea hadn't had time to get the bays open before a hit disabled the power in those sectors. Most of the pilots got out in escape pods, but we just left their planes behind.

As survivors came aboard, they told the tale of the ship's destruction, and I remember Mark Gunney's dire expression. Shaking his head, he let out a sigh, "Dammit, Aaron. Dammit."

That wasn't damning Aaron Ashby of course... it was more 'dammit, Aaron, why'd you have to get killed, after all this?' An apt question. As I said before, it was a costly day.

And we still had a few more things to do.

CHAPTER THIRTY-TWO
THE OTHER SIDE

Wolf and *Friendly* continued on to Sinope after we'd finished recovering *Honesty's* pods, while *Cheetah* went to look for the Martian that had seemingly survived its encounter with the Starlights. The destroyer escort was called *Bosporus Planum*, as it turned out, which I find amusing because the Bosporus Strait on Earth was one of the places over which the nineteenth-century sea battle of Sinope had been fought. Evidently, the name had also been assigned to one of the plains on Mars, which in turn had been used to name one of the *Planum*-class Martian destroyer escorts.

Well, *Bosporus Planum* was tumbling out of control away from Sinope when *Cheetah* found it, and Mark offered the Martians the chance to surrender. Some of this DE's small craft had already gone out and hauled in the life pods from the other, destroyed DE, but now the situation seemed dire for both crews... surrender, or tumble into oblivion.

They surrendered, but to their credit, they did so in a classy way: they abandoned ship, and their scuttling charges blew it apart, leaving us nothing to capture. I'm not being sarcastic when I say classy — that's the way professional spacers do it — but it left us nothing to bring back for study. Classy bastards.

The ship's life pods were immediately taken aboard *Cheetah*, where the Martian crews were greeted by many SF and crew armed with MAG-90s and sidearms. They were kept on the flightdeck for the time being.

Bosporus Planum's small craft — which fifty of the ship's crew had used to escape — were put under Starlight escort, and together they cruised to Sinope, arriving just an hour after we began our landings.

After all we'd gone through to get here, you better believe Karen and I were going down to Sinope ourselves, with the first team. Because we didn't know just how the Martian airlock-docking system would work, we decided not to travel in our fighters, but to go down with Rufus Chang's Special Branch squad. Matt was personally leading *Friendly's* SF and Special Branchers down as well. And get this: despite being shipwrecked literally hours before, all six of *Honesty's* Special Branchers, and nine of the ship's surviving SF — all Egesta veterans — demanded to go down as well.

We were thus landing with sixty-eight people, including twenty-four Special Branchers.

Boy, was I ever glad we'd taken Rufus Chang aboard back at Io — because we were missing *Lady Grace*, *Pictou* and *Trusty's* people, our landing force was very light.

Hopefully the Martians had abandoned the dome — if there were still Martians down there, it would have meant the ships that had run for Mars had left people behind. That didn't seem likely, considering the professionalism we'd seen so far that day.

We'd soon see, one way or another...

Anyway, it was a different experience, landing in Rufus Chang's boat. Karen and I almost felt as though we were betraying Charlie, invading a dome with another Special Brancher and all, but Charlie *had* told us to go in with Rufus — it was much better than going in with our usual irresponsible and independent flare.

Just as well, then.

It took the pilot of Rufus' shuttle about ten minutes to figure out the Martian docking controls, and then we eased up to one of the dome's airlocks and mated with its soft column with only minor difficulties. There was a fear, of course, that the Martians might have booby trapped this chute, so I wasn't without a healthy amount of concern as Rufus' 2IC popped the lock and stuck his head through.

Karen and I waited in the back of the shuttle, occasionally trading anxious glances, and then the Captain gave Rufus a thumbs up.

"Here we go, on me," Rufus said coolly. Like Charlie, he was a lead-from-the-front sort, so up he went.

We waited while the Branchers filed out into the chute, then Karen glanced at me, "Ready for this?"

I opened my mouth, closed it, then opened it again, "I swear to God, if this looks *anything* like Egesta, I'm going to kill somebody."

If you'd heard my tone, you'd know I wasn't kidding. I really wasn't in the mood to find a massacred population down there, though part of me was quite firmly convinced that I was about to see just that.

Karen smiled sadly and nodded, then drew her mag. I did the same and followed.

We got to the bottom of the chute and steeled ourselves, then I led the way out into the dome. It wasn't an elaborate entry arrangement — there were multiple chutes and they all just emptied onto the floor of the dome. A few tents — *tents*, really — were set up in the space beyond the chutes, but all in all, this seemed like a fairly crude dome.

The first thing I noticed as I came to a stop a little beyond the chute were massive bars stretching up to the low dome ceiling — a whole wall of bars, close together like jail bars, going floor to ceiling.

I then looked down, and found that Rufus' squad was moving forward in a broad line, MAG-90s ready and sweeping from side to side, checking for any hiding Martians.

No one seemed to be jumping out at them, so they were heading towards the wall of bars.

"Hey you two," Matt Baxter was suddenly beside us, and I had to smile at my friend.

"Matt..." Karen gave that first greeting, saying his name in the way you say someone's name as a hello.

"Glad to see you... in person I mean," I followed on.

Warmer than usual (good grief, I bet he was actually happy to see us after this long day!), Matt nodded and smiled, "Yes, I'm pleased to see you two, too. Hope it's not a bloody mess down here though, what?"

Karen and I nodded simultaneously, and then I sighed deeply, "Shall we?"

Friendly's Special Branch team, under Captain Gwen Jameson (remember, veteran of Egesta) moved forward past us, and then the SF from that ship, as well as the surviving security personnel from *Honesty* (who'd come down against doctors' advice to rest) also began arriving.

Matt, Karen and I headed for the wall of bars, not really eager to get there…

But we really, truly didn't need to be as anxious as we were.

By the time we arrived at the bars, Rufus' most technically-inclined officer had already shut them down — they were magbars (at least that's what we'd call them), and would stun anyone who tried to touch or get between them. Rufus had found a gate through them, which led to a smaller barred-in chamber, and that had a gate on its far side — it was like an airlock for captives.

Rufus' officer figured out how to open the gates, and on the other side, more than 2,000 Defense Command personnel and civilians began to stick their heads out of their tents.

Tents, like I said. Rows and rows of tents, all of them military grade, and containing cots for two adults (plus children) and good supplies of water and rations. There were disintegration latrines placed at regular intervals, as well as shower and washing facilities on alternating intervals, and the air smelled clean.

This was a budget POW camp — but it *was* a POW camp.

"Defense Command has taken control of local space, this dome, and Io," Rufus bellowed, "please remain calm for a moment while we sort out the situation."

Not bloody likely — Rufus knew it'd be pandemonium as soon as the announcement was made, but he had to try.

The first rush of elation at liberation would have to pass before we got these people under control again, but I have to say, the cheers were gratifying. Karen and I looked at each other, smiled, and holstered our mags.

Now we just had to figure out how to move everyone.

It actually took about an hour for us to find the senior officer in the camp, but when he emerged we met him near the entry chutes. It wasn't Commodore Prazsky, the commanding officer at Io; he'd apparently died in the defense of the base. Instead it was Captain Clive, erstwhile skipper of *Dominator*.

Clive was a roundish fellow, but seemingly good natured. He didn't carry the air of a Captain, though, so I had to assume he'd come to his position through political influence. I suppose it's not quite fair for me to make that comment, but his crew certainly hadn't performed well in his absence.

I don't know, perhaps he had a rapport with them — the ability to make them work where Andrea couldn't — but it struck me that neither Andrea nor any of the Belt Squadron officers could have gotten blood from those turnips…

Anyway, at the moment I really didn't need to critique Clive's style, I just needed to find out what he knew.

Shaking Karen's hand and then mine, Clive seemed a little star struck for a moment, "Well sir… *Admiral* sir, I see… we never thought they'd send the likes of you to our rescue. All of our thanks to you."

Right at that moment, those words were a bitter pill to swallow. I didn't feel like I'd done much at all today — compared to Andrea, Mark, Matt, Elise, Nancy, or the much less fortunate Kris, Giovanni Calzatti, and of course Aaron Ashby. All I'd done was talk a bit.

It was later pointed out to me, of course, that it was important talk — issuing of orders and such — but it's hard to feel like you've done a hell of a lot when other people have paid a much higher price.

But I wasn't going to get into that sort of discussion with Captain Clive, "We're glad to find you so well. We've secured Io, and we believe the Martians have taken off for good. Now we just need to figure out how to get you home."

"To Io?" he asked, an honest frown on his face.

"To the Empire," Karen answered softly. "Io's too much of a liability to try to hold right now, and the Martians took everything of value. But between your people here, prisoners we've taken and crews who've lost their ships, we're probably going to have a few thousand people to move. I'm not sure the combat storeship we have will be able to haul that many."

Clive nodded slowly, "I see, I see. Well there may be more of my squadron's frigates out in the moons, they could certainly help. Many were running with reduced crews."

It was incredibly good that he was being unquestioning and helpful — the last thing either Karen or I needed was to go through all this effort to find a petulant officer who started second-guessing us out of a need to compensate for his being captured.

Captain Clive just seemed plain grateful, and as shallow as this'll sound, I was glad he appreciated what we'd done.

"But don't let us get ahead of ourselves… tell us what happened here, Captain," I put the question to him after a moment, and Clive nodded.

"Please, please sir, call me Johnston. And to answer your question, approximately seven months ago… we think, I may have lost track of the time, you see… that Martian force turned up, and they blasted our squadron out of Io orbit. I believe my ship must have been hit and withdrawn… the battleship *Dominator*, sir. It was gone when I tried to return to it…" he paused, the implied question being 'have you seen my ship?'.

"We found it, and under the command of Captain Andrea Kiley, it was wrecked while destroying the Martian battleship. It was scuttled due to the damage, but you should have seen the other guy," I said, couching that in terms to avoid criticizing his crew and his XO.

Clive frowned again, "It was in fighting condition?"

"Your XO seems to have left dock prematurely, and failed to engage the enemy," Karen said quietly, and Clive seemed to straighten bolt-upright in shock.

"Mazur… I should have guessed… the honor of my ship, my crew…!"

I held up a hand, "Your crew was doing the lion's share of the work when *Dominator* destroyed the Martian battleship. The honor of your ship is restored, Johnston. Now, we think we've already been able to fill in a lot of the blanks about Io's occupation and the shipping off of equipment… what's been going on here?"

I didn't need a day-by-day report right now, just the highlights, and looking somewhat relieved that his ship had given a good (or decent) account of itself, Clive stopped to think for a moment, "Well, they did ship out much of the equipment and experimental research kit from the labs. And they weren't sure what to do with us, because the Martian

Admiral, one Benjamin Conflans, didn't have adequate transport for us. He was a proper gentleman, though — he made sure we had all the supplies and logistical support we needed, even shipped in our own food and some belongings from Io. Good fellow. Did he escape from that battleship?"

I cocked my eyebrow, "No one did, from what we saw. No pods launched."

"Quite a shame, quite a shame," Clive shook his head, then got his mind back on track. "The last of them left a number of hours ago, taking most of their equipment with them. They said they were likely not to be returning. I thought they may have lost contact with their Admiral, as it was quite abuzz around here lately. Some of them apparently recognized your ships, and were quite eager to face you. Considered themselves the best in their fleet, these boys did."

Karen and I glanced at each other at that point, eyebrows up, and then looked back to Clive.

"So here we are," the Captain said finally. "I have taken it upon myself to organize officers and staff to facilitate egress when transport is arranged, but if we could be moved to Io, that might be best."

I nodded, "Yes, keep us from having to defend two moons, I'd prefer that. It's a day-long flight, so I'm not sure if we could fit all of you into the ships we have here. We'll have to see."

Clive nodded, "Very well."

That seemed like a natural place to end it, so with a nod to each of us, Clive stepped back, snapped his heels together, and crisply saluted.

Somewhat surprised, Karen and I saluted back, and then he went on his way.

Letting out a breath, Karen looked at me, "He talks to superiors well. And he's right, we get them back to Io, we can organize them from there. I'm sure Charlie won't have flattened everything."

I smiled, "We'll see. For now... three ships, that's at least 700 each... can our life support handle that?"

Karen's warm smile, absent in its genuine form for so much of the day, returned, "Let's call Andy and see."

We set about making preparations to evacuate this place.

CHAPTER THIRTY-THREE
WHAT DO YOU MEAN, 'CLEAN UP'?

Charlie had just come back to the DCHQ building from the hospital when Gina Bertram's voice came into his ear, "Message for you just in from Sinope, Major Peters. It's from Rear Admiral Barron."

"Ooh, guess they're done out there too," Charlie replied with a nod. "I'll be up in a minute."

He'd literally just stepped out of the car in which Ben Belete had brought him to the HQ, so now Charlie climbed the stairs to the lobby doors, but stopped for a moment, feeling obliged to turn around one more time and look at his handiwork. Dawn was breaking, and in the growing light there was a glow over the rubble of the block of stores, half the stadium, four apartment buildings, and the entry building to the underground complex.

The half-burned residential houses seemed almost serene, and the mall, which from outside looked alright, seemed to wink and say 'someone had a massive firefight in me'. They'd totaled this place — for a good cause, absolutely — and Charlie had to admit to a certain feeling of accomplishment. It wasn't often that you got free rein to do this much damage... hell, it wasn't often that it was necessary.

But it had worked, and the final word was in: only two Special Branchers had been killed, both officers from Marcus Atallah's squad. This, of course, is a huge testament to the quality of Special Branch, when compared to the Martian Commandos. They're both elite special forces, but a Special Brancher is a little more elite.

Well, that and Special Branch had heavy fire support on its side. Only about a dozen of the Commandos had actually been taken out in firefights — at least that many had been crushed by buildings Charlie had dropped on them. But that was fine, his Branchers had done well. Eight of them were still laid up in the hospital, some in serious condition, but he had faith they'd pull through.

Anyway, he could stand out here staring at the wrecked dome city, or he could go take that message...

Arriving in C&C a few minutes later, Charlie nodded to Gina Bertram, "Put it up on the main screen."

She nodded, hit a few keys, and I appeared, "Hey Charlie... we're here, we have the Martians running. *Lady Grace* lost a drive pod, and *Pictou* is missing. We lost *Dominator* and *Honesty*. Andrea got off *Dominator* with most of the crew, but only about half of *Honesty's* crew got out, and none of its officers. They took two DEs with them, though, and we have many prisoners from those crews. There are 2,000 people in the Sinope dome, all in very good condition... and they want to come back to Io, at least until we figure out how we get them home. Saves us from having to defend two different moons, so I'm for it. It'll just take a bit of doing… *Trusty's* out keeping tabs on the Martians who ran, so I'm trying to figure out if we can cram that many into *Wolf, Lion* and *Friendly* for a day. Andy thinks we can, we'll just pile them in the corridors. Anyway, what I need is some accommodation for 2,000 people. Maybe some of them can go back to their homes… whatever's left standing. Just let me know, and let me know what your casualty situation is. I'm guessing by now you have things under control. Talk to you soon."

As my face froze on the screen at the end of the message, Charlie seemed to be equally frozen staring at it.

"What, they want us to clean up?" Gina Bertram frowned, turning to him.

He actually smacked his forehead, "We are so dead."

Wolf was starting to feel *heavier* with all the civilians and Defense Command personnel being loaded in. If you'll recall, we'd sent all our SF away to *Artemis Agrotera* and Io itself, so we had room for fifty people in those guards' barracks. We put the civilians there (200 of them, since they didn't have to live that way, just travel in there for a day) and then spread another 800 throughout the ship, mainly sitting in corridors or cargo areas — even in the studio on the rec deck.

As Karen and I inspected some of these arrangements, we felt slightly awkward — everyone was looking at us with gratitude and such, and we didn't care for it, so we headed to the bridge.

When we got there, Andrea Kiley was standing before the main screen with her arms folded, looking at a vid feed of a wrecked dome being piped up from Io DCHQ.

Karen and I came to a stop, standing on either side of Andrea, and Captain Kiley glanced at me first, "How do you think our refugees will react to that?"

"To what?" I frowned, looking up at the screen. "Where is that?"

Then my mind did the necessary reasoning to understand Andrea's question.

"Wait, that's *Io*?"

Andrea smiled, genuinely I think, "Seems the Commandos put up a fight."

"We were only gone a day," Karen's eyes were darting all over the screen, "how did he flatten so much?"

"Apparently, he brought in two planes from Lionstar. And when they were both shot down, he turned one into a makeshift artillery piece strapped to a couple of cars," Andrea explained it with a little… *bounce*. Couldn't really blame her — Karen and I both laughed in half-surprise.

"Casualties for his forces were two dead and eight wounded. And all the Martians have now surrendered… it worked, so we'll just have to figure out what to tell those civilians we're hauling," Andrea looked back to the screen.

Yeah. I mean, after seven or eight months, they probably weren't expecting to go home and find the place just as they left it… we could blame the Martians for much of the mayhem… and if the civilians complained, perhaps we could let them loot the shopping mall. Yes…

"We could get them to bring their tents with them," Karen half shrugged, and I chuckled.

"I don't think we have the room to take tents."

"They'll be fine," Andrea shook her head. "We just rescued them, didn't we? They bloody well should be grateful."

Well, that was true. It just wasn't something we'd usually actually *say* out loud.

"Can't disagree with that," Karen said a little gingerly, and she and I exchanged glances again. Andrea... well, you know.

Problems.

Wolf boosted for Sinope three hours later, with *Cheetah* and *Friendly* in company with us. Our parting gift to that dome was a laser shot each, and by the time the gift was delivered, the dome was split wide open. The Martians wouldn't be using it again.

CHAPTER THIRTY-FOUR

ON IO

Ultimately, there were some complaints when we arrived back at Io a day later, but not too many. It seems that after seven months, the civilians and DC personnel who called Io home *had* expected there to be damage. They even realized that, had the damage not been done, the Commandos would still be controlling parts of the dome.

To be honest, the acceptance of the destruction surprised me — if this had been a Belt colony, we'd probably have been chased by torch-bearing mobs, but I think a lot of these DC and civilians really wanted to go home to the Empire. Some hard cases wanted to stay, but there wasn't going to be any of that. When we left, we were all going, and this dome was probably going to be opened up. But that's for next book.

And so are most of those Io personnel questions.

When we got back to the rock, both Nancy Whitehorse and Elise De Winter were there, their corvettes sitting protectively alongside *Artemis Agrotera*, even though *Lady Grace* was missing a pod. Nancy reported that the Martians had indeed continued to run, and that made sense based on what Captain Clive and some of the captured officers from *Bosporus Planum* had said; if Admiral Conflans had been killed, and his second in command taken over, chances were the Martians wouldn't stick around for a close action.

Just as well, I'd had enough shooting for the week.

We docked with Io and moved both the recovered Io personnel and our Martian prisoners down. Charlie had set up tents he'd gotten out of the mall's adventure store (why they had an adventure store is beyond me — the Io park was dead) and from DCHQ for the civilians. As it turned out, then, their living arrangements weren't all that different here than they'd been on Sinope. Some of the houses in the residential area — the least burned — were cleared to take families, and the quarters in the DCHQ building itself were filled with their original personnel.

All of that I can talk more about next book (though I probably won't); the point for now is we got these people off our ships, which finally meant we could sort of relax. With the Io sensor grid working for us, we could stand down from action stations and let our crews rest, and we could visit the dome too.

Now, 'we' meant me, Karen and Andrea; Mark was sitting down with the survivors of *Honesty*, talking to them and patting them on the back — making sure his former crew was looked after — and Matt was seeing to the prisoner transfer, because Commander and ship CO though he was, his roots in the SF branch ran deep.

It was thus we three *Wolf* officers who met Charlie on the front steps of the DCHQ building, and all of us, Charlie included, were smiling when we did.

No, not at the destruction, or at the civilians being put into makeshift accommodations, or any of that sort of stuff; we were smiling because here we all were. That whole couple of days, I don't think any of us had thought much about the prospect of our own deaths

— even Charlie, when he'd been shot by that sniper, had a healthy (perhaps unhealthy) detachment about his own existence. His job was to lead, and to worry about others.

And we'd all been like that, though Andrea was probably the only one of us who'd come anywhere near having to face her own mortality.

Anyway, we hadn't been thinking about our deaths, but now that this was done, we could be very glad that we were all still alive, and that we were able to see each other again.

So I shook Charlie's hand as we came to a stop next to him, and with flourish waved my arm across the horizon of the dome, "So you've finally seen the light!"

That comment earned me a quizzical brow from him, and Karen came down the steps to stand at his other side, "Well, Karen and I have been casually knocking down buildings for *years*… you didn't have to try to catch up all at once."

He laughed, as did we all, because it was very good to be back together again. We'd be less happy in a moment, unfortunately.

When we got to the hospital, another quiet settled over us, and Karen was particularly silent. She left the group, started working her way from room to room, seeing her old crew, checking in and giving words of encouragement.

What got to her were the apologies. I was getting them too, but she was hurt more by them I think.

I mean, how do you react when someone who has absorbed 800 REM of radiation and was blinded by a flash while trying to get people into escape pods grabs your hand and apologizes for not being able to do more damage before getting knocked out of the fight?

How do you deal with *that*?

Some people think it's romantic movie-making when they put that sort of stuff into the films, but it isn't — everyone I met from *Lion's* crew was saying the same sorts of things… 'we're sorry'… 'we should have done better'… 'we won't let you down again'…

That's the pride of the Belt Squadron and the Jupiter Force, you see… the pride of most of Defense Command. It's the high standards our people expected of themselves. They wanted to do their jobs, and to look after each other when the going got tough. They wanted to make sure the Martians remembered them… they wanted to do some damage before they were taken out.

The crew of *Lion* had been robbed of that chance, and now, as most of them lay in that hospital recovering from radiation sickness, it was one of the few things that plagued their thoughts in their traumatized state.

So for me it was incredibly difficult to listen to these earnest promises, because obviously I had nothing against these men and women and I knew they didn't have anything to apologize for. They were part of the Belt Squadron family, and I just wanted them to get well. They had let no one down.

For Karen it was so much more personal than that, because they weren't just part of the *extended* family. She'd built this crew. *Lion* had been fresh out of the docks when Karen had taken command, and she'd assembled a crew that had gone on virtually unchanged right up to that day, the same way I'd assembled *Wolf's*. Hers was a welcome face in every room in the hospital — she was someone who could really comfort all these people. But that meant she had to listen to apologies, and that wasn't easy on her.

However many times we said 'there's nothing to apologize for' I don't know, but we just kept repeating it over and over... and over...

While we were doing this rather grim job, Andrea had gone to Kris Jacobs' bedside.

Andrea and Kris had been friends, as all Belt Squadron officers tend to be, though they'd never had any special relationship... they didn't have the history that Charlie, Kris and I had from the old days.

I say that because, based on their relationship, I wouldn't quite have expected Andrea's reaction when Karen and I finally got in there to see Kris. It was an awkward situation, I suppose: we arrived, and Andrea was sitting in the chair next to Kris' bed, leaning forward with her elbows on her knees, and her forehead cupped in both hands.

Karen and I looked at her, then at each other, and decided we'd not even notice her body language for now — anything we tried to say to Andrea here would have an audience, and in the meantime, Kris was suffering from acute radiation syndrome. That had to trump mental trauma.

So I went up the left side of the bed, and Karen went up the right, and we looked Kris over as the Aussie skipper slept. After a moment, I looked across at Karen, "Think it's proper to wake her up?"

With impeccable timing, Doctor Rhee walked past the foot of the bed, "You may, she has been sleeping for four hours."

See, I like doctors like Rhee. I find some doctors seem to think that we Defense Command officers don't understand that rest is necessary for healing. They're very, *very* protective — militantly so at times. But Rhee knew we wanted to talk to Kris, and he was willing to let us wake her up, as she clearly would have wanted. We weren't putting her recovery in jeopardy, we were just talking, and he realized that.

Reaching down, I took Kris' right hand and gave it a squeeze, "Hey, wake up."

What's interesting, now that I think about it, is that Kris' horrific appearance wasn't the first thing that struck me right then. In the car ride down, Charlie had informed us she was in the questionable camp when it came to survival — the redoubtable Doctor Rhee couldn't be certain they'd pumped enough drugs into her quickly enough to save her, but she had a solid chance.

Then we'd seen all of *Lion's* crew apologizing, and that had certainly changed our outlook for the day. I didn't even notice how ghastly Kris looked until she opened her eyes and managed a difficult smile.

"Hi skipper," she smiled, squeezing my hand back, then looking across at Karen, who'd taken her other hand. "Sorry I didn't take care of your ship better, Karen. Reckon it's unsalvageable."

You'll notice Kris' sentences were forming better; the swelling on her tongue had decreased somewhat... which we were pretty sure was a good sign.

Karen was keeping up her impenetrably brave face, but I could see her eyes twitch at that apology, and her smile tightened and thinned, "No apologies, Kris. Seriously, I can't take any more apologies."

That was one of the few times I'd ever heard an undercurrent of real, pure sadness and pain in Karen's voice — at least, in a voice she used in public.

"And *Lion's* up there. We're going to tow it home to get fixed up. A few months in the yard and it'll be ready for you when they put you back on space duty."

Kris looked back at me, and there was no way to read her expression through her cloudy eyes... actually, come to think of it, it was a good sign that she could see. But she squeezed my hand again, "You don't need to lead me on. I lost my ship."

She wasn't fishing for sympathy, she was sharing the guilt that the whole crew of *Lion* was feeling. I shook my head, "Even if you had, there wasn't a thing you could have done about it. My orders were to go in, and in you went. That battleship was waiting for us. But that's beside the point, *Lion's* up there, and you're going to be skippering it again. I'm an Admiral now, remember — I can make those promises."

I smiled as I said that, and Kris did the same — again with great difficulty.

"And Andrea destroyed the battleship," Karen added, filling in the news Kris may not have heard. "*Lady Grace* lost a drive pod, and we lost *Honesty* and we have to try to find *Pictou. Dominator* didn't survive the battleship fight, but the crew got off."

Kris nodded in short jerks, "We sent them running?"

"We did, and we got the Io people out of Sinope and back here," those words were added in a soft Irish brogue.

I don't know if Karen or I were able to contain our surprise as a warmly smiling Andrea Kiley arrived next to me and leaned down to see Kris, "Now you get yourself better, none of this dying business. We'll need you back in the squadron."

Kris nodded again, "I'll see what I can manage."

We continued to stand and make small talk for a while, hopefully just helping Kris with our presence. Eventually we left, heading for *Wolf* while she went back to sleep.

CHAPTER THIRTY-FIVE

EVERYONE SO TIRED

Fatigue was starting to set in when we got back to *Wolf*. Andrea made some excuse about having to do something and left Karen and me to ourselves, but as we watched her go we were becoming quite convinced that we needed to reconsider our approach with her.

"She's not in a good way," Karen said quietly, her voice strained.

I looked at Karen, and her face was drawn tight again, her eyes dark. She wasn't her unflappable self at this point. The strain of worrying about Andrea was compounding with the misery of her old crew and the fatigue after a long couple of days, to break down her façade in a way reminiscent of — but nowhere near as drastic as — Egesta.

"Oh no, not both of you," I said it bluntly, because it was Karen, and she frowned and looked at me.

"Come with me," I bobbed my head down the corridor, and started walking.

"What?" she asked, her voice still strained.

"We're not talking about this in the corridor!" I called over my shoulder.

Andrea retreated to her cabin, her head starting to spin. As she explains it, just the simple sight of Kris in that state had started a whole wash of emotions and thoughts that shook her understanding of herself even more.

Her word for her state of mind just then was 'fragile'. It was good that she had a bridge to stand on, and a crew she could trust, but even as these things helped reassure her, a new mix of Egesta guilt and guilt at failing her friends was starting to eat away at her. Progress made over the past months — if you can call it progress — was no match for all the dark feelings pooling inside her.

But she had her duty, and she was determined to hold onto that. No matter what was wrong with her inwardly, she had to be the strong and capable Captain outwardly. She didn't know if anyone was seeing through that mask — she wasn't even thinking in those terms. She just knew she had to do her best to hide her pain, and to deal with it herself, while she did her job.

This is what she was thinking as she closed the hatch to her cabin and left the lights off. Her mag belt was dangling temptingly from the chair, but in her stubbornness she refused to even look at it. That was a good development, at least — she wouldn't contemplate suicide now, that would be weak. That would reveal her problems to everyone.

No, she'd struggle on, because she had to. And no one would know. That was her pledge to herself. No one must know.

But at least two of us did. And ultimately, it was probably a very good thing for her, and for all of us, that we did.

Time would tell.

+++

While Andrea cursed her own weakness in the dark, I rather ungraciously led Karen to my cabin. This, of course, was out of character for me, but I was at a stage of being too worried to care any more... and I suppose that's saying something. I opened my cabin door, waved Karen through it, and then stepped in behind her.

As I closed the hatch behind Karen, I pointed to my bed, "Sit."

By now Karen was actually starting to appear frustrated, no doubt because of my brusque and juvenile approach in getting her here. I probably could have just asked politely and she'd have come, but instead I'd decided to be more difficult about it, and given our mutual fatigue, that hadn't been the best way.

She dropped onto the edge of my bed with some resignation, letting out a short sigh, "What?"

I stood in front of the screen in my wall and donned a stern expression, "Andrea's bottling up her pain or something, right? That's obvious?"

Karen swung her head from right to left, eyes narrowing as she tried to figure out what I was getting to, "Yeah, it seems like."

"Right, well if she's bottling it, you're buying it! Stop!"

Now I thought that line was brilliant. I really did. Look at that bottling metaphor. It's just so awesome.

Your reaction was probably the same as Karen's; she closed her eyes and then opened them, as if she'd just been exposed to some sort of noxious gas, "What?"

I wasn't to be dissuaded, though — I may be a ham-handed idiot, but I'm a determined ham-handed idiot, "No, listen, I won't be able to stand it if you start going all darker than night and broody. And don't deny it, that's how you're feeling."

"Well yes, my crew is—"

"Ah," I held up a hand to stop her. "Your crew is?"

Her frustrated expression started to loosen, "My crew's down there."

Admitting one's worries and problems out loud was important — or at least I believed it was, and it seemed I was right.

"Exactly. And that hurts. That hurts like me seeing Kris like that hurts, but probably worse, right?"

Karen bit her bottom lip for a second, then nodded, "Yes. Yes, it does."

"Right, so what seems like the best way to deal with that? In private? Does pretending it doesn't hurt seem logical?"

I felt like a kid saying that — it was so juvenile. And yet it somehow needed to be said. Command officers, in my experience, can get so wrapped up in trying to hide their own pain that they entirely bottle it, and it starts to turn them into different, more bitter people.

Perhaps it happens to some of us because no one forces us to talk. I don't know, I'm not good with interpersonal, remember. I'm terrible with feelings and all that intuitive relationship stuff.

But I was also damned desperate at this point — I couldn't afford to let Karen follow Andrea into a bleak state of mind. No way could I put up with more of that, Andrea could have the monopoly on it for now.

Karen — and Andrea will understand my meaning in this — was simply more important. I could *not* lose Karen, or... well, you know. Most of it, anyway.

So I was probably sounding a little distressed as I made my case, and Karen let out a very long breath, and slumped forward slightly, "They kept apologizing. And I know why they were doing it, but that's not easy..."

There, the gates were open, so I sat down next to Karen and put my arm around her, pulling her sideways against me so her head rested on my shoulder.

"Yeah, I hate it. If I'm ever down in the field, make sure I don't apologize," I said, trying to be comforting and instead failing to make sense. "Actually, scratch that, if I'm down it'll be my fault, so I should apologize."

"Oh stop, if you start blaming yourself for that whole Kate thing again, I'm going to smack you," Karen's voice was starting to soften, and I let my head fall softly against hers.

"Yeah, we should both just stop worrying about everyone else, I guess. For the moment, at least. Other people have much better reasons to be distressed about those things than we have," I could actually hear the fatigue starting to wear through my own voice when I said that, and Karen replied with an 'mmhmm.'

We sat silently for a couple of minutes, both of us replaying in our minds everything that had happened, both of us trying to put as much of it out of our minds as we could... not forgetting it, but... well... not being weighed down by it. Wasn't easy, and of course one bout of just sitting and thinking wouldn't remove all the feelings of guilt we were hoarding.

We'd just have to watch out for each other, as we always did. Keep ourselves from getting too caught up in those feelings, because that could only lead to bad things.

"I did like your bottling analogy," Karen said after a while, her tone smooth again.

"It was a metaphor, actually," I injected a little self-righteousness into that retort.

"Well, I liked the metaphor then."

"You lie," I replied with a smile.

"Well, yes. But it was a very strong effort. You may actually have a future in writing or something," she was now toying with me.

"Now you patronize!"

"*Now*," Karen pulled her head off my shoulder and looked at me, almost nose-to-nose, "I'm hungry!"

Of course she was, it was that time of day, after all.

We started to laugh, which was a very good thing.

AFTERWORD

The Dark Cruise comes next, and that of course refers to the infamous, slow, and deadly run home from Io weeks after this. Emptying a colony of its people and getting everyone safely back to the Empire is complicated, so I'll let you read about that when we get to the next book.

And of course, we have to deal with Andrea's state of mind, with trying to find those frigates that may or may not have gotten themselves lost out among Jupiter's moons, and finally with the establishment of the slow convoy home... all of that sounds terribly uninteresting, perhaps, but it isn't. Wasn't.

This mission to Jupiter had taken a lot out of us. The reporters being aboard — though I barely mention them this book, to my shame — had made the start of the cruise more tense than it should have been, and the long shadows of Egesta had manifested themselves as soon as we'd seen action again. I think it's safe to say we weren't the same officers who'd so handily won at the Battle of Belt Two, back in *The Rogue Commodore*.

And we'd paid dearly for our victory at Sinope. The Martians had lost a battleship, two destroyers (with another heavily damaged), and two DEs, not to mention all their pirate cohorts. We'd lost a battleship and two corvettes, with one frigate and one corvette very heavily damaged. On the face of it, then, we came away slightly better, but... well, I wonder sometimes — if we'd all been sharper, just a *little* sharper, could we have saved more of our own?

I don't know, and of course thanks to Jessica and Jocko, this mission was heralded (not unjustly) as a great success. It was just costly. It cost us ships. It cost us crews. And it cost us some more personal stability.

We'll see where all of that leads on the trip home, then. For now I think we're done, so thanks for hanging in. This has been *The Sinope Affair*, and I'll see you in *The Dark Cruise*.

Keep well until then!

THE DARK CRUISE

THE AUTOBIOGRAPHICAL REMINISCENCES OF ADMIRAL THE LORD KEN BARRON FOR 2232

THE MARTIAN WAR - 8

KENNETH TAM

FROM THE AUTHOR

Alright, I need to say this: I have a pet peeve with some science fiction (movies, shows, books... whatever) when it comes to the handling of the classic 'beast in our midst' story. A vicious alien turns up aboard a ship, or in a colony, and like a monster in the night, it (or they, if there are several) roams around, killing and terrorizing while any military personnel on hand seem helpless.

Or military personnel arrive at a colony or derelict ship and discover that it has been emptied by a creature, and then they get themselves killed in a vain attempt to stop it.

This, of course, is a recipe for great drama... but it always bothers me because it's often so ridiculous. Sorry, but it's true. I can only guess these stories are based upon the classic stories of Empire — for instance, the story of the man-eating lions of Tsavo. In those tales, 'civilized men' were pitted against 'savage creatures', and as far as I know, they usually had no military support. Such stories can be easily adapted to the science fiction genre.

The problem is that the adaptations haven't always been well thought out. There were never stories of exciting African beasts terrorizing a military camp, because the beasts wouldn't last long confronting well-armed troops. Some science fiction has recognized this — for instance, pitting vicious aliens against poorly armed crews of cargo ships instead of against 'elite' military units — but good military sense is not something that's always carefully considered.

I get into this subject now because, to a certain extent, *The Dark Cruise* looks at these issues — looks at how military personnel would deal with a situation as unlikely as some of those set up in these types of stories. Wait, you ask... does that mean... *gasp*... aliens?

Read on and see. The answer becomes pretty clear, I think!

The other thing I want to mention here is that planning and good judgment won't always keep you alive. Sometimes equipment is designed with a blind spot that developers either don't know is there, or overlook due to budget concerns. Those blind spots can cost lives, and usually they have to before they're corrected.

So there are a couple of different themes in this book.

Anyway, ranting aside, there are thanks to give! Many of the characters you'll read about in this book are based on real-world friends of mine. Thanks to all of those fine people — I hope your characters do you proud!

As ever, my good friend Peter Caron must be thanked for his insights and opinions. Wes Prewer must be given great credit as well, for being a perpetual sounding board for ideas, and for producing the images that really help give *Defense Command* its identity.

Of course most importantly, I must thank my parents and Iceberg partners, Jacqui and Peter. I've run out of clever ways to say it: they're just awesome.

And Atlas. As always, thanks.

— Kenneth Tam

FOREWORD

I suppose titles for books don't get much more ominous than *The Dark Cruise*, but of course I'm appropriating (stealing) that title from the numerous media stories done about our cruise from Jupiter back to Earth. So what was so dark about it?

Well, for one thing, we were out in the black, far away from the trappings of civilization we know and love, so that was probably part of it. You can still see the sun out there, it's just a lot smaller than we're used to.

But I think 'dark' comes more from what happened on that trip. It wasn't like *The Jupiter Patrol* — it wasn't a laugh-filled romp home. We found trouble, and at the time I didn't even know who had caused it. You undoubtedly know, of course, but I'm still going to be vague about it in this book, because I was vague about it then too.

Sometimes I wonder if we would have been more prepared for what came later if we'd known more about what happened on the way home...

Probably not. No, quite unlikely, really. Nothing prepared us... prepared *me* for what was to come.

But that's obviously in the future. For now we need to get home from Io, so let me set this up. If you remember from *The Sinope Affair*, the Jupiter Force had taken some hard hits in the encounter with the Martian squadron out at Io, and the Martians had already sent all the equipment they'd stripped out of our Io labs back to Mars.

We'd also recovered most of Io's population, and it was now living in the Io dome that Charlie Peters had unceremoniously wrecked (for good reason).

Worst of all — and it's not fair for me to call this the worst because we'd lost ships like *Pictou* and, of course, *Honesty* — *Lion* was severely damaged, and many of its crew, including our Captain Kris Jacobs, had suffered acute radiation poisoning.

We'll pick up with the story two weeks later. Yep, a whole two weeks. Seriously, you miss nothing significant with those two weeks. I'll explain as we go.

So... let's begin!

Chapter One

The Blips Arrive

To be honest, I wasn't sure what sort of tone the beginning of this book would have. My memory of this cruise, ultimately, is quite dark (not as bad as Egesta, don't worry), but I wasn't sure if I'd be able to find moments of humor and glad tidings with which to start.

Guess not.

Two blips approached Io almost two weeks to the day after we recovered the population from Sinope. Karen and I were both sleeping when they came in — it was our night cycle — but Mark Gunney had command during that shift, so it was *Cheetah's* bridge that bustled with action when they first appeared on scope.

Erica Martin, *Wolf's* Helm and Navigation Officer for many years, and now *Cheetah's* XO, was actually on duty at the same time as Mark, which is a little unusual. She was chatting with her Captain when the Sensors and Communications duty officer blinked and shot out of her seat in surprise, "Incoming, two unknowns... vector direct from Jupiter."

Mark and Erica frowned at each other and headed up to the main screen at the front of *Cheetah's* bridge, Mark bobbing his head towards it, "Let me see them. Look for IFF. Range?"

"About two hours out. We're getting the feed from Io's grid," the Lieutenant was back in her seat and working quickly, and Mark nodded.

"Alright, set up Battlelink, tell the officer of the watch on *Wolf* to wake Ken and Karen."

Mark, of course, was fully capable of dealing with two unidentified ships on his own, but it was good policy to wake us — if these two ships turned out to be the vanguard of a new Martian assault, having us napping would be bad.

Commander Matt Baxter appeared on *Cheetah's* screen two almost immediately. Matt never sleeps, I think. Again, as a reminder, he was no longer *Wolf's* XO, he was skippering *Friendly*, one of the only other ships we had intact.

Actually, I better give you a rundown of the squadron situation. Should have done this sooner, silly me...

Wolf and *Cheetah* were in fighting trim, so that's two *Predator*-class frigates. *Friendly* and *Trusty* (the latter formerly of the Jupiter Squadron) were also in good condition, and *Lady Grace* was missing a drive pod but, despite that, was in decent shape. *Lion* was an abandoned and irradiated hull, but was certainly salvageable. *Artemis Agrotera*, the combat storeship we'd taken out to Io with us, was doing just fine. We'd lost *Honesty*, *Pictou* and *Dominator* in the fights in *The Sinope Affair*.

So, to summarize, we had four active warships, and two damaged ones.

Trusty's XO appeared on the Battlelink a few seconds after Matt did, "Commander Whitehorse is on her way."

Nancy Whitehorse, like Karen and me, had been on a sleep period.

Then *Wolf's* representative appeared, our officer of the watch being our Helm and Navigation Officer, Shelby McLaws.

"Good evening, Captain Gunney. I've called Captain Kiley, Commodore McMaster and Rear Admiral Barron to the bridge," Shelby announced with her usual southern grace and charm.

Mark nodded to Shelby, then glanced up at Matt, "Matt, mind going for a look?"

Matt Baxter looked tired (you can see it in the Battlelink logs) but he nodded without hesitation, "Certainly."

Turning away from the viewfinder for a moment, Matt gave some orders, and *Friendly* began to push away from Io, heading out to intercept the two unknown ships. Io's long-range grid was only showing blips for the moment, so getting a closer look at the intruders would undoubtedly be a very good idea.

Mark folded his arms and watched on the main screen as the icon of *Friendly* moved out, and then glanced back as his Sensors and Communications Officer arrived on the bridge (looking like someone who'd just been woken out of a deep sleep) and dropped into his chair behind his consoles.

"Nice dreams, Numan?"

The Lieutenant Commander, Numan Nour, smiled without stopping his work, "Yes sir, she was very beautiful."

Mark laughed, "Well, sorry to interrupt. Can you get me anything on these two ships?"

Numan had only been promoted to Sensors and Communications Officer in the shuffles that took place in *The Gallant Few*, but he'd long ago gotten the hang of his job. He nodded now, keying a few buttons and then switching consoles.

"I can query them, if you would like," he looked up at Mark, and with a glance at Erica Martin, Mark shrugged.

"Couldn't hurt," Erica offered her simple reply, and Mark nodded.

"Record me," he looked back at the viewfinder. "This is Mark Gunney, DCNS *Cheetah*. You just woke up a lot of people, so if you're not friendly, you're going to have a bad day."

Nour grinned and keyed a few more controls. Seconds later, the signal was off.

Karen and I arrived on *Wolf's* bridge without much aplomb — we were nearly leaning on each other as we walked. We were thoroughly exhausted. I think I mentioned sometime in 2231 that, after periods of heavy action, fatigue can set in. That's what had happened to us; two weeks with nothing too major going on had finally convinced our bodies it was safe to switch back to 'deep sleep' mode to try to alleviate our cumulative fatigue.

Being woken up three hours into a six-hour sleep period was just cruel under those circumstances, but it was necessary.

"Status?" I could say that word without being actually awake, as Karen and I stumbled to the front of the bridge and started to look sleepily at the screens.

Andrea was already standing there, arms folded and an alert look on her sleep. Er. Face. On her face.

We were definitely tired.

"You wake up fast," I observed rather clumsily, glancing at her.

She favored me with a flash of smile, "Well, wasn't really sleeping."

If I'd been more awake, maybe I'd have asked what she meant. Of course, you remember all that had been going on with Andrea, and why she wouldn't be sleeping. I was just too tired at that moment to realize I should ask her about her statement.

Karen was looking the other way, because Jim Hannigan had rushed to the bridge with lipstick on his cheek. It was doubtless courtesy of Bunny, the sound technician for Jocko Kent, one of the reporters we had aboard. It was sweet, but, well, we were tired, so instead it seemed funny.

"Jim," Karen did one of those loud whispers, and as Jim looked at her, she pointed to her right cheek, "you should wipe that off."

Jim, too, was tired, and he frowned, thinking Karen wanted him to wipe something off her cheek, which was just strange. Then his mind started to function, and he wiped his cheek with the back of his hand, examining what came off.

Now, I would have expected Jim to have been flummoxed by that sort of 'embarrassing' moment, but he handled it quite deftly, "Two millennia of makeup, you'd think they could make lipstick that doesn't rub off on the kiss-ee."

Karen chuckled and Jim moved to his operations consoles and put our weapons on standby.

"Sorry to wake you all up," Mark acknowledged us on the Battlelink. "This could be good or bad."

"Most things are," I yawned as I said it, so my words were unintelligible. Mark smiled and nodded. We waited a little longer.

And then a little longer.

Felicia Khalid arrived on the bridge just in time to receive the message that came back to us from the unknowns. If you'll recall, Felicia took over as Sensors and Communications Officer after Kate Levec was shot during our first landing on Io.

"Message incoming… friendly tags, and vid attached."

I nodded and waved at one of the blank screens, "Any one you like, Felicia."

Terribly informal, I know. Did I mention I was tired? Come to that, am I ever very formal?

Felicia directed one of her techs to put the signal up on screen six, and the *WolfNet* buffering graphic flashed up as the transmission began to decode. It seemed to be taking an intolerably long time, but I assumed that was just me being impatient.

In fact, when I checked the time stamp on the logs I watched in prep for this book, I discovered the loading time was actually close to two minutes — quite long for any era of vid communication. This was probably because the old transmitter sending the signal didn't compress the message as much as our new processors would have liked.

Wow, you must have found that paragraph terribly interesting.

After those two minutes, a weary face appeared on the screen, poorly shaven with graying hair and eyebrows, and many deep wrinkles, "This is Captain Simon Kishko, DCNS *North Carolina*, to Captain Gunney of *Cheetah*. I am in company with DCNS *Kansas*, and we are the only remaining survivors of the Jupiter Squadron. We are most gratified to see assistance has arrived. We have need of many emergency supplies, please advise on an approach vector. Kishko out."

Kishko? Karen and I looked at each other, and she asked first, "Ever heard of him?"

I shook my head, then looked the other way at Andrea, "Name familiar?"

Andrea frowned and shook her head.

Now, obviously, the three of us didn't know every Captain in Defense Command, that'd be ridiculous. We still had to wonder, though — these two blips were coming towards us, claiming to be survivors of the Jupiter Squadron (remember, the Jupiter *Squadron* was the formation that was out here defending Io; we brought the Jupiter *Force* with us to relieve them), but what if they were Martians? Those blips could be Martian ships, trying to get into range of us through trickery, or they could be our ships with Martian crews.

The frigate *Quebec* had reportedly been taken by the Martians during the first attack. It was quite possible *Kansas* and *North Carolina* had been as well.

With impeccable timing, Nancy Whitehorse took her place on Battlelink screen four, "Good morning, everyone."

"Nancy," I nodded to her. "Captain Kishko, he one of yours?"

Nancy Whitehorse's eyes darted away from the screen for a moment, then she looked back and nodded, "Those two blips claiming to be ours?"

"They are," Mark Gunney replied from *Cheetah's* bridge. "Say they're *North Carolina* and *Kansas*."

"I have the message here now, I'll have a look," Nancy nodded.

If this was a Martian ruse, it'd be one based on the assumption that we didn't have anyone in our squadron who knew the skippers of those two ships. Nancy had been part of their squadron, though, so she'd be able to identify a doppelganger... what a strange word.

"That's him," Nancy nodded after a moment, then looked back at us. "He's aged a lot over the past eight months."

"Can't blame him," Mark replied again, "playing tag with those Martians all this time."

"And they'll be running low on supplies... they couldn't have been fully provisioned when they broke dock from Io," Andrea added quietly.

They were both quite right: these two ships, if they were who they claimed to be, had broken dock with reduced crews when the Martians had hit Io eight months prior — back when we were in *The Rogue Commodore*. Since then, they'd presumably been playing hide and seek between moons and rocks, rationing their supplies and praying for relief.

But, of course, this could still be quite a trap. The Martians could have taken Kishko hostage, or drugged him, done something to get him to say what they wanted. The only reason I didn't think it could have been pre-recorded was because he'd greeted Mark by name... the Martians couldn't have known who'd query them on their approach.

That said, better safe than sorry.

"Alright, let's hope he's on the level. All ships to general quarters. Matt, hold up where you are, *Wolf*, *Cheetah* and *Trusty* will come out to join you. Felicia, record me."

Felicia Khalid nodded to one of her techs, and the viewfinder zoomed in on my face and started recording, "This is Rear Admiral Ken Barron, commanding the Jupiter Force.

Captain Kishko, we're happy to see you alive. Of course, we can't be certain that your ship and your escort haven't in some way been compromised by the Martians, so we're going to come out to meet you. I'll need to be on realtime comms with you before I settle down a little on that count. See you in an hour, and welcome back to Io."

I nodded to Felicia and she compressed and sent the message.

Karen folded her arms and nodded slowly, "Well, here's hoping they're on the level."

"Yeah, if I'm going to be woken up in the middle of the night, I'd prefer it be for good news," I agreed.

A few moments later, Shelby McLaws had *Wolf* cruising out after *Friendly* towards the rendezvous with the blips. *Cheetah* and *Trusty* cruised right with us.

Chapter Two

The Redeemed Ships

About an hour later, we watched vid from one of our Starlights flying combat patrol ahead of our formation, and with that we could confirm the two frigates were indeed the ships they said they were — clearly two battered old *North America*-class frigates, first generation. *Old* is the operative word there, I have to say. These ships, had they not been out here at Io, would likely have been paid off years ago.

Instead, they'd been stuck out around Jupiter, playing hide and seek for eight months.

"Realtime range in two minutes," Felicia Khalid reported from Sensors and Communications, and I nodded.

By now, we were all reasonably awake — and I'll be honest, we weren't exactly thrilled about that fact. Though I imagine you gathered that from the last chapter. We weren't grumpy, really... just... hmm... tired.

I'm using that word a lot. If I wasn't so lazy I'd look up a different word for tired. Fatigued, perhaps. Weary. Somnolent. Ooh I like that last one. Have no idea how to pronounce it, but I suppose that's the joy of the *written* word.

"Decelerate to meet them. Jim, solution on *North Carolina*. Matt, target with us. Mark and Nancy, line up on *Kansas*," Karen was giving smooth orders despite her somnolentness.

Alright, now I'm pushing it, sorry.

Nods came back to us over the Battlelink as the targeting priorities were acknowledged: we had to be ready to shoot down these geriatric ships if it turned out Martians were commanding them, though I didn't get the feeling that Martians were involved in this little scene.

But my *feelings* weren't always reliable. Kate Levec would attest to that. Hence the aiming of the lasers.

"Have them marked," Jim Hannigan reported from behind us at the operations consoles, and we stood still, waiting again. Realtime range would give us the answers.

"Establishing," Felicia Khalid had now been in her job long enough to start predicting our needs, which was helpful.

We weren't really waiting with bated breath... more like with somewhat rude impatience. Screen nine flashed to a loading display, and the signal buffered slowly. I glanced at Karen, then at Andrea, and we all had that 'here we go' look on our faces.

Captain Kishko appeared, his face looking just as aged and exhausted as it had earlier, "Rear Admiral Barron, good day."

Kishko had, I found out shortly after this, joined the service *before I was born*. He was pushing sixty-five on that day, and had been in the service forty-seven of those years. He was a solid officer, but unremarkable, and worse, unconnected. He'd been doomed to Io in

2220, and he'd only been back to Earth twice in the twelve years between that posting and this day. He had the option to retire, but his life had been dominated for too long by the fleet. His only real family was the crew of *North Carolina*, and I have to say, it was to his calm and sturdy patriarchy that every man and woman aboard that frigate credited their survival.

That last statement, I suppose, betrays any cheap drama I could have built up: the ships were free and clear of Martian influence. They were loyal to the very last, and yet their stories are never made into movies.

I won't start ranting about that. Not yet, anyway.

"So, Captain, is there a Martian marine standing behind you with a gun to your back, making you talk?" I asked evenly, and the old Captain's eyebrows climbed.

"No sir, I am proud to say both our ships are free of Martian influence. We harried the Martians several times, though not as well as we might have hoped. We are in a critical situation for supplies."

He was trying to be awfully polite, but his main concern at that moment wasn't recounting his story to us, it was getting his crew off the one-fifth rations they'd been on for two weeks. Things were desperate.

Nancy Whitehorse, who obviously knew Kishko better than I did (they were squadron mates, after all), slid into the conversation now, "Captain, it's Commander Whitehorse. It's so very good to see you."

"Nancy," Kishko replied quite warmly, with the kind of affection a grandfather has for his granddaughter, "I am glad you have survived this."

The way he said it, I could tell the emotional follow-up was going to be too much — and I don't mean that in an insensitive way. Kishko deserved every chance to feel a warm homecoming, but even in my tired state, I'd caught the undercurrent of his desperation. It would serve no one to have him start to break down over the comms — he had every right to after all he'd been through, but he wouldn't have wanted it, and neither did we. I wanted relief teams aboard *Kansas* and *North Carolina* immediately, and then when we led the two frigates back into Io orbit, the reunion could begin.

"We'll send relief teams over immediately, Captain. For the moment, I need to cut the Battlelink with you," I interrupted quickly, perhaps too abruptly.

Kishko nodded slowly, "Of course. I look forward to shaking your hand, sir."

Again, the classic formality of the old days — the early days of his career.

With that he cut his own feed, and I looked up at the other screens, "Alright, send relief teams to the ship you were targeting. First shuttle is Special Branch only, just in case there *are* Martians aboard. And keep mags locked and Starlights on patrol. No chances."

The precautions ultimately proved unnecessary, but better safe than sorry.

We were back over Io an hour later, and twenty minutes after that Captain Kishko and Captain Lanakila Akuma were sitting in *Wolf's* briefing room across the table from Karen, Andrea and me, both of them looking decidedly unwell. Kishko had the gaunt face of a man who'd lost a great deal of weight for lack of food, and Akuma, who looked as though she'd already been fairly slight, was equally malnourished.

Both were clearly struggling to keep their composure.

"We're so glad that you've come," Akuma was the first to say it, and the way she said it, I knew it was going to be an awkward few minutes. She and Captain Kishko had been through many different kinds of hell, and we were going to be given their gratitude for bailing them out... when we hadn't even known if they were alive or dead to begin with.

I don't know about you, but I feel very awkward accepting thanks at the best of times. I absolutely hate accepting thanks at the worst of times, particularly when I've done nothing to earn them. The stadium on Egesta that first day... you know. So I was starting to get uncomfortable in my seat, and as I glanced at Karen, she was wearing an artificial expression that hid her equal discomfort.

Andrea, on the other hand, wasn't tongue-tied, "We're glad to find you both still alive out here. We were worried the rest of the Jupiter Squadron had been lost, but we didn't have enough ships left to go looking without risking Io if the Martians return."

We'd sent over our logs from the past few weeks so Kishko and Akuma could get up to speed on what had happened over Io, and so now they both nodded a little more hurriedly than they might have under better circumstances.

"You did what we could not do, Captain Kiley," Kishko, if you're wondering, was a real old-school, classy officer. He was much more formal than Karen and I ever were, and don't take that to be a criticism. He was a gray-haired gentleman-patriarch, and while he wasn't as casual as we usually liked to be, we certainly wouldn't hold that against him. His genuine good intentions were evident in his tone.

"Well, they had the drop on you, didn't they?" Andrea asked the rhetorical question, then followed up quickly. "We already dealt with Commander Mazur for running out on you. That you've kept your crews alive out there without a battleship's stores to feed yourselves is a heroic feat."

Andrea wasn't wrong about that, either. If you think back to *The Jupiter Patrol*, you may remember that I went off on Commander Mazur, who'd assumed command of the battleship *Dominator*, abandoning a solid chunk of her crew and running away from the Martians, even though she had the only ship capable of really hurting the attacking force. Well, these two skippers had been stuck without the supplies *Dominator* had aboard — and had shared with *Trusty* and *Pictou*.

Hence the malnourished appearance after eight months.

Eight whole months of *hiding*.

Anyway, at Andrea's use of the word 'heroic', both Captains looked down, shaking their heads. You know how it is, good skippers never take credit for a damn thing.

This conversation could definitely descend into a therapy session, though, if we didn't move forward to the more pressing matters, cold as that sounds. We needed more information before we could let it get that far.

"So, your two ships were the only ones to escape the attack?" I leaned forward and asked the question, perhaps too abruptly (again).

Kishko looked up and gave a quick nod, "Yes sir. No. No sir, my apologies. DCNS *Idaho* also escaped, and though we all escaped separately, we were able to rendezvous with each other within three weeks of the attack. We pooled our supplies, and determined that reinforcements from Earth would be needed were we to retake Io. Captain Turner of *Idaho* volunteered her ship to return to the inner planets. I take it her return is why you came?"

I stiffened slightly at that one — Kishko said 'her return' with a measure of relief. Obviously, *Idaho* had not arrived in the Empire: we'd come out here because of the dead silence from Io. If Kishko had been well fed and thinking clearly, he probably would have realized that the very fact we hadn't known who'd survived the initial attack was a sign that *Idaho* hadn't come in. Don't take that as a criticism — again, after eight months of strain, the man was entitled to forget whatever the hell he pleased.

It just made the next words tough… which is why Karen took them.

"No, Captain, I'm afraid Captain Turner didn't arrive," her soft, comforting words were still like daggers, and Kishko and Akuma's eyes both fell to the table again.

I don't know if I can adequately describe what they must have been feeling. They'd been lost, alone in the black for eight months, their single hope being that their friend and colleague would safely return to the Empire and get help. Help was now here, and that was a huge relief, but their friend was not.

Bitter business.

And they were not in condition to talk about it. That was clear enough.

"Alright, look, we'll do this later. We're getting supplies over to your ships now, and anyone needing medical treatment can go down to the Io hospital. Once your people are squared away, we'll debrief more. Take whatever time you need," I bailed us out of the meeting.

With slow, uncomfortable nods, both Akuma and Kishko rose from their chairs. They started to back away from the table, and then with the old school formality that never fails to impress, Kishko came sharply to attention, his heels clicking together and his hand coming the long way up to give a palm-out salute. A proper Defense Command salute. Akuma immediately followed the lead, her boots clicking together as well, her salute coming up.

Well, you don't answer that sign of respect sitting down. Karen, Andrea and I were on our feet in a flash, and our boots clicked together almost simultaneously as we brought up our own salutes, then lowered them again.

With parting nods, Captain Kishko and Captain Akuma left the briefing room.

Letting out a rather deep breath, I glanced at Karen and then Andrea, "I… I'm going back to bed."

"Couldn't agree more," Karen nodded.

We'd deal with this in the morning.

CHAPTER THREE

FRIENDS IN TOUGH PLACES

When I got up the next morning, I was obviously thinking about the two ships that had joined our force. We'd have engineers look them over and get them ready for the cruise home. They'd certainly help when it came to moving the population of Io back to the Empire — the more hulls we had for hauling people, the more space each of those people would have. Their crews would need to be assessed… I didn't like the thought of mixing up those complements of women and men after all they'd been through together, but if there had been breakdowns, we couldn't afford to leave broken people in key positions.

A lot to consider.

But I think I've talked enough about *Kansas* and *North Carolina* for the moment, because there are obviously two stories you might be wanting updates on. Conveniently, I can use the events of this very morning to provide them.

Karen was already awake, freshened up and dressed by the time I was pulling on my tunic over my ship fatigues. She smiled as she waited at my door, "What, didn't sleep well?"

I grumbled something, smiled and shrugged, "Had the strangest dream… and you were there…"

She smiled her winningest smile (which is pretty damned winning, as you know) and zipped up her tunic, "How inappropriate!"

I chuckled, zipping my own tunic and shaking my head, "Andrea was there too."

"Aha, how racy," Karen said with a twinkle, and I nearly groaned.

"Speaking of our Captain," I bobbed my head towards the hatch, and with a curt little nod, Karen opened it and gestured for me to step out.

"Why thank you," I walked through, looking both ways, and found the corridor empty. Karen came out behind me and shut the hatch.

"Speaking of our Captain…" she said in quieter tones, her smile fading.

I nodded at the words, and let go a sigh.

We were still worried about Andrea, but over the past two weeks, we'd done nothing about that worry. Part of our inaction was due to the fact that Andrea had been back aboard *Wolf* and had seemingly been improving… her state of mind appeared to be similar to what it'd been in *The Jupiter Patrol* — not too bad.

Part of our delay was simple anxiety over trying anything.

I know, I know. We should have been all over the problem. Once the dust settled after *The Sinope Affair*, we should have poured some old scotch and sat down with dear Andrea, and gotten her to open up and have a good cry, and then everything would be alright again.

Well, probably not exactly that. We should have done something, though. Instead, Karen and I both were afraid to rock the boat, to do the wrong thing. Andrea was improving. She wasn't having any sorts of strange outbursts in public, she wasn't losing her temper or her ability to communicate… so maybe she was getting better…

Yeah. Maybe.

Thing was, Karen and I were (obviously) still quite concerned. We just didn't know what more to do. We wanted to know where Andrea's head was, but that's not something you just ask someone. Well, that's not something Karen and I were too eager to just ask someone.

So we were waiting and watching, not actively trying to help. We should have been trying to help… but, well, we failed in that.

"We could ask," I tentatively answered Karen's unanswered question, and she nodded, her mouth thinning into a line.

"We could."

That was as far as we got, because down the corridor, Andrea's hatch opened and she stepped out, zipping up her own tunic. She looked our way with a smile that did not seem forced — and at this stage, Andrea tells me it wasn't — and waved.

"Good morning, how's that for another bad night's sleep?"

Smiling instantly the way you do when you don't want someone to realize you were just talking about them, I proceeded up the corridor, "Seems whenever we try to sleep, fate throws us something to interrupt it."

Not the snappiest reply, and had Charlie been there he'd have said so.

"Not the snappiest reply," Charlie Peters seemed to appear out of thin air behind Karen. Damned Special Branchers and their ability to appear out of thin air.

It's been a while, I think, since I've mentioned the tradition Charlie and I started back in our days on *Friendly*, to try to keep our verbal repartee top-notch. Snappy, clever, quick comebacks and such. Not easy, believe me!

Turning, I shook my head, "I know it was bad, because *I* didn't get a full night's sleep. Only five hours last night, with a two-hour interruption in the middle."

Charlie frowned, nodding somberly, "Well, that is terrible. I got three hours."

He then smiled, and I let out a groan, "Oh fine, I'm the only tired one, you all are fresh as daisies. Can we go now?"

Charlie came to a stop next to Karen, his eyes narrowing slightly. The two exchanged a glance, then shook their heads simultaneously, "He just doesn't have the repartee this morning."

I huffed a sigh and walked away. These jovial spirits weren't destined to hold.

Doctor Conrad Rhee was *Artemis Agrotera's* surgeon, and as you might remember from *The Sinope Affair*, he was running the Io hospital for us. Presently, he was looking after any sick and wounded from amongst the Io colonists we'd pulled off Sinope, any of the *Kansas* and *North Carolina* crews who needed attention, and, of course, the crew of *Lion*.

Remember *Lion*? Kris Jacobs' ship was irradiated in our first real scrap with the Martians. Kris herself pulled four people out of the outer reactor chamber while the ship's engineers and much of the medical staff sacrificed their lives in a frantic — and successful — bid to keep the ship from exploding. The reward for her life-saving efforts had been a radiation dose of over 2,000 REM, which put her on the bubble, so to speak.

I think by this time she was sliding off the good side of the bubble... which is a terrible attempt at extending that analogy. What I mean to say is that she was almost ready to start her recovery.

Yes, of course she'd recover. You probably know that already, because of how famous she has become. But it was very much touch-and-go at that point, and while Doctor Rhee had lately told us the chances of her dying now were slim, we were still on pins and needles about her.

She was, and is, one of the Belt Squadron family. I mean, sure, we were mostly called the Jupiter Force now, but we'd all come up together, fought at Deep Black together. We were really quite worried about her.

And, for anyone out there who thinks that somehow her virtually-guaranteed survival takes the drama out of the next two years of her life, think again. Sure, the question was no longer 'will she live'... it became, 'will her skin go back to its original color', 'will she be able to have children', 'will she get early-onset Alzheimer's', and so on. If radiation doesn't kill you, it sure as hell tries to tear you to pieces.

My grandfather, for instance, was exposed during his days as a combat engineer, and later in life it destroyed his mind. He didn't have the advantage of gene therapy back in his day, so there was no way to undo the damage that went unseen when he was exposed. That was a fate worse than death — and one that still ended in death. When a person loses all memory of who he is, and what he's done, it is the greatest tragedy. You die alone, even if you're surrounded by loved ones. You die wondering who you are, and why you're dying. It's a terrible, terrible fate.

But Kris, hopefully, would be much better off than my grandfather had been. Her annual physical had been done in January, just before *The Gallant Few*, and every physical exam ends with the taking of a DNA sample for your file. That sample can be used by gene therapists as a template to work back to, undoing the mutations radiation poisoning can cause. At Kris' dose level, she was looking at about two years of treatment, once we got her back to the Empire, but even that didn't guarantee a full recovery.

Sometimes gene therapy can't fix *everything*.

Incredible blotches on the skin (almost unbelievable — a lot of them are so colorful people don't believe they're real), sterility and destruction of the brain cells are possibly irreversible.

What I'm getting at here is that Kris had a very long, very brutal road ahead of her. And we all knew that.

Sorry, just realized I lost the narrative thread of the chapter in all that. But it just... well, I think we're often conditioned by movies and such to think that surviving an injury means everything's okay. We don't like to think about how bad our lives could get if we were injured or exposed in the way Kris had been. I understand not wanting to think about that... I really, *really* don't like thinking about such things, and you can probably appreciate the level of my reluctance.

But the fact is... and I think we all really do know this... a major injury is in some ways more torturous than death. The pain and strife goes on and on, and trying to heal takes long hours, hard work, and a steel core of determination.

It is, though, entirely worth it. It's harder than dying, but the payoff is (obviously) a hell of a lot better.

Kris was facing that situation now, and as Karen, Andrea, Charlie and I filed quietly into her room in the Io hospital, she was awake, staring at the ceiling, and thinking very much about what was to come.

I was going to describe our visit, recount what we said and how we stumbled our way through uncomfortable small talk for an hour as we kept her company, but... well, it was just an hour of awkward conversation. I'm sorry, as I think I've already said, I'm very, *very* bad when it comes to dealing with people in hospital. I never know what to say to offer comfort... I always end up thinking too much, sounding stilted and uncomfortable.

Charlie, I don't think he'll mind me saying, shares some of the same challenges, so in this case he and I ended up just standing there, letting Karen and Andrea find reassuring words, a task they seemed much better able to manage. Someone once asked me if Karen was better at that because she was a woman. I don't know, maybe? The neo-suffragists might club me with placards for suggesting that a woman is better at something because she's a woman... I don't know. What mattered right then was that Karen knew how to comfort Kris.

And so did Andrea.

That was a little weird, given the circumstances. Andrea's first visit to Kris' bedside was mentioned in *The Sinope Affair*, and you'll remember it was essentially wordless, and involved Andrea nearly losing her composure. Now she sat next to Kris' bed, and she and Karen were going back and forth, saying just the right things with a natural rhythm. It was impressive to watch — which, again, Charlie and I did, knowing when not to get in the way.

After an hour, we had to get back to our respective jobs, but Mark Gunney and Matt Baxter came down at alternate hours over the course of the day. We made sure Kris had a visitor every time she came out of her sedated sleep periods. It was the least we could do for one of the family.

On the second draft of this chapter, one of the editors asked a good question: was it really fair for us to be giving Kris all this attention, when there were so many other wounded people who we could have been visiting?

Well, yes, we were being cliquish, I suppose. The problem with having a family of officers as closely-knit as the Belt Squadron's is that people can be left on the outside — we end up playing favorites. I don't know what I can say to defend our focus on Kris herself...

I don't know if I have to defend it, come to think of it. I did feel pangs of guilt every time I walked through the hospital, and all sorts of people looked at me. Perhaps I should have tried to visit with all of them, to thank each of them personally for all their work.

But I didn't. The officers and crews of the Belt Squadron were my extended family. But... but Kris was immediate family, like a sister. And as much as all the crews of the ships that served under Karen's and my command mattered, we were so much closer to Kris.

Sorry, I really don't have any justification beyond that. If I were a better commander

— like Mik Mikaelsen or Wes Pellew, perhaps — I'd have been better able to spread my concern around to every man and woman in that hospital. As it is, I hope those people who were in that hospital and watched me walk past with little more than a nod of acknowledgment can forgive my distance.

CHAPTER FOUR

THE BUSINESS OF GETTING HOME

While wounded like Kris were being cared for, and while *Kansas* and *North Carolina* were being examined by engineers and their crews checked by medics, Karen and I went to the Io base headquarters building to meet with Captain Clive, the most senior remaining officer of the original Jupiter Squadron.

Actually, let me back up here: because getting from the hospital to the HQ building was a real experience. Remember how Charlie had essentially flattened just about everything in the Io dome when he was driving out the Commandos? Well, there were now tents in the streets, there were people living in the industrial buildings... the dome had the feel of a refugee camp.

And people were starting to get over their elation at having been saved from the Martians. There was plenty of food, the dome was nice and warm so they were comfortable, and so on... but having come home to see their houses and apartments wrecked wasn't easy on them. And some of them were getting a little vocal.

But — and this is the part I wasn't expecting — for every person who jeered us as we walked, two or three came to our defense. There were a lot of military and ex-military people at Io, and they knew very well that they'd have had no dome to come back to had Charlie not pulled out all the stops in removing the Commandos. Living on the street in a tent was a hell of a lot better than living in the corridor of an overcrowded frigate.

You might think that was good: the Io crowds were defending us more than they were jeering us. Well, slight problem was that jeers and counter-jeers often led to shoves and counter-shoves. Kyle Stranks, *Wolf's* Lieutenant commanding SF, was responsible for keeping order in the dome, and he was having a tough time. Two or three minor brawls had to be broken up, and then one really big brawl a few days prior to this had ended with one man trampled to death.

We needed to get out of Io. Soon.

If we were moving, with the people of the dome spread between all the ships of the squadron, including *Artemis Agrotera*, there'd be less chance of trouble breaking out on a grand scale.

Hence the meeting with Captain Clive.

We arrived at the Io HQ building after a brisk walk, then climbed the stairs to the front entrance, nodding to an SF as we passed him. The HQ building itself had become a temporary accommodation building for some of the Defense Command personnel we'd brought back from Sinope. Civilians were kept out in the street, but officers and ratings could sleep in the lounges, offices, and few actual living quarters in the building.

To those of you living on Earth, that might sound heinous — forcing the civilians to live out on the street, at the mercy of the elements. Remember, though, that we were in a dome. The elements were all firmly under our control, and it was very nice 'outside.'

We'd also put the infirm in the Defense Command barracks next to the HQ, so those most in need would in fact have the luxury of beds. We weren't heartless, you know!

Anyway, we passed many people in the busy HQ building as we entered the lobby, and we headed for the elevator and took it up to floor ten, the level Clive had taken over for his Jupiter Squadron offices. It was a complicated command situation... Clive was officially now Karen's opposite; she commanded the warships of the Jupiter Force, he commanded the warships of the old Jupiter Squadron, and I commanded both. We were still sorting all that out, though.

As we arrived on the tenth floor, we found some of the staff officers' kids playing in the corridor, and after exchanging some make-believe mag fire with them in the kind of imaginary gunfight kids excel at (they even got Karen!), we chuckled and headed into Clive's office.

I have to say, in my snobbery as a Belt Squadron and Jupiter Force officer, I'd first expected Clive to be inept and useless. I never had the chance to see him command a ship in action, but here on Io he was definitely impressing me with how he had taken hold of the new situation, and was organizing his people. I'd underestimated him, and I don't mind pointing out my own stupidity for that oversight. Johnston Clive was distinguishing himself.

Clive was going over a few pads with a couple of Lieutenants when we slipped in, but he looked up as we arrived and came quickly to his feet, "Admiral, Commodore, welcome!"

He came around his desk, "We're having a look at the stores reports from *Kansas* and *North Carolina*. They'll need a great deal of topping up for the cruise home, but I'm confident we'll have what we need."

I nodded slowly, "That's good to hear... actually, that's what we were coming to talk to you about. We want to start moving people out of here soon."

Clive nodded emphatically, "Yes, yes, I have to say that would make sense to me, too. We think there'll be some resistance by a handful of people who love it out here... but they can be stunned and carried off if worst comes to worst. And I think going home soon would make the most sense. We have to be where we can make a difference in the war!"

There was a certain honest enthusiasm in the way Clive said that — it came in the same sort of tone he'd used when he asked us about the *honor* of his ship (*Dominator*) back at the end of *The Sinope Affair*. Man definitely knew his duty, and held it to be quite important.

"That's it, definitely," Karen agreed with his words. "Last report I saw from the engineers said we'll be ready by the end of this week. What do you think about that?"

Clive looked up over Karen's left shoulder and literally grabbed his chin in thought, then nodded and looked back at his two Lieutenants, "Well, I think it will take hard work. But after all those months languishing on Sinope, I think a little hard work will go down nicely!"

The Lieutenants didn't look as enthusiastic as Clive did at those words, but they nodded in agreement.

"We'll have things ready!" Clive turned back with more emphatic nodding.

Well... good. You know the open-mouthed half-smile, half-look of astonishment that's somewhere between surprise and amusement? Maybe you don't... well, Karen and I both had that. Sorry I can't describe it better.

Clive took a couple of steps towards us, "So, I can begin work on personnel distribution by ship, if you don't mind."

My nod was much less emphatic, "That'd be ideal, Captain. You know your people better than we do, so if you could split them in such a way that we can avoid... you know... murders and things?"

It was a joke — yes, I know, a bad one — but Clive frowned seriously, "Of *course*, sir! I'll do my very best to avoid murders."

I nearly started laughing. Nearly. Again, let me restate here that by then I'd come to respect Clive, but you have to admit, his earnestness bordered on amusing at times. That or I'm just a sick sort of person, joking about murder. Or a little of both.

Karen knew my joke was terrible, so she didn't go anywhere near it, "We'll also need to work out the division of the squadron, your ship commands and mine."

Clive looked for a moment like he didn't understand what she was saying, and then he frowned in his animated way, "But Commodore, I assumed all Jupiter Squadron ships would be folded into your Jupiter Force. I thought I was to take command of my personnel in transit."

It didn't sound to us like he was afraid of commanding ships for the run home, though it may read that way. Karen's eyebrows went up and she glanced at me, just as my eyebrows went up and I looked at her. Must have appeared as though we practiced that, but we hadn't.

"Well... that'd work out well," I was the first to look back, and Clive nodded emphatically again.

"Very good to hear, sir!"

Karen and I kept talking for a few more minutes, but the details would mostly be sorted out over the course of the coming week of preparations. Getting all the people who'd lived on Io back home would take a lot of work — and stuffing all that work into a week wouldn't be easy... but Clive was right, there was a war on and we needed to get back to it.

In case you're wondering, we'd waited those two weeks because we'd been repairing damage. If you recall, *Lady Grace* was missing a drive pod, and *Lion* had of course been irradiated. Both ships had once been Karen's, which I suppose is weird... but anyway, it had taken two weeks for engineers to adequately patch up the stub of *Lady Grace's* drive wing to make it safe and secure for the long voyage home, and it'd take another week for engineers to finish venting radiation from *Lion*, and to secure the frigate for the tow home.

Theoretically, we *could* have left *Lion* out there... yeah right. I mean, it was possible to do so, but with the war on, we weren't going to leave behind a salvageable hull (or more precisely, we weren't going to blow it up, as we'd have had to do to make certain no Martians or pirates could find and salvage it).

So anyway, we'd be ready to go in a week. And Clive would have a week to figure out how to get all these people back to the Empire.

And speaking of 'back to the Empire'...

CHAPTER FIVE

THE OTHER END

The Independent Squadron was given a hero's welcome as it pulled into Hawke One space, and rightly so. As you no doubt have heard, Wes Pellew had gone out into the Barbary Cluster of asteroids (ironically named, you have to admit... if you know the obscure bit of history I just thought of...) to destroy the large pirate base that had been the jumping-off platform for a lot of the troublemaking during 2231.

Arriving with his squadron, less one frigate he'd lost on the mission, Wes found the press ready to pounce on him. It took a military escort from Commodore Christian 'Mik' Mikaelsen and the battleship *Cyclops* to get him safely in to dock at the Government Dome, and then it was another two hours of press in the docking lounge before he could get safely to Hawke Command and Control.

When he stepped into the huge C&C chamber — not unlike the one under Admiralty House on Capital Island — he had to stop and take a deep, calming breath, wiping his brow with the back of his sleeve.

"Oh, can I have your autograph, Commodore Pellew? Please?" an excited lady hurried up, waving a pad of paper and a pen (yes, pen and paper) at him, and he nearly backed into the door behind him in surprise.

He fumbled for words, "Uh... I... no... I mean sure... but why... I..."

She was nearly bouncing up and down, this lady. Lady, I mean. Poor Wes.

"Lia, behave, he's had a long few months!"

That was Mik, who had, over the past few months in co-command of the Hawke Force with Lia Hawke, become something of her keeper. He was much better at it than I was, so when she stopped hopping and turned around, planting her hands on her hips, her retort bounced off him.

"You're just jealous I'm not asking for yours!" she protested.

Mik was leaning over the vid plot table, not even looking her way, "Mmmhmm."

Wes, poor Wes. What a way to meet Lia. No, Wes really hadn't met Lia before this, which is quite incredible, when you think about it. Marshal Samuels knew her, and so did Mark Gunney, but until the war, Wes and Karen hadn't had the pleasure. Of course Lia had heard all about Wes, because he was a hero of the Empire, and my friend (even though I didn't know that he liked soup and didn't like heights).

So she decided to give him the sort of welcome she's really, really, impossibly good at.

Wes, of course, handled it with as much aplomb as anyone being accosted by Lia can, "Nice to meet you, finally, Lady Hawke. I've heard a lot about you."

He said that, I'll add, while still backed up against the door, and Lia extended her free hand, "Well, that's more boring, but probably more appropriate. I'm very pleased to meet you, too."

Someone tried to open the door Wes was flattened against from the other side, so he had to step forward as he took her hand, "Well. That went well."

Lia frowned, "Could it have gone badly?"

Wes shrugged, "Everything can go badly."

"Especially with Lia involved," Mik had left the plot table and was walking over. Lia backhand-slapped him on the shoulder.

"Hey!"

Mik chuckled and extended his hand, "Nice work out there, Wes."

Wes and Mik didn't know each other *that* well at this point, but they'd crossed paths a few times over the years before the war, and knew each other's quality by this time. Of course, this was just the start of the long spell when they... hell, soon enough, when *all of us* would be working together a good deal more.

Taking Mik's hand, Wes nodded, "Good to see you again."

"And you. Just in time, too. I just got a package from Admiralty House, and we have work."

"Ooh, work," Wes nodded, and then with a flourishy (is that a word?) game-show 'come this way' gesture from Lia, they all proceeded to the plot table.

Lia, of course, was suddenly all-business again. The way she does that transition from insanity to sanity is commendable — at this point it was actually helping her deal with the situation with her father. Neither Mik nor Wes knew about that predicament... No one knew what was going on, and that was in no small part thanks to Lia's ability to turn on the madness. I'm going to stay coy about the situation with her father for now — there'll be much more on it in the next book.

"John sent us the predicted course for the Martian ship carrying the experimental kit from Io," Lia was the one to start the explanation, and I realize now that I need to do some exposition so this will make sense to you.

Remember, the Martians had stripped all the experimental toys and weapons out of Io's labs by the time we arrived, and sent them back to Mars? That was the ship Lia was talking about. I'd sent as much information as I had about that shipment to John Fiora at Admiralty House — when it left Io being the key fact. From that, John had ordered Admiralty House's thinkers and computers to try to figure out where we could intercept the Martian ship.

Because Io is so far out from the inner planets, we could assume the Martian ship would make a straight-line run for Mars — not try to weave around to cover its tracks. It's generally a bad idea to start bending and weaving out in the black of the solar system. If anything happens to your navigation calculations, you could get yourself lost rather easily — even with the sun to use as a reference point for navigation. So the Martians would be going home on a straight-line course.

Taking that fact, the Admiralty thinkers added two others: the relative positions of Io and Mars. Put all those together with the approximate time of the Martian ship's departure, and you could extrapolate the course it was probably taking to Mars. *And* you could figure out where it would approach the asteroid belt.

In other words, they had a good idea where the Martian ship carrying all our experimental technology could be intercepted by Defense Command warships. So as

Lia pointed to the plot table, Wes looked down and noted a stretch of the Belt that was bracketed in red — a stretch that wasn't far out beyond Furnace Rock, one of those independent asteroids aligned with the Empire (you might remember it from *The Hawke Mission*).

"They're going to have to come through here... or *over* here," Lia said evenly. "Based on the amount of trouble those Martians gave Ken, I'm guessing they're not going to be so stupid as to try to run right through the Belt. They know we run regular patrols... it'd be risky."

Mik and Wes nodded at Lia's very sound assumption. As much as she can seem insane, Lia's also brilliant at her job.

"Was thinking much the same..." Mik nodded in agreement.

"Sure you were," Lia interrupted with a smile, and he grinned before finishing his sentence.

"... so best plan might be to try to get to them before they hit the Belt."

Wes and Lia both nodded, though Wes was still not fully up to speed on what was being said. He understood that the ship coming in needed to be stopped, but no one had told him *who* John had assigned to do that stopping. Was it to be the Independent Squadron, or the Hawke Force, or both?

"How many ships do we have to work with?" he asked simply, and Mik looked up.

"Oh, sorry, this is top priority for both our forces, so if you count all the Hawke Force and your squadron, I think it's... twenty-seven?"

"Twenty-eight," Lia corrected with a smile.

"Mmmhmm," Mik agreed. "What do you think, Wes?"

The question was a little more loaded than it sounds, because Wes had been cruising through some of the bracketed area in his hunt for the pirate base. He had more current insights on it than did Mik or Lia.

"Hmm," he leaned over the plot table now and pointed at the black just beyond the last of the Belt asteroids in this area, "You're right, Mik... they won't expect us to leave the Belt. They'll think their troubles are going to begin when they arrive inside the Belt perimeter, so as Lady Hawke said, they might take time and go *over*. But they'll have to stop out in the black to get their bearings before trying that. So we can catch them out there, if we're lucky."

"Call me Lia."

Wes hadn't realized that Lia was leaning close to his shoulder until she whispered it, and he nearly jumped, "Um. Will Charlie kill me?"

Lia shook her head sadly, "He doesn't seem to kill *anyone* for me."

Wes chuckled, "Unless they deserve it."

Mik wasn't put off stride by the banter, "So you're thinking we take a force out there and scout for them in the black, Wes? And then have a second layer of interceptors in the Belt, in case they slip through?"

Wes nodded, "Exactly. Two lines. If we catch them on the first line, great. If we get them on the second, just as good. How long do we have?"

Lia smiled again, "Well, we don't know how fast they were coming, so as much as *two months*. Aren't you excited to be here for that long?"

Eyes widening slightly, Wes nodded in a very slow and diplomatic manner, "Can't wait."

Mik started to laugh, and Wes wiped his brow with his sleeve again.

Alright, a pretty good question from the editors here: what about the 'but space is so big it's easy to miss someone when you're looking for them' argument that I seem to like so much? Well, shockingly, space was still big. There were no guarantees that Wes, Mik and Lia would ever see this Martian ship, but their plan gave them the best odds of running into it.

See, space is big, but the hazards of navigation do still lead ships to follow direct routes. They were banking on the Martians being more inclined to make it back to their Imperium quickly and with few navigation risks, and were thus deploying in a way that gave them the best chances of successfully intercepting the shipment.

It was by no means a sure thing, but it was better than no interception net at all.

CHAPTER SIX

AN UPDATE FROM AROUND THE EMPIRE

While I'm away from Io, I might as well fill you in on the goings-on around the Empire, now that we were into the summer (Imperial Standard Calendar) of 2232. I forgot to do any such updates in *The Sinope Affair*... sorry. Now we'll just do a quick survey before we get back to Jupiter space.

So, Earth first.

John and Daragh had things pretty well in hand at Earth by now. Obviously a number of months had gone by since Glorious February, and while the afterglow of the big win had faded, headlines were being made as new ships were being launched on a regular basis. The first new ships being commissioned were the *Australia*-class corvettes, the new twins to the old *Canada*-class. A few of those were in service by this time, but whenever a new one was delivered and commissioned, it was a big media event, as it was another sign of the great power of the Empire.

Some of the *Asia*-class frigates were about to come online, and the first of these ships was going to one of two places: either to Greg's command at Belt Two, or to Shauna Cass at the Forge (that Vulcanoid asteroid base I'm sure I've mentioned — Daragh's old stomping ground). Marlene was slotted to get a number of the new ships, but the Forge was a slightly higher defense priority, because where its orbit lay between Mercury and Venus, the plan was to turn it into our staging base for the assault on Mercury that was due in 2233. John and Daragh were thus building up the squadron at the Forge as much as they could afford to.

Marshal Samuels' squadron at the Belt was quickly increasing in strength. Remember, Marshal commanded the Belt Squadron, but that formation was a bit of a mess. Admiral Greg Noyce, commanding the whole Belt Sector, had ships at Belt Two that were not in fact attached to Marshal's squadron... namely his two battleships, *Warspite* and *Goliath*. Marshal was getting additional frigates and corvettes, though — mostly veterans detached from work in the Independent Belt on the Coalition side, and a couple from Mik's Hawke side.

With those ships, Marshal was finally able to get a handle on the convoy system he wanted. All told, he had about twenty ships of various ages and classes ready to escort the convoys that moved across the Belt, and others that headed to Earth and even Venus. Now, let's be honest, he really needed about sixty ships to run the system as he'd have liked — with enough ships to rotate them on and off convoy routes for servicing — but this was still much, much better than nothing.

The number of individual pirates who were robbed of their pillaging fun by Marshal's carefully deployed escorts runs into the dozens — and that number just encompasses the months when we were at Jupiter. Our commerce was safe, and by extension, our Empire's prosperity was safe.

Greg, in the meantime, was holding his battleships at Belt Two for two reasons: first, they were the only constant guardians the Belt colonies had, with Marshal's frigates and corvettes always moving to and fro. Second, they were to become the nucleus of his new assault squadron, about which you'll obviously hear more later.

Anyway, Greg's constant presence at Belt Two was what was allowing John to assign Wes' squadron to Hawke One, to keep an eye out for the Martian ship hauling our experimental equipment, though the Independent Squadron was also John's reserve force — if something went seriously wrong somewhere important, they could be pulled out of Hawke space and redeployed in short order.

Hmm. This chapter so far is just a bunch of impersonal paragraphs. For some reason I feel like I'm cheating… like I should visit a scene from one place or another. But where? Or who? I mean, this was a pretty run-of-the-mill time back in the Empire. I'm not kidding — you crack your average history book and it'll give you maybe a page or two on post-February 2232, unless it mentions Wes and the Barbary Cluster, or the Jupiter Force.

We had very low casualties for the rest of this year, and while the Martians evidently spent most of their time and resources consolidating defensive positions and preparing their famous Operation Sunbeam (I won't start complaining about the name until it happens), we spent the time holding our positions, setting up the convoy network, and launching new ships.

So how about this… if my editors demand a little dialogue scene in here to cap off this rather impersonal summary, I'll put one in. If they don't… well… then you're about to start a new chapter. How's that sound?

CHAPTER SEVEN

LOADING UP

I'm now going to skip ahead five days (from our last meeting with Captain Clive) to start on the embarkation (ooh, big word) process. It was a headache, and I suppose by many standards it was pretty boring, so I'm not going to get too deep into it… not *too* deep.

It was a strange feeling, though, I have to say: you start bringing civilians aboard your warship in large numbers, and you start feeling like you have to play host to them — try to be kind and whatnot. It shouldn't really cramp anyone's style, but it is a bit disconcerting.

Sorry, I'm not sure if that'll make sense to you. You know how it was an aggravation for us to take on Jocko and Jessica during *The Jupiter Patrol?* Well, these civilians didn't have camera crews with them, but they were nonetheless outsiders, and we had to look after them on *our* ship.

We had 2,000 civilians to move, in addition to the Martian prisoners we'd taken. There were also the scientists who we'd already settled on *Artemis Agrotera*, along with the survivors of *Lion* (who obviously couldn't return home on their own ship) and those who'd escaped the loss of *Dominator*. To carry all those people home, we had the following ships: the frigates *Wolf, Cheetah, Kansas* and *North Carolina*, the corvettes *Friendly, Lady Grace* (even though it was shot up) and *Trusty*, and *Artemis Agrotera*. So, doing the math (yes, with a calculator for me) that meant 250 civilians per ship… or, as we decided, 100 per corvette, 200 per frigate and 900 on *Artemis Agrotera*, because the storeship had that much more room.

Any way you slice that, though, it's a lot of civilians. A corvette crew was only about 200 people to begin with, a *Predator*-class frigate around 400. As you can see, we were adding many, many civilians to the mix.

Then throw in the extra Defense Command personnel, scattered across the ships of the squadron, and add the prisoners taken from Martian escape pods and from the Io dome during *The Sinope Affair*. There were a lot of bodies to move.

Technically, our ships could handle this many passengers. It said so right on the spec sheets. Every ship in the fleet is designed with an 'additional personnel transport capacity' built in, but often that capacity is sort of like the back seats in a sexy convertible hovercar: they allow the builder to say "sure you can carry four people!", but you'd have to chop the legs off most people to get them to fit.

Predator-class ships were supposed to be able to move as many as 600 people over and above their crew complements for extended trips, so our life support and water reclamation systems were not going to have any problems coping with 200…

But where were they going to sleep?

That, in fact, was the question being put to me in that instant, as Karen, Charlie and I stood at the bottom end of the lock that connected *Wolf* to the Io dome, and the waiting room before us started filling with civilians.

"So, where are they all going to sleep?" Charlie sounded somewhat skeptical, and rightly so.

I rubbed the back of my neck and donned one of those expressions that people get when they really aren't as certain as they should be, "Jim was sorting that out."

As XO and the head of *Wolf's* operations department, sorting out the civilian presence aboard ship was Jim Hannigan's job, and I didn't envy him.

"I think they're converting two of the cargo bays. Means we'll probably have to stop halfway back to bring on new supplies from *Artemis*," Karen added softly, obviously having paid much more attention to this problem than I had.

Charlie took a deep breath and nodded, "Well… remind me to stay out of the cargo section. I think they recognize me now."

I chuckled, "Hey, that bastard knocked down my apartment building!"

He shrugged in reply, "Yeah."

We watched for a few more minutes as the room filled, and then the reason Charlie was waiting with us arrived — twenty prisoners who were being thrown into *Wolf's* brig. Charlie noted their entry into the far side of the lounge, under the escort of a few of Rufus Chang's Special Branchers, and waved three of his own people forward to collect them.

"Our honored guests have arrived," he said sideways to Karen and me before following his people.

The civilians collecting in the waiting area hurled jeers at the Martians as they were led to the lock in single file, their chins dipped downward and their hands bound in front of them. Karen and I silently watched them pass — these were spacers off *Bosporus Planum*, one of the destroyer escorts *Honesty* had fought, and we'd hopefully get intelligence from them during the cruise home.

After the Martians disappeared, the crowd finished filing into the waiting area, and Karen and I stood rather quietly, staring at them. We weren't actually running this embarkation, I should say — other people would tell them where to go and how to get there. We were just here to be nice and welcoming to the people who'd be sleeping on air mattresses in our cargo bays for the trip home.

And, I have to admit, because we knew Jocko and Jessica were going to be recording this scene, and we figured it was a good idea to be in it.

I don't think I did any justice to Jocko and Jessica in *The Sinope Affair*. To be honest, I didn't notice Jessica's presence on *Wolf* much during our battles, probably because I was so very preoccupied with the fighting. Charlie tells me the same about Jocko — though Jocko had also been confined to the safety of the Headquarters building, out of the line of fire the whole time. Either way, they were out of mind for most of the last book.

It goes without saying, though, that while I might not have mentioned them much, they were still with us… hmm, I said that even though I said it went without saying. Sorry. I probably don't even need to tell you how this ended… but I will later, all the same.

Just now, as we stood and stared at the refugees, and as they stood and stared back at Karen and me (and the twenty other DC personnel in the lounge, preparing to help them embark) Jessica and Jocko were roaming quickly with their crews, taking statements and shooting B roll.

All of the interviews they did then — or at least, all the ones I saw — were quite positive. People were happy to be heading home, though some of them promised to come back out here to their beloved Io. Those were the crazy people. No offense if you're one of them, but you're crazy. Please don't challenge me to a duel, just accept that I'm right and get counseling.

The interviewees, it seemed, were also pleased to be heading home aboard *Wolf*, with the *celebrity officers* in charge. Yeah. Yeah, that was just weird. But it was said.

Anyway, I add all this stuff to my wobbly narrative because I hope it illustrates that the people we had coming aboard, while civilians, weren't troublemakers. Captain Clive's efforts to strategically group the passengers for the trip had been very well executed: the people who came aboard *Wolf* were all like minded, and thus not inclined to get into scraps with each other. This particular group was actually made up of civilians in the service industries on Io — the people who ran the coffee shops and fast-food joints, who stocked shelves and sold clothes. Good, regular people — not high-ego business types who expected the sun to revolve around them.

Those business types all ended up together on *Cheetah*, where Mark Gunney knew how to deal with them. His family is big in Imperial business, he speaks their language... I probably would have shot some of them if they'd been bothering me on *Wolf*.

We got the workers — 200 people who were used to getting up in the morning, going to jobs that were thankless, making modest money, and paying their bills. Regular people, if that doesn't sound bad, cliché or condescending. It's not meant to. I like regular people. I don't know if I've ever really explained that in these books.

So as they all stared at Karen and me, I raised my right hand and waved at them, "Uh... hi."

Big talk, I think you'll agree.

"Hi there," Karen waved her left hand, and sounded much less foolish as she offered her greeting.

We were off to a great start, as you can see. After more stellar dialogue, we started funneling people into the ship.

And there were no complaints. I don't understand why there weren't — we were cramming these people into big, cold, empty warehouses (for all intents and purposes) and yet they weren't asking us why we weren't giving up our bunks for them (don't even get me started on why that would be a bad idea) or giving them more privacy. They just put up with it, realizing that there wasn't much more we could offer.

I was pleased (and even a little surprised, despite the tirade I just went off on) by that tolerance, and I quickly came to respect all of them for it. I figure — and I could be quite wrong about this, but here goes — that it was because they'd lived so long on Io... they were used to not having everything just the way they wanted it.

They were good people — regular people. They had dignity, self-respect, and the same understanding that good Naval personnel have: that sometimes things don't go the way you want, but you make do.

It was a real pleasure to welcome them aboard *Wolf*.

And I think I've talked enough about the embarkation for now. I need to get us away from Io. Time for a new chapter.

CHAPTER EIGHT

THE FIRST STEP

"All ships are now clear of the Io dome," Felicia Khalid made that report from behind her Sensors and Communications consoles, and standing in the middle of the bridge, Karen, Andrea and I all nodded simultaneously.

The skippers of every ship we had with us were up on Battlelink, and over the preceding minutes they'd all reported when their ships had cleared the local orbital space over Io. Felicia's words thus wrapped up the departure process.

We were pulling out. It had been a day since we'd brought the civilians aboard *Wolf*, and with all the supplies we needed for the cruise back to the Empire safely in our holds (mostly in *Artemis Agrotera's* hold, actually) we were ready to leave.

"Jupiter Force prepare for cruise," I said the words rather blandly — I was tired, I have to say. As much as I probably should have dressed this up for the cameras that were on the bridge, I just wanted to get moving.

The sooner we left Io, the sooner we'd be home, and the sooner the civilians would be off our ships. The sooner people like Kate Levec would get their treatment, and the sooner Kris Jacobs could begin her gene therapy.

Oh, that's actually an important aside I need to explore (sorry about the break in flow): Kris and all the worst cases from *Lion* were aboard *Artemis Agrotera*, being monitored by Doctor Rhee. His ship's medical facilities had been augmented by all the kit he could steal from the Io hospital — if it wasn't bolted down (or if the bolts holding it could be cut), he had it aboard, just in case he ended up needing it.

Gee, that almost sounds like foreshadowing.

Anyway, that's where Kris was, along with Kate Levec (Kate was starting zero-gee physiotherapy on the cruise back, to speed her recovery once she got home).

Now, back to us leaving.

Karen began to order the warships in our squadron into cruising formation: *Wolf* would lead with *Kansas*, then *Friendly*, *Lady Grace*, and *Trusty* would cruise in the middle, with *Cheetah* and *North Carolina* bringing up the rear.

"Zail, slot yourself in behind *Lady Grace*," I gave my one requisite order in all this, and Captain Patel of the combat storeship nodded on Battlelink.

It was all rather complicated, now that I think on it. I'm not sure why we were keeping up the artificial divide between our jobs… Karen and me, I mean. She was officially the commander of only the warships in the squadron, while I was commander of the whole force… I think I explained this in *The Jupiter Patrol*. It was really needless duplication of orders, but for some reason we kept it up.

Ah well, as regrets about Karen and me go in this book, duplicating orders comes in pretty damned low.

"Andrea," I turned to our dear Captain Kiley as soon as I finished my orders to Zail

Patel, "would you do the honors?"

I'm not sure what she was about to do qualified as 'honors', but she nodded without batting an eye at my poor word choice.

"Jim, give me a solution on the Io dome, please. Stand by laser four."

Of course, we were going to destroy Io. The base was fully evacuated and stripped of its equipment. Any personal effects that survived Charlie's run-and-gun fest had been rescued. Now all that remained of the dome was an empty shell, and we were about to crack it. We'd have used a torpedo, but if you remember back to *The Sinope Affair*, we'd exhausted our supply.

"If any Commandos were hanging tough in the underground complex, they're going to be holding their breath for a while," Mark Gunney commented on one of the screens, and I nodded.

The dome above their heads was about to be blown wide open.

"We have a clean solution," Jim Hannigan announced behind us, and Andrea nodded.

"Shoot."

There was no ceremony. I suppose, had we been more energetic, we might have passed a quiet, somber moment in memory of the great history of Io, but we just didn't have it in us. I don't know if I can effectively explain why that was. We just wanted to leave, and we were finally getting our chance.

Laser number four was the one on the stern of *Wolf*, and now it erupted and lanced angrily out at Io. Domes, no matter who builds them and how tough they claim to be, cannot handle a sustained blast from a laser of that strength. It took half a minute of direct fire, but at last the shell cracked, and all the air trapped in the dome was set free, to dissipate in the black void.

Had this been a Belt dome that we were destroying, we'd probably have had to get in there with mags to render anything of use truly unsalvageable, but that was because the equipment needed to rebuild a dome was reasonably easy to find in the Belt. It had cost Defense Command over $430 trillion (adjusted) to get that dome built in the first place. Didn't seem likely anyone would be investing that much to come out to Io again.

"Alright, that's done. Let's get out of here," I looked up at the skippers on Battlelink. "Long cruise ahead."

Sober nods came from each of the people on the screens — this would be a much longer flight back due to our injured ships. *Lady Grace*, with only three pods, could manage just 141 kps, and *Artemis Agrotera* was towing *Lion*, and thus could do no better. We were looking at a little more than three months of cruising to get home.

But, as we'd seen in *The Jupiter Patrol*, we could at least expect the cruise to be uneventful. We'd have time to relax, treat our wounded, and to interrogate some prisoners. I suppose it'd be rather obvious and cliché to say we had no idea what was coming — it's pretty rare that we ever know exactly what's coming.

Anyway, this seems to be a pretty short chapter. I'm going to move ahead, now that we've gotten off Io, to start talking about the trip back.

CHAPTER NINE
PRISONER OF WAR

In the first week of the cruise back towards the Empire, Karen and I had something to keep us occupied. Those prisoners aboard *Wolf* had useful information, of that we were sure, so it was time for our patented, brutal interrogation techniques.

"I have the fiery mutilator of doom and excruciating pain next door, and I'm not afraid to use it," I offered my most terrifying ultimatum to Lieutenant (the Martians pronounce it *Lieu*-tenant instead of *Left*-tenant, by the way) Jason Rodney Fitzmonthenry.

Fitzmonthenry... damn that's a long name — typical Martians. Since independence, many of the families of their lower classes (the ones who end up as junior officers and spacers, though not High Admirals like Garvey) have apparently been merging old Earth names to give them a unique Martian sound... they thus end up with long ones like Fitzmonthenry. Anyway, he just stared at me.

"Look, Mister... Fitz..." ha, I shortened it on him! Take that!"...we have a long flight back to the Empire. That gives you lots of time to think. Once DCI gets their hands on you, I can't promise you'll be given such an easy time."

Fitz crossed his arms and shook his head, his mouth a narrow line, "Under the Ceres Accord, no torture can be carried out against a uniformed member of a recognized military force in wartime."

Karen, I should say, was standing next to my chair with her arms folded. We were, of course, in *Wolf's* interrogation room, which I don't think I've mentioned since *The Rogue Commodore*. Fitz was sitting at the far end of the table in his overbearing and impractical-seeming Martian uniform, and he was sticking to his guns.

That determination to be loyal to his flag should have earned him my respect. Unfortunately, something about the man also irritated me, so the respect wasn't exactly bubbling out of me.

"Under the Ceres Accord, Mars had no right to use pirates as combatants in a war," Karen said smoothly, tilting her head from one side to the other and drawing Fitz's attention.

Every time the young Martian officer looked at Karen, his face seemed to sour slightly. He hadn't said anything, but she and I had both noticed his reaction. We were pretty sure we knew what was causing it — the subtle clue being that, of all the Martian prisoners we took, none of them were women — but he hadn't been overt about it. Yet.

"Well then you can be *petty*, and use command decisions I wasn't a part of as an excuse to mutilate me," Fitz's reply was stern.

At those words I frowned, "Wait, you think the fiery mutilator thing is real?"

I probably shouldn't have blurted it out, but it didn't matter, the Lieutenant shifted himself in his seat and puffed up his chest more, "I know what you Empire types are like. We hear all about it. Those black-clad Special Branchers of yours, your secret police, they take people in the night, silence them if they speak out against your Empire. And you torture and terrorize. It's how you work."

He said that with a lot of conviction, and not a lot of good grammar. I let out a sigh and my chin slumped. One thing about being an Empire: it's really hard to get a good reputation among those outside your borders. Historically — and we don't always realize this today — the word 'Empire' has been used as an insult by people who want to paint all Empires by the actions of a few. Or by people who just think we should keep our noses out of other people's business.

But then who would we get to beat up and steal money from?

That was a JOKE, you 'small-Empire' people. A JOKE.

Anyway, Mister Fitz was showing off some of the Martian propaganda against us, and of course we know it's laughable. But there are always people, Martians and Imperial citizens alike, who buy it. Well, they're wrong.

Karen, by this time, was losing patience with our sport — and who could blame her? I should have mentioned this earlier, but we'd been working on Mister Fitz for over an hour. That in itself is probably an indication of how much time we had to kill on the cruise home.

But after all our work, he was still giving us the runaround.

"Look, who was your Admiral? Who was I tangling with?" I leaned forward and planted my elbows on the table, looking across it at Fitz again. The Lieutenant shook his head once more, and I groaned, "He's *dead*, he's not going to care."

"I have my honor," Fitz replied curtly.

Again, I should have respected that stalwart adherence to one's duty.

Karen let out a long sigh, then rubbed her forehead and murmured, "Honor…"

She repeated the word in the way you repeat someone's completely unbelievable answer to a question — you know, the kid burns down his house and you repeat his excuse, "It was my birthday."

That may not make sense, but Fitz heard the single, uttered word, and that got his blood boiling a bit. Touchy fellow, this Fitzmonthenry. Might be because of the name…

"Yes *honor*, not that I'd expect *you* to know what honor is, concubine!"

If there's one stereotype I'm oh-so-happy to highlight in these books, it's that many bad guys (note there, 'guys') are idiots when it comes to women. We in the Empire are now more or less spoiled by the equalities that were won decades and centuries ago. It was written into the Articles of Empire that all races and genders of humanity would be treated as equal persons, and of course, as we spread the Empire, that policy went with us. There was the recursion for a few decades during Lord Hawke's time, when women were 'put back in their place', but that obviously didn't last. By and large, we had the equality thing pegged (despite what the neo-suffragists might scream at you).

But the Martians were different. Some anthropologists and sociologists suggest their treatment of women is rooted in the times when the colony of Mars was founded (when men were traveling space far more frequently than women), and that seems possible to me. Their society could have developed from core notions that suggest women didn't leave their planet, or some other dumb thing.

Or, perhaps, there might have been a lower percentage of women in their population when they separated, and it could have been decided that they all had to stay at home, so the reproduction of Mars' population could be assured. How very Pion of them.

Anyway, I digress (what a surprise). Fitz's little snarl there had caused Karen to raise an eyebrow, in her charming way that says so much, and to move down the table.

I just sat back. This would be good.

Karen swung her hips a little as she walked, and then with her usual, incomparable grace she sat on the table, contorting her body to make it look like she was showing off. Well, she was showing off, but it was for effect. Not that I, being a shallow person, minded watching.

She then leaned down close to Mister Fitz, bringing her nose level with his, and speaking in a soft, intense voice — basically trying to do her best impersonation of a seductress (a weird motif for her, really), "Mister Fitz, I know you didn't mean anything by that."

Fitz — and this is brilliant — swallowed in a gulp. Keep in mind, the single-gender military meant the men of the Martian Navy didn't see women much at all. For those who are attracted to women (as Fitz clearly was), that made any close encounter... uh... you know what I'm getting at. They didn't see women much, but they wished they could see them more. They should have joined Defense Command — over half *Wolf*'s crew was female, and as I think has been mentioned, there were no regs against fraternization aboard ship.

But that sort of regulation just gets us branded as 'decadent hedonists' by the Martians. They think crews on eight-week hauls through the black should be monks. Yeah, tell that to the mag crews, the engineering teams or the flightdeck personnel. Not in this century, thanks.

Back to Karen, who had just thrown her hips around and was now talking all husky-like.

As she got her nose down close to Fitz's, he actually held his breath. Can't really blame him — you know Karen has the breathtaking skills — but it was amusing to watch the little bastard squirm.

"You know how I know you didn't mean anything by that?" Karen followed her first words with that line.

Fitz, now slightly overwhelmed, shook his head hurriedly.

Karen reached slowly up to her neck, her fingers stopping briefly on the zipper on her ship fatigues. Fitz swallowed again, probably hoping that zipper was going to come down a little bit, so he could see more.

But Karen's fingers kept going past the zipper, and then they gripped the side of her collar and pulled it sideways.

"Because," her tone instantly became sharp, "those are *Commodore's* bars I'm wearing, Mister. And you wouldn't be fool enough, or *dishonorable* enough, to refer to a *Commodore* in any service as a concubine, *would you?*"

Fitz's eyes widened slightly, and he didn't reply. He was quite confused now — she was beautiful, but she was an officer... he was supposed to respect officers, whatever service they were in...

I could almost see the smoke pouring out of his ears.

"Now," Karen let go of her own collar and reached out, her hand closing gently around his throat. "Who was your commanding officer?"

He started to shake his head again, but her fingers tightened around his neck very slightly.

"You can't torture me," he rasped as the grip started to interfere with his air flow.

Karen smiled and glanced back at me, then leaned down close to him again, "You going to try to convince your buddies in the brig that you were intimidated and tortured by a *concubine*, mister?"

See, as calm as Karen appeared, you could sorta tell she didn't like that kind of disrespect.

About five minutes later, and without any bruises at all, Lieutenant Fitz had started talking. He revealed what Captain Clive had already told us — that the Martian Admiral we'd faced off against was named Benjamin Conflans — and had gone on to explain that Conflans was one of the best officers in the Martian Navy. I couldn't disagree with that quality assessment. He'd made us pay to get Io back, and at the same time he'd taken good care of our people on Sinope.

Then he'd been killed when Andrea rammed his flagship, the battleship *Utopia Planitia*, with *Dominator*. A shame — I'd probably have enjoyed meeting him more than I did meeting Fitz.

Quick sidebar here: my editors were most panicked to discover that we've referred to the Ceres treaty as both the *Accord* (singular) and the *Accords* (plural). Which is right? We must be consistent!

Well, I commed around to some contacts in the Foreign Office, and in the Admiralty, and in the media, and depending on who I asked, I a got different answer. Some were sure it was the Accord, others that it was the Accords. Determined to get to the bottom of the question, I went to the actual signed treaty.

The title at the top is: "The Ceres Accord."

Okay.

Then the first line says: "These Ceres Accords represent a new era in solar relations..."

Oh. Kay. So... I guess both are right?

I blame the diplomats.

Anyway, I'm just going to keep using whichever one I remember people having said, or which one sounds better in the context. Please don't lose any sleep over it... as some of my editors may have...

CHAPTER TEN

IN FRONT OF THE CAMERA

In *The Jupiter Patrol*, interviews were something to be prepared for and feared, or at least to be anxious about. But now, having been through the whole Sinope affair with Jocko Kent and Jessica Qing, I have to say our perspectives had changed.

A couple of days after Karen and I had been conversing with Mister Fitz, Jessica and Jocko started conducting interviews for their next reports, and there was no awkwardness at all. After the big production we'd made about having to deal with them on the way out here, now we were comfortable having them around, and answering their questions.

That being the case, I was pretty relaxed as I walked into the conference room they'd taken over. They were interviewing everyone separately… hm, I don't think I said that right. Basically, how this worked was like this…

Oh great, I'm just mangling every sentence now.

How this worked was simple: each of us was booked for an hour for an interview. We'd go to the conference room at the appointed time, where Jocko would interview us for half the time, and Jessica would interview us for the other half. While the one correspondent was doing an interview, the other would wait in an adjacent cabin. Simple.

When I sauntered into the conference room that day, it was Jocko's turn to be up first.

"Won the coin toss, Jocko… or lost it?" I smiled at the reporter as I sat down and Bunny clipped on a wire microphone.

"Won it, of course," Jocko grinned with his brusque reply.

We were referring to the order of interviews, not sure if I made that clear — I was joking that to have to interview me first, he would have had to have lost the toss, because no one would want to interview me.

My editor assures me that by trying to explain this, I've killed the joke. Whoops.

"You doing many interviews with the civilians?" I asked as Bunny finished her work, and I nodded to her in thanks.

Jocko nodded, "Yeah, a lot of civvie stuff. Everything's pretty complimentary about you, though. I was surprised people weren't bitching more about having their homes flattened."

"So your report about us will be glowing," I said smoothly, and Jocko laughed.

"Like radioactive waste," he assured.

I chuckled, understanding the joke he was making. Had this been the cruise out, I would (obviously) have been suspicious of him, but now I knew him better. He was a bastard, but he was a good bastard.

"If you want to interview any of the POWs, they're all yours," I made that offer just as he was gathering his notes, and Jocko looked up.

"Really? Isn't that a violation of the Ceres Accords or something?"

I shrugged, "I doubt it. It's not torture, you won't be trying to humiliate them. If they want to talk, that's their business."

Jocko nodded, "I might do that, then. And I guess I'll have to tell Jess."

I began to nod (lots of nodding, we were doing), but then I stopped. In retrospect, I have no idea how I read anything into 'I guess I'll have to tell Jess', but for some reason it sounded suggestive to me. So, because I now had a jovial, friendly relationship with Jocko, I narrowed my eyes.

"*Jess*, eh? Something going on there?"

Jocko's eyes jolted up from his notes, his face blank for a few seconds as he tried to figure out a response.

"Hey... when I asked about you and Karen, all your skippers nearly threw me into the void," he protested with a grin.

"That's true... But meaning no offense to Bunny, Summer, and Destiny, you don't have enough people to toss me out of this room," I smiled at the camera crew.

Jocko laughed and leaned back in his chair, "Jessica's turned out to be a real nice woman."

He left it at that, and I was pretty sure I had my answer.

I have to say, I was enjoying this new relationship with the reporters. Jocko conducted his interview, and then Jessica came in and did hers. It was just that easy... much easier than their attempts to interview the Martians.

"You'll never get me to spew your propaganda!"

Jessica Qing, I'm told, actually looked quite offended at the word 'propaganda'. Remember, she was still getting established as a top-rung journalist at this time, but her big break — the one that got her this job (for better or worse) — had come when she'd exposed the woeful social security system in Germany.

In other words, she'd chopped right through German government propaganda saying that retirees were having a grand old time (when they were in fact living below the poverty line in many cases).

So when one Ensign Calvin Cartmorrisondez (ugh, the names) accused her of spewing propaganda for the Empire, she rightly took offense.

I wasn't there for this attempted interview, and it was by no means the only attempt, but if you ask me, it's a typical case of the Martians' stubbornness... and it's entertaining too.

Anyway, they were in the interrogation room, with two of Kyle Stranks' SF guards to make sure Calvin (no way in hell I'm typing that last 'name' over and over) didn't get aggressive, and Jessica had just asked him if he'd like anything to drink.

So, to put that dialogue into context for you, here it is again: "Good morning, Calvin. Would you like something to drink?"

That was Jessica asking, I should say.

"You'll never get me to spew your propaganda!" Calvin hissed back immediately.

Jessica looked somewhat disbelieving, say the guards (her camera was in there but it was pointed at him), though she replied smoothly, "We don't *do* propaganda, Mister Cartmorrisondez."

Calvin gave her one of the 'yeah right' looks and let out a snorted laugh, "Yeah. Right."

See, he was just being rude. It's unfortunate, too, because all this was being recorded — and he was actually one of the most cooperative prisoners we had. As such, this footage mostly made it to air... in fact, you've probably seen it, just with Jessica's questions re-recorded after the fact to make her seem less shocked by his rudeness.

"Mister Cartmorrisondez, we don't want you to make any statements about your mission. Our viewers *would* like to know *why* the Mars Imperium elected to start a war with the Earth Empire, though. We offered no provocation."

This gets rich, as you may know.

"Why? You know why. I don't need to tell you why," Calvin replied, I'd say almost petulantly.

Jessica stared at the Ensign blankly for a moment, then in a properly unimpressed tone went after him again, "Why don't you help me out with that?"

"What, your government hasn't been honest with you? Come on, the attacks on Asteroid Delta? Like you weren't behind them. Your Belt Squadron as much as left fingerprints."

Whoa, stop the presses! *I* started the war! Well, it wouldn't be the first time... oh wait, no, the other one was later. This one I didn't do.

And to all you conspiracy nuts out there, *no*, we did not attack Asteroid Delta. The entire suggestion that we started the war is absurd. If we provoked and they just responded, how did they set up that alliance with the pirates so quickly, and how did they organize their multi-pronged attacks of 2231 in such short order?

Easy. We didn't attack Asteroid Delta. Some think they know what happened there, but I remain skeptical. That's for a later book, though not for now.

It's informative to know that an Ensign in the Martian fleet believed we did attack Delta. And the Martians were accusing *us* of propagandaneering? That's probably not a word... but just goes to show, we couldn't be doing propagandaneering, because we don't even know the right term for it. Yay us.

For the skeptics, it's true, there's no way you could know that all my books up to this point haven't been huge, entertaining lies. You just have to trust me (which, I'll admit, is not always wise... alright, my editors say it usually is wise). If you want to believe we somehow started the war, and that every piece of history about the beginning of hostilities produced over the past twenty years has been a lie, you go right ahead.

Anyway, sorry, this is just driving further and further away from the narrative.

"We didn't attack Asteroid Delta," Jessica said cautiously.

Just guess how Calvin responded to that... with another snort and a shaking of his head, "Of course you didn't."

Nothing like a discussion where both sides are convinced the other is either totally wrong or lying.

"Lord Fiora probably just covered it up. We know about Lord Fiora. He's a murderer and a womanizer, but you people never report that either."

John, how could you step out on Anne like that? You bastard.

Jessica, by now, was getting somewhat intrigued. Obviously she wasn't believing the Martian's 'credible' information.

"Lord Fiora is an honorable man," she shook her head slowly.

Calvin let out a groan, "Well then I apologize, you're not their propaganda mouthpiece, you're just an idiot."

Jessica's intrigue waned. I'm sorry, calling a person an idiot like that is just a mood-killer.

And the SF guards standing behind Calvin, one of them a man named Eugene Sengooba, who Jessica had interviewed in *The Jupiter Patrol*, decided to adjust his attitude.

I know, smacking prisoners 'up side the head' is not a very polite thing to do, and it might be against the Ceres Accords, so I'm not saying they did that.

Ensign Calvin did inexplicably squeal, though, and Sengooba leaned down, "Mister Cartmorrisondez, please show respect to Miss Qing."

Calvin went on to spew more rhetoric, and of course he gave no straight answers to anything, but I think we've had our fill. Well, I have. If you haven't, access the fleet archives and you'll find the original interview reccie — Jessica kindly handed it over to us so that we could deconstruct it for intel, and so that she could use it in our recruiting ads.

Sorry, I meant in our propaganda. Right.

John, you womanizer! And damn me for attacking Asteroid Delta. I don't know how I can sleep at night.

Alright, my editors are saying I'm laying it on with a trowel. I'll stop. John is *not* a womanizer — he's like the 'anti-womanizer'. And Asteroid Delta? Well, you've probably heard the theories about that. I'm not the most likely suspect, if that place was actually attacked at all. More on that much later.

Now, it's time to fast forward. I can't maintain the coyness.

CHAPTER ELEVEN

SO WHY WAS IT DARK?

I'm going to level with you: up to this point I've basically been sticking in filler. I mean, the stuff to do with getting off Io was important — it set the stage for our cruise home. The stuff about Wes, Mik and Lia setting up the intercept force was also important. The prisoners were just interesting filler (to me, anyway).

And I haven't really been able to justify to myself (or my editors) continuing with it.

The trip back from Sinope wasn't fraught with the same sorts of juvenile romance tension the trip out had been. The first twenty days of cruising were pretty run of the mill. I cracked bad jokes and worried, Charlie trained with his Special Branchers, Karen occasionally danced, Andrea stared at her mag and woke up with night terrors, Jim wooed Bunny, Jocko and Jessica were seen having dinners and spending time together in other social settings... I could drag that all out, but really, I don't want to.

My reluctance isn't tied to missing all the entertaining stories... no, I'm skipping all that because it's stuff you already know. Nothing in those first twenty days really changed — when we came across *Idaho*, we were the same people we had been when we left Io.

This book isn't about those regular-seeming twenty days.

Idaho, and the darkness that ensued after we found that poor ship... that's what this book is about.

So with the patience of a kid waiting for his birthday presents, I'm going to jump straight to it. Hopefully my editors, and more importantly *you*, will approve.

"What the hell..."

Not the usual thing you hear from your Sensors and Communications duty officer when you're on day twenty-one of a boring cruise in-system from Io, so Andrea frowned and came out of her chair when she heard it.

"What's that?" she asked quietly, crossing the bridge towards the Sensors and Communications consoles. Felicia Khalid didn't have the shift, so it was Xavier Sanchez running the section.

"I see... confirm that... yes, that's a frigate adrift ahead. DCNS *Idaho*. Emergency transponder active."

Andrea's brow creased into a deep frown and she nodded towards the screens at the front of the bridge, "Put everything you have up front. Bring us to standby alert and call Admiral Barron and Commodore McMaster to the bridge. Activate Battlelink with all ships."

Was this an overreaction? Not even close. Finding a derelict ship under these circumstances was nearly as bad as running across a Martian battle force... but nastier in so many ways. Andrea had every reason to assume we'd just come across a world of trouble, and I really wish she'd been wrong about that. But personal demons notwithstanding, her tactical instincts were still spot-on.

See, finding a frigate adrift with its emergency transponder going was a very rare thing — and statistically near-impossible considering we were out beyond the Belt. For one thing, it was pretty uncommon that a frigate would have a failure that led to it being adrift without being destroyed. Possible, but uncommon.

More curious than that, though, was the fact that *we* were coming across it. *Idaho*, Andrea knew, was the Jupiter Squadron ship that had been sent back to Earth for help, but the ship had left months ago, when Jupiter was in a different place in its orbit. We were thus taking a different route home than *Idaho* should have… so how had *Idaho* gotten over to our base course?

It was suspicious on many levels. That said, it could have been quite innocent too. A navigation problem combined with a catastrophic engine failure. Having both things happen at once would seem quite unlikely, but then, many strange occurrences in history are so unlikely people think them impossible… until they happen.

I call it bad luck.

Well, usually I do.

This wasn't a late hour — Karen and I weren't sleeping — so we were in our uniforms and on the bridge within about three minutes of getting the call. As we arrived next to Andrea in front of the main screen, she nodded at the scans being put up.

"We've found *Idaho*."

My eyebrows rose, and when I looked at Karen, hers were up too. For all the reasons I just explained, this was a surprise.

Now the question was whether the ship was a trap. If there hadn't been errors in navigation and engines, a trap might be the only reason for the frigate to turn up on our base course.

Shelby McLaws passed us as she arrived on the bridge and stepped up to her bank of consoles, and Andrea immediately glanced at her, "Shelby, let's prepare to decelerate."

I nodded in confirmation, "All ships reduce speed. Bring us alongside when we're in range."

"Aye sir… that'll be about twenty minutes, sir," Shelby replied immediately, then tapped the appropriate people in her section on the shoulders to confirm.

We watched on the screen and waited while we got closer to *Idaho*.

"Everyone to action stations, this could be bait in a trap," I gave the orders much too late for us to effectively respond if Martian ships had been waiting to pounce, but thankfully, none were.

It was twenty minutes later, and our squadron was sitting in the blackness of outer-system space around the drifting hull of *Idaho*. All the skippers were on Battlelink, and now Mark Gunney opened the discussion.

"Smells like a trap to me. They shouldn't be this far over… they should be days to our relative right."

He was referring to the point made earlier about *Idaho* leaving Jupiter when the planet was at a different place in its orbit.

"Low level emissions… something's still running over there. Could be basic life support," Nancy Whitehorse observed quietly. She and Captains Kishko and Akuma were looking quite strained — *Idaho* had been their squadron mate, and as I found out later, Captain Phoebe Turner, the ship's skipper, had been considered one of their most daring and capable officers.

They'd sent their best ship on the dangerous run for help, and it hadn't even made it half way home. They were naturally, and rightly, hoping Phoebe and her crew were still alive in that hull.

But they weren't fools either. They knew, as Mark had said, that this had 'trap' written all over it.

"We have to have a look," Karen said softly, frowning as she spoke. "If there's anyone on that ship, we can't leave them trapped."

I nodded again, just as Matt Baxter made the completely appropriate counterpoint from the bridge of *Friendly*, "Yes, but if the Martians seized that ship and turned it into a trap, it's because they *know* we won't leave anyone out here. We must be incredibly cautious."

Both the Briton and Karen were right. We were in a proper conundrum… and I'm not sure if I've explained it well enough. Sorry to club this point to death if you think I already have…

You get the part about *Idaho* not being where we'd expect, fine. But if it looked so much like a trap, why weren't we just lasering the hull and moving on? Simple, what if it *wasn't* a trap?

Come on, they make movies about plights less dramatic than what the crew could be going through over there. Their navigation fried, their engines down, the brave Captain Turner and her women and men manage to survive for months on scant rations, praying that somehow their drifting ship, lost in the depths of the solar system, can be found.

If there was even a fraction of a percent of a chance that there were Defense Command personnel alive on that derelict, we had to check it out.

Even if the odds seemed quite good that the minute we stepped aboard a Martian scuttling charge would blow the ship to high heaven.

"We're also sitting in one place out here… I don't like that," Andrea observed quietly beside me — another good point.

Martian ships hadn't jumped us so far, but they could be nearby, ready to pounce as soon as we sent people over to *Idaho*. If we had small craft out, or teams aboard the ship, we were much less likely to run from an attack — we wouldn't flee and abandon our people, so the Martians would have a much better chance of bringing us to action.

See how much trouble finding a derelict Defense Command ship can cause?

"Alright, I want full fighter sweeps right now — all ships, rotating squadrons. I want eyes in as many directions as possible. We're staying at action stations… and we need to check it out."

There were nods on the screens and from Karen and Andrea on either side of me. The orders were logical enough, but they left a rather obvious question: who was going to check it out?

It wasn't going to be me. Not even I was stupid or brash enough to be first aboard a derelict like that. Rear Admirals aren't allowed to be so reckless, and as you've probably noticed, since Egesta, and then again since Kate Levec had been shot, I was getting too twitchy to be brash.

No, we'd have to find someone who could look danger in the eye and laugh… and who could keep his people alive inside a nuclear reactor, through sheer force of will.

We needed Charlie Peters.

Charlie has asked me to point out that he is *not* in fact immune to nuclear radiation — an admission which I have told him makes him sound less cool, but which he hopes might keep him out of stupid dares in future.

CHAPTER TWELVE

WHEN YOU KNOW IT'S A TRAP

Charlie looked at me with an open mouth, "We have to…"

He let the words trail off and looked up at the ceiling, shaking his head.

Karen and I had called him up to Andrea's day cabin to give him the news, and now he scratched his forehead and looked back down at the floor, mouth open and eyes wide as he contemplated the endless number of ways this operation could kill him.

Believe me, the same thoughts were running through my head, which was why I wasn't joking about what I was saying.

"Could be people in there. Could be full of nerve gas. So we start by sending in a bot, and if that works, then follow in for a quick sweep. We'll monitor all emissions, and I'll pull us up close alongside so you won't have far to run if it starts to blow…" I was running through the harried ideas that had come to my mind about how to do this as safely as possible, and as they started registering with Charlie, he began to nod.

"Yeah… that'll cut down some of the risk…" his voice trailed off again, and Karen, standing with arms folded and wearing a dark expression, lowered herself to sit on the edge of Andrea's desk.

"It might be a big trap… ship rigged to blow or a bio-weapon… or there could be a lot of small booby traps, designed to kill crew when they go aboard again," her words were grim.

As you're probably seeing, the complications and potentials for bad outcomes were infinite. Turning a derelict into a deathtrap just wasn't that hard.

"Or," Charlie looked up at last, making eye contact with Karen and then me, "there could be survivors over there. It's worth any risk."

In just about every movie you'll see, lines like that are accompanied by a subtle (or sometimes blaring) cue of brave, heroic music, to emphasize the self-sacrifice the hero is prepared to make.

It's a lot — a *lot* — more powerful when it's said simply and directly, the way Charlie says it. Some people don't believe that officers like Charlie Peters exist — they believe that no one *really* says the stuff he just said, or that if they do say it, they don't *really* mean it. They're either puffing themselves up or too naïve to realize the risks they're promising to take.

Well, Charlie means it. This is what he does. I've said it before, I'll say it again: Charlie may not like a situation, be it for political or practical reasons, but if there are lives on the line, he's going to do what he has to do to try to save them.

"Jeeze…" he shook his head slowly, "I really wasn't bored. You guys didn't have to find something to keep me busy. Or, you know, blow me to tiny pieces."

I tried to smile, and I'm rather sure I failed, "You know us, all giving, all the time."

Charlie managed a laugh, "Giving grief, apparently. I'll go tell Carly, and get the bot ready."

With that, he left, and as he walked out of the day cabin, Karen and I shared a concerned stare. There was nothing about this that felt good. Nothing at all.

A pertinent question my editors asked at this point was why we had to risk Charlie — why not Rufus Chang or Marcus Atallah? I don't really have a good answer for you on that one. Rufus, of course, would have done an excellent job as a first boarder, and so would Marcus. Any Special Branchers, you can be certain, would do well.

Well, my editors weren't satisfied when I tried to shrug off the question with that deflection, and then in the next draft when I tried to explain further, they said my answer was contradictory. (I'd said that we had absolute faith in Charlie, and that sometimes you have to put your friends on the line when you're in command… I'm not sure if those points actually contradict, but it doesn't matter.)

The reason we were sending Charlie, when it comes down to it, was simple: it was his job. I'd been sending him into messy situations since I'd taken command of *Friendly*, and while I don't recall any situations back in those days as potentially lethal as this one, it was still his job to go.

Friend or not, it was his duty.

Charlie didn't feel in any way offended by our choice. This was his job. He knew it was his job, he knew the risks associated with it, he knew that we'd need him to go into dangerous places at times… and this was one of those times.

He had lives to save, or a trap to spring. He hoped it was the former, he expected the latter, and when he boarded his Special Branch shuttle two hours after the meeting, he knew there was a good chance this was a one-way mission.

A hero of the Empire, no two ways about it.

"We're coming in closer to dock now," Chet Srisai was still flying Charlie's assault shuttle, and now he was deftly pushing the small craft up closer to the slowly drifting hull of *Idaho*.

As promised, I'd had Andrea move *Wolf* close to the spinning frigate, so that if a detonation began and Charlie and his squad needed to break dock and run for it, we could get between them and the explosion as quickly as possible. *Wolf* could shrug off a blast that might crush their small craft, though if the bang was big enough, it could damage *Wolf* too. Probably not the smartest maneuver, then, but I wasn't going to stand off while Charlie went in close and took all the risk.

"Seal up the suits. Chet, lock off your compartment," Charlie was on his feet in the rear of the shuttle, giving orders. He and his entire squad were wearing Class-A tactical suits — the annoying but effective environment suits that one could also fight in if necessary.

They wouldn't be breathing the air, or exposing their skin to atmosphere, or *anything*. There was a triple-layer sealed suit between them and any contaminant or biological agent on *Idaho*.

Chet Srisai sealed his pilot's compartment off from the rest of the shuttle, too, so he wouldn't have to wear the same suit while the small craft idled at the lock.

"Bot is ready," Ben Belete, another of Charlie's officers (remember him from *The Sinope Affair?*) was at the front of the cabin with a small, hover robot that was used for occasions like this. Remote-controlled and packed with sensors, the little bot could spring many types of trap... though if someone was nasty, they could certainly come up with weapons that would ignore it, and wait for warm bodies to arrive.

"Extending soft dock chute. We're going in on the forward pod, upper quarters deck..." Srisai's voice was coming over Charlie's headset, and the Major nodded.

"Roger that. Ben, get that bot ready..."

The shuttle moved in to dock.

On *Wolf's* bridge — and on the bridge of every ship in the force, I should add — we waited and watched with anticipation. Charlie and a few of his officers had tied their headset cameras into their shuttle's comm grid, so we were getting live visuals of what they were seeing on a number of our screens.

Yes, just like you see in the movies.

Remember how stressful watching the battles of Glorious February was for me on Belt Two? This was as bad, or worse. Because I was so damned close here, and because it was Charlie. And because Karen and I had been the ones to send him over...

We were standing ramrod straight, arms folded. I was grinding my teeth together and trying to control my breathing.

"We're locking on... five... four... three... two... one... lock on."

Chet Srisai's reports were also coming over our voice comm, and the cameras of circling Starlights from Wolfstar Squadron gave us live images.

The shuttle's lock extended and connected with the hull of *Idaho*, power relays linked and the computers attempted to interface with the onboard systems to open the hatches.

Then five words stopped my heart.

"Is that a power spike?"

CHAPTER THIRTEEN

NO

There are moments in your life when your heart seems to stop, and then there's a pounding in your ears and your brain feels like it's bristling. Adrenaline probably starts pouring into your veins, too, and time itself slows down. You can't believe that something as bad as you had feared was actually happening...

Then it turns out to be a false alarm.

"Not even close, that's just the juice for the hatch," one of the techs corrected the nervous question of another ('is that a power spike'), and I nearly dropped dead.

I broke the chapters between that question and its answer to give me a chance to do a little rant here: we've all become accustomed to the moment of seeming disaster turning out to be not a disaster at all... what I mean is, we're used to the show going to commercial just when our heroes are in peril, or the cliffhanger ending to an episode, or to the break in scenes in a novel leaving you dangling.

We all know that the hero comes out the other side, because if they were going to kill said hero, they'd have done it before that break, so that the impact could resonate with you for a while before they tried to carry on with the plot again. There are some exceptions to that rule, but by and large that's the way it goes.

In reality, though, moments of such terror — moments when you think *oh God, I've just killed Charlie* — don't come with the reassuring certainty that, no, he'll get out of this scrape alive. On the ground, in the moment, when your brain seems to tremor with a simple question like 'is that a power spike', you aren't apprehensively inhaling the popcorn or sitting on your couch going 'whoa' (things I normally enjoy doing, by the way), you're hoping desperately that everyone makes it out alive.

Instead of the warm certainty that there'll be an exciting escape on the other side of the commercial break, you have long seconds in which you can question the very fabric of who you are, and what you've done.

Those moments are tough... not as difficult as the moments when people *do* die, but tough all the same. They shouldn't simply be overlooked as exciting scene breaks.

Anyway, speaking of scenes...

"Bot's going across," Charlie's voice came up to *Wolf's* bridge, and on his headset cam, we could see Ben Belete shepherding the small thing into the airlock and closing the hatch behind it.

"Put the bot feed up on screen nine," Andrea ordered quickly. "Felicia, keep an eye on its data too."

As we watched the bot's feed on the bridge, Charlie watched it on a small screen at the back of his shuttle. Under Belete's remote control, the small robot drove across the chute and, as *Idaho's* airlock door was triggered, it passed into the ship.

"Inner door now," Charlie ordered softly, and Belete overrode the interior hatch of the lock, and rolled the bot inside.

The ship was pitch dark.

"Zero light. Switch to night vision," Charlie continued his commands.

The green tint of night vision flickered across the monitor, and then Charlie released an uncharacteristic comment, "Shit."

Lying meters from the lock was a body — or *parts* of a body. There was no way to get a good look at it, but Charlie could see the outline of an arm lying next to a leg, in a way that nature never intended.

"We have dead. And it looks like messy dead," Charlie reported softly, as though he was sneaking through the ship himself.

"Atmosphere scan is… clean. The air doesn't look like it's been circulated for a while, sir, but no Schedule 1, or Schedule 2 contaminants are present," Felicia Khalid reported into Charlie's ear.

Schedule 1 contaminants were (and are) the active bio-weapons of the period, and Schedule 2 contaminants were contemporary chemical weapons. Use of both types of weapon were outlawed in the Ceres Accords, of course, but that was no guarantee that someone hadn't tried to deploy them. Any compound that had been used as a weapon since the twenty-first century — right down to that damned 'Omega Strain' that had very nearly been released — was thus recorded in our database, and the atmosphere was checked for it.

All clear.

"Radiation levels are normal," Felicia continued her observations. "Everything here looks clear for going aboard, Major Peters."

Charlie nearly said 'easy for you to say' but he stopped himself.

He paused, then turned back to his squad, "Alright, we have mangled bodies and clear air. We're staying in the suits. No risks at all. We go for the bridge, try to get logs. Don't turn anything on without asking… booby traps could be anywhere."

The Special Branchers nodded evenly at Charlie's words, and then they each hefted their MAG-90s and headed for the lock.

Standing on *Wolf's* bridge, we looked silently at the pieces of the body the bot had found. There was an abundance of tension, our concerns that Charlie and his people would get blown up were turning into much more gruesome but much less likely ones.

Your mind is probably already skipping sideways into the movies you've seen. You know how the formula goes: a civilian ships finds a derelict pod or piece of technology, they bring it aboard and discover it's either not human in origin, or it has been contaminated with some unknown radiation, or (inexplicably) it's a Pion escape pod. They open it, one or a few monsters break out and start hunting the crew through the darkened corridors of the ship.

Defense Command officers all know better than to find much credibility in such stories… but then, we're all human too. We know there are no aliens in our solar system. We know that massive amounts of exotic radiation don't turn humans into fanged beasts (they liquefy humans, as some of the brave crew of *Lion* discovered). We've fought Pions, and we've been down to their rock (and we're actually going there next book).

But we still have fears. We know better, but sometimes we can't help but take a moment to wonder — just wonder — if the movies might have somehow got it right.

So a derelict ship, darkened and with body parts lying around... with Special Branchers boarding and us watching through their headset cams... yeah, this was the script from a horror movie.

"I don't like this movie," I muttered quietly.

Karen glanced at me, "I wish it was a movie."

We were, quite honestly, waiting with bated breath.

Charlie led his team through the lock, and was the first to put a boot inside *Idaho*. He had the visor of his tactical suit displaying a night vision feed, so he could look down and see the four mangled corpses in the corridor as he arrived.

His heart rate was up, but as a Special Brancher, he was able to contain his fear that he was the sacrificial offering to an alien monster in a horror movie.

"Watch the bodies. Chet, back the bot into the lock and if anything, human or otherwise, tries to cross the chute, break contact," Charlie's orders were just above whispers now. "Watch all angles. Let's go to the bridge."

Charlie and his squad left the bodies behind as they moved cautiously through the corridors of *Idaho*. They were only a couple of decks below the bridge, so they'd only have a few ladders to climb (lifts were down, though gravity was functioning).

Those few ladders, though, took them almost an hour — and rightly so. They came across a total of twenty-one corpses on the way, all mangled and torn apart the way they are in the movies — the way that makes the characters say 'no human did this'.

Well, Charlie's squad had been on Egesta — they could say with authority that humans could mangle bodies even *worse* than this. Not that such a statement would be in any way comforting to anyone.

"Dammit, I'd like to have some lights on..." Carly Henderson, Charlie's 2IC, commented as she rounded a corner next to him.

"Afraid of the dark, Carly?" he asked, not in a snide way, but a genuinely sympathetic one.

She snorted a laugh, "Today I am."

The team continued to move slowly and steadily up through the ship.

"Power output is staying level," Felicia Khalid was keeping an eye on every emission *Idaho* was giving off, and Karen, Andrea and I were like statues in the middle of the bridge, our eyes darting back and forth between screens while our bodies remained frozen.

"They're getting up to the bridge deck now..." Karen was nearly whispering.

Normally I would have made some crack about there being no need to whisper, but I tell you, I would have whispered saying it. I can't pretend that we — standing in our well-lit bridge, separated from *Idaho* by the safe cushion of vacuum — were under the same stress as Charlie and his people, but damned if we weren't getting caught up in the tension.

"Bridge hatch is just ahead," Charlie's whisper was, of course, completely appropriate.

"Good luck," was my lame offering in return.

♦♦♦

Charlie didn't reply to my words as they came through his ear. Using hand gestures (visible on night vision to his squad) he spread his people into two columns, one leaning up against each side of the corridor that approached the hatch to the bridge. He then waved them to move forward.

Silently, and stepping over the remains of two more crew — with mags lying near those bodies, I should add — they moved for the bridge, silent but quick.

Reaching the hatch, Charlie didn't waste much time. He gestured to his people to make sure they understood the sweep they'd do upon entry, then he grabbed the hatch crank and levered the door open.

Everyone on the bridge of *Wolf* could have used a few seconds of delay to ready ourselves for the horrors we expected to see on the other side, but Charlie moves fast.

Swinging in with his MAG-90 still raised and ready, he covered left while Carly, coming instantly behind him, went right. The rest of the squad poured in, and the hatch was slammed after them.

The bridge was reasonably gruesome. I suppose it's ridiculous to call something that's gruesome only 'reasonably' so... but that's how it seemed.

There were about a dozen bodies lying around, all mangled and torn, and because it was a tall, enclosed space, it was somehow scarier than a corridor.

You know how in the movies, the teams sweeping rooms always seem to forget to check the ceiling for the alien monsters? The ceiling was checked immediately by two of Charlie's Branchers. Two more checked the day cabin, and the rest were sweeping around *Idaho's* consoles.

A chorus of 'clears' was issued, and then the Branchers started to relax... a tiny little bit. They weren't about to let aliens drop out of ceiling ducts on them, so they were keeping their MAG-90s in hand.

"I'll see if I can get the computer online," Ben Belete said, heading quickly for the operations consoles. Charlie nodded, and for a moment he waited as Ben found a spot, pushed a body out of the way, and tried to activate the console.

It turned on immediately, and a log started to play.

Ben watched for a moment, then paused the log, rewound it, and plugged his comm in so it could be broadcast to all the waiting ships.

"I think we have a log, here," he said as he started playing it again.

Karen and I looked at each other with deep frowns — that had been awfully easy — and then screen ten flickered to life with a panicked person on it, a bloody gash on his head.

"I am Lieutenant Carl Devoir, of DCNS *Idaho*. I am the last surviving officer. We found... we found a pod. We brought it in. It was... it was *not human*. There was a creature in it... it's killing us! It killed the Captain. EP-5s don't seem to hurt it. We're making our stand in engineering... if I can get there... if you find this, we might be down there. If you have the firepower, come help us... please..."

The log cut, but already Belete was feeding other pictures up onto the screen through his comm: a silver, winged ship that looked vaguely alien, and what looked like surveillance camera footage of a beastly black creature with four bladed arms cutting through a squad of SF, and shrugging off mag fire.

"What... the hell?" I think I managed to actually utter the question first.

This was... well, confusing.

"Someone check fleet records for a Lieutenant Devoir," Karen was already being coherent, of course.

"Charlie, stay put for the moment. Look out for any gnarly tall aliens with four arms... but... well..." my words trailed off.

"Yeah," Charlie replied.

We were all confused, because to be quite honest, this sounded pretty ridiculous. After seeing all the carnage on the way to the bridge, we'd been expecting something a little more credible.

I'm sorry, that must seem harsh, but there was something about all this that didn't ring true. It had 'movie' written all over it... which was to say, it had 'pathetic ruse' written all over it.

"I have a record of Devoir on *Idaho*. No current picture... old one looks close to him," Felicia put the image of Carl Devoir up on the screen next to the image of the man in the log, and she was right, they looked similar.

Similar.

"Get that image of the 'alien' pod down to Andy, see if it looks alien to him," I ordered next, and Felicia nodded.

We were very skeptical about all this, and I hope you understand why.

"What about the possibility of survivors in the engineering section?" Captain Kishko asked dutifully on Battlelink, and I looked up.

Charlie beat me to a reply, "No offense to them, Captain, but I'm not ready to take my team on a walk through a potentially booby-trapped ship just because a conveniently-placed log entry tells me to."

Kishko nodded slowly, as did I — though I was nodding to no one in particular.

I looked at Karen again, "This is... a lot of theatre."

She nodded, "Slim chance it's true, I suppose... but they're asking us to go to the engines. Means either the trap is there, or they're trying to get as many of us aboard as they can."

"Yeah, so what do we do?" Charlie asked over the comm.

I shrugged.

"Did Ken just shrug?"

"Yes," Karen replied.

"Great."

CHAPTER FOURTEEN

WHAT NEXT?

So what do you do when one of your frigates has supposedly been invaded by an alien soldier with a black carapace, bony blades sticking out of its *four* arms, and an immunity to mag fire?

Send more troops, obviously. Because, to be frank, it's either true, total bullshit, or something in between. And putting more Special Branchers aboard is just about all you could do.

Well, that's not true: we could have pulled Charlie out and lasered *Idaho* apart, but what if there was an alien aboard... or survivors? Granted, we didn't think that likely (especially the alien part — I mean, *come on*) but for the same reason we couldn't blow past *Idaho* when we first detected it, we couldn't leave without at least looking to see if any of its people were still alive.

What we could do, though, was be very smart about where we put our Branchers.

"Alright, I've released the doors on bay two. You should be able to override and get in," Charlie was working at one of the operations consoles, talking through his headset to Major Marcus Atallah, who was on his way over from *Cheetah*.

"We are approaching the airlock near main engineering," Rufus Chang reported immediately after.

We were sending one squad to check out the supposedly alien craft in *Idaho's* landing bay two, and another to check engineering for survivors in the ship's engine section. While those squads were coming in, Charlie's shuttle was shifting its position to an airlock closer to the bridge, just in case one of the two new teams triggered a massive booby trap that detonated the ship.

It was about as smart as we could be about this.

"The pod looks human enough to me... looks like it's a horror movie rendition of an alien ship," Andy Jenson gave his expert opinion over the comm.

"Thanks Andy... we're all thinking the same up here," Andrea replied, then repeated Andy's opinion to Charlie. "Andy thinks the silver ship is human in origin."

There was a pause before Charlie spoke, "I'm not sure if that's a good thing or a bad thing."

Either there was actually an alien hunting people on this ship, or some bastard really wanted us to believe that — probably meaning there was a big booby trap waiting to be sprung.

"Docking now," Rufus came over the comm.

"And we're forcing the doors... now," Marcus Atallah added.

Well, we were about to find out.

+++

Rufus docked first, and as his team forced the lock and crossed into *Idaho's* engine section, we all watched on the bridge screens, again with bated breath. The section was dark and full of bodies — a by-now familiar sight — but it was a short trip for Rufus and his team to the main engineering bay.

The door was welded shut (they always seem to weld the doors in movies, because apparently that makes them stronger?), and there was a lot of blood spattered around.

"Looks like a last stand point," Rufus observed as he swept his headset cam over the deck around him. "Or something designed to look like one."

"You need to get into that bay, Rufus," I replied quietly. "Could be a trap though."

"It's that kind of day, sir," the Major observed wryly. "Everyone back around the corner."

With no ceremony at all, Rufus pulled a blastpack off his vest and slammed it against the corridor wall next to the welded hatch. He tripped its countdown trigger and sprinted away.

Bang, new door. Just like that. No finesse, no morse code knocking to see if anyone was in there, just simple, effective hole. I like Rufus' style.

As his team came back around the corner after the blast, their MAG-90s were up and ready.

"Special Branch, we're coming in!" one of Rufus' Lieutenants barked, and then led the way fearlessly into the engine bay.

The giant chamber wasn't quite carpeted in bodies, but there were many. At least thirty. All in pieces.

There were also many potential hiding spots, so Rufus' team slowed as they entered the bay, their weapons sweeping up and down, side to side, looking for any movement. There didn't seem to be any.

But then, rather suddenly, there was.

Marcus Atallah was kneeling down next to the wing of the silver 'alien' ship, shaking his head.

"It says 'Made in the USA.' I'm not kidding. Right here on the side," he reported over his comm.

"What?" I was almost incredulous in my reply. "You said you're not kidding... nothing like that's been manufactured in the USA for years..."

Of course I wasn't shocked that the craft wasn't alien — whether it was made in the USA or not, English 'made in the' writing sorta ruled out extra-terrestrial. How likely would it be that a completely alien species out there would be able to speak and write English? That's either lazy fiction or a lot of explaining to do.

No, there was no alien aboard *Idaho*... a fact that made the next yell over the comm very confusing. The way most of this little operation seemed to be.

"What *is* that?" one of Rufus' officers asked the question rather loudly.

He had every right to speak loudly, of course, because on his night vision visor, he was seeing the lumbering approach of a seven-foot-tall 'alien' with four arms and blades attached to each of them. It was hissing loudly (they always hiss in the movies) and seemed to have one large eye on its dinosaur-like head.

So… there *was* an alien?

Made in the USA?

"Hit it," Rufus didn't even sound worried, being a good Special Brancher. Twelve MAG-90s cut loose instantly, and not a single one missed.

The thing didn't even slow down.

This was weird. It was doing what the guy in the log had said it was doing — shrugging off mag fire — and it was coming at Rufus fast.

"Pull back. Don't know what this thing is, but I don't want to let it get too close until I find out," the Major said evenly, and with smooth nods, his officers fell back through the hole he'd made, covering each other with streams of mag fire as they went.

Rufus was the last one out, so the creature got closest to him — and his headset cam — before he turned away. I have to say, one ugly bastard… but largely humanoid (aside from the four arms). Now, if you ask the scientists, they'll tell you the chances of real aliens out in the galaxy being humanoid are not very good, so already I was wondering whether this was just a guy in a suit.

A really insane, hissing guy, probably on drugs.

Rufus gave the monster thing another full burst of mag fire to the chest, but the shots didn't seem to do much. If it was a guy in a suit, then the suit was wrapped in plenty of the fibers that Special Branchers used in their vest plates — the ones that keep you from dying when you get a full mag shot in the chest.

Since that didn't work, Rufus plucked another blastpack off his vest, retreated through the hole and dropped it in his wake. As he sprinted around the corner after his team, it went off, but seconds later the creature/guy in the great suit lumbered after him.

Well then.

"This is annoying. Jake, find a room we can hole up in," Rufus issued those orders to one of his Captains. "Adéla, get ready to break dock. Keep their airlock wedged open."

See, I like Rufus' style. That's taking nothing away from Charlie, you understand — I'd never dream of taking anything away from Charlie, largely because he'd hurt me. But no, Rufus was doing what every sole survivor in the horror movies only figured out in the end… he was just doing it before any of his people got eaten. Or mauled. Or whatever this guy in the suit was going to do.

Coming around the next corner, Rufus saw Jake Strutter holding a hatch open for him. Without pause, he went through, and then Jake shut the hatch behind him. The whole squad was inside, so Rufus gave the next order.

"We're all locked down, Adéla. Pull the chute."

Rufus' shuttle pilot complied immediately. While her override kept the inner and outer hatches of the *Idaho* airlock from closing, she detached her chute and pulled away under light thrusters.

Having listened to what was going on, Adrienne Thompson had moved planes from Wolfstar Squadron into escort position around the shuttle, and now they waited and watched as the atmosphere from the engine section was sucked out into space.

Rufus and his squad waited too — a little anxious, Rufus later admitted to me. This *should* work — there weren't many men in suits who could beat an explosive decompression, but if it really *had* been an alien, *maybe* it could hold on with all those blade things…

Nope. After about twenty seconds — and amidst the remains of many mangled crew members — a black, four-armed 'alien' burst out of the lock, and Wolfstar Squadron put the man in the suit out of his misery before he bloated too much. Or, if it was an alien, before it could do something alien-like.

Two Starlights went after the figure, just using their thrusters, and both pilots swear the thing was still moving, virtually unaffected by the vacuum. They claim, too, that when they sprayed it with their powerful mags, it exploded not in a puff of red guts (as it should when there was a human in a suit) but in a squish of black.

Now, I know these two pilots, and damned fine fliers they both are… but come on, it was a guy in a suit. At *most* it was a genetically engineered creature (though that'd be one hell of an engineering job). These two pilots just want to go on record as being the first humans to successfully kill an alien soldier.

I suppose if, in a few centuries, we run across a race of aliens that looks like that guy in the suit, they may get credit…

Anyway, that curious diversion dealt with, Rufus' shuttle returned to its position at the lock, docked, and the deck repressurized.

In his room with his squad, Rufus reported in, "Alright, we dealt with the 'alien.' There might be more, so keep an eye out. Now checking for traps in the engineering section."

"Roger that," Charlie came over the comm. "See if you can get lights for us, too."

"Will do," Rufus replied immediately.

Without further delay, he swung open the hatch and led his team out onto the repressurizing deck. The question on his mind — and on all of our minds — was why had that guy in a suit been trying to distract them?

CHAPTER FIFTEEN

TRAPS

The lights throughout *Idaho* flickered back to life as Rufus' most tech-savvy officer reactivated the basic mains from a panel in engineering.

Rufus looked curiously at the Lieutenant as he switched off his night vision, "All they had to do to bring up lights was throw a switch?"

The Lieutenant, Vesna Mandic, shrugged and nodded, "Just one button, Major."

"Hear that?" Rufus asked the question, directing it to those of us listening in. "There's no power problem with the lighting grid. Someone took it down to spook us."

"I bet if you saw the 'alien' under full lighting it'd look like a guy in a suit," I offered over the comm in reply, and Rufus nodded.

"Probably. So the question now is what was he trying to keep us from finding," Rufus turned his attention back towards the engine chamber. "He was holed up in the engines. Could there be a bomb down here?"

There were countless logical questions running through Rufus' mind — the first one being *why bother* with an 'alien' in the first place. We'd start pondering all the questions later, but for now we had to check to see if *Idaho* was getting ready to explode.

"I'll get Andy online and see what he says," Andrea came in over the comm next.

"Meantime, Marcus, why don't you move over to forward environmental controls and make sure there isn't a bio-agent waiting to be released," Charlie suggested. "With lights up, should be easier to spot traps."

"Roger that," Marcus agreed. Being in the landing bay, his team was closest to one of the environmental control stations — the one that managed atmosphere in the bow pod.

"We'll check the aft environmental control," Charlie went on.

Quick explanation here: on newer frigates like *Wolf*, there was only one environmental control center, with three redundant plants that didn't run unless the main was knocked out or you were carrying a ton of extra passengers. In the older *North Americas*, there were two plants that ran full time in order to keep the air exchanging. Simple differences in technology, really — our later plant was more efficient, so we only needed one to take care of the air in *Wolf*.

Anyway, the two systems weren't isolated from each other. It was more like having two fans going in a large room: one couldn't reach the other end easily, but eventually the air it was pushing could get over there.

The reason that was significant is pretty obvious, I think: a trap aboard ship could involve one of the Schedule 1 or 2 weapons I mentioned earlier, set to release once the atmospheric plants were started up again.

A canister of bio-weapon could be hidden at either plant and still be lethal, so both Charlie and Marcus had to look.

Anyway, sorry, back to Rufus. He had his mismatched eyes fixed on the far end of the engine chamber, where something looked fishy to him.

Rufus, I should say, isn't an engineer as such. He knows how to blow things up, but in his spare time he doesn't exactly build engines for a hobby. However, he has a knack for knowing when things aren't quite as they should be...

"Does that setup look regulation to anyone?" he asked in a flat tone as he began crossing the large bay towards the rear wall.

A couple of his people began to follow him immediately, one of them being Mandic.

"No sir, that does not look regulation at all."

There was something purposefully innocuous-seeming about the setup: a relay hatch had been pulled off the wall, and some cables were running from the innards of that access point to a nearby console. It could have been anything... a diagnostic procedure that had been interrupted by our 'alien' friend... an attempt to bypass command circuits during a boarding... something entirely innocent.

But the flimsy little drama that had been set up for us was making us rather attentive to detail.

"Route Rufus' headset cam to engineering," Karen's voice came into Rufus' ear. We'd have Andy Jenson (our engineer, I should have reminded you of that earlier) take a look at those connections.

Rufus and his fellow officers stopped about four meters short of the panel, their MAG-90s pointing at it. No, I'm not sure what good shooting it would have done —people often laugh at Special Branchers when they point their mags at things they're paying attention to. Those people don't get it: that's training. You see something unusual, no matter what it is, you point your weapon at it, just in case.

Maybe it'll do you no good, but having the weapon ready and in place gives you one more option if you need it — if you don't have your weapon on the thing, then you have one less option if it acts up. Certainly, there are times when shooting something — a bomb or whatnot —might make a situation worse... that's why Special Branchers just *point* their weapons, and don't shoot freely. Anyway, training your weapon on something unknown is just a good habit.

Rufus eyed the console cautiously. It appeared to be dark, and there was no hum coming from the relays. Seemed dead enough.

"That's nothing," Andrew Jenson was patched onto Rufus' comm a moment later. "That's set up as a diversion if it's anything. There's no way you could get enough charge through that relay into a reactor to do any harm. Look around, for me, show me the room."

Headset cams and great chief engineers made for a very useful combination on days like this.

Obeying the engineer's words, Rufus started looking slowly from left to right, and his officers did the same.

Everything else seemed to be in place. Was there a trap in here after all?

"Stop. Right there... Lieutenant Mandic, right ahead of you. Towards the corner, you see that?" Andy's voice was quickening slightly on the comm. "Why the hell would they leave that on?"

Rufus turned to the wall but couldn't see anything out of the ordinary, "What's the problem, engineer?"

Andy had his comm covered for a moment —Rufus (and all of us) could hear the muffled sounds of him consulting with a couple of his people. Then he replied, "In that corner, there's the number fifteen access panel. When a ship's running, you leave that off. It's the easiest way to keep an eye on the main relays. Only ever put it on for inspections and that sort of thing."

"It connected to something potentially dangerous?" Rufus asked as he started to approach the corner.

"You cross the relays in there, it'll overload when main power comes online. That's one of the reasons you leave the panel off," you could almost hear Andy's quick nod.

"Aha," Rufus came to a stop in front of the panel and leaned in close. "There are streaks in the grease over here. Looks like someone could have taken it off and replaced it."

By this time, everyone listening was holding their breath again. Nothing like finding a booby-trapped derelict to ruin your blood pressure.

"They could have booby trapped the panel itself... you pull it off, there could be an anti-personnel bomb," Charlie had been listening, and now he offered that sober advice over the comm.

"Was thinking the same," Rufus agreed. "Engineer, are there more panels like this one, with similar relays?"

The confirmation was quick, "One other, opposite corner. They regulate the flow between the reactors, before they get to the shunts for the engine pods."

"How volatile are they without power running through them?" Rufus dropped his MAG-90, letting it hang from its harness on his vest, and waved Mandic to look for the matching panel in the opposite corner.

"Not... they're just relays. But if you cross them and then switch on, the power flow will blow the reactors..."

"So they're just relays. Easy to cross, easy to fix?" Rufus was building up to something, but because we didn't know him quite as well as we knew Charlie at this point, none of us were getting it.

"That's right," Andy answered, clearly somewhat confused. "What're you thinking, Major?"

Rufus did some hand gestures, then pulled another blastpack off his vest and pressed it against the panel. In the opposite corner of the engine bay, Mandic found the twin panel and did the same.

They both backed off, and as we watched in surprise, Rufus triggered the bombs he'd just placed.

Just like that.

And it's a good thing he did. The panels were shattered, but as the Special Branchers dropped behind consoles for cover, secondary explosions came from both —bangs from anti-personnel mines.

Explosive mines, not mag mines.

As Rufus looked back up over the console behind which he'd taken cover, he shook his head, "Engineer, I think your people will have to do some fixing here."

✦✦✦

Moving through *Idaho* was, as Charlie expected, much easier with the lights up. The Special Branchers were still in their environment suits, so they weren't smelling or feeling anything different, but they could look for tripwires, suspicious clumps of bodies that might have hidden explosives, and so on.

It was, of course, rather gruesome (again). The dead were, upon closer examination, clearly members of the ship's crew. They'd either been mangled and murdered horribly by the man in his suit, our they'd been shot and cut up to look as if they'd been mauled. A

Either way, what had been done to them was starting to sink in on a real level. A Defense Command crew had been mutilated. Remember how well I took the destruction of the DCC ships like *Marconi*? This was on a more grizzly level than that, and as I watched more fully-lit headset cam footage from the corridors of *Idaho*, my anger started to build to new levels.

My anxiousness was changing — no longer was I feeling the grim worry that came with sending people through the dark corridors of a derelict to fight a monster. Now I was starting to entertain pure rage at seeing what had been done to these men and women. The visceral deaths suffered by this brave crew just to put on some damn show for us… that was making me *very* angry.

As we watched Marcus Atallah's team sweeping through corridors on their way to the forward environmental control, I was starting to try to figure all this out. So far we'd seen a false log, a fake alien, many dead crew, and a booby trap in the reactor relays. What kind of plan was this? What was really going on here?

All those questions had to wait, though. Whatever the Martians — and let's be clear, by now we were all assuming that this was the sick work of the Martians — had done to make this ship a trap needed to be discovered and deactivated. Then we could put more people aboard the ship to do deeper checks of its systems, and then *maybe* we could consider sending people over to bury the crew in space, and *possibly* restore the ship.

Yes, we were obviously thinking of restoring the ship. More on that later.

Marcus' team arrived at the entrance to the environmental control center, and through his headset feed, we watched him open the door and lead the way in.

The chamber was empty — not even any bodies present.

"Check for any obvious signs of tampering," Marcus directed quickly, and his officers began to move around the chamber, examining the various atmospheric processing units and pumps.

Andrea glanced over at Felicia Khalid, "Send these pictures down to the duty officer in environmental control."

Again, having pictures sent to the experts was a great way to save time on operations like this.

After a moment, Marcus' officers collected around him, each reporting nothing that seemed unusual to them.

One held up a scanner, "Atmoscan says we're at zero for all Schedule 1 and 2 contaminants."

Marcus nodded, "Good. Doesn't rule out the possibility of canisters somewhere in the ducts, but it looks like there's nothing in position up here for a central spread."

If you wanted to poison an entire ship of *Idaho's* size, you couldn't just open a canister of gas in one compartment and expect it to spread. Instead, you needed to get it into the system of ducts that supplied the crews with their essential human needs — things like air. As such, you'd patch some VX (if you want to get all retro with a nerve agent) into the system somewhere between the filtration scrubbers and the pumps... but there was no sign of any such tampering.

That didn't mean there *was* none... but the atmoscan coming up clean was a good sign.

Charlie entered the aft environmental control chamber about twenty minutes later, after a much longer walk from the bridge down through the neck of the frigate. More bodies were discovered, but no anti-personnel traps at all.

Coming to the entrance to the chamber, Charlie slowed his team and then used hand gestures to position them for entry. They were definitely able to move more smoothly with the lights up, but even though the 'alien' had been dispatched and no traps had been found so far, they were being very cautious.

"Going in now," Charlie narrated his actions for us as Carly Henderson opened the door and swung in first.

The team flooded the chamber, covering all angles and moving with that tactical sense Special Branchers seem to naturally possess. Within minutes, they'd swept the equipment in the room and reached the same conclusion Marcus had: all clear, atmoscan clean.

As the team collected around Charlie, he looked at one of the officers with a headset cam being fed to the bridge and nodded, "All the obvious places for traps have been cleared. We'll need more bodies and experts to check for the less obvious ones."

On *Wolf's* bridge, I hadn't moved from where I'd been standing, and my legs were getting sore.

I nodded (even though Charlie couldn't see that), "Yes. Alright, we'll send over shuttles of SF, technicians and medical personal. All in environment suits, I'm taking no risks. Don't change the atmospheric settings until the grid is checked out."

Charlie nodded again, "Alright. Warn them to dress warm, it can't be more than five degrees over here. I'm even feeling it through the suit."

"Roger that. You stay put for now," was my reply.

"Aw, I was hoping to go into the underbelly of the ship to see if our alien friend laid any eggs," Charlie protested with a smirk. The fact that he was feeling comfortable enough in the situation to crack such a joke boded well.

Soon we'd know if Rufus had stopped the only trap aboard *Idaho*.

Chapter Sixteen

Reasonable Paranoia

For the next twenty hours, security forces, technicians and medical personnel from *Wolf* carefully examined *Idaho*, looking in all the likely danger spots. The air ducts were completely explored by bots and by crews climbing around in environment suits. The reactors, the drive pods, and everything in between were examined foot by foot.

After the major systems and sections were cleared, the other, more creative possible points of sabotage were explored. Matt Baxter suggested the weapons — particularly the lasers — might be a good place to create an overload, so Andy Jenson's people went through those carefully. Andrea thought there could be explosives in the cargo bays, so those were unceremoniously emptied into the void.

It was also hypothesized that some unknown bio-agent could be planted with the bodies — some sort of new disease that had been engineered for the trap. Alicia Morgan thus came over from *Wolf* with most of her medical staff, and volunteers from the rest of the Jupiter Force.

First all the bodies were gathered into one of the empty cargo bays, then they were scanned carefully, and tested for everything Alicia could imagine — which was a lot. As it turned out, the bodies had been cleaved and mutilated post-mortem, after the crew had been killed by mags.

Except for one group, who'd apparently been cleaved apart pre-mortem by the 'alien', probably for the gruesome log entry we'd seen. The Martians must have staged that somehow… a horrible way to die.

While the sweeps were done, a team started going through *Idaho's* database, looking for any clues as to what had happened. We didn't find any. Whoever had taken the ship from its crew — intact, with no outward or inward signs of a fight — had also taken the data from the ship out with them.

And when I say taken, I don't mean they copied it and wiped the data. No, they actually *took the drives*. We had absolutely nothing left to access.

So all we knew was that it had not been an alien monster attack. The alien was a guy in a suit…

It probably isn't a surprise to you that the more we uncovered aboard *Idaho*, the less sense things seemed to make. As such, here's a conversation Karen and I had over dinner, as we tried to come to grips with all our findings.

Karen, of course, was lying in her usual spot on my bed, absently stabbing some fish sticks with her fork, "So… they move the ship onto a course they expect us to be taking home, on the one-in-a-million chance we'll actually see it and stop…"

She was still stuck on the unlikely interception — the fact that we'd found *Idaho* in the first place. I'd given up trying to figure out how the Martians had known where to put the ship for us to find, but it definitely seemed that they had been confident we'd come across it. After all, you can't convince a guy in a suit to stay aboard if you can't give him a reasonable guarantee that he'll be found.

Then again, anyone crazy or drugged-up enough to wear an alien suit would probably be game for any risk.

But why had they bothered with the alien suit?

"Yeah… but… why the ruse? Wouldn't an empty ship with no apparent threat be more likely to bring us aboard in larger numbers?" I was stuck on that. If you wanted to get as many Defense Command personnel as possible aboard ship before they turned on the reactors and blew themselves to kingdom come… why the alien ruse? If anything, that'd make us more suspicious.

"Well, you heard the Martian interview tapes… they might think we're so dumb we didn't realize it was a ruse. Could have put hundreds of people aboard the ship to hunt down that alien…" Karen offered, laying her fork down and toying with her ponytail.

I frowned and dropped my own fork onto the tray in my lap, "Maybe… but if it was a real alien, and we bought it, wouldn't we just pull our people and cut that hull to ribbons?"

Karen nodded slowly, "I sure would. But maybe the Martians didn't think we would."

With a sigh, I picked up my fork again and stabbed a fish stick, "This just doesn't seem that well thought out."

"No… not unless we're missing something. It's too foolish… or it's brilliantly overcomplicated for some reason," she picked up her own fork again before looking at me. "Like one of Grant's schemes, almost."

She just had to go and say that. I nearly lost my appetite at the thought. 'Grant', of course, was Grant Merger — our former classmate from the very old days, and… well, you know the rest. Grant had always been prone to maddeningly complex plans that hinged on a large number of moving parts doing just what he expected them to do, exactly when he wanted them to do it.

Usually plans like that fail, but Grant had a frustrating track-record of having his schemes actually work.

This plan, however, hadn't…

"The Martians have been getting over-complicated lately," I mumbled as I chewed. "Those coordinated attacks for the Battle Over Earth and February… they seem to like plans with multiple moving parts, too."

Karen nodded as she took a bite of fish, "Mmmhmm."

She chewed for a moment and seemed to be thinking.

"Well," she said with a resigned tone after she swallowed, "maybe Grant's working for them."

I'm glad I wasn't trying to swallow when she said it, because I probably would have started to choke.

"Let's really, *really* hope not. Last thing we need is for that bastard to have a real fleet," I think I was a little too emphatic, and Karen frowned at me.

"He's still under your skin, after all these years?" her question almost sounded rhetorical.

I shrugged, "Yes."

I didn't need to say any more than that — Karen knew, and I think she even shared my feelings about Grant Merger. We both hated him with the bitter intensity reserved for someone who has betrayed you.

I suppose I might as well do a little Grant Merger rant here, even though it's not part of the story. Grant had been our classmate, our friend. He and Karen and I had been unstoppable on our way through the Academy, at least to begin with.

Then, as we reached our final years, his perspectives began to shift… completely. We never stopped getting along personally, but he started wondering about the fidelity of this Earth Empire — he started to see shadows where there were none. The Empire was the 'evil doer', or so he 'discovered'. The Black Sun represented everything he hated.

Well fine, if he decided he didn't like the Empire, that was alright. He left the Academy before graduation, having been the only other cadet in our year to keep up with Karen and me in the tactical sims, but deciding he wasn't meant to be an officer. We were still friends (being young and hopeful, we agreed to disagree about some things) — we just lost touch with him.

Then, when Karen and I were out in the asteroids with Greg Noyce's old Belt Squadron, Grant turned up skippering his own private ship. He said he was a hunter of pirates. We actually thought that was a good thing — he'd be out there with us, not in the service but still on our side. We could count on him to do things DC couldn't do, go places where a frigate would be too obvious.

We vouched for Grant, and Greg trusted him because of our recommendations.

Then he'd started sabotaging us, and recruiting pirates. And then attacking ships from Imperial corporations that were supposedly trying to subvert the rights of free belt citizens. He fancied himself a freedom fighter, building his own little syndicate of pirates. Then he'd gone insane with the power, started attacking those innocent 'free' colonies. Of course, Grant's defenders — and there are far too many — say we're lying about that. They say he didn't attack the colonies — it was his pirates, refusing to obey his noble freedom-fighter orders.

Uh-huh.

I can tell you for a fact that Grant Merger was not a noble freedom fighter. Not a good man. Want to know how I can tell you that? Easy. He and I were very alike. *Very* alike. Similar in the way we thought and how we acted… we'd just been brought up in different situations. Funny how a different 'nurture' can affect how one's 'nature' plays out.

We're a lot alike, anyway. And he's not a good person because *I'm* not a good person.

As I sat there, frowning deeply and looking at Karen, I didn't know where that bastard was. He'd vanished after Greg and the rest of us had destroyed his fleet at Deep Black. All the same, I hoped like hell he hadn't joined up with the Martians.

I mean, how could he? They were an *Imperium*, an Empire by another name. He couldn't sign on with those bastards.

Even if it would explain a lot about how this little trap had been set. And about why it was so gruesome.

Karen slowly shook her head, "Don't worry. Can't be him."

She didn't sound convinced, and I knew I wasn't.

Great, the last thing we needed: more reasons to be skittish.

"I guess we'll see," I muttered and continued eating.

Chapter Seventeen

All Clear

For all the worrying we did, it seemed a day later that our fears were largely unwarranted. Sitting in *Wolf's* briefing room with Alicia Morgan, Andrew Jenson, Charlie, Rufus, Andrea and Karen, I was hearing that things on *Idaho* were checking out.

"We're warming the ship, the atmosphere is still reading clean," Alicia Morgan was giving the medical perspective, and I was nodding — along with Karen, Charlie and Andrea.

They'd swept *Idaho* from top to bottom, using atmoscans and surface samples to make sure no sort of passive chemical or biological weapon was present. There was nothing in the air circulation system or patched into it — all of the ducts had been visually cleared, *and* atmoscan sensors had been placed in the central conduits. Anything on the dangerous list would fire off a nice loud alarm through the ship.

"Engines check out. Nothing tied into the major power systems that could do harm... nothing at all tied in, I should say. We repaired the relays that Rufus... er... removed. Other than that, we can't find anything else wrong," Andrew Jenson's words seemed to come with a certain reservation, but they were still confidence-inspiring.

"Basically, we've looked the whole ship over... unless it's possessed with the soul of satan, it's probably safe to put people aboard," Rufus offered casually.

I tilted my head, "Satan? He's not going to get in my way. He learned his lesson last time."

Karen and Charlie both leveled glares at me.

"A bit predictable and *sad*," our intrepid Major wasn't going to let my poor offering get past the repartee standards committee.

I shrugged, "Well... he did."

Karen wasn't going to indulge me too much, so she looked back at Alicia, "You think it'd be safe to put people aboard?"

Our Doctor never took questions of peoples' health lightly — most doctors don't. Confronted with that basic question, she frowned and slowly began to nod, "I have a strange feeling about that ship. But we've been thorough."

Andy Jenson agreed with a nod of his own, "I'm creeped out by it. But that's part of the reason I'm confident. We're looking *very* hard for something wrong. We're not seeing it."

A silence descended over the table after Andy made his remarks, and everyone started looking at each other. I suppose under other circumstances it might have seemed funny, us all looking around at each other to confirm our thoughts.

It was decided. We had another frigate to bring home.

"Alright, we have a new ship," I said after that pause. "We'll start figuring out who to put aboard while your teams make sure it's ready for cruising, Andy. We'll also have to move some supplies across."

People began to nod, and Karen frowned, "Should we get *Artemis Agrotera* to move the supplies?"

This question haunts me, even today.

I shook my head, "Nah, be too tough for Zail to get a clean dock with *Idaho* until we get its engines running and its drift stabilized. We'll dock, move a skeleton crew over and start moving basic supplies. We can both top up afterward."

Because *Idaho* was drifting unpowered, it would have been very difficult for the massive *Artemis Agrotera* to securely dock with the frigate. For *Wolf*, much more nimble and about the same size, it would be much safer.

It was a very logical decision.

"I'll see to it," Andrea nodded, standing slowly. She seemed tense, but then so did we all.

"I'll get a list of the supplies *Idaho* will need, sir," Andy nodded, then came to his feet as well.

That was it, the meeting broke. Rufus and Alicia left right behind Andrea and Andy, so Karen, Charlie and I were left sitting alone at the briefing table.

"Bad feelings, anyone?" Charlie asked quietly.

I nodded, "Of course. But we all have them. The sweeps were thorough, the ship is safe."

I wanted saying it to make it so.

I also wanted to lighten the mood.

"Unless," I clutched my chin, "a squad of Martian-aligned *raccoons* is down in the bowels of the ship, ready to spring forth when we put a crew aboard."

Charlie scowled, "You promised never to mention that day!"

He then looked past me at Karen, "Back in the *Friendly* days, a crack squad of raccoons wearing mind control halos beat my team to its objective, and booby trapped the place behind us. Lost four people that day, and my favorite pair of pants. Still miss those pants..."

As his words trailed off, Karen applauded sympathetically, "He gets ten points for turning your joke into... *that.*"

I shrugged, "I don't know where he gets this stuff."

We shared a half-hearted laugh. Just as well we were getting them in while we had the chance.

CHAPTER EIGHTEEN

DOCKING

The process of docking two frigates together is not easy. Look on the front cover of this book and you'll see what I mean. Look at those angles… and you have to match drift direction, rotation and speed. Requires a sure and delicate hand, which is why Shelby McLaws personally took over the manual controls for *Wolf's* thrusters for the procedure.

You may have seen the footage, because by the time we were doing this link between frigates, both Jessica and Jocko were on the bridge, demanding (politely) to be let aboard *Idaho*. The bodies had been cleared, but they figured there was still a grim ghost-ship story to tell.

So, while Shelby wore a lady-like, confident-but-not-cocky smile, and complimented her co-helm operator with her southern grace, two camera crews were covering her. This footage, I'm pretty sure, is what made Defense Command Public Relations pounce on her when they saw it. Let's be honest, she's a beautiful young woman, she's completely capable and she's charming. She is, as the marketers say, the kind of woman 'women want to be, and men want to be with'. Well, they say something ruder for the last half of that slogan, but I'm not Daragh Ryan, so I won't use their foul words.

Anyway, that famous piece of footage of Shelby was being recorded, and as Andrea was supervising the docking procedure, Karen and I were being accosted by our eager correspondents.

"You have crew over there, out of their environment suits. It's safe enough," Jocko was the most determined. "We'll have an escort. We can carry atmoscanners if you like."

"Atmoscanners will do you no good if the ship starts to detonate and we need to do an emergency breakaway," Karen's reply was swift and smooth.

"We'll take that risk," Jessica insisted.

The fact that these two were growing personally closer was making them argue in tandem. But that was fine, because Karen and I could argue back in tandem.

"Until the ship is cleared of all possible dangers, we're only putting military personnel aboard," I'm sure I sounded firm and certain about that.

Jocko didn't look impressed, "You'll never clear that ship of *every* danger you can imagine. Look, just a few hours. Let us get some footage, we can cut that with the Special Branch feeds you gave us… we'll even stay close to the lock."

"No," I said it flatly.

"Come on," Jocko insisted a little more.

Jessica remained quiet, watching my expression.

I don't know what was going through my head at that moment. I looked at Karen, and her resolve was clearly starting to crack, "Well, I have to go over to see if it's suitable to put passengers aboard…"

"We could be guinea pigs!" Jocko seized the tiny opening.

Karen, I should explain, was going to check out the cargo bays to see if they had been sufficiently cleaned for us to turn them into living quarters without violating the Ceres Accords. No, we weren't going to be putting civilian passengers from Io in *Idaho's* hull, but we were strongly considering moving a few hundred prisoners off *Artemis Agrotera* into the ship, and locking them in the hold. That would free up more space on the storeship — space that would allow us to move civilians off warships. *Artemis Agrotera* was more spacious anyway.

Well… it wouldn't be *too* dangerous…

"Kyle, get over here," I gave up and called for my officer commanding SF. As he hurried up behind me from his station at the operations consoles, I glanced back toward him. "Get a team together. Carry atmoscanners and breathers for everyone in case something gets released. You're accompanying Jocko and his crew aboard *Idaho*."

Kyle nodded, "Aye sir."

Jessica started to smile, then realized she hadn't been named as one of the people going aboard. She opened her mouth to protest, but my hand flew up to halt her, "No, you stay. One at a time. If something goes wrong over there, I don't want to be accused of trying to kill both the reporters I took with me to Jupiter. Just the loud, ugly one."

Oh. Ha. Ha.

Jessica scowled but offered a grudging nod. She'd still get aboard, just later… and besides, she could probably coerce good footage out of Jocko, if it came to that.

Without further words, the reporters left Karen and me alone, so we strode up next to Andrea and watched on the main screen as vid feeds from orbiting Starlights showed *Wolf's* long docking column reach out to connect with *Idaho*. It was like watching ballet in zero gee.

Karen looked over at Shelby and then nudged me, "She's going to be famous, that pretty smile matching up with that pretty flying."

"I've seen prettier of both," I whispered back.

Karen smiled and — I swear — nearly blushed, "I'll take that as a compliment."

"I didn't mean you."

That got me an inconspicuous elbow in the side.

"Aw come on," I continued to whisper. "Just kidding."

"I'm sure there are other, better looking people out there who appreciate my charms," Karen bantered right back.

"I hear Shelby's pretty, you could try your luck with her," I chuckled.

Pausing with mock thoughtfulness, Karen narrowed her eyes at the southern belle, then purred, "She *is* pretty."

We both chuckled — it was a little light banter, reasonably typical for us.

It was the last light banter we did before Karen went aboard *Idaho*. I've always remembered it word for word, inflection for inflection, because of that.

"We have dock… now," Shelby punctuated her announcement with a glowing smile to the cameras. Even standing there, we could hear the DCPR officers melting in their seats and searching for Shelby's agent. Recruits would flock to Defense Command!

I swear, that woman's smile won the war for us.

Wolf and *Idaho* were linked in space.

CHAPTER NINETEEN

WORRYING ABOUT THE WRONG THING

A few hours later, Karen and a number of ratings were going through the cargo bays in the lower decks of *Idaho's* neck, while Kyle Stranks took Jocko Kent and his three camera girls around. All told, about ninety people were aboard *Idaho*, moving around freely without environment suits as the ship reached a comfortable temperature, and the atmospheric plants started running.

We were, needless to say, watching every power relay and atmospheric duct with insane vigilance.

Supplies were also starting to move from *Wolf* to *Idaho*, the first (rather important) one being fresh water.

A little more on that, because some people still don't seem to realize that having fresh water tanks aboard a ship is a good thing. Sure, you can have a closed system in which all moisture is reclaimed and funneled into your drinking system, but it's always a good idea to have a surplus.

When Lieutenant Sheldon Kong, one of Andy's engineers, led a team down to the three massive water tanks near the cargo bays, he found that each sealed container was reading empty. As such, we had to run a good old-fashioned water hose from the nearest outlet aboard *Wolf* into a direct line to the tanks. The water system was sealed from central control, and the water started pumping over to *Idaho*.

Crew were also using the oldest Naval method around — a human chain — to toss crates of foodstuffs up from *Wolf's* hold into the chute, where it was floated through to *Idaho*. We were very efficiently getting the ship loaded up with the essentials.

So, getting back to the narrative, let's join Jocko.

Kyle Stranks was leading the party of Jocko, Summer and Destiny through *Idaho's* crew deck, with Bunny and two other SF bringing up the rear. There were still some stains on the deck around here — bodies that had been mushy when they'd been chopped up and dumped for our benefit had left their mark. They were sure to get those spots on camera.

Sorry, that probably sounds horrible, but then I bet you've seen that footage. I bet it even stuck with you. One of the 'real' horrors of war.

"We should get a look in a cabin," Jocko said somberly, stopping near a door.

He then coughed very slightly, and sniffed the air, "Couldn't do anything about the smell?"

Alright, you're in a ship that you're *convinced* still might have a booby trap, and you hear a comment like that, what do you do?

"Breathers on!" Kyle barked immediately, and the reporter and the ladies with the camera and sound gear all rolled their eyes and did as they were told, as did the SF guards. After putting on his own mask, Kyle quickly lifted his atmoscanner and ran a check of the local air.

Wait for it... all clear.

"Alright... masks off," he said after a pause.

"I've smelled dead people before," Jocko shook his head. "Always makes me cough."

Kyle looked skeptically at the reporter, "We're not taking any chances."

"I noticed. But could we get some air fresheners in here?"

Kyle didn't budge at the joke. He was thinking of these smells and stains as the last lingering remnants of brave men and women who'd been killed in the line of duty. If it smelled bad, that was just the way it was. Him having to deal with the smell was a lot less difficult than them having died to create it.

Bunny coughed.

Kyle started to bark 'masks on!' but stopped as she turned away and vomited on the deck, "Sorry... I haven't smelled dead people before."

"Masks on!" Kyle barked as soon as her words trailed off.

Bunny wiped her mouth on her sleeve and pulled her mask on, "I'll keep mine on, I think."

Everyone else put their masks on again, and Kyle ran another atmoscan. Clean.

Jocko chuckled and prodded Bunny gently, "You're such a girl."

"You'd like me better if I was butch?" she asked innocently.

He laughed, and as Kyle ordered masks off, they continued down the corridor, looking for a room to enter.

"Water getting pumped in?" Karen had been walking by the hatch to the water-control chamber when she'd noticed the water hose, so she stuck her head in.

Lieutenant Kong nodded, "Yes ma'am. Tanks were completely empty when we checked them."

Karen flashed a smile, "Suppose we need to drink something."

The Lieutenant nodded, smiling back, "Yes ma'am."

With a parting nod, Karen moved on, leading her team of ratings to the next cargo bay.

"They cleaning the decks, ma'am?" one of the ratings behind her asked the question cautiously, and Karen stopped.

"Why?"

"You smell that... like grass or something? Smells like the scent they put on disinfectants."

Alright, you're on a ship that you think is booby trapped, and someone says they smell something 'grassy'. There's no grass on a ship, so what do you do?

"Masks, let's be safe," Karen pulled on her mask and her team did the same. One of the women with her pulled out an atmoscanner and ran a check.

All clear.

Sensing a theme here?

"Alright, off with the masks," Karen said, then pulled hers off. "You're probably right."

And just to be safe, she pulled out her comm, "This is McMaster... someone scrubbing the decks in *Idaho* with a scented disinfectant?"

There was a pause, then a sheepish answer, "It smells like pines, ma'am."

Karen frowned, "I don't smell anything. Where are you?"

"In the neck, four decks over the cargo holds, ma'am," the voice came back.

Raising her own atmoscanner, Karen ran another sweep of the local air, and it registered as clear, "Alright, thanks."

She then looked at the rating who'd detected the smell, "Grass? You sure?"

He scratched his chin nervously, "Uh. Could be pines, ma'am... I was born and raised on Venus Four... I ain't never smelled no real grass."

Karen smiled, "Great. I thought everyone was taught the Earth olfactories in high school."

He shrugged, "I didn't like science."

Taking no offense at the slight against her chosen field of interest, Karen chuckled and bobbed her head towards the next bay, "Come on."

They went on with their inspection.

"That's better," Jocko stepped into the cabin and took a deep breath. The stench of death wasn't so strong in here, and as Bunny stepped in she bravely took off her mask and breathed a deep sigh of relief.

The girls chuckled at her, and Kyle dutifully raised his scanner and tested the atmosphere in the room.

"Clear," he reported firmly.

Jocko laughed, "I swear, Kyle, you're going to take a reading with that thing and it's going to trip a scan sensor and detonate a bunch of mines or something."

Kyle froze in place, eyes slightly widened.

Could it...

Jocko roared with laughter, and the girls joined in. Poor Kyle, for so many reasons.

He put away his scanner and grumbled, "Just get your reccies. Be respectful, this was a person's home. Maybe one of those stains out there."

Appreciating the gravity behind Kyle's words, Jocko nodded, "Alright, alright."

The camera started moving through the quarters. Evidently, one of *Idaho's* Lieutenants had lived here, and she'd been interrupted in the middle of her sleep shift when whatever had happened went down.

Her ship fatigues were still in her closet, and a bloody pajama shirt was on her bed. Her mag holster was also out, the mag missing. If I had to guess, I'd say she heard boarding alarms, got out of bed, opened her hatch, and was shot in the arm (or something else not lethal) with a full power mag bolt as soon as she emerged. She stumbled back into her room, pulled her mag holster out of her closet, tore off her bloody pajama top, tugged on her uniform tunic and went out to help repel boarders.

She died out there.

Then her body was mutilated so it would look as though she'd been cut to ribbons by that 'alien'.

Jocko and the crew swept the cabin with their cameras, being sure to find the sympathetic imagery — a teddy bear that Bunny rescued from the closet (along with the Lieutenant's name, which I'm not including at the request of her family) so she could return it when she got home.

"This'll work," Jocko nodded, then looked at Kyle. "We're good."

Kyle nodded, and the crew left the cabin minutes later. This time Bunny was able to brave the smell without her mask.

So, nothing too terrible so far. Just a lot of worrying that something nasty might be in the air. I don't know why we were fixated on atmospheric problems, but we were. If only we'd known then what we do now.

Well, we didn't, so I best stop playing coy. New chapter.

CHAPTER TWENTY
BLINDSIDE

I met Karen at the lock as she came across from *Idaho*.

"Looks fine over there. We're getting the decks cleaned... still stinks, but I think the POWs are entitled to smell that."

Her words were unsympathetic without being harsh, and I nodded, "Agreed. They can put up with a smell. They won't have nearly as bad a time as the people who created it."

She nodded again, then coughed.

I frowned instantly, "Breathe in any deadly toxins over there?"

What can I say, we were hyper-sensitive.

Karen laughed, then smiled brightly, "If I did, Martian nerve gas just isn't what it's cracked up to be."

I smiled, "Good. Well, I'm on the bridge. You cleaning up before you join me?"

She nodded, "Crawling around stinking cargo bays hasn't improved my natural essence."

"No, it really hasn't," I grinned, then turned and headed away.

Now, if this were a movie, we'd cut to a scene of Karen stripping down and getting into the shower. Depending on the rating of the movie, she'd either do it modestly, sexily, or downright trashily. However, it won't surprise you that I'm going to cut somewhere else.

Jocko was satisfied with his footage, so he, Kyle and the camera crew were on their way back to the lock.

"So, you taking Jessica right back in?" the reporter asked the SF officer, and Kyle shook his head.

"I'll wait until they clean the decks up here. Should have it done in an hour or so, so tell her to be ready," Kyle came to a stop next to the chute that headed back to *Wolf*, then gestured broadly for Jocko to cross.

With a smile, the correspondent gave Kyle a manly handshake, "Thanks, buddy."

"Any time," Kyle was slightly resigned in his answer, but did offer a genuine smile in return.

Jocko and his crew returned to *Wolf*.

"First tank is full," one of the spacers working with Lieutenant Kong reported, closing the valve on the end of the water hose and pulling it off the port to the tank.

Kong was frowning as he knelt next to the valve on the second tank, "This one seems to be stuck."

They connected the hose to the tank and tried to open the valve into it. It wasn't budging — it was as though it had been welded shut. Being good engineers, though, Kong and his spacers didn't give up easily. First they used the classic method for moving jammed levers: a crow bar.

Still didn't budge.

"Alright, I'll go in through the top, see if I can unjam it from in there," Kong finally gave up on the brute force method.

"You sure, boss?" one of his ratings asked with a grin. "That alien the Branchers tangled with could have laid eggs in there. They could come after you."

Kong laughed, "Yeah, then I'd be famous, wouldn't I? They could take me over, make me their agent for communication with humanity!"

The spacers laughed, then helped Kong onto the ladder that ran up the side of the huge tank. At the top of the sealed enclosure was an access hatch for problems just like this one.

"Don't start the water until I'm *out*, okay?" Kong grinned as he popped the hatch.

One of the spacers tossed him a salute, accompanying it with an unconvincing, "Yessir."

Kong opened the hatch and pulled out his flashlight, pointing it down to the bottom of the container.

"A couple of shallow puddles, and a half dozen alien eggs," the Lieutenant said seriously.

The spacers quieted, one bravely asking, "Really, sir?"

"No," Kong laughed, leaning down to look around and make sure the tank was clear of anything that might explode.

Then his eyes started to get itchy, and he coughed.

"Stale air in here. I'm putting on my mask–"

He coughed again, violently, and his foot slipped off the rung. He'd been leaning over the edge of the tank, looking down through the hatch. Losing his footing dropped him stomach-first onto the rim, knocking the wind right out of him. He lost his balance and went head first through the hole.

The spacers reacted instantly.

"Masks!" one of them barked. The stale air probably meant nothing, but it cost nothing to be safe.

They scrambled up the ladder in a flash, and then immediately climbed down into the water tank, dropping to its floor next to the fallen Lieutenant Kong.

He was hacking and coughing violently, blood starting to come out as he did. His right hand was palm-down in a puddle, and as he pulled it away to bring it to his throat, one of the engineers saw something abnormal about it, and grabbed Kong's wrist. Shining his light on it, he saw a massive dermal burn.

Engineers are smart people, and they instantly started putting things together. The puddles all around them weren't water.

"We need a medical evac from the water chambers," one of the ratings roared into her comm. "We also have an unknown chemical contaminant down here! Isolate the ship!"

Karen was pulling on her ship fatigues when the emergency signal came over her comm, and she froze with her arms extended up over her head as she pulled her shirt on.

She stayed like that for a moment, then finished pulling on her shirt and sat on her bed.

Her heart rate climbed, and her breathing increased.

Trust bad feelings. Always trust bad feelings.

Chapter Twenty-One

Panic

I had been talking to Andrea when the call came in, and without thinking or saying anything to end our conversation, I immediately left the bridge. This was, for the record, the most irrational and *stupid* thing I could have done. Didn't matter, though, I was doing it.

Andrea watched me go, was certain she knew what I was doing, and didn't try to stop me. She was herself suddenly frozen, her heart rate climbing.

I haven't talked much about Andrea's state of mind in this book — I've just said it hadn't changed, and that's true. Remember how she'd been stable on *Wolf* before because it was an elite crew, people she could trust and be comfortable with? Remember how she'd become enraged when *Lion* had been severely damaged and its crew irradiated because (as far she was concerned) *Dominator* had been slow to join the fight?

Well, the same sort of anger started to loom within her, because *Wolf's* crew was her crew, and what she heard in that signal was pretty clear: someone had set a trap for her crew.

But she remained frozen in place on the bridge, because she didn't yet know exactly what was going on. Once she knew, then she'd react.

Alicia Morgan was in her environment suit and across the chute into *Idaho* so fast most of the security crew getting set to close our airlock hatch were surprised. She and her team got down to the water control chamber with all possible speed, and when they got there they found Kong on his back on the deck, rasping for every breath.

Through a feat of strength and determination, the engineers had hauled him up, out of the tank without ropes or counter-grav, then gotten him to the deck and closed the access hatch. They were all wearing masks, but two of them had contact burns on their hands from touching puddles in the tank.

As Alicia swooped in, she had her medical atmoscanner going. Her heart racing, she stopped to take a reading as her personnel moved to Kong's side.

The scan, which detected *all* Schedule 1 and Schedule 2 contaminants, and any derivatives of those compounds, came back clean.

You're probably thinking that the answer was obvious: we must have left something off the register. But those Schedule 1 and 2 lists are put together by DCI and DC Medical — *everything* we know about bio- and chemical-weapons is in them.

And we knew more than the Martians. We had ways I can't disclose of knowing we knew more than the Martians. There was *no way* the Martians could have invented something new that wasn't recognized on the Schedules…

"It's not showing up. Christ…" Alicia moved forward and dropped to one knee next to Kong. "Lieutenant, we're scanning you. Hold on."

He didn't. He died right there.

"Christ," Alicia repeated the word. "Alright, we need to get everyone out of here. Breathers stay on. Brooke, I need you to go back to *Wolf* and start a decontamination routine. We need to get all our people off this ship and into isolation in one of our cargo bays, right now. Rest of the team, get a counter-grav stretcher and let's get him up to *Idaho's* med bay. We autopsy here."

That was a whirlwind of orders, so I'll repeat and explain a little: something in that tank had killed Lieutenant Kong, and they needed to autopsy him to see what. They didn't want to risk taking him aboard *Wolf* because he might contaminate the ship, but there were living *Wolf* crew members aboard *Idaho* who were still at risk. They'd be brought back to *Wolf*, decontaminated at the airlock, and put into isolation. That was a fairly standard protocol.

The medics got to work, while the engineers were quickly ushered out of the water control chamber.

I threw open Karen's hatch like an overdramatic idiot, storming in three steps before stopping at her upheld hand.

"No," she said simply, her eyes locked on the floor between her feet as she sat on the end of the bed.

I didn't listen. I should have listened, but it probably won't surprise you to know that I wasn't exactly thinking rationally right then.

I dropped onto my knees right in front of her and put my hands on her shoulders, "You showing any symptoms? Anything at all?"

She shook her head, looking up, "No, but that doesn't matter. I just contaminated you."

I scowled, got to my feet, and closed the hatch behind me, "You contaminated me when we met at the lock. There are worse things than being trapped in a room with you, even if you're a plague carrier."

Karen's gaze was already back on the floor as I sat on the bed next to her and rubbed her back in a futile bid to offer comfort, "This is bad to say, but whoever went down, it happened fast. You're probably fine."

"We'll see."

Her words were slow and quiet, revealing the tumultuous state of her mind. I decided not to try to sound like I knew more than I did. I sat and waited next to her.

Jocko and his crew were sitting in Jocko's cabin, reviewing the footage they'd gotten aboard *Idaho*. They hadn't heard the harried comm call, they didn't know there was a chance they were all going to die.

Then Andrea overrode Jocko's comm screen with her priority alert, "Jocko, we just had a man die on *Idaho*. Something chemical, they're saying. You and your crew are to stay locked in your cabins… in your *cabin*, by the look of it… until we know more. You may be contaminated."

Picture that for a minute. You're sitting down, looking at your big vid screen, doing something mundane or even slightly exciting, and suddenly a signal cuts in telling you that you might have been exposed to something lethal.

Silence was Jocko's reaction, and after a few gasps, Summer, Destiny and Bunny were quiet too.

Alicia Morgan wasn't gentle as she helped her team heft the deceased Mister Kong up onto the surgery table. She was cautious as she pulled a scalpel off a nearby tray and started cutting, but not too cautious. As she told me later, she wasn't exactly following strict clinical protocols because she was in a hurry.

Anything that could kill a man that quickly after acute exposure and *still* not turn up on Schedule 2 was scary. That should have meant she took her time, but she didn't. Maybe that means she's a bad doctor, maybe it means she's a good doctor. I'm not qualified to judge, I'm just glad she went in fast and hard.

"Pulmonary edema… Jesus, look at this. His lungs…" she lifted one of the destroyed lungs from Kong's chest.

"What can cause rapid-onset pulmonary edema?" one of her medics asked, and she shook her head, continuing her work.

"Any of about fifty compounds… all of them on Schedule 2. Dammit, what is this…"

As she was looking at the organs, one of her team was checking out the burn on Kong's hand, "This looks like… frost bite. Contact burn from something he touched in that tank."

Continuing her rapid examination of Mister Kong's body, Alicia nodded, "Get blood, start running it for every sort of toxin you can think of."

Her medics continued to work as fast as she did.

Karen had her elbows on her knees, and was holding her forehead in both hands as she stared at the floor between her feet. She just sat and stared, keeping her breathing even and calm.

Her calm was as goddess like as she was.

I kept my hand gently on her back, but the waiting was killing me. It hadn't really sunk in that I might have exposed myself to a serious, nasty chemical weapon. Even if it had, I don't know if I'd have cared just then.

I can't adequately describe what was going on in my head. I suppose I'll have to get better at articulating just what I was thinking and feeling… I'll work on that. But, well, it was *Karen*. I defy any of you to have someone so close to you put in such nasty-seeming danger and *not* to respond as rashly as I did.

Well, many of you would probably keep your head. But as I think we've seen so far over the course of this year, I wasn't good at letting my mind retain control anymore. I was too damaged after Egesta, and too poor a specimen to begin with.

Those are my excuses, anyway.

What would I do if I lost Karen? That was the first time the crushing weight of that question really hit me. Without her, would I be able to stay balanced out here, in this war?

You know the answer, obviously.

But I didn't know — not then. So I wondered. And then I realized I needed to stop wondering and try to get more information, so I pulled my comm from my belt, "Andrea, what's going on?"

There was a pause, then Andrea's voice came back, "Alicia is opening him up now. It's Lieutenant Kong. He was in water control. We're pulling our people off and through decontamination. They're going into quarantine in bay five."

When Andrea said 'Kong', I could feel the muscles in Karen's back tense up under my hand, and her head tilted down so that her fingers could slide into her hair, get a grip, and tug at it. She let go after a second, then rubbed her eyes.

"What?" I leaned close and asked softly into her ear.

"I was in the room with him earlier. Good man, dammit," she whispered, her eyes jammed shut.

I leaned away slowly, then spoke into my comm, "Karen saw him earlier. What decon protocol are they using?"

Andrea paused and checked, "Number two. Shower and clothes change. They don't know what it is yet."

Karen smelled freshly showered… if that doesn't sound weird. And I could see a sealed bag with her uniform from her sojourn aboard *Idaho* over next to her laundry hamper.

"Alright, we've got that done. We'll stay here and wait for news. Patch me in with Alicia as soon as she reports," I closed the communication quickly, then holstered my comm and whispered, "Alicia's on it."

Karen nodded, and we continued to wait.

CHAPTER TWENTY-TWO

THE CULPRIT

"Nothing," Alicia Morgan nearly spat the word as she turned away from Kong's body, laying down her scalpel. "Anything in the blood tests?"

Her question was directed at the medic who'd drawn blood from the Lieutenant's body, and was now standing at a nearby scanner with it.

"Nothing conclusive," that man shook his head. "Low PaO2, that's it. Nothing reading as invasive on the scope."

That was obviously not what Alicia wanted to hear. Essentially, she'd cut open Mister Kong in a rush, taking risks and breaking protocols in hopes of finding out what had killed him, and what was endangering the rest of *Wolf's* personnel... and there was nothing conclusive.

She started to grow more concerned. If this chemical agent wasn't on our Schedule 2 chart, and it was doing this much damage, it had to be a totally new weapon — something that DCI and DC Medical somehow hadn't seen coming. She couldn't even *see* it... how was she going to cure it?

For now, she'd have to start worrying about the other crew members who'd been exposed. Some of the engineers who'd pulled Kong out had shown contact burns on their hands... they might be next. Perhaps their lower grade of exposure gave them more time. She'd have to get back to *Wolf* and start checking their symptoms.

Hopefully, she'd find something...

Andrea interrupted Alicia's thoughts, her voice coming over the comm, "Any news, Doctor?"

Shaking her head as though Andrea could see her, Alicia heaved a sigh, "Sorry, ma'am. Nothing. Lieutenant Kong died of massive pulmonary edema... looks like the work of a chemical agent, but I don't know which one. It's not on Schedule 2..."

"Not on the Schedule?" Andrea didn't quite contain her surprise. "Any signs at all of what it's doing to our people?"

"Low PaO2 readings in Kong's blood, ma'am... his respiratory system was taken down. We can start testing our exposed people for signs of that... maybe we lucked out and he was the only one to inhale whatever he did."

That sounds like a terrible hope, really... but then, Alicia had every right to entertain it. If we got away from our brush with this new agent with only one man dead, we could count ourselves lucky.

Unfortunately, she wouldn't be right. About any of what she was thinking, respiratory failure aside.

I hadn't moved from Karen's side when Andrea's voice came over my comm, "Ken?"

I pulled my comm out of my belt and held it up, "Right here. Give me some good news, Andrea."

She paused for a moment — just long enough for Karen to slowly raise her head and take a deep breath — and then repeated what Alicia had reported. Respiratory failure through massive pulmonary edema. Translated into regular speak, Kong's lungs had been somehow damaged and they'd filled with fluid, drowning him.

Karen looked back down as she heard the diagnosis, still managing to control her breathing through a feat of self-control beyond most mortals.

"Nothing on the schedule?" I asked the question softly, knowing Andrea would have already brought it up with Alicia.

"No," Andrea's answer was simple and cold. I could almost sense the chill that was coursing through her.

"Not on the Schedule..." I let out a sigh. "Keep us informed, Andrea. Send a medical team up whenever you need to check us for signs of respiratory failure."

I said 'us' and 'respiratory failure' without fully processing that I was in any danger, and that was probably just as well. Something odd was starting to occur to me.

Signing off, I slid my comm back into its position on my belt and then grabbed the remote to Karen's vid screen off the bed behind her. Turning it on, I pulled up a search window and began scrolling through data on Schedule 2 chemical agents. Whatever had killed Kong was not on this list, which meant it was either brand new... or *very* old.

See, this is the moment where the hours and hours of reading history books at the Academy tangibly paid off, and perhaps even saved a few lives.

Chemical agents that attacked the lungs were not new — far from it, some of the first chemical weapons ever used might fit that bill. Weapons that had been temperamental in their day, and that been abandoned before the Empire was even founded.

Mustard Gas? That was a blister agent that had seen some use in the First World War, doing a lot of harm... but nothing like this. No. Chlorine? Not likely... there would have been more symptoms, and I didn't know if it'd go after the lungs...

No symptoms.

Something came to mind from a lecture I'd once attended on the First World War battle of Verdun. A gas that was designed to have delayed effects against its target... what was it called?

Damned memory...

I pulled up a historical file on the Battle of Verdun — an epic attritional fight unlike anything we experienced in the Martian War — and started reading.

"Debut of metal helmets in warfare... draining of French Army assets..." I started reading quietly to myself off the screen, and my words drew Karen's attention.

Looking up with a frown, she noted the pictures and words on her screen, "You're thinking *old*?"

I nodded as I continued to read, "Worth considering, at least."

It was, because for once I was absolutely right about something scientific. As times to get things right go, this was a pretty damned good one.

My eyes fell on one word and I stopped reading.

"Phosgene."

Karen's frown deepened as her eyes swept over the text on the screen, trying to find the reference. Before she got there, I highlighted and opened the cross-reference file on Phosgene Gas.

There it was, all of it.

Phosgene was a nasty weapon on many levels. I don't understand much of the science of it (go figure) but I can tell you what it could do. Basically, in the First World War, they fired canisters of these chemical weapons at each other in artillery shells; the shell exploded and the gas spread.

By the time Phosgene came around, defending against gas attack was pretty old hat for both sides — soldiers were carrying gas masks at all times to avoid being overwhelmed by airborne poisons. Phosgene had been a creative German workaround to that problem: the gas was mostly odorless and colorless, and once inhaled, it didn't inflict its damage for many hours.

It was a heavy gas, four times the weight of plain air, so it stayed low, sinking into the trenches the war was fought in. That said, it hadn't proved terribly effective as a field weapon because it tended to disperse too much when not contained. It was hard to get enough concentration into a trench to do damage, so ultimately the weapon was abandoned. That's why it wasn't on Schedule 2 — no one had used it as a weapon for over a century before Defense Command even existed.

But that didn't make it any less lethal, if someone knew its history. Concentrating lethal amounts probably wouldn't be too difficult in an enclosed aboard-ship environment. When it got concentrated enough, it smelled like...

"Cut grass. It smells like cut grass..." Karen read those words in a whisper, then looked at me. "We smelled cut grass. We thought it was the scent on the cleaners they were using on the floor."

I stared at Karen as she said that. I stared and stared. Then I looked back at the screen, scrolling past the history of the weapon to its medical information.

Massive exposure led to death within minutes... pulmonary edema. Contact with Phosgene in its liquid form would cause frostbite-style burns. At temperatures over eight degrees Celsius, Phosgene turned into a gas that spread fast.

It all fit. It was Phosgene. The Martian bastards were spitting an ancient weapon at us because they *knew* it wouldn't be on our Schedule.

"Those bastards..." I wasn't exactly reserved in my commentary, but as I looked back at Karen she wasn't paying any attention.

"Exposure of two parts per million for eighty minutes can cause fatal edema within sixteen hours," she read the words quietly from the screen.

I looked back at the information with a frown, and then, at last, it clicked. Karen had been looking at those cargo bays for at least two hours. How much had she been exposed to?

As that registered, my mind ground to halt. I stared at the words 'fatal edema' and my head began to spin. I tried to force myself to think, to be coherent... it was a ridiculous, futile attempt.

I dragged my gaze back over to Karen, and her face was ashen.

"Symptoms may not even manifest for hours..." she said quietly. "It's like radiation. The latent period."

Remember the 'walking ghost' phase I talked about last book? Great, we had it again… this time for a totally different reason.

My hand on Karen's back slid across to her shoulder, and I pulled us together shoulder-to-shoulder. Her head tipped sideways to rest on my shoulder, and I leaned my cheek against the top of her head.

We stared at the information there for another minute. We should have called Alicia immediately, but we were both lost in the words.

My editors have asked me to be a little more clear about what Phosgene was, how contagious it was, and so on. Sorry I wasn't more explicit above… as I hope you understand, I wasn't thinking terribly rationally as I read those words in connection with Karen. And in repeating the scene, I'm only slightly more lucid.

Phosgene was a chemical weapon that was *not* contagious. You breathed it in, and the chemical sat in your lungs and slowly converted from 'carbonyl chloride' (no idea what that is, but it's what the information called it) into hydrochloric acid, which then damaged your lung tissues. If you'd breathed in enough, the damage to the lungs would be irreparable.

And there was no known way to stop the process from happening. Once Phosgene got into those lung cells, there was no getting it out. The only treatment was to deal with the symptoms — assist the victim's breathing, and if they lasted forty-eight hours, they'd probably recover.

That was the last 'current' medical advice on Phosgene, and it was from the early twenty-first century. Old school stuff. We, of course, had a better grasp of medical science, but that didn't help Alicia much. I'll explain that a little later.

Regarding exposure, I should let you know the parameters for a lethal dose. You know, having to talk about lethal doses of unseen killers in two consecutive books is not fun. Rest assured: the start of 2233 will see us leave behind these invisible blights…

Anyway, there were two ways to get lethal exposure to Phosgene (as there seem to be with most silent weapons): you either got a whole lot at once, or absorbed small amounts over a long period of time.

Kong had absorbed a lethal dose when he went into the water tank, because (and I should get to this later too) that's where the bastards had put the Phosgene (in liquid form). But it had been released throughout *Idaho*, *not* through the atmospheric system that we'd been so carefully monitoring, but through the *water* system. More on that later, too.

What all this meant was simple: chances were that everyone aboard *Idaho* had been exposed… there was just no way to tell who got how much in their lungs. Karen had smelled the grassy smell, which meant she'd definitely breathed in some. But, remember, Jocko had commented on the stench of death. Throughout most of the ship, the soft, often undetectable scent of the Phosgene had been masked by death.

That, I would guess, is another reason they'd set that gruesome scene for us.

Anyway, to wrap this chapter up, let me make this clear: anyone who'd been on *Idaho* had been exposed to one extent or another. The question was who had been given a fatal dose?

Had Karen?

CHAPTER TWENTY-THREE
TRIAGE

"Something that old?"

Jocko's question was understandably quite incredulous, and I simply nodded in reply as I paced past the foot of his medical bed. Now that we knew what we were dealing with, Alicia was rapidly switching from quarantine to triage — there was no need to isolate the exposed people from the rest of the crew, because Phosgene wasn't contagious.

Now we just had to force everyone who might have been exposed to stay in bed for a couple of days, and if (when) they started exhibiting symptoms, we'd have to try to keep them from dying.

Well, that was perhaps overdramatic, though not by too much: we didn't know for certain that anyone aside from Lieutenant Kong had been exposed to fatal levels of Phosgene, so there was hope...

Yeah, *hope*.

There were about ninety members of *Wolf's* crew to look after, so bedding arrangements for most had been made down in bay five, where they'd been quarantined in the first place. Only a dozen cases were in the med bay where I now stood, and these included Jocko (obviously), his camera crew, their escort, Kyle Stranks and Karen.

Alicia was moving from bed to bed, setting up vitals sensors to track their blood gases, and to examine their lungs for signs of damage from the Phosgene. The detectors were in place, we'd just have to wait for symptoms to manifest.

But we were only two hours from the end of their periods of exposure. That meant we might have quite a wait ahead of us.

"I'm going to start all patients on steroids, it might help," Alicia made that announcement almost offhand, and as she said it some of her medics began setting up IVs of the drugs for the patients in the bay.

I had no idea what good steroids would do, but I trusted that Alicia knew.

"How soon did you say we'd see the symptoms?" Jocko was handling his anxiety well, I have to say, and he didn't stop being a reporter as he did. Questions had to be asked, and answered.

"According to our info, it could be anywhere from three hours to forty-eight hours. After forty-eight, you're off the hook," I said quietly.

"If it's three hours, we're dead," Jocko's reply was frank — too frank for Summer, who broke into tears at the harsh words.

If I were lying where she was right then, I may well have done the same.

"If it's sixteen hours, you could still be dead," I didn't really help with my own frank words. "There doesn't seem to be any *real* correlation between how long you go symptom-free and whether you live..."

"If we're still fine by this time tomorrow, we'll probably live through this," Karen made that observation from behind me, her tone soft and almost resigned.

I turned to face her, and instantly her eyes found mine. I had never, up to that point, seen such a look in Karen's eyes. I don't know if I can describe it... she was terrified, and yet forcing herself to hide it from everyone but me.

Can you blame her for being terrified? I've said so often that Karen was superhuman... goddess like, really. But she was now being confronted by the human curse of mortality, in a mode entirely different to those she'd dealt with so many times before.

I don't know if this'll make sense to everyone, but let me try to explain: when Karen and I stormed a pirate house, or fought against raiders in our planes, or commanded battles from our bridge, we had some control over our fates. Chance might step in and let a Martian or pirate land the killing blow, but we at least had a chance to resist and evade — to try to save ourselves.

For someone like Karen to now be at the mercy of a toxin in her lungs — to be helpless before the actions of some damned ancient weapon...

We weren't built for this. We were people who needed to see our enemy, be able to fight our enemy.

Now we'd been robbed of that chance.

So Karen lay silently in her medical bed, and we stared at each other as time crawled slowly by.

While Karen and I stared at each other, Andy Jenson personally led a team in environment suits back across to Idaho. Nearly half his engineering staff was in bay five, waiting for their lungs to flood, and Andy was in a bad way because of it. As far as he was concerned, this was his fault — something he should have caught.

Of course it wasn't, but no one could convince him of that. Not with half his staff waiting to die.

So he and a picked team started going over Idaho with yet another fine-tooth comb. This time they knew where to start: the water control center, with its tanks of Phosgene.

"It must have been stored in these as a compressed liquid," Andy observed as he walked between the giant containers. "The ship was cold when we got here... when we warmed it up the shit evaporated and got into the system. That's why the tanks were empty when Sheldon checked them this morning."

He explained that for the benefit of his engineers, and later he explained it to me. It was a hell of a trap. Someone had figured that we'd check the engines for bombs and the atmospheric control systems for toxins... and had realized that we wouldn't think of something like the water supply system. Sure, we'd probably have tested the water for contamination once we started moving people aboard, but we wouldn't move people aboard until the ship was warmer than eight degrees Celsius, at which point the tanks would appear empty because the Phosgene had evaporated.

For all our caution, we'd played right into that bastard's hands.

Andy and his team moved on from the control center after about ten minutes of examination. For the gas to spread so effectively, it seemed clear that it had to be moving through the water pipes all through the ship, but that shouldn't have been possible: we'd closed that system when we began pumping in the new water.

Well, the bastard who'd planned this had been *very* clever.

Visual examination of all the valves and stoppers on the cargo deck revealed that *none* had actually closed. Someone had planted a bug in *Idaho's* operating system — a simple one that reported the water system to be closed when it wasn't. The result was... well, you know what it was. The Phosgene, as it evaporated, had spread out through the waterworks, pushing out into the shipboard air anywhere water would usually come.

The whole ship was hit, the bow pod worst of all because of the number of crew quarters (and thus water outlets) there. The spread was almost as complete as it would have been if the bastard had used the environmental control systems that we'd been so carefully monitoring.

It had caught us right out.

As Andy found yet another open water valve, he shook his head and cursed himself. It wasn't his fault, it wasn't really any of our faults. But at the same time it was. We all felt that we had to blame ourselves. And while we were feeling guilty, we had to continue working.

Jim Hannigan wanted to be in the medical bay, sitting next to Bunny's bed. As unlikely as a relationship between a blonde bombshell camera/sound technician and a communications specialist might be, those two had one — and, I found out during this day, a very strong one. They'd connected on many levels, and Jim really cared about Bunny.

But Jim had a critical job to do, and even Bunny had to take second place to it. Moving through the decks of *Wolf* with an atmoscanner, he was checking for any signs of Phosgene in our own atmosphere.

He wasn't alone in this mission, of course — *Wolf* is a big frigate, so he had most of the people from his department out with scanners, checking every corridor, cabin and crevice for any signs of the gas (now that we knew what to look for, we had programmed the atmoscanners to look for carbonyl chloride). All readings were coming up clear.

Of course, all the readings on *Idaho* had been clear as well, but Jim had cleverly gotten himself into an environment suit and taken the scanner he was now using across to the derelict frigate, where the new programming detected the Phosgene immediately. He'd created a quick-fix to the atmoscanner problem, but fleet R&D would still have to go back to the drawing board on the damned things.

That's a question my editors asked: why wouldn't the atmoscanners alert us to an increased concentration of a chemical they had the ability to detect? Simple: software. The atmoscanner was a small, handheld unit. To make it easier to use and more reliable, R&D hadn't developed it with the programming to scan and assess air quality, just to identify specific compounds and some derivatives. Up until this point, that had worked fine... we only ever used them to look for weapons we knew existed. It was an oversight — one, yes, that shouldn't have been made, but then, there are oversights like that all through Naval life. Sometimes the shortcuts get you killed.

Just ask the engineers from *Lion*, whose reactors were never shielded against surges from the secondary power grid.

Anyway, a clear reading on our decks boded well for us — it meant the gas hadn't managed to come through the chute that had linked *Wolf* to *Idaho*. That might sound a bit convenient, but there was a perfectly good reason for it: the chute was zero gee, and *Wolf's* atmospheric system was more powerful than *Idaho's*.

Think of it like two balloons, one slightly larger than the other, being squeezed and emptied so their air goes into a long tube. The air from one side doesn't have enough force to really bypass the air coming from the other side, and Phosgene, a gas heavier than air, would settle in the tube, not able to get pushed far enough.

At least, I *think* that's how the physics of it work. Whatever had happened, it had worked for us: the long, thin umbilical that connected the two ships had protected us from any serious contamination. Even if a few particles scurried across, they simply weren't enough to be a danger to the crew.

Good news.

The news from *Idaho* wasn't as encouraging, though: at that moment, the Phosgene had worked its way up to over fifteen parts per million in some areas. That amount of gas, inhaled for an hour, would likely kill a person. What we couldn't know, though, was how high the levels had been when our people had been aboard. The gas was spreading constantly, so the levels now had to be higher than they'd been... but how much higher?

No way to tell, and it wasn't something Jim could worry about — he had to take these readings...

Stopping before the hatch of the last chamber he'd assigned himself to scan, Jim took a deep breath, opened the door and stepped in. It was, of course, the medical bay. That's a privilege of being XO: you get to give yourself the plum assignments.

I looked over my shoulder as Jim came in, scanner held up in front of him, "A part per trillion in here. I think that's low enough to be safe."

"I'd say so," I concurred with his assessment as he approached. "They're probably all giving off a few particles. Tell Alicia the number, if she worries we might all end up in masks... but I doubt it'll come to that."

I gave those orders without too much thought, and then I looked back at Karen and tried to marshal a smile, "You're oozing Phosgene."

I don't know how that could have been interpreted as a light or funny comment, but I was smiling, and Karen wanted to be smiling too, so she laughed charitably.

"I have to say, that is probably the worst thing I've ever oozed," her answer was soft.

Jim lowered his scanner, then approached my shoulder, "I have people checking the whole ship. So far all we've seen are a few parts per trillion in bay five. We're cycling the air in that chamber through portable filters, and it seems to be catching the Phosgene."

I nodded, "Good. *Idaho*?"

Once the air got circulating aboard *Idaho*, the scrubbers in those two environmental centers *should* have filtered out the Phosgene — there was just so much of it that it'd take a while.

And there was a certain question as to whether we should even bother. Trying to save the frigate the first time hadn't gone well... what other surprises did *Idaho* have left in store for us?

That wasn't a decision for quite yet, though.

Jim looked past me at Bunny's bed, now, and as I realized he was no longer paying me any attention, I looked from her to him and noted their eye contact and their intense gaze. I'm sure if I was a more disciplined officer, I would have scoffed at *Wolf's* XO being at a lady's bedside while he was on duty… but I wasn't any better, was I? Since Kong had gone down, I essentially hadn't left Karen's side.

"Go on," I said quietly, and he nodded back.

"Thanks."

Jim went to Bunny's bedside, slipped both his hands around one of hers, and smiled reassuringly, "You'll be alright. Everything will be alright."

I watched Bunny's expression twist as she tried to decide whether to believe him, to pretend to believe him, or what. She seemed comforted, at least, that he was there.

I looked from them to Karen, and she was just looking from them to me. Again our gazes locked, and Karen smiled a slim, sad smile, then nodded. She knew I was no good at comforting people, but she knew too that I was there — and that, to her, meant a lot.

It had only been two hours since exposure for the people in the med bay. No one seemed sick… yet.

We waited.

CHAPTER TWENTY-FOUR

DEDICATED

You've undoubtedly seen the recordings Jocko took in hour three of his enforced bedrest. A few spacers were recruited to gather the correspondent's camera gear from his quarters and to bring it down to the med bay, because — as Jocko said to me — 'if I'm going to die, I'm at least going to get major awards for it'.

I had pulled up a chair next to Karen's bed as the camera was set up by the well-meaning spacers; Summer and Destiny explained what to do from their beds, using the distraction to keep their minds off themselves. It took a few tries to connect everything properly for the parabolic mics and such, but once it was set up, Jocko was ready to record his career-defining story.

"This is Jocko Kent aboard DCNS *Wolf*. Right now, I appear to be in normal health, but I have to report that I have been exposed to an ancient chemical weapon, left aboard a Defense Command ship the Jupiter Force found adrift yesterday. This weapon was clearly left as a trap for all Defense Command personnel who attempted to rescue that ship, and some ninety women and men are now under medical observation as we wait to discover how badly affected we all are," Jocko was sitting up in his bed for the whole speech, as I'm sure you've seen.

Waving his hand, he had the camera turn towards the beds of his crew, "Summer Mahoney, Destiny Philips, and Bunny Fox are my camera crew, and together we've been through some of the toughest battles in Imperial history. Earlier today, they were exposed to the chemical agent too. It is impossible to determine the level of our exposure, we just have to wait and see how sick we get, and how quickly."

The camera panned back to Jocko, "I may die today. I will attempt, though, to record for all you viewers as much information about this attack as possible, so that if I do not survive, this can serve as the last testament of myself and my crew, and so that it can reveal how far our enemy is willing to go. This is Jocko Kent, signing off for now."

On cue, the spacers switched off the camera, and Karen and I watched Jocko's face, then the faces of his camera crew, and we both marveled at the journalistic instinct they seemed to have, even now.

A few minutes later, Jessica Qing appeared in the medical bay with her own camera, though for some reason that didn't seem as opportunistic and self-serving as it might sound. She hurried over to Jocko's bed with a carefully controlled, impassive expression.

"How're your lungs feeling?" she asked directly, and Jocko shrugged.

"Right now, alright. Could start changing soon."

Jocko's frank assessment of his health drew a nod from Jessica, and then she bobbed her head towards her camera, "I guess you don't want to do an interview?"

He chuckled, "If I did and I lived through this, my director would kill me."

That drew a smile from Jessica, and as the sad expression crossed her face she discreetly reached down and squeezed his hand. They shared a moment all their own, then she turned towards us.

"Commodore McMaster, I'm sorry, but our viewers will want to know how it feels to be a victim of this sort of weapon," Jessica approached the foot of Karen's bed.

Karen stared at Jessica for a moment, her mind trying to decide just what to make of this request. She didn't want what could be her last hours immortalized on vid, but at the same time, if she answered the question, there was less chance that Jessica would bother other people with it.

Offering a slow nod, Karen sat up a bit in her bed, "Keep it short. And don't bother anyone else with the questions once you're done with me."

Jessica's eyebrows climbed slightly at the conditions, but she nodded. That was fine, having footage of Karen in a sick bed would more than make up for a shortage of other interviews. Sorry, saying it that way probably makes Jessica sound heartless, with a certain 'if it bleeds it leads' calculus governing her.

Well... I suppose there was some of that. But I couldn't hold that against her any more than I could Jocko's determination to record himself against him.

Jessica's camera crew got into position and framed Karen in their shot, and then she answered the questions. You've probably seen the footage.

"Commodore McMaster, I'm so sorry to hear that you've been exposed to this Martian chemical weapon. Can you tell us how you're feeling?"

Jessica's question was smooth, but Karen — for all that was going on right now — had a smoother answer, wrapped in a tired smile, "Right now, I'm feeling alright, Jessica. But from what we understand, the agent we're dealing with may not even cause symptoms for a day before it becomes lethal. All of us — myself and my crew who've been exposed — we're waiting now. We're all very anxious."

Of course, the tone Karen put on to say 'we're all very anxious' didn't seem anxious to anyone.

"How do you feel about the use of this sort of weapon?" Jessica's next question was pointed, and Karen's smile disappeared.

"We face the loss of our people in combat all the time, Jessica. You've already seen that. We try to fight our battles by the rules of the Ceres Accord, but sometimes rules get in the way... and at times like that, you end up with ninety people exposed to a chemical agent that never should have been deployed. I wish our enemy hadn't done this — hadn't broken the rules to get us. But I'm not surprised. I'm not surprised at all," Karen's answer wasn't quite a direct one, and Jessica noticed that instantly.

"Are you angry?"

Karen's chin sunk slightly, "I'm furious. But I can't do anything about my anger until I know I won't be dead by this time tomorrow. I hope and pray the rest of the people who've been exposed will recover. I don't want to see good men and women, my crew, die — especially not like this, unable to fight back."

Jessica nodded, then gestured to her camera man to open up his shot a little, pulling me — still sitting next to the bed — in frame.

"Rear Admiral Barron, this attack is a violation of the Ceres Accord. What do you think should be done in response?"

I should have expected a question to come my way, but as you've probably realized by now, I wasn't thinking clearly.

"What should be done?" I repeated the question with an edge. "I think I'll ask the Grand Admiral that, after we burn his fleet. Feel free to come along to ask him yourself, Jessica."

Jessica's eyes widened slightly in surprise, and Karen looked at me with a sharp 'watch it' expression, but imagine how much I didn't care.

Was I angry? Of course, I was bloody *furious*. I just had much less grace about it than Karen did. And if Garvey, or whatever bastard had taken over for him after Glorious February (I didn't know at that time) saw Jessica's report, I wanted him to know I was displeased.

Gee, would I go all maniacal and vicious if Karen died… if I lost her brilliant influence on my life?

Anyway, Jessica had what she needed, so with nods of thanks, she sent her cameras to take some B roll around the medical bay, while she returned to Jocko's side.

We sat and waited for another hour.

CHAPTER TWENTY-FIVE

IT BEGINS

Though the records showed that no cure or specific treatment had ever been found for Phosgene exposure, Alicia Morgan was determined to look for something to counteract the agent sitting in our people's lungs. However, unlike what you usually see in the movies, *Wolf* did *not* have some sort of magical chemical engineering lab aboard. We didn't have the equipment to start experimenting with the creation of a cure for Phosgene inhalation.

That was why Alicia was on the comm with Conrad Rhee from *Artemis Agrotera* when I slipped into her office. Her back was to me as she talked to Rhee on her screen, and I stayed out of the display's viewfinder range, so I wouldn't interrupt their conversation.

I have very little understanding of what they were talking about — they were bandying about words that I'd have needed four years of medical school to understand. I'll try to repeat as much as makes sense to me; sorry for the lack of detail.

"I do have the synth plant from the Io hospital," Rhee was nodding as I slipped in. "But to start from scratch... we could probably make it work over here. I have the space and the power, and I could scrounge the raw chemicals... but it'd take us days to go from concept to a drug ready for trial. And then we wouldn't have any way to run trials without injecting actual people."

Alicia's head was sagging, as she tried to nod. See, in so many movies, the brilliant doctors aboard ship at a time like this find the magic-bullet cure to the plague or whatever, then synthesize it and everyone is saved.

While I would have absolute faith in Alicia's ability to come up with a compound that could at least *help* our poisoned crew, she didn't have the equipment, or the *time*. That last one is critical, too. You don't just get an idea for how to fix something and then plug the formula into a machine. It takes time to synthesize, to blend, to produce high volumes of a compound...

It had been four hours since the last exposures aboard *Idaho*. There wasn't enough time to do any of that.

"What about trying to adapt something?" Alicia unfolded her arms and ran a hand through her matted, sweaty hair. "The Grendel Formula has to be close. It deactivates the chemical reaction in the alveoli."

"Yes..." Rhee started to nod, "we have stockpiles of that here... but we'll have to re-engineer part of the compound. You said the Phosgene converts into hydrochloric acid inside the lungs?"

Alicia nodded, "Yes, it's too late for us to stop that, but if we could deliver some sort of neutralizing agent we might be able to reduce the damage."

One of the Schedule 2 chemical weapons we did have a specific treatment for was called 'Grendel' (I guess because the chemist/weapons designer thought the name sounded cool). The weapon attacked pulmonary function in a way not dissimilar to Phosgene, going after the alveoli — the tiny sacs in your lungs that allow oxygen to pass through them into your bloodstream. Grendel did damage with an advanced corrosive compound that was almost instantly effective — breathe it in and the sacs burst within about five minutes, leaving you drowning in your own fluids. The Grendel treatment was thus designed to scrub the corrosive agent off without causing collateral damage... perfect for dealing with Phosgene.

Problem was, the compounds in the Grendel treatment shot were very specifically tailored to deal with biocorrosives — they wouldn't do a damned thing to something as crude as hydrochloric acid.

That said, having a base compound to work from would save a massive amount of time. Thanks to the lab equipment Rhee had liberated from the hospital on Io, he could start working on the Grendel compound, separating the chemicals that carried the cure to the alveoli from the actual scrubbers. Then he just had to come up with a new scrubber that would clean out the acid, and bond it with the Grendel carrier... easy.

Sure. Easy.

"I'll see what I can come up with. How long do we have?" Rhee was talking fast, and Alicia shook her head.

"I'm going to start losing the worst cases soon. A few hours, probably."

Rhee's mouth thinned to a tight line, "I don't even know if it's physically possible. But we'll do the best we can."

"Thanks Conrad..." Alicia turned and saw me. "Let me know how it goes."

The feed shut down, and Alicia came over to me, "I don't know... I don't think we can put anything together in time. And a rush job like this, I don't know if what we make will even be safe."

I studied the weary look on Alicia's face as she said those words. I don't think I've ever properly introduced readers to Alicia, but she was another young, dynamic, professional officer. Top of her class, Belt Squadron elite, and so on. She'd never encountered a medical case she couldn't come to grips with — she'd lost people, of course, but she'd always known what the trouble was, and what their odds were.

This one had blindsided her along with the rest of us, and the stress it was piling onto her shoulders was being revealed in the creases in her forehead, and the dark circles under her eyes.

"Do what you can," my reply was probably inadequate, but it was all I had. Obviously I wanted her to immediately come up with a magical cure — to inject Karen with something and send her on her way.

And, of course, to inject every member of *Wolf's* crew who'd been exposed with the same. That was a problem in and of itself... managing to create an experimental dose for one person might be vaguely possible, but *ninety?* That was a job for an experienced biochem lab, not for a team of doctors working with appropriated equipment in the belly of a combat storeship.

Anyway, I was going to say something more, but an alarm sounded outside the office, and without hesitation Alicia ran. I followed.

As we came to a stop in the center of the med bay, we saw that the observation panels over Summer's bed were flashing red, and we heard her hard, bitter coughing.

"Get a mask on her!" Alicia ordered instantly, and two medics arrived at Summer's bedside with an oxygen mask.

While that was done, Alicia pulled scans of Summer's lungs up on the screen over her bed, then softly swore to herself, "Shit... this is rapid. It's been four hours, right? Four and a half? She's going into respiratory failure. It's acute... get a spider into her throat, she's going to need all the pure oxygen she can get..."

She was giving those orders while already moving to the next bed over — Destiny's — and pulling up the same scans, "Almost as bad, you're getting a spider too. Christ, you must have gotten hit hard... all members of the camera team and escort need spiders right now!"

Medics started hustling, pulling the little robotic 'spiders' off a tray that one of them had pulled from a nearby cupboard. Dropping the eight-legged tiny bots into the mouths of each of the patients concerned, they attached oxygen tubes. The spiders then carefully guided those tubes down the throats of the patients, anesthetizing the throat lining along the way to stop gag and choking reflexes, and intubating them.

As the spider got into position in Summer's throat, her vitals began to stabilize — enough oxygen was getting into her lungs... for now. But this was just the first time the damage that had been caused was beginning to manifest. If there was more on the way, she wouldn't have a chance.

And neither would her crew.

"Wait!" I hadn't realized Jocko was struggling until he yelled sharply. I turned to him and he pointed at his camera, now sitting on a stand near his bed. "Someone record me!"

You might think that's ridiculous — a reporter always wanting to be on camera. But think about it from his perspective: this might be his last chance to report what was happening... his last chance to do his job. He didn't want to be robbed of it.

Without thinking, I walked over to the table, picked up the camera, turned it on him and hit record, "Go."

"No, we have to intubate *now*–" Alicia cut into the picture, but I stepped towards her.

"This could be his last chance, Alicia. He's earned a minute," I hear those words on the recording, but I don't remember saying them.

She looked at me and the camera, bit her bottom lip, then stood aside, looking at him tensely as he began to cough, and his lungs crackled.

"This is Jocko Kent, it's not looking good. Viewers, it's always been a privilege. To my family, and to the families of my camera team, we all love you. We're all sorry about this. So sorry. Mom, dad, Sam, Gwen... I love you all. I'm sorry. Goodbye."

He had started to lean up as he said that last line, then he began to wheeze painfully as he said his goodbye. His head dropped back to the bed, and seconds later the spider was dropped into his mouth and fitted with an oxygen tube.

I stopped the recording and put the camera down.

Then I turned to Karen, who was sitting up in her bed and staring at Jocko. Her jaw was clamped tight, her eyes a little wider than I'd ever seen them. She was determined not to panic, but damned if her brain didn't want to. I think we can all sympathize: you see what might be next for you, see how horrible it is... how do you react?

If you're Karen, you react with the grace I — we — knew to expect from her.

She looked from Jocko to me, opened her mouth, let out a breath, and then lay back. I came up beside her bed immediately, and leaned down close, "How're your lungs?"

Blinking a couple of times, and taking deep breaths, she looked at me again, "So far... so good."

I slid my hand under hers and sighed.

As I did that, Alicia hurried over and brought up Karen's chest scan, "Still clear. No edema started yet... your exposure was probably less than theirs, thank God."

Without further explanation, she turned and began to make her panicked rounds.

Five minutes later, doctors in cargo bay five called in to report seventeen patients with symptoms similar to Jocko's and Summer's, and another forty who were starting to get nasty headaches and less severe respiratory symptoms.

It had started.

Chapter Twenty-Six

Casualties

The next three hours — taking us out to seven hours from last exposure — were long and exhausting. On *Artemis Agrotera*, Conrad Rhee worked like a man possessed, using equipment he'd taken from the research hospital on Io to start splitting the Grendel compound, but as he feared, it wasn't fast work. Just splitting the agents in that existing compound took the entire three hours, and when it was done they had to start attempting to meld the carrier with a number of new hydrochloric acid neutralizers they'd selected.

That would take another three or four hours, if they were lucky.

In the med bay, all the members of the team that had gone around with Jocko started exhibiting increasing levels of respiratory damage, except for Bunny, who seemed to be in better shape than the rest. She'd been wearing her mask more, remember. She was too 'girly' to handle the stench of death.

She was still intubated, just to be safe, but while everyone in the beds on either side of her deteriorated, she lay there and watched, wondering when it'd happen to her.

Jessica came back to the med bay, but without her camera. She was standing next to Jocko, holding his hand, and unsuccessfully trying to restrain tears as her counterpart struggled to live. Jim Hannigan came down as soon as his duty shift ended, and sat with Bunny, holding her hand and trying to keep her calm.

Karen and I watched in silence.

Summer Mahoney died first. Her lungs were flooded as the alveoli were destroyed by the Phosgene. Alicia's team worked on her for ten minutes, trying to bring her back, but as that was happening, one of the SF from Kyle's escort team went into acute respiratory failure, and died as well.

Eleven minutes later, it was Kyle Stranks himself.

I did Kyle a great disservice by not mentioning him more in these past few chapters. He died with such honor that I should have said more, so perhaps I can correct that now. While he watched people panic, and while he had a tube shoved into his throat, he always made it clear to the medics trying to look after him that the civilians should be their priority.

The last thing he said to the medic who dropped the spider into his mouth was this: "If we start going at the same time and you have to choose, look after one of the them. It's my job to protect them."

You can call that blind, foolish devotion to duty if you like. Just make sure you don't say it anywhere close to me, Andrea, Charlie, or anyone else who would kill you in a duel for saying it. Kyle died hoping that some of the people he was supposed to look after would pull through. He died with quiet dignity, and all the honor befitting a Defense Command officer of his class.

His other SF guard went shortly afterward, leaving only Jocko, Destiny and Bunny alive from that camera team.

Bunny was beyond comforting as she watched this. She was getting enough oxygen to be quite lucid, so her hand was clamped around Jim's like a vice grip, and she was crying despite the tube in her throat. She'd lost one friend, two more were no longer conscious and were barely getting enough oxygen to live, and she was probably next.

A little more trauma than the average sound technician with a camera crew was used to seeing. She had every damned right to be upset.

Reports were coming in from cargo bay five as well: nine dead in the same time, all of them having had the bad fortune to be working in the same section of *Idaho's* bow pod that Jocko's crew had been going through.

Six more were in Jocko and Destiny's condition — barely hanging on.

Karen and I just watched.

What could we say? There have been a very few times in my life that I've felt totally helpless. This was one of them. There was nothing I could do to save these people — there was no enemy to fight, no way to cover them. They were dying from exposure to a chemical weapon so old we'd never bothered to create a treatment for it, and all I could do was watch.

Then Karen squeezed my hand, "Go to bay five. They'll need to see you down there."

Karen. God, what can you possibly say about Karen that's good enough for her?

I blinked a few times at her words, then nodded. Rising slowly from the chair next to her bed, I left med bay.

A minute after I walked out, Jocko Kent stopped breathing. Jessica called for Alicia, but knew as soon as the panels started flashing that he was gone. There seemed to be no coming back from this Phosgene poisoning. If it got you to the brink, you were probably going to die.

Jocko Kent, the reporter I'd come to respect despite his style, and who said his last goodbyes to his parents, ex-wife and son on camera, was gone. After all the battles he'd covered, all the stories he'd submitted from seedy pirate domes, all the action he'd witnessed, he'd been felled by a trap aboard a derelict ship.

When I arrived in bay five, the chamber was bustling. Medics were rushing from bed to bed as they tried to handle the large number of patients who were starting to manifest edema symptoms. It was nearly chaos, though some of the spacers who had been in the beds but were still feeling fine were on their feet, helping the medics however they could.

Those people were risking aggravation of their own lungs (rapid breathing from activity could apparently speed the Phosgene conversion), but they didn't care: they were helping their crew mates. To some of you, that probably sounds unbelievable. Again, this is a subject I will *gladly* fight a duel over: you want to get shot, try to argue that the crews of the Jupiter Force weren't in fact *great* people.

Anyway, as I started to move into the aisle between the beds in this bay, spacers started sitting up to nod to me, but I waved them down.

"How goes it here?" I asked as I walked, and deciding to show bravado before me, many tried to say it was fine.

That didn't work out so well because, at that very moment, one of the teams working on resuscitating a woman who'd gone into respiratory failure stopped trying.

"Need more hands down here?" I asked one of the medics as he rushed past, and he turned back to me and nodded once. "I reckon — any help we can get."

I pulled my comm from my belt, keying it to the bridge.

"Barron here, put out a general call to all off-duty personnel, we could use extra hands to help administer basic care in bay five."

I didn't wait for an answer from the internal communications tech who logged my message, just slid the comm back into my belt.

Seconds later, Andrea Kiley's voice came over the ship intercom, "This is the Captain. Our medical staff working with the personnel exposed to the chemical weapon on *Idaho* is spread thin. Any off-duty personnel who wish to lend a hand in basic care and monitoring, please proceed to bay five. I'm heading there myself. Kiley out."

I continued to pace between beds, not really sure what I was supposed to be doing. Was my simple presence supposed to make people with potentially fatal levels of Phosgene in their lungs feel better? I didn't know. They just smiled at me when I passed and nodded. Every one of them. I don't know why, they just did.

I tried to smile back. I patted some on the shoulder rather lamely. I occasionally said something pathetic like, "We'll get through this."

We. As if I was in the same state they were in. These people were heroes, bearing so well under their misfortunes that I have no words to describe their gallantry. We'd witnessed their quality when many of them had been saving lives on Egesta. Now we were seeing it again, and it simply never failed to strike awe into me.

And just to add to my speechlessness, both access hatches to bay five flew open a moment later, and the bay was flooded with off-duty personnel, and some on-duty personnel whose friends were covering for them. Nearly 200 people tried to get into the bay to help, so we quickly had to start sending some out. We'd keep sixty or so around, and rotate them through on shifts.

Among the new arrivals were Charlie and Andrea, both of them finding me as soon as they entered.

Andrea's face was gaunt, her eyes exhausted and yet somehow hard. She came up to me just to say hello, then moved on, talking to her crew in her softest, most soothing Irish brogue.

Charlie didn't move on so quickly, "How's Karen?"

I shook my head, "No symptoms yet. When I left, Kyle was gone. Summer too."

Major Peters stilled for a moment, and then nodded, "Kyle."

He didn't really say more than that — he didn't need to. Charlie had liked and respected Kyle Stranks, which was in itself a compliment from him.

"I swear," I shook my head slowly. "When he died, he was more worried about making sure Alicia didn't worry about him. Wanted her to focus efforts on keeping Jocko and the girls alive."

Charlie nodded again, his reply an exasperated whisper, "He was good."

We both took deep breaths, trying not to count the number of dead we already had. The number had to be in double digits by now. Then my eyes settled on the back of Andrea Kiley as she headed up the aisle, speaking to her crew.

"How is she?"

Charlie shook his head, "Haven't been on the bridge. Just now she looked…"

His voice trailed off. He didn't have the right word to describe what he was thinking, but I knew what he meant. She was close to snapping. I could just sense it.

This was worse for Andrea than being 'betrayed' by the crew of *Dominator*. Some Martian bastard had set a trap so underhanded that it had caught us all out, despite our best precautions, and now we were starting to fill body bags.

She was at this moment proving herself to be the powerful, loving, maternal figure to her crew… but how long before she went off?

"Keep an eye on her for me," I whispered that, to be certain no one overheard.

Charlie nodded once, "I will. Now, you've done your comforting for the crew. Get back to Karen. Let me know if her condition changes."

I like that he said 'if'. Almost made me believe she wouldn't be in a body bag by that time the next day.

I left the bay, nodding to the throngs of crew who'd come to lend a hand as I departed.

The officers and spacers of DCNS *Wolf* were looking after their own.

Chapter Twenty-Seven

The Next Stage

I got to the med bay as they were zipping a body bag up around Jocko. I stopped just inside the door and stared at that, then shook my head and closed my eyes. We were losing so many people… it was like a nightmare. Jocko Kent was a reporter — he was supposed to be immune to death.

Not really *immune*, obviously, but he wasn't supposed to die. If he got sick, we were supposed to be able to save him, to prove how good we were at our jobs, or to win his respect… you know how it goes in the movies.

But he'd died, just like the spacers and officers down in bay five were dying. Just the way Summer had died, Kyle had died.

I opened my eyes and refused to think about that — the same way I'd shut out casualties in a battle, I shut out thoughts of who we'd lost. There were still people waiting for their symptoms to surface, and until we knew how many we were going to lose, there'd be no point grieving.

Hold your applause to the end, as they say.

And 'applause' in that sentence is meant in an ironic, bitter, desperately sad way.

I returned to Karen's bedside and sat down, forcing myself to look away as they floated Jocko out of the med bay. Soon they'd be moving serious cases up here from bay five — they had the bed space now. Until they did, the chamber was less crowded than it had been… less crowded because five bodies had been removed.

"How're the crew doing? I heard Andrea's shipwide," Karen's voice still sounded strong as she asked the question, and I shook my head.

"They're doing what they always do," I think I sounded as amazed at their irrepressible spirit as I really was.

Karen nodded slowly, then rolled onto her side to look at me, "Good. How're you doing?"

I didn't answer that question for a moment — not entirely sure I processed it at first. Then as it started sinking in, I frowned and stared at her, "I'm sorry, you're the one who was exposed to the Phosgene. How are *you?*"

With a thin smile, she rolled onto her back and paused before answering, "Not dying yet."

Two hours later, Destiny Phillips died from acute respiratory failure. She hadn't been conscious for any of those two hours, so it somehow didn't hit any of us as hard as it might have. I suppose we'd expected it to come when she didn't wake up at all.

Bunny was the only one from that party left, and she was distraught. Jim hadn't left her side, which I think was helping her state of mind. New cases were brought in over those two hours as well, but Destiny aside, no one died in that period.

Nine hours from last exposure.

I alternately paced around the med bay, sat at Karen's side, and visited bay five to check on progress there. Things seemed to be stabilizing — all the people who'd gone into pulmonary edema at the seven-hour mark died, but no one else was starting to show symptoms.

I was starting to get hopeful — desperately hopeful, the way you get when you see the smallest respite in the face of immense tragedy.

I also slipped into Alicia's office when I heard her on the comm with Conrad Rhee. At this stage, I was beyond the point of being courteous about where I was sticking my nose: I openly eavesdropped.

"I'm sorry, Alicia, none of them are binding. We're trying again, but I'll need at least three more hours," Conrad was shaking his head, his face glistening with sweat and creasing with stress.

Alicia's chin had fallen slightly, and she shook her head, "Things are stabilizing over here for now, Conrad. You might have those three hours. Do what you can."

I have to marvel at the calm of medical professionals — in the face of all this chaos, they were keeping their anxieties and desperation in check, getting the job done. In the first draft of this book, I said there were no others like them for that kind of calm under pressure, but one of my editors very rightly pointed out that the whole crew was behaving with the same discipline.

Can't deny it. We had some of the best people in Defense Command aboard *Wolf* and in the Jupiter Force. Days like this one proved that, without any doubt.

I slipped out of Alicia's office before she noticed I'd been there to listen in, and on my way back to Karen's bed I stopped next to Jim and Bunny, putting a hand on the latter's shoulder, "How're you doing, Bunny?"

She had a tube in her throat, so answering with words wasn't worth attempting, but she lifted her head and nodded once.

I shifted my gaze to Jim, "Jim?"

All our years together on *Friendly* and *Wolf* had given Jim and I that rapport — I could say one word and he knew exactly what I was asking. He looked up at my question and half shook his head, "Not enjoying today."

I agreed with a nod, then offered what I hope was a confidence-inspiring smile to Bunny, and returned to my chair next to Karen's bed. There was nothing more to do now except wait.

Hour twelve brought with it seventeen new cases of pulmonary edema, none of them quite as serious as those that had come on at hour seven. Karen was not one of those cases, though Bunny was.

Again, all we could do was watch as patients arrived from the cargo bay and then deteriorated. By now the routine was becoming sickeningly familiar: the spider went in with the tube, and depending on the extent of the damage done by the Phosgene, blood oxygen levels either stabilized and the person lived, or there weren't enough alveoli left undamaged, and the person died.

Four of those seventeen cases died by hour sixteen — all of those victims having worked in the bow pod of *Idaho*.

Bunny didn't let go of Jim's hand for hours and hours. He kept encouraging her to fight, and fight she did. She did *not* die. Her decision to wear her mask during certain parts of that tour around *Idaho* had saved her from the worst moments of exposure, so the damage to her lungs was markedly less than it had been among all her compatriots.

The tube in her throat kept enough oxygen flowing for her to live.

In hour seventeen, Alicia stopped by Karen's bed to look at her chest scan.

"Lungs are starting to cloud, but you're holding your own," our exhausted physician managed an artificial smile. "We're seeing more stabilization with these cases. Fewer acute failures. I'm going to put you on a mask for now, just to make sure your oxygen stays high."

Karen nodded and sat up so the medics would have an easy time getting the oxygen mask fitted over her mouth and nose.

I continued to wait with her, but things going on in bay five were about to draw my attention.

The next seven deaths came in a flurry — seven of the nine patients still in bay five who had been suffering from pulmonary edema died within minutes of each other. As the medics there would be working on one, another would go into acute respiratory failure, and then they'd switch their resuscitation efforts from the one longer without vitals to the one who still had a chance… all without any success.

The damage that manifested in these later hours might have taken more time to show up, but it was no less lethal.

As these people were dying, too, they had an audience. Remember, there were dozens of volunteers in the cargo bay, along with the rest of the crew who'd been exposed and who were still in their beds, waiting to show symptoms, and praying that they wouldn't.

And, of course, there was Andrea.

Everything that Andrea had done to deal with her experiences on Egesta had, up until this point, been just a preview. She hadn't witnessed these sort of losses in person — she'd seen *Lion's* crew ravaged, but her only exposure to those people had been after the fact. Now her crew — the people she trusted and cared about, even after all she'd been through — were dying in front of her eyes.

That was too much for her to take without doing something about it.

But what could she do about it?

Charlie Peters was wondering the very same as he watched her stiffen at the last death, then turn and leave the bay with a very determined stride.

It took him all of a few seconds to realize where she was going, and then he was on his comm to me and to Carly.

CHAPTER TWENTY-EIGHT
NON-HERO MOMENTS

Andrea was moving through the corridors with a very grim expression. She wasn't armed — yet — but her face had murder written all over it. I imagine that's not too hard for you to understand, even if you don't agree with it. After all Andrea had seen, from Egesta to this very day, she was not in a terribly stable state.

In case my implications haven't been clear enough up to this point, she was now hell bent on killing some (or preferably all) of our POWs.

This is wrong. This is something that you *do not* do. No matter who you are, this sort of thing gets the book, with all its weight and might, thrown right at you.

Yes, if we so wished, we could probably cover it up, save reputations and avoid criminal prosecution, but that wasn't something we could do in good conscience. These weren't enemies of the Empire, they were POWs. Under the Articles of Empire, an enemy of the Empire had to be so branded by Parliament. These guys were all prisoners, not enemies.

We weren't allowed to kill them, whether we wanted to or not.

But that argument wasn't proving particularly convincing to Andrea as a tiny part of her brain made it. The Ceres Accords also forbade the use of agents like Phosgene, but that hadn't stopped the bastards from killing our crew with them…

The fact that the Martians had broken the Accords was no reason for us to do the same, angry as we might have been about it. And I should say that killing prisoners is wrong — it really is.

But I have some personal experience with the kind of anger and hatred that was bubbling through Andrea just then, and as wrong and evil as it makes me, I have sympathy with what she was thinking.

That does *not* (NOT) make it right. But I can understand why she was feeling the way she was. I can't condemn her for it, because I know how easy it is to get there. And to go further.

Fortunately for Andrea, though, she was surrounded by people with a better sense of goodness and decency than, say, me.

Well, *surrounded* isn't the word, really. But one of them suddenly appeared in front of her in the corridor, just minutes short of the brig.

If you have to ask how Charlie Peters figured out which route Andrea was taking, and how he managed to get past her and head her off, you haven't been reading these books closely enough. But somehow I doubt you have to ask — it's *Charlie*, after all.

Andrea came to an abrupt halt as he stepped into the intersection in front of her, his eyes locking with hers.

Whenever you see a scene like this in the movies, it's what I like to call a hero moment. A friend of the tortured protagonist stops that person from doing something bad, by saying profound things like, "You mustn't… you'll be no better than them."

Lines like those are all very cliché, and to me they've never made sense. The very reason that you're seeking to do those bad things is because you *aren't* any better than the other guys, and you intend on making those other guys regret every evil thing they did to your people. Someone saying, in mellow tones, that 'you'll be no better than them' isn't going to dissuade you.

But in the movies, the lines always work. Usually with violins playing, sometimes with a hug and tears (especially when the character getting ready to do the harm is female — movies love to have them break down in tears).

Fortunately for the prisoners, and particularly for Andrea, Charlie doesn't do 'cliché'. Well, that's a lie — he does the cliché of showing up at just the right time in the right place pretty well. But we'll let that one go.

"Charlie…" Andrea seethed out his name, and only his name, in low tones.

Again, in the movies the tortured hero tends to go into soliloquy mode at this point… 'they have to pay', and so on. Very moving, blah blah.

The way this really played out was much less verbose, and much more intense. Andrea's eyes did all the talking, and Charlie tells me they were *screaming*. Our intrepid Major had, by this time in his life, seen many people ready to kill, and many who'd actually gone through with it. He'd rarely seen someone possessed by the sort of cold fury that was seething from Andrea, though.

It was disturbing… this was his good friend Andrea, this was *Wolf's* Captain. Not really supposed to be the 'murderous rage' sort.

"Andrea," Charlie's only reply to the onslaught from her eyes was her name.

His tone was much more relaxed, but he folded his arms and squared off in the corridor before her, his body language making it quite clear she wasn't going to get to the brig today.

She didn't concede that point. Looking down, she visibly steeled herself, and began to move forward again.

First she stepped to the right, trying to pass him. Of course, he sidestepped and got in her way. Then she stepped left, and again Charlie moved into her way. By now, she'd closed the distance between them, and as her downcast eyes crawled up to his face, she blinked a few times.

"Charlie…" she whispered that softly, rather intensely, and he frowned.

She leaned a little closer to him, and put her hands on the sides of arms. He narrowed his eyes, understandably unsure of what she was trying to accomplish.

Then her knee jerked up into his groin. Hard.

"Sorry," she whispered coldly — not particularly apologetically — as that strike connected.

Now, Charlie may be a Special Brancher, but he's also a male of our species. And he was in ship fatigues — he wasn't wearing any gear to protect sensitive areas. Indeed, even in combat conditions, it was a rare person who could get inside his guard to deliver that sort of blow.

Andrea, though, was a rare sort of person.

As Charlie began to double over and wince, she stepped to the right and walked past him.

But fortunately (yes, *fortunately*) for her, Charlie wasn't *just* a male of our species, he was a Special Brancher. See how I reversed that line from the previous paragraph? Well, you can knee a Special Brancher in the groin — really hard, as Andrea had done — and get him to double over, but you can't take away his hand-to-hand combat skills, which in Charlie's case include moves you can perform while doubling over in pain.

He turned, and his left hand lanced out and grabbed Andrea's left wrist before she could get out of reach. She tried to jerk herself free, but with a grunt he hauled her back towards him.

By now she was getting a little more wordy, "Let *go...*"

Emphasizing that demand, she threw a punch at his jaw. Were it anyone but Charlie, that punch might have left him down on the deck and groaning, giving her time to make her escape.

But, to state the painfully obvious, it *was* Charlie. He didn't even block the blow, he leaned in so it'd collide with his shoulder and glance off. Then his right hand powered around and delivered one of those movie-like palm strikes to her temple.

You've seen pictures of Andrea: she's not built to absorb that sort of directed strike from Charlie. He knocked her into something of a daze — and gave her what turned into a formidable black eye in the process. She hit the deck disoriented, and that left Charlie to go back to his doubling over and wincing, as was his right as a male.

I showed up just as he was getting himself upright again, and looking down at Andrea with a frown on his face. He'd just punched out the Captain of the ship, which was generally considered a no-no in Naval circles. No spacers had happened by this piece of corridor, so he hadn't yet been forced to answer any awkward questions, but now that the instincts of the moment were starting to recede, he was trying to figure out what to do next.

Before I could open my mouth to offer any advice, Carly and the rest of Charlie's squad arrived, kitted with their tac vests and MAG-90s. They slid to a stop just short of Andrea as she struggled to get back to her feet, and Carly blinked a couple of times.

"Oh," she said, continuing this chapter's pattern of elaborate dialogue.

"Get her to her cabin, and sit on her door if you have to," I was pretty sharp with those commands.

Carly frowned, "What are we keeping her from?"

"The brig," Charlie didn't elaborate, but then he didn't need to. Carly's mouth opened to reply but she stopped as she realized what he was implying.

Without further discussion, the Branchers got hold of Andrea just as she found her balance, and then started for her cabin, clearing corridors of prying eyes as they went.

Charlie and I watched them go, then I looked at him, "She knee you in the groin?"

His face twisted slightly and he nodded painfully, "Imagine what she'd have done to the prisoners."

I swallowed, and was silent for a moment. Under other circumstances, there obviously would have been joking... but not now. Not this day.

Andrea Kiley, the formerly sweet Irishwoman known to the Empire for her seeming innocence, and often proposed to by adoring strangers, had just attempted to massacre POWs. And she'd even been willing to beat up on Charlie to get to that massacre.

Gee, do you think our plan of 'letting her be' so she could work out her issues was working?

"Well. We need to get her better help than we've been giving," I finally said that quietly, and Charlie nodded.

"In the meantime, I might need ice."

We headed for med bay, where the fun of this day was destined to continue.

Now, my editors are concerned about this chapter. At first I thought they'd be worried that I was wrecking Andrea's reputation.

Well, I still worry about that. But the editors were in fact worried about other things.

First of all, Charlie was *not* going to get court-martialed for striking Andrea. Even if she'd tried to file charges and her Flag Officer (me) had accepted the complaint, he had justification in acting to protect the lives of POWs. This made his action entirely defensible, given Andrea's state of mind (we could have proved her instability in court had we needed to). Anyway, that's a good question that I hadn't even thought of (silly me).

The second question bugs me, though. To quote one of the editor's notes: "Charlie punched a woman, gave black eye. You do not discourage this in your interpretation as written."

In other words, that editor seemed to fear that men reading this will take Charlie's palm strike as an excuse to beat up women.

Um. I don't know where to start on this. Obviously, what Charlie did has *nothing* to do with gender-based abuse. Nothing at all. Do I think men — be they brothers, fathers, boyfriends or husbands — should hit people they're in relationships with? Certainly not.

Am I against punching a woman? I'm against punching *anyone*, without a very good reason.

Keeping someone from executing POWs qualifies as a good reason. Frankly, a black eye was nothing compared to the damage that could have been done to Andrea's life if she'd gone cell to cell, shooting prisoners.

Charlie has a good palm strike, but it hits nowhere near as heavily as the book, when the book is thrown at you. Andrea could have spent time in prison, or even been hung. It would have been very *bad* for her. Not to mention the prisoners.

She had to be stopped, and Charlie did that the best way he could. Rightly so.

I don't understand why these absurd hang-ups about women in hand-to-hand combat still exist (or, to be honest, how that editor made this leap). We're a long way out of the 50s, for crying out loud. You think a 'pretty little lass' like super-spy Haley Briand couldn't kill most people — men or women — in a fist fight? Men: if a woman drops her gloves and decides to take you out, are you not going to punch back to save yourself? Women: if a man tries to beat you, aren't you going to take his head off?

Women, you should not abuse men. Men, you should not abuse women. Everybody, you should not abuse everybody.

But if all that doesn't convince you, then just reimagine this chapter and pretend that Andrea was a man. Hell, pretend it was me going to kill the prisoners, and that Charlie knocked me out cold to stop me.

It's alright now, I suppose? Because I'm a 'big strong' man, not a 'weak little' woman like Andrea, so it's okay for me to get knocked out when I'm acting like a psychopath. She should have been hugged and that would have made it all better.

Equality in action: you go crazy, you get knocked out, whatever chromosomes you have. Otherwise, men, women, don't hit each other — period!

Sorry, that developed into a rant. I'm sure the neo-suffragists will attack me with placards for saying all that... will I be allowed to fight back?

I better move on. Now I'm just procrastinating because I really don't want to get to the next scene.

Speaking of strong women in bad situations...

CHAPTER TWENTY-NINE

FALLOUT

"Wes offered to have a chat with her, though I think more than a chat might be needed."

Charlie and I were almost back at the med bay — Charlie walking now quite normally, the immediate impact of Andrea's knee having worn off. As I mentioned Wes' offer, he glanced at me, "Ah. Talk to her about grief and revenge. After Sara?"

I nodded. At that point, not many people knew about the bleakest times in Wes' past; many still don't know. And I'm not going to elaborate here. But Charlie knew what Wes had seen and done, and he knew as well as I did that hearing about those experiences might help Andrea.

"And if that doesn't work… then it's a desk," I chewed out those words. After all this — after all Andrea had been through, and all the time we'd spent ignoring her problems, hoping they'd go away, I desperately didn't want her career to be destroyed.

Well, I didn't want it destroyed in the first place, obviously… but now, if this outburst was any indication, there might have been no saving her.

"Let's not get ahead of ourselves," Charlie was being optimistic, probably for my benefit. "We'll give Wes a chance, and decide after that."

Charlie, as usual, was thinking steadily, while I was meandering. That wasn't about to change as we reached the hatch to the medical bay.

Keep in mind, now, that I'd been gone maybe twenty minutes dealing with Andrea's outrage. Just twenty minutes.

Charlie opened the hatch and then waved me through first — polite, that Major is — so I was the first to look to my left and realize Karen had a tube down her throat.

Charlie came in right behind me, closing the hatch, and he accidentally walked into me, as I'd stopped just inside the door to stare. If you'd asked me then what he and I had been talking about in the corridor, I wouldn't have been able to answer. I'm pretty sure I couldn't have remembered Andrea Kiley's name.

"It's precautionary more than critical," Alicia appeared beside Charlie and me, quickly trying to assuage my concern.

Yeah, best of luck with that futile effort, Alicia…

"She's developing respiratory problems, and some edema. It's not nearly as acute as others that we've seen… I don't think it's going to be fatal. But we didn't want to take any chances, so we intubated," she went on.

I shook myself out of catatonia as she finished her explanation, and moved rather ponderously over to Karen's bedside. She was still conscious, and had watched me stop like a stunned fool. Though she couldn't really smile around the tube in her mouth, she gave me a thumbs up.

Charlie passed me and rounded her bed, looking from me to Karen and back, realizing that he needed to say something, or I likely would just stare.

"Does that taste funny?"

Well, that's a question I wouldn't have thought of, and Karen looked over at him and nodded.

"You'd think in this fantastic modern era of spaceships and flying cars, we'd invent better-flavored tubes to jam down peoples' throats," he frowned and shook his head.

Those seemingly inane comments were useful — they forced my mind into a different gear, driving my repartee instincts to at least consider what he was saying, even if I couldn't manage a reply. I started thinking, not just staring.

After a moment and a few blinks, I looked from Karen up at Charlie and back. It was, I decided, a bad idea to be grim right now. The doctor had said she didn't think this would be fatal. Karen didn't need some idiot standing next to her bed acting like he was at a wake. I needed to get my head together, and try to defy the dire mood.

Starting to freak out about a tube in Karen's throat and a relatively good prognosis would be stupid, then. And insensitive to the plight of other crew members who were in much worse shape than she was.

And it would undoubtedly have hurt Karen's own state of mind.

With as much self-control as I could muster, I bent down and leaned in close to Karen's ear, "Andrea just tried to force her way into the brig. I think she was looking to do some killing."

If our goal here was to make Karen feel like she wasn't in any way incapacitated (despite the rather noticeable tube in her throat), then bringing that situation up with her was the best idea I had. Her brow creased now, and she shook her head.

"Can we get something for her to write on?" Charlie turned and asked one of the passing medics, who nodded and pulled a pad and a stylus from his pocket. Doctors carry those to take notes on, I suppose.

Charlie collected the pad and stylus, then put them in Karen's hand, and she started tapping out a message on the mini-keyboard on the pad screen.

'Someone beter go talk to he r.'

I looked at the message, then saw an opportunity — albeit a pathetic one — to lighten the mood, "You spelled 'better' wrong. And there's an extra space in 'her.'"

Karen's frown deepened, 'I hve a tuve in my throat.'

"And you can't spell," I'm sure it sounded like I was trying to be funny — as if the humor was forced. Karen was charitable.

'Just wait til im out of her.'

"Out of who?"

Karen didn't bother typing an answer to that, she just smacked me in the knee with the back of her hand.

Charlie then rode to the rescue, "Actually, when I tried to stop Andrea, she kneed me in the groin. Ken hasn't been harassing me about it yet… it's feeling like a lost opportunity to me."

Karen's eyes darted across to Charlie, her eyebrows carrying the message without a quick note. Someone had managed to catch Major Charlie Peters off guard, and get a shot like that in?

Shrugging, Charlie smiled, "She's crafty. Irish."

I managed to laugh at that, and the corners of Karen's eyes scrunched up, indicating her own amusement.

That was about all the amusement we could manage, though. Even Charlie didn't have enough tricks to keep the mood light while Karen lay there, intubated.

He and I — and Karen too — had all seen too many people die in that state today. We waited.

In hour twenty, Charlie left to check on Andrea — it made sense to have a friendly face with her, and despite the kneeing Charlie was certainly still a friend. I stayed next to Karen, and she remained awake.

I cannot effectively describe how slowly time seemed to move during those hours when she was awake with that tube in her throat. This was one of the longest days of my life — behind only the day we stormed the Geraldine Coilier Show and fought the Battle Over Earth, and... well, that *other* day.

I'm not talking about that other day now. I'm in a bad enough mood as it is.

Anyway, by the time hour twenty-one crept around, another spacer had died... but in a grim way, that was probably good news. Sorry, that didn't come out right: the good part was that only *one* spacer had died.

Eleven more were intubated in the same period, though. This Phosgene was horrid. It took its damned time manifesting, and the waiting for those exhibiting no symptoms was torture. Just imagine, feeling relatively fine, but knowing you *might* still have a fatal dose, and watching as people around you keep getting sicker, getting intubated, and some of them die.

Spacers have described to me the horrid ups and downs. The hopes that, if you're feeling fine now, you're probably alright... and then having someone in the bed next to you who thought the very same falling ill, then dying.

The fact that there were no incidents of outright panic is a sign of just how good *Wolf's* crew was. I know, I'm probably beating this horse into glue, but the crew on that frigate was just incredible.

Great women and men. Period.

Anyway, hour twenty-one also brought a more pleasant surprise, relative to the situation at least: Matt Baxter arrived in the med bay.

Matt, remember, was commanding *Friendly* now, but just about everyone on the crew remembered him as *Wolf's* XO, and he'd come over in his pinnace from *Friendly* with medical volunteers to give our people some relief... and to visit his old crew.

I should explain, actually, that the squadron was still out there, with Mark Gunney commanding. All ships were at action stations, just in case there was even more to this trap — in case the Martian bastards weren't satisfied with just poisoning our people. If any red ships arrived, Mark was ready for them.

The only ship not completely ready for that fight, of course, was *Wolf*. Andrea was in her cabin under guard, Jim Hannigan was sitting next to Bunny's bed, and I was next to Karen's. Shelby McLaws had the watch — it wasn't like the bridge was abandoned — but if trouble came in, it'd take Jim and I at least a couple of minutes to get up there, and for the crew helping with the care of the sick in bay five to get back to their stations.

You can call this a failure in ship command, perhaps. I say it was extraordinary circumstances, and that frankly, we weren't being negligent. If the enemy approached, chances were we'd have at least a half hour's notice, thanks to all the active sensors the Jupiter Force was putting out, and to the Starlights that were on patrol.

I need to get off this subject.

It's funny. The rant that I was getting onto — about failures of command — is absolutely valid, but as I'm writing it I'm realizing the reason I'm letting myself get on the tangent is simple: I don't want to describe Karen lying there with a tube in her throat.

I really don't. It's not something I like reliving, and I hope you can sympathize with that.

But getting past my own reluctance, let me describe Matt's visit in more detail.

The black Englishman, remember, had long been like a parent to Karen and me. He'd always told us not to do 'stupid stuff', and I suppose when it comes down to it, we'd started to listen. Throughout the war so far, we'd played things relatively safe, and I think he'd been satisfied that we weren't going to charge the guns like idiots, and die.

Now, Karen had a tube in her throat. And she'd gotten that without being foolish. The Martians had played a dirty trick, and put it there.

Matt saw her, and his expression told me all I needed to know about his reaction. Matt, as you've probably figured out, is an intense sort of man, and very protective. He expects people to be killed in war — it's a grim inevitability, and one he came to terms with back in the days of the Syndicate.

But traps and tricks run entirely against his sense of what's right. He'll kill the enemy in a stand-up fight. He'll even flank them or outmaneuver them or outwit them... but booby traps and poison? That was too much. That was too nasty.

A chill seemed to run through him as I studied him. He didn't have Andrea's Irish temper — he wasn't the sort of fellow to storm off to the brig.

Instead, he took a long, almost menacing breath. I don't know how a breath can really be menacing, in and of itself... but this one was. He then looked from Karen to me, "When this war is done, and we figure out just who planned this damned disgrace..."

He didn't finish the sentence. Did he really need to?

I nodded in reply, "You and me both, Matt."

We nodded to each other, and then Karen whacked us both on the legs. She then scribbled something on her pad, and held it up.

'Me too.'

I suppose in retrospect, that comment was ironic.

Matt left a few minutes later, and we continued to wait.

Chapter Thirty

Over The Hump

At hour twenty-four, anyone not showing symptoms of respiratory distress was released, though they were ordered straight to their cabins, and medics would check in on them regularly for the next day, just to make sure they were alright.

Conrad Rhee's next attempt at a compound failed too, through absolutely no fault of his own or his team's. They were trying to produce a treatment to a damned near ancient weapon, with equipment they'd ripped out of a hospital and set up in a hurry on their ship.

But damned if they didn't try. They didn't stop working. They didn't stop trying. But every compound they created fell apart. Even so, everyone on *Wolf* appreciated their efforts.

Two more were dead by hour twenty-four. Karen wasn't one of them, and neither was Bunny. This will sound sappy, cliché or just plain stupid, but I really think Jim's presence at Bunny's bedside was key to her survival. He was right there, whispering things to her that we couldn't hear from across the med bay, keeping his composure the whole time.

If I'm ever on a medical bed facing impending death, that's just the sort of support I'd want. It wasn't the sort of support I was giving Karen…

But then, she kept telling me after that it was very much what I was doing. I don't remember clearly enough to know whether she was lying about that or not, but I didn't much care then. And I don't much care now.

After all the drama, and after all the worry, her lungs were starting to clear.

'Starting to clear' didn't mean she was better, obviously. She was not cured, or healthy, but when Alicia came by in hour twenty-five, she looked at Karen's latest chest scan and started to nod.

"Looks like the worst is done. I'm keeping you intubated… but you'll be fine."

I should have drawn that out more — made it more dramatic. Sorry if I spoiled the dramatic impact of the 'she's going to survive' for you… but then, you probably knew she was going to come through this one.

If you've ever gotten that sort of good news at a hospital, you probably know the feelings that came in waves as soon as Alicia said those words — the relief, the happiness, and the exhaustion.

I remember staring at Karen — probably smiling, but I can't be certain — and staring. Yes, I repeated 'staring' in that sentence. Sorry.

If you haven't been there before, just imagine it. Just imagine watching all those people — people you care about — dying, and then seeing Karen, or whoever your equivalent to Karen might be, going through the same. You're wondering, worrying, hoping and even praying, completely without control, completely without any way to help…

Well, I suppose I've described all that already in this book. Imagine all that. Imagine that shadow, that weight pressing down on you.

And then imagine it being taken away in a flash. It's an emotional roller coaster, and I don't say that lightly. You're happy, upset, exhausted... every emotion you repressed while you were sitting at the bedside over the course of a day comes at you in one great flood.

I leaned forward and laid my forehead down on the edge of Karen's bed. I was completely beside myself.

Alicia walked away, and Karen lifted her hand and put it on the back of my head.

That woke me up. While I was mired in how rough all that had been on me, I'd failed to think of how she must have felt. For whole seconds I'd been thinking of myself, the fellow who *hadn't* been poisoned. Top marks again, Barron.

Picking my head up off the bed, I took Karen's hand in both of mine, and we stared at each other for a long while. I'm sorry if that sounds in some way ridiculous or overly emotional. Or not emotional enough, for that matter. But it's what we did. We just stared. You know us, we didn't need actual words to send messages to each other. So for an hour or more, we stared.

The final death count from the Phosgene came to forty-six. Everyone else made a full recovery.

Forty-six brave women and men lost their lives, though. A trap — an underhanded, dirty trap — had killed them.

Twelve hours later, Karen's tube came out, but she went back to an oxygen mask for twelve hours after that. As soon as she could talk, she sent me away to my cabin, and demanded I sleep. I must have looked like hell.

She sure did.

Yes, I just said that. She was asleep under the mask as soon as I turned to leave — she needed the rest even more than I did.

Bunny's tube came out about four hours after Karen's, and while she'd had much worse exposure, she was on the recovery trail. She didn't send Jim away to get sleep, so he slept in the chair next to her bed.

Alicia also got some sleep. Everyone did, more or less.

That was the end of the immediate crisis.

Sorry if that was an anti-climax. These endings so often are. I suppose if this was fiction, my editors would want me to 'sex it up'... have some inexplicable heart attacks, or have a Martian strike force come in to try to kill us, or make the Phosgene much worse than it really was and then stage a race for the antidote with Conrad Rhee.

There was none of that, though. Once people stopped dying, and once those still sick started to improve, we all passed out from exhaustion.

Well, the majority of us.

Andrea was sitting in her chair, and had been for most of the hours since she'd been escorted to her cabin. She'd slept for two hours on her bed, but hadn't really made herself comfortable. She was intermittently boiling with rage, and ashamed that she couldn't control that boiling.

To use the words she's lately become fond of, she was finally showing to the world all the 'emotional damage' she'd taken at Egesta.

Now, I need to make a point here — a crucial point Charlie mentioned to me. We have to remember that not everyone who came off two weeks on Egesta had *this* response to what they saw. Not everyone, in plain words, felt Andrea's rage, or were prone to being sent into violent outbursts by the horrors of war.

Combat stress reaction can manifest in many different ways, many of them much more destructive to the person suffering it than to those around her or him. Andrea's was a truly dramatic case, but others can be much more insidious. People can hide their pain, and never have Andrea's sorts of outbursts, until some of them actually kill themselves. They can have headaches, anxieties, paranoias, they can change in subtle ways, and never be noticed.

And no, they don't all suicide. In fact, most don't. Many end up making lives for themselves, forever haunted by what they've seen, but refusing to succumb to the hauntings. It's a question of personality — different people handle those experiences differently. You can't say any one person handles them better than any other... everyone is unique.

In some ways, I think it was a blessing that Andrea went so far to the extreme. We may not have stepped in and directed her to help if she hadn't gone so far. Those veterans who refused to inflict their pain on their friends and families, and who kept their problems out of sight, may never have gotten help with their memories. They suffer courageously in silence.

If they're reading this, I'm going to suggest they get help. That's Andrea's advice, anyway. Obviously, I'll have much more to say on that subject later... but for now, I want to drop into the narrative.

Charlie had sat with Andrea for several hours after he'd left the med bay. He'd then gone for a little sleep, and now, as Karen and I were both resting, he returned to Andrea's cabin and relieved Carly, who'd been sitting silently across from Andrea, making sure she didn't do anything rash.

There was a definite concern that she'd shoot herself after the day she'd had. We didn't think it was *likely*, but that's not the sort of thing you want to take a chance on.

As Charlie sat down, he studied Andrea's face. She wasn't looking directly across at him — she was seemingly staring into space, unaware of her company.

"They just pulled the tube out of Karen's throat. She should be fine."

Andrea didn't visibly react to that news at first, her gaze instead remaining fixed in mid air. Charlie decided after a moment's pause that she simply wasn't ready to react, so he leaned back in his chair and settled himself for a wait.

Then she surprised him — though without the knee this time.

"Thank you for stopping me earlier."

Now, if this was a movie (here I go again, I know), Andrea would have said that very emotionally, very gratefully. Charlie had saved her from becoming as evil as the bad guys and all...

But that's not how she said it. Her voice was icy, her words precise and controlled.

Charlie tilted his head slightly and frowned at them, and then Andrea turned her head to look at him, revealing the nasty black eye that had formed.

"If I'd killed some of them — and in retrospect, I think I would have — it would have ended my career."

According to Charlie and Andrea both, there was a very cold quality to those words. The implication was simple: she still wanted the POWs dead, but she was more concerned that she still had a career.

So, unlike the movies, she didn't care to be better than the bad guys. Just the opposite: she wanted to be worse, to hurt them more, and for longer. She wasn't going to be able to do that if she killed some POWs in a fit of rage, and lost her command.

To explain it the way Andrea did to me: "I started to get control of my rage. I was in a blind fury when I went for the brig, but after this I was much more thoughtful. I was ready to find ways to kill Martians that wouldn't be frowned on. So I could keep doing it. That's the mindset I had just then."

So unlike in the movies, she wasn't all better. She wasn't ready to cry and hug. She wasn't better than the bad guys. She was scary.

Charlie read all of this through her tone, and he leaned towards her slowly, "You're going to have a talk with Wes when we get back, or you won't keep your command. You might still lose it anyway."

She didn't know what the talk would be about, but despite that, she nodded.

That was it. For the next few hours they sat in silence, until Carly returned, and Charlie left again. New chapter.

CHAPTER THIRTY-ONE

LEAVING IT BEHIND

I was very much considering doing a chapter here about the funerals for the dead members of *Wolf's* crew... but I can't stand to write that. It was a very emotional day for all of us when we sent those forty-three people into the void. Among them, of course, were officers like Kyle Stranks, but I should mention that the bodies of Jocko, Destiny and Summer were not sent out. We brought them home so their families could bury them as they wished. All three were buried on Earth.

Two days after the medical crisis started, we were cleared to cruise. It probably feels like a hurried escape from the situation... I'll be the first to admit I have a hard time hanging in and writing about the fallout. I believe I fast-forwarded out of Egesta in *The Independent Squadron* too. Hopefully you understand.

Anyway, we were ready to leave *Idaho* behind two days later. And believe me, we were leaving it. It won't surprise you to know that thoughts of salvaging the hull were gone.

Standing alone on *Wolf's* bridge (well not actually alone, but Andrea and Karen were both in their quarters) with Battlelink up, I stared at the vid feed of that ship on one of the screens and shook my head. The ship had been sent on a mission to bring help to Io, with a brave Captain and crew determined not to let down their comrades around Jupiter.

Then the ship had been seized, and the crew had been brutally massacred in order to set up a disgusting farce of a horror movie, complete with an 'alien', to throw us off the scent of the real trap. Then the ship itself had been turned into a weapon against any salvagers.

Whoever had put this together had planned it very intricately — too intricately, even. It was the sort of ridiculous plan that I'd only ever known Grant Merger to produce, hinging on so many variables.

First the ship had to be put in our flight path, which was an impressive feat all on its own. It's hard to get two powered ships that are looking for each other to rendezvous successfully in the blackness of open space... to get a drifting ship right into position was a hell of a piece of work.

Then it counted on us actually stopping to check the ship out, instead of flying by. This, of course, was less of a leap... you don't leave a drifting hull beyond the asteroid belt if there's even a chance you have people aboard.

And then the plan had hinged on us being overly cautious, just as we had been. It relied on us to secure the ship, to see through the idiotic 'alien' act, and to search the ship top-to-bottom for traps we could recognize. It relied on us feeling we'd seen through the absurdity of the traps, and believing we'd checked *everything*.

And finally it counted on us putting people aboard, trying to make something of that ship, while our detectors failed to note the Phosgene because it was of such an antiquated chemical structure it wasn't on our lists.

As I say, the number of assumptions this plot made was ridiculous. And yet it had worked — worked to a goddamned 'T'. That's what made it worse. When a plan was that intricate and flimsy, and it still worked against you, and it killed forty-six of your people...

Though, thinking on it now, it could have gone better for the trap-setter. What if we'd done the cleaning and maintenance of *Idaho* in breathers, and no one had gotten sick? The Phosgene would have spread and settled throughout the entire ship undetected, because no one would be showing symptoms and the atmoscanners wouldn't have detected it. Then we could have put a crew aboard — a larger, skeleton crew for cruising — and they almost certainly would have died. Lieutenant Kong's sudden death had saved many lives.

That said, 'it could have gone worse' was in no way a compensation for what... for *who* we had lost. Matt Baxter really had decided he wanted to know the person who'd created this trap, and from the expressions on the faces of the skippers on Battlelink, he wasn't the only one.

"We're ready to cruise," Mark Gunney finally announced, drawing my attention. I nodded as I looked up at him.

"Get into formation, let's get out of here. Jim, finish off *Idaho*."

That last part was, of course, directed at Jim Hannigan, though I didn't look back at him as he stood behind the operations consoles.

"Aye," was his cold reply. He nodded to his technicians, and then a klaxon sounded in the number four laser room. The weapon was charged, and Jim's crew targeted *Idaho*.

"Goodbye, *Idaho*. May you find peace," Captain Kishko said over the Battlelink. Remember, *Idaho* had been in his squadron, and for him this whole course of events was painful in a different way. His friend's ship had not only been taken on the way home and its crew horribly killed (something we could all see was haunting him)... it had been turned into a tool of the enemy. For a spacer of the old guard, like Kishko, that was a fate worse than death for a noble ship.

"Shoot when ready, Jim," I was much less understanding of Kishko's sentiment then than I am now, so my orders had a very cold edge to them.

Jim took another few seconds to finish the targeting solution, then repeated the order, "Shoot."

Wolf's number four laser — that one's getting a lot of work this book — lashed out, the angry red energy dragging its way up and down the drifting hull of *Idaho*. The older frigate's reactors had been deactivated, so there were no power systems to overload: the hull was simply clawed apart.

"May we assist?" Matt Baxter's question was hard.

"By all means."

Friendly opened fire with its own laser, and together my two former ships cut *Idaho* apart. It took about five minutes to split the old frigate into unsalvageable pieces, a testament to the strength of Defense Command construction of any era.

But *Idaho* died. The only real revenge we got for all the pain of this trap.

The alien pod that had been 'made in the USA' died along with the frigate. But we did have pictures of that thing — we had evidence it existed.

"Let's get moving again," my tone hadn't softened. It didn't need to.

The Jupiter Force set course for the Empire, and we boosted away from the wreck.

Chapter Thirty-Two

Interception

About a week after we left *Idaho* behind, Wes Pellew was sitting in his chair on *Nova Scotia's* bridge, going through some forms on a pad. The Independent Squadron was, if you can remember from way back near the start of this book, waiting to intercept the Martian shipment of stolen R&D from Io, and as the weeks wore on, Wes, Mik and Lia were increasingly on edge, wondering if they were actually going to be able to catch the Martians.

Contrary to what our unlikely interception of *Idaho* might suggest, it was by no means a sure thing that you could successfully find a ship in the deep black. They could go right around you, just seconds out of range…

But you know that. And so did Wes, which was why he had his ships fanned out in the widest possible search grid, about twelve hours beyond the perimeter of the Belt. Starlights were cruising back and forth between the ships, and ahead of them, providing better coverage. Everyone was waiting.

Lia had her ships spread in a similar line right back at the perimeter of the Belt — the second line to catch the Martian convoy if it managed to get past Wes. Even two lines of ships, though, were not a lot in absolute terms: it was fifty-fifty that they'd catch sight of the Martians coming in from Io.

Well, you give Wes Pellew, Mik Mikaelsen and Lia Hawke fifty-fifty odds and they'll do something with them.

"Message coming in from *British Columbia*."

Wes looked up from his pad with a frown. *British Columbia* was three ships down the line from *Nova Scotia*, on the extreme left of the Independent Squadron's formation.

Wes' Sensors and Communications Officer had to wait a few seconds for the signal to decode, then he looked to his Commodore and nodded, "One of their forward looking Starlights has seen a DC frigate and a large Martian transport of some sort."

Getting to his feet immediately, Wes waved to the main screen at the front of *Nova Scotia's* bridge, "Show it to me."

Two ship description panes appeared on the main screen, one showing a DC frigate of the *North America*-class, the other showing a generic Martian large hauler.

"We don't have specific data on either, sir."

Wes nodded as he came to a stop before the main screen, and seconds after, his Flag Captain, Roslyn Young, arrived next to him, "Frigate's the right vintage to be *Quebec*."

"Indeed. Tony, send signal back to *Cyclops*, alert them that we have possible targets. Hold our position, though. I don't want to close the net if this is a feint."

You might have expected Wes to immediately order his entire squadron to pounce on the two-ship formation, but that would have meant shutting down their net. They had no idea how many ships the Martians had coming in from Io — if Wes pulled his squadron off its line, and there were more Martians following these two on slightly different vectors, those stragglers might get through.

The net had to stay intact.

Knowing that to be the case, Mik and Lia had positioned a four-ship 'intercept force' forward of the asteroid perimeter, about six hours behind Wes' line. If the Martians were detected, it would be this mixed Defense and Hawke Command unit that would maneuver to meet them, while the detection lines remained intact.

And Wes had just called them.

One of the neat features of the Hawke Force (that is, the combined Defense Command and Hawke Command force Mik and Lia were running) was that it had two commanders, Mik and Lia. Actually it had three, if you counted Rear Admiral Latisha Genda, Lia's senior flag officer.

Anyway, that wide availability of command officers meant that Mik was free to position himself wherever he liked... and for this mission, he and Lia had decided it'd make sense for him to be part of the intercept force, along with his battleship *Cyclops*.

Yes, I know (and he and Lia knew) that a battleship isn't the best ship for interceptions, not being as quick as a frigate or a corvette. But if you can remember all the way back to *The Hawke Mission*, *Cyclops* had been specially modified by Mik's orders — it was faster than the average battleship.

And — and this is the more important part — he and Lia were thinking, quite reasonably, that if a battleship intercepted the Martians, they'd be much more inclined to come quietly. Our noble enemies might figure they could out-fight some corvettes and a frigate, but if a battlewagon appeared, moving fast and accompanied by frigates or corvettes, they'd potentially decide their chances of getting away or surviving a fight were just too poor, and toss in the towel.

Anyway, all that background out of the way, we can join Mik about six hours after the initial detection. *British Columbia* had side-stepped out of line long enough to let the Martians pass right through without seeing any Defense Command ships at all. That kept them from changing course and trying to run for it.

Starlights shadowed the Martians the whole way, just to make sure they held their course towards the Belt... and they did. Those Martians were undoubtedly worried that they might have been detected, but in their place, I doubt I'd have done anything different. They could have skittered back and forth, side to side just beyond the Belt, always looking over their shoulder, but had there been no net waiting for them, that sort of behavior would have greatly increased the chances of them being detected by passers-by.

No, what they were doing here made sense: they'd picked their point for entering the asteroids, and they were just going to run it, probably hoping that *Quebec* could bluff them out of any problems.

To review, *Quebec* was the ship from the Jupiter Squadron (not the Jupiter Force) that had been captured at dock when the Martians attacked. Can't remember if I'd already mentioned that this book.

Anyway, they were coming straight in, hoping to go unseen, but they'd certainly been noticed.

Mik was standing before the screens on *Cyclops'* bridge those six hours later, as the Martians appeared on his sensors grid. He stroked his beard as he waited, and then he glanced at his Sensors and Communications Officer, Finn Yaalon, "If they start a course change, feed it direct to the others."

Finn nodded, and Mik looked back to the screen. The 'others' were the Defense Command corvette *Amherst*, under the formidable Commander Nikhil Jones, and the Hawke ships *Cassandra* (one of the mistress-named corvettes) and *Whirlwind* (essentially a *Predator*-class frigate in blue paint). If the Martians started to run for it, those ships would have to lead the chase, as they were faster than *Cyclops*.

"Still coming straight on," Finn reported after a moment. "We're in range of *Quebec's* sensors... now."

Because *Quebec* had been one of ours, we knew exactly what its detection range was — no guessing for Mik and his interceptors that day.

"Query *Quebec*, ask what ship and what intentions," Mik continued to stroke his beard as he watched the plot, and the query flew from *Cyclops'* signal array.

This was Mik's cunning plan: he'd give *Quebec* the chance to talk its way out of this — or at least, make the crew of the captured frigate think his intercept force didn't know it had been captured. Think about it: if you're in a stolen ship, and you're confronted by an overwhelming force with the ability to run you down, what will you do? You might fight to the death, leading to needless casualties.

But what if that overwhelming force gives you hope — if they don't realize your ship is stolen. Then you might try to talk your way out of the mess, or just keep them talking long enough to get around that force. If you go that route, it commits you to acting as though you're on the same side as your enemy, hoping they'll let you through.

So Mik was hoping that, if the Martians thought they could talk their way through, they'd come right into his weapons envelope, chancing that he'd be convinced and let them through. Then he'd have them.

But it didn't happen that way.

Mik continued stroking his goatee, watching as the Martian hauler and *Quebec* came on towards his force, and then Finn interrupted him.

"They just broadcast... general surrender, skipper."

Just as Finn Yaalon said that, the two icons on *Cyclops'* main screen began to decelerate. Seconds later, they were at dead stops, and their drives were powering down.

Uh. That was a surprise.

"Ask *Whirlwind* and *Cassandra* to take a closer look, and board if they feel it safe. Alert Wes that these might be decoy ships," Mik was already figuring out various angles to this unexpected action.

It seemed like an awfully easy surrender — no fight, no subterfuge — so they were either exhausted and weak after the cruise from Io, or they were just decoy ships, trying to tie up the interception force while the real Martian ships carrying Io's riches in R&D were coming in somewhere else.

Well, nope. As the boarding party from *Whirlwind* discovered when they went aboard the hauler, it was packed with our gear from Io — everything the Martians had stolen. Aboard *Quebec*, the boarding party from *Cassandra* (later reinforced by SF from *Cyclops*) found a crew of thirty-four Martians, running a ship that rightly needed four times that many people to have a barely-adequate skeleton crew. They were exhausted, and not ready for any sort of fight.

My editors (and probably you too) still have hard time believing they didn't even try to fight. To be honest, as much as I try to sympathize with how rough their flight from Io must have been due to their short-staffed situation... I probably would have tried to put up some sort of struggle. They didn't.

I suppose it's a window into the state of morale in the Martian fleet, when spacers from even their elite forces could be left with so little willingness to get into a fight...

But then, that's easy for me to say. I'm not the one who ran smack into a battlewagon and its escorts while aboard an old frigate with ten percent of its full crew complement and an unarmed hauler stuffed with R&D. That... actually does sound like a compelling argument not to fight and die for nothing.

Hmm. I think I've talked myself right back around. I can understand these spacers not wanting to fight.

After all that had happened out at Io, and on the way back, that interception seemed rather anti-climactic. The best ones always are, because no one dies and nothing gets destroyed.

Wes and Mik waited out there for another day, just to make sure there were no other ships for them to catch. Nothing showed up on their screens, so they closed down the blockade and headed for Hawke One.

Job done.

Chapter Thirty-Three

Pieces

Two weeks after we'd left *Idaho* behind, we still had a long haul left to the Empire. We were just over half-way, in fact, and spirits aboard *Wolf* were not exactly high. I've praised our crew enough for you to know that they were extraordinary spacers, but excluding Jocko's team, there were forty-three fewer of them now than there had been when we'd left to come home. That was difficult to deal with.

Usually, when you lose people in warships, it's in battle. Two things are different about those sorts of losses: first, those left alive can feel (maybe) at least as though they gave as good as they got... that their friends who died fell doing their jobs, fighting as a team... all those clichés that the movies really do get right, but people watching from the outside don't always realize are true.

But that's only part of it. No matter how you lose a comrade, there's always grief. If it's in battle, you may get to feel a bit better about it, but really, it's still an awful, awful feeling.

What was making this so much worse for the crew was the long, boring haul we were still on. There were no major activities on this cruise home, so people had nothing to do but sit around and think about who they'd lost. If we'd been in the Empire, we could have taken *Wolf* out on patrol, or given the crew shore leave, or *something* to help them get past it.

Instead, all they could do here was go about their jobs, every day remembering who'd been killed, and then as importantly, how underhanded and terrible those deaths had been. It wasn't good for morale. *Wolf* wasn't a happy ship, or an angry ship... it was a sad ship.

Part of the problem, it has to be said, came from the top. I was managing to do my job — I was visiting compartments throughout the ship on a regular basis, talking to people and trying to brighten their spirits. Only a year prior to this, I'd been their Captain, so I still had some ability to help the mood.

But Karen was missing. And so was Andrea. And the crew knew it.

Karen was on bed rest, recovering from the Phosgene. That wasn't so bad, because she could still occasionally venture out to greet some of the crew. But she wasn't on regular duty, and so she wasn't able to brighten moods very much.

Andrea was remaining in her cabin, and rumors were starting to spread in the lower decks about the circumstances surrounding that seeming confinement. Some people were convinced she'd killed POWs and that we were covering it up. Some thought she'd been psychologically broken by seeing so many of her crew killed in such a cowardly way, and that her career was over. I don't think people blamed her — she was one of the family — but many were losing their own confidence because their Captain had been so badly hurt by the *Idaho* trap.

This is why Captains are not supposed to reveal any doubt or concern to their crews:

we're the leaders, the example-setters. When the going gets tough, and lives are on the line, it's our responsibility to make the heavyweight decisions. Spacers work themselves to death for us, trusting that we actually know what we're about. As many times as I'll tell you now that I screwed things up, back then I couldn't be so honest. These men and women had put their trust in the command structure, and during those two weeks, the structure hadn't been there.

So while I went from section to section, showing confidence and trying to buck people up, it wasn't the same as it would have been a year prior. The crew knew that I was no longer their Captain… they knew their Captain was missing. It just added to the malaise.

To answer the question before someone asks it: fights weren't breaking out between members of the crew. This wasn't a case of, as Andrea explained it in *The Jupiter Patrol*, an unhappy ship. Just a sad, depressed ship. No one had high enough spirits to get into real fights… though if we let this general malaise continue, they undoubtedly would get there. Jim and I were worried about that.

So, to summarize all that rambling, *Wolf* needed an injection of good spirits… or at least a resuscitation of the old ones.

Two weeks after *Idaho*, we'd get that.

I was sitting in the conference room with Jessica Qing when it happened. Jessica had been cutting together the last of Jocko's footage, and she'd just shown me the story. It was brilliant, as you'll undoubtedly know because you've probably seen it. Jessica never took credit for the editing — it has Jocko's name on it, and it won him many posthumous awards.

To be clear, it's the story that ends with his last words, then fades to black.

I'm not going to repeat the contents here, because frankly, I don't want to relive that yet again. You can look it up in the archives if you want to… if you haven't seen it, it's worth a watch.

I suspect, actually, that the reason no one has ever tried to make a movie of this dark cruise is because they're afraid the attempt would pale beside the real horror of that piece. It's hard for any actor, no matter how good, to be completely convincing in 'death' when everyone's already seen the real guy die on screen.

Anyway, Jessica wanted to show someone the story she'd cut together. She'd worked for thirty-six hours without sleep assembling all the pieces, and she needed a second opinion, as I'm sure you can understand.

"It's brilliant. Does him proud," I probably sounded robotic when I said that quietly. You know how I'm poor at articulating feelings.

Jessica, who had teared up (as was definitely her right), nodded, "It's the best I could do."

I should have said something comforting right then, but I had no idea what I could say that would do any good. Fortunately for me, my comm chirped, so I pulled it from my belt, "Barron."

Jim Hannigan was on the other end, and he told me I was needed in the Captain's day cabin.

On the way out of the conference room, I put a comforting hand on Jessica's shoulder. That was it, though. I left her to grieve on her own.

When I stepped into the day cabin, I was slightly surprised to see Andrea standing there, her hands linked behind her back as she faced a picture on the wall with her back to me. Charlie was sitting on the edge of her desk, and Jim was standing with his arms folded next to the door. I frowned immediately upon entry, and glanced first to Charlie.

He was looking cautious.

Yeah *cautious*, can't think of a better way to describe it. He didn't look worried, angry, or happy... he looked like he didn't want to commit to any emotions at all.

Which wasn't much help to me as I tried to figure out what was going on.

Andrea, I should say, had been staying in her cabin voluntarily (unofficially relieved of command). We hadn't had anyone in there with her making sure she didn't kill herself for ten days. She'd seemed non-suicidal, but she hadn't been ready to face her crew again.

Her black eye was gone, at least.

"So... what's this?" if I couldn't figure out what was going on, I'd just have to ask.

Turning around, Andrea locked eyes with me. Her face was neutral (appeared to be a theme in this room — people's expressions betraying nothing), though her stare seemed a little warmer.

"I'm not in good shape," she said slowly. "When we get back, I'll get help. But I've left my crew without their Captain for too long. That's been my greatest failure of all, and I want to rectify it. If you'll give me back my command."

I distinctly remember the thought that popped in my mind as soon as she said those words: *well thank god for that.*

Of course, there was still a concern that her first act after being put back in charge would involve shooting and prisoners, but the tone of her voice was slightly different than it had been before. I didn't think she was in quite the same place she had been two weeks before.

Never hurt to ask, though, "So. Planning on killing any prisoners?"

Andrea, bless her, actually twitched out a little smile, "I wasn't *planning* to the first time, I think I was just going to. But no, I won't kill anyone. That's my word."

I believed her. You might not have, but I did. I saw where she was, and I thought then I had a pretty good understanding of it. She'd gone right to the brink, and only through Charlie's perfect timing and use of force had she been saved from going off the deep end. And she knew it.

Since it had been care for her crew that had led her off that deep end in the first place, it seemed to me that her sense of duty to *Wolf's* personnel would give her back the focus she needed to stay on an even keel, at least for the rest of this cruise. She wouldn't let herself act out the rage she felt, because if she did it would hurt her crew.

Her first attempt had already hurt them, and now she had to fix that.

Maybe you buy that, maybe you don't, but I certainly did. I think I understood back then. I certainly understand now.

"Command never actually stopped being yours," I said that matter-of-factly, and Andrea's smile broadened a little.

"I appreciate that. I'll start now, if you don't mind."

I managed a slim smile of my own, "We have a lot of pieces to pick up. Get to it, skipper."

With a nod, she started forward, waving Jim to join her as she left the day cabin. I watched her pass me, and nodded to Jim as he followed. Then, as the hatch shut, I looked at Charlie, "You got someone at the brig?"

"One person on with the security staff at all times. I'm saying it's to make up for the people we lost," he came off the edge of the desk with a nod of his own. "I really want to believe her. She seems to realize… her limits. Is that the best way to say it?"

I shrugged, "Probably. I hope she has. This crew needs its Captain back, and I don't cut it anymore."

Charlie understood what I meant, and we just stood there for a moment, wondering what was to come for our friend Andrea. We'd have part of our answer soon enough.

Alright, I've frustrated my editors greatly on this subject: they don't understand what Andrea's status had been over these two weeks, or what consequences there were for her.

First of all, Andrea was unofficially removed from command. To remove her officially would have ended her career for the same reasons that having her see a professional psychologist would have — Caldecott's people were still around in DC personnel, and they'd take out any of us if we gave them the chance.

Andrea didn't deserve that fate. She was in this state because she'd tried her damndest to save people on Egesta, and I was going to give her every chance to recover from that.

The important point that allowed me to give her a chance to recover was simple: Charlie had stopped her. The only offense she'd committed was striking a junior officer, which was not in fact against any regs. Charlie was willing to 'forget' her likely destination, *if* she talked to Wes and got herself under control.

She'd be given another chance. A chance she'd *earned*.

I don't know if you agree with this thinking on my part. You might see this as us covering up for a seriously unstable person because she was one of our circle.

Well, that's exactly what we were doing.

We were giving her chances — first the chance to take time away from her command duties to re-focus herself, then a chance to retake command and prove that she was back under control.

Some of us, I will say, weren't wild about these chances. Mark Gunney was obviously sympathetic to her plight, but he was rightly concerned about having someone with clear psychological problems commanding a ship in his squadron. He didn't mount a crusade against Andrea, but he quietly — and appropriately — mentioned his concerns to me.

I think Charlie had his own reservations, but he was also keeping a close personal eye on her. If she'd made a move that seemed unstable, he'd have swept in and removed her from command again, this time officially.

We were there, and we were watching. But we were giving Andrea a chance to come back. And she was making the most of that chance.

So to specifically answer the editors again, this wasn't having an impact on Andrea's career because we were covering it up. The only reason we could actually cover it up was because she'd committed no crimes... if she'd shot the prisoners, there'd have been no hope.

But she hadn't. We had hope. And we were doing everything we could off the books to help her.

If you disagree, I'm sorry, but it's what we did.

The Belt Squadron looks after its own.

CHAPTER THIRTY-FOUR
RELATIONSHIPS

A few hours later, I visited med bay, and was there when Alicia finally released Bunny Fox to her cabin. The damage to Bunny's lungs had been considerable, so Alicia had taken no chances in keeping the last survivor of Jocko's camera team under close observation for two weeks. Now she was being sent to her cabin for bed rest, much as Karen (and the other recovering victims) had been.

Jim was there to help her on her way, and I have to say, there was something... what's the word... refreshing? Yes. Something refreshing about seeing how happy she was to be on her feet, and walking next to Jim.

I don't know what you think of relationships aboard ship. Up until this point, I'll say that I'd been largely indifferent to members of my crews trying to find romantic liaisons or intimates aboard ship — if they wanted that sort of companionship, I certainly wasn't going to stop them, as long as their work wasn't affected.

Obviously, my opinion had changed. Jim had, I thought then (and I know now) found himself some happiness, and Bunny the same. Given all the death and injuries we'd been surrounded by lately, I thought that was a very good thing.

This will sound cliché, but in our business you could die any day. That being the case, I was definitely in favor of people finding as much happiness as they could while they had the time.

Kate Levec, Kris Jacobs, the entire crew of *Lion*, and the survivors of our encounter with *Idaho* would all probably agree with me. The people we lost on the Jupiter patrol would too. People like Aaron Ashby, who'd died with *Honesty*, or Commander Calzatti of *Pictou*, and their crews...

We'd lost a lot of people. Many had been hurt.

And as the war went on, we all figured (not wrongly) that our number could come up next. There was no point, then, waiting until after the war to find a bit of happiness, if we could get it now without failing in our duty.

Of course, this was all moot for me. I already had as much as I needed, despite a recent scare. I could keep making the most of my time with Karen, before... well. You know. *Before*. Before everything really went to hell.

Speaking of Karen, she was sleeping soundly when I slipped into her cabin that evening. Her lungs were largely back to normal, but as with all the recovering victims of the Phosgene, Alicia had her on extended rest, to avoid any permanent troubles. As I realized Karen was resting, I decided to slip out and let her sleep. Would have been rude to wake her, you see.

So Andrea was the rude one, then.

The intercom chirped as I was turning for the door, "This is the Captain. I have returned to regular duty after two weeks away. I must apologize for my absence. It was unavoidable."

Karen didn't wake up when I crept into the room, but when the intercom went, it was like flipping a switch: she was up.

"Hey," she rubbed her eyes groggily as she spotted me, but I didn't reply as we kept listening.

"I understand that the mood on this ship isn't good right now, and I understand why. But I cannot let that continue to be the case. We need to move on. I'm going to come around and visit all of you, and then we're going to start an intensive period of battle drills. We're going to work through this, and while we may never be the same as we were, we'll get better, a little at a time. Drills begin at 0900 tomorrow. Get whatever sleep you can in the meantime. Kiley out."

Karen sat up in her bed, pushing a hand groggily through her hair, "Andrea's back in command?"

I nodded, "She's ready for it, I think. And in case she isn't, Charlie has people at the brig. Just to be on the safe side."

Still not completely woken up, Karen simply nodded.

To quickly answer some questions about Andrea's address there, *no*, she didn't have to explain where she was for two weeks. The crew had no business knowing that. They didn't want to know. All they needed to understand was that their Captain was back, and that she knew something of what they were going through. *We* were going to get through this together, and such. That was all she needed to say.

It's strange. Part of what makes a happy ship work is the division between the commanders and the crew. We're close, we look after each other, and yet we know not to try to overstep certain lines. The crew cared about Andrea, but they weren't going to try to sit down and counsel her through her problems. That was for her fellow command officers to do. By the same token, we officers had no business telling the spacers how to feel, how to deal with their specific personal losses, and so on. We could go down and offer words of reassurance, or advice when asked, but we had to give them space to make their own recoveries, and vice versa. It's a quirk of Naval culture that may never go away... I think it has existed since ships on the sea had more than one deck.

When it comes down to it, a happy ship worked because everyone cared about everyone on one level, but focused their efforts on those around them. A rank-based division of labor, I suppose, made highly effective in our case because we had great women and men at every level.

So tomorrow, Andrea would start working everyone ragged with drills. In the absence of a new mission, drills were all she could offer to keep people busy, and they'd be enough. Over the next few weeks, the crew would start feeling more like its old self again. As Andrea had said, they wouldn't feel quite the same as they had before, but they'd be just as good, and just as ready.

Just as she would be.

But all that is getting a bit ahead of the story.

Karen looked at her clock and shook her head, "I've been sleeping way too much."

I chuckled at that, moving back towards the bed, "Much more beauty sleep and you're going to start blinding people."

"Ha."

Our repartee wasn't in good shape, as you can see. She was groggy, I wasn't really on my game, and we were out of practice.

"Not doing so good with the banter, are we?" my smile faded.

She looked up with a frown, "Well, I'm tired. That's not helping."

I nodded, "We're also out of practice."

As I said that, I went around the side of her bed to the chair that sat there, and lowered myself into it, "Suppose we'll have to practice."

Karen looked sideways at me, a smile sliding across her face, "What, you think we're just going to stay up all night practicing our banter?"

"People expect our banter to be at a certain level, we can't let them down," I countered with mock earnestness, and Karen laughed and flopped back onto her bed.

"Besides," I went on with as much fake seriousness as I could muster, "can you think of a better reason to stay up all night?"

Oh *snap*, as they used to say. My editors absolutely loathe double entendres, and this one is just killing them.

Closing her eyes, Karen smiled, "You know, I don't think I can imagine a better reason."

I laughed, and she kept smiling. *Wolf*, in company with the rest of the Jupiter Force, cruised towards home.

AFTERWORD

We got back to Belt Two without further event, so I'll leave it there. The next period of activity you'll need to concern yourself with starts in December of 2232 and January of 2233, and obviously, that'll be next book.

We got home in mid-October of 2232, I should say. When we did, our serious casualties from the mission (everyone from Kate Levec to Kris Jacobs to some of the more serious cases of Phosgene poisoning who were having a tough time recovering) went to hospitals at Belt Two and Earth, and *Lion* and *Lady Grace* both were sent on to Earth to go into dock at Luna for extensive repairs. We sent our prisoners to Luna, as well. At the same time, we delivered all the civilians from Io to Belt Two, where they were debriefed and given assistance in setting up new lives.

We parted ways with *Artemis Agrotera* shortly after getting back — Zail Patel's ship was sent to the Forge to assist Shauna Cass' buildup there, meaning just *Wolf*, *Cheetah*, *Friendly*, *Trusty*, *Kansas* and *North Carolina* ultimately stayed in Belt Two space.

Kansas and *North Carolina* were soon assigned to Marshal Samuels' Belt Squadron, and they began to run escort missions after two weeks of rest. It was felt that giving them important (and straightforward) work to do would be good for their crews, who for all those months had been forced to hide from the Martians around Jupiter. Now they had a chance to make a difference, and I'll always remember how thankful Captain Kishko was when I told him of the posting.

If only he'd known. But that's for next book.

Nancy Whitehorse and *Trusty* were drafted into the Jupiter Force, and we were all ordered to stay put at Belt Two — John was going to need us as a cohesive combat unit in 2233, so he wasn't going to have us do anything exciting for the rest of the year. Not that there was any excitement, really — we weren't missing out on much.

As you know, 2232 ended quietly. The next year would be the most brutal of them all, at least from the perspective of raw battling. There were many hard slugging matches, as we sought to finish off the Martians. For all you readers who love the big battles, there are plenty coming, as you probably already know. For you readers who like the character side of things more, not to worry: 2233 was the year when, as I like to say, we lost Charlie. Nothing was ever the same after that.

So for now, I'm going to sign off. I won't lie, I'm happy to have this year's worth of books behind me. Thinking back, I see now that 2232 forced me to look very closely at my own character, and to see the flaws that later would cause so much trouble. It's not easy to write about, honestly. Over the next couple of years, things would be moving too quickly for me to do much of that same self-critiquing, for better or for worse. The slowest year of hostilities was done, and the hard slugging was just about to begin.

Next year, we'll start with *The Canary Wars*, and then *The Forge Fires*. After that it's *The Mercury Assault* and *The Fleet Clash*. I hope to see you then, for more exciting adventures… or whatever the hell you call these. Until then, keep well!

ALSO AVAILABLE FROM ICEBERG PUBLISHING

THE
EQUATIONS NOVELS

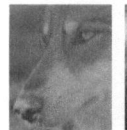

The Earthers evolved after humans were driven from the Earth by an intelligent bio-weapon dubbed 'Omega'. They are faster, stronger, smarter, wiser, *better* than humans, and they are the only hope for the survivors of the human race as an interstellar war between two great alien powers absorbs the galaxy. But all is not as it seems, and the humans and the Earthers face challenges that overshadow the wars of alien empires and threaten to destroy their civilizations...

The Equations Novels by Kenneth Tam

Book One: THE HUMAN EQUATION (Oct 2003)

Book Two: THE ALIEN EQUATION (May 2004)

Book Three: THE RENEGADE EQUATION (Dec 2004)

Book Four: THE EARTHER EQUATION (July 2005)

Book Five: THE GENESIS EQUATION (July 2006)

Book Six: THE VENGEANCE EQUATION (July 2007)

Book Seven: THE NEMESIS EQUATION (July 2008)

Book Eight: THE DESTINY EQUATION (July 2009)

The Equations Novels are complete, but there are spinoff series and new stories in the Earther universe still to come!

For more information, please visit
www.earther.net

ALSO AVAILABLE FROM ICEBERG PUBLISHING

HIS MAJESTY'S
NEW WORLD

by Kenneth Tam

1919. The British Empire and the United States have been
colonizing a new planet for nearly 40 years. But there are secrets yet
to be uncovered on His Majesty's New World...

His Majesty's New World novels by Kenneth Tam

Book One: THE GRASSLANDS (April 2008)
Book Two: THE FRONTIER (April 2009)
Book Three: THE REPRISAL (Forthcoming)

For more information, please visit

www.newworldempire.net

About the Author

Born in 1984 in St. John's, Newfoundland, Kenneth Tam holds both a Bachelor's and Master's degree in history from Wilfrid Laurier University in Waterloo, Canada. His MA thesis examined the creation and operation of the Caribou Hut, a hostel for Allied servicemen in St. John's during the Second World War.

In 2006, Kenneth received a prestigious Canada Graduate Scholarship from the Social Sciences and Humanities Council of Canada. He was also awarded a Balsillie Fellowship at the Centre for International Governance Innovation during 2006-07. In that capacity, he worked for Mr. Paul Heinbecker, Canada's former ambassador and permanent representative to the United Nations. He presently serves as a Communications Consultant for Kitchener–Waterloo's federal Member of Parliament, Peter Braid.

Since releasing his first novel in 2003, Tam has promoted his books across Canada, speaking with junior and high school students, delivering writing workshops, and doing book signings at bookstores and Iceberg-organized events. He frequently appears as a guest author at science fiction events across the country.

Kenneth is a partner in Iceberg Publishing, the company he and his family started in 2002. He has authored many of the company's existing titles, and is also responsible for graphic design, including the company logo, website, banners, advertisements, and other marketing materials. He acts as a primary contact with printers and suppliers, and is also key in new author development and recruitment.

He remains very lazy about writing his author bios. When they told him to make this one longer, he mostly copied and pasted it together from the Iceberg website, www.icebergpublishing.com.

www.ingramcontent.com/pod-product-compliance
Lightning Source LLC
Chambersburg PA
CBHW030744030726
47497CB00001B/124